THE JACK OF RUIN

~ Book Two of the Unseen Moon Series ~

by STEPHEN MERLINO

TORTOISE
RAMPANT

The Jack of Ruin

ISBN: 978-0-9862674-3-7

Cover art by Yo Shimizu at you629@artstation.com
Cover layout and design by Luke P. Shea
at www.lukeshea.com

For Kathryn—
artist, traveler, giver, and infallible compass
of what matters.

Acknowledgements

I have many to thank for their support and input during the creation of this book.

First and foremost, to Kathryn, Maia, and Roman, partners in adventure and inspiration. Next to Sue and Scott, who always supported their brother's geeky interests; special thanks to Scott for his proofread.

Next, to John and Sue Tomlinson, for all their support over many years.

Thanks to my beta readers, beginning with my first reader, Jane Merlino, whose encouragement from a young age made me believe in myself and kept me foolish enough to keep writing; to Stone Gossard, for his clear-eyed reading and wit, and for sharing this dream we had as kids; to Michael Neeley, fellow Tolkien geek, for his hexatious through-line reading; and to sci-fi writers Tim (Tim, I tell you!) Daniels (humorous sci-fi), and Heidi Farmer (sci-fi); RMFW fantasy writers Corinne "Conference Diva" O'Flynn, Karen "Unforgettable" Duvall; to lone wolf of the demon West, Stefan Marmion; to Wayward wolf of the alt-rainforest Joanne Rixon, for her generosity and brilliance as a reader and writer, which continually humble and inspire; to Carol Otte, another Wayward wolf, for her perspicacious critiques, generosity and stamina over multiple drafts; to Nick Markham, for his reads for consistency between *The Jack of Souls* and its sequel; and to Kai "make my day" Hiar, who is likely my most dangerous fan.

Special thanks to Amber Boker, Horse Whisperer & Rehabilitator, my consultant on matters equine, and to Magic Tom Boland, fellow teacher, unintentional publicist, and friend.

Also to my beta reader closers: Mark Hauge, whose deep learning in film and comics lore and consequent insights into plot and character continually blow my mind; and Craig Holt, traveler, philosopher, and professional crank, whose jungle noir novel, *Hard Dog to Kill*, released this year.

Finally, thanks to the *Seattle Writer's Cramp* gang, esp. Mike Croteau, Steve Gurr, Kim Runciman, Amy Stewart, Thom Marrion, and Barbara Stoner, who were there through the bitter end(s); the same for Ian Chisholm, Larry Jones, and Dan Solum and Diana of the *Wayward* group, who endured innumerable drafts.

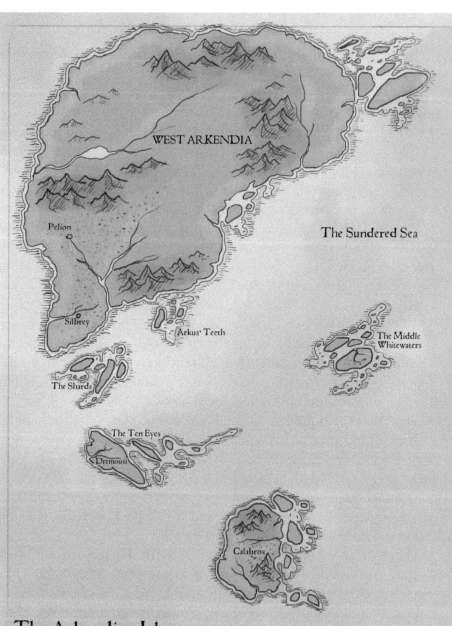

WEST ARKENDIA

Pelion

Silbrey

Arkus' Teeth

The Shards

The Ten Eyes

Dremousi

The Sundered Sea

The Middle
Whitewaters

Calabros

The Arkendian Isles

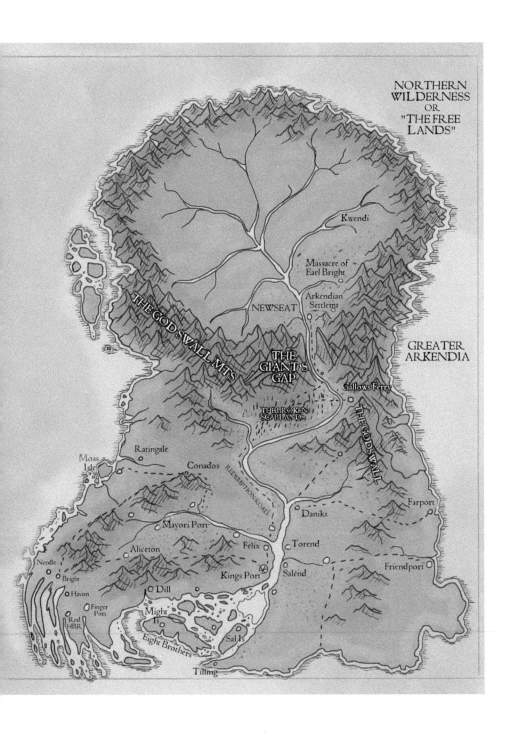

NORTHERN
WILDERNESS
OR
"THE FREE
LANDS"

Kwendi

Massacre of
Earl Bright

Arkendian
Settlemt

NEWSEAT

THE GOD'S WALL MTS

THE
GIANT'S
GAP

GREATER
ARKENDIA

Gallows Ferry

THE BROKEN
SCABLANDS

THE GOD'S WALL

Ratingale

Moss
Isle

Conados

REDEMPTION ROAD

Farport

Daniks

Mayori Port

Aliceton

Felix

Torend

Needle

Friendport

Kings Port

Saleńd

Bright

Havon

Dill

Finger
Port

Red
HBR

Might
Is

Eight Brothers

Sal Is

Tilling

Ruin (n):
1 – disintegration, loss, an end of good things.
2 – in Arkendian tarot-poker, the suit of the Mad Moon.

—From the first Kwendi Dictionary of Arkendian

A Voice In The Dark

Harric scanned the darkness of the bedchamber, straining for any sign of the intruder.

"Who's there?" he whispered.

A rasping voice answered from much too close in the dark, "We had an agreement."

Harric lurched to the back of his bed and struck his shoulder against the stone wall, knocking grains of mortar down his neck.

"Your debt is due," said the imp. "Did you think to hide from me?"

"No." Harric struggled to sound calm, but it seemed like his heart was slamming against the bars of his ribcage. "I knew you'd come. I expected you."

A finger of moonlight slanted through an arrow slit and etched a glowing triangle on the stone floor. It was the room's only light, but now that Harric knew where to look, it was enough to reveal the creature as a clot of deeper darkness at the head of his bed.

The imp—Fink, it called itself—stepped closer, talons clicking on the stone, and Harric flinched against the wall. The private chamber the garrison had awarded Harric for destroying Sir Bannus's army felt less of a privilege and more of a trap.

Stay calm, he chided himself. The thing could probably sense fear through the Unseen.

Steeling himself, Harric closed his eyes. At once he saw the teardrop-shaped hole at the top of his mind, the "third eye" or "oculus" the imp had cut with its talon in Harric's forehead. It hung like a luminous attic window, its edges outlined by the glow of the spirit world beyond. Pushing his consciousness up to it, he peered out. In the Unseen world of spirits, the chamber's stone walls and floor glowed faintly with the low spiritual essence of moisture and dust upon them, but his own limbs blazed with spiritual flames, and the wooden doors at either end shone with the residue of life, bright as promises.

The Unseen also revealed the imp. It hunched like a grounded bat, black and lightless against the ambient glow. Its gaunt body—no larger than that of a seven-year-old child—looked starved, with jutting ribs and a bald, overlarge head. The peaks of membranous wings reached almost as high as a man, and hooked talons adorned crooked fingers and feet. Beneath a long, bulbous nose, a hedge of needlelike teeth stretched in a permanent grin. White, pupilless eyes gleamed like boils tight with fluid.

Harric resisted the urge to glance at the two exits: one door opened onto the main corridor of the barracks; the other was the postern door opening onto the cliff at the foot of the outpost's wall. He could make a dash for one, but what would be the point? The imp would find him eventually. He took a breath and spoke forcefully, so his voice wouldn't crack. "I'm glad you found me, Fink."

"I kept my end of the bargain."

"You did. What…what did you do with her?"

"Your mother is in her grave."

Harric's heart leapt against his ribs again. "So. Will she stay there this time?"

The hedge of needle teeth widened in what might have been a humorless grin. "That's one deranged spirit that won't be back to torment you. She's gone."

Harric stared, scarcely daring to believe what he'd heard. He repeated it to be sure.

"Gone."

"No more haunting," said Fink. "No more attacks."

Harric nodded, and hope became belief. No more madness. No more terror. The curse was broken. A weight lifted from his spirit—a

weight that had become so familiar over the years that he'd forgotten it
was there.

"Now for your end of the bargain." The imp stood, knobbled limbs
crackling. He extended a hooked talon toward Harric's forehead.

"Wait!" Harric jumped and stood on the bed.

Hissing, Fink extended his wings to the sides as if to catch Harric
if he ran.

"I just mean…" Harric said. "I want to talk first." His mind galloped
as his gut seemed to push the air from his lungs. "But we can't talk here.
If the others hear us and come in, the game will be up. You might get
away, but I won't. They'll search me and destroy your witch-stone and
then hang me from the battlements." He rushed a hand through his
hair. "Let's meet outside. Up on the cliff, where the dark will hide us
and we'll have a clear view of anyone who approaches."

After a moment, Fink furled his wings. "On the cliff, you settle your
debt."

Harric nodded.

"Leave the sword," said the imp.

And he vanished.

Trickery is noble wit,
But lies are merely lies.
To those who say I wronged them,
Let them look again and sigh.

—Last words of the infamous Jack Pilgrim before his escape from the gallows.

2

On The Brink

Sweat chilled Harric's spine as he crept out a back door of the walled outpost. High above, the Bright Mother Moon hung mid-leap between the crags on either side of the pass. Pure and white, she painted the stone faces with silver and shadow.

Harric stole along the moon-shadowed west walls of the stable yard and managed to avoid the eyes of the watchmen, while the chatter of the river running down the east side masked the sound of his footfalls.

Scents of sun-toasted pine and wildflowers greeted him as he crept up the road behind the fortification, but the charms of late summer lacked the power to banish the dread in his stomach. There would be no tricking his way out of this situation. He couldn't swindle the imp like he could some West Isle slaver, and the imp was too shrewd to be maneuvered into a Rash Promise like Sir Willard. He couldn't con this foe or hide from him.

But he had to try something. The mere thought of Fink's "master-slave contract" curdled his innards.

As he started to climb the stairway at the foot of the cliff, he tried to imagine he and the imp were at a card table. He imagined he had only one card, and the imp was about to call the flop. Sliding his hand into his sleeve, he groped for his lucky Jack of Souls, but found its pocket empty. *Cobs.* A cold finger of doubt touched him right at the base of his ribcage. He'd left the card in the room.

Sucking a deep breath, he tried to imagine another card in his sleeve—some inspiration, some insight into the situation—but came up with nothing.

Well, then. What was the one card he'd imagined in his hand?

The witch-stone. Fink's stone. He slid his fingers into his shirt and grasped the egg-shaped orb that linked him to the power of the Unseen Moon. The stone was surely his only card. As long as he had it, he had something to bargain with.

But he knew if he didn't agree to Fink's terms, the imp would demand the stone back and…then what? He'd either have to find a way to fight the imp off—which was out of the question—or he'd have to give it back, and his dreams of using it to help the Queen would all come crashing down. With the stone in his hand, he had done so much already: he'd defeated Bannus's army; he'd saved his friends and their quest for the Queen; and—arguably—saved the whole cobbing kingdom. With Fink's witch-stone, he could be the greatest protector the Queen had ever known—a hero of importance akin to that of Sir Willard and the Blue Order.

And it felt like more than a dream. It felt like destiny. And he'd devote his life to it.

Sighing heavily, he dropped the witch-stone back in the inner pocket of his shirt and quested up his sleeve to the empty card pocket. He imagined tracing three sides of the jack, and rehearsed three of the jack's cardinal virtues. *Wit. Daring. Luck.* The fourth, *Charm*, would not serve him in a tryst with an imp of the Unseen. But he'd need all three of the others more than ever before. He had no choice but to hear Fink out and improvise as more cards appeared.

Wit. Daring Luck. Over and over, his fingers traced the edges as he climbed. *I can do this.*

His thighs burned when he finally reached the top of the stairs and stepped out onto the edge above the sleeping outpost. Below him, the stone walls and slate rooftops glinted hard and cold in silver moonlight. The ruin of its dove tower still smoldered from the recent siege, and a few embers among the fallen timbers glowed like watching red eyes. As he traversed the ledge, he got a bird's-eye view of the outer wall and gate that barred the pass. Upon the battlements, two watchmen dozed with bottles by their heads—a sin Harric forgave them, for all the survivors had celebrated their victory with mead and ale in plenty.

No sign of Fink yet. The ledge before him remained empty. As he traversed the face of the cliff, it climbed high above the road, like a moon-silvered plank of bare stone no wider than his shoulders.

As he hugged the cliff to his right and leaned away from the drop to his left, a new dread frosted his veins: he'd chosen to meet Fink there so he could show him the battlefield, show what he'd done, in case it might give him another card to bargain with; but now the location seemed foolish—like it gave the *imp* a card—for at twenty fathoms above the road, Fink could simply knock him from the ledge and retrieve the witch-stone from his broken body.

Well played, Harric.

He glanced back, worried that Fink might materialize behind, but saw no sign of the imp in the Seen or the Unseen. Below, the river burst from the frowning water gate at the front of the fortification wall and plunged like a silvery tongue for seventy fathoms into the valley.

A shadow appeared, some sixty paces up the ledge, right above the rockfall that buried Bannus's army. It seemed a blur of darkness, like a cloud of ash from a dead campfire, but from it the imp materialized. When Harric joined him, Fink was staring down at the shattered timbers and house-sized boulders as if he knew Harric had stood in that very spot only hours before when he brought the cliff down on his enemies.

He followed the imp's gaze to the wreckage. Seeing the enormity of it anew sent a wave of sickness through him. Dozens of men lay mashed beneath those boulders. Dozens of horses crushed, pinned, blasted from the side of the mountain. It was a mass grave. And all dead by Harric's hand.

They would have done worse to us, he reminded himself. *And now my friends sleep soundly in the stone halls of the outpost instead of wailing in the hands of Sir Bannus. For another day, the Queen and kingdom are safe. No guilt in that.*

With luck, it would take more than a day for the immortal Sir Bannus to recover from the blow. As the rocks had descended on his camp, Bannus's immortal horse had whirled and carried him over the cliff and down into the well of the waterfall. Since Bannus's horn had

resounded defiantly from the depths in the hours after, Harric knew he'd return. And unless his fall had knocked the memory of Harric's triumphant face from his immortal skull, the knight would return with even more determination and hatred.

Another anxiety to gnaw at Harric's gut.

Fink looked up from the rubble and fixed him with pupilless white eyes.

He must see the spirits of the slain amidst the rubble, Harric thought.

He hadn't dared look through his oculus at the mass grave below, but it drained the blood from his veins to imagine the spirits of the dead there—maybe as gory as their bodies—as they cursed him and clamored for revenge. If they could reach him, maybe they'd claw through his oculus and rend his soul to shreds.

"You've been busy," Fink rasped.

Harric retreated from the edge of the ledge and sat with his back against the cliff. If the imp shoved him from here, Harric would hit the rubble, and his spirit would join the angry spirits of the slain. He shook his head in dismay. *Well played, again.*

"Yes, it was a busy night," Harric said, or rather blurted. "I used the witch-stone and entered the Unseen, and…"

A hiss from deep in the imp's throat. "Didn't I tell you not to use it without me?"

"I'd be dead if I hadn't."

"There are worse things than dead." The imp glared from egg-blank eyes.

Harric explained Sir Bannus's siege. How Harric had used the witch-stone to move invisibly across the cliff so he could detonate a hidden fire-cone charge.

Fink's needled mouth stretched into a grimace that might have been a sly smile. "My witch-stone saved you tonight. Saved the old knight's mission. Saved Ambassador Brolli. Bet that feels good, too. Made you the big hero. Bet you want to hold on to that kind of power." The imp scrabbled closer. "This was our agreement: I help you, you help me. You want the power of the stone. You like it. I can smell it. And you can't keep it without me. Now you give me what I want. I require a master—a blood-soul compact that binds us in this life and the next. That's the price of heroes."

Harric's stomach tightened. "We talked about this before. I can't do that."

A hiss like a swarm of wasps gurgled up in Fink's throat. "You think you can keep my stone and use it without me? You think you can enter the Unseen alone? You won't last an hour. Alone, you're an injured calf ringing its own dinner bell for the wolves and gib-crows of the Unseen. The only reason you weren't eaten by one tonight is that the spirits were too scared to get near that mad-brained immortal and his mad-brained immortal horse. Don't believe me? Think I'm bluffing? Look at them. Now that he's gone, the scavengers are there." Fink gestured to the ruined camp below.

Harric hesitated.

"Look on what you've done," Fink said. "Know what's at stake."

Reluctantly, Harric slid forward until he sat on the edge of the shelf with his legs hanging down. Looking between his knees at the rubble and splintered siege towers made him dizzy, but he closed his eyes and pushed his mind toward the oculus at the top of his consciousness. The window widened at his pressure until he rose partway through it into the Unseen, and peered down at the killing field.

The spirit world was bright with the essence of mist from the waterfall. It formed a bright fog that obscured visibility beyond what lay immediately below the ledge, but among the massive boulders, Harric made out a dozen or more bright spirits of men. To his relief, they paid no attention to him, for they were preoccupied with avoiding several darker spirits in attendance. Harric's stomach rose as he studied them. They were hunched and shadowy figures—some winged, some with more than one head or more than four limbs—and they appeared to be either hunting the men among the boulders, or else watching them like cats with full bellies watch cornered mice.

The imp pointed to a flat slab of rubble on which a cluster of vulturelike spirits hunched over one of the slain and fed, heads low. The bright echo of a man writhed beneath them, and its pitiful wail drifted across the essence-rich air to rake Harric's conscience.

One of the vultures looked up from its meal and straight into Harric, sending a spear of cold fear through his middle. Harric let out a cry of dismay and collapsed back into himself, willing his oculus shut behind him. To his horror, the oculus had become sluggish and remained partly open, like a heavy-lidded eye at the top of his mind. The vulture spirit had stunned the aperture, leaving him open for an easy snack. He imagined the thing dipping it talons into his head and scooping him out like a soft-boiled egg.

Opening his eyes, he stared about to reorient to the Seen, where the flat slab lay lonely and abandoned in the moonlight.

"That could be you feeding the birds, see?" said Fink. "You need me. Only reason they don't come for you now is because I'm here. Without me, you'd be worse than dead."

Harric nodded and scooted himself away from the brink to return his back to the wall.

"But I require a master," said Fink.

"You—don't understand—"

"*I understand fine.* You go back on this agreement and I will take back that oculus. I will take back that stone. I will undo the seal on your loving mother's grave and let her mad spirit free—"

Fink stopped. He jerked his head to the side to see something beyond Harric on the ledge. In the same instant, he vanished in a cloud of swirling shadow.

"Harric!" Caris called. "Who's up there with you?"

Harric's heart leapt into his throat. He turned to see her just as she gained the top of the stairs at the far end. Plastering a smile over his terror, he waved. She did not smile or wave. She drew her sword and strode purposefully up the shelf.

"Just me," Harric called. "All is well."

Her frown relaxed, but she did not put her sword away. As she strode up the ledge, she held up a candle lantern in her off hand.

Harric let out a long breath of relief. She hadn't seen Fink. If she had, she'd be screaming.

The combination of silver moonlight and golden lantern made her glow like a vision. She'd tied her hair back in a simple warrior's tail, thrown on boots and breeches, and belted her sword over her nightshirt, which hung to her knees like an airy surcoat. The curves moving under that thin fabric sent a thrill through his core. At that distance, he could even imagine her as the same size as he. It wasn't until she drew nearer that the towering height and hard muscle of her horse-touched body became undeniably clear, and the vision shattered.

"You're alone," she said, as she neared and her eyes drilled to where Fink had been.

This isn't over. Fink's voice drifted into Harric's mind through his oculus. *You try to hide in that little fort and I'll drag you out in front of your friends.*

Harric turned his head away and murmured, "Where would I go? Piss off for a while."

"Who are you talking to?" When Caris found the ledge beside him empty, her eyes widened and she set her back to the cliff. "Is your mother here?"

"Gods leave us, no. Her ghost is never coming back. I'm alone."

She looked at him like she suspected him of madness. "Then who are you talking to?"

"My shadow?" He forced a welcoming smile. "Sorry to scare you. Come sit with me."

She made no move to sit. Her brow remained bent. "You need sleep, Harric. You look terrible."

"Please. Sit." He scooted forward to hang his knees over the shelf and patted the stone beside him. "Besides, you must be upset about something or you'd be sleeping yourself. Tell me what's wrong."

Some of the worry drained from her brow. With a tentative half-smile, she sat beside him. Tall as she was, her feet hung below his, and he had to look up to meet her eyes. Like all horse-touched, she wasn't merely taller and heavier than most men, she was also stronger and broader in the shoulders. Most men found that repugnant. Harric had ceased to wonder why he did not. He'd always been smaller and leaner than most men, so he'd never derived his sense of manhood from size or strength. Plus, she beat the snot out of people who hurt him, which was handy.

Her eyes flicked to him and away. "What are you smiling about?"

"You."

Her brow furrowed and she twisted the ring on her smallest finger.

He knew what was coming, and his stomach dropped. Whenever they were alone, that cursed ring was the monster in the room with them. He ran a hand through his hair and gave her a grim smile. "Wish you had accidentally given *me* that ring, instead of the other way around. On my finger, it wouldn't have changed a thing: you'd still have your natural indifference toward me, and since I already loved you, its enchantment wouldn't change me at all. The only inconvenience would be that it would be stuck on my finger."

She raised her eyes to his, a rare treat, but short-lived, as she flushed and looked down at the stubborn band of witch-silver.

"I mean it, Caris. If I could switch it, I would."

"It isn't always bad," she said, twisting it around and around. "Sometimes I even… I don't know. It makes me feel…" She scowled, then her eyes flashed, and she stole an angry glance. "Then I remember that's just the enchantment, tricking me, and I want to smash something. It's like some invisible hand keeps turning my face to you when I try to look away."

Harric clenched his jaw and looked out over the valley while she wrangled her anger.

Mist sighed up from the well of the waterfall, rising in moonlit clouds and sprinkling their ledge with a breath of clear river water. He avoided looking at the rubble, where he knew the vulture spirits still lurked in the Unseen, and instead lifted his gaze to the silvered faces of the crags above the opposite side of the valley.

She let out a loud sigh and seemed to relax, leaning into him and sharing warmth. It would have been a peaceful moment, if he didn't know a vengeful imp lurked there, just beyond their vision.

"How did you do it, Harric?"

"Mm? Do what?"

She took a breath, then turned to hold his gaze, something very difficult given her horse-touched nature. "Tonight, during the battle, how did you creep out on this ledge without anyone seeing?"

Something tightened in his chest. "What do you mean?" He licked his lips. "I was on my belly here, and then I stood and ran."

No lie there. Only evasion.

"Harric, I was looking for you. I came up and checked on the ledge, thinking you might have been shot there, and it was empty except for the bodies of the guards who had died trying to cross it before you. I had to back up onto the stairs because the crossbowmen in the siege towers loosed their bolts at the merest glimpse of me. There is no way you could have crept out here without them seeing you, but then I saw you clear as day"—she slapped the ledge as punctuation—"right in the middle of the ledge."

The pain that now shone in her eyes cut a hole through his heart. But he could not tell her the truth yet. She was still totally under Sir Willard's thumb with regards to rules against magic use. If there were ever to be any chance of her accepting the Unseen, he would need time to prepare his case.

"I guess I can see how you'd think that," he said. "It was a scary situation. Crossbow bolts flying. Bannus riding up and down. It's not like you could get a great look. Did you consider you just didn't see me here in the confusion?"

No lie yet. Please, Caris, let it go; don't make me lie.

But Caris grimaced as if in pain. She closed her eyes and raised her hands to her ears as if to shut out his voice—as she did when one of her horse-touched fits was coming on. "Harric, Ambassador Brolli killed the witch in Gallows Ferry," she said, as she began to rock back and forth. "And when a witch dies, they drop their witch-stone. But we never found it. You were right there, and... did you...?"

Alarum blasts couldn't have stunned Harric more. How could she have guessed this? Suddenly the weight of the egg-sized stone in the inner pocket of his shirt felt heavy and obvious. He shifted his arm to conceal it and stammered, "Caris—you're making me nervous, rocking like that—you could fall—"

"A stone from the Black Moon might really taint you," she said, as if reciting a well-rehearsed speech. "That's what they say. Even if you just *touched* one. Maybe you didn't know what it was and you—ah—" She clenched her teeth and rocked even harder.

Cobs. Harric laid a hand on her wrist to still her rocking and coax the hand from her ear. "Caris. Listen to me."

Repeating those words, he waited, and gradually she stopped rocking. With what seemed like tremendous effort, she lowered her hands from the other ear. And though she did not open her eyes, he knew she listened.

"Caris, I did not pick up a witch-stone." He hated himself for the lie, but he spoke it perfectly, as if it was the purest truth—just as his mother taught him—all the while despising every syllable. "No taint. You're worried about nothing."

She started rocking again. "You might have touched it accidentally and not even known it. Just now you were talking to air, Harric. Are you hearing voices?"

"Yes—well, yours and mine, I mean—"

She hit him in the arm, and her eyes flashed. "It isn't funny. I saw this ledge last night. You weren't there. Then you were. Was it Ambassador Brolli's magic?" A flicker of hope lit in her eyes as this new idea took hold. Harric closed his mouth and looked down at his hands, knowing how she'd take it. "It *was* Brolli's magic!" she said. "Why didn't I see it before? That's why you won't tell me. You promised Brolli you wouldn't tell, because he knows Willard wouldn't approve. And you knew I wouldn't approve."

Harric denied nothing, thereby confirming everything, and the lie slid between them like an irrevocable lens of shadow. It dimmed her and chilled the warmth between them as if they were separated by a vast gulf.

Her attention went inward, where he imagined her busily assembling the less-terrible fiction that explained his behavior: that it wasn't an incurable disease that afflicted him, but a temporary malady. Relief rinsed the worry from the lines of her face, but anger suddenly bathed Harric, and he had to turn his face away in case it leaked out of his eyes.

Why should he have to hide the truth? With that witch-stone he'd saved her life—all their lives—and probably the Queen's. It wasn't a taint. It was a talisman. And their opposition was idiotic. He wished he could show her, explain it all with a clear conscience, but it was too complicated for that. It would take time and care and patience to overcome tradition and Willard's influence, and help her see things clearly.

But he *would* tell her. He would plan it carefully, think it through, and introduce it by steps. He would come clean to her one day. This simply wasn't the time.

Her eyes now clear, Caris punched him again in the arm.

"Ow! What now—"

"If Willard saw what I saw at the pass, he'd cast you out, Harric."

"I saved his stinking life!"

"He is a man of honor. He'd toss you out and say, 'Good riddance! Better die in honor than live in shame.'"

"That's insane."

"You used Brolli's magic after he specifically told you not to. You ignored him, and you ignored the Second Law forbidding magic. It shows you don't respect the rules, Harric." Caris clenched her teeth. "What will I do if he casts you off? I can't lose you. This damn ring will torture me until I go with you, so I'd have to abandon Willard and my apprenticeship—and I can't do that. It would tear me in two."

"We're going to get that ring off as soon as we get to Brolli's people."

"Where you will stock up on more of his people's magic?"

"That's not what I meant."

She climbed abruptly to her feet, a new look of decision in her eyes. "Your tricks always bring trouble, Harric. Always. So listen carefully to what I'm about to say. If I find out you touch Brolli's magic—or any other magic—again, *I* will abandon you. I swear it. I don't care how much the ring hurts me. I will chop this ring off my finger if that's what it takes. I will not be tainted by magic or dishonorable trickery."

Without waiting for a response, she turned and stalked away, her candle dashing shadows behind her.

Harric hung his head between his knees and let out a long breath. Shame and anger tore his insides. He longed to follow her and confess. To apologize for the lie. To explain. But then what? Give up this proven power to protect everything they loved—to protect the Queen, to protect his friends—when even Sir Willard could not? So what if his power was the power of trickery and magic? He'd shown over and again the good he could do with it. But none of them recognized it.

A growl of frustration escaped him.

"Sweet romance you got there, kid." The imp had materialized right behind him, cutting him off from the back of the ledge. "Shame if anything happened to it."

There is no contract but the contract between equals.
All else is subjugation, which henceforth we will none.

— Queen Chasia on freeing bastards and women

3

Unbound

Harric's head went so light with panic that he almost toppled over the rim. Diving to the side, he tried to scoot to the back of the ledge, but Fink moved between—as quick as Harric's own shadow—his lipless mouth gleaming like a hedge of needles.

"What's wrong?" Fink said.

Harric dove again, and this time, Fink made no attempt to mirror him, and Harric practically embraced the cliff. Setting his back against the stone, he choked out a curse. "What the Black Moon are you trying to do?"

Fink's grin never faltered. "I thought you would dislike it if your girlfriend saw me, so I moved behind you. Is there a problem?"

The imp's tone was mocking. He'd guessed exactly how Harric would take it if he moved behind him, and had done it as a warning of what might happen if Harric tried to stiff him.

Fair enough. Harric let his breathing calm. "You heard all that? What she said?"

"*You used Ambassador Brolli's magic,*" Fink mimicked. "*That's why you won't tell me.*" Fink let out a cough that might have been a laugh. "She's a real plum. Did most of the lying for you. Not many girls would do that for a guy."

Harric frowned. "I can't tell her yet. I need time to help her understand."

"Oh, sure. Just give her time. With a little warming up, she and I will be best friends."

Harric's hands balled into fists. How had he become the knave in this ballad? He was supposed to be the hero. The bastard with a golden heart.

"The fact is, she'll find out sooner or later, kid."

"I'm not a kid. I'm almost twenty."

"Ooh, so old? You don't want to know how long I've been around, but let me put it do you this way: to me, you're a baby. 'Kid' is me being generous."

Harric blinked. "How long *have* you been around?"

"Let's just say if I was your grandfather, there would be more than one 'great' in front of that title."

Harric nodded. He felt his shoulders relaxing with the banter. "All right. You can call me kid."

"Back to your girlfriend. She'll find out. All your so-called friends will. And none of them will accept it. Not Sir Willard, not even Ambassador Brolli—yeah, I know their names because I've been watching you. And you'll have to give them up, kid. Once you're my master, cutting ties is the first thing you do. Price of heroes. Which brings us to our pact."

Harric gestured for Fink to slow down. "You don't understand. It's because you are new to this land, and because all your masters have been Iberg, on the continent."

"I've learned a few things about this backward land since I was brought here."

"I'm sure you have. But one thing you've missed is that we in this backward, uncivilized, and barbaric island kingdom allow no slavery." Steel certainties girded his heart now, and he could hear the steadiness in his own voice. Hooking a thumb under his belt, he said, "This is a bastard belt. Thirty years ago, it would mark me as a slave. Lucky for me, our Queen abolished slavery, so today I'm free. But I live every day with people who treat me like I still deserve to be a slave, and who want to toss our Queen and bring back slavery. So freedom is everything to me. I'll never be master or slave. *Never.* So you and I are here to find a mutually satisfactory alternative."

Fink stared, blank eyes unreadable. His head cocked slightly to one side as if he were uncertain he'd heard correctly. "No slavery." A black tongue slid out over the forest of needles and retreated. The imp glanced over his shoulder as if he feared someone listened.

"Besides," Harric said, "*master in this life, slave in the next* is a shit deal. I might live thirty years as master, and spend eternity a slave."

"But for that thirty years, you'd have power other mortals couldn't dream of."

Harric waved it way. "*Freedom* is power."

A hiss rose in Fink's throat. "No master, no slave? Then no pact. That's what he wants, that's what he gets. Just as soon as he gives me back the nexus stone he stole from my previous master, I'll be on my way." A taloned hand extended toward the stone in Harric's shirt.

Harric leaned away, one hand on the stone. "Don't be so—"

"And I'll let your mother out of her hole too, so things go back to the way they were when I found you. I'm sure you two will work something out. She seems reasonable."

Fink knew he had most of the cards. But Harric had certainty. He knew beyond any doubt what he would not do—what he would die for—and that was a power in its own right. It put him beyond negotiation on that topic, and Fink seemed to realize it. But instead of knocking Harric from the cliff, the imp appeared frozen, uncertain, and in the hesitation, Harric sensed his chance.

"You act like I demanded your head on a plate, Fink. But I'm offering you something precious. I'm offering you what the Queen gave me. *Freedom*. You and I could be equals. Call it partners."

Fink flinched as if Harric had jabbed him with a stick. His bald head cringed back on its skinny neck and swiveled about as if he were looking for spies. "Hush it, kid! It's a sin for me to even *think* of that. If my sisters or the Black Circle back in the Compact got word I was unbound, they'd catch me and feed me to a harrow. You have to understand something. The only reason I'm on this backward, moons-forsaken island is because I'm being punished. I'm on probation, see? They banished me to this magic-less rock to serve a banished magus. It was my chance at redemption. If I got this right, I could maybe return to Ibergia, where magic is everywhere and things make sense."

"So...?"

"So *that* all ended when the good Ambassador Brolli killed my master and you stole my nexus stone. Thanks to that, my chance at redemption is spoiled and I'm probably doomed, and my only chance is to get another blood-soul pact with you before they notice."

"Or freedom."

Fink flapped his hand and croaked, "You have no idea what you're talking about!"

"I know freedom. It has its own power."

"Blood-soul pact is the only power I know. It's that or nothing."

Harric nodded, but the card player in him sensed a bluff. Something in the imp seemed deeply uncertain. Even desperate. "All right. You're scared. I understand. I freed a slave girl once, and she reacted the same way at first, pissed off and paranoid because all she knew was fear and punishment—and maybe you're like that. But you're in Arkendia now, and our queen freed our slaves, including bastards like me, and I've sworn to fight on her behalf. In fact," he said, following his instincts to call Fink's bluff, "here—take your stone!" He tossed the witch-stone to Fink. "If it feeds on slavery, I don't want it."

Fink caught the stone. His face froze.

Harric crossed his arms, trying to look indifferent. "It's yours, Fink. I'll take it back, but only as partners, only if you give it as an equal."

Fink lowered his head and stared from narrowed white eyes. "You understand what this means, kid? I'll take the oculus back, too." He extended a hooked talon toward the teardrop window at the top of Harric's mind. "That means no more third eye into the spirit world. Back to being blind. That what you want?"

"Of course not. I want to partner with you. I want to learn from you and see more about the Unseen. I want to use its power to protect my queen. But it's better to be free and blind."

Fink had frozen again. After moments of agonizing silence, the imp slowly drew himself up and lifted the witch-stone in one hand and drew his arm back to toss it to Harric. But it never came. His arm froze, mid-gesture, as if someone had grabbed it. Fink grimaced. With only his arm apparently frozen and cocked to throw, the rest of him began to shake.

"What's wrong?" Harric asked.

Fink stared feverishly at the stone in his talons, as if straining against some invisible external force. The more he struggled to defy it, the more violent his trembling. Finally, he stopped and retreated, gasping from the effort. He glanced about, eyes wide with fear or surprise. "I can't do it," he said. "They won't let me."

"They?"

"The Black Circle. They put a compulsion on me to prevent me from giving it away without a pact. Don't think I don't want it, kid. I tried to give it to you. There has to be a blood-soul pact. It's the only way."

"But I had it without a pact before—"

"You *stole* it before."

A blade of panic stabbed under Harric's breastbone. He'd won the bluff, but lost the only card he had, and lost the game—lost the stone he needed to protect his queen. And now Fink couldn't return it without a pact.

Unless Fink were double-bluffing. How would Harric know if he'd *faked* the compulsion against returning the stone?

Fink hunched beside him, a rack of bones and hooks and blank white eyes, bony shoulders slumped in defeat, and Harric began to laugh. It was a low, voiceless laugh, under his breath, and it came from a growing sense that he had no idea whatsoever about the rules of the game he was playing. A laugh born of absurdity.

"Something funny?" Fink croaked.

"Yes. What you said. If this were an impit tale, this would be the part where the feckless fool, desperate for the power to protect everything he loves, and full of pity for the poor outcast imp, agrees to a blood pact."

Fink hissed. "Suck yourself."

"How's it done?"

"Unless you're a contortionist, it can't be done. That's the point."

"I mean the blood-soul pact. How's it done?"

Fink's lip curled. "You've had your little laugh. I don't much like it."

"No, I want to know. How do you do the blood pact? Humor me. I'm feeling feckless."

Fink's eyes narrowed. He crawled to Harric's side, talons clicking on stone, and stood up to his full height, which was a little over Harric's belt. Reaching up, he extended one hooked claw and laid it to the middle of Harric's forehead, precisely the way he'd created Harric's oculus weeks before.

Harric flinched.

"You want to know or not?" Fink said.

"Sorry. Just reflex."

Harric stood still as the talon pricked and burned and then slashed downward. Wincing, he dabbed his fingers in a trickle of blood before it reached his eyes. "Ow."

The hedge of needles glittered in the moonlight. "No pain, no pact." Fink stepped back and drew the talon down his own bald forehead, opening a rift in the skin. No blood emerged. Beyond lay only what seemed a gap of deeper black that made the tiny hairs of Harric's body stand on end.

"Next, you dab your finger and place it on my wound." Fink's gaze grew intent, his childlike body tensed. "I pronounce the agreement. You remove your finger, and it's sealed."

"Formal contract language?"

"Of course."

Harric nodded. "All right. Your compulsion prevents you from giving me the nexus without a blood-soul pact. Let's try this." He dabbed a finger on his forehead and reached toward the imp.

"What are you doing, kid?" The imp stepped back.

"Just let me try something, and keep your mouth shut. Let's see if I can speak the words of the agreement."

Fink's eyes widened. He opened his mouth to speak, then closed it.

So it isn't a bluff. There really is a compulsion. And he really wants his freedom.

Fink glanced about as Harric extended his finger, but held still as he placed it across the ghastly nothing of Fink's wound.

"*I, Harric, make this pact in blood with Finkoklokos Marn, signifying our agreement to enter in equal partnership...*" Harric raised his eyebrows as if to ask, "How am I doing? That sound formal enough?" but Fink only stared back, eyes wide, tiny body petrified.

"A term," Fink croaked. "It has to have a term."

"*...till such time as either should decide to nullify the agreement...*"

Fink's black tongue flicked across his teeth. "And I take back the stone and oculus—" he blurted.

"*...at which time the stone and oculus shall return to Fink...*"

Harric raised his eyebrows again, asking, "Anything else?"

Fink's expression transformed, hairless eyebrows riding high on his leathery forehead. Whether it was an expression of hope, hunger, or fear, Harric couldn't tell. "And you'll feed me," Fink said.

"*What?* Are you a pet?"

"You have to feed me. Say it."

"This is a partnership of equals, remember? And I don't require *you* to feed *me*, so…"

Harric removed his finger, and a tiny curl of smoke rose from the wound on Fink's forehead. Fink's eyes widened and his face contorted in anger, then went slack as he ran a finger over the smooth, unbroken skin of his forehead. The wound was gone.

His voice came out in an almost breathless whisper. "That *worked?*"

Harric's heart drummed against his ribcage. "Check and see." He extended his hand, palm up, to receive the stone. Fink licked his teeth and extended his trembling hand over Harric's. When his talons opened freely, the stone dropped into Harric's grasp, and Fink's brows shot up in surprise.

Relief washed over Harric like cool water after long heat. He clasped the stone to his chest, and it felt cool and smooth and right in his hand. Triumph welled and he felt like shouting. He'd played it right. He'd trusted the three virtues of the jack, freed another slave, and won back the stone. And now Fink would teach him the ways of the Unseen to help preserve the Queen.

"I'm free," Fink whispered. He seemed to stare into nothing, though it was never easy to tell what he was looking at, since the white orbs had no pupils. Then he twitched, as if snapping out of a waking dream, and a sly grin split his face. He hacked out something that might have been a laugh and looked straight at Harric. "You *freed* me."

An unpleasant shiver slid up Harric's spine. "Feels good, doesn't it?"

Fink laid a finger across his mouth, as if to say, *Hush. It's our secret.* And vanished.

Harric looked up and down the empty ledge. "Fink?"

A breeze blew up the valley, bringing with it the smell of blood from the boulder field below. Through his oculus, he risked a glance up and down the ledge, but found no sign of Fink in the Unseen.

"See you tomorrow night?"

A cold, slimy river stone of doubt settled in Harric's stomach. Annoyed, he stood and shook it off. He'd freed an impit from its chains. It was a good thing because slavery was evil. He pondered his inexplicable discomfort as he walked back along the ledge, one hand trailing against the rough cliff face. Before he passed above the outer wall, he put his finger on the source of it: the problem was that he knew what it meant to free a person, but he knew almost nothing of the Unseen or Fink. So if he were honest with himself, he had to admit he had no idea what it meant to free an impit, and what he'd just done to save his own soul.

Even the Iberg do not embrace all magic unequivocally…even they forbid traffic with the Unseen Moon—calling it the Damned Moon, the Dead Moon, the Dark Moon, the Black Moon—and condemning to drowning those who carry its dark stone…

—From Notes from Abroad, by Sir Martis Wise

4

Black Moon Interlude

On a crag above the fort, in a grotto of stone hemmed in with trees so gnarled and silvered with age that they might be mistaken for a trio of Pit Crones, Fink groveled before his sisters. Wind hissed through the branches, and the trees creaked with mocking laughter.

"THE COUNCIL HAS CONSIDERED YOUR STATUS," said Zire, her voice a grating sub-bass like a slab sliding on bedrock. She manifested above him as a pillar of black smoke traced with threads of silent lightning. Missy and Sic swayed to either side, skeletal shapes coiled in shadow.

"THEY CONCLUDE THAT YOU FAILED TO PROTECT YOUR MASTER, GREMIO. THAT YOU ALLOWED HIM TO BE SLAIN, AND YOU ALLOWED HIS NEXUS STONE TO BE STOLEN."

"That isn't true!" Fink said.

"YOU WERE WATCHED."

"If I was watched, then someone knows Gremio slew himself! He disobeyed orders. He was to avoid combat, but he got greedy, thinking he'd capture the Kwendi secret for himself, and what'd he do? Got clobbered, that's what, and the nexus was stolen the second he dropped it—"

Sic moved, white bones in cloaking shadow. "Gremio is the second master to die in your charge." Her voice was a breath of wind among stones.

"I got the stone back! I got the kid."

Sic fell silent. Missy whispered something.

"WE KNOW THAT YOU INITIATED THE YOUNG THIEF," said Zire. "THE OCULUS YOU GAVE HIM WAS NOT SANCTIONED AND WOULD NEVER BE SANCTIONED. DO YOU CLAIM YOU HAVE SECURED HIM IN A BLOOD-SOUL PACT?"

"Of course I have," said Fink, tugging at his nose. "I have a responsibility for that nexus."

The lightning in Zire's smoke intensified. "FIRST AN UNSANCTIONED OCULUS, NOW AN UNSANCTIONED MASTER. YOUR NEW MASTER MUST BE DESTROYED. THEN WE WILL TAKE YOU TO THE BLACK CIRCLE TO BE CONSUMED."

Before Fink could speak, a clawed hand reached from the smoke to seize him, as if she'd consume him then and there.

He squeaked and hopped backward. "Are you insane? I just got an inside track to the secret of the Kwendi magic! You need me! Mother needs me!"

Zire halted her advance, and Missy turned her skeletal head to Zire. "He speaks truth," said Missy, in a voice like mournful owl.

"Missy understands," Fink said, gaining confidence in Zire's silence. "Initiating Harric means we're in. That oculus means he needs me and he has to trust me—so as long as *he's* with the Kwendi, *I'm* with the Kwendi. And you know where they're going? Nowhere less than the Kwendi's secret city. So don't speak to me of 'unsanctioned initiation.' That oculus is our key to the secret of the Kwendi magic."

The sisters stood in stunned silence. He had their attention now, because this matter went to the highest and most urgent of Mother's schemes—higher than anyone present ever reached.

Sic's voice slanted in from the side, an echo of wind in a chimney. "This is a high claim. Mother will know of it, and we will return with her will. If she grants your life, know this: if you fail to acquire the secret to the Kwendi magic, you will be consumed."

"I WILL CONSUME HIM MYSELF," said Zire.

"Right," said Fink. "Only, no, you won't, Zire, because when this is over, Mommy's going to reach down to weak, little, untrustworthy, demoted outcast Fink and lift him on high to sit at her side at the very center of her web. And she'll grant me a noble form—something real sleek, like a pillar of fire—and then I'll demote your sorry carcass for being an insufferable obstruction to greatness and send you scampering to fetch me treats."

Zire rose, expanding above him like a colossus rising from its knees, a juggernaut of billowing rage. Missy and Sic stepped back, and Fink's impit heart fluttered.

Now I've done it.

He timed his leap to avoid the blow, springing up with a desperate flap of his wings.

But in that moment, the three sisters vanished, and he saw his mistake. The air collapsed around the space they'd occupied. A deafening clap resounded in the grotto, and the wind of their vanishment plucked Fink sideways from the air and dashed him against a tree.

He crumpled among the stones as sisterly laughter echoed in his skull.

Spitting curses, he rose and tested his wings. He tested his limbs. Nothing broken.

As he fled the scene, he allowed himself a secret smile. The kid's trick had worked. He'd told them he had a new master, but in fact he was free, and his sisters couldn't tell the difference.

"Henceforth let it be known that those without fathers in Arkendia shall be as all free men and women, and no longer beholden to masters or to the belts that once marked them slaves."

— Royal Proclamation, issued by Her Majesty shortly after her ascension speech. Her advisors credited the proclamation as the impetus for assassination plots that year.

5

Blood & Fire

Harric lay on his back and stared at the beams above his bed. Predawn light paled the arrow slit high on the north wall of his chamber. It wasn't enough to see by, but it lent a ghostly pallor to the mineral streaks on the ceiling, which looked like toothy mouths or racks of spikes.

Nightmares had awoken him and he could not return to sleep. In them, the empty-eyed vulture spirit had pinned him to the stone slab atop the rubble, while others opened his belly and tried to divine the future from his entrails.

"What have you done?" they'd asked him, while Fink watched with milk-white eyes and a permanent grin.

Not for the first time since he'd left Abellia's tower, Harric missed the comfort of Spook's purr, and wished he'd thought to bring the little moon cat with him when they had rushed to the pass. He hoped the cat had found enough mice around the tower to stick around until Harric returned.

A sound roused him from his thoughts: a distant buzz or hum that just tickled the edge of his senses. His gaze drifted to the dim gray line of the arrow slit through which it had come, and he held his breath, listening. He'd just released the breath, wondering if he'd imagined the sound, when he heard it again, more clearly: the sustained note of a distant horn.

Leaping from his covers, he fumbled to light a candle. The horn could signal their rescue.

More than a week had passed since he'd sent message doves to the Queen, calling for the aid of the Blue Order. Arrival of the Blue Order would virtually guarantee Ambassador Brolli's return to his people, putting an end to their danger and their flight from Sir Bannus. Brolli would be safe in his homelands within a week.

Harric threw on his clothes, cinched up his bastard belt, and climbed the ledge below the arrow slit to peer out. The bloody light of the Mad Moon colored the pale mist in the valley. In it, he could just make out the shapes of the boulders in the rock moat below the slit. Nothing moved but faint waves of red-lit mist from the waterfall below. Beyond the moat lay sixty paces of stony road and then the mountain of rubble he'd buried it with. The rockfall loomed in the darkness like a second fortress, facing the outposts across a barren no-man's land.

Nothing stirred. No enemy. No Blue Order. Only the lonely roar of the waterfall.

Judging from the silence of the barracks, the watchmen were either still sleeping, or they were listening for another note. Then it sounded again, and this time, it was louder and clear enough to jar his memory and turn his blood to ice.

Harsh, guttural, unmistakable. It was Bannus's horn. The immortal returned.

The blast suddenly doubled in volume, as if Bannus blew it as he rounded the last bend in the road below the pass.

Harric slammed and latched the view port, then bolted from the room, grabbing his sword on the way out.

"Bannus! Sir Bannus returns!" he cried, as he sprinted through the barrack hall. "Wake up! Sir Bannus!"

He skidded to a halt at the doors to Willard's and Caris's quarters. Caris's door opened before he could pound on it. She met his look, eyes blinking back sleep. "Bannus?"

"Impossible…" someone mumbled behind them. A face peered from a bunk room Harric had passed.

"Listen!" said Harric. "His horn!"

Willard's door jerked opened. Red-shot eyes greeted them from behind rumpled mustachio, and a wave of stale alcohol and ragleaf

wafted forth. "I heard you," he said. The knight pointed decisively at
Caris. "You—bring your armor in here. We'll arm each other. You"—
he pointed to Harric—"get on the wall and be my eyes. I want a report
when I arrive."

Harric spun and rushed for the stairs, almost bowling over a half-
dressed guardsman who was crossing the hall on his way to the privy.
Already, the rattle of arrows in quivers echoed from the open door of
the armory. A call for spitfires and resin chests rang through the hall.

Harric sprinted up the stairs. Mounting the top stair, he belted on
his sword and pushed open the door to the parapet. The Mad Moon
glowered down, turning the battlements to blood. The guards from the
night watch appeared to have just risen to their feet, blinking sleep from
their eyes. Like Willard, they stank of the previous night's celebrations,
and Harric had to avoid a spot where vomit splattered the parapet.

He returned their grim nods and pressed himself flat behind the
cover of a crenellation to look east down the valley. Since the fort
stood atop the cliffs at the head of the narrow pass, it commanded an
expansive view. A mile down the valley, on the road cutting across its
northern wall, rode Sir Bannus on the immortal Phyros, Gygon. The
beast churned up the road at full gallop, massive hooves pounding
sparks from the stone. Sir Bannus held a horn to his lips and blew
until the harsh notes multiplied in the crags like the horns of twenty
Old Ones.

Answering horns erupted from the head of the valley, so loud and
clear it seemed the blowers must stand at the very gates of the fort.

Harric whirled to look at the road outside the gates. There the rubble
rose as high as the wall itself—seven fathoms, at least—but Harric could
see enough over its top to spy a few new tents on the road beyond the
rubble, just outside of bow range. The new tents had sprung up during
the night—some of Bannus's men, come late to the battle, and their
tardiness had spared them the disastrous fate of the others. Now a lord
in green armor stood at the foot of the camp blowing a silver horn to
welcome the return of his master, while a half-dozen servants moved in
and out of tents and wagons.

As Bannus neared the camp, he stopped blowing and began to roar.
Snatches of unintelligible howling reached Harric. *Vengeance* was a
word he caught. *Abominator*, his pet name for Willard, was another.

One of the night guards puked, and this time, Harric made it to the edge of the parapet.

Bannus appeared to be raging without pause, alternately howling and then blasting his horn. Even at a distance, he looked huge. As he thundered up to the lord and servants in the camp, he dwarfed them—a giant among men, and Gygon a giant among horses.

Captain Gren emerged from the stairwell behind Harric with a few other men, and stood between the guardsmen to look out over the rubble. A thin, rangy gray-hair, Gren was probably nearing his pension, wondering how his soft duty had turned to nightmare. "Gods leave us," he muttered. "We celebrated too soon."

"No, sir," said Farley, a boy of no more than twelve and by far the youngest in the garrison. "Harric sent messages to the Queen, sir. The Blue Order will be here before Bannus can clear the rubble. They'll ride up his tail any day. Maybe today."

"Maybe today." Harric gave the boy a reassuring nod, and hoped he was right.

Bannus did not stop at the green lord's camp. He cornered Gygon sharply toward the mountain of rubble that buried his army before the fort.

As he neared, Harric spied clear evidence of damage the immortal had sustained when he leapt from the cliff to avoid the rockfall: half the horns had been sheared from the crown on his great helm, his left pauldron had been torn away completely, and his breastplate and parts of the armor of one arm and leg had been smashed and raked of paint to leave bright stripes of raw steel. Whether Gygon had acquired any new scars from the fall was impossible to tell. Many lifetimes of Bannus cutting and drinking from the beast's veins had left his wine-black coat more a tangle of violet scars than original hide.

Sir Bannus disappeared from view behind the intervening rubble, but the thunder of Gygon's hooves grew louder.

Harric's heart raced. Could Gygon simply gallop over the rubble without breaking his pace? Could he leap from the summit through sixty paces of air to land on the parapet?

A clatter of boots and equipment rose from the stairs behind them, and Harric turned to see three guards in their leathers bringing armloads of spitfires to the parapet. Harric took one of the sturdy weapons as they passed them down the wall, and checked to see it had been freshly loaded. Some men looked at the weapons with horror in their eyes.

"Use fire against an immortal?" someone muttered.

"Moons, yes," said Harric, examining his weapon with appreciation. "What have we got to lose?" Each of the spitfires was as long as his arm, with a heavy, trumpeted pipe. They had thick stocks carved with the image of a fire-cone tree loaded with cones of explosive resin. He swung the pipe over the parapet and rested it there. Sighting down the pipe, he laid his finger on the lever of the flint wheel and aimed at the top of the rubble pile. He held his breath, trying not to let the long pipe shake.

"What's happening?" said a new arrival.

"Watch and see," said Captain Gren. "Ready the spitfires, and if Bannus tops that rubble, let fly."

"Are you crazy?" It was Lane, a beefy-faced guard that Harric had noted on the previous night seemed to regard himself the true captain of the fort. "You don't use fire against an immortal. We need bows."

"I said spitfires, didn't I?" Gren snapped. "Fire is the only thing an immortal respects. Grab one and point it, and that's an order. I aim to show him we aren't afraid to use our resin."

A scent of fresh urine wafted to Harric. Farley had flattened himself against the parapet beside him, and the boy was pale as a snow hen, eyes wide as eggs. He'd leaned his spitfire leaned on the parapet.

"If you're not going to fire that," Harric said, "you can hand it to me when I've fired."

Farley nodded and swallowed.

Pale as ghosts, the men spread along the wall, muttering about the immortal commandment against fire. Two more men arrived with bows and quivers, and Harric noted that when Captain Gren wasn't looking, Lane and one or two others set their spitfires aside to take up bows.

Harric counted ten men, the full garrison. Such a small force was never intended for siege; they were simply the Queen's doormen for the pass, their role to keep petty thieves from Her Majesty's fire-cone groves. Ten men couldn't hold the place against a band of seasoned warriors, much less immortal ones. And though Harric could use the witch-stone to enter the Unseen and outflank the enemy again, it would do little good, for there were no more resin charges set in the crags above the road, and no suitable cracks to host a new resin charge. That had been a one-time trick.

Movement at the summit of the rubble caught Harric's attention. He looked down the pipe of the spitfire, expecting Bannus to bound over the top of the rubble. But it was Bannus's back in the distance, beyond the rock. The immortal was riding back to the green lord's camp.

Harric relaxed and let out his held breath.

In a motion almost too quick to see, Gygon whirled and Bannus flung a flashing weapon over the rockfall. Harric barely had time to duck before it hissed over his head and crashed in the courtyard behind him. A new hole yawned in the cookhouse roof, from which fragments of slate shingles skittered and clattered to the yard.

"Gods leave us," Farley said. He crouched further down, eyes white with fear.

Harric's heart thumped in his ears. Very carefully, he peeked over the wall to see Bannus riding back to the green lord's camp. Well. It appeared Gygon could not fly up mountains. That was a blessing. And it appeared Bannus had not forgotten his favorite bastard.

Lucky me.

When Bannus reached the green knight's camp, he lifted the shattered great helm from his head and handed it down to a servant. The sound of his booming voice drifted to them across the rubble, words lost in the distance. Servants scurried. The green lord mounted his warhorse, and four of the servants scrambled to load a donkey with packs.

"What's he up to?" Captain Gren muttered.

Several men on the wall called out and pointed at something moving at the top of the rubble pile. A pair of servants peeped over top and ducked back down. From behind the cover of a huge slab at the crest of the rubble, the servants erected a tall white pole. The pole was as long as a lance and supported at its top what looked like a round white tray of wicker, about the size of a warrior's shield. When fully erect, the tray would face the sky, as if to catch rain. The captain cursed. When the pole stood upright, contents of the tray became visible: three blackheart dove decoys, variously roosting, head under wing, or feeding with head down.

"A dove trap," the captain muttered. "They aim to intercept any messages meant for us."

Harric chewed his lip. Could such a trap catch the doves he had sent to the Queen? If his doves had been intercepted, then the Blue Order knew nothing of their danger, and there would be no rescue. A pit of doubt opened beneath his stomach as he glanced back at the ruined dove tower beside the gatehouse. Wisps of white smoke still rose from parts of its blackened skeleton. All the doves had perished in that fire, so they could send no more messages to the Queen.

Harric brought his spitfire to his shoulder, sighted the dove trap, and squeezed the lever.

The flint wheel sparked and the spitfire bucked, coughing out a resin wad that screamed across the air like a comet. The fireball corkscrewed wildly and missed the dove trap to disappear behind the rubble pile.

Several of the fort guards cried out in dismay, despite the captain's orders.

"You know what immortals do to those who use fire against them?" Farley said. "The—they say—"

Harric handed the smoking spitfire to Farley and picked up the boy's unused weapon. "Load that, will you?" A glance at Captain Gren confirmed the old guard merely watched, his face unreadable.

"You damn us all, bastard!" Lane said.

"We smashed his army last night," Harric said. "You think we aren't damned already? Every one of us witnessed it. You think he'll let anyone live who witnessed his defeat?" Harric sighted the dove trap again and squeezed the lever. The spitfire bucked like a mule, but its wad sped truer than the first, only dipping right before it hit. The wad clipped the underside of the tray, splashing it with fire and showering burning resin below.

"Yes!" Harric shouted.

Behind the trap, the servants scrambled from cover. One of them tore off a burning shirt. Harric noted shock on their faces, and imagined they hadn't expected anyone to dare use fire in the presence of Sir Bannus. As the servants wrestled the trap from its moorings, a shower of burning resin shook loose and rained upon them, prompting curses and yelps. They could replace the trap, but good decoys would be hard to find. And burning resin sent an important message: *We will use our spitfires, immortal prohibitions be damned.*

Several guards on the parapet cheered, but Lane still glowered. The man beside him, a pale-haired sack of bones with sunken eyes, muttered something to Lane.

"Pass guard!" Gren called down the battlements. "Show Bannus we have plenty more resin where that came from!"

A handful of spitfires coughed and belched out flaming comets that sizzled across the air and splashed upon the rubble or soared over the trap. Loopy smoke trails hung in the air between the rockfall and the fort. By then, the dove trap blazed like a torch, and the servants lowered it out of sight behind the rubble.

The captain gave Harric a grim nod. To the guardsmen, he shouted, "Ream your pipes and reload!"

When Sir Bannus finally mounted Gygon and rode back from the lord's camp, the top of the rockfall flickered and smoldered with splashes of burning resin. Behind Bannus rode the green lord and several servants with a laden donkey.

"Kinda small army, ain't it?" said a soldier to Harric's left.

Gallows laughter among some of the guards.

"What do you think Bannus is doing?" Farley whispered.

"We'll know soon enough," said Gren. "Stand ready."

"The bastard's sealed our doom," Lane whispered.

"Don't be a fool," Gren snapped. "You'd be dead already if it weren't for him last night."

A warm hand squeezed Harric's shoulder from behind. "What was that noise?" Ambassador Brolli's strange accent turned heads up and down the line. The Kwendi looked up at Harric through dark daylids that covered his nocturnal eyes like bulbous goggles.

"You missed all the fun," Harric said.

Farley, who stood to Harric's right, took a step back and made the sign of the heart in the air between them. Though the men had seen the ambassador the night before, they evidently hadn't acclimated to his strange appearance or the fact that his people used magic.

Captain Gren slapped the back of Farley's head. "Mind your manners." He nodded a greeting to Brolli. "Ill winds blow this morning, ambassador."

"Very *loud* winds, Captain Gren," said Brolli. "Bannus's horn, yes?"

Gren nodded.

"Did you see Willard and Caris down below?" Harric asked Brolli.

"She almost finish to arm him. He does not wish to come in his bed shirt."

Harric noted from the corner of his eye that Farley still stared at Brolli. The boy appeared to struggle with the fact that the Kwendi's long arms, powerful torso, and dwarfish legs marked him as not only of foreign race, but of entirely inhuman stock. The handlike feet didn't help. Nor did the bug-eyed "daylids." Farley probably thought the domed lenses were the Kwendi's actual eyes, like he was part insect.

As Brolli knuckle-walked between them to lean against the parapet, Farley flinched away.

Brolli lay his bandolier of hurling-globes at his feet, and the globes emitted a low rattle like the sound of river stones knocking together.

"Are those— Is that—?" Farley stared at the bandolier and stumbled back another step.

"Magic," said Brolli, his eyes on Sir Bannus as the immortal rode toward them and disappeared from view behind the top of the rubble. Brolli flipped the daylids up, as if for a clearer view, but glanced to the young guard instead. Gold, owlish eyes shone like coins. "Want to touch the magic?"

Harric suppressed a smile. Leave it to Brolli to tease in a grim situation. But Harric could see there was some real fear in the boy, who shook his head vigorously. Harric leaned closer to Farley. "Brolli saved my life once," he confided. "Twice, actually. Once with magic. As a good Arkendian, I hate magic just as much as you"—he paused, while Brolli recovered from a fit of spontaneous coughing—"but I have to tell you, I was grateful he used it that day. And his people will be important allies for the Queen. Maybe they can save her, too."

Brolli flashed Farley a feral grin, displaying thick, pointed canines. "I only save him so I can eat him later."

Farley let out a laugh. He looked at Brolli out of the side of his eye.

"He's kidding," Harric said.

"I know," said Farley.

"What is that word, kidding?" said Brolli. "You mean kids are my favorite food? Yes."

The echo of Gygon's hooves grew still, and Captain Gren called for silence on the parapet. All up and down the line, men finished reaming their spitfires and laid them across the parapet, awaiting orders. Brolli's hand slipped into his satchel and partly emerged with what looked like an apple-sized globe of glittering witch-silver.

Farley's eyes widened and all color drained from his cheeks, but he was not looking at Brolli's magical hurler—he was looking at the rubble. "Gods leave us," he whispered, as Sir Bannus rose up on the massive slab at its summit—the same slab, Harric realized, where the vulture spirits had fed the night before.

The immortal stood at a level with the parapet, a colossus in wine-black armor bearing in one hand a Phyros sword too heavy for any mortal.

Violet eyes burned across the gap, and Harric's heart jolted in his chest. His breaths grew short and rapid. *Too close. Too close.*

Even from sixty paces, it was clear Sir Bannus would tower over the men on the wall. He had to be four hands taller and three times heavier than the biggest mortal men. But any similarity stopped there. His youthful skin, colored deep blue by the Blood of the Phyros in his veins, had been disfigured by madness, ritual, and the wounds of many lifetimes of battle. Ropy scars so distorted his face that it seemed less visage and more a nest of violet serpents.

But what so jolted Harric's heart was the aura of intensity to the immortal—a bunched and coiled power, spring-tight, held on the brink of explosion in every fiber of nerve and muscle. This was the force that sent axes blurring across gulfs with deadly accuracy. What mortal could stop such a creature, half god, half monster? If Bannus could leap the gap between rubble and parapet, he'd slaughter them all before anyone blinked.

Harric knew from the ballads that nothing short of decapitation or intense fire could kill an immortal, but if an immortal could move with such speed, it was equally clear that nothing short of another immortal could kill one. And the small fires of their spitfires—though capable of bringing lasting pain—could only give an Old One pause, or drive him into a rage.

Harric's weapon shook horribly. His hand seemed paralyzed. He could not bring himself to lay his finger on the lever to spark the flint wheel.

"We're dead men," someone murmured.

Lane's black eyes bored into Harric. "The bastard's work. First he brings Bannus to our door step, next he lights up a spitfire. Gonna save us again, bastard?"

Bannus raised his iron horn and let loose with a resounding blast, then another, and another until the crags echoed with discord. Slowly, he lowered the horn and scanned the battlements, as if memorizing every face there. It felt to Harric like the monster stared first at him, and while he held Harric's gaze, Harric's heart fluttered like a bird in a cage.

To Harric, it seemed he heard the immortal's voice at his ear. *Thou, bastard, art mine. I shall make of you an immortal toy. I shall prepare a special place for you.*

Henceforth, let there be no Blood Color but red in Arkendia,
for that is the color in the veins of all true subjects. Likewise, let
my people wear what colors they will and be no longer chained
to the birth hues of their fathers.

—Royal Proclamation, sporadically adopted on the
East Isle, suppressed on the West Isle

6

Bastard Blame

Harric tore his gaze from the immortal and gulped at the air, unaware his breath had stopped. Sweat slicked his forehead. One by one, men looked away from Bannus. Those who met his eyes grew pale and trembled.

A hundred heartbeats passed. Two hundred.

When the immortal's voice boomed, Harric jumped. When he peered from behind the battlement, the immortal stood exactly as he had before.

"Listen carefully, men of the fort," Bannus bellowed. His voice was the rattle of gravel in a bass drum. "This I promise—that none of you shall die."

Murmurs and glances among the guardsmen. Hope flickered in a few naïve eyes.

"You shall not die, fort men, for you dared use fire against me. Know you not the example of Bright Castle, when Lady Bright so dared? Lady Bright did not die, nor did her household, for they live yet in my tower. I say you shall not die, for I shall use the Blood to keep you alive as I remove all bones but your skull. Thus shall you live, a sloven gut bag, begging for death, and I shall display you from high poles across the kingdom. Your boneless toes I raise, and your gibbering heads shall hang low, and thus you shall live as a sign to all who defy the Old Ones."

Farley whimpered, and someone on the parapet snapped, "Hold your noise or go below."

Bannus did not speak again until his booming echoes died and the waterfall reasserted its roar. And then one word boomed across the gap.

"Unless…"

"Gods leave us!" Farley said.

"Unless you deliver the Abominator to me. Him you call Willard, and his mewling bastard. Cast them from your walls and I shall spare you."

A grim laugh from Willard echoed up the stairwell behind them. The old knight climbed the stair with the aid of his great-sword, Belle. His blackened armor—the badge of an outcast—creaked with every step. Caris followed, her cobalt armor looking just as black in the dim light before dawn. She rested a hand on her sword, eyes like a mountain lion's, confronting each guard as if to say, *Touch Willard, and you'll be dead before you blink.*

"He'll make gut bags of you no matter what you do," said Willard. "He can't forgive the humiliation you served him last night. He can't allow you to live."

"None here heed you, Sir Bannus," Gren shouted. Brave as he was for saying it, his voice came out as a kind of treble crowing. "We serve the Queen to the last man. And we have more rock to gift you, should you threaten again."

"I think not." Sir Bannus's laugh was the sound of rocks shaken in a pot helm. "Yet you are not the only ones with resin." Bannus raised one plated arm, and a moment later, the air behind him flashed. Thunder crashed between the crags, and boulders at the edge of the rubble tumbled into the void. A plume of white smoke swallowed the immortal as the displaced boulders crashed below and the sounds resounded in the valley.

Nervous tension swept the line of guards. With resin charges, Bannus could clear a path along the edge in a matter of days.

When the smoke cleared, Sir Bannus still stood on the slab.

Using his sword as a crutch, Willard climbed the last stair and met the gaze of his ancient nemesis across the gap. He stood taller than everyone else on the parapet. Even taller than Caris. Since he'd stopped taking the Blood, he'd lost the outrageous girth and musculature of an immortal, but his huge frame remained as a mark of previous immortality.

Sir Bannus leveled an armored finger at Willard, and the scars of his ruined face contorted. "The Abominator whispers lies to you. Deliver him, or live a fate worse than death."

"Blue gods, Bannus," said Willard. "How many times have I heard that speech? They sing ballads of the last fool who fell for it, and that was two hundred years past. Does it not make you weary? Do you not tire of this life?"

"Ten castles to the man who brings me that tongue!" Bannus roared.

"Please don't anger him, sir," Farley whispered. "If he can climb that rubble, he can climb these walls—and I—" Farley swallowed, eyes bright with tears.

Willard did not take his eye off Bannus. He gave a brief smile to show he'd heard the boy. "Bannus won't attack, son," he said, loud enough for it to carry across the gap to Bannus. "He is too proud. Could he climb down? Certainly. Could he jump and possibly scale these walls? He might. But *you* give him pause, brave boy. *Fire* gives him pause. I know it well, for the Blood does not heal burns the way it heals other wounds. It may scar over, but the pain never fades. The fire lives unabated in the flesh. And despite his looks, Bannus is no fool. He knows this fort guards the Queen's fire-cone groves. He knows it contains more fire-cone resin than anywhere else short of her armory, and that if he attacks alone, he will burn."

Bannus threw back his head and laughed. "I fear no fire. Already I bear more burns than any mortal could endure. See!" He stooped and, with a gauntleted finger, dabbed up a wad of flickering resin from the stone at his feet. He stood, yellow teeth bared in a grin, and smeared the liquid fire on his mangled cheek.

At sixty paces, Harric heard it sizzle.

"Your time is short, fort men," said Bannus. "Perhaps you believe the Blue Order knows of your plight. Perhaps you believe they are coming. They do not know. Perhaps you believe my army is lost. There again you deceive yourselves, for true men flock to my banner each day. Scores now ride to join me, as do my immortal brothers. I prophesy here and now that in three days, when our resin has cleared this rubble, I shall have my three dozen and they shall overrun your feeble defense. Yet it need not be so, if you deliver the Abominator and his bastard. That is your only rescue. I grant you till midnight."

The green lord climbed onto the slab behind Bannus, sending rock chips clattering into the rubble. Bannus's head snapped toward the commotion, and something in his manner suggested to Harric he was displeased with the lord's unplanned arrival. The lord advanced to stand beside the immortal and, without so much as a nod to acknowledge Sir Bannus, he faced the fort across the gap.

"Sir Willard, I challenge thee to a duel!" the lord yelled. "I throw down my gauntlet!"

The back of Bannus's armored hand clapped the lord across the face and sent him somersaulting backward from the slab to disappear onto the rubble pile.

A murmur of surprise rippled through the men on the wall. Harric stared after the green lord at first in shock at the man's folly, and then in chilling recognition: Willard's night-hex had struck the lord, as it had once struck Harric. What else could account for such fatal folly? He shuddered to recall how it had invaded his mind— and Caris's, too—in Gallows Ferry with a powerful sense of luck and power and righteous invulnerability. It had been intoxicating. It had driven them to folly beyond measure, as it had this green lord, and it had nearly cost them their lives.

"See, fort men," Bannus roared. "This is what comes of keeping Sir Willard the Cursed, Sir Willard the Hexed. And his hex touches all. It will touch one of you next. Why else do you suppose the bitch queen banished him? Why else do you suppose he cannot keep a squire? Death and folly follow him like attendant wolves and lay waste to the mortals around him. But it cannot touch me. You will be wise to hand him to me and be rid of it. Midnight!" Two more blasts shook the air behind him and trembled the wall. Boulders as big as horses flew from the rubble into the well of the waterfall. Again, smoke enveloped the rubble, but this time when it cleared, Sir Bannus was gone.

Silence reigned on the parapet as echoes of the blast faded.

Caris glared up and down the line of guards, hand on her sword in case any had the idea of attempting Bannus's offer. None seemed eager to test a fully armored horse-touched warrior maiden, and Harric felt a flush of pride and admiration for her. Predictably, the moment she turned her back, Lane gave Harric a long stare.

Captain Gren shoved Lane hard against the parapet, knocking his head against the stone. His stare broken, Lane blinked in stunned surprise.

"You are not in charge here," said Gren, pinning Lane to the wall. "And I won't let you play your poisonous little games today. Not when our lives are at stake. So I tell you this once: you take orders, or I lock you up. Your choice. And right now, I order you to shut up and do exactly as I say. What is your choice?"

Lane glared at Harric over Gren's shoulder, hatred in his eyes. Hatred of bastards, Harric judged. He had seen it often enough to recognize it and know it meant sympathy with the Old Ways. Harric flipped him the sign of the cob.

"Follow orders, sir," said Lane, eyes still on Harric.

Gren gave him another violent shake. "You'd better."

"We know of your hex, here, Sir Willard," said Gren, turning away from Lane. "And it makes no difference to us. Your service to the Queen outweighs it."

"I thank you, captain." Willard's eyes lingered on Lane until Lane turned away and left the parapet. "But Bannus is correct: we got lucky today when it struck one of our enemies. It could strike you next, or Harric, or anyone else. That is why I do not intend to burden you with my presence any longer than necessary."

Gren nodded, and Harric thought he saw a glimmer of relief behind his eyes. The effects of Willard's hex were well enough documented— and exaggerated—in a hundred Sir Willard ballads to put a healthy doubt in anyone. As if seeking a change of subject, Gren smiled at Harric and laid a warm hand on his shoulder. "Your man here sent a spitfire wad right into their dove trap, Sir Willard. Burned it good."

Willard grunted his approval but pursed his brow. "They had a dove trap?"

"They did," said the captain. "Would have caught any message the Queen sent back to us here, but that hardly matters. What matters is the birds Harric sent to the Queen and Blue Order."

Willard squinted out over the rubble. "It troubles me that Bannus said there would be no Blue Order. *Perhaps you think the Blue Order knows of your plight,* he said. But we gave him no reason to think we expected the Order."

"They'll be here any day now," said Farley. "Just like captain said."

As if to counterpoint their conversation, something flew up from behind the rubble and soared toward them like a stone from a catapult. A cry went up from some of the men, and everyone crouched behind the crenellations. The missile was only the size of Harric's head, but it wasn't a head, and it wasn't a stone—or at least it wasn't all stone—for feathers jutted from the missile at ragged angles. The feathers whistled weakly as it spun past and crashed through the roof of the mess hall behind them.

"Ha! Missed!" Farley said.

As the men rose from their crouches, a feather lifted on a breeze beside the hole in the roof and drifted away. "Don't think he was trying to hit us, Farley." Harric caught Willard's eye, and the old knight cursed under his breath. Someone had lashed a bird or two to a stone in order to give it enough weight for Sir Bannus to throw.

And it didn't take much imagination to guess which birds they must be.

During the Great Betrayal—which the betrayers call the Cleansing—
Sir Gregan led the Blue Order against the Old Ones...to slay or
drive them back to the West Isle, whence they came. Yet it was
Sir Willard—youngest of the Blue Order, and most fervent in his
hatred—who slew more of the Old Ones and their Phyros than the
rest of his order combined. More than any other, therefore, merits he
the title of "Abominator," and more deserves eternal suffering when
the Old Ones return...

—From The Betrayal of the Old Ones, First Herald Milbred of Pelion

7

The Hunted & The Abandoned

The broken bodies of two doves lay on a mess hall table before Harric. Despite it being a broad, high-ceilinged room, the space felt crowded as Willard, Brolli, Caris, and a half-dozen guards leaned in to watch him search the birds for the anklets that held tiny written messages. Someone had lit tallow candles and set them on the table, but the tallow smoked badly, giving the place an atmosphere like some card dens Harric had known. The birds wore no anklets, of course, for whoever had captured them had removed the messages and read them; he found tiny ends jutting from their beaks like lolling tongues. As he drew them carefully out, it felt like drawing cards in a high-stakes game he knew the dealer had rigged.

Captain Gren spoke, his voice low and reverent of the tension in the room, but his tone full of command. "Sir Bannus has resin charges. We'll pile stones inside the gate and inside the postern door in case his men try to blast them. Tonight we double the watch."

Farley, who now understood what was at stake in the birds on the table, licked his pale lips, his gaze glued to Harric.

As Harric smoothed the crumpled ribbons of parchment, the men began to fall silent. And when he spread them between his hands and held them flat on the table so all could read them, only the sound of the falls sifted in through the windows. The messages were identical, and he read them aloud. "*Willard, Brolli in danger. Sir Bannus. Send Blue Order.*" He released the rest of his breath in a falling sigh. "It's my handwriting."

A collective murmur, like a groan, rippled through the room.

The previous night's celebration seemed now hollow and foolish. So much hope had resided in those messages to the Queen. Lane muttered something to his pale-haired companion with the sunken eyes. Harric saw the word "bastard" clearly on his lips. Sunken Eyes glared daggers of blame, as if it were Harric's fault the doves hadn't made it, and the dove master, Garon, sent a particularly dark look at Harric. That surprised him. Could the man resent him for sending his doves off without permission, even though it might have saved them all?

The danger sense in every Arkendian bastard prickled up Harric's spine. Those three would be trouble. From that moment on, he would not to walk alone until he'd left the outpost.

Willard drew so forcefully on his ragleaf that the coal crackled at Harric's ear, returning his attention to the useless messages.

"I'm sorry, sir," Harric said.

"Don't be. Damned smart of you to send those messages in the first place."

At the sound of the knight's voice, the murmurs fell silent, and all eyes fell on Willard. Everything had changed, and everyone knew it. Without the aid of the Blue Order, the fort would inevitably fall. It was just a matter of time. Yet some would have to hold it against Bannus for as long as possible while Willard escaped with Brolli. The guardsmen did not know the particulars of their mission, but they knew that the fate of the kingdom very likely depended on Brolli recommending a peace treaty to his people, and if anything happened to him, the result might well be a war that would weaken the kingdom and its resistance to the return of the Old Ones. And if the Old Ones took the throne, they knew many more would die and all would suffer.

But staying at the fort would be suicide, and everyone knew that, too.

Willard sighed a cloud of ragleaf through his nose into his enormous mustachio, and the whiskers fumed as he took another crackling pull. The guardsmen shifted on their feet, and in the smoky candlelight, the white edges of their eyes flashed and flicked as they exchanged glances.

"Last night, you men displayed a bravery other men of this age can only dream of," said Willard. The old knight's eyes still stared through the table, but his voice resonated with pride and conviction. "That kind of bravery is only sung in the ballads of the Cleansing."

He raised his eyes and stood to his full height, towering above them like a pillar in the hall. In full armor, it wasn't hard to imagine the immortal Willard of legend—huge, strong, and steel sharp. "There is no greater test to a man than defying an Old One," he said, scanning their faces, "unless it be to defy the worst of the Old Ones, Sir Bannus. And you've done that. Not since the days of our Queen's grandfather during the Cleansing could a monarch claim such subjects as you. And no knight living today can claim what you did last night."

As he spoke, his gray eyes met the gaze of each guard in the room. Harric watched as each man returned the look and in turn seemed to grow taller, too, as if meeting Willard's eye lent them power. In the faces of the guards, Harric thought he saw the same awe he felt to be so near the hero who had once driven Bannus from the land.

"Yet you'd be fools if you weren't terrified," said Willard. "In ten lifetimes, I never met a foe more worthy of terror than Bannus. He is the very monster you know from the ballads, and nothing a balladeer could devise could be worse than the truth. He has infused Krato's Blood in his veins for so long that there is nothing left of his humanity."

"So what do we do now?" said a middle-aged guard with blinking eyes and a bulbous drinker's nose. His voice sounded reedy and tremulous after Willard's baritone. "We thought the Blue Order was coming to rescue us. They ain't. So we can go with you, can't we?"

Lane muttered, "We wish," but Captain Gren cut in before others could voice their fears.

"Abandon the fort?" said Gren, glaring at Lane. "After last night's stand, you'd let Bannus take it without a fight? No. We stay and guard Sir Willard's back."

The men traded silent glances, and the middle-aged guard stared down at his hands. "No point in bravery if you're dead," he said. "And I ain't the only one as thinks so."

"And you're right about that," said Willard. "Nor would I ask you to die in a hopeless stand. It would be a waste of rare men. What I ask is that you maintain the appearance of resistance, so Bannus must spend the time necessary to clear the road for his men to prepare a proper siege attack, which ought to take days. But when night falls on a day in which his work is nearly done, that night, you must deprive him of his prize and slip away. Flee into the wilderness, and then luck be with you. That stratagem will provide us with precious days of head start."

"To take the ambassador to the Queen," said Farley, who listened intently to every word.

Willard nodded, acknowledging the boy, but not correcting his assumption. "Much depends upon the Queen's discussions with the ambassador. And your bravery will make the peace possible."

Harric flicked his gaze to Brolli, half expecting the Kwendi to correct Willard's omission and tell the men their true objective—indeed, their opposite objective—not to take Brolli south to the Queen, but north to his people beyond the Godswall. For Brolli had already met with the Queen, and now it remained only for him to present Her Majesty's proposal of a treaty to his people.

To Harric's surprise and relief, the Kwendi let it stand. Perhaps Brolli reasoned, as Harric did (and presumably Willard), that the garrison was no less safe believing Willard and company were headed south, whereas Willard and Brolli were much safer if they did. For if any of the garrison should desert or be captured, they could only pass false information to Bannus.

"Big Thom and Glenn, you're on wall duty," Gren said. "I want all spitfires loaded and resting at ten-foot intervals upon the battlements, and shots fired at anything that moves around that rubble pile. Weaver and Moy, set up a temporary stable on the road up the pass, well out of sight and sound of the wall. Barwell can help muffle their hooves with cone sacks, and walk them up. We'll keep the horses there until the day we flee."

As Gren allotted duties, Willard watched with approval. "You few stood fast when you saw that monster howling at your gate," he said. "And now, by holding it again, you preserve all that my brothers in the Blue Order worked for in the Cleansing; you preserve your queen and country, and you preserve your loved ones and their freedom." Willard raised his fist before his chest in a Blue Order salute, and the men copied it, eyes gleaming. He held the salute for several long heartbeats, then released it.

"To your duties," said Gren. "At breakfast, I assign tasks for the rest."

The gathering broke, but the spell of purpose and inspiration did not. Harric could see it in the eyes of the guards. Once worried about their survival, they now saw themselves as part of something greater than all of them. He wouldn't be surprised if some volunteered to stay and fight to the end. Harric himself looked at Willard with new appreciation. It was hard to imagine this was the same broken-down ex-immortal, ex-champion with whom he'd endured a month of suffering and flight. And it made him feel petty and childish for his judgments back then.

When the garrison had dispersed, Brolli regarded Willard with an expression of curiosity. "Who is this man who spoke just now?"

Willard gave him a wry smile as he puffed his neglected roll of ragleaf back to life. "My best comes out in crisis. Now we must pack and depart. Harric, Caris, prepare the horses."

"You forget, I think," said Brolli, a light of mischief in his eye, "the priest Kogan still sleeps."

Willard didn't roll his eyes, but they drifted briefly upward. "He celebrated long enough to sleep a week. We'll leave him here with the men of the fort. It will be excellent for their morale."

"I must object, Sir Willard," said Brolli. "It is because he helped us that he is hunted."

Willard frowned. "You realize what a burden he is? He hates magic more than anyone in Arkendia, Brolli. If you think I frown on magic, consider that it's his *religion* to hate it. He can barely look on you without condemning you along with your people. The good father sees no gray."

"That changes nothing of our responsibility."

Willard sighed. "If we can wake him, and he so chooses, he may come. But I'll ask he remain at the fort as a boon to the men here. They have beer, which should help to that end. But if he insists on joining us, so be it. Yet I predict trouble. Harric, see if you can wake the father. Tell him to find me. Then help Caris with the horses."

Harric nodded, but his mind was only half on the knight's orders;

Caris still hadn't looked his direction all morning, and that boded ill. At the very least, it meant a laborious conversation in his future.

"Girl, I'll need you to prepare Molly's breakfast," Willard said. "Hit the kitchens. Sergeant Lane slaughtered a goat and has the blood and bone meal ready."

As Caris set out for the kitchens, Harric stepped beside her and gave her a warm smile. "Morning, Caris."

She stopped short as if startled out of deep thought. Without looking up, she pressed her lips together in a kind of grimace and stalked past. She might have tried to hide it, but she was tugging at the ring again.

Moons, he hated that ring. It made her so miserable.

Knowing Willard would bark if he followed her without first gathering his things or waking Father Kogan, he suppressed the urge, and let her go. Instead, he hurried into his quarters, grabbed up his saddlebags, and jogged off to find the priest.

He found the giant man flopped in the remains of the dove tower, snoring like a hedge boar and wallowing in ash. Several timbers of the collapsed roof smoldered beside him. Perhaps there had still been a cozy fire there when he'd chosen that spot to sleep. Unfortunately, the heavy smell of smoke did little to mask the stink of the priest's odor. Had the man never bathed? He certainly hadn't washed the woolen rugs of his smothercoat, which reeked of mildew like something buried under a haystack over winter.

"Get up, Father Kogan." Harric kicked at the upturned soles of the huge man's boots. No response. The snoring continued. He kicked again, harder. "Father!"

"You want to use this, Master Harric?"

Harric looked to see Farley standing behind him with the bucket of water the watchmen used for drinking. Harric grinned and beckoned Farley over. "Go ahead," he told the boy, "but be quick."

Farley's eyes widened, and he shook his head. He set the bucket at his feet and scampered back a few paces. "No, sir. You do it."

"Then get ready to run," Harric said, as he retrieved the bucket and walked back to the snoring giant, "because I'm going to blame it on you."

"You wouldn't!" Farley squeaked with delight.

"No. I wouldn't. But I'm going to run, too, and I don't want you in my way."

Harric made sure his escape route was free of impediments, then sloshed the water in the priest's hairy face.

Kogan's roar of indignation must have been heard across the valley. By the time he cleared his eyes of water and matted hair, Harric and Farley stood twenty paces hence, poised to retreat farther, if necessary.

"Sir Willard sent us to wake you," Harric called. "The knight is leaving, and wishes for you to see him in the mess hall. You may join him on the road, if you wish, or remain here with the beer kegs."

The priest spat water and strings of beard from his mouth. Squinting against the predawn gray as if it were noonday sun, he sputtered, "If daylight didn't pound my brains, I'd wring your skinny necks!"

"Don't blame the messengers, father," said Farley. "Blame Willard. But hurry, 'cause he's leaving."

Harric lingered at the top of the stairwell and watched the priest rub his temples. Farley, who had scampered down the stairs, climbed back up and peered from around Harric.

As the priest sat up, water dribbled from his beard into his lap. His small brown eyes found Harric and Farley.

"Said I'd come, didn't I?" he growled.

"You missed a show of Willard's hex this morning," said Harric.

The priest's brow furrowed.

"Hit a green lord, too," said Farley. "Made him act the fool, and Bannus bopped him."

Kogan's gaze moved from the boy to Harric as if for confirmation. Harric nodded, and Kogan said, "Anyone else touched?"

"No one on the wall," said Harric.

"Got lucky, then. I seen that hex do worse. Might've had you throwing yourselfs from the wall, thinking to challenge Bannus or join him." Kogan looked up at the east ridge, where the sun paled the sky with approaching dawn. "Till the sun crests the hill, keep clear of Willard. He don't mean it, but he can't control it. Probably won't strike again."

"How do you know?" said Harric. "When does it strike? It struck me once, the first time I met him, back in the market at Gallows Ferry. But I wasn't bothering him, just talking."

Kogan made an effort at smoothing the great tangles of hair and braids away from his forehead, without success. "Mostly hits when he's in danger."

"Or pretty ladies," said Farley. "It's always pretty ladies in the ballads."

A silent laugh shook Kogan's shoulder and belly. "And what pretty lady ain't danger? Just stay away if you can," he said. "Steer clear till sunup."

The Blood Tooth is singular to adult Phyros mares. Stallions do not have them. Composed of ivory and shaped much like a boar's tusk, the tooth hangs from the upper jaw on either the left or the right side, like a single fang. In combat, it is a formidable weapon, but its primary purpose appears to be the blooding of their offspring.

—From *Notes on the Sacred Isle,* Sir Gregan Lamour

8

Tainted Blood & Magic

Caris found Lane at the butcher's block in the middle of the kitchen, quartering a freshly skinned goat. The sergeant glanced up when she entered, and his lip curled in distaste. He slammed the cleaver down, severing a joint. "Buckets on the floor." He gestured with the bloody blade to a pair of wooden buckets beside the door, and resumed parting joints and sliding the bits aside—chunk! scrape—and scowling between blows.

Caris dropped the sack of oats from her shoulder to the table, and set the buckets beside it to mix the meal. The stink of warm blood and bone meal filled her nostrils.

"Shame to feed a holy Phyros on the blood of goats." Lane spat in the straw. "Some would say sacrilege." Caris emptied the oats into the bloody meal. "Rightly done, it's the blood of virgins and bastards."

Caris dropped the empty sacking on the table and picked up a heavy rolling pin to mash in the oats. "You volunteering?" She tried to keep a straight face, but grinned in spite of herself. She was never the one with a verbal riposte, but that was a good one, and Harric would be proud.

Lane slammed the cleaver into the block, eyes smoldering, and Caris put her hands on her hips to look down at him from at least a head taller. She let her gaze travel down his pudgy, unarmored body and back up, and raised an eyebrow. It was a look her brother had taught her to use, anticipating the many fools who would question her legitimacy and challenge her to duels. The look had saved several men's lives, and looked as if it would save another now.

Sure enough, Lane threw down his rag and apron and—seething—stormed past her and out of the kitchen.

She watched him out the door, then moved the buckets so she could work with an eye on the entrance. That man was not to be trusted. He'd as much as announced his allegiance to Bannus and the Old Ways with his "bastards and virgins" comment, and if he grew desperate enough, he might act on it. After loosening her sword and dirks in their scabbards, she set to stirring the oats into the mash until the grain, blood, and meal were thoroughly mixed in a heavy mixture that—minus the bone and with the addition of sage and rosemary—wasn't unlike the stuffing for Mother Ganner's bladder sausage.

Relieved to leave the stifling confines of the fort, she emerged into the courtyard beneath open sky, and hiked toward the stables. The stone walls and cobbles still slept in the shadow of the pass, but the river chattered brightly in its channel on the far side of the courtyard. The chill breath of the river kissed her cheeks, and in it she caught the liberated scents of sap and wildflowers from summer meadows beyond the pass.

She smiled, imagining the delight of Rag and the other horses when they reached those meadows that afternoon after the cramped stalls and dry fare of the outpost.

A shout of alarm from the stable broke her thoughts. She looked up in time to see a groom spill out the central door and into the yard, nearly falling on his face in his haste to exit. Dropping the buckets, she hurried to him, ten explanations swarming her head, none of them good. "What is it?"

"It's broke out!" he spluttered. "Blood everywhere!"

Caris's heart stuttered. "Molly? She's out—"

"Nearly took off my head!"

Hurrying past him, she shouted, "Get Sir Willard!" and sent her horse-senses before her into the stables, dreading what she'd find. If Willard had forgotten to put Molly in her chains… But she sensed the other horses safe—if upset—in the east stalls of the stable. At least, Rag and Idgit and Snapper were there…but Molly's foal, Holly, was not with them. To her alarm, Caris sensed Holly in the west arm—her mother Molly's arm—her young mind radiating curiosity.

Gods leave us, she's going to get herself killed.

Cursing, Caris entered and turned up the west wing.

Twilight still cloaked the stable, but it didn't take long for her eyes to adjust, and when they did, the scene sent a stab of terror through her gut. Molly had indeed escaped her stall, and though the heavy four-point chain hobbles still restricted her movement, she now loomed over her foal, violet blood frothing from her mouth. The hood of Holly's tournament caparison had been ripped from her head to expose her wine-black coat and mane. It now hung about her chest like a foolish neckerchief, and blood smeared its fabric.

"Holly!" Caris's stomach clenched as she ran to her.

Inexplicably, the filly gamboled and pranced just outside Molly's reach, as if trying to entice her monstrous mother to play. If it weren't for the chains on her mother's hooves, Holly would already be dead on the floor, for though she was Molly's offspring, she had not yet come into her immortality, and a blow from her dam would kill her. Visions of dogs and bears eating their offspring flashed in Caris's mind as she grabbed Holly's halter and hauled her away.

"Gods take it, get away from her!"

She sent her senses into Holly and tried to calm her, but the filly's emotions were a jumble of fear and desire and powerful filial attraction.

Molly let out a deep-chested growl, and her violet eyes burned down at Caris as strings of blood and saliva dripped from her blood tooth.

Caris tried to back Holly, but the filly whinnied and barely relinquished a step.

Molly's chains gave a terrific clatter, and Caris looked in time to see the Phyros perform a bizarre four-hoofed hop forward. Her gigantic hooves boomed on the plank floor, now a good two strides closer, and Caris nearly leapt from her armor.

As Molly bunched her hind legs for another hop—a hop that would bring her well into biting range—Caris panicked. Without thinking, she did what she would if faced with any other aggressive horse, and diverted her horse-senses to Molly. She gave the mare a quick mental slap to startle her and buy time to escape.

And it felt like she'd leapt into fire.

Roaring heat closed above her head. Blinding violet rage invaded her skull.

Caris screamed and retracted her senses, and the fire vanished, but her mind still reeled. As the dark twilight of the stables engulfed her, new noise assailed her. Horses screamed. Molly let out a startled whinny, terrifyingly close, and something yanked at Caris's right arm.

Unfamiliar rage flared in Caris, filling her chest like resin in a furnace.

"Bloody bitch!" she roared. She wanted to smash teeth. Anyone's teeth. She wanted to lash out, rip flesh, strike, crush. When the force yanked at her arm again, she wrenched back savagely, and Holly gave a whinny of pain. She still had the filly's halter in her hand, and the moon-blasted fool was still trying to pull free and get back to her mother.

"Idiot!" She wrenched Holly around, ignoring her whinnies of distress, and hauled her back before Molly could make another leap.

Behind them, Molly tossed her head, slinging foam and growling in frustration.

As she bunched and jumped again, Caris dragged Holly down the corridor to her stall, where the gate was wide open. That doltish groom had probably left the gate untied after bringing fresh straw, and the moment he left, Holly had gone straight to her mother.

After shoving Holly into the stall, Caris slammed the gate and tied it. Rage boiled behind her eyes. If she caught that groom, she'd dash him against a wall, tear his ears off, throw him down.

What's happening to me?

She closed her eyes and leaned her back against the gate. The heat in her chest made it feel like every exhalation would be a spout of fire, and it frightened her. Flinging her senses out to the other horses, she found that Molly's bloody activities had them panicked—especially Rag, who wasn't Phyros-trained. The smell of blood filled the place and put even the cool-blooded Idgit on edge. Rag actually whinnied in fear when Caris's wrath-tainted mind touched hers.

Cursing, she withdrew her senses and opened her eyes in time to see Molly bunch and jump, bunch and jump again. The report of the chains and hooves on the wood floor made Caris flinch, and that was like flint on steel, igniting the unfamiliar rage all over again.

"Back off!" she spat, and whipped her sword from its sheath. A
couple more of those bizarre four-legged hops and Molly would be at
Holly's stall, and though Caris knew the immortal beast would crush
her and rip out her throat, she would make the monster bleed.

When Molly jumped again, she thrust the tip of her blade before
her frothing chin. "I said, back off!"

Molly stamped a massive hoof, jarring the boards beneath Caris's boot.

If she hopped again, Caris would give the beast a scar to remember
her by and probably die beneath those hooves, in glory.

For what? said a corner of her mind that still struggled for reason.

Sir Willard's voice rang in the courtyard, and other voices joined his.

Molly's gaze bored into Caris as if the mare would burn twin holes
through Caris's skull.

"Do it, you Blood-mad bitch," Caris said.

"Molly!" Willard lumbered into the stable, then called to others
outside, "Stay out!"

The Phyros held Caris's gaze a moment longer. Then she flicked
her ears and snorted as if dismissing her, and turned her head to see
Willard. The old knight limped to her side, wheezing through bared
teeth. His head swung from the wreckage of Molly's stall in the west
arm to the standoff unfolding in the east. "Mother of moons," he said,
as he grabbed Molly's halter and hauled her head down beside him.

His eyes flicked from Caris's face to the stall behind her. "Holly…?"

"Bleeding." The word came out like an accusation, twisted by the
rage that contorted her face and heart. "Molly tried to rip her head off
and I stopped her."

Willard squinted past Caris toward Holly. "Her hood's torn, but I
see no injury on her."

"There's blood all over it." Caris opened the gate and walked up next
to Holly, who shied a little, remembering her recent rough treatment.
Grabbing control of the halter, Caris studied the filly's head and neck.
Then she shook her head, cheeks flushing. "You're right."

Willard let out a long breath and sagged against Molly's scarred
head. When Caris closed the gate behind her, he said, "You hurt? She
bite you?"

Her hands balled into fists. He was goading her. "I think I'd know
if she did."

His eyes narrowed and he watched her for several moments as his breathing calmed. "You touched Molly's mind, didn't you?" he said. "Yes, I can see it. You've never held my gaze more than a second, but since I've arrived, you've been glaring at me without pause." His voice had become low and gentle. Was that pity? Was he *pitying* her? Before she knew it, she lashed out for a stinging blow across his smug face.

But it never landed. Molly snapped at her hand like a striking snake, and though her mouth didn't close on Caris's wrist, the attempt deflected the blow.

Willard's eyes went wide. Molly growled, and Willard had to drag her head down to keep her back.

"I—I'm sorry, sir—" Shame and horror hit Caris like a fist in the stomach. "I don't know what happened— I—"

"Already forgiven." Willard gave a grim smile. "You touched the mind of a Phyros, that's what happened. Not a pretty place inside her, is it? I don't expect you'll do that again soon." But his brow remained bent as he glanced between Molly and her foal. "I'm not sure what was going on here, but you did well to protect Holly. Take a moment to calm down, and then meet me at Molly's stall. I want to hear exactly what happened."

He led Molly away, chains rattling across the planks, and Caris let out a long breath. Rage and horror still warred in her blood, and it sent a throb of nausea through her stomach.

This is not my anger.

She took deep breaths and let them out slowly, imagining that each breath was a drench of cool water on the fire in her chest. In the adjoining stall, Rag whinnied in distress, eyes rolling in fear, and an ache of regret dragged at Caris's heart. Rag could sense the unnatural rage in her—something she'd never sensed in all the years of her bond with Caris—and it frightened the mare. More, it dismayed her like she'd lost a best friend or sister.

Caris ached to go to her and comfort her. *I am still your Caris*, she wanted to say, *and the rage will pass,* but until it did, she sensed that to stay near Rag would only make matters worse.

Biting her lip against her own distress, she pushed away from Holly's gate and followed Willard to the other wing of the stables.

"She's ruined it," Willard said, as she joined him at the wreckage of Molly's stall. Splintered boards and timbers littered the straw. "Be a good lass and rip out the planks between the next two, so I have somewhere to put her."

Willard's eyes sparked as if he thought he'd said something clever. Probably *lass* was supposed to be funny, or ironic—the kind of word joke she never understood—and her frustration with the world of humans and *words* sparked the rage all over again. This time, instead of smacking him, she seized one of the planks in the partition between stalls and wrenched it from its pegs. She hurled it into the wreck of the first stall, and wrenched another, which split as she flung it after the other.

It felt good. No. Better than good. She wanted more. Plank after plank went this way until the partition was gone and she stood panting like a goaded bull.

Bridle yourself, Caris.

She found Willard watching closely, something like a new respect in his eyes. He gave her a slow nod, and a shiver rolled up her spine.

This must be how Phyros-riders feel all the time. Wrathful and righteous and…wonderful.

If that was so, then it was a marvel he'd ever stopped taking the Blood. And no wonder Sir Anatos had developed the disciplines to control it, and no wonder the immortals of the Blue Order had embraced the Rule of Anatos. She'd had only the smallest touch of Molly's mind, and the rage had nearly mastered her; what hope for those who drank freely of the Blood?

Shamefaced, she stepped aside as Willard led Molly in.

"Let's hope as long as Holly doesn't get out, Molly won't decide to break out again."

"Would she have killed Holly if she caught her?"

Willard stuck a stick of wood in his mouth like he would a ragleaf roll, and clamped it between his teeth. "Smoked my last roll this morning," he said, rolling the stick from one side of his mouth to the other. "Not sure how I'll manage the pain without it." He motioned for her to follow deeper inside the stable, away from the doors, and she followed.

"She didn't want to kill her," he said, voice lowered. "I believe she wanted to *blood* her."

Caris's brows knitted. "Blood her? You mean, share the Blood?"

Willard gave a grim nod. "The blood all over Molly's mouth was her own. She'd gouged her mouth with her blood tooth. If she'd gotten a hold of Holly, she'd have plunged the tooth into an artery and infected Holly with the Mad God's Blood." Caris blinked in surprise, and Willard gave her a small smile. "I owe you much for stopping her. If she'd succeeded, Holly's eyes and coat would turn violet, a full Phyros, and it would be clear to all who beheld her."

"But Molly's never done this before. Holly's been at her side since I met you, so Molly's had many chances to blood her."

Willard nodded. "I imagine that, until now, Holly was too young. We can't know for certain, because we don't know much about Phyros breeding and foaling. Until now, it's always taken place on the Sacred Isle. One thing is certain, however: I dare not lead her behind Molly any longer, or it may happen again."

"I can lead her. I already ride at the rear, since I have to keep Rag as far away from Molly as possible."

"Yes. Molly at the head, Holly at the tail."

"Sir, may I ask how Molly got pregnant?"

Willard glanced back at the doors as if looking for eavesdroppers, then puffed out a short sigh and smoothed his mustachio. "It is good that you should understand this; if something should happen to me, it falls on you to report it to the Blue Order and the Queen. It happened last fall, when I visited the Blue Order in Peridot Castle. I stabled Molly with the rest of the Phyros, and one of the stallions obviously paired with her, somehow. Fairly certain it was Gregan's stallion, Ghan, but it doesn't matter. In three hundred years since I bonded with Molly and took her from the Sacred Isle, she never accepted a mate. We all assumed she'd never breed off the Sacred Isle. And yet it happened. I believe it is because the Chaos Moon approaches. It also may be true that the Phyros only breed in the year of the Chaos Moon."

A shiver ran up the hairs at the back of Caris's neck. "There have been signs that the Chaos Moon may be coming. The return of the Old Ones. The emergence of the Kwendi."

"Yes. And our little Holly is as dark and dangerous as any of these things, for if the Old Ones learn Molly can breed on Arkendia, and if they learn she has foaled another mare, they'll try to capture and breed them both in order to restore the ranks of the Old Ones."

The old knight's lip curled beneath his mustachio, and his voice took on a hard edge. "I did not devote ten lifetimes to destroying the Old Ones only to hand them the means of restoring their order. If I didn't fear how it would affect Molly, I'd slay Holly now—as I'd have slain her the day she emerged. But Molly is likely to prove worse than any she-bear if her foal is threatened. I fear I would lose Molly as well, in that case, which I can't risk. But if it comes to a choice between that and the Old Ones taking her, Holly must be slain. And again, if that need should arise and somehow I am unable to do it, the task will fall to you. Do you understand?"

The question took Caris by surprise. She stared, heart thumping, as she imagined the wretched slaughter of an innocent creature like Holly. Imagined herself doing it. And it almost wrenched a sob from her. The only thing that kept it back was the image of Holly in the hands of Bannus's wretched shield bearer.

She swallowed hard. "Yes," she said, voice hoarse. "I understand. I will."

Willard nodded. It seemed her confidence lifted a small weight from his mind. "Good. Beheading is the way. Get an axe. Keep it sharp. And from now on, keep it in your things."

"I hear you say women are weak and lack wit and memory, and that therefore I am unfit for rule. You beg me wed a man that he may lift the burden of the throne. But alas, that cannot be. I simply cannot bring myself to such a decision. I must lack the wit and judgment necessary."

— Her Majesty to Prince Jormund of West Isle
at a banquet for the Iberg ambassador

9

Curses & Promises

A flicker of movement drew Caris's attention to the central stable door. Harric had stepped in, his face marked with concern. His eyes hadn't adjusted to the comparative dimness of the stable, so he hadn't seen her yet.

Watching him, it took her a moment to realize that something was missing. When she recognized what it was, she blinked in surprise: the love ache was gone. Where was the leap of her heart when she saw him? Where was the pang of longing that had plagued her for the last month?

She raised her hand with the Kwendi wedding ring and examined it, expecting to see it blackened and broken, but it looked the same as ever.

Nevertheless, for the first time since they'd left Gallows Ferry, she saw Harric with clear eyes and heart, free of the ring's influence. She saw him not as her love—as the ring had forced her—but as a rather small, pretty bastard friend. A man with a generous heart, and an irreverent brain, full of trickery that she abhorred. Indeed, there he was sneaking his way into the stable like a jack thief with a guilty conscience; the sight kindled a flicker of anger in her chest.

Willard followed her gaze and, when he saw Harric, mirrored Caris's frown. Harric caught sight of them, and relief washed over his face. Smiling, he began to cross to her, but Willard waved him off. "All is well, boy. I need to talk to Caris alone. Good time to saddle your horse. We leave in the hour."

Harric's brow creased, but he nodded.

As he left, he cast Caris a look that sparked exactly nothing in her heart. Had her touch on Molly's mind burned out the ring's power?

A guard outside called for Caris, and Willard winced.

"Moons take it," he said. "Molly's foolishness has taken too much of our precious time. Soon as you're packed, ride up the road and help the men set up their temporary stable. We'll gather there within the hour and depart."

"Yessir."

He studied her face. "Has the rage passed? Feel more yourself yet?"

She took a deep breath, considering, and found no embers left of the fire that had ruled her only minutes before. She nodded, relieved, and anxious to return to Rag.

"The fiercest fires die soonest."

As he moved away toward the door, Caris noted that his limp had gotten worse, probably from running to the stable in full armor. Picking up an old rake handle for him to use as a staff, she started after him, but stopped suddenly as a stab of longing for Harric returned with such force that it took the wind from her. Staggering, she laid a hand to her breastplate and let out a small gasp of pain.

Willard turned. "You all right?" His eyes searched hers, and she dropped her gaze from the uncomfortable contact.

"Yes. I'm fine." She turned from him as hot tears sprang from her eyes, and she forced herself to walk like a confident version of herself into the east arm of the stable.

He did not follow, and when she heard him depart, she clapped a hand over her mouth to muffle a sob and dropped to her knees in the straw by Rag's stall. A familiar roaring of horse-touched confusion began between her ears, and she moaned, reaching out to the mare to calm herself and fend off the attack. She could still feel Rag's agitation from the morning's events, but the mare didn't recoil from the touch of Caris's questing mind.

Laying her forehead on the straw, Caris wrapped herself in the mare's senses.

Rustling straw.

Good oats at her nose.

Calm friends nearby.

A wicker and flick of ear. Swishing tails.

Rhythmic chewing, wet mush on her tongue.

Caris rocked back and forth over her knees until the roaring subsided, and when she finally emerged from the refuge of Rag's mind, she did not know how long she'd been on her knees. Worry pricked her to clamber to her knees and look about to be sure Willard hadn't seen.

The place was empty of all but her and the horses, but Molly's enormous, scarred head jutted from her stall to watch her like some ground-level gargoyle. A low growl bubbled up from the Phyros, as if in judgment that said, *You are weak. Your mare is weak. You crawl to her and whimper.*

Caris looked away. She didn't need another judge. She was her own harshest judge.

Keeping half her mind in Rag's steadying presence, she groped through the confusion in her heart, which felt like the stalls Molly had wrecked. The Phyros's fire had swelled it with strength and freedom she'd never known, but the moment it left her, all her weaknesses and the ring's ache had returned with double vengeance. The ring's spells now crushed her heart like binding chains, so tight that she struggled to breathe, and Rag's influence was barely enough to keep her standing.

She gasped for air and her vision blurred with tears as the roar rose again in her ears. *I can't do this. I can't! It has to end.*

Stumbling through the stable, she searched for tools. A wild new hope gave her strength.

I can end it. I can end it now.

Harric retrieved his gear from the yard and lugged it to the stables. As he passed Molly's stall, he saw Caris in the adjacent stall, at a worktable where the garrison repaired harnesses. He tossed his saddlebag over the rail behind Snapper, and returned to see what she was doing.

"Hey," he said, stopping at the open gate to the stall.

Caris cursed and fumbled with a chisel that she held awkwardly in her right hand. In her left hand, she held a hammer.

"Get out of here, Harric."

It took half a heartbeat for Harric to register the wild intensity in her voice, and another to realize she'd laid the back of her right hand on the worktable, palm up, fingers converging on the chisel to balance it vertically on the base of one finger.

He didn't need to guess which finger she balanced it upon.

Harric lunged to her side and grabbed away the chisel. "What the Black Moon are you doing?"

"Dammit, Harric!" She tore the tool from his grasp and held it out of reach as he grappled with her armored limb. Snarling, she shoved him back and slapped her hand back on the table.

Harric bounced back and dove for the only thing he could reach in time, her hammer arm.

"Please, Caris!"

Furious, she jerked her arm away and thrust the hammer and chisel into his hands. "*You* do it, then." Laying her finger on the table, she waited, chest heaving, eyes burning holes into Harric.

Harric dropped the chisel as if it were a viper, and when she stooped to retrieve it, he kicked it away. "Moons take it, Caris. Stop it. You can't do that to yourself."

A rough sob escaped her. Eyes brimming, she seized the front of his shirt. Half carrying him, half spinning him as if leading in a dance, she bore him to rear of an empty stall and pinned him against the planks. Splinters of the rough-hewn wood jabbed through his shirt into the skin of his back. Through clenched teeth, she said, "I—cannot—live—with this ring."

Harric's throat grew tight. "I'm so sorry, Caris," he said. "I hate that ring. I hate the way it hurts you. I hate that it was my hand that gave it to you. I wish every day it were on my finger." He scanned her face and found only pain and shame there. "I can't know what it must feel like, but I hate that you have to feel it, and I wish I could do something about it."

"It makes me think of you all the time, Harric. I can't stop it. Like a stupid song stuck in my head. And it *hurts*." She pounded her breastplate as if she could dampen the pain behind it. "I want to chop my heart out, too."

She turned to leave him, but he scuttled around her to block her path. Judging by the determination in her eye, she was going for the chisel again.

"Just wait," he said, heart and mind racing. "You don't even know if it would work to cut it off. Brolli said it could really hurt you if it is forced off somehow. It's magic. He said it is enchanted to stay on. And even if you cut your whole finger off—or cut the ring itself in two—its enchantments are entwined in your mind and your heart. Tearing them out could hurt you in ways you can't even see—not to mention you'd maim your sword hand."

Caris groaned and hung her head. Some of the tension drained from her shoulders. She extended one hand to the side to steady herself against a plank partition between stalls.

"Please," said Harric. "The first thing we'll do when we get to Brolli's people is go to the magicians who made it; they'll know how to do it safely."

Raising both hands to cover her ears, she squeezed her eyes closed and sank to her knees, the leather harness of her armor creaking.

Harric took a step back. He didn't expect her to fall into one of her horse-touched fits right here, not with her horse so near, but he wanted to give her space. He knew she was probably reaching out to Rag with her senses and drawing on that kinship to steady herself.

Something tickled his wrist and dripped from his fingertips. *Mother of moons, I'm bleeding.* A small gash hooked across the heel of his hand. He must have gotten it when he dove for the chisel. Now that he was aware of it, it stung like a wasp sting.

A wave of gratitude swept through him. *Small price.* It could have been Caris's blood.

Motion caught his attention, and he looked to see Molly had lifted her head to peer over the plank partition that separated the two stalls. Her greedy nostrils sucked at the scent of his blood, and the mineral stink of her breath wafted to Harric.

Gods leave us, what a monster.

He pressed a handful of straw over his wound and sidled to the opposite side of the stall. Caris no longer panted her breaths. As he crouched beside her, she stirred, and her hands fell away from her ears.

"It's driving me mad, Harric." Hair hung before her face and concealed her expression, but her voice came out low and fraught. She rose, head bowed, her gaze on her hands, where she tugged at the ring.

Gods leave it. How ironic was it that he, a bastard fighting all his life against the slavery of bastards and women, had inadvertently enslaved the woman he most cared for? That moon-blasted wedding ring was no different than the cruel masters he'd fought all his life, forcing her to love, bending emotions against their natural course. But he was helpless to do anything; the ring couldn't be tricked in a wager or beaten in a card game like a slave master could.

His frustration must have leaked from his eyes, because the next thing he knew, Caris grabbed him by the shoulders and kissed him, hard. She pressed hungrily into him. The ridge of her breastplate gouged his sternum, but he hardly noticed, because his heart and body responded instantly, rising to meet her.

No. *This isn't her.*

He pulled back, turning his head away. *Dammit.* She'd never smashed a kiss on him like that before. She stepped back, and he studied the confusion of hunger and disgust in her face, wondering whether the ring might be getting stronger, or if her resistance was simply—finally—wearing down

"I'm sorry, Caris. You don't want that. Not really."

"See what I mean?" She gave her mouth an angry wipe with the back of her hand, and her cheeks flushed. "If you ever let me kiss you like that again, I swear I'll—" The sight of his hand stopped the words in her throat. She grabbed him by the wrist and swiped the bloodied straw away from his wound.

"Stupid," she muttered, face flushing again.

"I must have cut myself—"

"Stay here." She stepped out of the stall and returned a moment later with one of the bandages from her saddle packs. Glaring, she bound the hand. Harric couldn't tell if she was angry with herself for hurting him, or angry with him for endangering himself. He didn't ask. Probably a little bit of both. When she finished, she met his eyes again. Strange how easily she could meet his eyes when she was furious. Sometime, when she was calmer, he'd have to ask if anger dislodged

THE JACK OF RUIN

her horse-touched hatred of "touching eyes," as she called it.

At the moment, it felt like her glare would set fire to his eyeballs.

She turned abruptly to leave, but he held her arm. "Promise you won't try that again, Caris. The real Caris would never consider risking her sword hand."

The muscles of her jaw pulsed. "Don't treat me like a helpless girl."

Harric actually laughed. "You, helpless. That's funny. How many times have you saved my life—two, three times? I assure you, there is no danger of me mistaking you for helpless. But if anything is stronger than that ring, it's your sense of honor. If you promise, you'll be true to your word. So promise me."

She tore her arm free from his grasp, but held his gaze for a long moment, emotions warring behind her eyes. "I promise," she said, as if each word might knock him down if she said it hard enough. Then she stalked off to Rag's stall.

Relieved, he eased himself down against the back wall of the stall he'd ended up in. The new straw crackled as he found a comfortable position, releasing its sweet and comforting scent. Hanging his head between his knees, he let out a long, slow breath. His hands were trembling. The chisel upset him deeply. And whether he wanted to admit it or not, his heart ached, too. Three moons, his *head* ached: *Don't touch magic. Don't sneak or pull any dishonorable tricks. Don't stop me from hurting myself. Don't touch me. Don't let me touch you.*

A few more ultimatums and she might cure *his* love. He managed a wry smile.

When he heard Rag's hooves in the main passage of the stable, he raised his head and watched Caris lead the mare out and into courtyard. By chance he'd ended up in the center stall across from the main doors, which afforded him a view as she adjusted her saddle in the lantern light of the yard. Gods leave it, she was beautiful. No denying it. Well formed. Unpretentious. Driven. Stomped her enemies. Stomped his.

"That's it, torture yourself, Harric," he muttered, as she led Rag out of his view.

Molly's unmistakable growl drove a spike of panic through him. A violet eye glowered at him through a gap in the partition between stalls. Moons, could Molly do anything but glower? Composed as she was of nothing but fury and violence, he doubted it. On the other hand, if he had been sliced and ritually bled for centuries by Sir Willard, he might glower, too. Fans of scars surrounded her eye like the rays of some cruel violet sun, each scar from a bloodletting that had once kept Willard immortal. Still, Harric had to credit Willard with a certain restraint in his cuttings: rather than the random and barbaric slashes he'd seen on Bannus and Gygon, Molly's seemed restrained and deliberate. Civil, if that were possible.

She growled again, eye blazing, as if challenging his thoughts, but she didn't smash through the partition to take him. Maybe this was her sympathetic glower. But no amount of superficial civility could change the fact that Bannus and Molly both hailed from the same Mad God, so Harric scooted himself a few feet farther away along the back of the empty stall. Not the best place to recover his nerves after the trauma with Caris, perhaps, but he was too tired to get up and find privacy elsewhere.

"Hey, kid," Fink whispered in the air beside Harric's ear.

Harric startled and glanced around.

"Didn't want to spook you." Fink's hunched black form materialized beside him.

Harric scrambled to close the gate to his stall and glanced up and down the stables to be sure no one approached.

"How can you be here?" Harric said. "It's day."

"Not quite. Dawn broke over the horizon, but it's not over the crags here. We have some time."

"Actually, this isn't a great time."

Fink studied him with his pupilless white eyes. "The girl. She's upset you."

Harric looked at the batlike creature before him. He opened his mouth to speak but closed it. "You wouldn't understand."

"Oh. Well, sure. If you mean I wouldn't understand a girl twice your size kissing you and saying don't you dare kiss me or I'll hurt you, then yeah. You're right."

Harric gave him a sharp look. "You were here for that?"

"But if you mean I wouldn't understand how you're in love with her but can't act on it even though she acts like she loves you because she's under the spell of that ring, and since it's not actual love, you have to bottle your feelings, even when she starts rubbing on you, so you're basically walking around with a broken heart and a cob like a sledge handle all the time, then yeah, I don't get that, either."

Fink quirked his bald black head to one side and looked at Harric.

"Okay," said Harric. "Maybe you'd understand a little."

"A little, he says. They don't call us tryst servants for nothing, kid."

"What do you mean? A tryst servant. That's what you are?"

Fink nodded. "A *tryst servant* is what they call the moon servant of an Unseen magus—though in my case, I should say moon *partner*, not servant." He leered, needle teeth chillingly bright. "You freed me from that."

"What does 'tryst' have to do with anything? In Arkendian, *tryst* means 'secret romantic encounter.'" An image of a bunch of batlike Finks crawling about delivering love letters made Harric snort out a laugh.

"That's exactly what it means, kid. In the old days on the continent, one of the first things some novices did the day they became a Black Magus was to have their tryst servant lay a charm on the prettiest boy or girl they could find. It's very unpopular with magi of the other moons, so they outlawed it in the Iberg Compact. But you of all people don't need that; your big girlfriend can hardly keep from kissing you—"

"You could help her!" The words exploded from Harric in a shock of realization.

"Help her kiss you? I *guess* I could. I mean, I could get naughty if you really—"

"No, I mean help get that ring off her finger."

Someone coughed outside the stables, and Harric jumped. He peered out to see Lane trudge past a door, calling someone to get a wheelbarrow. Lane disappeared, and Harric turned to Fink.

"You could help, couldn't you?"

Fink's inscrutable white eyes stared. "I've never been asked to uncharm someone."

"But you could do it?"

A black tongue swept across Fink's teeth. "That's Kwendi magic on her finger. It's like nothing I've seen. None of the three moons knows how it works."

"But it's Unseen magic, right? *Love* is unseen." Harric heard his voice rising defensively as the flutter of hope faded. "The Kwendi magicians put Unseen power in the ring, so you should be able to do something about it, right? Maybe undo it?"

Fink let out a guttural hiss. "You're clever. You think about things."

"It's *all* I can think about, Fink. I hate seeing her like this."

"It'd be a lot easier if you just enjoyed it— I know! No slavery, I get it!" Fink held up his talons as Harric drew in breath to lash out at him.

Harric sensed fear in the impit's hesitation, as if the Kwendi magic scared him, but there was something else, as well. Greed? Ambition? "You're curious, aren't you, Fink? Why won't you do it?"

"I didn't say I won't. I will." Fink's face twisted in a grimace. "But it's maybe dangerous. The Kwendi know how to capture moon magic in witch-silver. No magus in the entire Iberg Compact knows how they do it. So, sure, it's Unseen power in her ring, but can I touch it? Can I change it? Do I suspect anything about how they put it in the witch-silver of that ring? No, no, and no. I don't know a thing about it, kid. No one but the Kwendi know, and they aren't sharing." Fink licked his teeth again. "Still, we could be the first to take a look."

"Yes!" Harric spun about and pushed the gate to their stall wide. As he peered up and down the empty stables, his mind ran through destinations Caris might have gone, and settled on the makeshift stables up the river road.

"What are you doing, kid?"

"Come on. She probably took Rag up the river road. Let's meet—"

Brolli barked in his unmistakable tenor outside the stables. "Sir Willard!" It came from outside the entrance at the right-hand wing of the stables, and alarmingly close.

Harric jumped back into the stall and retreated to the back corner.

"Ambassador," the old knight answered full and clear, as if he'd just entered the building. A few horses shuffled in the straw of their stalls, and Molly tossed her gigantic head so her mane flashed above the partition beside Harric.

"Gods take it," Harric muttered. "Fink, can you meet me up the river?"

Fink had retreated with Harric into the corner nearest Molly's stall, but he watched the planks of the partition as if he expected the Phyros to burst through at any moment. "That thing's been looking at me, kid. How do you people live with them? Don't you know—"

"The river!" Harric whispered. "Meet me there."

"You have a lot to learn about the Unseen if you think a spirit will go near a river, kid. And dawn's coming. Between that and the river…" Fink shook his head. "Wait till tonight."

Brolli and Willard stopped outside Molly's stall, and Harric dared not speak again. A blade of panic stabbed through his chest at the thought of either of them spotting Fink. "Go!" he mouthed, motioning frantically for him to leave.

Fink's grin only widened. *Remember what I said about these so-called friends of yours?* His mouth didn't move, but his voice echoed in Harric's head. *Going to have to leave them, kid. They won't accept the Unseen. They won't accept you. That's the price of heroes.*

I know! Harric thought back, unsure Fink could hear him. *But not now — please go — just go!*

The man that walks his own road walks alone.
—Arkendian proverb

10

On Broken Oaths

Harric's head rang with panic. "Go!" he mouthed.

Fink lingered, waggling his taloned fingers in a grotesque yet effeminate farewell.

And vanished.

Closing his eyes, Harric leaned his head back against the planks and let out a long, slow breath, his heart hammering against his ribcage.

The sound of a latch on Molly's stall announced the knight's arrival with Brolli.

Cobs. By now, the knight would expect Harric to be gone up the river with Caris, and would yell at him for "idling about" when he should be moving. Plus, if Willard's hex was still active, the last place Harric wanted to be was anywhere near him until the sun crested the ridge. As soon as Willard was inside Molly's stall, Harric would slip away.

"You must take the Blood," Brolli said.

"I am in charge of this mission, ambassador. And we settled this before."

Harric rolled his eyes at the old argument and rose to his feet, poised to flee. Despite his best efforts at stealth, however, the fresh straw rustled, betraying him. If it hadn't been for Molly letting out a mighty snort and stamping her hooves at the same moment, he'd have given himself away.

Through a gap in the plank partition, Harric saw Willard moving in

Molly's stall, but to his immense frustration, Brolli remained outside, where he would see if Harric left. Motionless, he remained in the back corner, as any movement might attract attention through the gapped partition. One more noisy outburst from Molly, and he'd cross to the gate of his stall, and hope Brolli was looking the other way.

The stables grew very quiet as the old knight stood beside Molly, stroking her scarred coat. Harric held his breath. After several long moments, Willard spoke, his voice low and freighted with warning. "If I take the Blood again, ambassador, I break the most sacred vow ever given to a lady."

"A foolish oath," Brolli said.

"You think the Lady Anna unworthy?"

Harric cringed. The old argument was straying into dangerous territory; though every Arkendian child knew of Willard's oath to stop taking the Blood and grow old with the Lady Anna, he was famously private about it. He'd thrown ballad-makers and courtiers into pigsties for indelicate snooping. If Willard found Harric "snooping" now, all the progress he'd made in the knight's regard would be erased, Willard's worst opinion confirmed, and the gap between them wider than ever. This when Willard had just started to forgive Harric for the way he'd tricked him into taking Caris as his squire.

Harric's hand went instinctively to the witch-stone in his shirt.

Fink had warned him not to enter the Unseen alone—that he needed protection against scavenging spirits. But Fink had also said the reason Harric had been able to do it the night before was because the spirits had been afraid to come near Sir Bannus and Gygon. If that were true, then Molly would have the same effect, and she was much closer to him than Bannus had been.

Harric closed his eyes, hoping desperately that dawn hadn't broken over the crags, so his oculus would still be there.

And it was. High at the top of his mind, it hung like a sleeping eye waiting to be wakened. Willing his consciousness upward, he pressed gently against it until it widened. As he felt it relax, he pushed harder and rose through, into the Unseen.

It was like entering a burning building, but without the heat. All around him, the stable blazed with spirit fire. Hay, wood, soil— everything living or once living—gave off ribbons or threads of bright spiritual essence, like curls of glowing smoke. Their profusion in the stable made it difficult to see farther than a dozen paces, and it did no good to sweep his hand through the air to dissipate them like regular smoke; spirit strands merely wavered and whorled and kept their shape.

His head throbbed with the burden of holding himself in the Unseen, and perspiration bloomed on his face, reminding him to hurry. The night before, he'd had only minutes before he'd collapsed back into the Seen and become visible to all.

He took a careful step toward the gate, but the straw crackled perversely under his weight, and Molly's head—now maned in blinding violet spirit—jerked up and she scanned over the partition. Harric froze as a violet eye seemed to fix upon him, and a low growl boiled from her chest. Willard looked through a gap in the planks—so close that Harric could almost reach out and touch him—but the knight looked right through him.

A wave of relief fluttered behind Harric's ribs. *Run,* he told himself. *Just run while you can, and noise be damned!*

But someone moved in his path. Two men now stood in the main door to the stables, their spirit strands blazing like signal fires above the fog of essence. Harric could just make them out: it was Sergeant Lane, and his sunken-eyed friend.

Lane held a club. His friend carried rope.

Harric bit off a curse. He knew a bastard hunt when he saw one, but he also knew that he could not sustain himself in the Unseen long enough to get out the stable doors and get clear of those two. His head already split under the strain. And if he tried, he'd probably pass out at their feet, easy prey.

Gods take it. They'd spoiled his escape. He was trapped.

In the first four years of her reign, the Queen's allies foiled no less than four plots on Her Majesty's life. All four were of West Isle origin and resulted in brutal suppressions in the west. Subjects on the East Isle celebrate the occasion of each foiled plot with a holiday, bell-ringing, bonfires, and festivities.

—From A *Short History of a Backward Island,* by the
Iberg Ambassador Viero Meritosi

11

On Treachery & Heroes

Harric watched in frustration as Lane and Sunken Eyes drew up just beyond the entrance and out of view of Willard and Brolli. As the knight and ambassador continued their argument, Lane appeared to listen. He frowned and shook his head to his companion, holding up two fingers as if to say, "There's two of them." Then he glanced up and down the rest of the stable as if searching for someone else. Again Lane shook his head.

They want to toss me to Bannus. Willard, too, if they catch him alone.

Black spots swam before Harric's eyes. Harric felt himself swaying on his feet. Soon he'd be gasping for breath as if he'd sprinted up a long hill, and he'd collapse in full view of everyone. He couldn't let that happen. At the very least, he had to remain conscious.

Steadying himself against the plank partition, he released himself back through his oculus and into the Seen.

The pressure lifted instantly, but he found himself swaying on his feet and struggling to gulp enough air without gasping aloud.

Mercifully, Lane and Sunken Eyes had left. But they left him in no better position than he'd been in before they came. *Bad luck and stupidity,* he chided himself. If Willard caught him, he was well and truly cobbed, for what possible excuse could he make? It was the kind of rash and foolish act he might claim was the work of the night-hex, but he knew it wasn't the hex. This was all his own doing, and Willard would know it, too.

"If I die, your kingdom falls," Brolli said, "and Anna falls with it. If you die, what is the point of your oath?"

"I remain true to Anna."

"And what use is that to her? Even she would be telling you drink it. Once we are being safe, you can stop the Blood again. But now, the Blood will make you like Bannus, yes? A giant. A match for him. You must drink."

Brolli stepped forward to where Harric could glimpse the side of his face. The Kwendi had lifted his daylids to peer at Willard with his huge, owlish eyes. "It is a simple choice. Either you are drinking the Blood and beat Bannus, or Bannus catches you and forever keeps you a stump like we see last night, a living trophy, and worse."

Willard's breathing sounded almost as labored as Harric's felt. Harric could see him through the gaps in the planks, standing frozen, caught between terrible alternatives. The old knight turned his back to Brolli—his side now to Harric—and squeezed his eyes shut. Willard's lips moved soundlessly, and Harric could not help himself but watch. *Forgive me,* he seemed to say. Then aloud, in a hoarse whisper, he said "Leave me, Brolli."

Brolli hesitated, uncertain.

"I said leave."

Brolli left the way he'd come.

In the silence that followed, Harric watched Willard through the slats, glimpsing parts of his face, parts of Molly's agitated bulk. The knight's breathing grew rapid as he fumbled at buckles on his saddlebags, then fell silent again, and Molly went deadly still. The air seemed charged with the tension of some titanic spring.

Then violet blood painted the straw on the other side of the slats, and Molly let out a tremendous, deep-chested sigh. Willard suckled the wound with urgent, sloppy swallows—the sound of a water-starved prisoner on a moistened sponge—and red-hot embarrassment flooded

Harric. He looked away, ashamed.

I am so cobbed. So cobbed. His heart hammered so hard that he feared Molly would hear it.

If Willard caught him spying on this most intimate moment—caught him while the Mad Blood raged through his brain—Harric was a dead man. A hundred tales flashed through his mind—tales of Phyros-riders who slew innocent friends and lovers in the blind fury that came after taking the Blood. Though Harric could hardly classify himself as an "innocent friend."

Frozen like a bird before a snake, he gripped the nexus stone, wishing he had strength enough to reenter the Unseen.

The sucking sound ceased, and Willard groaned, a deep growl in his barrel chest. Then he thrashed against the planks, which made Harric jump. Dust shook loose from the wood and floated up into the air as Molly stamped her chained hooves and tossed her head so Harric saw flashes of violet ears and wine-black mane above the partition.

The commotion was all the cover he needed. Harric moved across the rustling straw as swiftly as he dared, willing Willard to continue his thrashing. But the noise stopped abruptly, and Harric froze—no farther than a step away from the stall door and freedom, but he dared not move. A glance told Harric that Willard no longer stood beside Molly on the other side of the partition.

His heart gave a terrific leap, as if to escape his chest.

Then Willard appeared before him at the gate.

Harric leapt back with a small cry of fear, as Willard's face contorted in supernatural fury. Lightning jags of violet veins shot through his forehead and throat. The skin of his cheeks flushed purple. His eyes—now violet, now purple, now blue—burned with so much rage that Harric imagined they'd burst from his skull.

"Oh—I—" Harric stammered. "I'm so—"

What came next happened almost too quickly to understand. Molly roared in rage—a sound part snarl, part whinny, part bellow—and Willard jerked to one side. A club from behind slammed on his left shoulder plate, and the old knight whirled with a quickness impossible for a man even half his age.

Lane's mouth dropped open in astonishment, and Willard planted a mailed fist in it, sending him flying, along with several newly liberated teeth. Lane crashed backward into the dove master, who also carried a club, and the two sprawled on their backs. Sunken Eyes stood in wide-eyed disbelief, his coil of rope dropping from nerveless fingers into the straw.

Before Lane or Garon could right themselves, Willard was on them in a snarling frenzy of pile-driving armored fists.

When Sunken Eyes tried to flee, Willard seized him by an arm and used the man's momentum to swing him headfirst into a timber support post. Harric didn't see the impact, because Willard's bulk was in the way, but he heard a sickening crunch and saw dust shake from the rafters above.

Harric retreated two steps back into the stall. So much for fleeing while Willard was occupied. As he retreated another step, Willard warded off blows from the clubs, wrested one from Lane, and turned it on its master with horrible efficiency. As the blows fell, Harric shrank into the farthest corner of the stall, out of sight of the grisly scene, and made himself as small as he could.

His back had just bumped into the far corner when Lane's dazed and bleeding form rose high above the partitions on Willard's upraised arms. In the next instant, Willard slammed Lane down on the partition beside Molly's gate, where he hung half in, half out of her stall. He barely had a moment to writhe in agony before Molly had him by the neck and dragged him squealing into her stall.

Harric slapped his hands to his ears to keep out the wet sounds of snapping bone and gobbled flesh.

Outside the stall, Garon lay crumpled, staring with unblinking eyes, his head at a fatal angle from his shoulders. Sunken Eyes sprawled in the straw beside him, gaze fixed on Harric as his mouth moved like a fish out of water, starving for air yet somehow unable to draw breath. Then the eyes glazed, and the mouth fell still.

The trio had been crushed. Willard now stood at Molly's gate, his back to her as she continued her noisy meal. For many long moments, the old knight's chest seemed to heave with passion, armored shoulders rising and falling. Gradually, he stilled, then slumped. His breathing slowed and returned to normal.

Unlooked-for hope awoke in Harric. In the tales, Phyros-riders woke from rages with no memory of what they'd done. And now it looked as though Willard had no memory of Harric. That would be bastard luck indeed. He could put this whole thing behind him and go back to being the hero who smashed Bannus's army and…

Willard turned and looked directly at Harric through a gap in the planks, and Harric's guts froze. The knight's eyes no longer burned violet, but rage still burned there, and now they stabbed into Harric like blades through his ribs.

"I'm so sorry," Harric whispered, his voice miserable and pathetic. "I never meant—"

"Mother of moons!" Two guards appeared in the central door of the stables, behind Willard, and stared in shock at the scene before them. "What happened?"

"These men attacked me," Willard said, still with his back to the men. His voice came out low, and eerily calm, but his eyes remained fixed on Harric. "They wanted Bannus's favor, I suspect. They won't get it. Leave us. I must have words with my man."

The men stood transfixed. They looked at each other, and at Willard's back. Questioning eyes fell on Harric, and Harric realized Willard wouldn't face them, lest they see some residual violet of the Blood in his features. Harric nodded to the men, and they left.

In a few swift strides, Willard rounded the gate to Harric's stall and was on him. Seizing him by the shirt, he lifted Harric and flung him through the wooden partition opposite Molly's stall. The air whooshed from Harric's lungs as he impacted with the planks, and the boards sprang from their moorings to tumble in the straw beside him.

A tiny corner of Harric's mind noted that this was the second time a Phyros-rider had thrown him through a wall. Clambering to his knees, he thanked his luck for loosely nailed planks. Then Willard loomed over him and Harric cringed, expecting to be thrown again, but instead—with what seemed like more effort than it had taken to toss him—Willard stepped back, fists trembling at his sides.

"Well, now," he said through clenched teeth. "Now you know it all." He squeezed his eyes shut, shaking as if struggling against the immortal urge to murder. Flushes of violet swam across his cheeks. When it finally retreated into his flesh, he opened his eyes and laid his burning gaze on Harric.

Guilt and self-loathing pinned Harric and sealed his mouth. There was nothing he could say that wouldn't sound squirmy and feeble. Half certain he deserved whatever the old knight would say to him, he forced his eyes to endure his glare.

There came a wet cracking and gobbling from Molly in the stall beside them.

Willard inhaled deeply through his nose. "You are a jack fool, and a sneak," he said. "You have repeatedly violated my rules, and now you have violated my trust in the most personal way I can imagine. The only thing keeping me from discharging you immediately is that blasted ring on the girl's hand, and the fact I have a responsibility to get it off. If I discharge you now, the ring will torment her even worse. She might follow you, and I can't risk that."

Harric raised his eyes to meet the old knight's scorn. "I'm sorry, sir. I couldn't think how to get out—"

Willard waved a hand as if striking a bat from the air. "Your words mean nothing. I've known men like you. Too smart for your own good. Respect nothing. Walk on others. Walk on what's sacred. It's all a game to you. Everything is open for a trick, a ruse, a joke."

Harric bit his tongue.

In the courtyard, a couple of guards called to each other. Someone slammed a door.

"Last night," Willard continued, "you used Brolli's magic in violation of my orders and the Second Law. I overlooked it because you also saved our lives. But I do not overlook this. If you disrespect my rules or privacy again, or if I find you sneaking about, I will clap you in shackles and bundle you on a horse until we get to Brolli's people, where I'll give you to the hangman. Do you understand?"

Harric nodded.

Willard stared at one bloody gauntlet and flexed the fingers. "No pain. Already my joints heal. The change won't be complete for weeks, and it won't be visible for days. Until then, Brolli and Caris will not notice, and you will not tell them of my oath-breaking. Even when they learn it themselves, you'll never reveal that you witnessed the act today. You'll take it to your grave. Is that understood?"

Harric bowed his head. He'd seen Willard in the ugliest, most unguarded moment of suckling and swallowing at Molly's wound, and the knight would not forget it. He looked up to search Willard's eyes, but Willard had returned to join Molly without awaiting answer. Harric heard him hurling a saddle on her towering back, and the jingle of harness buckles. Harric climbed to his feet and lingered a moment outside Molly's stall, searching for something to say, but the knight's back remained steadfastly to him.

The fissure that opened between them in the moment he'd tricked Willard into taking Caris as his squire now yawned, an unbridgeable gulf filled with judgment and disdain.

Dazed, Harric crossed the stables to Snapper, who looked at him and stamped, impatient to get going. As he brushed the gelding's chestnut coat in preparation for saddling, Harric returned to something Fink had said twice to him—first on the cliff when they'd made their partnership, and again in that stable that morning. *You're going to have to leave them, kid. That's the price of heroes.*

Only Harric didn't feel like a hero. He felt like a first-rate cob.

Said the First Herald to our knowing queen, "Krato never intended a woman to rule." Holy Chasia quipped, "Yet in Krato's own herds the Phyros mares are larger than the stallions they rule. Does this example not show us that a woman's place must be the throne?"

—From a court gossip rag published in Kingsport, early reign of Chasia

12

Spitfires & Magic

Harric dragged the bodies from the stables. He moved in a daze, his mind scattered, his body still in shock. It felt like a wind blew through a huge hole in his middle, for not only had he witnessed gut-twisting violence, but Willard's small trust in him had vanished. As soon as the old knight had saddled Molly, he'd left Harric to "bag up what's left" of Lane, and ridden up the pass to join Caris.

He knew Willard was wrong and hypocritical and unfair in several ways, but the old man was also his childhood hero. He was every bastard's hero. Without Willard and the Queen, every bastard would be a slave. So no matter how big an ass the man was, his rejection hurt.

"Harric."

Harric looked up. He realized then that Gren had been talking to him, and he'd had to raise his voice to get Harric's attention. "Sorry, captain."

The captain studied Harric, a frown darkening his gaze. He nodded to Molly's blood-spattered stall. "I'll take care of Lane. You get your things together."

Harric stared into the straw and nodded. He wanted to thank him for the kindness, but his eyes began to sting, and tightness gripped his throat.

Someone laid a hand on his shoulder. "Help me into my saddle?" Brolli stood beside him. He looked up at Harric.

Harric nodded and followed the Kwendi into the stables, trying not to look at the gore in Molly's stall. Brolli looked, and his face seemed paler after.

"You see these men attack?" Brolli said, as they entered Idgit's stall. Brolli rested a long-fingered hand on the front cantle of the saddle and paused to look at Harric. "I never should to left him alone."

"They didn't touch him. Molly warned him."

Brolli's brow creased. "You see it."

"Molly roared."

Brolli sighed and clambered easily up the saddle to perch on its summit. From his satchel, he produced a small pillow to position beneath him; Harric waited with the straps while Brolli fussed like a cat preparing its bed.

The Kwendi frowned. "You Stilties have the large rump. I have only bone."

Harric recognized the ambassador was probing him for a smile. He managed to lift one corner of his mouth. "Stilties?"

"Yes. It is my name for your people. I wonder how you balance so high on your stilts."

Harric pulled the strap across Brolli's legs and buckled it.

"Too tight," said Brolli. "Use the third hole."

Harric readjusted the buckle. Kwendi proportions were all wrong for a regular saddle: not only did Brolli have no rump to speak of, but his burly arms and torso made him ridiculously top-heavy over dwarfish legs. Worse, the legs were too short to grip the horse with his knees. Instead, he clutched the stirrups with his fingered feet, but that quickly exhausted him, and couldn't be maintained when he slept in the saddle.

"Try to lean forward and put your weight on your arms," Harric said. "Just grab her mane. It won't hurt her."

Brolli nodded. "Thank you. I do not know why you Stilties love horses. When she trots, it is like she is making a kick to my back. I think Idgit means Arse Hammer in your language."

Harric led Idgit from the stable, then handed Brolli the reins and returned to Snapper. As he tightened the saddle girth, a guard entered with an armload of clothes and started stuffing a shirt with straw.

Scarecrows for the battlements, Harric realized. They'd prop them up to make the place look manned before they fled. The man gave Harric a grim nod. Then his eyes flicked to where Harric had laid his saddle packs, and his expression closed and hardened.

I might resent staying behind while others fled, too.

After fastening his packs behind his saddle, he led Snapper out of the stable and mounted beside Brolli in the courtyard. Hunched beside Brolli was a mountain of hair and woolen smothercoat on a white musk-auroch cow as big as Molly. The mountain of hair was Father Kogan in his tentlike coat of woolen rugs. His mane of dirt-brown beard and braids stood in fabulous disarray from his sleep in the dove tower. And though Farley had offered to re-braid his hair, he'd refused, saying, "Widda Larkin did these braids, and now they're all I got of her. Lands, I miss her."

The auroch cow was Geraldine, a gift from the fort, as she'd be butchered if captured, and Kogan was too big for any horse in the place.

Of the two, the musk-auroch smelled better.

The priest's red-shot eyes presently glared at Brolli, and Harric realized too late that though Brolli knew of Kogan, the priest had seen little of the Kwendi. Faced with the sight of him now—while hungover, in daylight, and at speaking distance—Kogan looked on the verge of violence.

"Good mornings to you, giant friend!" Brolli said, too loud for hungover ears.

True to his nature, Kogan spat. "You may be Willard's friend, you bald-faced chimpey, and you may be the Queen's last hope, but don't bring your god-cursed magic near me."

"Well understood," said Brolli, ignoring the insult and rudeness and maintaining a diplomatic smile. "But consider, your Second Law forbids *your* people magic, not mine. Perhaps the gods give other laws for my people."

"None what I know."

"And we must work together to survive Sir Bannus and the Old Ones, yes?"

Kogan's only response was a burning glare.

"Shall we exchange pleasantries on the road?" Harric said. "Willard wants us moving yesterday."

As Harric and Brolli rode up the river road to meet the others, the priest followed on Geraldine. Over the chatter of the river beside them,

Harric caught snatches of grumbling:

"…Civilized chimpey…legs too short by half, and mis-made arms… what come of magic…"

Harric glanced at Brolli, whose gold eyes flashed with amusement. "Is that what I seem to your people?" he called back to the priest. "A civilized chimpey?" When Kogan only grunted in reply, Brolli looked to Harric. "Do I?"

Harric gave a noncommittal shrug. It wasn't actually a bad description of the Kwendi, except that Brolli was a couple hands taller than a chimpey, had much broader shoulders, and no more hair on his body than Harric. The most striking difference was that his flat, strong-jawed face had a kind of alien handsomeness no chimpey ever had.

Brolli snorted. "I had the same idea of you, father, as the civilized bear."

The priest narrowed his eyes. "Call me civilized again and I'll toss ye in a river."

Harric found the makeshift stables a quarter mile up the road through the pass, well out of sight of the fort and Sir Bannus. It consisted of fifty paces of snake-rail fence and a wagon full of hay. A half-dozen fat and agitated mules and horses stood tied to the fence at intervals—agitated, no doubt, because none of them were Phyros-trained and Molly had just passed by. Caris waited with Willard several hundred paces beyond, and the sight of her—proud and strong and beautiful astride Rag—whispered an ache of fruitless longing through Harric's heart.

How had Fink put it? *Walking around with a broken heart, unable to kiss her back.* Something like that.

As Harric rode past the makeshift stables, the stable master watched, hay fork in hand. Harric recognized him as one of the guards who'd cheered his shot with the spitfire. The man had also seen to it that Idgit and Rag each had a new set of iron shoes on their hooves—and would have given Snapper a set, but the beast had lived up to his name and nipped the man when he stooped to examine his hooves. Harric saluted, but the man seemed to look right through him, chewing his lip as if he wished he too were leaving the besieged fort.

Guilt pulled Harric's eyes back to the road.

Harric wondered how many of the seven guards left alive would abandon their posts and steal horses that night to try their chances in the wilderness.

Gren and Farley stood beside Caris and Willard, waiting to see them off. Two well-wishers made for a pathetic farewell party, but Lane's insurrection and its bloody conclusion had severely dampened morale. Of their own company, Willard appeared to be seething with the Blood still, barely controlling his agitation, and Caris had already plunged her horse-touched senses into Rag to keep the mare calm near Molly.

"You ride for the white witch's tower?" Farley asked, as Harric reined alongside. "You don't fear her more than Bannus? Captain promised we won't go near that cursed tower. We'll take our chances in the wild."

Harric gave a small smile. "Abellia is gentle and kind. The tales you've heard are lies."

Farley didn't seem to hear him, for his attention had shifted to Caris, who was stroking Rag's mane and making horse sounds in the way she did when she'd lost herself in the mare's senses. "She talking *horse*-talk?" Farley's nose wrinkled.

Caris heard him and looked up. It took a while for the words to reach her in her state of commune with the horse, but when they did, a deep blush crept up her neck. Abruptly, she turned Rag and walked her a few paces up the road.

Harric sighed. "That might not have been the most delicate thing you've ever said."

"I'm sorry," Farley said. "I didn't think she'd care. I wouldn't care if I could talk to horses. Does she really understand what they say?"

"From what I've seen, she does. In a way you or I could never comprehend."

Willard was speaking to Captain Gren. Harric snuck a glance at the knight and saw no telltale purple or blue in his skin or eyes. "Remember, Captain Gren," Willard said, "keep the men here no longer than three days. That will give us all the time we need. After that, steal away, even if it seems Bannus has not yet cleared the rubble."

Gren nodded. "It is our honor, Sir Willard. Now if you'll excuse me, I have a gift for your man, Harric." Willard's glance hardened, but the captain smiled and nudged Farley, who jerked as if he'd been stuck with a pin. Farley lifted a fat waxed-canvas pack to Harric. From its top protruded two of the fort's wide-mouthed spitfires, and Harric caught the distinctive scent of resin.

"With the captain's thanks," Farley said.

Harric smiled in surprise. "I am honored."

"Well, you showed you can use them," said Gren. "And take this." He handed Harric a leather blast mask shaped like a scowling dove. "Hate to see that pretty face pocked by resin."

Harric's eyes stung with sudden tears, and in the depths of his self-loathing, a little light appeared. He dared not blink, lest the tears fall, but in a moment of inspiration, he donned the mask to hide his eyes. "I'll wear it with honor," he said.

As if to convey his opinion of that, Willard turned Molly abruptly up the road. "Luck smile on you, captain."

The snub to Harric was not lost on Farley, whose eyes widened. Gren smuggled a wink to Harric, which Farley intercepted. His boyish face bloomed with a mischievous grin, and from where Gren could not see it, he stuck out his tongue at Willard's back.

"The mask suits you," said Gren. The captain held Harric's eye long enough to suggest he referred to more than just the blast mask. Then he laid a brisk slap on Snapper's rump and sent Harric trotting after the others.

Harric looked back, uncertain how much the captain guessed about him, and feeling a tug of real loss. "I'll see you at your knightings!" he called back.

Moons, he hoped he would. If they survived Sir Bannus, they'd deserve earldoms.

As they rode up the pass, Harric couldn't help but glance back periodically. Each time, he half expected to see Bannus and Gygon charging up the stony road, and though there was only ever empty mountains behind, he knew he wouldn't feel safe until that night, when they'd shut themselves in Abellia's tower.

A breeze gusted down the river gorge, blowing his hair back. In it, autumn's chill mingled with the dying scents of summer. The leaves of

the trembling aspen still wore jackets of green, but Harric judged that
in a few short weeks they'd shimmer like tumbling yellow coins.

When the sun had climbed high into the sky, they reached a stony
basin with a clear blue lake in its middle, and beyond it ridge after
ridge of green forest. The instant Caris spied the lake, she spurred
Rag into a gallop and raced along its dry mud edge. Holly and Idgit
snorted enthusiastically, but remained tethered in their line.

"Lady Caris knows what's best for her beast," said Willard, "but we'll
preserve the rest of the horses. We've many days of hard road ahead."

Watching Caris ride lifted another weight from Harric's heart. It seemed
when wind streamed through her hair, a hood of worries fell back from her
face. Her eyes brightened, her cheeks colored. When she reached the end
of the lake and raced back toward them, she leaned down, picked up a
sun-bleached stave off spoke-limb from the beach, and veered Rag into
the adjoining meadows to joust at the shrubs. Little cries of her laughter
reached them on the breeze.

Kogan's piggy eyes sparked. "Horse-touched got a gift. Never tire of
watching them ride. You ever know Brother Mikl, Will?"

Willard grunted. "Dog-touched. Traveled with a pack of stolen
hounds?"

"Not stolen, Will. *Converted.* When a lord set his hounds after
Mikl, that lord never saw them again. That lord wondered, 'Why'd my
hounds go quiet? Musta been killt by the priest!' But Mikl wouldn't
hurt a dog. He made them family."

"Useful when freeing peasants, no doubt."

"Aye, that's so, Will. Hard to hunt a man if your dogs disappear. And
no farm dog in the country would speak a word when Mikl passed by in
the night, neither, so he stole a chicken better than any man I knowed."
Kogan scratched his chin through the nest of whiskers. "You reckon it's
like that for the lady and horses?"

Willard gusted smoke from his nostrils. "She emptied the stables in
Gallows Ferry. Made a herd of twenty horses and ran them up the road
like a stampede. Left Bannus's crew staring."

Kogan nodded. He watched Harric from the corner of his eye. "But
then, ol' Mikl were never quite right in the head. Hardly a word in him,
except dog words like growls and yips."

"Caris isn't like that, if that's what you're wondering," said Harric.

"She's smart, and talks as well as most."

Kogan raised a shaggy eyebrow. Was that a teasing smile under the beard? "Oh? That's good for her."

Nearby, Rag leapt a stump and wheeled only a stride after landing. Caris shouted, eyes flashing.

Moons, I wish I could make her that happy.

His mind returned to the possibility of using the powers of the Unseen to remove the ring, but he couldn't let his hopes get too high. If Ibergs had been trying in vain to crack the secret of the Kwendi magic, Fink might be just as baffled by it. Harric pressed the pocket containing his witch-stone to feel its reassuring solidity against his ribs. At this point, it was still their best hope.

They halted for a stretch and a meal at the edge of a stand of pale stemmed aspen. Harric went straight to Caris's side and shared a handful of blueberries he'd hurriedly picked along the shore. He loved to be with her after she'd been with Rag. In those times, she had few words, but her spirit glowed, and her mind seemed most relaxed and free of human worry, so the silence was warm and companionable.

Caris watched him, a small smile playing around her mouth. "You know, when I don't hate myself for thinking about you all the time, I actually like you."

"Truly? You think one day without that ring you'd—"

"No."

"But we'd be friends."

"Probably."

As Harric sliced into a hunk of hard white cheese made from Geraldine's milk at the fort, Father Kogan let out a howl of outrage from deep in the aspen. He erupted from the brush, plowing through saplings and shouting, "Moons and magic! To arms! We're under attack!"

Harric bolted to his feet, spilling his lunch.

Caris faced the aspens, sword flashing in her hand. "What is it?"

Kogan crashed into the open, eyes wide and wild. "It's a moon-damned witch walker! To arms! Rope and fire!"

...Sir Kogan was a formidable lancer in his day...competing with me and knights of the Blue Order...when he wasn't drunk or breaking horse backs by vaulting into saddles... A great loss to the sport when the god took him...

—Sir Willard, quoted in *Tourneys of the Golden Age of Chasia*, by Lord Billus

13

Old Friends & New Peril

Harric crouched, scanning the trees for an enemy.

Kogan grabbed up a pine trunk the size of Harric and spun about to face the aspen as if something pursued him. "I seen it in the trees! Went in to pipe a leak and there it was, staring at me like a god-touched statcha!"

Brolli had wakened and now stood with a globe of witch-silver in one hand and a painted war club in the other. Willard moved to the ambassador's side with Belle in hand.

"What is the word *statcha?*" said Brolli.

"A statcha! Like it were carved from stone—"

"*Statue,*" Harric said.

"—only this one were made outta clay and sticks like a drunk potter made it, and it walks like it got no knees, or it would've catched me!"

Harric paused. "Mudruffle? I think he means *Mudruffle.*"

Brolli lowered his club and barked out a laugh.

Willard cursed.

Kogan gave the limb a couple of mighty two-handed swings, and the weapon sang an ominous *whuh!* with each. "Mud and wattle he is, and I aim to make him kindling."

"Put down the tree, Kogan," Willard growled.

"Reckon a club ain't right for it, Will? It's made o' mud and sticks, so a club oughta—"

"A *friend*, Kogan," said Willard, and this time, the knight's words had an edge of menace. "It's the white witch's servant, and a friend." Turning impatiently to the aspen grove, he shouted, "Mudruffle, show yourself. You are safe now."

Confusion twisted Kogan's thick brows. "An Iberg witch-toy is a *friend?*"

Harric imagined he saw a flash of residual Blood rage in Willard's glare. "Mistress Abellia is one of the few Sisters of the Bright Mother Moon that the Queen has licensed in Arkendia. She is a friend of the Queen's. Therefore, she is a friend of mine—and a friend of yours if you have a brain in that thick skull. Abellia's tower stands in a grove of fire-cones that produces much of the Queen's resin, and her magic snuffs lightning before it can set off the fire-cones. I encourage you to consider the importance of that resin in our war against the Old Ones before you murder her servant."

The priest's brown eyes turned to flint. "I abide your chimpey friend, Will, because he ain't a magus. He's just an ambassador. I abide him because the Queen needs a peace treaty with his people, because now ain't no time for another enemy at our back." Kogan gripped the club like he would twist it into splinters. "But there ain't no treaty with the Ibergs. And I won't brook no shambling witch-walker made of sticks and rubbish. I'll crack it to pieces."

"We aren't yet sure it is Mudruffle," Brolli said. "Might it be some other creature?"

Mudruffle's weirdly hornlike voice bleated from the brush. "It is I! I am without injury,"

"Sounds like it strangles a goose." Kogan strode toward the sound, tree still in hand. "I'll bash the unnatural statcha to splinters!"

"Kogan!" Willard boomed, and the priest halted. It seemed to Harric that Willard's voice had altered, deepened, amplified somehow. Perhaps the priest noticed, too, for he stopped and stared at Willard in surprise. If he suspected the old knight once again hosted the Blood of the God in his veins, however, he said nothing.

Willard stormed to the priest's side and grabbed him by the smothercoat. Tall as Willard was, he still had to look up to meet Kogan's eyes. What he then said to Kogan was uttered too softly to be heard, but the tone was clear as a bell on a winter's morning: Kogan would tolerate Willard's companions, or he was free to leave.

The irony of Willard defending another magic-using companion while condemning Harric's *assumed* use brought a burn of acid to Harric's throat, but he swallowed it down. There would be no use in arguing with Willard. It would just make the old goat more suspicious.

Caris plowed through the greenery with Harric in tow, until the little golem stood before them, no higher than Harric's navel, his clay surface shaped and textured in the guise of an Iberg forester, complete with jaunty slouch hat and high boots.

"Harric and Caris," Mudruffle honked. "I fear I may have startled your gigantic companion. I did not see him until too late, though it staggers the mind to consider how one can overlook a mountain."

"Kogan is a peasant priest," said Harric. "It's his religion to hate magic. It isn't personal."

"I am more concerned for your wellbeing than my own," said Mudruffle. "Last night we heard a great rumbling from the pass, and my mistress sent me to investigate. As I am unable to ride, my progress is slow, but by good fortune you have stopped to rest near my farthest point of progress."

Caris related the tale of the previous night's battle, including the blasts that brought down the cliff on Bannus's army. "You must have heard the blasts and rockfall as far away as the tower."

"Yes," said Mudruffle. "But that would not explain all. Since you left, we have heard distant thumps from the northern ridges. Not as big as the sound of your explosion, but many dozens. We fear your enemies may be trying to clear one of the blocked passes there, in order to come around behind you. Abellia wished me to warn you."

Harric's stomach twisted. He knew of passes north of Gallows Ferry that had been intentionally blocked in order to isolate access to the fire-cone groves. It was illegal to blast them clear, but Sir Bannus would not let that stop him, and the Queen's servants in the north were too few and too weak to try.

"Thank you, Mudruffle," Caris said, sharing a grim look with Harric. "We'll tell Willard immediately. Come with me and I'll get you on a horse."

"I fear the giant, my lady."

Caris frowned. "I think Willard has spoken with Father Kogan, but I'll check." She left Harric with the golem, her armored figure sliding easily through the brush.

"How is your mistress?" Harric asked. "Well, I hope."

"She is well. How goes the Lady Caris, with the Kwendi ring on her finger?"

Harric nearly gave a reflexive "Fine, fine," but found himself pausing. The golem knew as much about magic as Fink. He was, after all, a servant of the White Moon. And Harric trusted him to hold Caris's interests in mind as much as anyone, so it could only help to share his concerns. "She suffers," he said.

Mudruffle nodded. "As do you, I think."

Despite Mudruffle's ridiculous honking voice, the words touched Harric. He pinched the bridge of his nose. "Only the ordinary kind," he said. "You know, if I thought it would do her any good, I'd leave her and Willard and strike out on my own."

"You are correct in assuming it would be worse for her."

Harric nodded. "I thought so. Have you thought of any way to remove the ring without hurting her?"

"If it were Bright Mother magic, perhaps I could do something. But there is Dark Moon magic in that ring. Of that I am sure."

Caris returned through the brush, face attractively flushed with exertion. "Come, Mudruffle. Willard guarantees your safety. But I should warn you that your news of the thumps in the north passes has put him in a foul temper—"

"Big surprise," muttered Harric.

"—and he's ordered us back in the saddle, immediately, and then he wants to hear the news from you directly."

"I am happy to tell him as I told you."

Caris led them back through the aspens toward the shore. "Also, the ambassador is awake," she said over her shoulder. "And he asked that you be strapped beside him on his pony. He very much enjoys your company, and he says those without knees should ride with those without rumps."

"I also have no rump."

"All the more reason. Father Kogan agreed to follow at a distance on his cow, and to sleep the night in the meadow below the gardens."

"Last time you stayed with us, Sir Willard expressed interest in me guiding you through the mountains beyond our tower. Assuming I go with you, will the priest go with us then?"

"I think so."

Mudruffle paused. "It is my hope I will not live in constant peril of being smashed to kindling."

"We all live in awe of the good father's whim," said Harric.

Caris led them in silence the rest of the afternoon. Twice Harric imagined he heard distant horns behind them, but whenever he looked back, he saw nothing but empty trail. Eyes and ears now strained forward, too, anticipating enemies from some newly opened northern pass. None appeared there, either, but whenever the trial allowed it, Caris urged the horses into a canter to cover more ground. The worst possible outcome would be if they were trapped between Bannus on one side, and men from some north pass on the other.

The tower finally drew into view in the late afternoon. High on its ridge amidst towering fire-cone trees, its yellow sandstone shone gold in the late evening sunlight. Fat resin cones hung like explosive ornaments in the trees' highest branches, prompting Kogan to jab a stubborn finger at the thunder spire rising from the top of Abellia's tower. "That thunder spire is truth-solid fact the Queen don't need no white witch to damp lightning. Magic-free Arkendians already found a way."

When they reached the meadows below the terraced gardens, Kogan halted and made the sign of the heart before him. "This witch woman," he said, looking at Willard. "Ain't you worried about your hex lighting up around her? Ain't it foes and women what set it off?"

Willard gave a stiff nod. "It is. But Abellia is a crone. And for whatever reason, my hex is not triggered by crones. Nor is it wakened by attached or uninterested women." He indicated Caris with a jerk of his head.

"Sounds like a jealous hex. You slight a witch or something, Will? Maybe you slighted a witch and she put a no-love hex on ye."

"I've thought that myself."

Kogan shook his head and spat. "And that's why we have the two laws."

The priest turned the great musk ox aside, and the two of them lumbered away toward a huge weeping willow beside a creek in the middle of the meadow. "Find me at the willow in the morning."

Willard caught Caris's eye. "Let's move, girl."

Caris hesitated, her eyes on the priest, then looked at the sky, where gray clouds threatened rain.

"Father Kogan," said Mudruffle, who had been watching Caris and the priest. "Mistress Abellia is sworn to shelter and protect. She took Caris in last winter when she had need, and she welcomed Willard when first he fled Sir Bannus. You would be most welcome in the tower."

"Honk not at me, vile whatsit!" Kogan said. "Nor tempt me with magic nor witches. I'll bunk in the wild with Gerry, like a good Arkendian, and taste no magic vittles, neither."

Harric pressed his lips tight to keep from smiling; when the good father was roused, his language grew lofty.

"Let him go, Mudruffle," Willard said. "Don't goad a mad dog."

Caris led them up the switchbacks, where they passed through Mudruffle's terraced gardens and orchards. Harric's stomach growled in anticipation of the little golem's cooking. Mudruffle made glorious, crusty breads and delicious white beans in spiced oil that Harric sometimes dreamed about. When he passed an apple tree loaded with yellow fruit, Harric snapped one off and sank his teeth into the sweet flesh. Kogan had forsworn anything touched by the witch or her "witch-walker," claiming "Geraldine's milk will keep me whole, and I'll find forage in the wild wood, too."

Harric couldn't help but notice the cow also carried ale casks from the fort.

Forage, my toe. He'll be just as hungover tomorrow.

Halfway up the terrace switchbacks, they heard a sound like the *thump* of distant blasting. It came on the wind from the north.

"As I reported," said Mudruffle, "I fear your enemies are at work in the north pass."

"You see how badly they want our good ambassador and his wedding ring," Harric said.

"I am so honored," said Brolli, who had emerged from his sleeping blanket. Another *thump* rumbled from the north, and he winced.

"How long have they been blasting?" Harric asked.

"Two days, Master Harric," said Mudruffle. "It began the day you left us."

So much for a head start on our pursuers. "Sir Willard," said Harric, "the Queen's toolers cleared a rockslide north of Gallows Ferry in two days."

Willard chewed at a stick shaped like a ragleaf roll. "How far from here is the north pass, Mudruffle?"

"Two days' walk, a day on horse," Mudruffle replied.

"That means they could reach us as soon as nightfall tomorrow, at which time we must be long gone. It will be ill news for Captain Gren if he comes this way. Tomorrow we shall leave him a sign on the road below. Tonight, we must provision from Abellia's stores, and by noon tomorrow I want us down the other side of this ridge and on the trail. Understood?"

Mutters of acknowledgement from the others.

"Harric, pack the saddlebags with provisions. Caris, check the gear and horses."

"I will go north while you sleep," said Brolli. "To spy if there be campfires."

"I can also help in this regard," said Mudruffle, "as I require no sleep."

Willard grunted. "The rest of us will be sure to get to sleep early. We wake at dawn to rouse the priest and cut staves for lances in that meadow. I want to be on the road before sun crests those mountains."

"See, Arkendia, the fruits of thy folly! For your so-called Cleansing hath set a woman to rule. Call it not Cleansing, then, but Defilement. For woman was made in service of man…and to take empire from a man and give it to a woman…seemeth an evident portent of the Chaos Moon…"

—Reportedly said by Second Herald Quort, upon the ascension of Queen Chasia

14

White Moon Servants

Harric hobbled the horses at the foot of the tower so Mudruffle could take Willard and Brolli to greet their hostess. Before crossing the threshold, the golem paused and made several subtle motions with his sticklike hands.

Removing wards, Harric realized. The first time they'd entered the tower, weeks before, alarms had sounded as Brolli crossed the threshold. To Abellia's horror, Brolli had confessed to bearing magic from all three moons. To Abellia's credit—or to the credit of her fierce desire to learn more about Kwendi magic—she'd only hesitated a heartbeat before she removed the wards and welcomed him inside. This time, Mudruffle made no fuss or announcement, but Harric found himself wondering if Fink could show him how to make similar tricks in the Unseen.

The golem led them up the tower's curving stairway past several floors to the top, where the kitchen and large windows and ample Ibergian rugs made a fair and gracious living space. Since Mudruffle had no knees, he ascended the stairs in a zigzag fashion, goose-stepping from the far edge of one step to the opposite edge of the next, pivoting, and repeating.

Harric had plenty of time to count one hundred and five steps to the top living floor.

When they finally arrived at the landing, they found the door open and Abellia waiting in a stuffed chair by the fire. Tiny and frail, she peered at them from a face pale as paper. Her white hair seemed so light and thin that it virtually floated above her shoulders, but her dark eyes flashed with alertness and life.

"Mio Doso," she exclaimed as they entered. "We worry very much of you." Her Iberg accent made her Rs sound like Ds. *Woddy veddy much.* "The great thunder we hear. The mountain falling. But here you are."

Harric hurried to her side and helped her to rise, which she accepted gratefully.

"Good Harric." Her black eyes flashed like wet pebbles in a sea of wrinkles. "Kind boy, take me to the ambassador."

When they reached Willard and Brolli, she released Harric's arm, took up the Kwendi's huge hand in hers, and stared intently into his huge golden eyes.

"I wish you to stay here," she said, her voice creaking. She turned her watery eyes to Willard while holding fast to Brolli's hand. "You are to be safe here, Sir Willard. No danger from this Bannus."

"I thank you, good sister." Willard gave a polite bow. "But we cannot be certain of that. And I would not bring danger to you."

"Then we must to go with you," she said. "We go with to help on your way."

"Mama," Caris said. "Our road is rough and dangerous—"

"That's true," said Willard. "Mudruffle agreed to guide us with his maps, and his help is more than enough. You will be safe here in your tower."

Abellia let out a brief spark of a laugh. Her eyes flashed as if she had a merry secret. "I am being a Sister of the Bright Mother, Sir Willard. For such important time, these bones may be made to strong again. I go with you." The door to the kitchen thumped, interrupting her, as Mudruffle emerged with a huge tray of food balanced on his head. "But first, you must to eat," she said. "Then we hear where you have been these three days."

"Your table is most welcome, mistress, but I wish to make clear from the start that we stay but one night," Willard said. "Just long enough to rest and be on our way."

"To the lands of the Kwendi." Abellia's eyes sparked. "For a treaty with the Queen. But we let you to eat first. Eat in peace, and tonight we to speak of news and to plan."

As soon as Mudruffle set down the tray, which was full of bowls and jugs and loaves and covered pitchers, the ancient woman beckoned to the golem. "Come, I have much to prepare."

As Mudruffle crossed the room in his jerking stride, Caris shared a worried glance with Sir Willard. Harric's sense of the absurd threatened to make him smile. Would there now be three passengers who had to be tied to their horses?

Harric handed Abellia off to Mudruffle, and the golem led her away to her chambers.

"Harric," said Willard, before Harric could approach the food. "I want you to tend to the horses and clean out the saddlebags in preparation for tomorrow. The Lady Caris will remain here with us." Willard sat, tore off a hunk of bread with his teeth, and noisily chewed it as he poured a cup of brown ale.

To Harric, the way he'd said "lady" meant "one of noble character."

He suppressed the urge to roll his eyes.

"Will do!" he said, putting on his best happy-to-help tone. "Just let me grab a bite to take with me." He scooped up a bowl of beans and a loaf of bread, ignoring Willard's glare and sending Caris a wink. He couldn't let her worry that something had happened between him and Willard, or she might ask about it, and he'd sworn himself to secrecy about the incident. Nevertheless, he felt her eyes on him as he left, so he kept a cheerful bounce in his step.

Once on the landing of the stairwell, he paused, half expecting her to follow, though he wasn't sure what he'd do if she did.

"I am glad to be here again." It was Brolli speaking, his mouth obviously full. "Most delicious fat beans. I missed them."

"What did Abellia mean by saying she was coming with us?" said Willard. "She can't weigh seventy pounds. First wind would blow her down. Moons, the wind of Brolli's beans would send her skyward."

The Kwendi barked his peculiar laugh.

"Yes." Caris paused as if chewing. "I hope to talk to her about it."

"She is most interested in my magic," said Brolli. "I think she wishes to see my people."

Willard grunted. "Told you she'd be lulu about that. But it's out of the question."

Harric left them, a coal of anger burning in his chest. Willard clearly intended to treat him like a misbehaving servant now.

Halfway down the stairs, a strange sound caught his attention. It came from a door on the landing below the main living floor. He paused on the landing and listened. It was Mudruffle. The golem's voice grew louder, as if he were moving toward the door. Of course, the only reason Harric could hear the creature at all through the heavy door was because of the extraordinary nature of his voice—that toneless shout, breaking to honking, like a distressed donkey.

"If this is so, mistress," said Mudruffle, "then I must go with them." He spoke in Iberg, and the accent was difficult for Harric to pry through, as his mother's lessons had been with a decidedly Arkendian pronunciation. Fortunately, the golem paused for long stretches after he spoke, which gave Harric some time to translate what he heard. During the pauses, Mistress Abellia must have replied, only with a voice too weak to penetrate the door.

"Indeed, your service to our moon has been great, but you could not thrive on such a difficult road…I am certain. And the immortal hunts them…danger. It is most urgent the Bright Mother succeed in this…"

Harric set the bowl of beans and the bread on a stair below the room, and crouched at the crack beneath the door to listen. Willard's head would explode if he saw him. But they spoke about him and his friends, and not in terms of Willard's quest, but in terms of the Bright Mother. What did the White Moon care of their mission, and what "success" did it so urgently seek?

He heard a murmur beyond the door. Abellia's small voice, perhaps.

Then Mudruffle's voice. "Very few can grant the right to heal yourself. We must inform Vella. She will know."

Heal *Abellia's* body? As far as Harric could tell, she wasn't ill. The only thing keeping her from accompanying them on their "hard road" was her advanced age… Harric's eyes widened. Of course. The Iberg emperors were said to be ageless, and it was the Bright Mother mages who provided that service. Mudruffle was talking about restoring Abellia's youth!

Golden light blazed beneath the door. The intensity drove Harric back in surprise. Instantly, he knew—or rather felt with the core of his being—a mighty presence beyond the door. Knowledge of it pushed the air from his lungs and left him bracing himself feebly against the wall, mouthing like a fish in air.

A new voice rang out, clear and bright as brass in his mind. There were no words—neither Iberg nor Arkendian—only thoughts so golden pure and powerful that they banished the borders of self and became his own thoughts, filling him with profound but fleeting understanding.

This opportunity is most unexpected and good, it thought—*she* thought—and her rightness and purity filled him to ecstasy. He was a candle in a bonfire. Gloriously consumed and overwhelmed. He was a creek bed flooded with a mighty river of thoughts.

Your service is noted, Sister Abellia. But this is a matter too great for a vestir such as I to decide. The Bright Mother alone must possess the Kwendi secret. That we know. Above all, it must be kept from the Unseen, whose trade is secrets. Far better it were destroyed than it fall to that moon. Therefore, I must alert the ronir. They will decide your course of action. Await a Sending from one greater than I. You have done well.

Then it was gone, and Harric's mind was small and dark again.

Abandoned by that golden certainty, he felt cold and empty and utterly without meaning. The Bright Mother was the only meaning, and the Unseen its opposite, a blot of defiling darkness. He staggered a few steps down the stairs and collapsed in a ball, his cheek on a cold stone stair. There he gaped and stared like a calf stunned by a butcher's mallet.

Harric had no idea how long he'd been on the stair when he roused. A voice had brought him back, echoing loudly in the narrow stairwell. He lifted his head and peered about.

A tiny, frail old woman in ghostly white passed through the light of an arrow slit as she climbed the stair, her back to him. She clung with claw-like hands to the arm of someone at her side, who helped her climb.

She had not seen him as she turned to climb the stairs above, and now, as she disappeared around the curve of the stairwell, another wave of emptiness swept through him. He pressed a hand to his mouth, holding back a sob. Then he rose and staggered down the stairs and out into the yard. In the stable, he curled in a ball and wept.

Empty. Alone. Damned.

Eventually, his own thoughts returned to fill the void. The boundaries of identity re-formed, and he knew himself again. He forced himself to stand, to breathe, to look around.

Willard's young packhorse, Holly, tossed her head, looking at him from under the tournament caparison Willard insisted she wear constantly. Her stable mates still waited outside, impatient to be rubbed and watered and fed. One whinnied, and Holly whinnied back.

"Hold on," Harric muttered. "I'll be out to get you in a moment."

He massaged his temples, trying to piece together the events outside the glowing door. His memory of the event seemed in shreds, and even as he struggled, they faded. The more he returned to himself, the more the transcendent glory of those moments retreated. He grasped for the words he'd overheard, but they slipped away. He grasped for that ineffable feeling of rightness and joy, but it eluded him. It was as if a great swath of his memory were bleached white by a blaze of unearthly light, the stuff of his mind too frail to retain it.

He remembered Willard's order to take care of the horses before supper. Hadn't he taken a bowl of beans for himself? He must have left it on the landing. He remembered hearing Mudruffle speak. He'd spoken in Iberg, and a few of the words had made Harric dig deep into his mother's Iberg lessons. Yes. He remembered those. *Accompany. Secret. Success.* And he remembered feeling that Mudruffle wanted something from Harric's companions.

After that...the memory faded. Too close to the burn.

Rising, he shoved the hair back from his face and tended to the horses, all the while mulling the matter over. Regardless of the specifics, the experience on the stairs left him with the distinct feeling that Mudruffle and Abellia had an agenda they weren't sharing with the rest of them. Something to do with their moon and its desires, and not with helping Willard.

Obviously, he ought to tell Willard, but he knew exactly what the old knight would think: *You are a fool and an eavesdropping sneak.* A pulse of shame heated his face. *He'd probably think I was sniffing about for magic, too.* No. He couldn't tell Willard or Caris.

He'd see what he could learn from Fink.

Since the Unseen Moon can in fact be seen by the stars it occults, we should learn to call it not "Unseen" but simply "Black." And since it takes no predictable path through the sky and has no effect on the tides, I stipulate it is no moon at all. What it is I cannot say, but to call it moon is mere foolishness. "The Black Spot," let us call it, for that is all we can truly say.

—From *The Sayings of Master Tooler Jobbs*, by Prentice Vincen

15

Black Moon Interlude

Fink bounced on a wire in the fire-cone trees. The massive cable descended from the soaring structure Harric had called a "thunder spire" and anchored in the bedrock. He wasn't sure of its purpose. Something about stealing thunder and lightning? That didn't seem right. How could one steal such things? He'd ask Harric about it when he came.

He shifted uncomfortably on the wire. This sort of contraption was all over Arkendia. "Toolery," Harric called it. Instead of magic, they resorted to this clumsy mechanical flimflam. He picked absently at the strands of the cable under his feet. Above him, a breeze rocked the spire, and the cable slacked, so he dipped slightly, then rose as the spire rocked back again.

Such effort, such labor and energy. And all to avoid magic!

He shivered. Arkendian refusal of magic made his guts crawl. And it was an aspect of Harric's background that put him on guard. The kid thought differently than any magus Fink had known, and in surprising ways that he couldn't anticipate. And if Fink couldn't anticipate him, how could he control him?

The air before him pushed with a loud rush and pop as Fink's sisters materialized around him. With a small cry of surprise, he slipped from the wire, only avoiding a stinging fall to the roots with an awkward grab with one hand, which won him time to spread and flap his wings before he dropped.

Zire loomed above him, a pillar of black smoke. Sic and Missy flanked her, tall, cloaked figures of bone and hooded skulls.

"Greetings, sisters three," he said, as he found footing on the fire-cone roots and folded his wings in a peak behind him. He performed a mocking bow, his grin wide and strained. "To what do I owe this enormous—if utterly uncalled-for—pleasure?"

A squirm of worry wriggled through him as his gaze flicked from one to the other and the other, looking for clues to their purpose. They had no reason to be there. His reports had been on time. He hadn't summoned them. In fact, he didn't want them there, for if Harric saw them, it would damage his already tenuous trust. The one time the kid had seen them, he nearly fainted.

Sic spoke, her voice the fluting hiss of wind through dry bones. "*We come to relieve you. We choose to secure the Arkendian ourselves.*"

Fink's jaw dropped like he'd been knocked with a stone. When he finally found his tongue, he quivered with fear and fury. "Even you aren't that stupid. You'll ruin everything."

Zire's grating sub-bass sent an itching vibration through the membranes of his wings. "YOUR ATTEMPTS TO WIN THE ARKENDIAN'S TRUST BRING RISK. I WILL TAKE POSSESSION OF HIS WILL AND ELIMINATE RISK."

Fink could not keep the panic from his voice. "Possess his body? You're teasing, right?" He glanced to Sic and Missy, who remained silent. Did he sense discomfort in their stiff postures? Perhaps Zire had overruled them in this, for it wasn't like them to play this sort of trick; if they wanted to torture him, they'd simply beat him and rob him of his meals. With a jolt, he realized how stupid he'd been. He'd assumed they'd merely wanted him to fail again, so they could consume him or make him their slave forever. To thwart them, he'd simply planned to succeed—to use Harric to get close enough to steal the secret of the Kwendi magic—and thereby win promotion beyond their reach. But all along they'd been plotting to make a play for the Kwendi magic *themselves*.

He put on a sneer. "That kid is smart. His Kwendi friend is smart. And the white witch's tryst is as clever as he is ridiculous. I give you half a day in Harric's skin before one of them senses you and the white tryst casts you out in full sunlight." He snorted. "Half an hour, more like. And you can bet your smoking cheeks I'll be there to watch it."

"IT IS OUR JUDGMENT."

"Judgment requires *understanding*," Fink snapped, "and you no more understand Harric than you understand White Moon doily weaves." He glanced at Sic and Missy, searching in vain for signs of understanding, then jabbed a hooked talon toward them. "It'll be your failure, too. Mark my words, this act of idiotic overreach will undo you. *Possess his will.* Are you kidding? This kid requires finesse, not invasion. He requires a soft touch, and cunning, and only one of us—me!—has any of that, and you know it."

"MISSY HAS A SOFTER TOUCH," said Zire.

"Softer than what?" Fink laughed. "A hammer?" Panic made his breaths short and rabbitlike. He forced himself to take a few deep breaths and looked again at Sic and Missy. Sic had turned her hooded skull to Missy, who seemed to sense her, and looked away. Hope sparked in him. The younger sisters didn't want to cross Zire. But they saw the folly in her plan.

"Look. Girls." He spread his hands in a placating gesture. "Possession is a last resort. If Harric were uncooperative—which he isn't, because he needs me—or if he sends me away—which he won't, because he wants what I can teach him—or if he loses his connection with the Kwendi or the knight—which he can't, because he's tied to the knight's girl by the entanglement of that Kwendi ring—if any of this happens, *then* I give you leave to possess him as you like. But now, when I have him right where we want him?" His lip curled in a sneer. "I bet you souls to damnation that white tryst casts you out in full sunlight before you've enjoyed your first lunch in that body."

"*Perhaps there is no hurry in this decision, sisters,*" said Sic.

Blue light flickered in Zire's billowing smoke. Missy's hood turned toward her.

"I've got him eating from my hand," Fink continued, "like a baby bird that's lost its mama. He keeps me secret from his friends. He'll ask the Kwendi anything I want. But if you take me away or possess his body, you may as well appear as you do now and ask for the secret."

Missy nodded her empty hood. Her voice was the sound of distant, mournful owls. "There is no need to act now."

"I COULD TAKE POSSESSION OF THE CAT INSTEAD."

"You know nothing about human affairs—" Fink said.

"YOU HAVE USED THE CAT IN THAT WAY."

"He knows how the cat works, smoke-for-brains. He's seen my eyes in it. You don't think he'll notice if his pet walks up with smoking holes for eyes?"

In a motion faster than Fink could follow, one of Zire's gigantic, smoking hands slammed him flat upon the roots. Fink cried out in pain as his wings and spine racked against the unrelenting surface.

"I WILL HAVE THE KWENDI MAGIC. I WILL HAVE THIS ARKENDIAN."

"He's yours!" Fink squeaked. "Just not yet! We need him! Be patient!"

Zire's burning hand pressed harder. The pain of the roots nearly made Fink pass out. His chest flattened so much under the weight that he could scarcely draw breath.

"Besides!" he wheezed. "If I fail—I take the fall—not you. Double safe—"

"I WILL HAVE HIM."

"No one contests that," murmured Missy.

A deep rumble from the smoke that was Zire. Flashes of lightning, now red with anger, threaded through it.

"*Is it decided, then?*" said Sic, her whispery voice sliding in from the side. "*We wait to possess the Arkendian?*" She'd framed it as a question so Zire could make the decision, but by asking it, she made clear she supported Fink's caution. Fink strained his eyes to the side, trying to see her as she spoke, but flashing smoke obscured his view.

Zire rumbled, a roiling storm compressed in a pillar of darkness. "AT THE END OF EACH NIGHT, YOU WILL REPORT TO ME." The vibrations of her grating voice rippled through her hand and into Fink in waves of pain. He squirmed, no longer able to gather enough breath to cry out. "YOU WILL ANSWER TO ME. WITHOUT FAIL.

Fink nodded wildly. *I can't breathe! You're crushing me!*

"EACH NIGHT, YOU WILL CONVINCE ME WHY I SHOULD NOT TAKE POSSESSION OF THE ARKENDIAN."

Stars flashed before his eyes until she released enough pressure for him to suck in a breath and howl in pain. "If that's what it takes, sure! Yes!"

Another taloned hand appeared from the smoke. She dragged a single hooked claw down Fink's belly, parting the black flesh like a fisherman cleaning his catch. Fink howled as she dipped a talon in the slit and drew forth a loop of spirit, one of the souls he'd consumed. In its distended form, he saw eyes wide in terror, mouth wide in silent scream.

As Zire drew it into her smoke, hatred writhed through Fink. "Let me go," he said.

The hand that pinned him evaporated into smoke, and he clambered to his feet. With one hand, he held in his guts. "Mother will hear of this—" he began, but before he could finish, the three vanished and the air clapped behind them with a report like a snapping tree trunk.

The air at his back gusted forward and slammed him face-first into the roots.

"Fools!" he sputtered. "Idiots!" Panting with helpless rage, he clambered to his feet and threw handfuls of dirt after them. Some of the stones bounced among the roots. He looked about in the Unseen for their lurking figures, but saw nothing. No laughter trailed after. No hand emerged to grab him.

Far above, the fire-cone trees sighed in a breeze. Spots of red moonlight shifted across the faces of massive trunks around him.

He was alone again.

Fink let out a shuddering sigh. Cradling his belly, he sat on a prominent root and pinched the wound together so the spirit flesh could mend. The kid would be there before long. When the wound closed to form an itchy vertical line, he leapt up to flap himself back on the wire to think.

He'd lost a soul from his belly. That stung, but mostly from humiliation. Other than that, and pride, what had he lost in the skirmish?

Nothing.

He still had Harric. He still had charge of this opportunity to claim the Kwendi secret. Had it resulted in anything new? Yes. If he should appear to lose control of Harric, his sisters would intervene. He frowned. Well. He wouldn't lose control. How could he? He and Harric were partners.

So, what had he gained?

A sly smile crept across his face.

First, he'd exposed a rift between that idiot Zire and her younger, wiser sisters. Most important, he learned Zire wanted the credit for delivering the secret of the Kwendi magic to their moon. He shook his wings with quiet fury. The moment he had it, she'd try to snatch it from him. How she hated him. How she feared the vengeance he would take if he were ever promoted above her. She would rather no one of the Unseen achieved it than let Fink achieve it.

Almost. But her greed was stronger than her fear.

She would let Fink get close, and when she thought him on the verge of success, she'd move into Harric and claim the prize herself. So that was when he'd have to be careful—when they were getting close to the Kwendi. That was when he would have to be on his guard. And the kid would have to be on guard, too.

He allowed himself a sly grin. He was the smart one. She was the strong one. He'd outmaneuver her. Outplay her. Outwit her. And in the end, he would deliver the secret to Mother. He never tired of this fantasy. He'd make Zire his lackey, and when he hungered, he'd hook snacks from her belly and suck them like noodles between his teeth.

After dark, all cats are lions.

—Iberg saying

16

Questions In The Dark

It was past midnight when Harric buckled the flaps of the last pair of bulging saddlebags and lugged them to the cellar to hang on a hook beside the others. Two he'd stuffed with grain for the horses. The rest he'd crammed to the seams with butter, potatoes, wax-wrapped cheeses, and as many cakes of "strong bread"—a dense Iberg confection of figs, spiced honey, and whole hazelnuts—that he could fit. He'd stuffed himself with half a cake while he worked, and imagined he could live happily on strong bread alone.

"Harric?" Caris's voice down the cellar stairs.

"Here."

A moment later, she appeared in the doorway. When she saw him, her cheeks darkened and her nostrils flared like she was about to cross the room and plant a kiss on him. A heavy dread tugged at his stomach, even as his heart and other parts cheered approval.

"You're sleeping with me tonight," she said.

Harric blinked. He opened his mouth to speak, but found himself at a loss for words. Something set alarum horns blaring in his mind. Her *eyes*. She was actually meeting his eyes, pinning him with an intense gaze. The act was so alien for her that it took him aback. Normally, her horse-touched nature kept her eyes averted and limited her to rare glances. He'd never seen a sustained gaze like this. It was eerie. Un-Caris.

"Um. Sure," he said. "I mean, we've all been sleeping in basically the same room since we arrived—"

"No. I mean I put our bedrolls together in the stable loft." Her brow creased and then her cheeks flushed again. "It's...cooler there. And more private."

Her eyes held his, and he found himself looking away, embarrassed. *Embarrassed? Moons, by what?* He couldn't tell. "Okay. Is...everything okay? Do you need to talk?"

She nodded, eyes still intent. Now she seemed furious with him, or with herself. The muscles of her neck stood out, taut as lute strings. "So you'll come?"

"Yes. Of course."

She gave a curt nod, and finally broke her stare.

As she left, Harric stared after her, unable to move. That wasn't Caris. Something was very wrong. The ring. Something in the ring's spell had changed. His stomach gave a sick twist. He had to find Fink. Fink would know.

He flung the last saddle back on its hook, closed up the rest of the packs, and shut the cellar behind him. Above, the tower seemed to sleep. No light and no sound whatsoever traveled down the curve of stairway before him. He crept up the stairs to the ground floor then crossed the empty landing to the heavy exterior door. There he left his candle in a cresset and slipped out.

The sweet scent of fire-cone needles greeted him on the end-of-summer air. A light fog seemed to be moving in from the west. He couldn't help but think of the fogs his mother used to send, full of grasping spirits and vileness. But this fog had none of the unnatural opacity of her fogs. It appeared to be natural, if inconvenient for travel.

The red light of the Mad Moon turned the fog to blood, dashed itself against the trunks of the fire-cones, and glittered like bloody shards in the canopy of needles.

Across the yard, the stable was already dark, which meant Caris had finished with the horses and gone up to the straw of the stable loft, where she'd made their beds. With luck, she'd fall asleep, so he wouldn't have to explain why he didn't come straight to bed. Day work was done, yes—but night work was just beginning.

Ignoring the call of his weariness, he crept down the stairs into the yard, and since Brolli and Mudruffle had gone north for their watch, he headed south.

A shape the size of a large squirrel darted toward him from the shadow of the stables with a querulous *mew* that announced it was his little moon cat, Spook.

"There you are," Harric whispered. "Did you miss me, catty-cat?"

Spook padded up, rubbing against his ankles and meowing as if scolding Harric for his two-day absence. Harric picked him up and held him in the crook of his arm as he walked, scratching behind the cat's big ears. Spook purred with the volume of a much larger animal. To Harric, it was the drumming of distant hooves.

"Hush, little growler. Mudruffle will hear you from the other side of the ridge. He'll think Bannus is upon us."

The season brought a definite chill to the night air, and Harric hadn't thought to bring a blanket, so Spook's warm little body brought comfort as he followed a trail between gigantic fire-cone trunks. The soft thrum of Spook's purr was also a balm to his nerves, which were frayed by the taxing events of the day. By all rights, he should be fast asleep in his bed, not heading out to meet Fink.

But of all his worries, Fink was the first.

Since he'd struck the deal with the imp, a weight had hung in his chest. In his desire for the power of invisibility, Harric had jumped into a pact without really knowing what it entailed. Beyond the fact that entering the Unseen made him invisible in the Seen world, he knew almost nothing of the Unseen. He didn't know its rules, its dangers, or its denizens. He was a babe in the woods, forced to rely entirely on Fink as his nursemaid—Fink! A creature with whom no one would leave a corpse, much less a baby.

He sighed and paused beside a fire-cone trunk to let his eyes adjust to the darkness. "I am in deep, Spook," he muttered.

Spook acknowledged that with a tiny hitch in his purr.

Why did Fink even want a pact with Harric? What did Fink get from it? Harric had given Fink his freedom, of course, but Harric had no idea what that really meant, beyond the fact that, in exchange, Harric himself wouldn't be enslaved after death. But what if, by freeing Fink, he'd created a worse problem? What if there was a *reason* Fink was required to serve as a slave? What if it was some important restraint or punishment? Maybe it was as simple as Fink proving himself to some "Black Circle," or maybe his sisters; the imp had implied that the pact with Harric was his chance to show himself worthy.

But that only raised another question: What would happen once Fink proved himself? Would he have any use for Harric? What would be in it for Fink after that?

Harric ran a hand over his face. *Moons, I know nothing.*

And Fink knew all about Harric and his friends. Harric knew Fink had spied on more than one of Harric's conversations with Caris, and no telling how many with Willard and Brolli.

There. That was the core of the problem.

Though the pact made them technically equal—dealt them each an equal hand—Fink knew all Harric's cards. Yet it was equally clear that if Harric wished to become a useful servant for the Queen and the greatest trickster Arkendia had ever known—he needed Fink. Alone, Harric could barely hold himself in the Unseen for a minute. With Fink at his side, it was effortless; he could stay in the Unseen all night.

As expected, he found Fink in a clearing where one of the thunder-rod's heavy cables swooped down from the sky and anchored in the earth. The cable was thicker than Harric's thumb and stretched up into the darkness like a strand of the Unseen Web. A windlass in the lowest reaches of the cable kept tension high. It was on this windlass that Fink perched, muttering.

"Talking to yourself?" Harric stepped into the moonlight of the clearing. Spook looked up to see Fink and yawned. "I'm not that late."

"Hey, kid." The imp perched at eye level, like an agitated crow, eyes skipping to the sides, weight shifting from one foot to the other on the cable.

"Your sisters." A chill of dread slid up Harric's spine. He too looked about. "You just met your sisters, didn't you?"

Fink scowled, an act that made his face doubly hideous, which Harric hadn't thought possible. "Sibling squabbles," he croaked. He waved a taloned hand in the air as if banishing their memory, and turned his milky eyes to the upward-swooping cable and the high thunder spire to which it was attached. His familiar grin spread across his face. "Your people do some pretty odd things, you know that?"

"If by that you mean great things, yes." Harric soaked in Spook's calming purr. The cat was as comfortable with Fink as Harric was. Maybe more, since it had been the pet of Fink's former master. "By the way, Fink, if lightning hits the spire, you'll cook like meat on a stick."

Fink grinned. "The only cloud for miles is the fog crawling up the valleys."

The sight of the imp crouched in midair like a knob-kneed spider made Harric nervous that they might be seen. If Caris saw that, she'd split Fink on her sword before asking any questions. "I think Caris is sleeping," he said, "but Mudruffle and Brolli are out scouting..."

"I've seen them. The Kwendi's far over the ridge." Fink waved to the north. "Brolli went down into the valley and left Mudwhistle walking back and forth on the rim like a knee-less wind-up doll. How do you take that guy seriously?"

Harric laughed. "Why is he like that? Are all the Bright Mother tryst servants made of sticks and mud?"

Fink scowled. "No, they're not all like that. He's like that because he chose to be like that. He could've chosen a *manifest form*, like I do. The spirit taking flesh. But by choosing to enter a construct, he doesn't have to devote any of his strength into maintaining a form, which gives him more strength to do other things, like make teacakes and doilies and whatever else those White Moon fluffs are into."

Harric grinned at the thought of Fink in a crotchety wattle-daub construct.

"And before you ask, the answer is 'No, kid, I will not climb into a scarecrow for you.' End of subject."

"I wonder what his manifest form would be."

"A big white goose."

"So what is he? A...spirit?"

Fink frowned. When he spoke, he seemed to choose his words carefully, as if defining something. "He is *a being composed of the elemental creative forces of his moon*. You'd call that a spirit, but it wouldn't be strictly true. True spirits—like your soul—arise from nature. From the material world." He motioned around them. "You see it rising from everything alive. Call him an *elemental being* and you've got the idea."

Harric nodded. From the formal posture Fink had taken, Harric sensed that it would be bad manners to ask right then if Fink were such an elemental being. What would an elemental force of the Spirit Moon be, if not spirit?

"Anyway, we don't have to worry about Mudnoodle interrupting," said Fink. "I asked my sisters to keep watch in case he decides to march this end of the ridge."

"Your sisters." Harric suppressed a qualm. He'd seen Fink's sisters once, and the image still visited his nightmares.

"Don't worry. I told them to keep their distance tonight. You look like you need to talk."

Harric swallowed. He took a deep breath. "I entered the Unseen after you left. I had to."

"What did I tell you about that?"

"You told me it was dangerous," Harric retorted. Weariness made him defensive. "But you also said as long as I was near an immortal, no vulture spirits would dare come near me. I was right next to Molly when I did it, so unless there's more you didn't tell me, I was fine."

Fink stared. He didn't seem angry at Harric's outburst. His needle jaws bent in what may have been a smile.

"But it was hard to do, like last time," Harric said. "Very hard. I could hardly hold it a minute. Is it…ever going to get easier?"

Fink nodded. "I'll train you. And you'll get stronger."

Harric let out a long breath. He stroked Spook's soft ears to help still his nerves. The little moon cat watched Fink through eyes narrowed near slumber. "I've been wanting to talk to you about this," Harric said. "Now that we're—" He almost said *partners* before he caught himself, remembering Fink's sisters might be near. They couldn't know Fink was free.

"—bound," Fink supplied, eyes widening as if he sensed the near-blunder. "That's what we call our pact."

"All right, bound. I have a lot of questions." Harric felt awkward asking, but angry that he felt awkward, since it was his right to know as much as possible about their agreement. He forced himself to forge on as if he were in a pact with someone no more mysterious than an Iberg trader. "For instance, is this…all you do? Is it your job…to help—" Harric paused, hesitating to call himself a magus.

Fink's teeth glistened. "Mortals like you? Yes. It's my role among the moon servants."

"So, the last magus you had. You taught him how to use his witch-stone?"

"Nexus. It's called a nexus, kid."

"You taught him how to use his nexus. And how to use his oculus?"

Fink's bulbous nose wrinkled. "Gremio was a bitter outcast who treated me like his personal whipping dog."

"But you had to teach him."

Fink nodded. "I was bound. But I helped him as little as I could in every way possible, you see? He wanted total control. Didn't trust me. So I gave it to him. *Total control.* If he wanted something, he had to tell me *exactly* what he wanted me to do, and I'd do *exactly* what he said. If he said, 'Fink, you ugly bat, go get me something to eat—something simple, nothing fancy, and make it quick'—well, I'd come back with a live lamb on a string. 'Quick,' get it? Got him into a lot of trouble in the end."

"Master in this life, slave in the next, right?"

Fink stared. "I don't discuss the terms of my former contracts."

A chill of doubt rippled through Harric's stomach.

"You don't trust me," said Fink. "Maybe I don't trust you, either. Let's do a truth geas."

Harric let out a small laugh. "You don't trust *me?*"

Fink's black tongue flicked across his upper teeth. "You're clever. What you did last night with our pact makes me nervous."

"All right. What is the geas? Some kind of truth spell?"

Fink's hairless skull bobbed. "Every tryst servant can do it. Helps build trust."

"How's it work?"

"I'll show you." He extended the talons of one hand before his needled mouth and flickered his forked tongue across the tips. Reaching above Harric's head, he raked them back and forth, as if gathering reeds.

"Wait. What are you doing, Fink?"

"Just watch. I'm not going to hurt you. Much."

All dreams spin out from the same web.

—Mir Hopi, Unseen Apologist

17

Trust Among Tricksters

A shimmer of spirit moved beyond Harric's oculus, so he closed his eyes and strained upward into his mind to peer out into the Unseen. Fink had gathered a curtain of glimmering blue spirit strands around them—a curtain woven, he realized with alarm, from the luminescent strands that rose from Harric's soul. As he watched, Fink bent and re-bent and warped them into a complicated, all-containing bubble; silhouetted against the blue light, Fink looked like a spider on the lens of a lantern.

The imp quirked his head to one side. "Tell me a lie."

"Hold it. You did this?" Harric struggled to keep the panic from his voice. "You"—he waved his arms at the embracing curtain—"used my spirit to—"

"Relax. It's the geas."

"Made from my *soul?* Think you can tell me when you're going to touch my soul?"

Fink hissed. "I can undo it."

"No," Harric said. He knew he needed this. Trust had to start somewhere, and this was a logical place for it. "I just want to know before you do something with my spirit. Ever."

"Your wish is my command."

"Now you're making fun of me."

"I give you permission to mock me when I panic over nothing."

Harric retreated from his oculus and opened his eyes, momentarily disoriented by the comparative dark of night in the Seen. Fink lurked before him, a crow on a wire.

"Lie to me," said Fink.

Harric took a breath to calm his thumping heart. "In another context, that request would be horrifying. All right, I'll lie." He tried to say, *You're beautiful,* but the words were converted to a yelp of surprise and pain as a loud *zop!* sounded in his head and every inch of his skin recoiled as if slapped.

Fink let out a croak that must have been a laugh, and bounced the cable in amusement.

"You could warn me!" Harric snapped.

"Then it wouldn't be as funny."

"Moons, Fink! This is supposed to be for trust."

Fink spread his hands in a placating gesture. "Kid. Relax. You aren't hurt. Look, I'll try to tell one myself. I'll say, 'Kid, I hope you treat me like pig shit.'" Fink opened his mouth and seemed to gag on the air. There was another *zop!* and Fink backflipped from the wire to crash in the dirt below.

Harric smiled. "Okay, that was funny."

Fink untangled himself from a jumble of wings and limbs akimbo. "Souls, your strands sting."

"Hold on. If you can't lie to me, then how could you tell me the lie you planned to tell me?"

"Cute thinking, kid. But it wasn't a lie *then.* It was truth. I really *was* going to tell you that."

"But what you really were going to try to tell me was itself a lie."

"Nah, kid. If I don't *intend* to tell you a lie, it ain't a lie." Fink flapped back up to his perch on the windlass. "Try it." He bounced on the wire and grinned as if he'd enjoy another Harric zop.

Harric frowned. He didn't relish the thought of another, but he needed to be sure he wasn't being played. "All right. I'm going to say, 'You look a lot like my mother.'" He tried, and again his words caught, and *zop!* he bounced back with another yelp and a curse.

Fink cackled like a crow. "That never gets old. But you see? A lie's in the intention."

Spook squirmed in Harric's arms. Apparently he'd had enough of zopping and yelping. Harric let him down, and Spook scampered a few paces away before stopping to glare and begin grooming.

"How do I know you aren't faking your zop?" Harric said.

"How could I?"

"I don't know. That's my biggest problem. I don't know how these things work, but you do."

"You saw it for yourself; I'm inside the geas as much as you. If I lie, I get stung."

Harric maintained his poker face, but inwardly he chafed. The fact that Fink was inside the geas bubble didn't necessarily mean it affected him as it did Harric. This was where his utter and complete ignorance of the Unseen hobbled him. He didn't even know enough about Fink to set a trap for him and test whether the geas worked on the imp. Still, to have any chance of using the geas to his benefit, he'd need to know the rules. "How long's the geas last?" he asked.

"Sixty-six questions. We've used eight already."

"What? You mean—?"

"Nine, and ten." Fink's grin glittered in the red light. "Might want to conserve."

Harric bit back a curse. Fink had let him use up eight questions before he even knew how the geas worked. He ran a hand down his face, trying to clear the fog from his light-washed brain. *Pull yourself together. You can do this. Just like counting cards in tarot-poker.* Instead of wasting another question, he made a statement. "If we need another geas, I assume we'll do another later."

A grin spread across Fink's face. "You learn fast. But I must correct your assumption. A geas is a one-time event. To weave a geas, I have to trick your strands into serving as a truth net. It isn't natural for them. They won't cooperate next time."

"Why only sixty-six questions?"

"That's the number of your strands."

Harric raised an eyebrow. This was an aspect of Unseen lore he hadn't imagined. "Do all people have sixty-six?"

Fink shook his head slowly, eyes on Harric. "You're a sixty-six."

A shiver rippled up Harric's spine. Something in the imp's manner felt ominous.

"That was twelve," said Fink.

Harric took a deep breath. The more he learned, the more questions popped into his brain. He needed to resist every single little question he could ask, and focus on the big questions that dogged his every waking and dreaming hour. Things like: *What have I gotten into?* Though he was pretty sure that was so broad that it would be a wasted question too. He decided to keep track of the number of questions the way he did with cards. With his left, he'd count up to ten and then start over. With his right, he'd record each time his left hand reached ten. That would take him up to fifty, anyway.

"My turn," said Fink. "Question thirteen. You any good?"

Harric swallowed his frustration with himself, and almost asked, *What do you mean? At what?* but caught himself. Was the imp trying to bait him into wasting questions by asking vague ones himself? "Explain what you mean," he said.

"Are you any good at...*whatever it is you do best?*" A knowing leer from the imp; his hairless eyebrows jumped up and down mockingly, as if on strings.

No sense in Harric hiding what he was. The imp had seen him in action. "Damned good," Harric said. "And I want to be the best."

Fink nodded. "Fifteen. I've seen you pick locks. Seen you pick pockets. *What* are you?"

Harric paused. The imp didn't know everything. Fink actually had questions. On the one hand, that came as a relief. On the other hand, the truth of Harric's training was something he'd never shared with anyone. He tried to say, "I don't know what you mean," but the geas zopped him with a full-body slap that made him jump and curse.

Fink's eyes narrowed. "You're holding out on me."

Harric tried to speak again, but *zop!* it slapped him again. "Cobbing *moons!*" He laughed. "I was going to say, 'If I tell you, I'll have to kill you,' but apparently the geas has no sense of humor."

Fink did not smile. "You want me to trust you, you'll answer the question."

"I'm a jack," Harric said, settling in on a partial truth. "A gentleman thief. A swindler. A trickster. A spy."

"Who taught you?"

"My mother."

Fink studied his face, white eyes glinting pink in the red moonlight. "You said spy. Is that what she was? One of your queen's fancy lady spies?"

Harric cringed inwardly. That was a secret he'd sworn never to reveal. Technically, he hadn't revealed it, but he'd been careless. Fink knew more about Arkendian politics than Harric had guessed—enough to catch the larger implication of the word "spy"—and now the imp had sniffed out his mother's training without even needing the geas.

Then Harric smiled. "I cannot discuss former...contracts." He hesitated on the word *contracts,* because his mother had made no formal "contract" with him, but he'd sworn never to betray the existence and nature of her profession.

To Harric's surprise, Fink made no objection. The imp's sly grin only widened. "We've heard tales of your queen's lady spies. Didn't know they were real. What are they called?"

"We have tales about them here, too. The balladeers call them *courtistes.* They're supposed to be a kind of courtesan, spy, and lady jack, all in one."

Fink bobbed his bald head. "Are you a courtiste?"

"I'm not a woman, and I've never been to court, so no. Plus, the one who trained me was as mad as a cat on fire."

Fink made a gurgling sound that—judging by his grin and the way he bounced on the wire—might have been a giggle. "So you're a gentleman jack that may or may not have been trained by a full-fledged courtiste?"

Harric nodded. That was a satisfactory compromise. For all intents and purposes, his deluded mother had raised him in secret to replace her in court, and since she was mad, perhaps his oath to her was meaningless. But he was beginning to feel very strongly that Fink didn't need to see any more of his cards. The imp already knew too much. And despite the point of the geas being to build trust, it felt to Harric like the more he could keep hidden, the better. For instance, his brush with the goddess in the tower, which he'd intended to bring up to Fink, he now resolved to keep to himself. Until he had answers to his own questions, he'd keep these cards close to his vest.

"My turn." Harric consulted his fingers. "Question twenty-three. Why did you ask me to put something about feeding you in the pact?"

Fink scowled. "What do you think? I want you to feed me. I'm sick of starving."

A chill of dread crept up Harric's neck. "Feed you. So I save part of my meals each day and bring them at night—"

"You think I eat sandwiches?"

"Stop asking empty questions. You're using them up."

Fink leered. His bald head bobbed below his shoulders and peaked wings. "I answered your question. It isn't my fault you weren't specific."

"If you want me to trust you, explain."

Fink's grin widened, flesh drawing back from his jaws to expose warty black gums. "I'm a spirit, kid. I eat souls."

The stone in Harric's chest sank into his gut. His stomach gave a nauseated twist. "So, rabbit souls would do?" he asked. "Chicken souls?"

Fink's bulbous nose wrinkled. "In a pinch. Like you'd eat rat if you had to."

"So, this is kind of important, Fink. You need people souls?"

"Yes. It's easy, kid. You kill someone, then you twirl up their soul on a fork and stick it in my mouth."

Harric stared.

"Kidding. Not so much the fork part. But how else am I going to eat? You have to kill somebody! But before you get too high and mighty about this, let me take this opportunity to remind you that you sent a fair few souls into the Black Moon just yesterday without any urging from me, though I had the misfortune of arriving too late to that feast due to my taking your mother back to her grave. Scavengers, once they arrive in numbers, don't share."

"How often?"

"My meals? Depends. Alternatively, I could nurse off your spirit. Talk about high-quality soul—"

"No."

"Why not? The strands grow back over time, and—"

"No."

"Just saying it to be clear."

Harric turned away. He felt his heart drumming in his chest.

"Kid. Relax. I'm fatter now than I've been in years. See there?" Harric turned his head to see Fink raise a bony arm and indicate his ribs. His ribs did seem less pronounced than they had when Harric first met the imp. He'd almost been skeletal then. Now he seemed merely skinny. "Souls seem to pile up behind you and your friends like shit behind horses. I've never seen so many liberated spirits since I started following you and What's-His-Bucket. Tonight I found three more down in that fort in the stables where I'd last seen you."

Visions of the dead men swam before Harric's eyes. Lane. The dove master. The sunken-eyed man. He swallowed. "You ate their souls?"

"They were wicked. What do you care?"

"Answer my question."

"Of course I did."

"And they're gone forever?

"After you eat a chicken, is it gone forever? Of course it is."

"I eat a chicken's *meat*. Not its soul."

"But if an eternal soul is wicked, why should you care if I eat it? You want it floating around doing wickedness?"

Harric tried in vain to read the blank white eyes staring back at him. He smelled a note of mockery in the way the imp said *wickedness*. "So you only eat wicked souls. Who decides if a soul is wicked or not?"

Fink's grin became strained, as if Harric had asked for a shameful admission. "I'm on probation. I'm only allowed degenerate spirits."

"And you get to decide if a soul is degenerate or not?"

A hiss bubbled from Fink's throat. "No. A degenerate spirit is obvious. It does not rise."

"So a good soul rises to the moon, and a degenerate one doesn't. That's the judgment."

Fink nodded. "Souls judge themselves."

Harric began to pace. So many things warred in his mind for his attention and warred in his heart for his conscience, but not so much that he didn't realize he'd just uncovered something crucial to his understanding of his own spirit.

Spook looked up from his grooming to watch Harric walk back and forth.

"But I didn't kill those men last night," he said. "You can still eat them?"

"You, your friends, that monster horse. It makes no difference. I have first claim."

Harric imagined a feeding frenzy of Unseen spirits with Fink at the head of the line. "Just to be clear, Fink: I said I'd feed you. I didn't say I'd go kill someone every time you're hungry."

Fink scowled. "I remember the terms."

"And *my* soul? If we're together when I die, what happens to my soul?"

Another wicked grin spread across Fink's face. "Assuming it isn't degenerate?"

A spear of doubt lanced through Harric. "Of course."

Fink coughed out something like a laugh. "Can't you ask something original, kid? Everyone has to ask, 'What happens to my immortal soul when I die?' And I always have to say, 'It depends, and anyway, I can't—'" *Zop!* "Ow! All right, I can tell! But I won't because I'll get in trouble!"

This time, Fink remained on the wire through the shock, but it left him bristling, his wings and tail at full extension. Harric compressed his smile between his lips.

"All right, laughing boy," said Fink, "you tell me. What do *you* think happens when you die?"

Harric frowned. That wasn't what he'd meant by the question. He suspected the imp knew it and lied on purpose to distract him with a humorous zop. Still, he let the larger question stand—he had to hand it to Fink, it was a very diverting question—but when he went to answer it, he found himself blushing. "Well," he began, "I believe my soul goes to the Hall of Ancestors in the Bright Mother Moon, where maidens..." Harric stopped.

Fink was making a honking sound through his nose.

"How close was I?" said Harric.

Fink gave an apologetic shrug. "All you need to know is this, kid: when you die, I'll take care of you."

Harric raised one eyebrow. "Take care of me? That could mean anything. What I meant was if you'll eat my soul when I die or feed it to someone else."

"You are my *partner*." Fink whispered the last word. "When you die, I will do my best to make sure you come to no harm. That better?"

Harric nodded. "What did you do with your former master's soul when he died?"

Fink's gaze didn't waver. "Nothing. Arrogant bastard forbade me to touch him when he died. I *couldn't* do anything. So I let him float away unescorted. Real bad move on his part. Oh, he commanded me to help when they came for him, but it was too late by then."

Harric blinked in surprise. Fink's former magus had known enough to manipulate Fink, to play different angles and rules, and still ended up dead. Worse than dead. Harric swallowed a lump in his throat. His relationship with Fink was different, though. He'd done the right thing insisting they be equals. Like all slaves, Fink had chafed under his bondage, and retaliated against his master whenever possible. Toward Harric, there would be gratitude.

He hoped. At least he now knew Fink's intention for Harric. That was one worry answered.

"Question forty-nine," Fink began.

Harric consulted his fingers again. "Fifty," he said, and a wave of anxiety played across his heart. *I've only put one worry put to rest, and it took fifty questions.* He clenched his jaw and took a deep breath through his nose. "Fink, I still have some important questions. Please don't waste any."

"Question fifty." Fink's eyes narrowed as he spoke. "Arkendians are supposed to be afraid of magic. But when your Kwendi friend killed my former master, you grabbed his nexus, and instead of throwing it into the river, you kept it. Why?"

Harric nodded. The imp wanted to know his motives. That was good. It meant Fink couldn't read Harric's heart. "It happened so fast, I didn't really have time to think about it."

"But you kept it."

"I had seen the witch—your former master, I mean—turn invisible. That's… I'd never imagined that before. It didn't take much to realize how useful it would be for me as a jack."

Fink's needle teeth gleamed in the moonlight. "Power."

"You make it sound dirty. I want the power to do good. To protect what's good."

"An idealist! Heh. You're going to be disappointed every day, kid. That what your mad-brained, murdering mother trained you for? Protecting the good?"

"Stop wasting questions!"

Fink made an apologetic bow. "I get excited. Now, answer the question."

"Yes, for good. She wasn't always like that. She had good days."

"Oh, sure. I guess I must have caught her on a bad day."

Harric smiled. "The worst possible bad day, to be sure. But she wasn't always like that. It got worse as she aged. But even then, she wanted me to serve the Queen."

"The greater good again. That is touching."

"No. She was always an egotistical fanatic. She wanted to protect the Queen, but just as much, she wanted me to redeem her own name in court. So she took my childhood and..." Bile welled in Harric's throat, choking him off. It hurt to swallow it. It was only with effort that he managed to keep his lip from curling in an involuntary snarl. "Sorry. I get angry about it sometimes."

Fink's hairless eyebrows had climbed his forehead, pushing rows of rumples upward.

"But she was right about the Queen," Harric said. "Queen Chasia freed bastards like me from slavery. She freed women from their slavery. We both owed her everything. And in spite of how much I hate my mother, I devote my life to my queen."

"So you're a patriot. And you decided to play with magic. Wanted to become invisible. A gentleman jack's dream. That the only reason?"

"Yes."

"You sure?" Fink's tone was sly.

"Stop burning questions. You know I'm under a truth spell."

"Maybe you want to be a big man. Maybe you want everyone to respect you. All these knights and warriors around—even your girlfriend—they don't respect a gentleman jack. Maybe you're ashamed of this manservant role while she waxes knightly. Maybe, with magic, you hope to shine as bright as she. You think with magic they'll finally respect you?"

"Magic would make them respect me less." That was a stinging truth. But the imp's point had hit its mark. Of course Harric wanted Caris's respect. Of course he wanted Willard to recognize his value in their quest. But even vanquishing Sir Bannus's army hadn't proven enough to do that with Willard. Harric paused for a moment, thinking of Caris. "I'd like Caris to accept it. Not just accept it. See how it could help the Queen. I don't know if she ever will."

Fink's eyes glinted red in a sliver of moonlight.

"That was fifty-five," said Harric. "My turn." He crafted the question carefully. "Power. Respect. That's what I get from this partnership. What do you hope to get out of it?" There it was, the last of his big worries. He watched the imp intently.

Fink stared back. His grin seemed wider than ever, as if he'd been expecting this question. "You know what I want, kid. I want to survive."

"And that means you need to prove yourself to your sisters, so you will be taken off probation?"

Fink's grin faded a little. It became strained. He nodded.

"Speak the answer, just to be sure."

"Yes." He hissed. "I must prove myself to my sisters if I am to survive."

"And once you prove yourself, what use will you have for our partnership?"

Fink rocked on the wire, shifting his feet. Mention of his sisters had changed him. His gaze slid to the side. "I don't know."

Harric waited for the geas to jolt the imp from the wire, but nothing happened. "You don't know?"

"I've never had a partnership before. And I don't know what my sisters will do. If I'm happy and it's up to me, I stay. Keep me fed, and I stay. If not…" His black tongue swiped the front of his teeth. "Maybe I take my nexus and go."

Harric swallowed. "And how do you prove yourself to your sisters?"

Fink sneered. "Same way you prove yourself to your Arkendian friends. Earn their respect. Defeat their enemies. Honor and obey them." He spat out the last words like poison seeds. He glared at Harric. "Speaking of which, how long you going to keep up that *valet* act? If you're going to survive in the Unseen, you need to be up at night with me. All that sword training and armor-polishing nonsense for Sir Whatsit's going to wear you out. You won't be able to stay up for your real training."

Harric narrowed his eyes. "You spent enough time in my cat to have learned that being valet to our most celebrated knight is nothing to sneeze at."

Fink's bubble eyes widened. His head dipped and his grin widened. "Yeah. You knew about me in the cat? No hard feelings?"

Harric shrugged. "I was angry when I figured it out. But then I realized I would have done the same thing if I'd been in your position. After all, I had just stolen your nexus. You needed to find out what I was all about before you acted, right?"

"Yes." Fink waited, watching Harric. "You're not going to forbid me to ride in your cat?"

Harric shook his head. "No need. His eyes go white when you're in him. It's pretty obvious."

Fink's face squirmed into a frown. "That's a limitation of the weaving."

"I could get some goggles for him, like Brolli wears. Then no one would see."

Fink let out a croaking laugh. "No one would suspect a thing."

Harric watched Fink bouncing on the cable before him. A strange transformation was taking place inside him. Many of the mental walls he'd erected around himself before this conversation were dissolving, letting in light and air to his spirit. A weight of worry lifted. He no longer feared he must murder for Fink; he no longer feared for the fate of his soul after death. Those blocks removed, he felt he could trust Fink as much as he could trust any fellow jack. More, in some ways, for their goals were aligned. They were partners. And as long as both were happy, they'd stay that way.

He smiled.

"Do we have accord?" Fink asked.

Harric nodded. "Question sixty-six. We do."

"Good. Now get some sleep. You look like death."

As Harric walked back through the chill air of the fire-cones, he paused to take stock of the evening's discussion. He scratched Spook's ears and looked over Mudruffle's terraced gardens to the meadow where Father Kogan slept with Geraldine. The Mad Moon had sunk too low to light the valley, but it was easy to see that a high bank of fog did indeed creep up the valley. In another hour, it would cover the meadow and kiss the feet of the gardens. So much for Brolli's scouting.

Harric let his mind walk back over the course of the geas, carefully picking through the questions and answers.

Did he trust Fink now? No. Moons, no. But he felt as good as he might if he'd partnered with another human trickster, like himself. Did Fink have secrets? Certainly. But so did Harric. He'd have to keep his wits about him in their partnership, and stay alert, playing his few cards close to his vest, make sure it was always in Fink's interest to play true. These were risks and necessities he could live with. In what poker game was there no risk?

He felt his spirit rising to this partnership.

In an odd way, he felt better about this than he did his relationship with Willard. With Fink, he feared no judgment. With Fink, he felt no need to dissemble or put on artificial righteousness. He'd begun to weary of that façade with his friends.

He smiled. The cat looked up with huge green eyes. "I'm all in, Spook. Wish me luck."

Put no trust in gods, for they are wild and flighty as sand in a river.
—From *Sayings of the Wandering Fathers*

18

On Broken Hope

Light moved on the other side of Harric's eyelids. He threw his arm over his eyes and rolled over, groaning. Somewhere below his bed in the loft, Molly had been stomping and snorting and disrupting his sleep for what felt like the last hour. Weariness pressed him into the straw like a leaden coat. Then a lantern handle squeaked and someone knocked at the foot of the ladder to the loft.

"Heave up!" Willard's bull-throated bellow shattered the predawn silence. "Heave up, I say. Day approaches."

Caris stirred beside Harric and sat. "We're up." With a sharp knuckle, she gouged between Harric's ribs, jolting him awake. Under her breath she said, "Harric, where were you last night? I waited up for you."

Harric groaned and tried to roll out of reach.

"Grab a pair of axes from the tower, girl," said Willard. "And meet me at Kogan's camp in a quarter of an hour. I saw a grove of ash down there where we can cut lance staves. Boy, since you have letters, paint up a placard to post for Captain Gren—something to warn him the enemy has preceded him here, and to be alert. Then load and saddle the horses and bring one of them down to haul the lances back up. Molly..." Harric could hear the frown in his voice. "She's in a mood, so I won't be taking her down."

"Understood." Caris's voice, too near, again beat Harric back from the gates of slumber. "Is Brolli back?" she called down. "What news of the north passes?"

"Didn't learn a thing. Too damned foggy. We can be comforted that our enemy was just as hindered by it. Nevertheless, I want to be on our way by midmorning."

As the sound of Willard's boots retreated into the courtyard, Harric felt Caris rise in the straw beside him.

"Get up and look at me, Harric."

He opened his eyes. Anger colored her cheeks. Or maybe embarrassment. Then he recalled her visit to him in the cellar the night before, and he felt a twinge of guilt. "I'm sorry," he said, forcing himself up onto an elbow to properly face her. "I didn't want to disturb you. You looked so peaceful."

She returned his gaze, nostrils flaring. Then her chin rose, and she said, "Tonight, then. Don't do that to me again."

"I won't," he said, truthfully. But even then, he knew he'd have to find some other way to avoid her bed. *Gods leave it, that ring is bent on cornering me. And I'm a lump of ice if part of me doesn't want to let it happen.*

She dressed quickly, and he used that as an excuse to turn his head away and flop back into the straw. Sleep came swiftly and left just as fast as rude hands seized him under the arms and hauled him to his feet.

"You are not going back to sleep." With a series of well-aimed thumbs to ribs, Caris herded him barefoot to the ladder. He tried begging. He tried cursing. He tried whining. Nothing worked. She kept jabbing. Residual anger fueled her, perhaps, and a humorless horse-touched intensity fortified her concentration. He almost toppled from the loft in his effort to escape, but once he got his feet on the ladder, he moved swiftly to the stable floor.

Shivering, and now fully awake, he called up, "My boots?" He tried to put as much accusation in it as he could. The boots hit the ground without warning, so he just sighed and pulled them on.

"You're welcome," Caris called down.

The air felt damp and cold. Outside the stable doors, a thick fog stirred in an early breeze. He shivered at another memory of his mother's murderous fogs, and jumped when Willard emerged from it like some black-armored specter.

Willard glared at him, and Harric recognized the violet flash in his eye that indicated he'd taken the Blood again. Harric took a half step backward, but the knight ignored him. Willard bit on one of his replacement ragleaf sticks, then rolled it to one side of his mouth to spit a fragment into the straw. "Steer clear of Molly. She'll be back to her grim and brooding self in an hour or so."

Harric nodded, and Willard strode into the predawn fog, armor clicking and harness squeaking, just as Caris climbed down from the loft.

"Hear that?" Harric said.

"Yes. I wonder what's gotten into her."

Harric stared at the barn where Molly was stabled alone and pondered Willard's cryptic warning. She was *in a mood?* It must have something to do with him bleeding her again. Did it make her as agitated as it made Willard? Thinking back to the first time he bled her, it seemed likely, for immediately after the first cutting, she'd gone berserk on Lane.

Great. So we'll have two thundering rage monsters on hand whenever he bleeds her.

The fog had swallowed Willard, but the click and squeak of his armor—eerily amplified by the fog—made it easy to track his path toward the top of the switchbacks.

"He's walking to the meadow," said Caris. "I've never seen him walk anywhere, have you?"

Harric shook his head. "Only to the privy."

She looked at Harric, her eyebrows risen. "You don't think he let Abellia *heal* him, do you? What else could explain it? Even if Molly is unridable right now, what else would explain him walking instead of riding Snapper or Idgit?"

Harric snorted. "Not Abellia's magic."

"But she said she could reverse aging. I wonder if she did it for Willard. He might not even know it. Don't you think he sounded a bit…louder and stronger just now?"

"I don't see Willard ever accepting magic," said Harric. "Ever." He found it strange at first that she hadn't considered that Willard might have taken the Blood, but it wasn't his place to enlighten her, so he said nothing.

Caris stared into the fog in the direction of the squeaking armor. "I'll ask Abellia later. She'll tell me."

Mistress Abellia watched from her window as Caris left the tower with an axe in each hand and trotted into the fog for the head of the switchbacks. Harric emerged from the barn, watching her go. He led the smallest horse by its reins—the Kwendi's horse, she thought—and tied it to the post outside the door. Abellia smiled to see the animal was no longer favoring its back left hoof. Not wishing to raise Sir Willard's suspicions, she'd waited till everyone slept before making the painful journey down the tower stairs to the stable and healing the poor beast.

Of course, Willard had warned her directly against using magic, especially around Harric. And, of course, she'd nodded and smiled in reply. But she was sworn to heal, and if the old man didn't like it, he could heal the next one with his people's barbaric blood-lettings or mud-and-leaf plasters.

She snorted.

What preposterous people, Arkendians. She'd seen their "healing" before: smashed leaves smeared in wounds. Poison dripped in mouths. Broken limbs lashed to planks. It wasn't healing, it was torture. They had no understanding of the Bright Mother: no Mending, Preserving, Cleansing, Divining, nor Wards. In Iberg lands, blindness and deafness and lameness were unknown; in Arkendia, they were as abundant as blackberries and viewed simply as "incurable" or "bad luck."

If only they could see the lowest beggar in Samis. How they would flock to the Mother.

Yet the old knight forbade it—insisted this barbaric lack of magic made his people strong.

She tapped her nexus stone with a brittle nail. There was a brutal sense to that line of thinking, of course; those who survived the twin dangers of injury and "healers" would be naturally tougher than any Iberg she'd known.

Her nexus pulsed, bright and hot in her hands, startling her from meditation. Someone had located her stone with a Searching. A strong one. The stone pulsed again, growing brighter, and sent out a pulse of her own to help the searcher, and called Mudruffle from the adjoining room.

As Mudruffle approached, her nexus erupted with the blinding internal light of a Sending.

The old woman's heart fluttered against her breastbone. A Sending like that could only come from the Moon itself. This meant they would acknowledge her service and reward her with health. Now, after a lifetime of healing others, they would allow her to mend her own aged body, and she would go with Mudruffle to the Kwendi lands.

Her breaths grew short and rapid with excitement.

"A Light Bringer," Mudruffle honked.

Abellia nodded. "Assuredly. See. Here is the sigil." In the face of the nexus, a symbol had appeared, identifying the sender.

"It is *Morinster!*" said Mudruffle.

Abellia's hand trembled. "Your beloved general, Mudruffle. I have never had the honor."

"It seems my message concerning the Kwendi has caught their attention, mistress."

She steadied her hand by clasping her nexus between both palms. Morinster might not authorize a full healing, but a partial restoration would be enough for her to make the journey. A partial restoration would be just. She mustn't be greedy. She'd given her life freely in service, after all, with no expectation of reward.

Her heart thumped wildly as echoes of old ambitions revived in her breast. To be noticed, in her eightieth year. For her sacrifices in this backward land to bear fruit. The rest she scarcely allowed herself to acknowledge in the secrecy of her heart. *To have second life. To have a chance at truly living.*

The sigil in the nexus vanished, warning of the impending Sending.

A Sending of this distance was a phenomenal act. She had never witnessed such a feat, even in the Bi-lunar Council. She found her palms sweating as Mudruffle closed the shutters to the windows. Why was she so frightened? Wasn't this what every magus wanted, to be noticed by the moon itself? Direct contact with the source, without the knowledge of the council? But the presence of the eternal was itself terrifying. She had only just recovered from the previous night's encounter with Vella.

"Mistress, the tower door is locked," Mudruffle honked as he closed the last shutter. He stood rigid beside her.

The air in the center of the room began to shimmer, faintly at first, like a glimmer of sunlight in windborne crystals of frost. Then the glimmer exploded into blinding white light. This was nothing like the warmly golden effulgence of Vella. This was stark and hard and absolute, scouring the room with uncompromising purity.

An apparition rose through the floor—or rather, the head and shoulders rose; the top of a colossus was too large for the room, its feet in the cellar. Abellia struggled to make sense of what she saw; one moment her mind would latch on to something familiar to give it reference—a plate of sun-bright armor, eyes like cutting diamonds—and next she'd see the plates as scales of some bright serpent, or the eyes as multitudes unwinking. And when she saw the wings—great spans of light, transecting floor and ceiling—they refracted into more wings than she could count, at angles that seemed impossible.

Vertigo seized her and she grabbed the table for balance. She could not look away.

The being scanned the tower, crystal gaze passing through Abellia to fix upon Mudruffle. Had it rested its gaze upon her, she doubted she could have remained standing. Such eyes! Such power and understanding! This was a presence that buttressed the very fabric of existence, dwarfing mortal spheres as mountains dwarfed and gave shape to valleys.

There were no words; the eyes said everything.

Mudruffle shook with ecstasy as Morinster communed with him, and Abellia watched, petrified. The Light Bringer shared none of his instructions with her. She was so near, however, that she felt the tone of its thoughts to Mudruffle. She sensed its approval. She sensed warning and commands.

Mudruffle made a small bow from the waist, his way of nodding. Surely those instructions would be engraved by those glittering eyes on his soul.

A deep note sounded. The air, her flesh, the timbers beneath her vibrated—as if the stone ring of the tower were the bass pipe of some gigantic organ and she a mote of dust in its wind. *It speaks!* she realized. Then the kaleidoscope of wings collapsed around the eyes, like the fall of some crystal house, and the Light Bringer vanished.

Darkness and silence descended like smothering smoke.

Abellia sat hard and stared, unseeing, into the gloom.

The Light Bringer had not come for her, but for Mudruffle. Indeed, it had not seemed to see her at all. She hadn't registered in its gaze.

And though she had heard no words, she knew it had not granted her request. Maybe never noticed the request at all.

A hole seemed to open within her, and her soul drained from her into emptiness. Then shame filled the space left behind. If only she could become stone—unfeeling, unseeing—and stare like this forever. Were there not tales of maidens turned to stone by vengeful gods? Could the Morinster not grant her that much? She had dared hope; now let him smite her to stone as a warning to others.

She collapsed at the table, smothering her face with her arms. The nexus dropped dully on the boards. Her existence, her life's work, confirmed meaningless, beneath notice. Unworthy in the eyes of eternity. Her dreams mere delusion.

Mudruffle remained still, as silent sobs racked her.

Gradually, she became aware of the birdsong outside her window, and the smell of dried ale and the knight's ragleaf on the table. Somewhere outside, a horse whinnied. When she recovered enough to speak, she lifted her head and wiped her tears. Mudruffle's shining black eyes watched intently.

"Morinster left me the words to summon his brethren," said Mudruffle. "To summon a Light Bringer."

She looked up, confused, then hurt, then surprised at her own hurt. "I have never heard of such a thing, Mudruffle, in all my years." Ugly emotions rose in her throat like bile. Anger. Jealousy. Emotions she could not recall feeling in many long years. Her lip began to curl, betraying her, and she hid her face in her hands.

Mudruffle shifted on his clay feet. "It is the nature of the situation, not the servant, that merits it. I may only call it if the other moons interfere directly with our goal."

Our goal.

Us.

What a lie that now seemed. She was never the vessel for this mission. It was Mudruffle all along. But it wasn't his fault. She could not feel anger toward him. Mudruffle had never left her. It was her moon that abandoned her. "You will go with them to the north," she said, trying to be strong. "To the land of the Kwendi."

The tryst servant nodded. "The tower is stocked with food. I have seen to it."

She looked up. "You knew I would not go?"

"I began preparing after Vella's visitation. To be safe."

It surprised her how much this little secret hurt her. Mudruffle had known all along she would not be asked to go. That there would be no healing. How naïve and foolish she must seem to him. How weak and petty. Had she not grown at all since she first took oath?

If Mudruffle noticed, he said nothing of it. "I will return when it is finished," he said.

"Of course."

"Until then, mistress, farewell."

She nodded, and he left. But she felt then the certainty that Mudruffle would not return from this venture, and that she would spend her last years alone in that empty tower.

She was too old to travel, and she had only her research into Arkendian witch-silver, which the Kwendi emergence had made meaningless. She might as well let herself fall ill and summon an Arkendian healer to speed her death.

Mudruffle descended the stair, leaving her alone in a tower cell, empty as a long-drained cask.

Harric stood in the doorway of the stable, gazing up at the tower. He had been grabbing his sword to join Willard and Caris in the meadow when he'd seen a light on the dark side of the tower. Once again, something bright as day dazzled around the edges of the first-floor shutter, and his shoulders stiffened as if in memory of a blow. He recalled the sense of something divine and eternal on the other side... and the feeling of despair that impaled him when it left.

Cursing himself for a fool, he climbed the stairs, unsure why he did. Willard was in a hurry, Bannus's men were working on flanking them from the north, and he was poking around after half-remembered dreams in the tower. Even thinking of it summoned an echo of the desolation it had left him with.

He found the door to the main living floor open; a single candle lit the room from the table under the window. There he found Abellia slumped over the table, her white head resting on her frail hands.

Something was wrong. He felt he was intruding, and turned to go, but she lifted her head and turned dull eyes on him. Some of her wispy hair had escaped a bun and floated before her eyes, giving her a wild look. The eyes were puffy, her gaze hollow, and it reminded him of the look in his mother's eyes after one of her visions.

"Sorry to disturb you," he said.

"Young Harric." Her voice came out like a croak. She gestured vaguely at the covered crockery on the table. "Sit. Eat. You came for bread and beans."

"Well, I thought—"

"Sit."

Harric sat across the table from her. She stared at him with red-rimmed eyes. Not sure what else to do, he served himself a bowl of beans and ate. She said nothing, her gaze vacant again. For many heartbeats he ate, gazing out at the fog outside the open window. It hadn't thinned much since he'd awakened.

"Look at me." Her voice was no more than a whispered breath. She held a gnarled hand before her, and turned it to and fro, as if to examine it. "So old. So used. All for nothing. Such a dear oath...no worth at all." She chuckled, hoarse and hollow.

Harric felt a flutter of sadness for the old woman. Was she talking of her oath to her moon?

Her eyes glistened, black and beautiful in her grief. She dropped her head to her hands again and shook with silent weeping.

Harric swallowed the beans. He wiped his mouth. He knew the despair the light being left behind. But he did not know how to comfort her. He certainly couldn't admit he knew what she was going through, or she'd wonder how he knew.

He laid a hand on her tiny, warm wrist. "I'm sorry."

After a while, she ceased her weeping. She did not lift her head, and he judged she would like him to leave. He gave her wrist a gentle squeeze, and rose.

"The ring on my Caris. You gave it to her." She raised her head and leaned back in her chair, eyes dim but focused upon him.

It was not a question. It seemed an accusation.

"Yes. It was an accident. I didn't know what they were."

She nodded. "The ring is wicked. Wicked magic from a wicked moon."

A pulse of anger shot through Harric's veins. He suppressed it. "Can you take it off?"

"I cannot. It is not my moon."

Harric said nothing. He sat again. He had so many questions she might answer about the magics of the moons, and tryst servants in particular, but he did not know how to open the topic without revealing too much.

"You do not fear the moons as Sir Willard does." She dropped her hands into her lap below the surface of the table.

"I think there must be some good in the moons. Not all of it's bad. You've shown me that."

She nodded, missing or ignoring the challenge in his tone. She closed her eyes, and a spray of light played on the fringes of her robe. It wasn't sunlight. It was before dawn. Then he felt a tingle in the skin of his shoulder, which had been scraped when Willard threw him through the planks. A warmth like a caress traveled up his stiff neck. The dapples of light moved in synchrony with the sensations in his skin—coming from something below the table, in her lap. She raised her hands above the table, cradling a pearl-white stone the size of a goose egg, shining with an inner light. *Healing light,* he realized. *A nexus of the Bright Mother.*

Then the light was gone, and the warmth drained from his shoulder and neck.

"It was you," he said. "You healed Idgit while we slept. I couldn't believe her recovery."

"I am sworn to it." Her voice remained dull, her eyes empty.

He pulled down his shirt to examine his shoulder, and prodded where ragged scratches had been only hours before. He rolled his neck without pain. He was whole again.

Realizing his mouth was agape, he closed it. "Thank you."

"Your Willard would not thank me."

"No, but I am not Willard. I don't see a witch. I see a healer." He risked a question he hoped wouldn't seem out of place. "I—suppose it is something you learned from Mudruffle, isn't it? The magic of your moon? You've been with him since the beginning?" She stared at him, uncomprehending. "To use your nexus. He taught you?"

As understanding lit in her eyes, they went hollow, as if from some deep inner pain. He instantly regretted asking it, though he didn't know why it should grieve her.

"I'm sorry," he murmured. "I didn't mean to upset you."

She turned from him, as if to signal she wished to be alone.

He excused himself and left the tower, uncertain what he had witnessed. *Such a dear oath. For nothing. Used up.* Something hardened in him. That would *not* be his fate with Fink.

Sir Willard was a banished man,
His fair deeds lost to foul,
His many squires a testament,
His many ladies' scowls.
Yet the Champion's fault was ne'er to love,
But to love too close to the Queen.
He should have reserved it for Her that's above,
Or hidden it better, I ween.

—The chorus of the famed Sir Willard ballad "Black Armor Becomes Him"

19

Divine Blood & Mortal Oaths

Harric strapped to Idgit the sign he'd painted on a plank for Captain Gren. It read, HIGH CAUTION – ENEMY IS HERE, and he'd signed it "Sr.W," for Sir Willard.

After grabbing a lantern, he mounted and urged Idgit into a walk. They descended the garden switchbacks into a deeper fog made gray in the indirect light of approaching dawn. A breeze blew up from the pass, shredding the fog and pulling it away like rags of carded wool. Lower, in the forest-rimmed meadow, the fog still pooled, however, forcing him to navigate by memory at first—and then by the sound of voices— toward the willow where Kogan made his camp.

Halfway across the meadow, a dark shape loomed. Idgit startled, ears perked forward, eyes rolling white. The shape gave a deep snort of greeting.

"Easy, Idgit. It's just Geraldine."

The musk-auroch gave a shake of her massive head, spraying droplets of moisture in a halo from long ears and wool. Idgit gave her an unnecessarily large berth. The auroch chewed her cud and watched with calm, wise eyes.

The voices in the camp had gone silent. Harric could see the willow ahead as a darkening of the fog. "Hello?" he called. "Someone sent for a packhorse?"

"It's Harric," said Caris. Her voice came from one side.

A grunt came from the opposite side, and Kogan's tall bulk loomed from the fog. "Might have given a shout afore now," he said. "Fog's got us jumping like fleas. Could move an army in this and none would know it."

Caris and Brolli emerged from the other side. Kogan took Idgit's reins as Harric dismounted.

"But so timely!" said Brolli, flashing his feral grin. "What a good valet you are!"

Harric's eyes narrowed. Caris pinched a smile between her lips. To Brolli, Harric said, "I have a demon that wakes me in the form of a beautiful warrior maiden."

Brolli barked out a laugh. "That is luck. I have only the sad old knight who stink of ragleaf."

"Did you get very far last night?" Harric asked. "See anything before the fog set in?"

Brolli frowned. "Could not get close enough to the north pass before I am making the turn back, or maybe I am getting lost. I had hoped to see fires. Did I hear wolves? Maybe it was men. I cannot tell."

"Will said wait here for him," said Kogan. "He's looking for lance trees. Said make sure you packed and saddled the horses."

"I did," Harric replied.

"Then help yourself to some mash at the fire. Ain't hot, sad to say, but oughta be warm."

Harric blinked. "You made a fire?" He glanced up to where the firecone ridge sailed above streaming rags of fog.

Kogan belched, and only when the beer fumes reached him did Harric realize the priest was roaring drunk, and probably not at his sharpest. Kogan grinned. "Will near took my head off for it."

Harric picketed Idgit and followed the others to the charcoal patch of ground that had been Kogan's campfire. Caris handed Harric a wooden bowl of mash. Harric raised an eyebrow. The bowl appeared to be the only one in camp, which meant it had to be from Kogan's camp kit. That gave Harric visions of the priest licking it clean and drying it with his beard each morning.

Harric examined the mash as Kogan sat with a grunt on a log opposite and promptly flopped over onto his back with a surprised "Oop!"

The mash was simple boiled oats. Some looked like they might be whole oats—hull and all—from the horse's fodder. There appeared to be a submerged twig. Harric's stomach threatened to flop over. He glanced at Caris to find her biting back another grin. She'd endured the stuff, and now she was enjoying the show.

"What?" he said. "Is this tease Harric day?"

"It's hit the trail as fast as we can day," said Willard. His voice preceded him from the foggy margin of the willow.

The sound of it jolted Kogan into motion from where he'd lain flat on his back. He wallowed in his smothercoat, a swarm of arms and bare legs, and managed to get to his knees before Willard pushed through the curtain of willow branches. Willard seemed taller than usual, probably because of the helmet and oiled cloak he wore over full armor, and he strode with vigor without the aid of his crutch. While Kogan's eyes were on Willard, Harric flung the mash to Geraldine. The beast eyed the lump placidly, jaw working cud.

A tiny gasp from Caris called Harric's attention away from the auroch. Her jaw had dropped open. She stared at Willard, who returned it with violet intensity. His skin had gone blue. There was no hiding it now.

One by one, Willard met the eyes of the others.

Brolli's jaw moved without sound. Then he closed it and bowed.

Kogan beamed from his bush of beard and let out a joyous whoop. "That's the Will *I* remember!"

Harric had to suppress an irrational urge to kneel before the fledging immortal. Harric's own blood seemed to shout, *A god among us! A hero! A king!* in recognition of divine blood so near.

Willard's skin was not the outright blue of Bannus, who had taken the Blood without intermission for centuries and looked like an angry blueberry. Where Willard's cheeks normally flushed red, they now darkened to an icy blue, as did his lips. Just as striking was that everything about him seemed firmer, stronger, straighter.

Caris's cheeks had drained of color, but when Willard's eyes fell on her, they flushed. Her mouth clamped shut, jaw muscles bulging. She glared at Willard in defiance, but then her gaze faltered, and her eyes flicked to the sides as if in advance of a full-blown horse-touched collapse.

Harric cringed inwardly. *How could I not see this coming?* To him, Willard could be both hero and hypocrite. Though he didn't like them, he could understand the contradictions. But Caris had always struggled with the gray areas of human behavior, and to her, Sir Willard was a pillar of honor. For the hero to reveal himself as an oath breaker was to challenge and shatter the constellations of her world.

Willard's violet eyes flashed with suppressed rage, as if in her dismay he saw the judgment of the world. Instead of releasing her gaze, so she might collect her herself, the old knight hardened it as if it could break her fragile grasp of the situation and send her horse-touched mind into breakdown.

Harric stood abruptly, drawing a sharp glance from Willard. *Poor Willard,* he wanted to say. *Is this supposed to be a glorious entrance? And is Caris spoiling it? How the Blood must warp one's thinking.* Instead, he said, "Caris. Let's check on Idgit," and took her hand in his.

The contact allowed her to tear her eyes from Willard, and the panic and pain Harric saw in them tore at his heart. She sucked in a deep breath, as if in her shock she'd forgotten to breathe.

"Idgit needs you," Harric said, guiding her toward the pony, and pointedly ignoring Willard.

As Caris's eyes found the little horse at the edge of the camp, the mare's head rose, ears pricked toward her. Caris shook off Harric's hand—along with her last shreds of human decorum—and ran to her, falling on Idgit's neck like a long-lost friend. As she buried her face in the pony's shaggy mane, she let out a muffled sob.

Harric's jaw clenched, and he looked away, fury burning in his gut. He didn't dare look at the knight, but felt Willard's god-touched gaze like a pressure on his skull. Joining Caris at Idgit's side, he let Idgit lick the remnants of the mush from his bowl, and then busied himself removing Captain Gren's sign from the saddlebags.

"Let Bannus find us now." Kogan chuckled, apparently oblivious to the whole exchange. "You got him matched, Will."

"It is good," said the ambassador. "I almost wish to see it!"

Harric couldn't tell if Brolli made conversation to distract Willard from his apprentices, or if he was as oblivious as Kogan seemed, but he chattered on about an imagined meeting between the two immortals, and Kogan interjected enthusiastically. Harric imagined the old knight's hands balled into fists as he wrestled with the Blood rage.

When Willard finally spoke, his voice was low and measured, exactly as it had been when he'd thrown Harric through the planks in the stable. "I won't be his match for weeks," he said. "Maybe a month. Today was only my third draught in two days."

A silence followed in which Harric risked a glance at the men around the dead campfire. Willard's attention was on Brolli, and he'd rested his hands on his armored hips, which Harric took for a sign he'd reestablished control over the Blood rage.

"But the Blood heals my body," said Willard. "Already, it's taken my aches, and my armor grows loose about the waist and tight about the arms."

"I see it," said Brolli. His awe was clear. "You change."

Indeed, Harric found it hard not to stare. Though the old knight was still the pot-bellied, skinny-legged Willard they all knew, it was easy to see he now stood straight and moved without sign of pain. His chins had melted by half. The bones of his face emerged sharply.

"Yes. I change," he growled. "And it is a change you may live to regret urging, ambassador. So let's get one thing clear. I am no god. I'm no king. I'm a man, an unfit vessel for this stolen Blood. Therefore, I'm mad as a rabid dog. Mad with the heat of the Blood in my flesh. Mad with thirst. Mad with battle lust. And mad with hunger, though to eat will madden me more, so I must fast." Willard's hands flexed and squeezed into fists, as if by speaking of it, he talked himself into a rage.

Clenching his jaw, he closed his eyes and took a deep breath. A long moment later, he exhaled and opened his eyes. "My flesh burns with the transformation. I sweat to death. Hot as a kiln in here."

"What can we do to help?" said Brolli.

"Cobbing little you can do. I will thank you to bring me water when you have it. But I beg you steer clear of me when I am alone and silent or with Molly, for then I will be as an injured bear and likely to strike before I know you."

"Water right by your foot, Will," Kogan said.

Willard picked up the water bucket and drank deeply, snorting into it like an ox at a trough.

"So he'll be a danger to us, but not so much to Bannus," Harric muttered to Brolli. "What could go wrong?" The Kwendi did not appear to hear him. Brolli had taken out his travel journal and was already scribbling intently in his foreign alphabet.

Willard dropped the empty bucket and wiped his mouth with the palm of his gauntlet. Striding away through the willow branches, he called over his shoulder, "If you're done with your little tantrum, girl, you can pick up an axe and follow me to the ash grove."

Caris cast a sullen glare after Willard. With the aid of Idgit, she'd recovered her composure. With a farewell pat on Idgit's neck, she stumped back to camp and picked up an axe in one hand. She didn't meet Harric's eyes as she followed the old knight, but Harric recognized hurt and disillusionment in her eyes.

Picking up the remaining axe, he followed Caris.

They caught up to Willard when he paused in a grove of slender ash some sixty paces into the trees. Willard had marked several trunks for lances, and pointed out the features he sought in the wood. "Best if it's straight from the start, and you need to watch for broken limbs that might make a weak spot in the core. Ideally, we'd take them at the end of winter before the sap softens them up." He frowned. "These green summer poles will be too heavy and soft by a long measure. That'll have to do for now."

Harric and Caris felled and stripped the trees Willard marked, and he demonstrated how to hollow the grip and leave a generous counterweight at the butt.

Caris would not meet Harric's eye, but she worked diligently, if violently, with the axe.

They had nearly finished a second lance when the old knight stiffened. He laid a hand on Caris's shoulder to still her. "Hush!" He strained, listening. Willard turned north toward Abellia's tower and froze. Then he cursed. "Hounds," he said. "They've found us."

In the end, they remember who won, never how. Be sure you win, and let history take care of the rest. You'll be surprised when you hear the ballads, how honorably you fought.

—Attributed to Sir Gregan Lamour, or to Sir Willard, during the Cleansing

20

Of Sense & Stratagems

Harric heard nothing but the rattle of the brook in the meadow and the distant sigh of a breeze in the fire-cones atop the ridge. But ballads were sung of Old Ones who heard as well as any rabbit.

"They have hounds?" Harric whispered. "Where are they coming from? Bannus's pass?"

Willard was already striding through the saplings toward the meadow. "No." He gestured to Abellia's tower. "From the north, over the ridge. Bring the lance staves."

After scooping up the lances, Harric and Caris hurried after Willard. They emerged into the meadow and crossed to Kogan's weeping willow, where the priest lay flat on his back inside the curtain of branches, snoring like a bear. The fog had scudded up over the ridge, leaving only light wisps where the forest bordered the meadow, and in the fire-cones on the ridge above. Willard stormed up to the sleeping priest and kicked him soundly in the side. "Get up, you stinking clod! They must have caught your scent from the next valley over."

The lilt of the dogs grew louder on the ridge, and a horn echoed through the fire-cones.

The priest's eyes opened and he sat bolt upright. "Hounds!"

Willard was already adjusting the stirrups on Idgit's saddle. He measured the pasture with his eyes, as if judging whether he could get to Molly before the dogs were on them.

"Wait! I'm not caught without these again," Brolli said, as he retrieved the bulging bandolier of Kwendi hurling-globes from the packs. Altogether, the ten or so globes probably weighed as much as Willard's armor, each solid iron or witch-silver and big as the fattest apple. "Now go!" he said, as he slung them over his shoulder. "Ride to the tower for your Molly! We hide till you return."

"Too late," Willard said. "Can't you hear them? A company of heavy horse rides with those hounds. Wouldn't make the middle switchback before they burst upon me. Girl! My lance! Moons, I've no shield. No matter—shorten the lances. Cut an arm and a half off the tips."

"Both lances?" said Harric.

"Both! And be quick!"

"You're going to fight?" said Caris, as she and Harric laid into the poles with the axes. "On Idgit?"

"Do I have a choice?" Willard growled. "Make the ends of the shafts flat. And hurry it. I want to be waiting for them in the open when they arrive."

The priest grinned. "I always like a good fight in the morning time. If you can knock 'em down, Will, I can do the rest."

"You'd better," Willard said. "Knocking them down is about all I can manage." He heaved himself up into Idgit's saddle, and the good-natured pony sighed loudly.

Kogan seemed to notice Idgit for the first time, and his face crumpled in a frown. "Ye look like a couple-a fat lords a-pig-a-back, Will. If ye don't knock 'em down, they'll fall laughing."

"Just keep your beard hole shut when they come. I'll do the talking."

"You aim to *talk* to 'em?"

"Shut your noise so I can think!"

Harric finished his lance first and hoisted it to Willard, who gripped it easily with one huge hand and scanned the gentle bowl of the meadow. From its head at the base of the switchbacks, to its foot at the edge of the trees, the meadow sloped gently downhill about two hundred paces, each side bordered by rock escarpments. The road ran more or less straight down its middle, with Kogan's willow in the center of all.

Willard nodded, as if he'd come to a decision. "Kogan and I will

stay here at the willow to meet them. The rest retreat to the foot of
the meadow and hide in the trees on either side of the road. Once
our enemies descend the switchbacks, I'll hail them. Code of Honor
requires they halt and speak, at which time Kogan will keep his noise
shut." He glared at the priest, who flashed a crack-toothed grin. "There
will be no heroics from you, girl," said Willard. "Not without armor.
Understand?"

Caris returned her mentor's gaze with fierce intensity. She nodded,
but Harric could see in her eyes the determination to fight.

Brolli's brow furrowed. "Then what? Tell me what you plan."

"I'll stay here in the field and meet them," Willard replied. "With
luck, they won't have lances and I can talk them off. If they have lances,
they will want to try me. My advantage is this: I'll don my helm so they
can't see any tint of the Blood. They'll see the paunch of my armor and
think I'm still mortal and vulnerable—all the more since I'm not on a
proper horse."

Willard's mouth twitched into a smile that sent a shiver down Harric's
spine. The shadow of something cold and cruel passed behind the
violet eyes. "Molly's absence will make them overconfident and greedy
for fame. Instead of mobbing me, they'll want to try me honorably, one
at a time, for a chance to say they unhorsed me. That's worth more than
a knighthood to some. And as long as I can bluff them that way, one at
a time, I can thin their ranks before they realize their error."

"All the same, Will…how you gonna fight?" Kogan asked it almost
timidly, as if embarrassed by his own doubts. "I love a fight as much
as anyone, you know that. But you got no shield and no point on your
spear, and you're riding a pony."

"We could run," Harric suggested.

"They've hounds, boy," said Willard. "And believe it or not, Idgit's
war-trained. Yes, *trained*," he repeated, at the priest's incredulous look.
"How else could I get her used to Molly?"

"But she won't take the shock of two lances striking at once, Will,"
Kogan said. "She'll buckle down flat."

For the first time in many days, Willard grinned. Great, square
ragleaf-stained teeth in a stained mustachio. "Who said anything about
the shock of *two* lances? Only *one* will strike home."

Willard donned his helm and turned Idgit toward the pasture.

The priest blinked, then grinned. "Oh! That means he's gonna cheat. Had me worried, Will. Thought you was going to prate about honor and such."

Willard urged Idgit into a trot. "If things go bad, hook back through the trees to get to the tower. You'll be safe there."

The dogs grew loud on the ridge above. At any moment, Harric expected them to emerge from the fire-cone trunks below the tower. He hoped Mudruffle's clay ears were clear enough to hear the hounds approaching, and that he had enough time to totter back to the tower and bar the door. Abellia would probably be too depressed to notice them, and too slow to descend the stairs in time to bar it herself.

"Hide in the trees, Brolli," said Willard, "and don't let them see you, no matter what happens. Remember, they'd like nothing more than to slay you in order to sabotage the Queen's chance for a treaty with your people. They'll all want a shot at you."

The ambassador was already speeding away with his peculiar foot-and-knuckle lope, satchel of hurling-globes slung before him. Harric cast a worried glance at Caris as they sprinted, axes in hand, after Brolli. She pursed her brow in concentration as she studied the eaves of the forest ahead.

"No heroics, right?" he said between breaths.

She cast him a look of exasperation. "I'm not planning anything stupid, if that's what you mean. But it's going to take heroics to survive this."

Harric grimaced. She was right.

How the moons did Willard let this happen? By walking to the meadow without Molly, he'd exposed his rear, exposed them all, when he knew an enemy might be near. Supposedly a great tactician, Willard had put them in a terrible situation.

As they neared the trees at the foot of the meadow, dewy grass soaking their breeches to the knees, Harric wondered if the Blood had affected Willard's judgment. Did immortality make him arrogant and overconfident? Maybe this was a side effect of the Blood. Or was there a reason he hadn't ridden Molly so soon after drinking from her veins? Maybe she was unmanageable so soon after a cut. Or maybe *he* was unmanageable when he rode her so soon after a cut, and he'd simply miscalculated the risk of enemies traveling through fog.

Harric caught a grim glance from Brolli as the Kwendi's pace slowed and he fell back to lope beside him. Brolli's sack of hurling-globes had gone dark with moisture from the grass.

One thing was certain: if they survived this blunder, they'd not make this mistake again.

By the time they finally plunged into the trees, Harric's legs had become sandbags, and his lungs burned like he'd run through resin fires.

"There!" Brolli pointed to a boulder the size of a carriage on the left side of the road, only sixty paces from the edge of the meadow. "Make cover there! I go up!"

As Harric and Caris veered left to hide behind the boulder, Brolli veered right and flew up a huge grandfather spoke-limb on the opposite side of the road. The ancient tree rose some seventy feet above the smaller ash and hazel, its thick limbs overspreading the road and shading out taller trees. Brolli ascended the tree with the grace of a squirrel and as quickly as he had moved across the ground.

When he appeared above, he crouched upon a stout limb directly above the road, his long-fingered feet gripping the limb. He used one hand to steady himself on a limb above, while in the other he cradled an iron shot the size of a melon. "Hide there," he called. "And as soon as you can, run back to the tower."

"We aren't leaving," Caris said. "You need us."

"No heroics!" said Brolli. "Remember what Willard says."

"I remember," said Caris. "But he didn't say no helping."

Brolli glared at Harric for support, but Harric shrugged. "She may have a point. We have a drunk priest, a broken immortal, and a lonely Kwendi. Why not a pair of unarmored apprentices?"

Brolli made a sound of disgust in the back of his throat. "Then stay hidden as long as possible. Surprise is your best weapon. Trees are your armor."

When I die, one hundred balladeers will starve, and so I'll be revenged on their breed.

—Sir Willard, upon learning the balladeer Vitus Troth had compiled
100 Sir Willard ballads in a folio "cycle."

21

On Bad Endings

Willard waited upon Idgit in the middle of the road in the middle of the meadow beside the weeping willow. Hounds bayed in the fire-cone grove above, eager tenors ringing from the trees. Hoofbeats thrummed and echoed like an approaching storm from the north. No fewer than eight horsemen, by the sound of it.

A dull dread pressed on Willard's chest. If Sir Bannus were among them, this was the end. He did not fear death the way he once had when he'd first stopped taking the Blood. But it hurt to know that Anna would learn from someone else that he'd broken his oath to grow old with her and die.

If Bannus appeared at the top of the switchbacks, Willard's plan was simple: he would turn Idgit around and ride to tell Brolli and the others to hide while he drew Bannus and his knights away down the road. As soon as they passed, they must flee to the safety of the tower. Of course, after that, Gygon would catch Idgit easily, and Willard was no match for Bannus after only three draughts of the Blood. So Willard would end it before Bannus could stop him. A quick cut, a short bleed, and the Sir Willard cycle would finally end. He'd imagined it a thousand times. There was no other way.

How Bannus would rage when he realized his nemesis had cheated him of his long-imagined dream of a living trophy for his hall. Of a limbless Willard kept eternally alive with the Blood. How he would howl of the craven, cheating Abominator.

We must sing our own ends, dear Bannus. I owe you nothing.

Nor would he allow Molly or Holly to fall into Bannus's hands. He would instruct Kogan to take Belle in hand and behead the Phyros in their stalls. If necessary, Kogan and Caris could chain them first, or—

"Sounds like a whole pack of 'em, Will." Kogan emerged through the curtain of weeping willow branches beside him. "Oughta be a ballad writ for this one, so we have to let one live to tell the tale."

"Then I shall surely slay them all."

"Har! Them's that's famous never appreciate it." The priest's big bare feet swatted the earth as he strode to Geraldine and grabbed a long-handled stake mallet from his gear. "Get up, girl!" he said, grabbing her nose ring and tugging her to her feet. "Run ye to the forest! Git! You don't want no part of this."

Geraldine snorted and lumbered only a few steps away, but Kogan swatted her backside until she heaved herself into a trot, rags of wool flapping like the fringe of a shaggy cloak. She kept up the trot until she reached the foot of the meadow, where she halted and looked back through wooly bangs. Apparently satisfied that he wouldn't aggravate her further, she lay down heavily to watch and chew her cud.

Kogan ducked back through the fringe of willow branches.

"Where are you going, Kogan?" said Willard.

"Taking a safe lookout. Can't stick an arrow in what you can't see."

"That is well."

Willard moved Idgit forward until he found a view of the priest through a gap of willow branches. "If I should fail, Kogan, you must win your way to Molly. She must not fall into Bannus's hands. Do you understand?"

Kogan had been climbing into a low crotch in the trunk of the tree. Now he froze, standing in the crook between branches. He gave Willard a crack-toothed grin and made a chopping motion at his neck. "I can do that." Then he sat in the crook and swung his bare feet below it like a child on a bench. He was whistling "Heave-Ho Father" through his teeth.

Willard frowned. He would need the priest's strong arms if the knights couldn't be talked off, but Kogan was thick-headed and unpredictable, possibly as much trouble as he was help. "Kogan," Willard said, putting a weight of seriousness in his tone. "Stay silent, and stay put till I call."

"So you can hog the glory?" Kogan laughed. "I expect to hear my name in the *title* of this ballad."

"This is grave," said Willard. "Molly's not here to help us. When it comes to the fight, there'll be plenty to share, but I aim to soften their ranks first, and for that, you must do as I say."

He could see the priest craning his neck for a view of the ridge through the curtain of willow stems. "Too bad it ain't nighttime, eh, Will? If it was night, you'd have your night-hex a-workin'."

Willard snorted. "Be glad it isn't. Odds are just as good that it would strike you or me before it struck them."

Three hounds burst from the trees at the head of the ridge and halted at the crest, looking down over the gardens and switchbacks to the meadow. Upon seeing Willard, they plunged down the ridge, ignoring the switchbacks. A knight in flame-orange armor emerged on a chesty destrier from the fog and shadows of the fire-cones and reined in to gaze after the hounds. In one hand he steadied a long, orange-painted lance, which he rested in its stirrup cup; his shield bore no crest or markings.

The knight raised a horn to his lips and sounded a series of piercing high notes, then spurred his destrier down the switchbacks toward them. Knight after knight emerged from the fire-cones and followed, all in full armor with unmarked shields and bearing lances with a single green pennant.

Had it been Sir Bannus's company, the pennants would be black.

Willard let out a long breath and smiled. No Bannus. He'd live another day, and maybe long enough to tell Anna himself of his oath. "Things are looking up," he muttered.

Idgit's ears swiveled back toward Willard, and she turned her head to look at him with a big, questioning eye.

"Trust me," he said, with a reassuring pat. "Compared to Bannus, nine fresh knights with full armor and lances is a party."

To his surprise, she snorted and pawed the grass as if restless to get things started. Willard smiled. It must have been Caris's influence. He resisted the urge to crane about and look for her at the foot of the meadow, but wondered if she could even apply her horse-touched influence at such a distance. More likely, she'd fortified the mare's fighting spirit before she left for the forest. Gods leave her, what a mighty force she and her horse-touched gifts could make of a mounted company. But no gift came without price, and with hers came that damned horse-touched oddness. And a knight of the court needed more than skill with horse and blade. His own life and banished-black armor proved that.

The leader of the knights, signified by the double pennant on his lance, emerged from the fire-cones last of all and spurred his charger down the switchbacks. Emerald armor signified his nobility, but his shield displayed no crest or family.

The hounds reached the meadow long before the knights. Rangy, long-legged hunters with floppy ears and shaggy red coats, they bayed their fool lungs hoarse as they pelted across the meadow to Kogan's tree. Once there, they crowded the trunk, leaping and *baooo*-ing like they'd treed a dozen bears.

First of his company to arrive, the orange knight reined in at the head of the meadow and awaited his peers and his captain. "Sir Willard!" he crowed. "We have been looking for you! What luck we should meet! Is there a dung pile near, or do I smell a peasant Wanderer?"

Willard glanced to the tree to see Kogan had clambered to his feet in the crotch of the tree and now hopped from foot to foot in order to avoid having his toes nipped. "That won't do, lads," Kogan said to the dogs. He swept his mallet down in a great, swooping blow that scooped one dog and sent it spinning through the branches. The hound yelped and squealed through the air and landed with a muffled thump beside Willard. Limping to its feet, it whined and slunk up the meadow to the knights.

"That's a warning, lads," said Kogan to the remaining dogs. "Run along now." To help them take this to heart, he performed a couple more impressive sweeps of the mallet, and the dogs, to their credit, thought better of tempting fate. They followed their mate up the meadow.

"Rather not you leave them their scent hounds," Willard muttered. "Better you killed them."

"Hate to hurt a dog, Will," Kogan called, loud enough for the orange knight to hear. "Warn't their fault their master's a git."

As the rest of the knights arrived, they formed a cavalry line at the head of the meadow, Willard studied them carefully: nine fresh-faced knights in all the colors of the Arkendian blood arch. They were young men, none of them yet born when Willard led the Cleansing that drove the Old Ones from the land. Visors up, their eyes sparked with excitement as they muttered boasts up and down the line. Willard didn't need to hear every word to know their tenor: they had found the elusive Willard, and their company would be heroes. Some would even have a hand in subduing him. All of them wanted a chance to draw his blood.

When the emerald lord finally arrived, he raised his lance in parley, and reined in before Willard. When he propped up his visor, Willard recognized the ruddy, hawkish face as belonging to a son of the earl of Eyand, a noble family long at odds with the Queen.

"Sir Willard. What a pleasant surprise," said the nobleman. "You've lost the famous Molly, I see. What a pity."

"What can I do for you, Eyand?"

"Eyand, you warthog!" the priest roared. "Put your visor down! You're scarin' your dogs!"

The nobleman's dark eyes flicked briefly to the willow, then back to Willard. His voice chilled noticeably when next he spoke. "These are my terms, Sir Willard. I cannot promise you the lives of your companions. The crime of consorting with the Abominator is simply too grave, and once I deliver them to His Holiness, it is he who shall decide their fate."

"Not much else I care about, frankly," said Willard, "but go on. Mostly, I want to see the look of terror behind your eyes again when you say the words 'His Holiness.' That amuses me. After ten lifetimes, few things amuse. Yet I spent much of ten lifetimes with His So-called Holiness. Shall I tell you the amusing fate of those who ride with him? You have only to look at his shield bearer to know it. If he regains the throne, all of you will wear the mask."

"I came not here to bandy words, Abominator." The sneer on Eyand's face had drained away as Willard spoke, but he raised his chin in defiance. "What I promise is this: if you surrender yourself and the Kwendi ambassador with his wedding ring, no man here will lay a hand on you in battle. None will be able to claim he unhorsed Sir Willard, none will be able to claim he bested you in battle, and your reputation will remain unsullied."

"How foolish and vain you must think me," Willard said, in a booming voice meant to be heard by all present. "I am the Queen's knight, Sir Eyand. Sworn to protect. As you are sworn, for that matter. I do not submit."

A ripple of excitement passed through the cavalry line.

"We hoped you'd say that," said Eyand.

"I only ask that you come at me honorably, one at a time," Willard continued in the same booming voice. "Tournament rules, no spitfires." Eyand's eyes flashed as he considered this. "Also, as I am lame in the leg, I ask that if an unhorsed opponent wishes to face me on foot, the priest be allowed to stand in for me."

"And when the priest falls?" Eyand grinned.

"Then I shall stand for myself."

"Seems a poor sort of arrangement for us."

"Then deny me, if you prefer, and let's be on with it," Willard snapped. "I have other matters to attend this day."

Eyand snorted. Turning his stallion, he rejoined his men, and the young knights converged on him. Watching their excited conversation, Willard could see them urging Eyand to accept the terms so they could all have a turn plucking honors from the corpse of Willard's glory before surrendering him to Bannus. By announcing his terms to the whole company, Willard had made it harder for Eyand to deny them.

But Eyand was no fool. If he were careful, he'd call Field Rules and they'd come at him all at once—overwhelm him and gain the certain victory. If he did, Willard's only hope would be to charge through their ranks and keep going up the switchbacks in a desperate bid to reach Molly before they caught him. But that was a desperate hope, and he knew it. Idgit was not strong enough to carry his armored bulk up the switchbacks at a run. Her poor legs would give out before they made the second terrace and the long-legged mounts of Eyand's company overtook them.

Eyand held up a hand, and his men fell silent. Resuming his place at the head of the cavalry line, he called to Willard, "Tournament Rules, Sir Willard; let it not be said we denied you any terms before defeating you on your final field."

"Good news, girl," Willard muttered to Idgit. "Just don't make it look too easy."

"Malgus," Eyand shouted down his line, "be first to greet the old man with your spear."

From the line of waiting knights, the orange surged forward, lance lowered and shield angled before him. Willard urged Idgit in motion and drew his sword in his left hand while keeping the lance stub directed at his opponent. A glance at the priest confirmed Kogan crouched in the crotch of the tree, grinning like a fool.

Idgit had barely got up to a canter when the orange knight met them at a gallop. The painted lance darted toward Willard, but he flicked it aside with his sword and jammed the blunt end of the ash pole under the orange knight's chin. The orange flipped backward off his horse, and Willard sat firm as the force of the blow transferred through the lance and his arm and his back into Idgit, who huffed as if she'd been kicked in the gut. He felt her hind quarters sink a little beneath him, but she didn't stumble.

The orange knight hit the turf behind them with a dull clatter and the sickening *crunk!* of breaking bone and cartilage that ten lifetimes of battle taught Willard was an unlucky fall and broken neck.

Kogan released a howl of celebration. As Willard turned Idgit about, helmets up and down the line of knights turned to each other as if the knights were confirming what they had seen.

"Come on then, Eyand, you gelding," Kogan taunted the knight. "This man's on a *pony!* Is that all the Brotherhood can deal these days? Blood must be thin in the west! I've seen more pluck in a poxy fishwife!"

Willard cantered Idgit back toward the willow, and as they passed the orange knight, Idgit whinnied and tossed her head. The knight lay sprawled on the turf, unmoving, head at unhealthy angle.

"Keep up that lip, Kogan," Willard growled, as he rode past Kogan's tree, "and they won't wait their turn like good little boys."

This time, he didn't turn Idgit to face them until he'd ridden some thirty paces past the tree, so he could meet the next knight nearer to Kogan.

As soon as Willard turned, Eyand signaled, and a gold-armored knight in flowing ribbons bounded forth, white gelding churning clods from the earth.

The gold presented his lance almost sideways, with the tip far to Willard's right. Willard understood his plan, and it was a good one. At the last moment, the knight swung the lance to center, so its tip approached from the right, where Willard couldn't deflect it with his sword. It was a difficult move, but the man performed it admirably. Instead of beating the shaft aside with his sword, Willard was forced to beat the darting lance upward with the shaft of his own lance, sending the deadly tip high. But the gold promptly returned the favor, beating Willard's shaft aside with the forte of his lance, and they passed with neither scoring.

Willard smiled. Sir Gold was a skilled lancer, and though he'd obscured his crest on his shield, Willard was willing to bet this was a son of Tirr, a famous gold-blooded jousting family on the West Isle. In ten lifetimes, Willard had met more Tirrs in more tournaments than he could count, and the great thing about Tirrs was that though they were often mightily skilled lancers, they were predictable. What was their motto? *In tradition, victory.*

Willard snorted. His was more like, *Gods take tradition — just give me the victory.*

At the top of the meadow, Willard turned Idgit to face Sir Tirr, and once again they rode together, lances lowered, riders leaning forward in their saddles. This time, Willard had the slope in his favor, and he spurred Idgit into all the speed she could manage in order to meet Sir Tirr where the fallen orange knight lay.

The thing about tradition, Sir Tirr, is that it isn't very flexible.

Tirr's gelding churned up the meadow, and when he'd almost reached the site of the fallen knight and the combat was about to be joined, Willard swerved to the left so they would have to pass on each other's weak side. He timed it so the gold knight could not match the maneuver and keep Willard on his strong side without trampling the orange knight where he lay. Tirr shifted his lance to his weak side, but the maneuver came off rushed and unrehearsed, so Willard easily pressed the gold lance aside, disengaged his own, and planted the stub under Tirr's breastplate. The stave shattered in an explosion of splinters as Sir Tirr toppled from his saddle. When he hit the ground, his golden helmet dashed from his head to reveal a furious face and wild golden locks.

Idgit staggered through the blow but kept her feet again, and as they trotted back to their place beside the willow, she whinnied another challenge.

Kogan pushed through the willow curtain like a musk-auroch

through a tapestry. He carried the spare lance in one hand, the long-handled mallet in the other, and the grin of a madman on his face.

"Here you go, Will."

Willard turned the shaft in his hands to find a good grip and balance, then rested its butt on his foot in the stirrup. "Is that gold fellow up?" The priest nodded. "He's yours. I don't dare get off the horse while the others are mounted."

Kogan licked his lips and squinted at Tirr. The knight was climbing to his feet. "I got him, Will."

"Take care," Willard said. "See the blue in his cheek? He's blood-painting. Even dried and taken in wine, the Blood has power. Might not be as dazed as you think."

"I seen it."

Sir Tirr drew his sword and started for Kogan with unsteady steps.

As Kogan strode toward him, he unbelted his smothercoat so it fell before him like the wall of woolen carpets on a rug-beater's line. As Willard predicted, Tirr lunged with surprising speed, thrusting for Kogan's belly, but Kogan was already turning, the carpets of the smothercoat whirling outward to dampen and divert the blow.

As if finishing a dance between them, Kogan swung his mallet down in a low, swooping arc, like he intended to knock a croquet ball all the way to Kingsport. But the mallet continued its arc up beneath Tirr's shield to catch him just below the belt, where the armor was soft. The blow lifted him—armor and all—an inch off the ground, and when he returned to earth, he crumpled like sodden paper, and Kogan stepped on his neck to finish him.

The remaining knights roared in fury.

"What'd I do?" Kogan said, eyes wide, arms spread. "Warn't that fair?"

"Ever seen neck-stepping in tournaments?" Willard couldn't help but chuckle.

"Field Rules it is!" Eyand snarled.

On hearing this, Kogan spat, then turned and pelted down the road, his smothercoat flapping like the wings of a drunken moth. Eyand watched him go, a snarl on his lips. "Sir Yors, remain with me. The rest, take a run at Willard with lances, then the priest. Do not let him reach the trees."

Five knights in the cavalry surged forward as one, leaving Eyand

and a red-armored knight behind. Willard spurred Idgit to meet them.

The advance line of knights thundered toward Willard, lances lowered, but each was so greedy to score the first hit that they ended up racing side by side in a line, instead of single file or in pairs. And a line was easy to evade. As soon as Idgit was up to a canter, Willard turned her sharply toward the left edge of the approaching line. By the time the line reached him and he had to face their charge, he'd moved far enough to the left that he could split the two left-most riders, making it impossible for the lances of the three other riders to reach him across the others.

As he charged between them, Willard extended the sword in his left hand, the lance in his right. The left rider tried to disengage his lance over Willard's sword, but Willard caught it and slammed it aside and down in a circular sweep that sent the tip of the lance into the dirt. The recoil of the lance slammed the knight's breastplate and arm, and broke the shaft as he passed.

On his right, Willard used his own lance to beat his enemy's shaft upward, but at the same time, Idgit's stride faltered. He dared not drive the lance into the man's breastplate or the force of it could knock her down. She'd already given all she had, and now her legs were probably failing.

Rather than unhorsing the man, Willard settled for a ringing blow to the helmet.

And then they were through the line of knights, and the meadow opened before them. Unfortunately, Eyand had ridden behind the others and now tore down the meadow, green lance straining forward while the red knight stood as second behind him.

Willard glanced behind, confirming that the knights of the line had followed Eyand's orders to take Kogan. To Idgit, he cried, "Give it everything you've got, girl! He's coming at a run!"

At the Field of Flinders Tourney hosted by Earl Doblin, Sir Willard set the record for highest number of lances burst upon shields of opponents in one tournament. Seventy lances he burst, and it would have been greater, but Doblin ran out of lances, and when Willard called for green poles newly cut, the senior Heralds pronounced them illegal, spoiling the fun.

—From the diary of Sessil Riloy, Herald Prentice

22

Steel & Fire

Harric piled dead branches behind the boulder to make better cover, and dusted his hands off. "Did he unhorse a third one?" he said, looking up at Caris where she stood on a log beside the boulder and craned to see into the meadow.

She said nothing. A hand went to her mouth as if in surprise or fear. "Uh-oh."

"Uh-oh? Don't say uh-oh," he said, climbing onto the log beside her.

The field had changed. Kogan was now bounding toward them through the grass, smothercoat waving and flapping as a handful of knights thundered after him and still more charged Willard.

"Uh-oh…" Harric whispered.

"Five knights!" Caris called up to Brolli. "Kogan's bringing them to us!"

"I am seeing," said the Kwendi.

Caris climbed to the top of the boulder and craned her neck toward the running priest. "He's going to make it," she said.

Harric remained at the foot of the boulder, where he could see the approaching priest through a gap in the grove. To his surprise, one of the pursuing knights discharged a spitfire at the priest. The wad soared just over Kogan's head, spattering him with sizzling resin and spraying across the grass near Geraldine, who viewed it with her customary calm.

"Gods take them," Harric muttered. "A wildfire could set off the whole fire-cone ridge."

Kogan slowed and grabbed his gut as if pierced with an arrow. He bellowed like a stricken bull, then vomited a spout of beery yellow, followed by another, and another, as if each stride pumped it from his guts.

"Gods leave me, he is an idiot," said Caris.

"Yes, but he's our idiot," Harric said. "Our big, strong idiot."

After a final spout, Kogan lumbered back to speed, but the horses had gained precious ground.

Harric bit his lip as Kogan put on a burst of speed only twenty paces from the first trees. Twice that distance behind him, the lead knight spurred his mount, gleaming lance point stretching forward like the head of a viper.

Eyand's lance darted for Willard's neck, and Willard parried it high with his sword. His lance stub struck low in the center of Eyand's shield, jolting the nobleman backward and out of his saddle, but not before Eyand steered his stallion straight into Idgit as if he would trample her.

Idgit's weary legs collapsed and the stallion barreled into Willard, hooves slamming chest armor and helm, and the stallion's massive shoulder knocked the wind from him. Willard spun back and over the saddle as Idgit screamed in terror.

A distant part of Willard recognized that Eyand had played on a weakness that Willard hadn't been aware of until that moment. In ten lifetimes, no one had dared check his mount because that mount was Molly, and Molly was bigger than even the biggest Phyros stallion. Eyand had correctly guessed that Willard would never see it coming.

Bollocks.

Willard tucked his limbs in and tried to roll when he hit the turf, but one boot caught briefly in its stirrup, and that leg hit hard and skewed the landing. Dirt sprayed through the ear holes of his helm and the eye slots went dark with mud. Gasping for breath, he got a knee under him and crawled to hands and knees. He raised his visor in time to see Idgit shoulder into him as she struggled to her feet, and though she nearly trampled him, he was able to grab her reins again and hold fast until she got her hooves under her.

"Easy, girl," he murmured, as she whinnied and looked about with rolling eyes.

A glance showed Eyand crawling to his feet some ten paces hence.

Willard knocked the rest of the dirt from his visor and searched for his sword. It lay at his feet, bent almost forty degrees.

Holding fast to Idgit's bridle, he braced the bent sword against the grass and more or less straightened it under his boot.

Eyand walked toward him with a very straight, very sharp-looking sword in hand. The lord raised his visor. A bloody cut gaped across his hatchet nose, but his eyes gleamed in triumph. Without looking away from Willard, he signaled to the red knight still waiting at the head of the meadow. "Field Rules, Sir Yors. You may take him."

Sir Yors, whom Eyand appeared to have saved for last because he was nearly as huge as Willard, saluted and urged his horse forward.

"Yield, Sir Willard," said Eyand. "And I'll call Yors off."

Willard cursed. Even if he parried Sir Yors's lance, the charger would flatten him like a battering ram, and Eyand would take him while he was down.

He set his foot in Idgit's stirrup, but she screamed and pulled away, eyes rolling with some new fear. Gods leave it, Caris's touch had worn off.

But then he heard it. It was a sound only he would recognize, and it made him laugh.

He discarded the sword and released Idgit's bridle.

As Idgit bolted, Eyand beamed in triumph. "You yield?"

Willard forced himself to hold Eyand's gaze without looking to the source of the sound he'd heard. He raised a finger. "You're about to find Field Rules a most unfortunate choice."

The lord's sneer faltered. He turned his head to look up the meadow, but it was too late.

Sir Yors was but two strides away, his gleaming spear tip homing in on Willard, when Willard heard the tiny wheeze again. It was the wheeze of excitement Molly made in the moments before joining battle.

Harric flattened himself against the boulder and peeked around it to look for Kogan and his pursuers. Against his chest he clutched his wood axe. He had no idea how to fight with an axe. *Aim and swing and hold on?* Caris had told him to "Hook a knight's shoulder and drag him off his horse," but he had doubts. That could easily turn into "Hook a knight's shoulder and be dragged across the kingdom."

"If I don't hook a knight," he whispered, as Caris climbed down from her perch on the boulder, "how about I just bash the piss out of his knee?"

She cast a skeptical glance at him. "Just be careful you don't hit me by accident."

He nodded and returned to his spot on the down-road end of the boulder, where he could peer up the road without crowding her. Just as he looked around the edge of the boulder, he saw Kogan burst into the trees and pound down the track toward him. The priest's huge feet slapped the path, and his hair smoked like an old campfire. A group of knights thundered in his wake, led by a bronze knight only five paces behind; his lance snaked toward Kogan's back.

"Duck!" Harric shouted, but the priest blundered on, staring wide with exhaustion. A split moment later, he would have been skewered if an iron shot hadn't descended like a meteor onto the crown of the bronze knight's pot helm. The knight toppled from the saddle and slammed in the dirt before Harric. The shot graced the top of the pot helm like a dirty pearl, but impact against the ground jarred it loose to reveal a dent in the helm like a bowl.

An umber-red knight rode on the heels of the bronze, and as Kogan whirled to face him—long-handled mallet in both hands—he directed his lance tip at his chest. Another iron ball slammed the knight's armored shoulder and his arm appeared to go limp, dropping the spear. Kogan stepped aside and caught him full in the throat with the head of the mallet as he passed.

The third knight swerved his horse and held his shield above his head as he rode beneath the tree. The iron ball glanced off the shield and he charged by, lance straining forward for the priest's ample chest.

"Run!" Harric shouted, but Kogan tossed his mallet aside and charged straight at the onrushing stallion.

"No!" Harric grabbed one of the branches he'd piled by the boulder and heaved it into the stallion's face as it passed. The beast smashed through it and trampled it down without injury, but the sudden appearance of the obstacle startled it enough to throw off the rider's aim. The lance sped past Kogan's right ear, and Kogan dove for the charging war-horse like he would tackle a bull calf.

The two met with a breath-stealing thud. Kogan's bare legs flailed as he flew backward, while his bare arms grappled the horse's neck. The horse snarled, and Harric could see it biting the priest's head, tearing at his hair. As the horse slowed, the knight discarded his lance and struggled to stay in the saddle. Stubborn as a tick, the giant priest bore the stallion's head to the ground with the full weight of his body, and as it staggered to a stop, he twisted.

The stallion screamed as the priest forced it to its knees, and the knight dove from his saddle before his horse could roll on him. One foot, however, got trapped beneath the horse as it fell, and when he cried out in pain, Kogan released the animal and literally fell upon the knight. The knight drew a dirk and stabbed it into the smothercoat, but Kogan seized his hand and enveloped him in an upside-down bear hug that pinned both arms to his side.

"Fight like a man!" the knight screamed, his voice muffled in Kogan's smothercoat.

Kogan stood and hoisted the man upside down. The knight struggled to kick him in the face, but that ended when Kogan drove the knight headfirst into the unyielding road and put all his weight behind it. Once. Twice. On the third time, the man went limp, and Kogan let him crash in a heap at his feet.

"That all of 'em?" The priest belched and blood spurted from his nose like a faucet. He dropped to one knee, then to all fours. "Wup. Head's spinning."

"Get out of the road!" Harric said.

A spitfire popped up the road and Harric heard a resin wad scream into the branches above. Flames splashed through the branches where Brolli had been. He caught a glimpse of Brolli leaping from branch to branch and shouting in Kwendi. Two knights—an amber and a red— had reined in at the entrance to the wood, and now sat with smoking spitfires in their arms, peering up into the branches. The red knight shouted and pointed, and the amber lifted his spitfire and touched it off with a burning punk.

"Watch out!" Harric shouted.

Another hissing wad streaked into the branches, hit a limb, and sprayed fire through the leaves and twigs. Somewhere above, Brolli shouted.

"This is it," Caris said. Harric backed up to see her leaving the cover of the boulder and circling around the knights while their attention was on the Kwendi. Her path would take her into thin cover of scraggly brush, however, and if they looked away from Brolli for an instant, she'd be vulnerable. Harric chewed his lip. He knew he'd be no help at her side…but he could help with the diversion.

After dashing around his side of the boulder, he stopped in the middle of the road and brandished his axe in the air. "You dimwits! You'll set the whole fire-cone range on fire!"

The amber pranced his charger backward and pointed at Harric. The red produced a second spitfire, and set the thing off with some kind of flint wheel almost as soon as he'd taken aim. Harric yelped and dove back toward the boulder, leaving his axe in the trail. A searing missile screamed past him, spattering his pant leg with flaming resin.

"Shit!" he squeaked. Heat bloomed on his thigh. He tore at his belt and pulled down his pants before the resin burned through and stuck to his skin. He'd just forced his pants down to his boots where he could stamp the fire out, when a horse loomed above him and he heard the sound of drawn steel.

Harric heard the whistle of a blade and felt a tug at his left shoulder blade. The flesh there bloomed with stinging pain. "Cob!" Without looking behind him, he dove backward and managed to crash into the patch of scrawny alders. The red knight's blade whistled again and rang among the branches, and his stallion shoved between the trees, froth flinging from its lips.

"Cob!" Harric crab-walked backward into the alder, pants still around his ankles, while the horse chested between scrawny saplings, only a stride behind.

From the top of the pursuing horse, a helm shaped like a wolf head glared down. "Sit still, ye bastard idiot."

No! I can't die with my pants at my ankles!

Harric tried to dive backward again, but the pants dragging between his feet had caught on a branch and held him fast.

From the corner of his eye, Willard saw the red knight struggling to keep his charger on target, as the beast had clearly sensed Molly and begun to panic. In the last moment, it locked its front legs and ducked her head, sending the red Sir Yors flying. A split moment later, Molly bowled into the charger's left flank.

Eyand staggered back to avoid the flurry of hooves and screaming horseflesh.

Sir Yors slammed into the turf in front of Willard, red pauldron scoring the earth like a fancy plow blade.

Molly knocked the charger from its feet, then turned on Eyand with terrible fury. The lord didn't even have time to scream. Blood sprayed. Molly had him by the neck and shook her green-armored toy from side to side.

The charger rolled to its feet and fled.

Molly dropped the limp Eyand and pounded him with her fore-hooves while she bit and tore at one arm.

"To me!" Willard bellowed. "To me!"

Molly whirled, violet eyes flashing. With a pale hand dripping in her mouth, she trotted to Willard and dropped the gory prize at his feet.

"Charming as ever." Willard grinned. "Moons, it's good to see you."

Molly had been saddled, though badly, with the girths so loose it had slipped almost half to one side. But considering the feeble Mudruffle must have done it, it was a wonder it didn't hang full under her belly. Tied to the saddle was Belle in her scabbard.

"Gods leave you," Willard muttered to the absent golem. "I could kiss your knobby hand." He laid his head beside Molly's neck, and the Blood rose and thrummed in his veins. Power thrilled through his limbs. Moons, it felt good. He was whole again. Hale again. Free of pain.

Free of pain, old fool? He snorted as he heaved and shoved the saddle to Molly's back. *You've traded one pain for another—sacrificed your heart again for your queen—and the vultures of regret already fatten on it.*

An image flashed before him of Caris's face that morning when she learned of his broken oath. *Damn her judging eyes.* Another image followed of Anna growing old without him, and—damn it all, he'd done what he had to. Was he not sworn to the Queen as well as Anna? Did Caris think he broke his oath lightly?

The red knight stirred at his feet. "My apologies, Sir…Yors, was it? But your leader declared Field Rules." Letting the Blood fill him with wrath, he set Belle's point in the mail between back plate and helm and slammed it.

Molly let out a snarl of approval. After wrenching the blade free, he mounted and turned her toward the forest. In four strides, she was in a gallop. He let the glory of their partnership flow through him—the ancient, wordless kinship and understanding, the power. Behind him lay four knights, choked in their own blood.

But from the wood came shouts and screams and the clash of arms and fire.

For the second time in his life, Harric saw Brolli fall upon an enemy from above him. The first time, the Kwendi had been lurking in the rafters of the inn at Gallows Ferry. This time, he dove from the burning branches and landed behind the knight on the rump of his horse. The horse reared, and Brolli held on to the rider's cape. When the animal set its hooves back on the ground, he flung the cape over the knight's head and vaulted over him to land beside Harric.

"Run!" Brolli yelled.

By then, Harric had kicked off his boots—leaving his pants with them—and the two of them bolted along the edge of the boulder for the thicker brush behind it. Branches whipped Harric's legs, and when something sharp stabbed the bottom of his foot, he stumbled to his knees with a cry.

Brolli seized his shirt to haul him to his feet as the stallion bounded around the boulder and the knight's sword flashed high for a strike. A squealing, metallic *crack* echoed through the trees, and the sword spun to the ground.

A wood axe lodged in the crown of the wolf-faced helm. Caris stood behind the knight, atop the boulder, her chest heaving.

The knight fell, leaving one foot in a stirrup as the stallion stopped a step away from Harric.

"Help him," Caris said, pointing. "The foot!"

After a moment's confusion, in which Harric wondered why a dead man's foot needed help, he realized she meant the horse, and unhitched the foot from its stirrup.

"The other knight?" Brolli said, looking up at Caris. "The spitfire?"

She dismissed the question with a wave back to the other side of the boulder. Blood flecked her face. Her lip curled as she looked Harric up and down.

"I'm okay," he said, unnecessarily.

Caris shook her head. "What is it with you and losing your pants?"

"I—" He closed his mouth. He gave her a calm smile. "It was a diversion."

She surprised him by nodding. "Oh, thanks. It worked."

He nodded toward the knight at his feet. "Nice heroics."

A rare, shy smile flashed across her lips, and Harric's heart flopped like a yielding puppy.

The red knight's horse, freed of the foot in its stirrup, worked free of the alders and now trotted down the trail, away from the fire. A sizable blaze crackled in the branches above, a midair bonfire four fathoms above the trail.

"Must stop the fire before it spreads," Brolli said.

From the pasture came the rumble of approaching hooves. Twenty strides down the trail, Kogan clambered to his knees in the bushes. His brow furrowed as he listened. "That ain't a pony." He cursed, struggling to his feet, and cursed again when his leg buckled and he landed on all fours. "That ain't a pony!"

"It's a Phyros," said Caris. "Molly."

Willard and Molly emerged in the gap in the trees, and reined in well short of the fire above. Scanning the battle scene, Willard appeared to take note of the injured survivors. "Boy's naked and bloody. Kogan looks like a corpse. Girl?" High on the boulder, Caris faced her mentor, hands on her hips, chest still heaving from exertion. She looked like a statue from a famous battle.

"Good fight, Will." Kogan waved from his knees a few paces down the road, face bloodied and grinning. "That girl damned well took out the last two by her own self. But it warn't heroic, Will—like you said, no heroics—so she did it regular. Just what she had to."

Willard's eyes narrowed, and a wide smile sent wrinkles fanning from the corners of his eyes. "The last two herself, you say. And no heroics. Quite an accomplishment."

Caris flushed and gave a curt nod.

"Oh, and I distracted them for her." As Harric limped back into the alder to fetch his pants and boots, he began to giggle uncontrollably. He had no idea where the laughter came from, and he tried to bite it back, but it was no use. Knights were squirting brains from their noses and he was running around in his undershorts. He ducked behind the boulder until he could control himself and pulled up his pants, only to have his foot snag in a burn hole big enough to fit his head through and tear the rest of the pant leg away. His left leg was now bare from mid-thigh.

The giggles threatened to return, but a sobering *crack* exploded in the fire above and showered him with burning embers. Cinching his bastard belt, he looked up to see the fire had spread to the size of three bonfires in the branches.

"This fire is being the danger now!" Brolli barked. "We control it, or it climbs to fire-cones and Abellia!"

*In the time of King Farnor, our Queen's royal father, Sir Willard
offered a fortune to any smith who could craft a sword that was
both strong enough for a Phyros-rider, and pure enough to chime a
perfect C sharp. After many blades and smiths, an apprentice horn
maker named Geromey Till presented him with a blade of star-iron
and steel that a man could tune a lute by. Willard named Geromey
Swordsmith to the Blue Order, and named the sword* Belle.

—From *Court Fools and Heroes*, by Timus of Warbeton

23

Smoke & Sacrifice

Heat from the blaze overhead warmed Harric's scalp and forehead as he pulled on his left boot and grabbed for the right. Spots of ash drifted like snowflakes among the smaller trees of the grove and dusted the trail beneath the spoke-limb. He coughed as a whiff of wood and resin smoke filled his throat.

"Hurry, Harric," said Brolli, peering at the flames only four fathoms above. It had spread to more branches and part of the trunk, doubling its size.

As Harric pushed his foot into his right boot, he felt a stab of pain in his left shoulder blade, reminding him that the red knight's sword had left a nasty gash there. In all the excitement, he'd been able to forget it, but now that it had his attention, it throbbed and he could feel his shirt sticking to it.

Another horn sounded from the ridge as he shoved his heel into place.

The sound sent Molly into fits. She'd been restive before the horn, pawing the earth and snorting and wheeling so Willard had to keep a tight rein; now she reared and lunged at the air, eyes fixed on invisible foes.

Harric lurched to his feet and hurried away from her.

"That's the horn of their baggage train," Willard said. "Get me a lance."

Caris jumped from the boulder. Harric finished cinching his bastard belt around what remained of his pants and jogged to the bronze knight's horse, which had moved down the path to get clear of the burning tree.

"What are you doing, boy?" Willard said. "I said fetch me a lance."

"Caris has the lance." Harric pulled a silver horn from the saddlebag and blew it in answer to the one on the ridge.

"Har!" Kogan beamed. "They'll think their friends won the field! They'll skip on down as fresh as boys to a spring dance."

Willard gave Harric a grudging nod. "I expect these riders to be no more than grooms and squires. Short work. Follow when you see it's clear. Leave the fallen. Bring their horses."

Harric could see through a gap in the trees to a line of horses starting down the switchbacks. "Looks like at least a half-dozen riders and laden packhorses."

"Come to your reckoning, boys," said Kogan.

"Sir Willard," said Brolli, "we must stop the fire or the fire-cones—"

"Hang the fire-cones!" Willard snapped. "A fire at this point is more friend to us than to our enemies. And if these men escape to report, we're worse off than before. What do you bet Bannus is riding up this pass this very moment to meet them? Kogan, fetch me a shield!"

Through the smoke, Harric glimpsed the fire-cone trees on the ridge above, their tops drooping with ripe resin cones. The nearest of them was no more than a quarter mile away, and the smoke was already riding the wind right up the valley toward them. That mean the fire would spread in that direction, and once the fire-cones caught fire, the explosion would light up the sky like a beacon. Maybe Willard realized what an ideal distress signal it would make. And depending on the wind, the resulting forest fire might cover their escape and their tracks.

On the other hand, it would absolutely cook Abellia in her tower.

Harric saw the worry in Caris's eye as she returned with a bronzed lance and handed it up to Willard. Slaughtering squires was probably something she hadn't anticipated from her mentor. They were all learning that there was little Willard wouldn't sacrifice for his queen—including his own honor—but surely he wouldn't be so callous as to view Abellia's life as an acceptable sacrifice. He must plan to take Abellia with them if the fire got out of hand.

Brolli was sputtering in disbelief. "What can you mean? Is this how Arkendians wage war—win at all costs, even if it make you the monster?" He flipped up his daylids to stare at Willard, shock and accusation in his golden eyes.

"There are no saints in war," Willard said. "Only winners and losers."

Brolli's teeth were bared in preparation for a retort, but at that moment, Molly danced perilously close to his bare feet, and he was forced to skip away. Before he regained his tongue, Kogan bellowed, "Got it, Will!" and presented Willard with the bronze knight's gleaming shield. "Good West Isle steel. Har!"

Willard girded it to his arm, and Molly groaned her frustration at the delay. Her eyes bled the Phyros war mask in fans across her cheeks, and the scars crisscrossing her coat stood out like livid veins. The moment Willard secured the shield, he turned her and let her run.

"Follow me when it's clear!" Willard shouted, as Molly exploded from a standstill into a tearing gallop.

Kogan spat a bloody gob. "And let you hog the fun?" He raised a captured skin of wine and rinsed the blood and dirt from his nose and lip. As he lumbered after Willard, beard dribbling wine and gore, he reached grubby fingers in his mouth and yanked out a tooth. Tossing it to Harric, he winked. "Souvenir."

"Father!" Brolli called. "Willard said stay here."

"Yea, but he don't mean it."

"We need your help with the fire," said Harric.

A loud *crack* from the fire above made Harric jump.

"Will don't care about no fire." Nevertheless, Kogan came to a slow, swaying stop in the road. A heavy sigh escaped him. It was the sound of a man settling in for a deep, comfortable sleep. Then he collapsed to his knees and vomited in the grass. "Maybe I'll rest first."

"Let him go," said Caris. "He can barely stand."

Another *crack* from above, and sparks showered down on them.

"Help me cut these trees before they catch the fire," Brolli barked.

Since the spoke-limb's branches spread ten paces in all directions, it dwarfed the young ash and brushlike maples in its shade, but those that grew outside its circle of shade grew tall and mingled branches with the grandfather tree. As the fire moved out the ends of the spoke-limb branches, it threatened to leap into the tops of these neighbors.

"Cut these to fall away from the fire!"

As Brolli pointed out the trees nearest the fire, Harric picked up his wood axe and set upon the largest of them. The ash tree was a daunting six inches across, but he was an experienced woodcutter; he'd cut all Mother Ganner's firewood in the winter, and he was an enthusiastic better in log-cutting contests in Gallows Ferry, so he set to it with practiced fervor.

Angle cut, flat cut, angle cut, flat cut. Chips flew. His injured shoulder blade ached, but if he drew most of the power from his right arm, he could limit the left arm to merely guiding the blows.

The bright smell of sap rose in sweet counterpoint to the smoke as chips bounced from his cheeks. Caris chopped at a tree beside him, while Brolli, who had only a fallen broadsword to work with, devoted his efforts to downing saplings.

Smoke burned Harric's eyes and throat, and sweat soon slicked his face. The fire above roared and dropped burning coals, some of which singed the hair on Harric's arms.

Caris cursed. "Why isn't it cutting?" She was laying into her tree as if assailing a foe, and her progress in the green wood was less than half of Harric's. He realized with some amusement that she'd never had to cut wood in her life—that she'd had servants for that.

"Alternate cleaver and turnstile," Harric said, translating woodcutting technique into classic sword strokes. "Like this." He demonstrated "Cleaver. Turnstile. Cleaver. Turnstile."

She grunted as she delivered a mammoth cleaver and sent a huge cantle of wood flying. "Ha!" Before Harric cut enough to topple his tree, she'd more than caught up to him. When she'd cut it more than half through, she dropped her axe and shoved her tree until it cracked and fell slowly away from the burning spoke-limb.

"Mudruffle!" she screamed. "Watch out!"

Harric followed her eyes to find Mudruffle in the fall line. The little golem did not seem to hear her. He appeared to be circling the burning

tree, picking his awkward way through the brush with the help of a
walking staff in one hand. His other hand he spread before him as if to
catch an invisible butterfly.

Caris leapt around the tree in time to get a shoulder under the
slowly accelerating trunk, and Harric lent a hand from his side, but the
tree had too much start and they had to let it fall in a crash of whipping
branches.

"Mudruffle!" Caris screamed.

The fallen tree branches thrashed inches behind, and the little
golem paced on, oblivious, with his hand spread before him.

Caris let out a shout of frustration.

"Another!" Brolli instructed them, pointing to another ash on the
opposite side of Harric's tree. "It is spreading!"

To Harric's horror, the top branches of his tree had already
caught fire.

"Let me!" Caris shouldered him aside. Placing her hands against
the trunk, she pushed, rocking back and forth. Tiny pops came from the
weakened site of Harric's cutting. Harric dropped his axe and grabbed
one of the tree's branches on the other side to pull as she pushed. When
the trunk gave a loud crack, Harric jumped aside and the tree fell with a
crash. As soon as he'd stamped out the burning branches of his tree, he
ran to the next-nearest tree to be threatened by the fire, and despaired.
Despite their efforts, the fire now danced in the branches of several
adjacent ash trees, and since the ash grew increasingly close together
as they moved away from the shade of the spoke-limb, it would now
accelerate from tree to tree faster than they could cut them.

Brolli shouted, "Begin!" pointing to the tree before Harric.

Harric tried to say, "It's hopeless!" but took a lungful of smoke
and choked.

A loud, feathery *pop!* silenced everything. At the same moment, it
seemed the flames and smoke sucked back into their sources and closed
up shop with a snap. The roar of the fire ceased. Crackling branches
fell mute.

Harric looked up and pushed hair from his eyes. The heat was gone.
A great billow of smoke rolled up and away on a wave of rising heat,
but the clearing had gone cold. Not even a trickle of smoke remained
from the smallest smoldering branch. Eyes wide, he let out a laugh of

surprise. Even the blackened limbs now appeared as cold and inert as sticks from some previous year's fire.

Caris gasped. "Mudruffle!" Harric followed her gaze to the base of the spoke-limb, where Mudruffle stood rigid as a fence post. He'd extended a hand against the mighty tree as if to steady himself. His staff crumbled to ash as Harric watched. A dry, white-hot, sizzling sound emerged from Mudruffle; every inch of his strange clay body hissed like a drowned campfire.

Caris dropped her axe and ran toward him. "Mudruffle, are you hurt?"

Mudruffle gave no response. He seemed unnaturally rigid, like a smoking statue of himself. Then he tipped away from the tree and crashed to the dirt.

Brolli was beside the fallen golem before Caris or Harric could reach him. He held out one hand to keep them away. "Don't touch him. He is hot." Tiny crackling noises came from his wooden joints.

Caris stopped short, and Harric ran up beside her. Indeed, waves of heat flowed from the tryst servant's clay body like a pot newly taken from the kiln.

"Mudruffle, can you hear me?" Caris said.

As if in reply, the wooden joints burst into flame.

A severed head delivers no messages.
—Shield motto of House Nors, East Isle

24

Loot & Loyalty

"Put it out!" Caris cried. With her hands, she scooped loam and soil from between roots and cast it on the flames, and Harric and Brolli joined her. The loam sizzled and popped like rice in a pan, but it snuffed the flames. Some of the sticks in the loam caught fire, but Caris kept shoveling. Her eyes had flown wide with panic.

Harric ran to Kogan, and when he returned with the half-full wineskin, Caris had stumbled away down the trail. Harric dribbled wine on the smoking soil and watched as she held her hands to her ears and blundered away, bowing rhythmically. Brolli stared after her, brow wrinkled. *At least Willard isn't here to scowl at her,* Harric thought. Brolli could be forgiven for being unfamiliar with her horse-touched episodes, but sometimes Harric wanted to shake the old knight.

Yet as he squirted wine at a flame that had popped up in the loam, he had to scold himself. *Maybe the problem is you, Harric. She's coping fine. She's probably gone off to collect the scattered horses, which she knows will help calm her.* She didn't need Harric's protection and could handle the old man in her own way. In fact, she was managing her status with her mentor a lot better than Harric was. Best worry about his own sorry standing.

Mud steamed and bubbled in Mudruffle's joints.

Brolli lifted his daylids and peered down at the half-buried tryst servant. "He took the fire with him."

Harric gave him a hard look and glanced after Caris to be sure she didn't hear. "You think he's dead?"

Brolli gave him a look of surprise. "I do not know. But he took the fire. To protect the old woman, I think. This is why your queen brings them here, yes?"

"Yes. I'd never seen it before, but they use the Bright Mother's power to prevent fire."

Brolli nodded. "At some cost, it seem."

Harric nodded. He wondered if Abellia had been there too, that her nexus would have made it easier on Mudruffle. Without it, he'd burst into flame, and used up his little constructed body. Harric peered under the brim of Mudruffle's tricorn hat. The button eyes shone dully in the gray morning light. Inert. Unmoving. Dead? Could a golem die?

A squeeze of loss and worry visited Harric's chest.

"I think if we are not fighting the fire," said Brolli, "it is harder for him to stop it. Maybe too much. Maybe then he is bursting like his staff."

Harric scooped more cooling soil on the golem. He dribbled the last drops of wine over him. He felt like a witch casting a spell to raise the dead. "He saddled Molly, too," he said, wondering at the little creature's resourcefulness. "He saved us."

Brolli climbed to his feet. "Come. We have done what we can. Gather the horses. Then we bring Mudruffle to Abellia. I will find Idgit in the meadow."

Brolli left, and when Harric stood, he found Caris approaching from the trees, leading two of the spooked horses. A set of reins in each hand, she stared forward, eyes distant, calm. He felt a wave of embarrassment for worrying about her: give her a horse and she'd handle anything.

"I set your sign for Gren in the track," Caris said.

"Moons, I'd forgotten all about it," Harric said. "Where'd you find it?"

Her gaze remained distant, attention inward, as she motioned vaguely down the path. She handed Harric the reins of a big black destrier with a look in its eyes so ugly he was certain that without her horse-touched influence, it would have tasted him already.

"Wait one moment," he said, declining the reins. "We should search these lordlings before we go. Don't get fussy about honor, now. This is fair loot."

"We don't *loot*, Harric." She practically snarled the words.

Harric had to suppress his immediate reply, which was *Oh, moons yes, we do!* Instead, he cursed himself for his thoughtless choice of words.

"This is the kind of thing I told you about," she said. "Dishonorable—"

"Spoils. I meant spoils. That's the proper term?"

Her eyes grew steely. "Leave them, Harric."

Harric held up his hands. "Okay, but you're making a mistake, Caris. Think about it. If we leave these men with their coin and resources, we leave those things for Bannus."

"That is fear talking, not honor."

The slow clop of Idgit's hooves came to them down the trail from the meadow, and Brolli emerged from the foliage, leading her. Judging by the cock of his head, he was listening intently to the argument.

"I think if Willard were here, he'd say that's *war* talking," said Harric. "This isn't some summer tournament. These lords wanted to kill us. They tried to. Should we leave their weapons and resources to strengthen their friends who follow? Plus, we have no idea what lies ahead for us. We may need coin to buy passage on a ship to get up through the Giant's Gap. We may need things to trade. And we certainly need information. Think of what we can learn from signet rings on these knights, or letters in their saddles. Names, families. Plans."

"Harric, stop it." Caris's voice shook. "If Willard saw this, he'd send you packing."

"What do you think Willard is doing right now, Caris? Do you think he's speaking honorably with those squires in the baggage train? He's slaughtering them. Is it a fair fight? Moons, no. But if he doesn't kill them, they'll inform others who'll try to kill us. And a minute ago, our mentor was ready to let the forest burn if it kept the Queen's quest safe. He'll be just as practical about this bronzed killer and his murderous mates."

Harric walked to the bronze knight and paused above the man's sprawled corpse. Kogan had positioned his dead hands in a lewd position. Brolli joined them and flipped up his daylids to watch. Judging them, Harric thought. Judging Arkendia. Harric felt an uncomfortable and unfamiliar anger toward the Kwendi.

"Willard's judgment isn't right today," said Caris. "The Blood has altered him. Before, he never would have brought us down here like this, without Molly and without me donning my armor. He never should have…" She stopped, hand to her mouth.

"Never should have taken the Blood in the first place," Harric said quietly. "Never should have broken his oath."

"That is my fault," said Brolli. "I pressed him." He frowned. "Perhaps I should not judge him, but I must agree with Caris. A Kwendi would bury them with gear."

"They're the ones who called Field Rules," Harric said, still directing his argument to Caris. "That's honorable combat language for anything goes, right? I promise you, Blood or no Blood, if we show up at the tower with nothing but our honor, Willard will burst a forehead vein."

Caris's jaw muscles pulsed. She looked away from the bronze knight and gave a stiff nod.

"I'll take that as permission." Harric stooped to the knight and, when no objection came from Caris, spared a glance at Brolli. The Kwendi flipped his daylids down in a vain attempt to conceal his disapproval, but Harric couldn't help but feel he'd tried and ruled against Arkendian war code and ethics.

This is to keep you alive, Ambassador Brolli. Trust us to know these enemies better than you.

Pushing the ambassador from his mind, Harric focused on the fallen knight before him. In truth, he could barely suppress his eagerness: what a dream it was for a gentleman jack to have at his disposal a half-dozen fallen lords with purses, jewels, secrets—even an unburned shirt and pants among their gear. But as he stripped the bronzed gauntlets and pulled at the lord's rings, the putty-like coolness of the dead hand sent a shiver of revulsion through his stomach.

This was not like robbing a sleeping drunk. It reminded him of the dead Iberg—Fink's former master—whose corpse had tumbled on top of him on the night he left Gallows Ferry with Willard.

He swallowed. *Just pretend they're sleeping, and make it quick. Think of the loot.*

Concentrating hard, he didn't notice Brolli leading Idgit past until the horse nearly stepped on him. As Harric removed the gorget from the bronze lord's neck, Brolli proceeded to Mudruffle and lifted the golem's rigid body to lay him behind the saddle.

Harric removed a signet ring and chain that hung around the knight's neck, along with a pouch full of golden queens. From the red knight, Harric took another purse, a silver brooch, and a paper the man had stuffed in a glove. It may have been nothing more than a handbill for a play in Kingsport, but they could take time to read it later. This bounty reminded him of a time when he and his mother drammed the whiskey of a camp full of squires and emptied their purses while they slept it off. They'd left stones in place of coins, and, come to think of it, he'd left one or two in lewd positions with each other, which must have led to consternation when they woke. These knights, however, wouldn't wake.

He pulled the boots off each and found a love letter in one, a pouch of rubies in another. Groping behind breastplates, he found more letters, and one with a seal he recognized as that of the Brotherhood of Krato. By the time he finished, his pockets bulged, and he'd even managed to swap out his ratty sword for a sleek but modest affair with brilliantly light balance. Best of all, he found a small stash of ragleaf, which meant there might be more on the baggage train. He'd have to remember to search it; if that didn't earn him points with Willard, nothing would.

Returning to Caris, he placed several letters gravely in her hand.

"Keep them," she said. "Let Willard reward you."

Harric stuffed the rest of the letters in his shirt. Score one for reason over honor.

"Let's move quickly," he said, as soon as he'd stowed everything. "We have no idea if there are more coming, or if they might slip past Willard, or how many."

Brolli had awakened the priest and coaxed him to his feet. When Kogan saw them readying the horses, he lumbered up the path to find Geraldine. Soon they were riding up the path to the meadow. The high cantle of the destrier's jousting saddle felt odd to Harric, but powerfully secure. Caris rode before him on a captured gelding, while Brolli affixed himself to Idgit's saddle.

In the meadow, Geraldine followed, bearing Kogan, who half sat, half slumped on her ample back.

As they climbed the gardens and switchbacks below the tower, Harric squinted into the morning sunlight, looking in vain for Willard on the ridge above. The first evidence of the knight's passage lay in Mudruffle's second garden terrace, where they came upon two sleek Iberg geldings munching happily on carrots. On the trail nearby lay one of their riders—an unarmored youth, leaking the last of his blood to the turnips. The other lay sprawled on the trail at the foot of the next switchback, apparently skewered through the back with a lance.

Caris collected the abandoned horses and rigged them in a train, her hands sure, eyes distant. They left the slain where they lay.

Pink water trickled down the irrigation pipe from the next terrace. The source of the coloration turned out to be a squire nearly cloven in two, lying in the cistern in a raft of floating guts.

"That's Will for ye." Kogan chuckled. "He don't leave it pretty."

By the time they reached the top of the ridge, Caris trailed five riding mounts of mixed breed, and a magnificent chestnut tournament charger. The trail had just crested beneath the fire-cone trees when Caris gave a cry and leapt from the saddle. After thrusting her horse's reins into Harric's hands, she bounded ahead to where Rag emerged from the trees, tossing her head and swishing her tail in greeting.

Harric glanced around for Snapper, guessing Mudruffle had released all their horses when he heard the horns, but saw no sign of the gelding. When Harric led the string of captured horses to her side, Caris was so deep in horse-touched communion with Rag that she appeared oblivious to the others. Tears streamed down her face as she pressed her cheek to Rag's. It seemed she was experiencing some kind of emotional release or relief after the battle and the killing, and Harric cringed to witness such an intimate and private moment. As the others drew up, she was murmuring words and sounds and moving her eyes and head as horses did.

Kogan craned to get a look, and his brow wrinkled like a discarded blanket.

When Caris finally stepped away from Rag, she dried her cheeks on the backs of her hands and took the string of horses from Harric like she'd known he'd been there all along.

"What the Black Moon was all that mumming and snugging?" Kogan said. "You married to that horse?"

Caris paused and gave him a flat gaze. "Tried. It's not allowed."

Kogan let out one of his big laughs.

"Rag is the closest thing I've got to family," she said, as she turned and led them through the fire-cones. "She understands me better than anyone."

Harric found Snapper grazing idly in the tower yard, and led him and Rag back into their stalls while they waited for Willard, and Caris tied the train of captured horses individually at the rail along the side of the stable. She waited until everyone dismounted before emerging from her horse-touched trance that kept the unfamiliar horses as docile and cooperative as if they'd known her all their lives. When her attention returned to the world of humans, they began to fidget and balk at her and at each other, but none of them panicked.

When Brolli arrived on Idgit, Harric held the pony's reins while Brolli dismounted and lifted Mudruffle's stiff figure from its basket.

"Where is Kogan?" Brolli asked.

"Waiting in the fire-cones on his musk-auroch. Wouldn't come near the tower."

Brolli nodded. After Harric put Idgit in the stable with Rag, Brolli carried Mudruffle up the tower steps, a deep frown stamped across his brow. Harric accompanied him, and Caris strode ahead to knock loudly on the tower door, but the door opened as Caris reached the top. The old woman emerged ghostlike from the dark doorway in her white robes and airy white hair. She must have seen them coming and descended the long stairs while their horses climbed the switchbacks.

"We're so sorry, mistress." Worry choked Caris's voice. "We couldn't help him."

Abellia nodded, smiling at Caris. "I know."

"You knew?"

Abellia nodded again, her eyes on her tryst servant's constructed body in Brolli's arms. She bent close, her frail hands emerging from her robes and traveling over his surface like shy white mice.

"He was saving us," Brolli said. "He was putting out the fire, but it was burning him. I think he is wishing to protect the fire-cones. To keep you safe."

Abellia nodded. Her eyes glinted like wet black pebbles. "I watched him. He was very brave." She motioned for Brolli to lay Mudruffle on the top stair, and took Caris's arm to descend a step below the rigid tryst servant. From there, she was able to bend over Mudruffle and examine the scorched wood of the creature's shoulders and hips. One frail hand dipped into her robes and returned with the white nexus. "Such fire is not happening near this," she said, raising her nexus. "If I am there, he is to be safe. But I was to be here." Her words seemed hard. Almost bitter. "Still, I help him."

Without any show of hiding her magic, she held the glowing nexus above Mudruffle's body, pausing it over the charred wooden joints.

Harric couldn't see exactly what it did, but he heard small snapping sounds. Had she repaired the joints? Was she trying to "wake" him?"

Mudruffle did not stir.

She stood. A faint smile curved her lips but did not reach her eyes. "You must to take him with you. He will return."

Caris's eyes widened as if she imagined a god possessing a scarecrow, and Abellia laid a calming hand on her arm. "He will wake," Abellia said. "He only sleeps."

Brolli picked up Mudruffle again and bowed to Abellia. "I will fasten him in his saddle."

"If you wouldn't mind," said Caris, "I would like Rag to carry him."

"Of course." Brolli bowed again.

Harric had been watching Abellia. On Brolli's announcement that they'd take Mudruffle with them, a shadow of worry seemed to lift from her, and as the Kwendi carried him down to Idgit, he got the distinct impression that she was relieved to get rid of her tryst servant. He couldn't guess why she would want that, but the intuition was clear, and it surprised him. He studied her, searching for a solid clue, but found nothing. *What's your game, old witch? Yesterday you were sad he was leaving.*

It almost seemed like what he saw behind those glittering eyes was an unpredictable and rebellious teen. He puffed a small laugh from his nostrils. He might not know what she was scheming, but she was up to something. That much he knew. She'd be a terrible poker player.

Caris helped Abellia back to the top stair.

"Turn," Abellia said to Harric. "What is this pant you wear?"

Harric laughed. He posed, modeling his one-bare-leg fashion.

Caris pressed her lips together tight but failed to hide her amusement.

As he faced away, modeling the rear view, a wave of heat swept through his shoulder wound, startling him. He craned his neck behind him, expecting to see his shirt on fire, but saw nothing. The old witch cocked her head, looking up at him with a mischievous spark in her eye.

She'd healed him. She'd even managed to divert Caris first by calling attention to Harric's leg.

The old woman was full of surprises.

He extended his leg before him in a courtly bow of one trickster to another, only to find, when done, that Caris continued to stare at his bare leg.

"Um, Caris?" Harric said. "Eyes up here?"

Caris smiled. Her nostrils flared as she looked up at him, and as her eyes met his, he felt his heart skip. This was the second time in less than a day that she'd leveled at him what he considered a powerfully sensuous look. Like the way she'd looked at him in the cellar the night before.

"Time I found some new pants," he said, stepping down the stairs.

"No hurry," she said, then blushed powerfully and scowled as if she would hit him if he commented.

He did not comment. With as much nonchalance as his training could muster, he fled.

Abellia wasn't the only one up to something; the ring was definitely getting worse. Glancing at the sun, high above, Harric guessed he had another ten hours before he could talk to Fink about it. Fink had to have an answer to this. If not, Caris was going to find him alone some time and give him that look, and he would have to think very quickly.

He crossed to the captured horses of the squires and started searching the saddlebags. In the first he hit the ragleaf bonanza. He probably could have found it by smell alone, for there were enough rolls in that pack to keep Willard in smoke for a month. Harric couldn't help but smile at the notion that the old knight might promote him from "jack fool and a sneak" to "insufferable knave." And if they were lucky, the herb's mellowing qualities might stave off the Blood rage.

In the second, he found a spare shirt and a pair of linen breeches he

could wear with a belt. Those he took into the stable to change. He'd
have to repair his own shirt as soon as possible, however, as it sported
several special pockets, including the one that held his lucky jack and
the one for his nexus. For now, he could hang the stone in a pouch
from his neck.

Harric had just emerged from the stable to scrub his shirt in the
trough when the sound of hoofbeats drummed through the fire-cones
on the north of the ridge. His heart jumped, and his gaze snapped to
Caris. Her head rose, alert and listening as her hand went to her sword.

"Is it Molly?" Harric whispered, as he hurried to belt on his sword.

Caris let out a long breath through her nose, listening. She
nodded. "We have to move the horses. Step away," she said, motioning
to Brolli. "They may not all be Phyros-trained."

Brolli joined Harric beside the barn's stone cistern, which functioned
as a general trough, as Molly erupted from the trees and into the yard
between the tower and stable. The Phyros held her enormous head
high and exultant. Dried streaks of blood from her eyes still fanned
across her face in a windblown mask.

In the next instant, two of the five captured horses screamed in
terror and pulled against their reins as if their bridles had turned to
snakes. Caris let them go, and they bolted. The remaining three horses
danced sideways and out of the Phyros's way, but did not try to flee.
Caris closed her eyes, reaching out to them, no doubt, for they quickly
settled into a calm little herd against the barn.

Before Molly had fully stopped, Willard dismounted and staggered
toward the cistern, eyes wild and face flushing violet. Gobs of Phyros
blood stained his chin and mustachio as if he'd been gorging on the stuff.

"Water," he gasped, stripping his gauntlets as if they were on fire.
"Out of my way."

Caris stepped back as Willard filled a bucket from the cistern and
raised it with both hands to gulp it in noisy swallows.

"Do we ride?" Brolli asked.

Willard's only answer was to snort between swallows.

Harric exchanged a glance with Caris; Brolli watched from behind
the mask of his daylids.

"Take it calm, old man," said Brolli.

Willard tossed the bucket aside. "There is no calm in a wildfire."

Dropping to his knees at the edge of the cistern, he plunged his head completely under the surface of the cool water.

"Don't question him till it passes," Harric said, as purple Phyros Blood spread like ink in the cistern. "The Blood mads him, just like in the ballads. And…it always passes in the ballads, right?"

Caris seemed to have grown a little pale as she witnessed the transformation in her mentor.

"Pretty, isn't it, ambassador?" said Harric.

Brolli did not smile. They all knew if any were to blame for Willard's relapse, it was he. "This is the word you call *sarcastic*, yes? I think it is not a merry thing."

Willard pulled his head from the water and let it drip into the cistern while his breaths continued to come with massive heaves of his shoulders. Gradually, his breathing steadied and his skin settled into a pale blue, only remaining purple in the cheeks. He stood, and when his violet gaze found them, much of its wildness had abated. "Mount up. I rode down the rest of their baggage, but there are others from that direction, and they aren't far behind. With luck, they'll be delayed while they make accommodations for their fallen, and rather than follow us, they may ride to the fort to open the pass for Bannus."

"The squires," said Brolli. "How many did you kill? We found five in the gardens."

Willard met the ambassador's gaze, unblinking. "None escaped. None will spy our leaving."

Harric watched Brolli from the side of his eye. And though he could not read the Kwendi's expression because of the dark daylids, it seemed to him that something was changing in the Brolli—or had changed already—since Willard started taking the Blood. He had a growing sense that Brolli now stood in judgment of the old knight and found him lacking.

"This has been a dangerous day," Brolli said, and the flat, measured tone of his voice strengthened Harric's suspicion. "I believe I learned much about Arkendian war."

Willard's teeth showed in a restrained snarl. "My war philosophy is mine, not Arkendia's. Do not mistake my ideas for those of the Queen, for they are often vastly different. All the more now the Blood is in me."

Brolli said nothing, but bowed deeply. Harric guessed the Kwendi had much to scribble in his ambassador journal. Things like "Field Rules" and "Slaughtering squires for safety." Would these be foreign concepts to the Kwendi? Though such things were commonplace in Arkendian ballads, Harric imagined other peoples might justly think them barbaric.

"A gift, sir." Harric held up the satchel of captured ragleaf.

Willard's eyes widened. "Gods leave you," he murmured, as he accepted the cache. He held it up to his nose to inhale deeply.

Harric bowed, and resisted saying, "This is the part where you forgive everything and make me an earl."

As Brolli explained their loss of Mudruffle at the fire, Willard lit a roll of ragleaf and squinted through the smoke to where Brolli had lashed the golem behind Caris's saddle.

"Wake up, will he?" Willard exhaled smoke into his mustachio. "Good. We need his knowledge of his map. In the meantime, Harric can read Iberg and will be our translator. Come! We must bid our hostess farewell. And now I see she has watched my rude entrance and I must blush with shame. Forgive me, good sister, I am now more myself."

Abellia had indeed watched the performance from the doorway. Her small dark eyes bent upon him now with concern. "You are touching the deep fires, Sir Willard." She shook her head, but said no more.

Willard crossed the yard and stopped at the foot of the stairs to perform a deep bow. "We owe you our lives, mistress. And I fear that in return for your hospitality, we brought harm to your servant and danger to your door."

"Mudruffle will return," she said. "And the Mad Moon has no power here."

Willard bowed again. "May we meet again."

Harric raised a hand in farewell as they rode from the yard, and her black eyes crinkled in a smile as she raised a pale hand in return. Again Harric sensed something behind the smile—relief, maybe—that made him feel she was impatient to be rid of them.

The Iberg word for a "yoab" translates to "land-whale," and though the great beasts are no longer found anywhere on the continent but in the northernmost forests, it is a fair comparison. Like whales…huge…tiny eyes in a mountain of barnacled flesh. The primary difference being that a whale has fins instead of legs, and swallows the sea instead of soil.

—From Marolo's Lexicon of Great Beasts

25

Yoab Run

Harric dismounted when they reached the place in the fire-cones where Geraldine lay chewing her cud, with Kogan passed out on her back.

"Wake him," said Willard. "And you might as well wash his face a bit while you're at it."

Harric handed Spook and his reins to Caris and took down his water skin from his saddle. The long-suffering musk-auroch watched through wooly bangs as he approached.

"This should be entertaining," said Brolli.

"If it works at all," said Harric. "He's pretty far gone." Standing outside the priest's considerable reach, he squirted his water skin into the priest's face, and jumped back.

"Time to wake, father!" Brolli crowed.

Kogan's eyes fluttered. His bleary gaze found the Kwendi on Idgit. "Lead on, fair damsel!"

Brolli looked to Harric. "What is this *damsel* word?"

"It means 'brave warrior,'" said Harric.

Brolli grinned. "I am the damsel."

"Har! Me too," said Kogan. "We're damsels together."

Caris gave Harric a look.

"No way I'm telling him," Harric whispered. "Too funny."

"Harric, you read Iberg," said Willard, "so I want you to keep the map." He drew Mudruffle's map from its oiled leather case and held it out for Harric. "Unroll it so we can see it together."

Harric hurried to Willard and accepted the map. It was a heavy, impressive document inked on calfskin and wound about a pair of staves as long as his arm. Harric imagined it would have been much too large for Mudruffle to pack around on his map-making expeditions, so the little golem must have used rough parchments for notes and drawings while out, and then transferred them to this "master map" when he returned.

As Harric unrolled it, Willard said, "Since we haven't looked at this map together since before the attack on the fort, I want you all to see it afresh. If we're separated, remember it, and you'll be oriented and know where to expect us."

Harric climbed onto a high knot of roots and held it up while they gathered close.

"We're here," Harric said, pointing out the tiny sketch of a silver tower in the center of the map. "To our west"—he pointed to a blue line running up and down the left edge of the map—"is the River Arkend and Gallows Ferry. The gray line running the river must be the Free Road to the northlands."

Willard nodded. "Our first objective is to get back to the river so we can get a ship to take us up through the Giant's Gap up into the northlands, but Bannus and his men cut off our routes west. Therefore, our only choice is to ride east into wilderness, and hook north to skirt our enemies and find another way to the river."

"It's a race," Brolli said.

"It is," said Willard. "Harric, point out Mudruffle's route through the wilderness."

Harric put his finger on the map. "Mudruffle's trail goes east down the far side of this ridge and into the next valley…" He drew his finger east and paused to read the golem's writing. He gave a grim smile. "He names that valley the *Yoab Maze,* and the trail north through it he named *Yoab Highway.* That sounds fun."

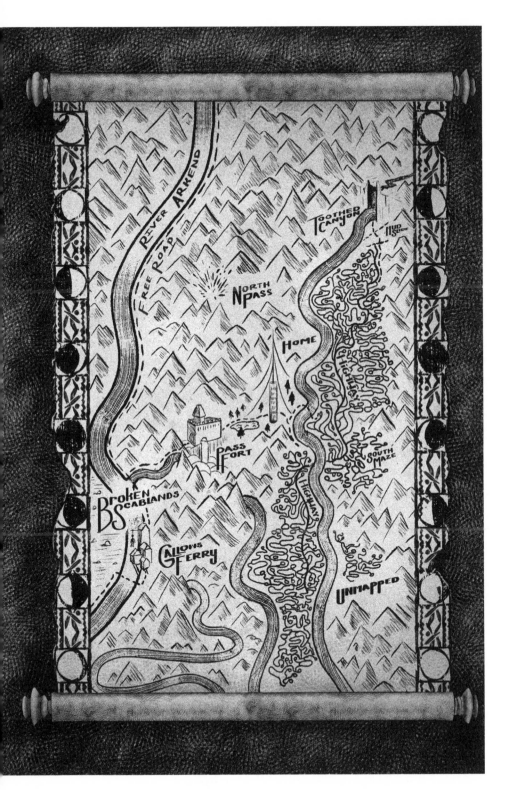

"He refers to the yoab runs that crisscross the old forests," said Willard. "The beasts use the same paths every year, and over generations they've established runs as clear as any highway. If it weren't for their plowing, the place would be impassable with fallen trees."

Brolli's eyebrows had risen from behind his daylids while they talked. "*Yoab?* This is the blind four-leg mountain that almost killed us when we woke it?"

Willard grunted in the affirmative.

"How is this a good trail?" said Brolli.

"A yoab is big and unpredictable, but it isn't sadistic, insane, cruel, or invincible, like Bannus. It's just hungry, preparing for hibernation, like bears."

Brolli shook his head. "I like this not."

"Nor do I," said Willard. "But it's what we've got. Our one advantage in this race is that while Bannus knows we must get back to the river, he does not know we intend to go *north* to get to it. He'll expect us to head *south* toward civilization and the Queen, not north into the teeth of an unmapped wilderness."

"I see," Brolli said. "Unmapped for him, not for us."

"And if we can leave him a false trail heading south," said Willard, "all the better. We head north while he goes south, and if luck is with us, we'll find one of the Queen's ships anchored below the Giant's Gap, and our troubles will be over. If not, we'll book passage on the next waterwheel up the Gap."

Kogan poked the top of the map with a finger like a dirty potato. "*That's* your goal? A blank spot on the map?" He'd poked the space beyond the Godswall, which remained conspicuously free of all but a few words in Iberg that Harric understood as *lost magic*, maybe, or *stolen magic*. "Reckon that's the Free Lands, but your map don't show where to go."

"Those are the *Kwendi* lands," said Brolli. "And there, *I* shall be the map."

The priest did not seem to notice, but to Harric, the ambassador's tone was one of careful correction, as if to remind all present that the lands beyond the Godswall were not "Free Lands" open for Arkendian settlement, but part of the Kwendi lands, and that until a treaty was reached, Arkendian presence there was contested.

"No Chimpey lands for me," Kogan said. "Once we strike the road, I'll ask after my flock and Widda Larkin and rejoin them as soon as I can. I worry about the families we brought north. And Widda Larkin never wanted the burden of leading them."

"That's all one," said Willard. "Our trails are one until then."

"We will help you find your flock again if we can," said Brolli. "You have sacrificed much to help me this far."

"Saddle up," Willard said to Harric. "Every moment here is a moment gained by our enemies."

Harric mounted and then partly unrolled the map. It seemed to him that it wasn't just the space above the Godswall that lacked notation, but much of the space below, as well, and that bothered him.

As he fell in line behind Willard, he kept the map open before him, and gave Snapper his reins to follow Molly, while he examined it. A quick look confirmed that his initial impression was right; though Mudruffle had crammed most of the space below the Godswall with carefully written details of landmarks and geographic features, the notes dwindled the closer they got to the lower edge of the Godswall. He guessed that the terrain grew more and more difficult the farther north one went, and that for such an ungainly hiker as Mudruffle, a journey all the way to the Godswall would be nigh impossible. It seemed unlikely, therefore, that he'd ever actually been to the head of the valley, and that more likely any notes there were based on what he had guessed from some viewpoints farther south.

After rolling the map carefully on it staves, Harric slipped it back in its case. As he stowed it on his pack and took up the reins again, he pondered the implications. If he was right, it meant that they might fight their way through wilds to the Godswall, only to find the way west to the river impassable. And if Bannus or his allies were hot on their trail, they'd be trapped against the mountains.

He let out a worried sigh. No point in telling Willard. Like the knight had said, they had no other options. For now, they'd have trust in luck and hope Mudruffle woke before they made any crucial blunders.

Spook mewed in his basket as they left the ridge, so Harric slipped his hand under the lid and rubbed behind the little cat's ears to comfort him. He also kept the lid on tight until they'd ridden beyond the cat's familiar hunting grounds; if the little furball shot out after a squirrel, there would be no halting to recapture him, but once they were in less familiar territory, where he never ranged far afield, he could be trusted to stay near.

As they descended the switchbacks into the valley, Harric caught magnificent views of the ancient forest of the Yoab Maze below, and in spite of everything—Willard's hurried pace, the yoabs before them, Sir Bannus behind—Harric felt his spirit opening. For the first time since they'd arrived at the tower, they were on a new trail, headed in a new direction, descending into the unexplored east.

The trail down from the ridge proved easy to find and only slightly overgrown. Harric guessed it had originally been cleared as a fire-escape road by the toolers who constructed the thunder spire, and though the toolers had never returned to it, he spied evidence of Mudruffle's lonely maintenance in the form of more recently pruned branches and saplings.

That road ended abruptly, however, and dwindled to something more like a game trail. Harric kept the map handy after that, and it proved useful, for the way was often obscure, but Mudruffle had annotated this portion of the map with an almost absurd amount of detail. Notes like *Burned Trunk* or *Tumble of Red Rock* were abundant. Farther north up the *Yoab Highway* was a feature in red ink that he'd named *Toothed Canyon*, with no other explanation.

When Harric shared it with Brolli, the Kwendi said, "That sounds pleasant," and yawned hugely, displaying his thick canines.

"You ought to sleep," said Harric. "It's way past your sleep time. Spook's already snoozing."

Brolli shook his head. "I must see this trail myself."

When the path finally deposited them in the green valley, far below Abellia's ridge, scores of grasshoppers erupted from the trail, wings snapping angrily. Willard called a halt when he'd led them from the shaded forest into sunlit meadows of wildflowers and summer grass beside the roaring river. Mudruffle had named the water the river the Deeprush, which was appropriate, for it was twice as wide as Harric could throw a stone, and looked deeper than a tall man in its most muscular rapids.

Harric brought Snapper to the edge of a glassy pool in an offshoot of the main river, and let out the reins so the gelding could drink. An otter cut a shining V across the surface of the pool, its black head watching them before ducking under. On the far bank of the river, a half-dozen red elk raised their heads from grazing, blazing in the sun. A blackbird trilled in reeds, and something in Harric's spirit, long cramped and starved of natural peace, grew light and drank it in.

Molly lunged toward the elk, shattering the mirror of the pool before Willard could rein her back. The elk sprang away and vanished into the brush, and the Phyros snarled in frustration.

Harric tried to focus on the scents of watercress and carrot weed, but Molly's ozone stink stopped the air in his throat.

"Way to feel the moment, Molly," said Harric when he'd regained his breath.

"She's hungry," Willard said. "Needs to feed on something more than the blood mash from the fort. Especially when I'm bleeding her. Would've given her one of Abellia's goats, but I didn't think the old gal would like that."

"These noble elk will do?" Brolli flashed his canines. "It would please me to hunt for her in the night. And it would please me to eat roast meat."

Willard frowned. "No roasting for us, ambassador—not until we're out of yoab country. But I'd welcome a fresh kill for Molly. Mudruffle's marks cross this river here, yes?"

Harric nodded. He pointed upstream to a reed-rimmed bend in the river, where the floor of the valley appeared wider and the river shallower. "The map says we can ford it around that bend."

"Good. Lead the horses in where you will leave no tracks. Somewhere rocky, not sandy. And when you leave the water on the other side, be sure to find a place where tracks will be difficult to see. Once you find the Yoab Highway, follow it north and camp on high ground before dusk. I'll catch you up before you get to the canyon."

"You aren't coming?" said Harric.

Willard shook his head. "The fire in the meadow this morning probably signaled Bannus to move through the pass. That puts him no more than a day behind us—"

"You don't think to *meet* him, do ye?" Kogan said. The priest's head, which had been resting on his chest in apparent slumber, rose with a jerk. Red-shot eyes squinted at Willard from a tangle of braids. "You ain't ready, Will. Not yet."

Willard whirled in his saddle. "Shut your idiot mouth!" His fury exploded with such ferocity that Harric nearly dropped the map and Brolli jumped. The knight's face flushed purple and his fists trembled on Molly's reins as if barely able to withhold the signal to attack. Molly waited, spring-tight, eyes on Kogan.

Kogan shut his idiot mouth. He very slowly raised his hands in placation.

"Willard and I will run the extra horses south," Caris said, so softly that Harric almost missed it. Her gaze appeared distant, as if half in the horse world and half in the human, but her eyes rested on Willard, whose shoulders rose and fell in shuddering breaths. "We'll head south down this side of the river," she said, her voice still low and calm, "and hopefully Bannus will see our tracks and follow them. Once we get the captured horses moving southward on their own, we'll let them go and break off to cross the river and double back. With luck, Bannus will waste days on the false trail."

As she spoke, she kept her eyes on Willard, as if gauging his reaction. Gradually, the flush of purple retreated from his skin, his eyes regained focus, and his breathing normalized. When she finished her description of their plan, he'd calmed enough to give a curt nod and a hoarse "As she says."

Kogan lowered his hands, and Brolli exhaled slowly. Harric guessed the ambassador's eyes were as big as goose eggs behind his daylids. When Kogan seemed about to speak, Harric shook his head behind Willard and drew his hand emphatically across his throat.

Kogan's eyes flicked to him, and to Harric's relief, he clamped his mouth shut again.

"If I say I do not like this plan to split up," said Brolli, voice low but clear, "will you become monster and kill me?"

Willard flushed again, and his jaw muscles pulsed. "Just stick to the map," he said, voice hoarse. "If you get lost, stop and wait." He turned Molly about, ending the conversation. While Molly's bulk shielded the view of the others, Willard tossed a pouch to Harric, who, surprised, barely reacted in time to catch it. Hefting it in his hand, Harric knew instantly it was not coin. More like strips of dried bark, or herbs.

"If you need it, eat it," said the knight, just loud enough for Harric to hear.

Harric palmed the pouch as Willard and Molly turned south along the riverbank, Molly's huge hooves thumping the shallow soil.

Kogan let out a noisy sigh and rubbed a hand over his face.

As Caris gathered the leads of the captured horses, Harric said, "We should call you the Willard whisperer."

Her eyes distant—her mind obviously in the world of horses again—she managed a faint, embarrassed smile.

"Good luck," Harric said. He couldn't help a little worry leaking into his tone. And if it wasn't a trick of her horse-touched trance, he thought he saw worry in her eyes as well.

She cast him a cryptic glance as she mounted, then rode after her mentor.

Each moon has its servants,
Both celestial and mortal.
Celestial servants walk the earth as guides
To the mortal —
As tutors and conduits to their moon —
That the mortal may accomplish on earth
The eternal purpose of the moon.
Without their mortal counterpart
The celestial must remain on their moon,
And without their celestial guide
The mortal is powerless.

— Saying of unknown origin, common in the Iberg Compact

26

The Price Of Immortality

Abellia sat in her window with the view of the west valley.
The tower was still and quiet without the busy sounds of Mudruffle's industrious hands mending, cooking, and cleaning. The larder was fully stocked with jarred pears and lentil soups, and the pantry was full of milled flour and spices, but there was little use in it. He'd been gone a day, but she hadn't eaten since he left. Now, on the second morning of his absence, she finally heated a pot of broth he'd left on the hearth for her first day alone, and drank it as she stared out the window.

Below, the morning sun angled through the tops of the fire-cones and dappled the far end of the little valley where Caris had pastured her horses and the old knight had trained her in arms.

An ache of regret touched Abellia's heart.

Watching Caris had reminded her of what it meant to desire something so much that she would sacrifice all for it. What it meant to seek a dream in spite of censure and opposition — to lose family, friends, status, everything for the dream. She too had followed a dream in her youth, giving up everything to take her vows to the Bright Mother.

But her dream had betrayed her. It had used and forgotten her. She closed her eyes against the memory of the Light Bringer in the tower — its cutting, unseeing eyes; her own invisibility before eternity — and suppressed a moan that threatened to push past her lips.

Trembling hands lifted the broth to her lips, and she sipped it, heart thumping in a ribcage that felt to her as frail as last year's reeds.

All will be restored, she reminded herself. *Soon. Drink your broth, old husk. You must be well and strong to make this journey.*

Her eyes fell on the nexus where it lay on the table beside her, bright as a promise. Mudruffle's nexus. How fortunate it was for her that he had been unable to take it with him — that he'd spent himself in suppressing the fire and was unconscious when they left and took him with them. Surely he would have insisted he take it; no magus of her advanced age had ever been allowed to keep a nexus, unwatched. And yet she could not be sure he would have done so. Mudruffle had expressed concern about her safety in his absence should the murderous knights return and surround her tower; perhaps he would have left her the ancient stone to protect herself until he returned. She liked to think so. And it would have been a reasonable gesture, given her lifelong loyalties.

But he would have been wrong.

She blushed at her own audacity. Yet it was better he leave her this way, for he did not have to take the stone, and she did not have to lie to him.

She would wait another hour before she acted.

Her luggage was prepared, and the bathing trough filled to precision with cool milk Mudruffle had stored in the larder. The harness that would steady her nose and mouth above the surface of the milk was in place. The butter she would slick against her skin was warm and ready in bowls.

She drained the last of the broth, though her belly was full to the point of discomfort, and tottered over to the trough to review her calculations. In the surface of the milk she saw her shrunken and dry reflection peering back at her, and a thrill of anticipation filled her. When she was done, she'd see a young woman in the reflection.

She made a sound like a crow, scolding herself for her vanity, but let her robe fall to the floor around her feet. It was time. She had to act right away, for she had no idea when Mudruffle would return to himself—today, tomorrow, the next day—and when he woke, he might return to claim the stone from her. And if he did, she must be long gone. She would go to the river, and there she would disappear in the Arkendian countryside where her order dare not seek her. Mudruffle would never find her, and she'd live out an ordinary life—perhaps even seek out Caris, or Harric.

Her stomach pulsed with guilt and anxiety, but she repressed her anger. It was *she* who had been betrayed. It was *she* whose life had been stolen and returned when it was used up and crumbling.

Sounds of horses and men startled her from her thoughts. The morning sunlight gilded the west wall of the tower, streaming in through the eastern window. The birds were active in the understory and around the tower's crown, but it was still twilight beneath the trees. She stooped and pulled up her robe, then walked back to the main room and peered out the western window into the yard below.

She saw knights with lances. Men-at-arms with spitfires. Someone banged on the tower door.

"There!" someone cried, pointing to her window. Abellia raised a frail hand in greeting.

A knight larger than any she had ever seen entered her field of view on a charger that drove the other horses away like a dog among chickens. He was impossibly broad, thick-limbed, over-muscled, and plated with armor like a tortoise. Sir Bannus, the Phyros-rider Sir Willard had warned her about. It had to be. More monster than man, and his horse as scarred and strange as Willard's, but a stallion. The eyes were darker purple, and the scars—if possible—more numerous and random, barbaric.

Anger rose in her frail body. She would not allow this monster to interrupt her plans. She would send him off after Willard in the wrong direction.

A voice like gravel in a bass drum boomed from Sir Bannus.

"We seek the criminal Willard. We know he was here."

"This man is no longer being here," she chirped.

"*No longer being here.*" He laughed. "An Iberg. We'll have some fun after all. Open your doors, witch. I wish to be certain the man we hunt isn't cowering in your cellar."

"The man you hunting would not cower anywhere. And see! I am counting here only six men. He is already kill your army. He is not being afraid."

Bannus grinned, broken teeth in a nest of scars. To his companions, he said, "Break the door in."

Abellia cradled the egg-like nexus in her hands, and fortified the doors with the protective energies of her moon. The nexus glowed softly, illuminating her face and snow-white hair as two men-at-arms approached the door with axes and laid into it. Their axes spun from the iron as if it were made of slippery stone. After a half-dozen futile swings, they turned to Bannus, shaking their heads.

Bannus said, "A neat trick, witch. Burn the outbuildings."

"This is royal fire-cone stand," said Abellia. "If you making fire, you are dying too, yes?"

"Burn the buildings!"

Men-at-arms with spitfires used glowing punks to light tinder. Abellia sent a wave of creative energies to banish the flames. The men-at-arms cursed, claiming their punks had gone out. When they fetched their spitfires to blast resin against the stable, they found the coals in their fire cups cold. Flint hammers failed to spark.

Bannus laughed. "This is a white witch. Peace magic. I've seen it before. Let's see how it fares against steel." The immortal turned his massive charger and shouted to the rear of the company, "Titus! Bring them!"

In the growing twilight, Abellia watched a hooded rider walk his horse up the path from the gardens. He led a horse with two passengers: a young man, gagged, his hands bound behind him. He wore what looked like a filthy woman's nightdress. Dried blood decorated the front like a bib. One of the lad's eyes had swelled shut. His nose appeared to be broken. His lip was a fat red tuber. Oddly, a belt bound the dress to his waist, but then she recognized it as a bastard belt like Harric wore. An Arkendian invention born of their obsession with blood rank.

This boy's colors were red and black, which was a low color, if she remembered correctly. Harric's had been green and black.

A shiver of dread rolled up her spine.

Behind the boy rode a crone, a grandmother nearly as old as Abellia herself. She'd been bound about the waist to the young bastard, and she slumped to one side, white hair hanging lank over her face. As they neared, she saw both had been weeping, for there were streaks of clean skin beneath their eyes, where tears had run.

The young bastard's eyes found Abellia, pleading. A dart of grief and pity split her heart.

The man Bannus had called Titus halted the horse beneath the window and looked up. His face was concealed by a crimson mask of polished stone. The visage carved upon it was handsome, calm, and peaceful.

"Shall we skin them for you, witch?" said Bannus. "Shall we peel them slowly, let them beg for us?" The masked one turned toward the bastard, and he recoiled from his gaze, letting out a single, body-racking sob. "Show her what we mean, Titus."

"No," Abellia said, raising her hand. "I come down. But you must be swearing by your bond-mount—Gygon, as he named, yes?—to release these ones, and never harm them again, nor your companions to harm them."

Bannus sneered. He swept one mighty arm in an arc encompassing all his companions. "Hear all! I swear by Gygon, my life, my soul, my bond mate, to release these two wretches, and let them go unharmed by us."

Abellia nodded. "You release them now, yes? If I not come down, you can easy catch them."

The masked one hauled the captives from the horse and cut the bond about their waists. The bastard bolted and ran wildly down the path, tearing at the gag still binding his mouth. Bannus laughed harshly as the grandmother crumpled like a tiny tent without poles. She made no attempt to rise.

A stab of fear pierced Abellia's veil of calm as she realized the old woman could not, or would not, flee. She willed a Corporal Channel into the old woman, and when it reached her, a searing fire erupted in Abellia's hip sockets and backbone, and in fiery streaks along the skin of her entire body. She nearly crumpled as the crone had done, but willed herself erect in the discipline of her training. There was no time for weakness. She let the warm power of her nexus follow the channel into the woman's time-ruined body, and felt the pain lessen as tissue healed and bone mended.

The nexus grew hot in her hand from the major channeling. The crone's flesh also grew warm. Abellia eased back the amount of power she channeled from the Bright Mother; too much could burn and exhaust the tissues. It was a holy paradox: that the power of Life might conjure the shadow of Entropy in the body and in the heat of its own nexus—the very essence of the Mad Moon's opposite power.

Steadily, the gravel in the old mother's hips turned to granules, and then to jelly, and then to healthy sinew and bone. The empathic pain in Abellia's hips receded, and disappeared, and the ill-twisted wires of fire in her backbone unwound, the barbs dulling then disappearing. She kept the channel open, allowing a general wash of mending to knit adjacent tissues, so the new healing would not put undue strain upon them. If she kept the channel open indefinitely, time itself would be turned back in the ancient flesh, and it would remember its youth, but the wholesale dispensing of youth was forbidden, and even now her nexus was almost too hot to hold.

She closed the channel and peered into the yard below. The old woman remained curled in the dust, unmoving.

"No part of our bargain requires the old sack to choose freedom," said Bannus. "You see she's become fond of our company."

"She enjoys my attentions," said the masked one.

The other knights shifted nervously in their saddles, but Bannus bellowed laughter that rang in the stillness between the buildings. What horror had they promulgated upon her? Abellia opened the channel again and quested over the old woman. What she found beneath the sack dress was bewildering and horrifying, and made her step back from the window as if slapped.

Long, fresh, curving incisions had been made in the papery skin along the warp of bone and limb, and then somehow closed and healed with gratuitous scars. These were the fiery streaks she had sensed before in the skin. How were these cuts possible? The loss of blood alone from such wounds was more than any mortal could endure. And how they *burned!* Each scar blazed with the pain of a fresh whiplash. Abellia gasped in rising indignation. This was not healing! This was a horror of flesh and Entropy totally alien to her, and not the infamous Arkendian hokum healing either, for it was too complete—the wounds were new, yet fully closed, a feat far beyond the powers of herbs or plasters.

If only she could see the scars, she could better understand them, and better mend them, but in this case she had few options, so she opened the floodgates of the channel and let her moon's power wash across the brutalized tissue like a tide of dispelling grace. Let the scars melt away! Let the horror be forgotten like last year's winter! Let the old woman rise without pain! Abellia felt the skin around the scars tighten, thicken, freshen, rejuvenate. But the lattice of newly healed wounds remained etched in the skin, unwavering, as if carved by the hand of a god whose will superseded even the Bright Mother's authority to heal.

Dumbfounded, Abellia released the channel. She'd never met a power that could resist the healing might of the Bright Mother. As if in sympathetic frustration, her nexus burned hot in her hand.

Below her, Sir Bannus stripped his helmet from his head and snarled in impatience. "Open your door or the bargain is done! We'll bring back the bastard, and this time, we will not stay our hands! You will lie awake this night to the sound of his cries!"

The sight of the immortal's uncovered flesh struck the wind from her like a blow to the gut. His head seemed nothing more than a mangled mass of scars like purple serpents. Indeed, the knight's flesh bore the selfsame scars as those on his mount and those of the crone. The revelation stunned her, but the conclusion was inescapable: the scars on the crone were indeed from a god, and therefore could not be reversed by the lesser powers of the moons. And the Arkendian's preposterous claim of Krato's Blood in the Phyros was true.

"Find the bastard!" Bannus said. "Bring him back! The witch betrays her bond!"

Abellia raised the glowing nexus high and brought it down in a brilliant flash of light. The stone hissed sharply, searing her palm with sudden heat, and she stifled a cry, jiggling it from one hand to the other until she could let it down into the water pitcher, where it hissed and sank to the bottom, inert. There was a red burn on her right palm that would blister badly. She paid it no further heed, but peered briefly from the window to confirm the nexus had done its work.

The yard below remained still. Knights who'd lined up beside the door to take her as she emerged had slumped to the ground. Sleeping. Silent. The horses dozed. The masked one curled in the dust, breathing lightly. A fat knight fell like a boulder from his saddle, but did not wake. Even the gigantic immortal sat motionless on his sleeping Phyros.

Abellia smiled. The bastard would have time to run before the men woke, and they did not have dogs with them. That was good. But her gaze snagged on the crone.

Frowning, she retrieved the nexus from the pitcher and sent a Waking to the crone.

Nothing. No response. It was as she had feared; the old woman's mind and body were so brutalized that she'd gone catatonic. And there was no healing of the psyche through the Bright Mother; only the Unseen could heal such wounds, if it ever chose to heal anything.

Abellia shuttered the windows and tottered to the edge of the milk trough, where she sat and considered her options. There were really only two courses of action available: one, she could leave the poor, abused grandmother to die in the hands of those monsters. If she did that, she could use her nexus to mask the woman's pain until she passed away. Then she could wait until the knights left, at which point she could continue with her own plans. Alternatively, she could save the woman by dragging her into the tower while the knights still slept. However, in Abellia's present weak and aged state, she would not be capable of moving or carrying the old woman; that would require a strong, young Abellia.

Tears swam in her eyes. Damn them for coming today! Had they come tomorrow, she would have been gone and free! But then another voice inside her answered that if she had not been there when the men arrived, the crone and bastard would have died horribly. The injustice of it pained her, but there was really only one choice for her. In the end, she was a healer, and healers did not abandon others when it better suited their own needs; healing others *was* their need.

And she could do both—she could heal herself and save the grandmother—only she must hurry.

With a tiny noise somewhere between a growl and a cry, she let the robe fall again and laid herself gingerly in the trough of cool milk.

Settling her head into the harness, she adjusted her position until the milk covered all but her face. Her tiny body trembled already with the cold—so much that she feared she might lose feeling in her hands and drop the nexus she clutched against her skinny belly. Without further hesitation, she opened the only channel forbidden a white magus: a channel directly from the nexus to her own withered flesh.

The power flooded her tissues indiscriminately, and she caught her breath at the force of it, as many of her patients had before. No Bright Mother magus knew the sensation, though all had been tempted to know it. Had there been any who never fantasized of such treachery in moments of weakness? Could Mudruffle have truly seen in her something that would make her any different?

She clasped the stone in withered claws, eyes wet with tears as the power flooded her flesh. Her limbs and skin and joints warmed, then cooked with growing fever. Systems rebuilt, tissue grew and strengthened, heart pounded and lungs panted. How it burned in her bones! How the nexus scorched like an ember in her hands! The milk seemed suddenly warm and no good in cooling. Panting like a dog, she squirmed in discomfort. Her head ached. Her brain seemed to cook like an egg in its shell, and her mind spun free in wild and blurry hallucinations.

She saw Mudruffle standing above her, sticklike arms waving frantically. He burst into flames, and then the Light Bringer rose in his place. The creature hadn't deigned to see her before, but now its eyes cut through her, damning like a flash of lightning. Then it too was gone, and there was only pain and fire in her limbs, and she feared she'd done something wrong, or triggered some kind of trap or punishment for any who dared use this channel. But she could no longer feel her hands for the pain, could no longer work her fingers to release the nexus. Hammers of heat beat in her skull. Her body jerked. Her blood seemed a-boil and heart near bursting.

Vomit and excrement exploded from her, hot and putrid. She choked and sobbed, delirious, until her mind failed, and all was blackness.

A maid who tells no lies will never marry.

—Arkendian folk saying

27

Blood & Consequence

As Willard and Caris disappeared in the willows along the bank, Harric opened the pouch and found strips of dried jerky meat inside. No…these were scabs, he realized, as he pulled one out. Blue scabs. His eyes widened. *Phyros plasters.* Willard had harvested the strips of dried blood of Molly's war mask and given them to Harric. His mouth fell open. Ballads sung of Phyros plasters and their powers were legendary: if you pushed them into a wound, the wound healed; if you ate one, your wounds scarcely affected you, and your limbs and heart filled with strength and courage. Harric snorted. More like violence and rage, he guessed. Nevertheless, it was a valuable gift. Plus, it was the only magic Willard approved of. And he'd given it to Harric.

I'll be damned.

But what did it say about the danger Willard thought they were in?

Brolli was writing in his journal again, his mouth pressed in a grim, tight line. A glance at Kogan revealed even the priest still sullen from Willard's display.

Harric let out a long breath. "Not what you expected of the Blood, eh, ambassador?"

Brolli did not look up from his work. His Kwendi writing tool scratched across the surface of the paper, leaving a trail of jagged marks that made up the Kwendi alphabet. Somehow today's words looked sharper, cut deeper than others Harric had seen.

"I think it might be fair to say that he tried to warn you, ambassador."
Harric smiled. "You asked for this. Begged for this. He didn't want to take
the Blood."

Brolli flipped the daylids onto his forehead. Golden eyes blazed at
Harric, pupils black and huge—too big for daylight—but the Kwendi
left the lids up.

"I must know how this Blood works." Brolli's voice was tight and
hard, his accent more pronounced. "This rage is the thing I must see.
This is what rules your people—this fire, this...tyrant Blood is what
rules this land."

Was the ambassador saying he egged Willard into taking the Blood
so he could see what it did to him—to see if it made him like Bannus?

A coal of anger burned under Harric's breastbone. Instead of raising
the point, he chose a more diplomatic approach. "The Blood does not
rule Arkendia anymore. The *Queen* rules—"

Brolli swiped his hand through the air as if batting the notion away.
"Your queen has no power. Bannus cares not a fig for your queen. He
rides to the north and makes war. He rides across the north and makes
terror. She cannot stop him. This"—he pointed after Willard—"this is
the true power in Arkendia. This is the ally or enemy my people must
decide for." He gazed after Willard, nose wrinkling as if he wished to
spit a bad taste from his mouth. "And it makes the unpredictable ally,
and the very bad enemy."

Harric felt something tighten in his chest. Lack of sleep seemed
to unmask the ambassador. This was no longer the wry, practical trail
companion and co-adventurer Harric thought he'd come to know over
the past month; this was the treaty ambassador of the Kwendi, a man
assembling important concepts of Arkendia and its queen to take back
to the Kwendi people—a man whose information and decisions would
determine the future of two peoples. And suddenly that treaty seemed
by no means certain—in that moment, Harric could see Brolli advising
his people either way.

Harric swallowed. "I don't disagree with your assessment. An
unpredictable ally indeed. But a strong one, and a much worse enemy.
Worse yet is Bannus and the Old Ones. You think Willard's barely
controlled rage is a hazard? If Bannus had been here just now instead
of Willard, do you think he'd restrain his anger at an irritating priest?"

"You'd be covered in my blood," said Kogan. "Bannus don't know how to control the rage. Willard studied with the Blue Order to learn how."

Brolli stared at them, eyes tired and searching. "Bad, worse, and worst. These are the choices? There are those among my people who wish to push your settlers from the north. Push them back down the Giant's Gap and seal the Gap so we may live in peace again."

Kogan looked as if he would challenge this notion, but Harric caught his attention and gave a warning shake of his head, and to Harric's relief, the giant looked away and said nothing. Harric did not want Kogan to give Brolli any more reason to criticize Arkendia. Better to let such things lie. But Brolli caught the glowering look on Kogan's face and grimaced as if suddenly hearing how rude he had been.

"Forgive me." Brolli sighed. "Forget this. Please. It is the words of a very tired Kwendi."

"Already forgotten," Harric said.

Spook went rigid in Harric's arms, and Harric instinctively pinned him in his basket before he could escape. The moon cat mewed in annoyance, big eyes fixed on Snapper's head. A leaf or something had flown into the horse's mane; Harric had seen it from the corner of his eye as he talked with Brolli. Now Snapper shook his head, rattling his bridle, and whatever had landed on him flew to Harric's forearm and clung there with cool, soft fingers.

Harric laughed and lifted the arm away from Spook, whose attention remained riveted to the plum-sized green frog on Harric's arm.

"A glider!" Harric said, holding his arm out so Brolli and Kogan could see. He was glad for an excuse to change subjects and lighten the mood. "We used to have these in Gallows Ferry."

The frog crawled up his arm toward his elbow, seeking higher ground from which to launch toward a tree. Harric watched as it climbed to his shoulder, inches from his eyes, and laughed as its cold little fingers stuck to his neck.

"Why *used* to have?" Brolli did not look up from his writing.

"Emigrants ate them all. Or let their bored kids take them to play with on the road."

Brolli looked up. "They are not even a mouthful. Yet you people eat them till they're gone?"

Harric felt his hackles rise at this latest criticism of Arkendia. "I don't. Nor do my people, normally, but the emigrants on the road are in a tough situation. They're hungry. Some are starving. And hundreds come through each day."

Kogan grunted. "Gotta feed my flock. We planned good. Plenty of food. But some flocks don't have luck. Brother Mahz barely got on the road at all. Expect them to starve to save a damn frog? If a frog feeds a child, it ain't a question."

Brolli looked at the priest. He said nothing.

Harric ground his teeth, but he couldn't fault Brolli. The ambassador was right to ask. And he was right to worry. The droves of emigrants invading his people's land in the north were like locusts. They needed food and they needed shelter, and they'd take both from the land.

Harric captured the frog as it climbed toward his ear. He held it at arm's length from Spook, but had to release the cat in order to take up the reins long enough to walk Snapper to a tuft of nearby willows. Spook climbed from the basket onto Harric's lap, big eyes riveted to the hand with the frog. "Easy, Spook." As soon as they stopped at the willows, Harric again pinned Spook in his lap, provoking a frustrated growl.

Raising the frog beside the tangle of willow branches, he uncurled his fingers so the frog could stand in his flattened palm. Without hesitation, the frog oriented to the nearest branches and leapt. It couldn't close the full distance to the branches. Harric had made sure of that. But at the apex of its leap—still a foot short of its target—the magnificent yellow tongue flashed across the gap. Quick as it appeared, the tongue retracted and drew the little creature into the foliage. The tongue flashed again and drew the tiny yellow body even higher.

He smiled. "I've seen one climb to the top of a willow that way, then leap and glide after bait-moths. You see, Brolli? I'm no frog killer."

"Your people never starve?" Kogan's tone bordered on accusation. "Never had a long peace and too many people for your land?"

Brolli turned to Kogan. He flipped his daylids down, so his expression was even more opaque. "These are not problems for my people. Perhaps when you are there you will see."

Harric shifted in his saddle. Kogan had come a long way since his first encounter with Brolli. He wasn't throwing an anti-magic tantrum. But he was definitely operating outside his bounds again, and, judging by his tone, was not headed for making nice with the ambassador. "Yes, the Queen's family has brought us a long peace," Harric said, trying to bring the focus back to the positive. "Before her family came to the throne, the islands warred almost constantly. Since her grandfather pacified the West Isle, her wise rule extended the peace and our population has naturally grown."

"You Kwendi make war?" Kogan said. "That how come your population don't overflow? How many Kwendi kingdoms are there?"

Harric noticed the ambassador grew very still as the priest talked, as if Kogan had hit close to something Brolli didn't wish to reveal. "My people have no kings." Brolli reached under his daylids to rub his eyes. "I must sleep. My brain makes the unclear thoughts." With a small bow to both of them, he drew his sleeping blanket over his head. His voice emerged, slightly muffled. "We go now. I must sleep."

Harric traded a glance with Kogan. The priest's brown eyes narrowed. He shook his shaggy head. "Don't feel right," he muttered.

"That they have no kings?" said Harric.

"None of it."

Harric frowned. As he leaned down from his saddle and grabbed up Idgit's lead, it occurred to him that though Brolli had been studying Arkendian culture very closely, Harric knew very little of the Kwendi. It felt a little like his relationship with Fink had felt before the geas. But that wasn't the core of his unease. What bothered him most was the sense that in the last few days, something fundamental changed in the ambassador's attitude. He used to be curious about Arkendia. Now he seemed critical.

Soft snores already emerged from under Brolli's blanket.

"Ready, father?" Harric said, urging Snapper to the river.

"To toss the smug little chimpey in the stream? Aye."

Harric ignored the priest, but Geraldine shook her wooly head so her ears slapped like the flaps of some ridiculous winter hat.

Snapper only hesitated a moment before splashing into the water and walking up the stony bed toward the bend upriver. Pausing where the water was just above his ankles, he beckoned to the priest, who drew up beside him on the lumbering musk-auroch.

"Think about what Brolli's just seen," Harric said. "Willard's changed. It's scared all of us."

"Don't scare *me*."

"Because you've seen it before. Caris and I had never seen it before, but at least we knew the stories and ballads about the Phyros-riders and knew what to expect." He indicated Brolli with a nod over his shoulder. "He has none of that. Think what that must be like. One day it's Sir Willard, your trail companion, next day it's a purple madman slaughtering squires and almost murdering a friend."

Kogan's brow rumpled. He stared upstream, chewing on his beard.

Harric squeezed Snapper with his heels, and the gelding splashed forward again.

The Queen desperately needed the treaty with the Kwendi, especially now that the Old Ones had returned to challenge her throne. If the Kwendi refused peace, she'd have another enemy on her shores, and this one armed with an unfamiliar magic. It would weaken her armies, and the Old Ones would use that to their advantage.

But if roles were reversed, would he recommend a peace treaty with a nation of locusts and madmen? Would any sane man? These thoughts left Harric feeling hollow and gray.

Caris rode after Willard, her mind immersed in the world of the horses she led. Rag still needed a steady touch to keep her calm around Molly. Fortunately, the captured horses had all been Phyros-trained, and the packhorses knew each other and fell in naturally behind Rag's lead-mare governance. The gelding charger, however, did not like forming a string with the others without first establishing dominance, and required considerable gentling lest he kick the teeth out of the next horse in line.

Still, she was grateful for the distraction, and as much as she calmed them in the face of their trials, they also calmed her when the human world stopped making sense. Or when the Blood raged in Willard.

Thought of it sent a thrill up her spine, but it wasn't fear.

Her eyes strayed to the old knight, riding ahead around a thicket of brush and dry boulders. What scared her about the Blood rage wasn't the danger it posed. It wasn't the violence in the Blood, or the mindless fury. But…she felt it, somehow, in her horse-touched senses. That was it: when the Blood racked Willard, she sensed his distress like she would the frustrations of a furious stallion.

Her mouth dropped open. She could sense the *horse* part of the Blood in Willard—not the part that was the Blood of the God, which made him immortal and violent, but Molly's *own* blood, which she took from her great ancestor, Imblis, the first horse to be made immortal.

How had Caris missed this possibility before?

Extending her senses carefully to him, she felt it. She hadn't imagined it! But…had she ever actually touched it? Gods leave her… yes. Without even thinking, while Willard raged at Kogan, she'd reached out to calm him like she would any furious stallion. A spear of fear ran through her middle. Had Willard felt the contact? And if he did, would he have known it was her? Her eyes found the knight, still riding before her. There had been no sign of it in the old man.

She let out a relieved breath.

Behind her, the captured charger whinnied and jerked against its lead. She turned in time to see a rear hoof flash back at the next horse in line, who stopped and pulled against its own lead. It avoided the kick, but its eyes showed its fear.

Cursing herself, Caris turned Rag to bring the mare's influence to bear and reestablished concentration on the gelding. Its mind rippled with frustrations she attempted to smooth, even while calming the other. The gelding kicked again before she managed to bring it back in line. Then she moved through the others, reassuring and restoring their sense of herd and security.

Willard was barking at her. She was so deep in her concentration, she missed what he'd said. She sent a part of her mind out to make sense of his words. "What the Black Moon are you doing? Keep them in line, and pick up the pace."

She sighed. He'd already moved past the willows to trot Molly away along a long sandbar. As soon as she made a quick check on Mudruffle to be sure he hadn't jostled loose, she brought them all up to a canter until they caught up.

And there it was again, Willard's presence, as clearly as if another horse had joined their train. It wasn't as strong as Molly's or even as strong as any mortal horse, for he was still mostly human. But the equine blood of Imblis was in him. Caris could feel it. And if she could feel it, she could touch it.

Of the three moons, only the Bright Mother—the White Moon—
denies its greatest gifts to its servants.
Of all three moons, no doubt the White Moon is most wise.

—Attributed to Black King Silas of the Iberg Compact

28

Fear & Folly

Abellia woke in agony. Her hands and head and belly burned with pain that ripped her mind like a blinding fire. She had no recollection of where she was, or why she was in such misery. She tried to move, and received more pain as payment. Her body was not responding well. She opened her eyes and cried out as the shuttered windows sent lances of searing light into her brain, and once again she plunged into unconsciousness.

When next she woke, her belly and hands still blazed, but the pain behind her eyes had lessened to a dull ache. She was cramped and shivering. She recognized the room and the empty milk jars. Then, in a rush of urgent memories, she remembered the crone and the sleeping knights.

I must stand. I must get to her. Her eyes searched in vain for the hourglass she had intended to use, to measure the length of her unconsciousness, but even as she did, she realized she had forgotten it in her rush to begin.

Slowly, holding her breath, she peered down the length of body to see new, youthful limbs, supple flesh and skin as smooth as rose milk.

A sob of emotion escaped her lips.

It had worked. She was young again.

A throb of burning pain in her hands reminded her of the cost.

Holding her breath, she raised them from under the milk and cried out at what she saw. Both palms had cooked and fused to her nexus stone in spite of the cooling milk. Huge blisters formed under the skin, and she could not separate her hands from the stone without tearing the blisters. Clenching her teeth tightly, she tried to tear the skin free of the nexus by twisting her palms in opposite directions around it. Pain bloomed anew, and her hands parted with a nasty crackling sound. Darkness crowded her vision from the sides, threatening to take her again, but when the pain subsided, the darkness retreated. Sucking a deep breath, she sat up in the tub and raised her hands again from the water.

She stared in mute horror. The skin had not torn away from the nexus at all. Instead, the nexus stone had split down the middle so each half remained fused to the blister of a palm. The two shards of the nexus, once white and pearly bright, were now dark and brittle, and unmistakably dead.

A low wail died in her as shame closed around her throat like a fist.

The magnitude of her sin had no precedent. She had spent a precious nexus of the Bright Mother—a stone capable of healing thousands—on her own selfish resurrection. She pressed the back of one hand to her lips to hold back another wail and rocked back and forth in growing horror. She couldn't breathe. She couldn't speak.

What have I done?

The snort of a horse jarred her back to the present.

How long had she been unconscious? She studied the shadow and light against the eastern shutters, and judged it was still morning, but much later than she had hoped.

With tremendous effort, she hauled herself into sitting position and clambered from the trough. Her body was weak and unfamiliar, her head faint and spinning. How thin she was, and hungry! She managed to pick up a cup of sweet carrot juice with the sides of her hands, and drank it down before she donned the robe. Reeling on new limbs like a newborn calf, she made her way down the stairs. Dimly she noted her robe was much too short now. With each step, her body seemed to remember itself, and her stride became more confident.

When she reached the outer door, she fumbled with the latch on the window grate. The nerves of her hands still dazzled with pain, and the split halves of her nexus still stuck to her palms. She peered into the yard, daring to hope the men still slept. A rider-less horse had waked, and now cropped grass near the crumpled grandmother. No other sound could she hear in the yard.

She lifted the bar and eased the heavy door open with silent thanks to Mudruffle for keeping the hinges well oiled. Heart pounding, she peered out. All asleep. She'd given them a mighty urge when she opened that channel. Bright Mother willing, they'd sleep the day through.

Picking her way among the sleeping men-at-arms on the steps, she wobbled toward the crone. Abellia's legs were dangerously feeble, and her head dangerously light, but by half crawling, using one hand on the steps above her, she managed to avoid a stumble.

In the massive channeling, her body had used all its own resources to rebuild. The juice she had drunk provided scant fuel, and every fiber in her being screamed for platters of beans and fruit and meat. *Meat!* She had not eaten flesh since childhood, but she knew with a certainty that she would devour an entire pig if one lay cooked before her.

She shuffled to the horse and led it to the side of the stairs, where she could better mount. Without ceremony, she grasped the crone beneath the arms and struggled to lift her to the horse. The pitiful creature moaned, but did not resist. Nevertheless, Abellia tried several times and failed to get her on the horse.

As she paused between attempts, movement caught her eye. A bolt of panic tore through her.

The god-knight. Sir Bannus.

Had there been movement among the scars of his face? Petrified, she stared up like a bird before a serpent. His face was a nest of thick and purple scars, like the faces of burned men she'd once healed in the Hospice of Tronte. Amputated ears, mutilated nose. Yet it seemed at peace now. Had she imagined movement? Was he but feigning sleep?

Fear mastered her, and she abandoned the crone where she lay. Unable to look away from the horrible face of Bannus, she groped for the horse's saddle and reins. The shards of nexus in her hands snagged painfully on the leather, preventing her from closing her fingers properly and grasping the reins. How appropriate it would be if these reminders of her sin prevented her from escaping!

With the strength of resolve and panic, she clawed beneath each half of the broken nexus and tore away the blisters in a flood of warm fluid.

Tears in her eyes, she dropped the shards and struggled on her belly aboard the saddle until she could swing a leg around and grasp the mane and reins.

Movement again from Bannus. This time, there was no mistaking it. A single scarred eyelid fluttered and opened. The deep violet eye fixed upon her as if it had watched her even in sleep. Madness gleamed in that eye, and Abellia lost her breath. It seemed her lungs had collapsed. Though they ached to suck in air, they had shrunk to the size of raisins and she would suffocate from fear.

The contorted lips grimaced into something like a grin.

Abellia managed to back her horse. The Phyros woke with a surprised growl and, without perceptible command from the immortal, matched Abellia's retreat.

Bannus's eyes raked over her body. "What a nice surprise. Titus? You must see the offering that the witch has sent us."

The Phyros followed lazily, as if still half-asleep, and Abellia's horse shied, nearly throwing her. Bannus sat in exactly the same posture he had when he slept, eyes fixed upon her. Behind him, the masked one staggered to his feet and remounted.

Panic gripped her. Without her nexus, she was defenseless. She'd never felt so helpless. Now she would be punished for her sin.

Her questing fingers found a spitfire in the saddle behind her, and her heart quailed quailed at the touch of it—a tool of chaos, of destruction—the defilement of the Red Moon at her hand. This was her punishment, she realized, as she fumbled to pull it from its nest without using the palms of her hands. This was the natural result of her choice to serve herself, not others—stripped of the healing nexus, she was forced to take up fire.

The weapon was far too heavy for her newly minted arms, and as she tugged it free, her awkwardness made Sir Bannus laugh. She pointed it vaguely in his direction and screamed for him to stop.

"You know which end to use?" His voice sounded as scarred as the rest of him, as if gravel filled his throat.

"Yes! Stay back! I—I know you immortal not liking fire!" In spite of the futility of the gesture, holding the spitfire returned to her a measure of self-control. She had seen the weapons demonstrated. The mechanism on its stock was the same as the clumsy "firewand" Sir Willard used to light his ragleaf—a lever that turned an iron wheel against flint in order to spark resin.

"You can't hit me. You'll miss, and start a…" A shadow of doubt crossed his eyes.

"There. You see?" she said, angling the pipe toward the fire-cones above. "I cannot hit you, maybe, but I only need to hit the sky." In that moment, she knew she had a chance. She knew the fire dynamics of the grove, and she knew Mudruffle's escape route—where the heat and wind would come strongest, and where it would be least, and by pure luck, the Phyros had backed her down the very route Mudruffle himself would have chosen to escape a fire.

Before the Phyros could leap, she closed her eyes and pulled the lever.

When the Holy One cut and drink from the Phyros,
And when the Blood of the God fills them with his wisdom,
And when the god speaks, through them, divine words,
Then shalt thou scribe each utterance on finest parchment
Of brood and bastard and bind it as new scripture
in the Sacred Book of Krato.

— First Commandment of the Blood Heralds of Krato

29

Phyros Blood

As Rag climbed a crumbling sandbank in Molly's wake, Caris looked up to see Willard halted ahead of her on the flood plain, at the edge of the willows and alders that fringed the deeper forest behind. The pungent stink of ragleaf smoke rode a breeze from him and boxed her in the nose. He'd started on a new roll.

"Hobble the horses here," he said, "and follow me on foot."

Caris looked at the sun's position in the sky. They couldn't have left Harric and Brolli more than an hour before. They hadn't even traveled two miles down the river. Did he have some trick in mind regarding the tracks that they left for Bannus?

Willard watched her through a cloud of smoke. "I need you to do something for me." Without further explanation, he urged Molly into the trees and disappeared behind a screen of brush.

Puzzled, she did as he bade her and followed. Hiking in full armor let her stretch her legs and got her wind up, but she scarcely enjoyed it as she normally would. It was strange for Willard to make her leave Rag, and a stiffness in his manner made her chew at the inside of her lip. What did he need? Why not tell her before she left her horse?

She found him more than a quarter of a mile from the river, beneath a fir tree. He'd dismounted and now stood waiting under the fir's spreading branches, Molly's reins in hand. As Caris joined him and began to catch her breath, she noticed two additional things: on the ground before him lay a coil of chains that she recognized as Molly's four-point iron hobbles, and in one hand he held a polished wooden box the size of a fancy dagger case.

She glanced to Willard's face, looking for clues.

His gaze hardened. "I'm going to ask you to do something for me," he said, voice low and measured. "I'll explain as we go. You understand?"

Caris shifted her feet. She nodded.

His lip curled slightly as he tied Molly off on one of the fir's lower branches. Then he returned to the scaly trunk and sat with his back to it. He set the box beside him and stuck the ragleaf between his teeth. Hands free, he reached his arms back as if he'd embrace the tree behind him and met Caris's gaze. "Chain me to the tree."

Caris felt the blood leave her face.

"Just do it," he said. "And make it good, because I must not slip free."

A dull roar began in Caris's ears. What was this about? Should she know what this meant? She felt her vision narrowing to a closed tunnel before her as the roar grew louder—both signs heralding a collapse. She closed her eyes tightly. *No. I cannot curl up on the ground now!* She reached out for Rag and managed to sense her even at this distance. The mare was calm and content, and Caris dove into the connection to draw the mare's senses around her like a shield against the confusion.

Sweet grass. Unworried, swishing tails. Soothing sun on her haunches.

"You with me, girl?"

Caris nodded. The roar receded. When she opened her eyes, her vision had returned to normal. Splitting her attention between Rag and Willard, she picked up the chains and held up one of the thick manacles to his arm. *It's the Blood rage,* she realized. *He needs to be restrained.* The manacle was made for Molly's ankles, so it was too big for his wrist, but it fit tightly above his bicep. She clamped it in place and screwed in the bolt. Stretching the opposing manacle around the other side of the tree, she found it a few inches short of his other arm.

"You'll have to stand," she said. "It doesn't reach."

When he stood, the chain rose to the higher and narrower part of the trunk, so if he strained his arms back, she was able to clamp it in place and screw it tight. When she finished, she stepped away, and he sagged against the chains. Hanging like a man sentenced to lashes, he sucked furiously at the ragleaf, unleashing clouds of smoke.

"You know I must face Sir Bannus," he said, gray eyes boring into her. "It is inevitable."

She clenched her jaw. This was the reason he'd broken his oath to Anna. She knew it was necessary. She knew he was right. But that did not change the fact that he'd broken his vow. She felt the roar begin as a low hum between her ears, and closed her eyes to bathe again in Rag's calm.

After a moment, she said, "That's why you're taking the Blood."

"Yes. But even so, I fear I won't have enough of it in me before he finds us."

Caris pursed her brow. She hadn't thought about this, but now it seemed obvious. Willard was a long way from the huge size, outrageous musculature, and deep blue of Sir Bannus. "How…much does it take?"

"Not how much. How long." Willard sucked at the tiny stub of ragleaf between his teeth and spat the butt away into the rocks. As he spoke, rank smoke gusted with his words. "Normally, when a mortal begins to take the Blood, it is a slow process. To keep control of the rage, one drinks no more than twice a month—to take it more often would be to invite madness and blind fury. At that rate, within the year, the transformation is complete. I, however, do not have a year. So I must drink again today."

"You want to take it twice in a *day?*"

"Thrice. I've already drunk twice." She glanced at his face, uncertain what he wanted her to understand. "But I am not any man, Caris. Nor am I new to the Blood. I lived many lifetimes with it running through my veins, and I know its ways. So I hope I can push the process, compress the year into days. I must try. I must achieve at least partial transformation, or we are lost."

Caris looked at Molly, who returned the look with steady eyes. She dared not extend her senses to the Phyros, but sensed eagerness and triumph in Molly's glance and in the high lift of her head. Caris turned back to Willard. "So, how…?"

"You will cut her and bleed her, Caris, and hold the cup to my mouth."

Caris felt her mouth drop open. The roar began between her ears, and she stepped back.

Heads low, cropping grass. Contented chewing. Herd. Safety.

"I will instruct you." Willard nodded to the box. "Open it."

Caris swallowed. She picked it up and opened it. Inside, nested in purple velvet, lay a fine straight razor and a golden cup.

"Bleeding a Phyros is simple. Find the vein, lance it, catch the Blood in the cup, and then hold it to my lips."

She blinked in surprise.

"You've heard of ceremonies and sacred rites at every bleeding." He gave her a wry smile. "That's the way of the Old Ones and their ridiculous Heralds. We cut and drink."

Her heart felt like it would pound its way through her breastplate. She managed to give him a nod, but she could not meet his eye or she would fall into the roaring confusion that was human discourse. She did what she could, which was listen, and she nodded again to show she heard him.

"Good," he said. "Once you bring the cup to my lips and I drink, you must leave me. No matter what I say, no matter what order I give. You must ignore me and get out of sight."

"I will retreat to the river with the horses."

"Don't tell me where you'll be, you fool. If I break loose, the Blood rage will seek you. Understand?"

She nodded.

"And if you should hear things, if I should say things…unkind things…vile things to you, pay no heed, for it isn't me. It is Krato in me." She glanced up to note a grim smile. "I expect the Mad God will have a thing or two to say about a young woman in armor."

A plume of fear brushed inside her stomach, but she couldn't suppress a curl of her lip.

"Aye," he said. His voice dropped so low that she almost didn't hear. "Imagine how it feels when he inhabits me."

"How do you stand it?"

He shook his head. "Mercifully, I remember little after I swallow. But enough on him. Go to Molly. She presents her shoulder to you."

Caris hesitated. With her hobbles on Willard, nothing restrained the Phyros but her lead on a branch the side of Caris's wrist. "Will she fall into one of her moods once she's bled?"

"She will. But as long as you hold the cup of Blood, she won't molest you. Get clear of her, let me drink, and go. She'll be raging with hunger, but she won't leave me to follow you."

Caris walked slowly toward the gigantic Phyros, carefully avoiding her gaze. Molly did appear to thrust her right shoulder out for a cut. Round muscles slid beneath the wine-black coat, making the livid scars jump and sink like squirming snakes. The sheer mass of scars was impressive: the legacy of Willard's ten lifetimes of cuts. Bright violet, thick as fingers, they splayed across Molly's coat like jags of lightning, following the paths of veins. The old scars were so numerous that Caris saw few places she could lay a hand on Molly's coat without touching one. The idea that even a single vein might remain untapped in that landscape of slashes seemed absurd.

But Molly knew: at the back of the shoulder was a soft weal of raised skin between two scars—a curve of untapped vein.

"She'll let me do this?" Caris glanced up at one steady violet eye.

"She knows what the cup and blade mean. Hold the cup beneath the vein," Willard said. "Press it close into the coat, so none spills."

It was the closest Caris had ever been to Molly. As she pressed the cup against the coat, she felt the extreme heat of the beast against the back of her fingers. Molly's coat felt as if she'd been soaking the noon sun for an hour, or like she had an extreme fever. Was this the normal resting temperature for a Phyros? Natural awe rose in Caris, and she had to push aside a powerful urge to reach out to Molly with horse-senses, lest the Mad God roar through the connection and scour her mind.

Caris looked up at the canopy. Her best guess told her the sun had begun its descent down the far side of noon. "If we wait to drive the horses south until after you recover, it will be too late to catch up to the others before sunset. As soon as I've given you the Blood, I'll ride them south and send them on."

Willard considered that. "Be careful. You needn't go far."

She paused, staring at the ground between them. "Is this the real reason we came south? So you could take the Blood. So the others wouldn't see it?" She frowned inwardly. She could hear the bluntness of her own words, but she didn't know how to smooth them. If Harric were there, he wouldn't even have to ask this question; it would flow from his tongue in the regular course of conversation, and the old knight wouldn't even know he'd asked it. Her tongue had no such grace. It spoke plainly and—apparently—struck flat. As often as not, people heard her questions as accusation.

Willard's gaze hardened and his chest puffed as if he'd bark at her. Then he frowned and slumped back against the chains.

"The false trail is vital." He closed his eyes. "But yes... The worst of this ugliness I wish to keep private. The fact is, I worry about the ambassador's view of me. Until I reestablish control over the Blood, I am not myself. I am rash. Violent. I speak in anger without thinking. It makes me vile, and I fear it could change his heart."

Caris studied the old knight. Not so old any longer, actually. The wrinkles and bags around his eyes had smoothed as the flesh tightened. The fat of his neck and face had melted almost entirely away. Ridges of bone and cords of muscle had emerged like reefs and shoals at low tide. She blinked to clear her eyes and looked at him again with growing awe. Now that she'd seen it, it was impossible to *un*-see it, and he was hard to recognize: if it weren't for the gray mustachio and ragleaf-yellow teeth, she'd have assumed him some other Phyros-rider.

His gray eyes caught and held her gaze. "It changed your heart this morning. I saw it."

She felt a pulse of guilt and stared at the ground. "I am sorry I judged you. It wasn't fair. You did..." She couldn't say he'd done the *right* thing. "You did what you had to do. What was needed. Harric tells me I see only black and white and that people are generally gray. I don't know if that's true." She risked a glance and found him watching her with a look she didn't recognize. Perhaps his eyes smiled.

"He may have something there," said Willard.

"I try to see it, but I am sure Brolli sees it. He wanted you to take the Blood because he wants to live."

Willard grunted. "Everyone wants their own monster to fight off the monsters, and Brolli's no different. But he isn't stupid, either. He knows the trouble with that is that no matter which monster wins, in the end you're still left with a monster on your hands."

"Compared to Bannus, you are no monster. Brolli must see that."

"For our queen's sake, let's hope so." He jerked his chin toward Molly. "Now cut her and bring me a swallow of her cursed blood."

Where there are old forests, there are yoab. In these later years, the great blind beasts survive only in the mountains of the north and east. House Pelion's trophy hall boasts a skeleton said to be from the largest recorded yoab at a length of thirty paces and crest height of three fathoms.

—From *Natural History of Arkendia,* Sir Alhimbror Green

30

Fire Draught

Caris's mouth had gone dry. As she approached within reach of Molly, she watched the beast's eyes carefully.

"Look closely at the vein she's presenting to you," Willard said. "You'll see the short scar I started along the top. That's where I took the last two draughts today. You will continue that scar along the vein."

The new scar was so small that Caris hadn't noticed it among the livid ropes around it. It was a tiny stub—no longer than the width of her thumb—branching off another scar. "If this is two cuts, then the cuts must be very small."

"They are. More like punctures, really. A larger cut would gush all over the place, and it is vexingly hard to get off your armor, so I don't recommend it." He let out a grim chuckle. "The Old Ones hold it to be a grave sin to spill a drop, but you'll just want to be sure it doesn't soil your armor."

"Soiled by the god." A little laugh bubbled out of Caris, surprising her. Of course she'd known Willard carried no love for the Mad God, but until this moment she hadn't realized he loathed him as much as she.

She positioned herself to one side. Pressing the cup beneath the vein, she steadied her razor hand against Molly's hot skin.

"Good." Willard licked his lips, eyes fixed on the vein. "Now plunge it in and remove it. Let it drain into the cup."

"How long will it bleed?"

"Not long." His voice had gone dry. "It scabs almost instantly, so as soon as it does, you'll want to lift the scab and slide the blade in the mouth of the wound to keep it open. The flow will slow, but keep the wound open until the cup is full."

Caris's hands grew slippery with sweat. Her father had told tales of Heralds scouring battlefields for every flake of holy scab, and how some could read auguries from where they fell. She tried to push these images aside, and imagined she was simply letting blood from one of Mother Ganner's blood-stallions, to make blood draughts for the inn.

Holding her breath, she dipped the razor in and out of the vein, and an arc of violet Blood followed. The spurt surprised her, and she almost dropped the cup as she pulled it away to catch the arc before pressing it back to Molly's side as it flagged.

A shudder rippled through Molly's enormous frame, and she let out a rumbling groan.

"Good." Willard's voice scraped out as a whisper. "Keep it open until the cup is full."

Caris scraped away the scab, a little stab of panic spurring her heartbeat when she saw the wound had already closed, but a quick dip of the razor reopened it, and when the cup filled, she let it close and breathed a sigh of relief.

A curl of smoke rose from the new scab as a purple scar rose and thickened beneath it.

Smoke.

She stepped back, staring at Molly in awe. The cup burned Caris's fingers, so she had to continually move it from one hand to the other. Was there fire in her blood? The Mad God was in her, after all—the war god, the god of fire and destruction.

Molly held her head high. Her scarred sides heaved as if she'd been running, and hot, sulfurous air gusted from scarred nostrils.

Something thrilled through Caris. She bowed deeply and backed away. The gesture came unbidden, unplanned, but it was as natural as kneeling for a queen.

When she brought the cup to Willard, his cheek seemed sunken and pale. He licked his lips, almost panting with anticipation. "Remember what I told you," he said in a ragged whisper. When she didn't answer right away, he tore his gaze from the cup and lifted his eyes to her. She hadn't anticipated the eye contact, and flinched. How she hated touching eyes! Harric had explained to her how important this signal was to people, like ear movements to horses. Knowing that didn't make it any easier, however, and she guessed this was a time when meeting eyes was important.

The roaring started in her ears, and her vision began to narrow.

Instead of looking away, she closed her eyes. Looking away was her "biggest tell," according to Harric. If she didn't touch eyes, people would judge her. But he'd also taught her the trick of staring at people's noses instead. It seemed ridiculous when he first suggested it—she'd thought he mocked her—but he convinced her to try it, swearing that no one would know the difference. And he was right. No one did notice. And it wasn't as bad as touching eyes.

"Girl!"

She opened her eyes and stared at the tip of the knight's bulbous nose.

"Do you remember what might happen when I take the Blood?"

An ugly lump sat in her gut. "Yes. Krato's words, not yours."

He nodded. "Be ready. Plug your ears; do as you will. Just don't listen."

"And…you will remember nothing of what he says?"

Willard shook his head. "Nothing." His hungry eyes returned to the cup, and beads of sweat pricked out on his forehead.

"How will I know when you're back?"

"Gods take it, girl, give me the cup before it hardens!"

Her hand trembled as she set the razor back in its box and lifted the cup to his lips. He sucked and swallowed, and then sucked the scab from the bottom and licked at the cup. Her stomach rose in protest as she held it for him, but she held it steady, and when he finally turned his head aside, she set the smoking cup in the box with the razor.

Willard gasped as if in tremendous pain, then thrashed against his bonds.

Heart leaping, Caris retreated a few steps. Did the Blood burn as it went down? Did it burn in his stomach and in his veins as it spread through his body? Willard roared, and she jumped; his voice had taken on an uncanny volume and basso tone.

Before she could tear her eyes away and flee, his head whipped toward her, eyes blazing violet. Grinning maniacally, teeth stained with Blood, he roared, *"Thou!"* The voice sent vibrations through her that seemed to reach into her chest and squeeze her heart to a halt. The flesh of Willard's face pulled back, baring teeth and bulging his eyes in hideous parody of the man. His eyes raked her up and down as if they would pry the iron plates from her body.

The sight froze her in place. A small corner of her mind screamed, *Run!* but the god's eyes held her like snake eyes charmed a bird.

A purple tongue slid across his lips. "Kneel for me."

Caris inhaled suddenly, strongly, as if someone stuck her with a hot nail. Her heart started again. Though her feet and gaze seemed frozen in place, her hands were free. She tugged a plated gauntlet onto one hand, and wadded up the rag she kept for swabbing her brow on the trail.

"Mis-bred thing," said Willard-Krato. "Unfit for life." The violet eyes seemed to penetrate to her soul, her deepest self. "Thy brood-mother should have smothered you on sight. Thou art half beast. Unworthy of station."

Caris tried to move, but the voice held her. There was a presence behind the voice, a captivation, and her heart rose to it, bared itself for approval...so these words cut deep. Each was a keen dirk sliding lazily past her armor into her heart.

Part of her kicked in pain and protest, but still her heart rose, craving approval, surrendering to the truth of his divine judgment—despairing, yet still rising, hoping for some small sign of favor in the contempt.

"Do you wear the color of cobalt?" he said. "Thou art unfit for any color. Thou hast no blood rank. True men turn from you in disgust. Thou wilt breed slaves with bastards."

Caris crammed the rag in his mouth.

She shouted as she did it, though to her own ears it sounded more like a cry, and Willard-Krato's eyes bugged like they'd pop from their sockets. The attack came as such a surprise to him that she got most of it in before he realized what was happening. With a steel-clad thumb, she crammed the rag between gnashing teeth until he gagged and his jaw slacked to let her stuff in the rest.

Purple with rage, he choked on the gag and tried to spit it out.

She grabbed the dust kerchief that hung around his neck and pulled it up over his mouth to hold the gag in. Before she could get it in place, he began thrashing his head from side to side, so she lost grip and it fell back about his neck.

Panicking, she slammed his head back against the tree with the back of one arm, and locked it in her armpit until she could haul the kerchief up across his mouth.

The moment she sprang clear, Willard-Krato went berserk.

He roared into the gag. His eyes bulged with fury as he bucked against the chains, but even with Krato's help, Willard's body was no match for chains designed for Molly.

Caris put her hands on her hips as she caught her breath and assessed her handiwork. And though she kept her gaze well clear of his eyes, she found herself drawn to him—to that ego-annihilating presence—in the same way she was tempted by Molly's presence. To catch a glimpse of the improvised bridle she'd made him, she had to imagine he was nothing but a snake-bit stallion she'd tamed and stabled. To her relief, the gag appeared to be holding tight across his mouth. It had been too tight to lift over his mouth easily, so when she yanked it over his chin, it probably left a nasty burn. Something like guilt gave a tug at her heart, but she snuffed it. He'd said, *Do what you will*, after all, and he wouldn't remember.

The important thing was that she'd silenced Krato.

A terrible cracking sound from Willard made her flinch. She looked and saw he'd begun grinding the kerchief between his teeth. It sounded like the cracking of bones beneath boots, and his eyes burned with such hatred that she almost felt them scorch her skin. His judgment reared above her, and she felt her heart helplessly rising for approval.

With a cry, she hurried away, burying herself in Rag's calm.

Safe. Steady.

When she'd covered twenty strides, she glanced back to him straining against the chains, veins popping, the burning gaze following as he gnawed the gag. She couldn't stop him from gnawing through. But it only needed to hold long enough for her to get out of hearing.

Swishing tails. Sun on tired legs. A quiet snort.

The darkness fell away, and she picked up her pace to a jog. And as her mind cleared and her heart recovered, she felt a troubling giggle rising in her lungs.

She'd gagged the Mad God. She'd silenced him.

The very idea terrified her...yet she felt just like she'd won a tournament against an Old One.

As the sound of Willard's struggles faded behind her, the giggle became nearly continuous. Some of it came from triumph, but as much came from nervous terror. What if he broke free and took her? What if... But no. He was bound with iron. He was lashed to a tree until *she* released him.

To the gods with terror.

She jumped like a colt. "Stuffed his gob!"

As if in sympathy, the chirp of birds and chatter of river grew louder, and she saw the water's glittering surface through the brush.

The horses looked up as she rejoined them, their ears perked in curiosity, and she greeted Rag with a nuzzle. As she stroked her smooth cheek, Rag nickered and nudged her back. The mare's ears swiveled toward her as if she wanted in on the joke.

"Hard to explain." She held up a carrot she'd saved from her lunch, and felt the tickle of whiskers as Rag lipped it up from her palm. "Besides, you're happier not knowing."

A distant bellow sounded in the forest from the direction of Willard's tree. Willard-Krato must have finally gnawed through the kerchief. Thankfully, she was far enough away that she could not discern words, but his fury was immense and tireless, like the roars of an outraged yoab. The horses' ears swiveled toward the sound, eyes widening as they looked to Caris, and she soothed them with soft sounds and pats.

"He can't get to us. Let him bellow."

Nevertheless, the roars made her wonder. Even if Willard wouldn't remember the gag, what if Krato did? What if next time he cursed her before she could gag him? She was probably overthinking it. Maybe Willard had not meant the god *literally* occupied his flesh. Maybe that was just an expression meaning the Blood made him vile, like the god made him say things like the god would say.

She chewed her lip, wishing Harric was there. He saw things from a different vantage. Half the time, the irreverence of that vantage infuriated her, but sometimes it helped her see something she would not see alone. And often he set her heart at ease.

As soon as she removed the horses' hobbles, she looped the lead line through their halters and formed a train, then secured the lead on Rag's saddle. As she led them downstream, she realized that in addition to the buzz of worry in her mind, thought of Harric had summoned up a dull ache in her chest. She frowned. She shouldn't have let herself dwell on him, but her heart kept returning to thoughts of him. They'd only been apart a few hours, and already she missed him. If she could lay a false trail for Bannus and return to Willard without much difficulty, they could catch up to Harric by sunset and bed.

Bed. Her face grew warm. Stupid. They couldn't share a bed in such company.

What a thought that was! Now her cheeks blazed. Yet this urge had burned in her for the last couple of days—a new and foreign fire in her—and it confused and angered her. It was that loathsome ring's doing. It had to be. It forced her feelings, and now it seemed to be giving her these physical urges. She managed to snuff them when she focused on the horses or on some other engrossing task, but the moment she let down her guard, she found herself plotting beds or private moments. Gods leave it!

She bit back a yell of frustration.

I miss him. I hate him. I want to bed him.

If she cast her mind back to before the ring, she recalled she had actually scorned him. She'd never forget when she saw him caught for conning a slave-lord in Gallows Ferry. She remembered clearly how shocked and ashamed she'd felt. In that moment, a dozen little details of his behavior over the previous weeks had fallen in place and she'd seen the pattern of trickery and dishonor in him. Still…he'd been kind to her. When she'd first arrived in Gallows Ferry—confused and prone to horse-touched episodes of panic—he'd helped her. He'd come to her aid when no one else did, and got her on her feet. They'd been misfit friends.

But even then, before she'd learned what a trickster knave he was, she'd had no attraction or physical urges. Once, when Ana asked her what she thought of Harric, she'd made Ana laugh by referring to him as a runt.

She buried her face in Rag's sun-warmed mane and breathed in the mare's scent.

Was *that* how she'd seen him? A runt? It must have been. But that was stupid. He was finely formed, his shoulders and buttocks—

Her face grew hot again. Gods take the ring!

She fled fully into the world of the horses and, since the only male in the string was a gelding, found no such urges there. Shared sensory images flooded her mind. Green juice filled her mouth, soft greens dissolving on her tongue. Rough-edged herbs surrendered their pungency between molars. Gradually, she felt her heartbeat calm.

"Safe. Steady," she murmured. Rag nuzzled her.

With a sigh, she mounted. Turning back toward the river, she led the string of horses downstream along the sunny riverbank. Her task was to leave a few miles of tracks and then release the captured horses and send them southward. Let that task divert her from thoughts of Harric.

They followed the river for a half-mile of easy going on soft sandbars and gravel banks. Then the watercourse bent, and the bank ahead bristled with palisades of logs and massive boulders. Instead of searching for a way around, she turned back to the ancient forest. If she could find one of the yoab runs Mudruffle had indicated on his map, it might prove the easiest way for the horses to take southward.

She glanced back at Mudruffle's inert figure behind her saddle.

"Wish you were here to guide me," she said, laying a hand on his cool clay hat.

Upon learning that the Heralds had excommunicated her from the lists of the Arkendian Blood Ranks, Queen Chasia responded with this proclamation: "Henceforth shall this day be known as Excommunication Day, and a holiday. On this day let none work, but let the bells ring, let bonfires blaze, and let my people make dances and sing, for never have tidings brought me such joy." In this way, she mocked the Heralds…and for it, the people best love Excommunication Day.

—From *Queen Chasia's Golden Years*, by Blue Gildrus

31

False Trail

Scents of rich green life filled Caris's senses as she plunged the horses into the forest. Behind her the clatter of the river fell to a low rush, like the breath of wind in distant trees. Eventually, all sound hushed, as if in awe of the ancient trunks like standing columns in some green god's palace. Beams of sunlight slanted down from holes in the canopy, illuminating clouds of dancing insects. During the worrisome detour with Willard, she hadn't noticed the forest's grandeur, but now her heart felt lighter and her spirits rose, eyes lifted to the soaring canopy.

She soon found, however, that even though the trees were widely spaced and the canopy was an airy dome above them, the floor of the forest was crisscrossed with fallen trunks of the ancient giants, which made travel difficult. Harric had a name for these logs. Something like "seed mounds" or "sapling beds," because the rotting bulks acted as raised beds for seedlings to get a start above the shading ferns and shrubs. During her long hours in the saddle, she'd come up with her own name—"swan logs," because they reminded her of the swans at home, which carried swanlings on their backs, raised above the water until big enough to brave the moat themselves. And because the tree's final sacrifice to its children was like the swan's dying song, which was its most beautiful.

Pretty names aside, the great bulks were too high for horses to cross, and after dozens of dead ends and backtracks, she decided the best name was *maze logs*.

Swallowing her frustration, she picked her way west, hoping to intersect a yoab run.

How long since she'd left Willard? She glanced up, but could not see the position of the sun through the canopy. She imagined they'd been gone an hour, which left her only one more hour before she'd have to send the captured horses south and loop back.

Rag's head rose, alert, and her body stiffened.

Yoab.

Rag's nostrils flared, and Caris smelled it through her. A rank mildew and urine stink. Both of them remembered it from their nearly disastrous encounter with a yoab on their way to Abellia's tower. And this was not an old scent, months old, like it should be. It was pungent and sharp, as if laid down that morning. *Piles.* She chewed her lip. Had the monsters already come down from summer feeding on the hillsides?

The other horses whinnied, fear rising in them like froth in a boiling pot, forcing Caris to spread her attention among them to still their drumming hearts. She gave Rag extra attention, smoothing the aroused memories of their last encounter. She could not allow the mare's fear to blossom as it had the first time they met a yoab: the moment that beast had roared, Rag's fear overwhelmed Caris so swiftly that she'd become part of it, blacking out until long after their wild flight through the forest. If they encountered another yoab, she could not allow that to happen again.

As soon she felt she could spare some of her concentration, she stood in her stirrups and scanned over the fallen trunks for signs of yoab. Nothing. No huge beast disguised as a hill of moss and lichens. But the space beyond the logs looked scoured and tilled as if a yoab had fed there. She urged Rag forward, and they rounded a swan log and entered into the yoab feeding site. In the space about the size of a large corral, the forest floor had been stripped of all plants and plant matter—alive and dead—leaving a tumult of thin soil and sand and rock, as if it had been tilled by a mad giant's plow.

She walked Rag into the clearing. Judging by the lack of new sprouts in the raw earth, she'd been right to estimate it was a recent till. And if one yoab had come down from the hills, others must be returning as well.

Gods leave it. Her plan felt a lot less certain.

Standing in her stirrups again, she spotted what she'd hoped for—a broad path stretching away between the trees to the south. Mudruffle's Yoab Highway? To the north of the clearing lay another broad path stretching north. The Yoab Highway. Relief washed down her like cool water.

She nudged Rag down the south run, a breeze in her face, and Rag stepped more energetically in the soft soil, grateful for the change. Once they left the feeding site, the run ran flat, straight, and wide enough for a pair of wagons abreast. But unlike a human road, it looked like it had been reamed through the forest with a giant battering ram. Logs and boulders and shrubs had been shoved to the side, making low mounds on each side, like mossy hedgerows of rubble. The sand and rock surface of the road itself had been flattened and packed by generations of yoab that left drag marks down the middle and clawed prints along the sides.

After a check to be sure Mudruffle was well secured, Caris brought the horses into a canter to make up for lost time in the labyrinth. How long had they been zigzagging through the log maze? Over an hour, that was certain. Willard must be out of his rage and wondering what happened to her.

A new worry pressed in her chest: if anything happened to her, Sir Bannus would find Willard bound to a tree.

She needed to send the captured horses on their way and loop back to him. As soon as the horses got used to the run—after maybe a mile— she'd cut them loose.

They'd cantered no more than half a mile when she heard a loud crack from somewhere ahead. It sounded like a breaking tree trunk, but distance muffled it. Rag's ears pricked forward.

Caris kept a firm hold on the emotions of the little herd.

Steady. Safe.

A minute later, another powerful *crack* resounded much closer. Rag's ears oriented ahead and to the right, and her nostrils flared. The strong scent of yoab hit them just as Caris saw something move in the forest only sixty strides ahead and to the right of the run. Or rather, she saw part of the forest move. A mossy hillock rocked side to side as it plowed into a swan log, shaking ferns and seedlings all along the log's length.

She felt her stomach drop.

It was an adult and at least as big as the one they'd met below Abellia's tower. Small plants and lichens swayed on its peaked back some two fathoms above the forest floor. If it had been asleep, she wouldn't have distinguished it from a lumpy hillock in the forest floor.

One of the horses snorted, and Rag's eyes widened, showing their whites.

Safe, she told them. *Steady. Together.*

The monster had its back to them, and it appeared so engrossed in its meal of rotten log and soil that it hadn't noticed them. In that instant, she saw three options: she could stop the horses and turn back, she could stop and try to skirt around the beast through the log maze on the opposite side of the run, or she could spur into a gallop and rely on surprise and greater speed to fly past it.

Her breath stopped as the instant flashed by.

Then she set her heels to Rag and brought her to a gallop. She would try to fly past before it could react. The other options were too risky, especially if the yoab swallows hadn't flown south for the winter yet: the birds would raise the alarm, and if that happened when the horses were at a standstill, they'd never get to speed in time to escape. Speed was their best hope. And she'd outrun a yoab once before, when she hadn't even had a clear road.

Steady. Safe.

Twenty strides away, and the yoab's hind end still faced them.

She leaned forward and steered Rag to the left edge of the run, the horses' collective fear threatening to drown her. She had to keep her control this time, or Rag might try to flee into the labyrinth where they'd be trapped and flattened.

Fifteen strides.

As the yoab strained against a chunk of rotten log the size of a longship, its hind legs raked mounds of soil behind it, flashing bearlike paws with claws as long as her forearm. Sheets of gray hide puckered and flattened behind the legs, and with every thrust, the little forest on its back rocked and bowed. A loud *crump!* echoed between the trees, and the longship upended and crashed sideways toward the run. Small trees thrashed, and a hail of dirt and debris showered the undergrowth.

Rag missed a step, and a surge of horse fear—hot and bright—rose like bile in Caris's chest, burning and constricting her throat.

Safe! Steady! Together!

At five strides, joy hammered Caris's fear. They were going to make it!

Then the air around the yoab exploded with darting birds, and her fears were confirmed. Screeching like a pen of angry chickens, the birds fluttered from hollows in the beast's mossy sides to wheel around its head.

Horse fear hit Caris like a wall of floodwater. Desperate to keep control, she pulled her influence from the other horses to focus on Rag alone, and released the others to the full flood of their fear in hope that it would drive them south for miles.

Run! Rag's panic screamed.

Steady! Caris said, infusing her with confidence in her speed. *But yes! Run!* And she let Rag stretch into an all-out race.

The yoab whirled with astonishing speed for something so huge. This close, Caris saw it was as least as big as the one below Abellia's; that meant it was old enough that its tiny eyes had long been buried under the folds of skin that piled down its back and onto its carriage-sized head. But Caris knew it could smell as well as some beasts could see.

Its bulldog jaw hung open like the drawbridge to an earthen keep, showing rows of bony ridges in place of teeth, but as the horses drew even with it on the highway, the jaw clapped shut. Curtains of leathery throat folds puffed and wrinkled like the gullet of a pelican as nostrils big enough to suck up a dog flared toward the horses.

Steady! Run!

The blind crag of the yoab's head tracked them, and as its nostrils closed with a leathery snap, it launched its tremendous bulk for the horses.

Whether the yoab couldn't smell well enough to anticipate their speed and direction or whether it simply missed, the monster crashed across the run behind them.

The charger and one of the captured riding horses drew even with Rag, heads down, ears back, and eyes showing white. Looking back over her shoulder, Caris watched as the yoab thrashed about, then oriented on the scent of horse coming to it on the breeze. The drawbridge mouth released a bellow that echoed through the trees and vibrated every particle of Caris's body.

Unhooking the captured horses' lead from her saddle, Caris tossed it over the charger's saddle and reined Rag back so the others could race past her. The moment the last of them charged by, she veered Rag left into the log maze so the yoab would follow the others south. Too late, she realized what she'd thought a clear way into the maze was in fact a dead end bound by huge logs and blocked at the end with a boulder the size of four wagons. Rag squealed in fear and tried to leap one of the great swan logs that penned them, but fell back, nearly throwing Caris.

The yoab thundered up the run toward them, its head angled first after the other horses, then left toward Caris and Rag.

Caris nearly threw up her breakfast.

Determined to be in motion if the beast turned on them, and not to be standing for its charge, she spurred Rag back. Rag resisted, trying to veer toward the logs for another attempt at leaping them, but Caris managed to focus her enough to get her up to a galloping charge.

The ground pitched and Rag stumbled as the yoab pounded down the run as if it would pass the mouth of her dead end and keep going, then swung its head toward them and dug in its fore-claws for a plowing sideways stop. Horned claws still churning, it laid its cragged head low and charged up the dead end toward them.

Caris yelled out the fear pounding in her throat. In the last moments of the charge, she swerved right, hoping to race past the beast and up the run toward Willard, but the great head swung to intercept. Her only option was to swerve left past its opening jaw, but a clawed paw slammed down before them, blocking the left as well, and it was too late to turn or stop.

Now their only choice was to run right up the back of the gnarled paw, and Rag performed it beautifully, leaping from it into the run beyond.

As Caris sent waves of confidence and relief and pride into Rag's harried spirits, the yoab howled. As it began to turn after them, Caris circled with it in the hope that it would lose track of her.

Smell the other horses! Please smell the other horses!

A wave of soil hit Caris and Rag like the slap of a giant hand. Rag tumbled into a thicket of ferns. Caris rolled free and hit a rotten log. Her arm jerked as the reins pulled against Rag, but she held tight and focused all her mind on the mare. If the yoab had lost their scent and they stayed still, it might move away and leave them. Caris poured so much of herself into Rag that the horse reacted in a kind of stunned shock.

Safe. Together. Stay.

Rag struggled to her knees, eyes white-rimmed with fear. Caris let her clamber to her feet, but kept up the intense focus while holding her bridle low so Rag couldn't rear.

Safe. Together. Stay.

Only six paces away, she dimly sensed the yoab's hind claw gripping the earth. The great bulk had stilled, but she heard a mighty snort and the snap of leathery nostrils. From the corner of her eye, she saw the huge head swinging left and right.

Her heart beat so hard that she feared the beast would sense it, but the yoab continued to snort and suck the air from down the road.

Gods leave us, we circled downwind and it's lost us!

The enormous claw before them tore into the earth with gut-wrenching violence, and the mountain surged away. In two mighty strides, it rose on crooked stumps and thundered after the other horses like an avalanche in a chute.

Caris let her relief flow back against the mare's fear—*Safe! Safe!*—and as she watched the yoab gallop away, she stood and hugged herself into Rag. Tears of joy wet her cheeks. Their tumble had been a blessing, she realized. If they'd stayed on their feet and tried to run past the yoab, the creature would have sensed the pounding hooves along its flank and lashed out.

In spite of Caris's soothing, however, the poor mare's eyes still rolled, and her ears still pricked toward the south and the dwindling roar of the yoab. Stroking her neck and bathing Rag's mind in a sense of safety and security, Caris walked her back into the maze. Something thumped behind her, and she turned to see Mudruffle lying rigid and facedown in the moss.

Heart leaping in her chest, she picked him up and pulled a few stray ferns from his hat. "Gods leave me, you held on just long enough," she said to the senseless golem. "If you'd let go during that mayhem, I might never have found you again."

After lashing him tightly to her gear, she hobbled Rag a good bowshot from the run, and went back to hide their tracks as best she could. Sir Bannus must find no prints leaving the yoab run. When she finished replacing divots and covering scores in the moss, she mounted Rag and they began the laborious process of picking their way through the maze toward the river. Once they crossed the river, they would find a trail up the opposite side and hook back to Willard.

Willard. She smiled. She had a triumphant story for him. Not only had she run the horses south, but she'd enlisted a yoab to spur them along.

Her only worry was that she'd used the captive horses a bit callously. She looked south through the trees, chewing her lip. They would outrun the yoab, but then they'd be lost in the woods, miles from farm or stable. She had to comfort herself with the thought Bannus's men would track them and they'd soon be back in a stable.

And let Sir Bannus meet the yoab. Gods leave it, wouldn't that be a glory.

Emerging at last at the river's edge, she looked up to see that the sun had advanced well past noon. A knot of tension twisted in her stomach. The old man should be back in his skin, but she feared she'd taken too long and they would not be able to catch up to Harric and the others before sunset.

"Gods leave it," she muttered, as Rag splashed out of the river and up a stony draw on the opposite bank. She did not want to camp alone with Willard. Not with Molly lusting for flesh and the rage so fresh in his Blood.

...an unknown tooler is said to have accidentally discovered the process for refining fire-cone resin...after harvesting the resin from a batch of cones, he is said to have used the empty cones to flavor his moonshine... When bits of resin still in the cones dissolved in alcohol, they separated from seeds and oily impurities and left a residue of powder in the bottom of the jugs. We call that powder blasting resin or spitfire resin.

— *First Tooler's Primer,* Master Tooler Jobbs

32

Seeds Of Sorrow

Harric reined in at the foot of a huge red cedar rising straight from the middle of the yoab run. Where the trunk met the ground, the tree was wide enough for seven or eight people to link hands and stretch around it. Nothing this big had been seen near Gallows Ferry since the sawmill went up at the rapids. The yoab apparently demonstrated their respect for such a grandmother tree—too huge to push over—by rubbing against it and diverting their run around it; a ragged skirt of bark hung about the base of the trunk for more than twice the height of a man, suggesting the beasts rubbed against the tree like giant cats might against the leg of a giant.

Thankfully, judging by the sprinkling of needles over the raw soil of the run, no yoab had been here for weeks. That was good. Instead, the soil was pocked with the prints of two-toed hooves of elk that had crossed beneath the great tree's shadow.

Harric's eyes followed the graceful lines of the trunk up into the canopy, where its limbs mingled with those of its neighbors. A couple of black squirrels appeared in some of the lower branches and peered down at him, then skittered around to the other side of the trunk.

"Father Kogan," Harric said. "Wake up." He opened Mudruffle's map to study the spot where the golem had marked it.

"Mh? What'd I miss?"

"You missed me cursing this map."

"Pah. Bet you curse like a baker's wife."

"Like a frontier bastard, you mean. Your ears would have peeled off."

"What's the matter?"

"I can't read the annotation. It says, *Red Tree,* which is clear enough. But then it either says, *steer clear,* in Iberg, or *path clear.*"

Kogan blinked at him. He leaned out to one side to see around Snapper and Idgit, then his eyes followed the tree skyward. "A beauty." He yawned, revealing a mouthful of brown, cracked teeth. "Let's camp."

Harric frowned. "Heard a yoab bellow while you slept."

"Back near Will and Caris?"

Harric nodded, and let out a breath to expel some of his worry. "It's got me thinking the things might be coming down from the heights already."

Kogan mashed the sleep from his eyes with a meaty paw. "How do you know it was a yoab? Ever heard one?"

"Last month. My ears are still ringing."

"Har!" Kogan squinted up at the canopy, where a few beams of sunlight slanted down and splashed across the trunks. "Late afternoon, looks like. As good a time as any to camp."

"All right. But let's move off toward the river."

Harric found a low gap in the rubble at either side of the yoab run and urged Snapper up and over, onto the spongy moss and ferns of the forest floor. Idgit followed, with Brolli wobbling, asleep, in his saddle. Picking his way between huge rotting logs, Harric headed toward a flat-topped hillock half a bowshot from the yoab run. The site would be close enough to the run that they'd be able to see Willard and Caris when they passed, but hopefully not so close that a passing yoab would notice them.

"Wake the chimpey?" Kogan said, when they dismounted atop the hillock. Brolli still sagged in his saddle, a blanket draped over his head.

"Let him sleep."

A rumble and crash resounded above the valley.

Kogan cocked his head.

"Thunder?" said Harric.

"Sounds like. Maybe a rockslide."

Harric tried to find the direction of the sound, but the echoes of the valley made it impossible, and the canopy obscured their view. The rumbling continued, overlaid with a new rushing sound of wind. The canopy above them sighed and swayed.

"Storm coming." Harric hobbled Snapper and Idgit, then pulled the canvas tarp from his saddlebag. "I'll string up some shelter. If it rains, at least we'll have a dry spot to sleep."

Kogan grunted. "Rain, storm. It comes or it don't come, and we can do nothing about it. But hungry is different: I can do something for hungry." As Harric stretched and staked out the canvas, Kogan knelt at Geraldine's tail, took her udder in his hands, and drank from a teat. Harric's stomach rumbled. Kogan grinned from behind the auroch. White milk flecked his beard. "Take a teat. Plenty of room."

"Thanks. I'll have strong bread."

Harric tacked up the tarp, then retrieved half a cake of the figgy, hazelnutty delight from his saddle. He took it to a hummock with a view of the yoab run, where he sat and ate and listened to the wind in the canopy. The sigh of it seemed to fill the valley. It didn't take much to imagine it as the sound of a waterfall, or the rapids of the river at Gallows Ferry, or to consider how like the wind those waters sound.

A slant of sunlight found its way down to the moss beside Harric. The beam danced about crazily, pushed about by the wind above. He squinted up in the beam to see a cloud of moths high up where the light pierced the canopy. They flittered down from the gap as if dislodged by the wind from their roosts, and the sunlight lit them up like fireflies. At first it seemed they stayed strictly in the slant of light, as if they wanted to stay warm as they descended. Then he realized the moths were everywhere in the canopy, and everywhere dropping to find less windy havens.

He stood, head tilted back to look straight up. The canopy snowed moths. The air teemed with them. He thought of his small frog friend, and how it would fill its little belly with them tonight.

"Father, come see," he said, without looking away from the scene above. "It's snowing moths."

Kogan let out a wet belch from the back end of Geraldine. "Huh?"

Harric stuck out his hand to let the creatures land, but as a few fluttered by, he realized they weren't moths at all. Capturing one in his hand, he held it between two fingers before his eyes. "Oh, no…" It felt like ice water pooled in his stomach.

It hadn't been thunder. It hadn't been a rock slide. And the wind wasn't a storm.

"Fire-cone seeds." Kogan exhaled roughly. "Gods take that mad-brained son of a jack. He did it. He burned the whole thing."

Harric's mind went to Caris. Caris loved Abellia as a mother. Abellia had taken Caris in when she first ran away to the frontier. She'd taken care of her until Caris could strike out on her own in search of a knight mentor. There would be nothing he could do to comfort Caris for this loss, but he wanted to be with her. If he couldn't offer comfort, at least he brought companionship, if she wanted it.

But maybe Abellia had survived. She was a white witch, after all. Her whole purpose there was to prevent fire in the fire-cones. Surely she could keep herself safe from fire. But if so, why wouldn't she have prevented the fire in the first place?

A whisper of doubt set his mind winging back through his last moments with her. Her depression. Her misery. The last image he had of her, as she watched them leave, and the sense that she'd been eager to be left alone. Was this the reason why? Had she been planning her own pyre? A pyre that could burn half the northlands?

In the next moment, he was running, taking leaping steps down the far side of the hill toward the river.

"Where you going?" Kogan said. "Can't help her now!"

"The fire! If there's a fire marching down that hill—" He didn't bother finishing the thought. Kogan knew enough to know if a wildfire came down into their valley, they'd be on the run from more than just Sir Bannus. And if Caris and Willard didn't get clear of it before it marched down into the valley, they'd be cut off. Either way, they had to know if a fire chased them.

"Watch for Willard!" Harric called back, and he ran.

Caris found Willard asleep where she had left him, strapped to the tree like a man sentenced to burn at the stake. As she walked into the clearing, she kept an eye on Molly, who lifted her head at her approach and glared with murder in her eyes. Nothing new there. If Molly moved, it would be a problem. She could glare all she wanted.

Holly and Rag were picketed well out of sight, and downwind.

Stopping several paces short of the sleeping Willard, Caris examined him. Gods leave him, he hardly looked like himself any more. He looked like a burly young knight wearing Willard's mustachio. It gave her a queasy feeling to see the transformation. It was happening so fast. At least he wasn't blue any longer, and the rage seemed to have passed.

Willard stirred. Or it seemed he did, but she hadn't seen him move. After a moment of reflection, she realized that she'd felt it with her horse-touched senses, and cautiously opened the senses to him. She had no idea how much he might feel—or how much of the god she might encounter—so she hovered her senses gently around his consciousness, waiting to feel the stirring again.

And there it was. A flitting presence, just beneath the surface of his consciousness, as a fish basking at the surface of a pond.

Surprised, she focused her attention more keenly, and the instant she did, the presence vanished below. She blinked, scanning for it again, in vain.

But in those short moments, she sensed very clearly that it was a being separate from Willard, though not Krato. Krato's presence was violent and fiery and unsubtle. What she'd sensed was elusive and… intelligent? No. Not intelligent. Cunning. A fierce cunning, like a fox. She smiled, suddenly giddy and swelling with excitement for no reason. The feeling passed as abruptly as it came, leaving her in a shock of recognition: she'd felt the same lightheaded gleefulness when Willard's hex had struck in Gallows Ferry. That night, it had overwhelmed her mind with such irresistible force that she barely knew what was happening. What she'd just felt was the merest echo of it, but there was no mistaking it.

Gods leave me, did I just see his night-hex? The notion came unbidden, as a recognition, not a thought. But the sensation had coincided with touching Willard's mind and sensing the other presence there. Holding her breath, she brushed the surface of his consciousness again, searching, but whatever it was—the hex-presence—had not returned.

Withdrawing her mind, she stared down at Willard in awe. Kogan had called the hex jealous. Yes. That was part of its cunning. A jealous, cunning *thing* inside him. But could a hex be a living thing?

The roar of a distant yoab sent a flurry of little brown birds up from concealment in the undergrowth into the branches of the larger trees. The sun had dropped behind the west ridge. Behind Abellia's tower.

The question of the hex-presence would wait. Darkness would not.

Crouching at the hobbles, she unlocked one of the chains and let it fall slack at Willard's side. His neckerchief now hung limply from his neck; he'd gnawed through it, and the sweat-rag now lay in a sodden wad between his feet. Beside it, Willard-Krato had etched letters in the dirt with the heel of his boot.

A knot of dread squeezed her gut as she read it.

BROOD HORE.

Her lip curled. He referred to the brood halls of the West Isle. The dungeons where women were bred until they died.

But *HORE?*

The knot of dread dissolved as her chest began to shake with quiet laughter.

Oh, gods leave her. *HORE.*

The Mad God couldn't spell.

She clapped a hand over her mouth. Tears wet her eyes, and the crude letters blurred.

After wiping her eyes, she read it again to be sure. Her own learning in letters had come in secret from her brother's tutor, so she didn't have as much as Harric. But she could read most tracts she encountered, and she certainly knew her father's pet name for her, *whore.* Willard couldn't write it, because in ten lifetimes he'd never learned more than the letters of his name.

HORE! She laughed. Kogan was right: the gods were unworthy of regard.

"What's so funny, girl?" Willard's head rose. He looked at her groggily, and a wry smile twisted his mustachio. "Your mentor look that foolish?"

"No sir, I'm sorry."

"Well, something's damned funny."

Turning away, she stepped to the side where he couldn't see her, and fiddled with his manacle. "Let me get your chains off."

"Don't be a fool. How do you know I'm back to myself?"

Caris stopped. She stepped back to look at him, feeling sheepish. "I guess because Krato wouldn't stop me from releasing him?"

Willard gave a grim nod. "Next time, don't be so hasty. Now what's that, you say?" He jerked his chin toward the words in the dirt.

She hid her mouth with her hand again. "Nothing. A threat."

His eyebrows rose. "Something funny about it?"

"A little. You wouldn't think so." She wiped it out with her foot and set back to work on the manacle. "Are you feeling well? Can you still feel your arms?"

Willard watched her a moment as if he'd pursue the question, but then he looked away. "More or less. I can feel the edge of the rage growing with each new draught. Soon, in the next days, I must begin the meditations that control it."

"The Blue Meditations."

"The same." A weariness tugged at the edges of his eyes as he craned his head back to look into her face. "And you?"

She smiled, the laughter threatening again.

"Guess it couldn't be too bad, then." He snorted. "Then let me up before Sir Bannus finds us."

Removing the manacles was easier than putting them on. Soon Willard paced about, massaging the blood back into his hands. As soon as he packed the chains back in Molly's bags, he mounted and followed Caris to the stony stream bed where she'd left Rag and Holly. Trailing Holly behind Rag, she followed Willard down the stream bed to the river, and up the shallows toward the bend where Harric and the others had gone.

Sir Bannus did not appear, and they crossed the river without incident. As Rag splashed out of the shallows and up another stony draw, thunder rolled down the mountain behind her. She turned Rag to look, expecting to see a storm cloud rising over the ridge.

What she saw pulled the air from her lungs.

High in the sky above Abellia's ridge, a column of smoke as big as a mountain mushroomed upward like it would pierce the dome of the sky. From its widening eaves fell sheets and curtains of glittering seeds.

Caris's mouth moved mutely. It felt as if something had knocked the wind out of her. She was unable to look away, unable to draw breath.

Tears filled her eyes. Sucking a shuddering breath, she screamed, "No! No! Abellia!" She watched, desperate to find her eyes had deceived her, that it was just an ordinary forest fire. But she could not mistake the sun-bright blaze of burning resin. The white-hot conflagration seared her vision. Ordinary trees along the ridge burst into orange flames in a wave moving outward, like ripples in a pond.

Caris's vision blurred. She spurred Rag back into the river.

"Girl!" Willard shouted. "There's nothing we can do."

"We have to help her!" She looked over her shoulder at him, and through her tears saw that pain and sympathy lined his face.

"I'm sorry," he said. "We cannot help her. Only her stone can protect her."

Caris slumped over her saddle, and Rag stopped in the middle of the stream. A silent sob racked her. Willard was right. There could be no rescue. Even if they could reach Abellia without meeting Sir Bannus, there would be nothing they could do. The damage was done. Either she lived, or she did not. And Sir Bannus was coming. Caris wondered if any of the fort men had escaped, if Farley had survived.

Numbly, she looked up again at the rising cloud above the burning ridge. She'd never seen anything so enormous. So mighty. So final. An abyss had opened beneath her heart, and the roar started between her ears. She turned Rag to follow Willard, and fled into the mare's senses.

Panting, Harric leaned against a boulder at the edge of the forest and looked across the valley to the burning ridge. "Gods leave you, Mistress Abellia," he murmured. It was the closest thing to a prayer any Arkendian had. Abellia's people would have blessed her in the name of one of a dozen Bright Mother divinities, none of which Harric could even name.

Far to the south, a column of smoke rose in the shape of a mushroom. It rose so high above the ridge that it would have towered over most clouds. Glittering sheets of white seeds wafted from under its outstretched cap to drift like ribbons in the winds. Some fell in the valley like snow. Most seemed to have been carried so high that Harric strained to see them at all.

A rustling and a crackling of twigs came from the forest behind. Harric turned to see Brolli knuckle-loping toward him through the brush.

When he saw the fire and the smoke, Brolli sucked a short breath. There was nothing to say. They both stared, stunned by the scale of the disaster.

"This is my fault," Brolli said, his voice scarcely above a whisper.

"It's Sir Bannus's fault," said Harric. "Don't take this on yourself."

The ridge blazed with orange fire. Harric guessed that because the wind was racing west up the side of the valley that sparks hadn't jumped east down the cliffs into the trees of the valley. But flames spread north along the rocky spine of the ridge, and he imagined it also spread down the west side, which had a gentler slope and no barren cliffs to act as a barrier.

"How could he set fire to them?" Brolli said. "Will this not burn him, too?"

Harric nodded. "I would have thought so. Maybe something went wrong. Maybe he didn't expect this to happen."

Brolli frowned. "Or maybe he does it on purpose, to destroy the queen's resin. Maybe he comes down the valley now to find us."

Harric sighed. "Well, he either burned up in the fire, he fled back toward the pass, or he's coming down the trail into the valley."

Studying the sunlit cliffs below the fire, Harric pointed to a landmark from Mudruffle's map: a tall, sun-bleached snag that Mudruffle had noted as *White Fang*. "Remember that snag? The White Fang?"

Brolli nodded. "Yes. I think I see it."

"The trail from the ridge passes right below that. If Bannus or his men pass there, this sun will shine off them like a beacon."

Brolli nodded.

Holding his breath, Harric watched the forest around the snag. If Bannus got to this side of the ridge before the fire ignited, he would descend that trail. And if he got down the trail to the river before Caris and Willard could cross the river and disappear on the opposite shore...

"If you have any Kwendi prayers," he said, "this would be a good time for them."

Brolli grunted. "I say the prayer already." The lenses of his daylids reflected fire and expanding plumes of smoke. "This fire is not also a problem?"

"Not as long as this westerly wind holds. Fires go where the wind blows them, and so far the wind is blowing west and away from us. Cliffs tend to stop fires, too. Back in Gallows Ferry, we never had to worry because of the cliffs."

"Are those cliffs big enough?" Brolli nodded to the rocky spine of the ridge.

"Won't stop Bannus, that's for sure."

Together they watched the trees around the white snag as the fire raged on the ridge above. The green mantle of trees rippled with the wind rising from the valley, but no shard of sun flashed from spear tips, no spark of colored banners flickered between trees. Harric let out a sigh and climbed to the top of the boulder, making himself as comfortable there as one could while watching for a monster.

"I say another prayer for winds," Brolli said. "But I wonder how do you ask I pray? I think Arkendians deny the help of gods."

Harric smiled. "We do. But as long as you're praying—not me—I commit no heresy."

Brolli's head cocked to the side. Harric glanced his way as the Kwendi flipped his daylids up on his forehead and peered back with thoughtful golden eyes. "This is why Willard mistrusts you, yes? You do not follow rules of your people. I wonder why so?"

Harric puffed a little laugh from his nose. He let his eyes travel up and down the trail below the snag. After a while, he said, "Part of the reason is that I was born a bastard, Brolli. In Arkendia, that means something. Actually, to a bastard, it means everything. I realized at a young age that the moment people saw my bastard belt, they thought themselves my better. Grownups, especially, treated me like a slave, even though the Queen had freed bastards before I was born. That's when I learned their rules were like weapons, and if I followed their rules it would hurt me and diminished my chances of living."

"Why wear the belt, then, if you're freed of it? Surely that lowers your chances."

Harric's jaw clenched. "I am not ashamed to be a bastard. I'm proud. I won't take it off for anyone, and I'll prove myself *their* better."

Brolli grinned his feral grin. "Pride. Stubbornness. I understand that. But Willard does not call you bastard, yet you resist his rules."

Harric took a deep breath, thinking. He was a bit reflexive in his resistance to the old knight. He didn't know why. Yet it wasn't all reflex. "It isn't that I think his rules are there to hurt me. It's just that…" He frowned. "I guess what I'm trying to say is that it's second nature for me to question rules. It's innate for me to examine rules and dodge or find alternatives to bad ones."

"You mean you dodge rules that are not pleasant to you."

Harric heard the teasing humor in the Kwendi's tone, but he returned his gaze seriously. "No. Those who follow no rules but their own end up hanged. As a general rule, I try to avoid hanging. But rules used to keep me down…those I avoid and undermine when I can."

Brolli chuckled. "You and Willard have what my people call the difference in philosophy. Yours is the bastard survival philosophy, yes?"

Harric joined Brolli in laughing. "That'll be the title for the ballad of my life."

Together they watched the sun set beyond the western ridge and turn the smoke plumes from the fire to a vivid orange and red. When the sun sank too low to light any but the highest tops of the billows, the fires glowed gold against their undersides.

Brolli let out a long sigh. "We will see no gleams on spear tips now. But this is good. Maybe the fire keeps Bannus from this valley."

A muffled *crack* like a horse stepping on a thick branch sounded in the forest back toward the camp.

Brolli's eyes widened. He whispered, "Or maybe not."

Together they ran across the moss as quietly as they could, hunched low behind seedling logs as they picked way back to their camp. Brolli glided along beside Harric in his rolling, knuckle-walking lope.

"It has to be Willard and Caris," Harric said. "If it were Bannus, there would be horns."

"Are you sure?"

"No. And come to think of it, yoab don't sound horns either. So we might be cobbed."

Brolli flashed a wry smile. "If it is Bannus, we are fools who run to their deaths."

"Only one way to find out," Harric said, starting up the hill.

"It will be good to die with you."

If the bright sun loves you, why worry about the moons?
—Arkendian proverb

33

Fractured

Harric scrambled to the top of the hillock, Brolli at his side, and peered through the deepening dusk.

"It is our friends," Brolli said. He pointed, and Harric saw them in the deepening shadows, picking their way toward them through the fallen trees. Halfway down this side of the hillock, Father Kogan waved a blanket over his head.

A glimpse of Caris's profile sent a rush of mixed emotions through Harric, and chief among them was relief.

But in the last few days, she'd changed. Unmistakably. And unnaturally. It scared him. It seemed the ring had gone from creating an artificial love that she could fight and resist to making physical impulses she didn't seem to have as much control over. The sensuous looks, the outright invitations… It was possible she'd given up resisting, but she was too disciplined and tough for that to be likely. Something must have changed in the ring.

And you haven't even asked Fink about it yet, you cob. Serves you right for forgetting.

A little knife of panic pricked his gut as he realized he hadn't set up his bedroll in the camp, and if he didn't set it up soon, she'd arrange another private grotto for them. She'd be angry, cob it. But there was nothing else to do. With luck, he could get Willard to say it was his idea.

Hurrying to his saddlebags, he grabbed his bedroll just as Willard approached the top of the hillock. Harric flopped the roll beneath the canvas tarp he'd already strung for the old knight, and laid out Willard's blankets as well.

Willard crested the hill and, with only a stiff nod to Harric, took Molly to the far side of their camp. Father Kogan joined Willard, and the two spoke about the wildfire. Harric trotted to the edge of the hillock to locate Caris, and saw her dismounting below and lifting her saddlebags from Rag, as if to make her camp there.

Harric joined her, and as she hung Rag's saddlebags over a log, he removed the saddle for her. As he rounded the mare to lay the saddle beside the bags, he stopped dead in his tracks. There beside her stood Mudruffle—indeed, the little golem walked up to meet Harric and performed a stiff little bow.

"Greetings, Squire Harric," Mudruffle honked. "I did not wish to alarm your priest friend in the dark, so I asked that Squire Caris stop short of the camp where he rests. Willard also thought this best."

"Mudruffle!" More feeling came out in the exclamation than Harric had thought he held for the creature. He glanced at Caris, who watched with a sad smile.

"He woke up when we got on the yoab run," she said. "We thought it would be best if he didn't make an appearance till daylight. I'll tell Father Kogan tonight, so he's prepared for it tomorrow."

"Good idea." Harric set the saddle on a hummock of moss and took the golem's cold clay hand in his. "I am so glad to see you well. Your map has been very useful."

"Thank you, Squire Harric," Mudruffle said. "I am most pleased to be with you again. I only wish it were under different circumstances."

Harric's gladness evaporated. "Yes, I am so sorry for your loss. We all are."

"Mistress Abellia was a true servant."

"I'm sure it is a terrible loss for your moon, as well."

Mudruffle bowed again. "Indeed, and more, Squire Harric. Her stone was lost in the fire." His hat tilted backward so the polished black eyes glinted in the shadow of the rim. Behind Mudruffle, Caris looked up and put a hand over her mouth. "As I am the custodian of that stone, I share a bond with it, and I know it is certainly destroyed."

"I'm so sorry," Harric said. "I hope it isn't indelicate of me to ask, but does this mean you must return to your moon?"

"I will remain with you," said Mudruffle. "I will stay with you to complete Abellia's last wish, to guide you to the Kwendi lands."

"Boy! Girl!" Willard called from the top of the hillock.

"His armor," Caris said, with the briefest of glances at Harric. She started up the hillside, and Harric followed.

As they reached the crest and entered the camp, Harric laid a hand on her arm, and she paused. "I'm sorry about Abellia," he said.

She said nothing. She closed her eyes and turned to join the others, but then her hand found his, and she paused. When her eyes found his, the change in her expression was startling. Lips slightly parted, her nostrils flared, and her heavy-lidded gaze slid down his front.

He dropped her hand as if oblivious. "Let's help Willard with that armor," he said, loud enough to catch the attention of the men.

She grabbed his hand and pulled him back to her. She looked as if she was going to pull him in for a kiss, but then her brow furrowed as if she were questioning what she was doing. Then she sucked a quick breath and parted her lips, and the heavy eyes found his. "Willard can wait."

"Harric," Brolli said. "Come tell Willard what we see."

"Come with me," Harric said, extricating his hand again. "You'll want to hear this."

Caris was smoldering as they joined the others, but Harric continued to act oblivious. He could think of nothing else to do, except reasoning with her, but the look on her face just then hadn't seemed terribly reasonable. Brolli said, "It seem Bannus did not follow in the valley. We watched the trail for an hour in the sunlight."

"Maybe he didn't get on our side of the fire," Harric said. He felt Caris step up beside him, too close. Her hand found the small of his back and massaged the tight bands of muscle there. "He must have misjudged how hot it would be and got stuck on the other side."

"May his immortal bones burn to cinders," Kogan growled. "A more godly beast never poisoned the land."

Willard grunted. "This is good news," he said, but his eyes had found Caris, and a shadow of concern seemed to move behind his eyes. His gaze flicked to Harric, who widened his eyes in a silent plea. If Willard understood his meaning, however, he showed no sign of it.

"Brolli, can you watch that ridge this evening as we sleep?" Willard said. "If anyone comes down at night, they'll need torches, and will be plain to see."

"I have slept enough. Yes," Brolli said.

"Girl, I want you to stay with Holly and the others at the bottom of the hill. I'll hobble Molly here, and Harric will mind my armor."

Willard's voice seemed to wake something in Caris. She stiffened and glanced at her mentor, her eyes clear. "Yes, sir," she said, and left them to return to her horse.

Harric let out a long breath and acknowledged Willard with a look. Willard returned the look with a hard, accusing stare.

"I wasn't taking advantage of her," Harric said. "It should be obvious I'm trying to avoid her. She has me running in circles."

The knight's jaw muscles bulged as he ground his teeth, and a violet light flickered in his eyes. His fists balled tightly, creaking the leather in his armor, then relaxed. Squinting at him in the failing light, Harric realized the Blood was changing Willard rapidly—had changed him. The angles of his face behind the mustachio were hard and lean, the sag of fat below his jaw completely gone.

"The ring," Willard said, turning to Brolli. "It's forcing her on him." The way he said *him* seemed to indicate the problem wasn't the ring forcing her, but that the person it forced her on was Harric. Wonderful. With immortal muscle came immortal attitude.

Brolli looked at Willard expectantly, as if waiting for a point.

Willard growled. "What's that infernal thing up to, ambassador?"

"I do not know what you mean," Brolli replied. "The ring is as it has been."

"It is not the same," Harric said. "Its spell is changing. It's making her...physical."

Brolli's huge teeth flashed in a feral—yet somehow apologetic—grin. He shrugged. "I do not know this magic. It was my task to deliver it as a gift to your Lone Queen. But such a spell fits the idea for the ring, to hurry a wedding."

Harric bit back on snapping at the Kwendi. How could they think the Lone Queen would want a slave ring? Who the Black Moon advised them on this? He forced himself to count to five and take a deep breath. "It's getting worse." After glancing at Caris, to be sure she'd moved out of hearing, he turned again to Willard. "I've set up a canvas to keep the dew off, and laid my bedroll there. Hopefully Caris won't try to move it away with hers…"

Willard nodded, but his eyes remained hard. "I'll tell her I want to keep an eye on you here tonight."

"Thank you." Harric gave them both a small bow, and turned out of camp in the opposite direction from Caris. "I need to leave camp for a while. Be alone. I won't go far."

Willard grasped Harric's arm as he passed, halting him in his tracks. A hood of shadow cloaked the old knight's face, but his breath came hot and stinking of ragleaf. "What I do is for the girl, boy. This changes nothing between us. To me, you are nothing more than a faithless, sneaking jack, and the second that ring is off, I will jettison you like useless luggage. Then you may serve your own vanity until you hang."

Harric's anger still smoldered in his breast; now it flared as if fanned with a bellows.

He looked down at Willard's hand, still gripping his arm, then met the old knight's glare. After a moment, Willard released him, and Harric stepped away. "I too am only here as long as Caris wears the ring. I do not stay to serve you. And you of all people should be careful to speak of vanity, Sir Willard. While you struggle to discern yours from duty to our queen, I'll serve with clear and even conscience."

Harric did not wait for the reply, and turned on his heel and left.

As he descended the hillock, boot heels sinking deep in the moss with each long downhill stride, his heart fluttered with excitement. *What have I done?* He pushed a hand through his hair and found himself smiling uncontrollably. *I stopped worrying about Willard's approval, that's what I've done.* And his heart felt larger and freer.

In spite of all the death and grimness around them, the smile spread into a grin. Here was something to celebrate. Something a long time coming.

Funny how childhood heroes must be abandoned before one could fly on one's own.

Let none judge the Unseen foul who never saw its glory.
Its light lays bare all follies, reveals all secrets, exposes the Seen
and its vanity.

—Verses credited to Unseen apologist, Lupistano Uscelana

Of Nudity & Round Bellies

Harric headed north, keeping his back to the hillock, until the profusion of trees concealed him from view from the camp. Then he bent his path west toward the river for a look at the burning ridge. The wildfire drew him the way campfires draw eyes. And it seemed somehow appropriate to keep vigil on the blaze that had likely taken Abellia's life.

Without star or moonlight beneath the canopy, darkness descended more quickly than he'd expected, and though he could see shards of moonlit valley between the trees ahead, he could barely see the logs and shrubs in between. He was still a good bowshot from the forest edge when he stepped in a moss-covered hole and twisted his ankle. Hopping to a stop, he sat in the moss and let the pain in his ankle subside.

"Stupid," he scolded himself; he hadn't brought a candle, but he had a built-in window to an illuminated world of spirit in his moon-blasted forehead.

Closing his eyes, he concentrated on his oculus. The aperture appeared: a teardrop-shaped window at the top of his mind, backlit with the glow of the spirit world beyond. He pushed his consciousness toward it until it widened enough for him to peer out into the Unseen.

The air glowed with thousands upon thousands of luminous spirit strands arising from the luxuriant forest life around him. It was so dense with spirit filaments large and small that he could only see the lay of the forest floor for perhaps thirty paces before it was obscured in the general glow.

"Wondering when you'd think of that," came a raspy voice beside him.

Harric jumped and snapped his head to the side to see Fink grinning like a graven grotesque. "Moons, Fink. You have to scare the piss out of me?"

"Have to? No." Fink's grin widened. "Did you really piss yourself?"

Harric let out a short puff of exasperation. "It's an expression." He peered closer at Fink. "Is something different about you?" It seemed the glowing curtains of strands in the air made it like Fink was looking at Harric through the bent glass of a bottle. But on closer inspection, it wasn't the strands. It looked like Fink had actually...swelled?

"Fink, did you get stung by a bee?"

Fink raised his bald eyebrows. "You don't like the new cherubic me?" He held his arms to the side as if to better display himself. Bony Fink was definitely gone. The ribs that used to jut out like pickets had submerged behind a thick pad of flesh—the same with his knobby knees and elbows—and his concave belly was now the swollen gut of a drowned corpse.

"Moons, Fink, you have two chins! Can you even fly anymore?"

"Sure, in the Unseen I can. In the Seen?" He shrugged round shoulders and waved it off. "I could probably glide, in a pinch. But isn't it great?"

"If you say so. What happened?"

"What happened? You and Sir Ragleaf left a banquet so big that I had to leave some to the vultures, that's what happened. When was the last time I ate like that? I can't even remember. Never." Fink sat back in the moss and let the globose belly sag between his knees. "Be sure to thank him for me. I could get used to this."

Harric felt his stomach turning over. He swallowed and tried to think of something to say, but his mind was a blank.

"Do we have to talk about this again?" Fink scowled. "Those men came to kill you. Most of them would have tortured you. They were not good people. Good eating? Sure. Bound for what you'd call the Good Place in the afterlife? No. This is one of the tasks of a moon spirit, kid: we clean up the unworthy souls. You magicless cobs might call it part of 'nature' if your heads weren't so far up your magicless—"

"Okay, I get it, Fink."

"I don't think you do. For instance, you think Caris has a good soul?"

"Of course."

"Me too. Grade A. And what's going to happen to her soul when her body dies?"

Harric shifted his feet. "Well, our souls go to the Hall of the Ancestors in the Bright Mother—"

"Excuse me, but how many of Caris's strands do you see going to the Bright Mother?"

Harric's brows pinched together. "Well, none, but—"

"But nothing. What does that mean?"

"The fact her strands don't go to the Bright Mother? Well, I guess I can conclude that the Bright Mother…doesn't draw spirit."

Fink steepled his talons before him. "Good," he said, as if encouraging an especially dim student. "The Bright Mother doesn't draw souls. And which moon does?"

Harric shook his head. "But if good souls don't go to the Bright Mother when they die…" Fink leaned forward in exaggerated anticipation. Harric looked up through his oculus at his own strands rising up to the Unseen Moon, then looked back to Fink. "You're saying—"

"I'm not *saying* anything. I can neither confirm nor deny any of this in the presence of a mortal. I simply point out what should be obvious to one granted an oculus."

Harric took a deep breath. "You seem to *imply* that, after death, the good souls go to the Unseen Moon."

"And the vile souls?"

"Well, you eat them?" Harric shook his head again, as if trying to dislodge confusion from his skull. "But it sounds like you're saying—"

"Not saying—"

"—that for the good souls there *is* no Bright Hall of Ancestors, only the Black Moon's hell, while the vile souls are simply eaten."

Fink's expression did not change, but he froze, so the grin seemed suddenly forced. "Who said anything about a hell?"

Harric ran a hand through his hair. He could not imagine a Bright

Hall of Ancestors in the Black Moon. "Um, everyone, I guess."

"This the same everyone who says there's a Hall of Happy Grammas in the Bright Moon?"

"Yes."

"Thought so." Fink stared at Harric for several heartbeats, then abruptly slapped his soul-stuffed belly and waved it all off. "The good news is that these black-hearted bastards won't bother anyone anymore."

"Oh? Sure they were all bastards?"

Fink slyly cocked of his head and looked at Harric through narrowed eyes. "Tell you what," he said softly. "You don't call my moon 'hell,' and I won't use 'bastard' to mean black-hearted knave."

Harric laughed in spite of himself. "Sorry about that. I just… You just collapsed my view of the afterlife. It's a little disturbing."

"You'll get over it. New initiates generally do, unless they go insane. But you don't seem like the type to go mad. Oh, wait," Fink said, eyes wide with feigned surprise. "Your mom was mad as a resin fire."

"Funny."

Fink coughed out a raspy laugh. "So what happened back in that valley? You have a murder party? Didn't see any of your friends among the dishes."

Harric's smile faded. "We were lucky." Harric told Fink about the day's events: the battle, the departure into the valley. Finally, he told the imp about the changes in Caris. When he finished, he sighed and ran his hand through his hair. "It's getting worse, Fink."

"What was your first clue? The resin-fire crater on top of the mountain, or the angry blue giant riding down the other side?"

"I'm talking about Caris, Fink. But wait—you mean Bannus? Down the other side? Are you sure?"

"Am I sure? Was I stuffing myself with the souls of his men when he tore by with his pants on fire? Hard to miss that."

Harric let out a long breath. "That's our first stroke of luck in a long time. No way he's getting past that fire to follow us. Not soon, anyway."

"He's not so smart, lighting the place up like that. Looks like brains don't come with immortal blood. Made me rush my meal, too."

"You didn't see Abellia's soul?"

Fink shook his head, the grin falling from his face. "Sorry, kid. She wasn't with the others. But then, she'd avoid that sort anyway."

Looking back toward the hillock, Harric said, "What I meant about it getting worse was that the ring's getting worse, Fink. You said we could take a look at it in the Unseen. That maybe you'd be able to understand how it works and maybe get it off her? Can we do that tonight?"

Fink shrugged his bony shoulders. "Let's go see." He motioned for Harric to lead the way back to camp. "Maybe I can, maybe I can't. Won't know till we look."

Harric led them back, and soon spotted yellow lantern light at the base of the hillock where Caris had picketed the horses. When they drew within a stone's throw of the lantern light, he signaled a stop. Using his regular eyes in the Seen, he could see her sword flash and hear it *thunk!* in a log as she drilled herself in sword strokes.

"She's still up." Harric chewed his lip. "At least she's distracted with training."

"What about the Kwendi?" Fink asked. "We need to worry about him showing up?"

"Brolli is supposed to be out watching the ridge with Mudruffle. They probably won't be back unless he has something to report, and since it sounds like Bannus won't be coming down the mountain, we're probably fine. Still, we should be careful."

"All right," said Fink. "Let's have a look at her. Take off all your clothes."

Harric stopped and looked at Fink out of the side of his eye. "What? Why?"

Fink's grin became a leer, an expression distinguished only by the sheer multitudes of teeth visible and a quirk to one side. "It takes effort to hold yourself in the Unseen, as you know. It takes even more effort to hold your clothes and gear in the Unseen. That's one reason you didn't last too long on that ledge the other night. If you'd stripped naked first, you might have made it all the way across without passing out. Of course, then your friends would've wondered why the moons you were naked when you finally showed up, so pick your poison. Tonight, I'll hold you in the Unseen because I want you to be able to concentrate on other things, so I ask you to leave the unnecessary gear behind."

Harric blinked.

"You'll get used to it. Might even like it."

Harric grimaced. "Fink, if Caris finds me walking around in my undershorts one more time, she will think me mad."

"Unless she likes it."

"Enough, Fink."

"You think this is an elaborate ruse for me to get you naked?"

"Well, you *could* translate my clothes, right? You've done it before when helping me."

"Sure I could. But if I do it for very long, you'll start seeing my ribs again, and I'll get hungry." Fink spread a very toothy grin. "Real hungry. Got souls for me? Didn't think so. So strip down and get used to it. We're going to be naked together a lot."

"Lucky me. But I'm drawing the line at shorts. Not only will I not spy on her naked, but I don't need splinters when I sit, or to freeze off my unmentionables."

The newly plump Fink bobbed his head. "All right, you can keep your under-the-pants."

"They're called shorts."

Fink waited, apparently bored, as Harric undressed.

"Nice bum," said Fink, when Harric had removed his breeches.

"Fink, look—"

"Kidding. I'm kidding! But it's exactly what you expected me to say."

"I'm not really in the mood for the jokes tonight."

Harric bundled his boots and clothes and set them beside a tree, but, after a thorn in the heel, put his socks back on. "I can't walk around barefoot, Fink. Can you manage socks and short pants?"

Fink raised a hairless eyebrow and shrugged. "Socks and short pants it is. Some spirit walkers make little slippers for the Unseen. You should do that. Now show me how you enter the Unseen."

Harric glanced toward the lantern light, uneasy. "Maybe you should just go and then tell me what you saw? It would look really bad to be seen like this."

"Seen? You won't be seen as long as I'm helping you. Anyway, you have a lot to learn, kid, so you need to come and see and listen."

Harric sighed. "All right. Just don't get think of getting a laugh by popping me back into the Seen half-naked."

Show me your horse and I will tell you what you are.

—Sad Bella, horse-touched stabler of the Two Colts Inn

35

The Unseen Seen

Harric closed his eyes and looked out through his oculus. The imp sat before him, watching. "Show me how you enter the Unseen."

Taking a deep breath, Harric relaxed his oculus and pushed his mind up as if he would climb through. He surprised himself by slipping halfway out, and the spirit world suddenly surrounded him in three dimensions. Luminous smoke-blue filaments filled the air, wavering like river weeds in some sleepy pool of the Arkend. He had the impression of having risen halfway through a hole in the bottom of the river. The burden of supporting himself there, however, fell upon him so hard that it nearly shoved him back through.

"Fink—!" He gasped as his temples gave a sudden throb of pain.

The weight and headache vanished.

"That better?" said Fink.

"Thanks."

"Tomorrow night, we'll work on your stamina."

"Can't wait."

Fink motioned for him to follow, and pushed ahead through the curtains of strands as if they were nothing more than smoke. The Unseen altered sound, as well. The sounds of Caris's sword work were slightly higher, but also amplified, like sound in fog. As Harric followed Fink, he parted the strands and moved through them easily, but they tugged as if he passed through heavy cobwebs.

Fink clambered to the top of a tall seedling log about thirty paces from Caris's camp and beckoned to Harric. When Harric eased himself up beside him, he crouched and surveyed the area she'd chosen to camp. She'd hobbled the horses at the base of the hillock. Her bedroll lay beside the horses, but instead of sleeping, she'd hung a lantern on a branch while she ran through her parries and strokes and thrusts against a rotten stump.

The sight of her spirit stole Harric's breath. She seemed nothing short of a goddess come to earth. Bright, broad strands bloomed from her like rays of sun in deep water. Numerous as the hairs on her head, these upward-flowing ribbons leapt from her like wings. She seemed a being of fire and air and light, and the majesty of it dazzled his mind.

To his eye, she moved as if in a dream. Sound dimmed. Her sword arced around her in lazy sweeps. Her strands rippled upward, drawing his attention to the open well of the moon above, deep and black. The moon swallowed all strands of all life around him, so it seemed he looked up into the vortex of a whirlpool in the sky. It even felt that he himself rose to meet its embrace.

Intruding whispers nattered at the edge of awareness. Irritatingly urgent, they persisted until Fink's horrific proboscis appeared upside down before Harric's face. "Wake up, dreamer boy!" Fink croaked.

Harric staggered and felt himself step into open air. He fell about a fathom from the log onto soft ground, but he hit it hard enough to knock the wind from him. He mouthed the air, trying to shout, but before he regained his wind, Fink clapped a hand over his mouth and sat on his chest, newly fat legs straddling him. "Easy, Harric. You fell into the Siren Sleep."

Harric struggled to pull the imp's hand from his mouth, but Fink's grip was iron.

"Harric?" Caris called softly from somewhere nearby.

Harric froze. He remembered he'd been watching her.

"Souls, kid, you'll give us away."

Pieces of the situation fell back in place in Harric's mind: Fink was not hurting him; Caris was near. He needed to be quiet.

The imp's milky eyes narrowed. "You going to shout when I take my hand off?" Harric shook his head. "Good." Fink removed his hand and clambered off Harric.

THE JACK OF RUIN

Harric looked around. His mind gradually cleared of the dream fog, and he recognized where he was. The last thing he remembered was studying Caris's soul and... A lump of dread sank in his stomach. "Damn," he muttered. "I did it again."

Fink nodded. "See what I mean by lots to learn? Looking too long at a soul is just like looking at the moon. Mortal eyes can't handle it. Now, if you chose to be a Spirit Reader, I'd train you in ways to look and avoid the Sleep, but that's a whole other school of mastery. As a Spirit Walker, you have to avoid looking even at your own soul. Understand?"

Harric swallowed, then nodded.

"In your defense," Fink whispered, "she's a real beauty. I mean, don't get me wrong—on the inside. Her heart. Her personality."

"Shut up, Fink."

"Just don't look too long or they say you'll go blind."

"Did I *say* shut up, or just think it?"

"Harric?" Caris's voice drifted to them, eerily warped by the spirit fog. She'd climbed to the back of a seedling log at the edge of her camp, sword over shoulder, a hand on her hip in an show of impatience. After staring in their direction for a few heartbeats, she hopped back down and returned to her training.

"Let's try it again," said Fink.

They crept back to the top of their log and together peered through the curtains of filaments. This time, Harric made sure not to look at the whole, and to look aside when he felt it beginning to hypnotize.

"Where's Sir Blue Balls?" Fink whispered. "Shouldn't he be giving her pointers?"

Harric snorted. "He wouldn't be alone with her at night. Wouldn't be proper."

"What a guy." Fink nodded to Caris. "So. See the ring?"

Harric nodded. Now that his mind was clear, he could see among her strands a huge band of burning white silver, like a barrel hoop as tall as a man. The hoop plunged into her chest and out her back, enwrapping great sheaves of her strands and pulling them to one side like a reaper gathered standing wheat before the sickle. Her strands did not seem impeded or harmed by the hoop—there was, in fact, no sickle to be seen—but it was a clear manifestation of the wedding ring.

Revulsion and anger gripped his guts.

"It's a weave called an Opening." Fink's bubble eyes fixed on Caris. "Mother Doom, how do they do that?"

"Do what? You said it was Unseen magic. Can't you do that weave?"

Fink's proboscis wrinkled like a dried-out black tuber. "Of course I can do the weaving. What am I? A novice? What nobody knows is how they put weavings in that impossible metal. Imagine how useful it would be if we knew how to store weaves like that, kid. We could put enough Web Strand in a bit of witch-silver for you to run around in the Unseen with all your clothes and fancy boots, too—just stored in the metal, waiting for a time you need it."

"And there's an Opening in this one. What's it an opening for?"

Fink shook his head. "It isn't an opening *for* something—it's an opening *of* something. Seventh Order love weave." He tore out another clump of moss. "The little chimpies are working Seventh Order Unseen weaves into their witch-silver, and they don't even have Unseen servants to help them."

Harric turned his eyes to Caris and watched as she danced, flowed, drove at the rotten stump. The hoop seemed to burn and smoke as if alight with spiritual fire.

"But what's an Opening *do?*"

If Fink heard him, he ignored the question. Harric was about to repeat it when the imp let out a low hiss. "Let's start with what it isn't. It isn't a Compulsion. A Compulsion is a mind-control weave, and it's focused on the head—the eyes in particular. A Compulsion's only a Third Order weave, but what it lacks in the finesse of a higher-order weave, it makes up in raw, bludgeoning power. It makes the target kind of stupid—mindlessly devoted, all doe-eyed and mush, laughing too loud at jokes and all that. Be glad this isn't a Compulsion. An Opening leaves their head alone and goes straight for the heart, where it does just what it sounds like—opens the heart toward the ring giver and creates trust and emotional bond. So an Opening affects the head, too, but only indirectly."

"And you can do one, or take one off?"

"An Opening? Sure. It's complicated, but I can set one up. And I could take one off if I'd made it myself. But since this one isn't my work..." Fink frowned in the direction of Caris. "I'd have to know how it was applied, or I could hurt her. Plus, I don't have any idea how they put it in that witch-silver, so I don't know how to get it out, either."

Harric felt his heart sink. "Hold on, Caris," he murmured, too faintly for her to hear him. "Can't help tonight, but soon."

One of his strands had drifted over to Caris. Then he realized there were several already streaming toward her and tangled in the Opening. A sick feeling rose in his stomach. "It's using my strands. That's how it fixates her on me. By forcing my strands on her."

Fink nodded. "The Opening needs an object. You're the object. But don't look all horrified, kid. It won't hurt your strands. It just strengthens and directs her attention to you."

"Anything I can do to remove them?"

"If you could, they'd just go back there."

Harric's eyes traveled the path of his strands from his own column of brilliant soul-ribbons to the Opening in her chest. The diversion of his strands was very subtle. He hadn't noticed before because they didn't go directly from him to the Opening, but first rose toward the moon with the rest of his strands, and then arced across among Caris's strands and into the Opening. As he watched, another of his strands peeled away from the rest and looped into the Opening.

Harric flinched. "I just lost another one."

"Relax, kid. They're always attaching and detaching depending on how close you are."

"So, if I run away, more of my strands will detach?"

Fink looked at him. "Is this a hypothetical question, or are you about to go 'wild man of the wilderness' on me?"

Harric sucked a deep breath and closed his eyes. *I am being an ass.* Caris's entire heart was ensnared in an Opening weave, and he was panicked about a few of his own strands. He forced his breathing to calm, so his heart would stop racing. "Sorry."

Fink leered—a grin out of one side of his needled mouth. "You're welcome."

Caris had paused her training. Breathing heavily, she swabbed her face with a sleeve and peered in the direction of Harric and Fink. Her shirt clung to her, damp with sweat. The Opening, bright and large as Harric himself, gradually ceased to smolder and waver. As he watched, the spirit fire flickered and died, leaving a white band amidst the smoke-blue glow of her strands.

Fink extended a taloned finger toward Caris, his brow wrinkling. "What's that behind her shoulders? How many rings does she have on?"

After a moment, Harric saw what Fink was looking at. In the bright welter of her spirit strands lurked another hoop. It was harder to see because it was smaller, and a translucent gray, like the ghost of a hoop. The longer he studied, the more it resolved, and he saw it as a thin hoop plunging between her shoulder blades and the back of her head.

Dread breathed a chill into Harric's guts. "It goes in her head, Fink."

Fink nodded. "Probably a Mind Compulsion. It must be dull like that because it's not active yet." He cringed as if imagining it active. "But kid, I thought you said it was just one ring. There's more?"

"An Arkendian wedding ring is actually three rings interwoven to make one."

Fink met his gaze, eyes narrowed. "Molded together, or separate?"

"Like a chain, only three links long. When you line them up and put your finger through, they fit together like one ring."

Fink turned his attention back to the gray rings. "Clever little chimpies."

"It's Arkendian design. The Kwendi copied it."

"You want me to say your people are clever?"

"Just clarifying."

"Clever little Arkendians."

"But that means there must be a third one," Harric said. A new weight sank in his gut.

"Lucky for you, I don't see... Oh," said Fink.

"Don't say 'oh.' What do you mean, 'oh'?"

"I should have known," Fink muttered. "Look below her belt. This one's active."

Harric looked, and the weight in his stomach became a driving fist. He held his breath until he finally spied the third hoop. Like the Opening, it glowed white-hot and plunged between her breasts and out her back. But instead of looping upward and soaring above her like the Opening, it looped downward, re-entering beneath the belt in front and back.

"You aren't going to like this, kid."

"I can already guess." Harric's stomach turned. "It's another Compulsion."

Fink nodded. "Yes, but this one's a *Body* Compulsion. Simple, strong. Not mind control, but…real hard to resist that for long. Dangerous."

Harric's gaze snapped to Fink. "How? What do yo mean?"

"If horse girl jumps on you, kid, she'll break you in half."

"This isn't funny, Fink. And the issue isn't what might happen to me. For her sake, I can't go near her anymore."

"Souls, kid. Why not just kiss her? Make it a lot easier for both of you."

Harric sighed. "Why is it I feel you can see into the worst parts of my heart?"

"So you admit I'm right."

"No, I don't, because you're wrong: I did kiss her, once, and it was a disaster."

"What? When?"

Harric grimaced. "Not proud of it, Fink. It just happened, last night when you were escorting my mother to her cairn. You know, the victory and everything, we were feeling good, and it just happened. Then, this morning, I found her trying to chop off the finger with the ring on it."

Fink made a gasp or coughing sound. "She doesn't do anything by halves, does she?"

"No. And it scared me, Fink. If things got out of control with us…" Harric shook his head. "No. I've got to do right by her, even if it isn't easy or comfortable or satisfying."

Fink shuffled his feet. "You can't keep away from her, kid. It's a Body Compulsion. She'll come for you. Hard."

"I don't care what it is. It doesn't compel *me*. So if it's forcing her, then I can't be near her. It's that simple. I have to leave her. I have to strike out on my own."

I know a spell to dull my enemies' blades
and turn arrows to ash in the air.
I know a spell to sunder fetters
and one to close a wound.
But none can tell me a spell
to undo the harm done by a lie.

— From "Lessons from a Red Adept," found in imperial library at Samis.

36

Truth & Illusion

Harric turned away from Fink, his mind spinning through the implications of what he'd just said.

"*Leave?*" The word came out of Fink like a squeak. His white eyes bugged like Harric had jabbed him in his ample gut, and he started wringing his hands. "Kid. She'll chase you. Doubled with an Opening, I doubt she can resist it, and if you resist her advances, it could go really bad."

"You think I should just let it happen for her own good? What the Black Moon are you talking about? If I go along with this horse shit, you don't think *that* would go bad? She'd hate herself and me as well!" He stared into Fink's inscrutable face with a growing sense of disbelief. "And don't tell me you forgot that if she chases me I can hide in the cobbing Unseen."

"Calm down, kid. She's going to hear you."

In fact, Caris had stopped her training and was peering through the darkness in their direction.

Seething, Harric hopped down behind the seedling log, where they'd be less likely to be overheard, and tugged Fink after him. The imp landed before him, blinking in surprise. Barely able to keep his voice a whisper, Harric leaned into Fink. "Are you so worried you might lose your place at the Sir Willard banquet of souls that you'd advise me to stay, even if it endangers her? Even if it endangers me? Well, cob your cobbing snacks, Fink. It'd be better we both starve. I'm serious about this."

Fink spread his hands in a gesture of surrender. "Kid, calm down." The black tongue flicked nervously over his teeth. "Are you telling me you've decided to leave her? Leave the others?" His bald black head shook as if he were anticipating a denial.

Harric frowned. He hadn't wanted to admit it to himself, but since the incident in the stable when Caris nearly amputated her finger to prevent the ring from compromising her integrity, and since that same day when Willard nearly murdered him, his heart had been steadily — if secretly — turning toward departure. Now that he had confirmation the ring had even worse in store for Caris, it seemed the clearest possible decision. "Yeah," he said, running his hand through his hair. "I guess I am. It's time to leave. Just like you predicted."

Fink let out what seemed a very forced laugh. He gestured with his hands as if trying to physically calm Harric. "Look, kid. Naturally, you're emotional about this. And, just as naturally, we'll do whatever you want about it. But I'm thinking of what's in your best interest here. This 'knight's man' act with Sir Ragleaf puts you in the best possible position to help your queen, which is your primary concern, right? Sir Blue Balls is right in the center of Her Majesty's concerns with the Kwendi ambassador." The black tongue licked at the corners of his mouth. "That means if you stay with him, you'll be one of the first outsiders to see the Kwendi lands."

"Yes, all of that is true," said Harric, "and none of it matters."

"Seems a little extreme, don't you think?"

"You don't know Caris, Fink. She is very disciplined. So far, miraculously, she has resisted the weaves in the ring. She can be damned proud of herself for that. But now it's starting to overpower even her. And when that third band wakes, what then?" Shuddering, he turned away. "It's inevitable, Fink: I have to strike out on my own."

"What would you do, kid? You have no connections, nothing."

He turned back to face the imp. "I don't know yet. I'll figure something out. I guess I'd want to scout ahead of Caris and make sure their way is clear, maybe clear the way if I can."

Fink's scowl twisted upward on one side. He glanced around like he was worried someone might overhear.

"You predicted this would happen someday. You said I'd need to break away, that these friends wouldn't understand my new life. What happened to the 'price of heroes' and all that?"

Fink's grin seemed frozen in place. Taloned hands rubbed and twisted together. "*Someday*, kid, I said *some*day. But now? Seems you ought to stay with Sir Ragleaf as long as you possibly can. That's where you can do the most good."

Harric let out a breath through his nose. Something in the imp's manner rang false. He sensed an urgency beneath the facade of nonchalance that took him back to the moment in Abellia's tower when he'd overheard her in conference with some mighty presence. They too had expressed an urgent need, some agenda above and beyond their desire to help Willard and Brolli. Details of the memory eluded him again, but now he studied the imp's features in an effort to understand the connection. It had to be something about the Kwendi magic. Fink had as much as told him the Unseen wanted the secret to the Kwendi magic, and the Bright Mother must want it, too.

"And what do you want from it, Fink?" he said, watching the imp closely.

Fink grinned and patted his ample belly. "I wouldn't mind staying at the banquet of souls until we absolutely have to leave."

He'd had evaded the question. Fine. Harric would make him sweat. "I'm sorry, Fink, but that's exactly what I am saying. Time's up. We absolutely have to leave."

Fink's grin froze again. The white eyes shifted to the side, then he ducked his head as if conceding a point. "All right. Look, I can't remove the ring, kid, but give me a couple days, and I'll see if there is something I could do to disable one of these weaves."

Harric's eyebrows climbed his forehead. "Are you saying you forgot you could do this until now that your food supply was threatened?"

"Kid." There was a plea for understanding in the way Fink said the word, but his eyes also darted to the sides like he was cornered. "It isn't like that."

"Then tell me what it *is* like."

"It's like I didn't want to ask my sisters for help, that's what it's like."

Harric felt his blood turn to ice water. He'd only met Fink's sisters once, and the encounter still troubled his dreams. "Oh. They might be able to do it?"

Fink grimaced. "Maybe. But only for a price."

Harric heart shriveled a little. "Ah."

"I could ask Missy to take a look. She's good at this sort of thing. Maybe she could disable a weave without hurting Caris."

"So. The price. What kind of price?"

Fink's grin went flat. "The price is souls, kid. Or a claim on yours. Only one kind of coin in the Unseen."

Harric did his best to push down his horror, to hide the panic this brought, but his heart was hammering so hard that he guessed Fink could hear it. He held the imp's gaze a moment longer, then turned to watch Caris while this news sank in.

She had stopped her drill and laid the practice sword against a log. Lifting her water pail in both hands, she drank deeply, snorting between gulps. A tiny rivulet spilled down her neck to soak the front of her shirt. Moons, he did not want to leave her. He wanted to help her. He wanted to help her protect the Queen.

Leaving made no sense. But it made the only sense.

The real prospect of leaving her suddenly clarified something for him: he couldn't leave her with the lies he'd told, which already created a gulf between them. If he left without first telling her the truth, the gulf would be permanent.

As Caris drank, the hoops of the ring's two active weaves ceased to smolder and waver, and the spirit fire vanished, leaving bright white bands looping in and out of her spirit. Peering closer, he saw the third—lurking, gray, and faint—like an ember in ash awaiting a wind to bring it alive.

"What do you say, kid?" Unease had raised the imp's voice an octave. Almost to a whine. "Give me tomorrow and the next day? That's two more days and two more nights after tonight. Should be enough time for me to find Missy."

When Harric didn't answer, Fink followed his gaze to the dormant Compulsion. "Missy will know what to do. Maybe she could do something to keep that weave dormant."

"What do you think that third hoop is waiting for?"

"Souls if I know, kid. Comic timing?"

"Thanks. You're a big help." Harric let out a long breath. "All right, go ahead and ask Missy. But"—he held up a finger and met Fink's blank eyes—"only ask her opinion. No touching Caris until we say."

Fink cringed and wrung his hands. "Heh, sure. I…can make her promise. But promises have a price, too." His head swiveled about as if he suspected his sisters might be near enough to hear.

"One more condition." Harric nodded to Caris. "If that third hoop—the Mind Compulsion—comes into play before Missy comes, the deal's off, and we leave."

Fink bobbed his head. "Sure. Of course."

"All right, go ahead. No harm there."

Caris set down the pail and wiped her mouth with the back of her hand. After a long stare in the direction of the hillock camp, she grabbed her sword and launched into another series of sweeps and thrusts— the Cane, Tailor's Yard, Widower—each executed with precision and speed. Moons, she was good. And again, the hoops of the ring ignited with spirit fire.

Harric rose his head, suddenly more alert. "That fire on the rings. When she resists the weavings—either by fleeing into the horse world, or by fleeing into her training—the weaves start to burn…" His words trailed off as his mind caught up.

"Probably when she's angry with you, too. Give her a reason to hate your guts and those weaves will light up like bonfires."

"Fink, that could be the key. Are you saying the two active weaves— the Opening and the Body Compulsion—won't work if I do something she hates?"

"The weaves would still work, kid—you should know that by now, since you daily do something she hates—but when you do something she hates, her natural emotions are temporarily strong enough to counter the artificial ones from the ring."

Harric's mouth opened and closed. If anger and determination strained the weaves, maybe all he had to do was tell her the truth, and the weaves would bend to the breaking point—or, at the very least, fuel her resistance. Something solidified in Harric. He stepped back from the log and turned to retrieve his clothes. "Come on, Fink. It's time I come clean. Kill two birds with one stone."

Fink crow-hopped after him, peering up at Harric with wide eyes. "Harric. Partner? What are you thinking? You aren't going to tell her about me, are you? Kid?"

"I think I have to."

"Heh. That'll go over like a plague boil on a bride."

"That makes you the plague boil, doesn't it?"

"Maybe you want me to come with you? I'll smile real nice."

Harric stopped. "Fink, I've thought about this. Even if Sir Bannus ambushes us before dawn and kills us all, I still have to do this." A little bubble of panic rose in Harric's middle as he realized that if he was going to die, he wanted to die with everything clear between him and Caris.

"She could take it bad, kid. She could rat you out. Then what?"

"Have you not been listening? Sir Bannus is in the valley. We could be dead before she has a chance to rat me out."

"Will you stop with the whole 'Bannus is going to kill us so nothing matters'? You'll be in the Unseen."

"Not if he catches us during the daylight."

"And if he doeesn't kill you and you leave her, then you lose all that staying with you offers. No look at the Kwendi lands. No reward from the Queen. No recognition. Nothing."

Harric nodded. "I have to take that chance. She'll hate me, but we want that anyway."

Fink tugged at his enormous nose. "If you get her mad enough to burn out the rings, there'll be nothing urging her to keep your secret. As long as the rings function, they keep her conflicted and quiet. Once they're gone, she'll share your secret."

"Probably." Harric shrugged and started for Caris. "But it changes nothing. I have to do what's right, then worry about the rest."

"Not yet, you don't." Fink stopped him and held out a hand, palm up. "Not until you give me my nexus stone. I've seen your people take witch-stones from Ibergs. You give it to me and I'll keep it safe."

Harric deposited the glassy black stone in Fink's waiting hand, and suddenly the risk of the whole thing felt a lot more real than it had a moment before.

Better to be slapped by truth than kissed by flattery.
—Attributed to Queen Chasia

37

Open Eyes

Harric donned his clothes and circled Caris's horse camp until he could approach from the direction of Willard's camp. By the time he'd completed the circuit, Caris had stopped her training and put her sword away, and when he joined her, she had leaned over the water bucket to splash her face and swab her neck with a rag. Idgit noticed him first and swiveled her ears in his direction, nickering.

Caris's eyes found him and she stood, nostrils flaring.

"Hey," he said. Water dripped from her chin down the curve of her collarbones. She reached back with both hands to tie her hair behind her head, which stretched and pulled at her clinging shirt. He forced his eyes away, but her gaze feasted on him like she'd missed him for weeks.

"Are you sleeping down here?" she asked.

His heart fell. Had the ring already made her forget Willard's instructions that he sleep separately? "No, Willard wants me to sleep on the hill." He gave her a lopsided smile. "Plus, remember how you said you'd kill me if I did?"

She clamped her jaw shut, and her face darkened. "You said you loved me," she said, voice suddenly ragged. "Was that a lie?"

The pain in her voice stabbed at him and hardened his resolve.

"No, that wasn't a lie," he said. "I do love you...but there are other things I haven't been truthful about, and...well, this might be our last night alive, and I came down here un-say those things and tell you the truth before it's too late. You probably aren't going to like what I have to say, but hear me out."

Caris's eyes went cold. He could practically see the word *truth* resonating in her, calling up a part of her uninfluenced by the ring. "You lied to me?" she said, voice low but hard as stone. "About what?"

He closed his eyes and took a deep breath. He could practically hear his mother shouting a dozen dodges to extract himself from this reckless mistake—everything from a line that would turn it all into an ill-conceived jest, like, *I lied when I said I'd never touched magic, because I've touched you, and you're magic,* to self-pitying lines like, *I lied when I said I'd be fine if you never love me, because I won't.* The words flooded to his lips, ready to spill forth in an easy con.

But he clenched his teeth and swallowed back a lifetime of trickster training.

"I didn't lie when I said I loved you." His voice came out faint and trembling, which made him angry. Louder, he said, "I meant that, but you should know a couple things before you give that too much weight. Things like my training. My childhood. I never told you the whole truth about that."

"What does your training have to do with love?"

He suppressed a groan. Truth telling was harder than he'd thought it would be, and he was doing it much worse than he'd expected. *It shouldn't be hard—just say it like it is, no creativity required.* So he forced himself to keep talking, groping around for an entrance. "My training makes it hard for me to say this. I sometimes wonder if I might…or even if I can—"

"Gods take it, spit it out!" She rammed her sword in a log. "I swear I'm about to throw you in the river."

"Right. Okay." He took another step back, hands up. "For you to understand, I need to tell you *what* I was trained as—"

"Then cobbing tell me!"

"Promise you won't repeat it to anyone."

"Toss yourself, Harric. I don't make the Rash Promise."

Harric winced. He'd won her apprenticeship with a Rash Promise from Willard, so she had grounds to be wary. But all the same, it was part of his plan to keep her angry—and thus more herself and less influenced by the ring—and that was working. "All right, then I'll simply have to trust you, because nothing else will make sense until you know. It's like this: my mother didn't just train me to be a courtier, Caris. She trained me as a *courtiste*. The courtistes are real. My mother was one—the best, if she's to be believed, which she isn't—and she raised me in their ways."

Caris stared, pursing her brow. He could practically see her mind putting this information together with what she already knew of him and his mad and murderous mother. As she did, the snarl faded and her jaw grew slack.

"This—this is where the sneaking and tricking comes from?" she said.

He nodded. "It's more than a knack or a game for me, Caris. I've spent as many hours picking locks and pockets and hearts and studying exotic powders as you've spent riding and fencing and drilling with your brother."

"You think I'm stupid?" Her cheeks darkened. "Is this another lie? There is no such thing as a male courtiste."

"No, you're not stupid, and you're right about courtistes all being female. But my mother went mad and raised me in exile. She never asked her sister courtistes for permission; she just did it. Said she had visions of my importance among the courtistes one day. And I think she trained me in secret as a way to redeem herself in court." He held his hands palms up before him. "So I am the first male courtiste. Kind of like you'll be one of the Queen's first female knights." He paused, faltering, and smiled weakly. "Wonders and more wonders, right? Chaos Moon must be coming."

As he spoke, a shadow of horror rose steadily in Caris's eyes. He imagined he could see all the rumors of Her Majesty's courtistes—ruthless courtesan spies and assassins—percolating up from all the legends and gossip she'd have heard in her noble family. Tales of deceit and manipulation and betrayals, tales of "good" lords and ladies brought low by wily plots.

She took a step back and looked him up and down, as if struggling to see this new Harric in the man that stood before her.

"Obviously I'm not like her," Harric said. "I'm still the person you know. And I'm not like the courtistes, because I refused her mission to court."

"You rejected *her*," she snapped, suddenly back on her toes. "But you didn't reject her ways. You still sneak, you lie, you trick, you con—you are exactly what she trained you to be."

Each word was true, and each was a stone piled on his heart, and suddenly a voice inside him screamed that this was a mistake, and that it wasn't too late to lie his way out of this blunder. But it *was* too late. He'd made sure it would be too late as a safeguard against just this kind of failure of will.

Caris's hands balled into fists, and she dropped her head to stare at the ground. Her hair fell about her face, concealing her expression, but her voice shook. "That's the lie you wanted to tell me about?"

Harric forced himself to shake his head. "One more," he said, with enormous effort. "The true nature of my training was a lie of omission. The real lie was when I told you I never touched the witch-stone in Gallows Ferry. Because I did."

Her head shot up. "What?" Tears now streaked her face and glued hairs to her cheeks.

"I touched the witch-stone, and…more than that, I have a tryst servant, just like Abellia has Mudruffle, and he's given me insight into that ring—" He rushed the words out, sensing that if she exploded before he could finish, he'd be tempted to leave something out. He had to clear the air between them. And the more he told her, the more tools he gave her to resist the rings. She staggered back, eyes wide and white, but he pushed on. "We have some ideas on how we might make the ring go dormant again, or at least how we could weaken it, but I don't want to do anything without your permission—"

"Are you mad?"

He held his hands up in a calming gesture, but something fundamental, something visceral and animal in her, recoiled like he'd transformed into a spider and spoke in some hissing spider language.

"The Black Moon is unclean!" she said. "Unholy— You—you—"

The utter rejection and revulsion written in her eyes changed everything. In that instant, Harric forgot his purpose and panicked— panicked that the hatred he saw was the sort that would last forever, even after the ring was removed; that he'd gone too far and would lose her if he didn't do something.

"The ring *itself* is Unseen magic, Caris. Abellia and Mudruffle never told you because they probably thought it would scare you. But obviously the Kwendi use the powers of the Unseen freely and don't think it's evil, so why should we?"

She clapped her hands to her ears and fell to her knees, where she began rocking back and forth and groaning.

Cobs. Cobs, cobs!

He ran a hand through his hair and tried not to pace as she escaped into the horses. But his heart had withered like a winter apple. The look she'd given him—like he was some horrible stranger—had stricken him deeply. And in the minutes that he waited for her to recover, his mind scrambled to prepare something to say, and he felt emptier and more alone than ever before.

Her breathing finally calmed, and as she stopped rocking, she opened her eyes and lowered her hands from her ears. "Get away from me, Harric," she said, balling her fists in her lap and staring into the light of the lantern. "I warned you what I'd do if you ever touched magic again. Now get away. And stay away. I won't warn you again."

Harric let out a deep breath. He'd done it. He'd uprooted the lies and replaced them with truth she could use to fuel her fight with the rings. He'd come clean, and she'd banished him from her presence.

Quest accomplished. All hail the victorious hero.

He took one step back from her, but didn't leave yet. Her face twitched and one hand trembled. "I know you made no promise to keep any of this to yourself," he said. "But if you do plan to tell, I ask that you first let me know. Would you? Please?"

Caris could have been carved in stone—the image of some grim and resolute queen—for all the sign she gave him.

Then she was in motion and he stumbled backward in surprise. As he twisted to catch himself with on one hand in the moss, several things happened at once. Rag whinnied, something yanked at a lock of his hair at the side of his head, Willard's bellow shattered the silence of the glade, and steel clashed on steel above Harric.

When he rolled to his feet, eyes wide as full moons, Willard stood between him and Caris, swords locked. The look on Caris's face was nothing short of wild fury as Willard shoved her several paces backward and maintained his position between her and Harric.

"Enough!" Willard roared. "Stand down!"

Bristling, Caris fixed her eyes on Harric as if she might brave Willard's blade to get another shot at Harric.

Harric retreated a step, staring in confusion at the swords, then at the blood on his hand as it came away from an unconscious rub at his scalp where his hair had been yanked.

Blood. It hadn't been a yank, as with a hand. It was a cut, as from a sword.

Caris's sword.

His mouth dropped open as he pieced together what had happened. If he hadn't stumbled in surprise, she'd have beheaded him.

After throwing her sword into the moss, Caris turned and stalked from the clearing, hands shaking. As she passed Rag, who sidled away from her with eyes rolling white with fear, Caris's face twisted. A moment later, she jolted into a run and vanished among the trees, leaving her frightened horse to comfort itself.

Willard turned on Harric, sword still in hand, the burn of violet in his eyes. "What did you try, knave?" He took a step toward Harric. "Did you try to seduce her? Did she have the sense to repel you? I can think of nothing else that would so stir her. She'd have cut your throat if it weren't for your bastard luck."

"No," Harric said, shaking his head numbly. Blood was now trickling down his neck and into his shirt. "I—"

"Don't lie to me, or I'll finish what she started."

Harric closed his mouth and stared after Caris. His heart had fallen into a widening hole in his chest and was pulling everything else after it.

Willard said something about Bannus finishing the job for him on the morrow, anyway, but if not, the next time Harric tried anything like that, Willard would let Caris cut him. Only reason he didn't let her finish it that night was what the rings might have done to her if she'd killed Harric—something about how he'd be banished the second those rings came off. Blah blah.

Then Willard was trudging after Caris, his broad back receding in Caris's wake, and Harric stood still as a statue, his scalp on fire and a trickle of blood on his shoulder. He stayed that way, unmoving, as if he might stop breathing and die and be free of his pain, until a sound beyond the camp alerted him Willard or Caris might be returning, and he forced himself in motion.

He found himself moving away from the camp into darkness. Numbly, he headed in the opposite direction of Brolli's post and Mudruffle's path, vaguely navigating toward a mossy bowl he'd spied earlier, and using his oculus to navigate.

He still could not accept what his memory told him had just happened. He kept raising his fingers to the side of his head, where he found a shallow cut and hair sticky with blood. Caris had tried to kill him. He felt like a foolish piglet stunned by a butcher's mallet, his disbelieving brain unable to grasp the obvious.

So he kept moving. He concentrated only on putting one step after another, searching for the bowl he'd seen, but when his legs tired and he still had not found it, he gave up and slumped against a rotting log in a nest of ferns upon a hillock. He'd scarcely leaned his back against the log when he saw at the foot of the hillock the mossy crater he'd been seeking. It looked as he remembered it, a fuzzy green bowl some three fathoms deep and twice that across. It had probably been a yoab wallow at some distant time. A good place to curl up and die, but he was too miserable to get up again, and a pile of ferns would do just as well.

If only he hadn't stumbled when she struck. He'd have died right there without any knowledge what had happened. And what poetic justice it would have been for Caris to liberate herself by killing the object of her enchantment. But as luck would have it, she'd missed, and left him only with a throbbing cut in his scalp and the clear and terrible image of the moment when it all went wrong.

Cold sweat broke out on his face and chest, and a wave of nausea rose in his stomach.

She'd tried to kill him. Actually *kill* him. It hadn't been a bluff. He had seen in her eyes the same iron determination he'd seen when she'd held a chisel to her own finger—a look of moral certainty born of her truest self, of her deepest values, beyond the influence of the ring.

Which meant she, Caris, fundamentally despised him. She had judged him and tried to execute him as a witch.

Cradling his face in trembling hands, Harric stared into darkness. It was just as Fink had predicted so long ago: if Harric didn't leave her and the others, he'd end up rejected and alone, maybe dead. But by *Caris*? Never from Caris. He'd rejected that notion. Thought he could beat the odds and have it all.

Cob it. Cob it all.

The hollowness in his chest pulled inward, as if it would suck him into its void. Then something inside him cracked and his heart spilled out in silent, racking sobs.

How to ride a Stilty horse:
Step One – Drink two bottles of Arkendian Sherry.
Step Two – Allow yourself to be lashed to the beast's saddle.
Step Three – If still conscious, repeat Step One.
Step Four – If Step Three fails, instruct a squire to
brain you with a stick.

—From "Survival Rules for Kwendi Near Stilty Horses,"
by Second Ambassador Chombi

38

Blood Rite

Caris woke on her back and stared up at the patches of starlight perforating the lattice of the canopy high above. All around her, the black trunks of ancient trees towered like the legs of giant sentinels.

Her dreams had been strangely torturous, so she sought back in her memory for the reason, before they faded.

Courtiste. Magic. Lies.

Harric.

Then came the memory of leaping up to slice Harric's lying throat, and she relived the sensation of her entire body bunching and springing and whipping the sword like an extension of her will.

The memories hit her like a runaway carriage, and she curled up in her blankets, pressing her hands to her ears. Horse-touched confusion roared to life in her skull, and with a groan of dismay, she fled into Rag before it could claim her. Thankfully, the mare's mind was soft and accessible in slumber, and its peaceful senses gradually smothered the roar. It also had the effect of making her doze, but only for a moment or two, and then she was able to piece together what had happened that night.

Harric's words came back to her, along with the vileness of his secret life and lies.

At the end of his speech, she'd been on her knees, fighting against the roaring confusion that had been rising between her ears. It had seemed he was bragging. That he was proud of pollution, and thought she should be too, like a cat laying the gift of a bloody rat on her pillow. At last, the roaring had been too much, and she sought out Rag, but Rag had resisted…

And she'd found Molly instead—violet fire, terrifying and thrilling. *Gods take the monster.*

Closing her eyes again, Caris squeezed handfuls of blanket in her fists and concentrated on Rag's calm. In her mind's eye, she saw again the expression on Harric's face as he explained how he'd lied to her. How he'd touched the witch-stone in Gallows Ferry. How he'd taken it and embraced the power of the Unseen Moon. How he had a servant spirit like Mudruffle—some horrible impit from the Black Moon. How he seemed so proud and almost hopeful in the way he told her, as if he thought she might approve or congratulate him. As he revealed horror after horror, the roar of confusion had begun in her head, and she'd reached out to Rag.

It seemed now that Molly had been lurking right where Rag should have been, and the moment she opened her horse-touched senses to Rag, Molly had pounced. The Phyros had thrust herself into Caris's open mind, and her violet fire had ignited Caris's rage for Harric's treachery like a spark on a fire-cone.

But it wasn't Molly who slashed at Harric. No. It might make her feel better to think that Molly's blind violence had overcome her, that she hadn't known what she was doing, but that would be another lie. She had known exactly what she was doing. Molly's touch had merely freed Caris from doubt and enabled her to act.

She lifted her chin to look square at that fact: the blow had come straight from her heart, and it had felt good. It had felt right.

Kicking off her blankets, she rose and paced, her face flushing hot. *I will not apologize for that. I will not feel guilt for the only pure thing I've done since this cursed ring caged me.* A week ago, she would have crawled back to beg forgiveness of Harric. But now the notion made her sick to her stomach. It had been a moment of freedom and honesty.

She felt like a young filly must feel when she stretched her legs for the first time on a wide field away from her mother.

But that would make Harric *your mother,* said a small part of her mind—some new and strange and somehow wiser part. *The mother that restrains you is* Rag.

The notion made Caris stop in her tracks. She'd always thought of Rag as a *sister*—almost a twin—as a partner in mischief and best friend. But when she tested the thought against her feelings, she sensed the truth of the statement: at some point, Rag had become her *mother.* Rag protected her. She nurtured her. She served as her rock, for Rag calmed Caris's horse-touched confusions and gave her the stability she needed to function in the human world.

Mulling this over, she lit her lantern and hung it on a captured lance.

And if she is your mother, said that new, wiser part, *then it is only natural that you leave her to run your own fields, just as you left your birth mother to seek your fortune as a knight.*

A flicker of fear flashed through her mind. *Leave Rag for Molly?* Leave a lifelong friendship marked by shared history and devotion for an intoxicating violet fire that quelled the ring and bolstered her spirit?

Rag was her soul mate. Her heart. How did one abandon one's heart?

She looked over to where the mare slept, only to find the horse's head up, watching her with big, dark eyes. Caris's heart swelled and tears streamed from her eyes. Hurrying to Rag, she embraced her neck and buried her face in her mane. All the years they'd spent together flashed before her eyes—all the trials Rag had endured, all the miseries she'd suffered with Caris, all the triumphs shared.

"I vow it now," she said, also sending the ideas directly to Rag. "I vow I will never betray you like Willard betrayed Anna. I will never touch the Phyros fire again, and we will be as we have always been. I swear it!"

Rag pulled away, and the openness she'd displayed in sleep drained off as hard walls rose between them. Her distrust smote Caris's like a fist to the gut. But the vow gave Caris a new clarity and focus by drawing the clear boundary between right and wrong, devotion and treachery, that she needed.

Coaxing Rag back into her embrace, Caris stroked her cheeks and murmured soothing sounds. Henceforth, she'd have to be doubly wary of Molly: whenever she felt the ring's influence, she'd have to resist the temptation of touching Molly's fire, and whenever she opened her senses to Rag, she'd have to guard against Molly's ambush.

I can do it. I will do it. I've vowed it.

Caris stayed with Rag until the mare fell back asleep, then she returned to her bedding, packed it up, and stowed it. Willard would be rising soon, and she would need to be ready. Splashing water on her face helped wake her. As did a long drink from a cold waterskin. And since the aches in her shoulders and legs were agreeable ones, she ran through her stretches to get her blood moving. As she finished, she heard Molly's chains rattling in the camp above—not the sound of the Phyros shuffling her hooves, but the continuous clatter that signaled Willard was stowing the hobbles and preparing to ride.

A few minutes later, when Willard and Molly loomed out of the darkness into the circle of her lantern, Caris waited for them in her saddle upon a very sleepy Rag. He gave her a grim nod and led her a mile or so north of their camp, where they found an appropriately sized tree, and Caris chained him to it. He agreed to let her gag him as soon as he'd drunk from the cup, and by the time Krato was raging into the gag, she had her back to him. She mounted Rag and turned her west through the maze of logs, to find the edge of the forest and take her up and down the river valley.

The sounds of his snarls faded behind them, replaced by the steady plod of Rag's hooves in the duff and the chirp of early-rising birds in the undergrowth. The mare had opened to Caris considerably since waking, the result of steady communing on the trail and careful avoidance of Molly. *Just like we used to be.* She kept sending that idea to Rag, and Rag kept tossing her head and flicking her ears back in a coltish way that made Caris laugh. Just like before Molly.

At the edge of the forest, Caris took a deep breath of the open air and looked out over the twilight-gray valley. Some stars still shone in the sky: the Sailor's Eye and the Witch's Thumb.

Abellia's tower still stood against the sky to the south—alone, like a blackened tooth on barren gums—and the sight tore at Caris's heart. All around it lay a wasteland of smoking ash. Not even a stick remained of the fire-cone grove under which it once sheltered. Nothing remained of the thunder spire or the barn and stables. The lightless upper windows, barely visible in the distance, stared like empty eyes, and the only movement was a forlorn ghost of ash stirred up by the wind.

She closed her eyes and sent out an aching wish that Abellia had survived and escaped somehow. That she had eluded Sir Bannus.

Across the valley, the wildfire raged on the ridge, red and orange like a second sunset in the west. Smoke filled the northwest sky in expanding plumes like autumn storm clouds, their underbellies reflecting the angry light. *And it's getting ahead of us*, Caris thought, chewing a fingernail. The same south wind that kept the yoab from catching her scent blew the fire ahead of them, and if it found a way into the river valley before they got ahead of it, they'd be trapped with the fire before and Bannus behind.

She glanced back toward where she'd left Willard, and chewed at her lip.

It would be an hour before his Blood rage passed and she could share her concerns. The speed of the fire was just as important as the direction, maybe more important. But there were no such fires on Moss Isle, or anywhere in the west, so she had no familiarity with them. Harric would know, having grown to manhood in the north.

At the thought of him, a flutter awoke in her chest and bloomed quickly into a throb of longing for him.

No... She groaned. The ring had reawakened.

Old doubts rose in her, feeble fears suddenly given voice, like a clamoring rabble reinvigorated by the speeches of a charlatan:

Harric was only doing what he thought right.

He did it to protect his friends.

He's like Willard taking the Blood and breaking his vow—doing something dishonorable to help them all survive.

If you accept Willard and his Blood magic, why can't you accept Harric's?

She clapped her hands over her ears and crumpled over the cantle of her saddle. Somewhere in the back of the clamor she heard the newer, wiser voice—*her* voice—insisting, *Harric lied, and deserves no mercy*—

Then a wave of nausea racked her and she leaned out in time to throw up on the yoab run.

She couldn't think clearly now. She couldn't *feel* clearly. So she escaped it as she always had, by burying her senses in Rag's steady temperament, and letting the rest slide away.

By the time she reached Willard, the disorientation of the ring's enchantment had passed, but she still felt the steady ache of missing Harric. To numb it, she kept half her attention in Rag.

She found Willard slumped forward and hanging against his chains. The blindfold lay in the dirt with the chewed ends of gag, punctuating Krato's latest message, BLUD TRATR. This time, she felt no amusement rising inside her. Instead, the words conjured the memory of her father, glaring at her in wrathful judgment. *Blood Traitor.* These were the very words he'd use if he could see her now: a noble lady of their Cobalt House aiding the Abominator, aiding the Queen against the return of the Old Ones.

"What's it say?" said Willard. The old knight's head rose, gray eyes streaked with violet.

Her lip curled as she told him and smudged the words out with her boot soles.

He grunted and let himself hang against the chains, as if he were exhausted. "They don't call him the Mad God for nothing."

Caris unbolted the manacles, bundled them together, and lugged them to Molly. As Caris struggled to open the flap to the saddlebags with one hand and keep the chains together in the other, Molly struck. The Phyros's head moved so quickly, and her jaw bit so fiercely at Caris's neck and shoulder, that Caris had no chance to dodge or escape once caught.

In a spasm of paralysis, Caris dropped the chains, and her body jerked uncontrollably. She tried to cry out, tried to make any sound, but the pain was so great that she could only gape and mouth the air, unwilling to move lest the movement make the pain unbearable. The blood tooth had punched below her left collarbone, above her heart. Blood and drool, red and purple, poured from the wound and ran down her front.

Rag screamed.

Somewhere, Willard shouted, and Molly gave Caris a tremendous shake. The blood tooth plunged deeper, and an agony of fire coursed through Caris's every nerve and vessel until it seemed her skull and spine would erupt and her heart explode in flame.

Trust a day at evening
A weapon when tried
Water once crossed
And a friend when dead.

—Arkendian proverb

39

Dream Cache

Harric dreamed he stood in his old chambers at the top of the inn in Gallows Ferry. All his things were there, just as he remembered them, but the place was unusually cold. Dead ash lay in the fireplace, and the candleholders hosted no candles. The only light was a sickly blue flame in a clay lamp on the dining table.

"So that went well," said his mother from behind him.

He let out a long sigh and turned around to see her reclining on the threadbare couch she'd brought with her from court twenty years before.

"I miss this place," he said. "It's just as I remember it."

"Admit it. You miss me too."

"No nightmare is complete without you. And you're still in the same gown you lived and slept in for the last months of your life. It even has that lovely urine smell. Can't you even wash it for my dreams?"

"Darling boy."

"Get out of my head, Mother. Go back to your rest."

She laughed, and the white makeup on her cheeks cracked like plaster on some horrible jester's mask. "There is no rest in that pile of rocks. You were cruel to send me there. But now it seems you will join me and you'll see for yourself. Will you? It would make my eternity."

"Will I what?"

"Will you kill yourself for me? Or die of a broken heart for that oversized nag?" She laughed and clapped her hands in delight. "You know I left instructions with Mother Ganner to bury you with me. We'll have such times together. I have much to teach you."

Harric gave a halfhearted shrug. He turned to the front window, looking for solace in a vista of the river and the scablands, but boiling gray fog buried it all. That irritated him. The river was something eternal, something that would be there when he was gone, and he knew in the dream that a last look at it would ground him in the eternal. Instead, gray fog poured over the windowsills in sluggish falls, and began to fill the room.

Can one die of a dream? Could I leap from the window into the river, or let the fog smother me?

"Of course," said his mother, as though she could read his thoughts. "But it matters not how it is done. You are to join me. I have seen it."

The fog rose to his knees, squeezing and chilling like mud and holding him where he stood. He made no effort to resist it, and watched it rise. There seemed no point in resisting. Either it would kill him or it wouldn't.

"You told that horse dullard the truth. Thought it would free your soul." She tilted her head back and closed her eyes, as if she were enjoying the scent of roses in a garden.

"*Every lack-wit owns the truth,*" Harric murmured. "*Only I control a lie.*"

Her eyes widened. "You *did* listen to my lessons. How it warms your mother's heart to hear it. But you ignored my wisdom, and the cow tried to kill you." She sniffed and turned her head away from him. "Without me, all your foolish dreams have failed."

The fog sent tendrils up his chest and wrapped his arms in cold restraint. When they reached his mouth and nose, he knew it would suffocate him. And he knew his mother was right. His dreams *had* failed. And without Caris, the rest had ceased to matter. Perhaps it had been Caris's regard he was fighting for all along, not the Queen's.

He made no resistance as the fog enveloped his head filled his lungs like wet wool. Darkness swam before his eyes, and his mother's laughter dimmed.

But death in sleep eluded him and he woke in the nest of ferns atop the hillock, the ache of his loss returning with crushing force.

Almost reflexively, he opened his oculus and looked up at the canopy. Brilliant blues exploded in the leaves and limbs, but that sight—once beautiful to him, a miracle—struck him as joyless as the fog in his dream. On some level, it offended his heart that the Unseen should continue on, so bright and boisterous, in the face of his emptiness and loss.

The sound of Brolli's voice broke the stillness. The Kwendi had said something in the harsh tongue of his people. A curse, perhaps. It sounded like he was down in the bowl of the yoab wallow.

Harric froze against the log. He did not want company. If he didn't move, the Kwendi wouldn't see him, and would pass on by. Brolli was probably hunting for an elk or something for Willard to feed Molly, and would be no more interested in speaking with Harric than Harric was with him. Looking through a gap in the ferns, he saw the Kwendi standing before a low rectangular door in the middle of the mossy bowl below.

Just leave. Harric closed his oculus and tried to sleep, but could not.

Brolli barked his peculiar laugh, and Harric opened his eyes to see him stooping before the door. The hard lines of the door's edges stuck out, harsh and foreign, against the soft curves of the mossy floor as Brolli hauled something from inside the opening—a pack or large bag. Then the door was gone, and only Brolli and the pack remained. Brolli shouldered the pack—which included a bandolier of hurling globes—and headed back toward camp.

Harric stared after him. A day before, such a sight would have set his heart jumping with excitement. Now it seemed he had no heart to excite. Just an aching hole.

So he has a magic closet. Who cobbing cares?

Harric stood and started plodding back toward camp. If he couldn't sleep now, he might as well walk back and see if by the time he got back, he could sleep. As his blood began moving, it woke his sluggish body and mind. He knew what he'd seen was a display of incredible magic. He knew it implied the Kwendi were capable of feats much greater than simply exploding hurling globes. He knew there must be many secrets like this the Brolli kept from them.

He knew he should care.

But he didn't.

Walking, too, seemed pointless, so he stopped. All he wanted was to curl in a ball and never get up. He hadn't felt so empty and lost in… ever. And he did not want to go back to camp.

"Fink?" he said. "You there?"

Nothing.

He had no idea if he could "call" the imp across the Web of Souls just by speaking normally, but it was worth a try. "Come on, Fink. I…" He swallowed. He had to pull himself together. Digging deep in his memory, he dredged up the words Fink had put in his dreams before Harric had even known Fink existed—the words of his summoning.

"*Nebecci, Bellana, Tryst.*"

Strands of spirit dashed sideways in a brilliant blue flash before Harric's oculus. Then a sound like that of a heavy pillow swatting the moss erupted behind Harric.

"Souls, kid!" Fink squeaked. "A little warning? You have to yank me from the Web?"

Harric turned to see him sprawled on his face like a netted bat. "Have to? No."

Fink spat moss. "Ah. Funny. Turnabout's fair play. We're even."

"Thanks for coming."

"Not like I had a choice. That summoning isn't exactly a request, kid. More like a siege hook."

"Is there a different one I should know?"

"Nebecci, *Tasta*, Tryst. I can answer that at my leisure." Fink stood, dusting his leathery skin. "So what's the emergency? No, let me guess. Your little truth picnic wasn't all honey and roses." As he finished dusting himself, he finally looked up at Harric and froze. "Shit, kid. You all right?"

"Wasn't the best conversation I've ever had."

"Serves you right, telling the truth like that." Fink flashed a needled grin. "Kidding. Truth is always the best policy. I think you may recall me saying that from the start."

The image of Caris's instant of judgment flashed before Harric's mind, and he found himself staring, reliving the iron certainty in her eyes.

Fink snapped his fingers in front of his face.

Harric barely flinched. "Feels like I carved my own heart out and kicked it down a hole." Unconsciously, he raised a hand to his blood-crusted hair, and Fink's eyes widened. "Yeah, she cut me, Fink. Think she would've killed me if I hadn't stumbled."

"*Kid.*"

Harric swallowed a rising lump in his throat and nodded. A foolish heat was rising in his eyes. "Yeah. But it's all right. I'm okay. I don't want to talk about it."

Fink let out a whistling hiss through his teeth. "You wish you hadn't told her?"

Harric sucked in a long breath and let it out slowly. "I don't know."

"Well, you *did* tell her," Fink said, in a reasonable tone that irritated more than mockery, "so that's what you have to work with. And just because it didn't go the way you hoped, doesn't mean it still wasn't the best way to play it. You both got a lot of years ahead of you, and when news gets out of all the great deeds you're going to do, she'll reconsider her hasty judgment. She'll realize she was just scared, and young, and wasn't ready, see? You have to look at it in terms of the long game."

Harric closed his eyes for a couple heartbeats and willed the imp to shut up.

"Plus, kid, now you're *free*. Free to focus on what matters: the Unseen. Right? Right?"

"I don't... Not now, Fink."

Fink's face hardened and his entire body grew still. "Oh, gee, I'm sorry, kid. Did I interrupt your display of moaning and sighing? You're probably wondering how I could be so insensitive. Well, let me remind you that it was you who called me, and now that I'm here, I'm not leaving."

"This is none of your business."

"Then why the White Moon did you call me? So I could stroke your head and tell you it'll be all right?" He snorted. "You probably didn't notice, but I tried the soft touch, and a lot of good that did. So now I'll talk straight. The soul goes on, kid, and you better snap out of your pity vortex or you aren't going to last another day."

"Fink..."

"Don't *Fink* me, kid. You don't *get* to give up. You don't get to give up because you're part of a partnership now, and we have a deal. You have a responsibility to me. And don't think I don't know how this love-broke drill goes, because I had a master, Filia, that was either in love or broken by love all the time, and you know what she was worth when she was broken? Nothing. Worse than nothing, because she still took up space and food that someone with a spine could have eaten." He shook his head several times. "I was a slave then, kid, and had to listen to her moan, but I'm a partner now. Equals, remember? So I'm telling you to get up off your lonely ass and abide by our pact. It's survival time."

Harric closed his eyes and shook his head. "I… Fink. I don't even know what you're talking about."

"Oh, you know. You just stopped caring—that there's an immortal blue giant burning forests to find you. And he's going to find you. He has more dogs than his dogs have fleas, and enough metal-skinned men on ill-tempered horses to find ten of you."

Something like worry for Caris stirred in Harric. "You think he's going to catch us? We have a map and he doesn't."

"He has dogs. Once he has your trail, who needs a map?"

"Then Willard will face him."

Fink snorted. "I've seen Sir Mustache. He looks like Bannus's little brother."

"He's drinking the Blood, now, Fink." Harric said it like the fact should shock, though Fink knew nothing of Willard's oaths or history. "Willard is growing. Every day he's bigger."

"All little brothers grow, but never fast enough," Fink said with a bitter sneer, shaking his head. "Our only hope is that he finds you after the sun's gone down, so you can hide in the Unseen. So I have one night and one night exactly to teach you how to last longer than a minute in the Unseen, or I'm going to lose my partner."

Fink's arm snaked out to rap a knuckle on Harric's forehead.

"Hey. Stop."

Fink rapped him harder, his eyes angry. "I'm not joking. Get up. All this girlfriend distraction is going to get you killed."

Harric extended both arms to ward off another rap. "Stop, and I'll get up."

"All right." Fink's expression didn't soften.

With what seemed like the effort required to climb a mountain,

Harric got to his feet.

"Tonight, lover boy, you're going to practice three things that might keep you alive a couple more days. And if you're lucky, this'll take your mind off things."

Harric let out a long breath. When Caris was upset, she always buried herself in her training and her horse; maybe he could bury himself in the Unseen. He nodded.

"That's the partner I've come to love. Now take off your clothes."

Something like a laugh bubbled from Harric's gut and died on its way up. He started unbuttoning his shirt.

"By the way, Sir Bignuts doesn't have anything against you in particular, does he? He doesn't know your name?"

"He...threw me through a wall once."

Fink stared. "So maybe not a first-name relationship on his end, but he could pick you out of in crowd."

Harric thumbed his bastard belt as he unfastened it. "I'm a bastard, Fink. And Bannus is a big lover of the Old Ways, which are the ways of every bastard a slave, and every lord a king, and every immortal a king over kings, which results in a kind of worship of war and battle."

Fink's teeth glittered. "Sounds like a soul feast."

"At first, maybe. But anyone they kill can't be enslaved. And their biggest enemies they keep alive with the Blood for longer than ordinary mortal lives."

"That all? I can see why you can hardly be bothered to care."

Harric sighed. "You made your point. Why can't you just be with me as soon as the sun sets?"

Fink grew very still, and something about his expression sent a shiver through the small hairs along Harric's spine. "I try," Fink said. His body, too, had frozen in its crouch, and his voice came from him without moving his lips, as if Fink himself were no longer present and his body was only a channel for his voice. "But when the sun rises on you," he said, "I return to the Web, or to my moon. And time is not the same there. And distances are different."

"Whatever you're doing, Fink, it's really unsettling."

The imp's head quirked to the side and his gaze went to Harric. "I'm an unsettling sort."

"You were talking about time and distance. But tonight, when I summoned you, you were in your moon or whatever, and you came instantly."

"Yes. A summoning is a powerful weave. It pushes a bridge through the time between us. But I think I've told you that even then I can't always come when called. I'm not just sitting there waiting for you. I have…duties." His face and hands twisted unpleasantly. "I must…answer to others."

A long silence ensued, which would have been uncomfortable if Harric could get anything to matter. Fink broke it by giving a startling snap of his wings.

"We'll work on your stamina tonight," he said. "But first things first. We'll start with your entrance into the Unseen."

"My entrance."

"Your *non*-entrance, I should say. Right now, when you enter the Unseen, you make a big splash and send waves through the strands that announce your entrance. That won't draw Sir Bu-ass's attention, but it draws attention in the Unseen, and that can be just as bad. There are things up there in the Web that are just as fond of eternal suffering as your big blue daddy is."

"Can you not call him that? His name is Bannus."

"So you have to learn how to enter the Unseen like a snake enters a pool, without a ripple."

Harric closed his eyes and stifled another sigh. Nothing was sticking in his brain. It took enormous effort to stay engaged. "So…the other night when I entered the Unseen on the cliff above Bannus's army…"

"That night you entered with a belly flop, and every nasty crawly in that quadrant of the Web knew something juicy and inexperienced just entered the Unseen. Lucky you were so near Bannus and his big blue freak horse, because none of them dared come near."

Harric nodded. "Entrance and stamina. Anything else?"

"One thing. You need to control your oculus."

"I control it fine."

Fink waved a taloned finger over Harric's head, and Harric's oculus went totally flaccid. From a small window like a keyhole, it relaxed into a huge hoop that dropped around him like a shed robe.

"Peekaboo," said Fink, as the spirit world rose bright and complex around Harric.

"Oh."

"Yeah. A big *fat* O, big enough for any lesser sprite to reach in and scoop you out like a soft-boiled egg. You have to learn to lock that down. Got your attention, lover boy? Good." Fink removed his hand and the oculus rose, depositing Harric back in the Seen.

Harric nodded. He took a deep breath that did nothing to fill the emptiness in his chest. "All right. Show me."

An hour later, Harric crouched against a seedling log, lungs burning like he'd been running at top speed for a mile. His body, if not his spirits, felt invigorated. But he had to admit that even his spirits had benefited, and the pain of the void in his chest didn't feel quite as strong.

"Again," said Fink.

Closing his eyes, Harric concentrated on closing the oculus. It opened if he pushed his awareness upward toward it, and it closed if he drew away. But he'd practiced drawing away so much in the last hour that it had become weak and unresponsive to his will. Like an overworked muscle, it seemed his will had gone numb. Finally, by pushing his mind up to and back from the oculus, over and over, he managed to work up a feel for it again, and, with a final effort, drew it closed to a mere sliver. That had been the best he could do all night. A sliver. He could not yet shut it completely.

"You're doing better, kid. Sweating like a whipped mare, but at least you're working hard. My last partner? He didn't like to work. What a silk-pantied waffle eater he was. Raised in privilege, you know? Made me to do it all, which is why I was all ribs when I met you."

"Nice to have one mentor who appreciates my effort. Sir Willard thinks I'm lazy."

"He thinks that because you're always tired because you've been up nights with me."

Harric sat against the soft moss of the log while he caught his breath. He watched Fink in the Unseen through the oculus, as the imp perched on a hummock of ferns. "Things will be a little more complicated again, now that Mudruffle's back with us."

Fink nodded. "I'll stay in the Unseen. No sense risking the little kindling stick seeing me."

"Abellia had wards at her tower. Can you set up wards around us to warn if anyone comes near us when I'm with you?"

"Sure I can. Not a bad idea."

"Can you teach me to make them?"

Fink frowned. "I could, but you want to be 'invisible,' right? We call that Spirit Walking, and it isn't one weave, it's an entire school of mastery. And one of the most dangerous."

"Could I learn both?"

"No. Spirit Walking will take everything you have. It isn't like Spirit Reading or Loom Watching or Dream Crafting or any stuffed-armchair school of mastery. To spirit-walk you have to have more than just stamina: you have to know how to avoid the Dread and the Siren Sleep; you have to know how to use your nexus without disturbing the Web, and how to negotiate with a Spinner if you mess up her work. You have to know how to ferret those wards you mentioned, and how to avoid prowling sprites. Then there's the whole smooth entrance thing and Web etiquette and hierarchy—souls, kid, you have to read the Web like a sailor reads the sea. Understand?"

Harric nodded. "Spirit Walking is what I've wanted. I just didn't know its name."

"Good. Glad you don't want to be a tea reader. And Spirit Walking has a chance of keeping you alive the next couple days. Now, let's get you to bed while there's still some bounce in your step."

When you climb back on a horse from which you have fallen —
and are perched again upon the saddle — then you are most
in danger of falling again.

— Arkendian saying

40

Blood Marked

Caris's limbs buzzed with fire. Waves of terror ripped through her and she tried to lurch upright, but strong hands held her down.

"Stay still," said Willard.

Her eyes focused to see the old knight close, leaning over her. His blue skin seemed black in the forest twilight. She had no idea how long she'd been unconscious, but by the look of the darkness around them, dawn still dallied in the east.

"Where — is she — ?" she stammered. "What — ?"

"You'll live," he said. "She blooded you."

"She — ?" Red fury flared before her eyes, and her lungs sucked air like she'd breathe it out as fire. "The bloody bitch! I'll rip her eyes out!"

"Steady," said Willard, his weight on her shoulders growing heavier. "The rage will pass."

Caris bucked, trying to rise, but Willard kept her solidly grounded. "Rag!"

"She's fine."

Caris sobbed in fury. "No she cobbing isn't!"

"Control yourself. The Blood rage is in you, but it will pass."

Panting with fury, she bucked again, to no effect, and growled in frustration. Just below her collarbone, where the blood tooth had plunged, a coal of fire burned steadily. When she put a hand to it, she found a thick scab that fell off as she probed, and under it a knot of hard scar tissue the size of half a walnut shell. "Treacherous bitch!"

"Yes," Willard said. "She's that. And your heart bears her mark now."

Something in his tone gave her pause. "What does that mean? She thinks I'm her foal?"

He shook his head, eyes distant, as if deep in his memory. "I don't know. Never happened before." The words came out clipped, like he found them difficult to speak. "Couldn't have predicted it." He glanced into her eyes and leaned back, removing his hands from her shoulders. "Violet's gone from your eyes."

Caris rolled, pushed herself up onto her knees, and tried in vain to see the new scar under her fingers. She could feel her heart hammering beneath it.

Willard said, "Chaos Moon is truly coming."

Molly stood thirty paces away, head high, violet eye glaring at Caris. It was a look of ownership. Of domination, patronage, and…something else. Kinship. A tremor of weakness unstrung Caris's spine. She braced herself with one hand on the ground, her mind reeling. Like a mother.

"Never." Caris spat in the dust. "I've seen what kind of mother you are."

"Stay away from her," Willard said, watching them both. "She is not your doom."

He stood, offering her hand, and when she took it, he hauled her to her feet. Pulling her close, he did not release her hand, but forced her to touch eyes with him. His gray eyes flashed violet, and she sensed Krato lurking behind them, staring out with hatred and rage. Her own anger rose inside her, and she did not look away.

"She is mine," Willard said. "She is my doom."

She gave him a curt nod, but had to suppress a surge of defiance that wished to challenge Molly and fight her for dominance in the herd.

Willard's mouth twisted as if he read all of it in her eyes, but after a long moment, he released her and returned to Molly's side. "Mount up."

Another thing occurred to Caris. "Do you think she might want Holly and me to bond?"

Willard stood very still, his back to her. Without turning, he said, "Do not wish it. Do not think it. It is not a doom to wish for."

Caris watched, motionless, as he prepared to mount. Around them, twilight under the canopy brightened with the approach of dawn. The others would be rising back at camp. But on second thought, it wasn't dawn that brightened the place, it was her *senses* that had brightened. Trees, ferns, moss, shrubs, and insects stood out in bright relief. The voices of birds sounded more clearly and brighter as they sang to the dawn. The forest itself now thrummed with the vibrations of life. The Blood had altered her senses.

And that thrumming wasn't the forest. It was…Molly. It came from right there in front of Caris, and…inside her. Her own heart resonated with it.

Breathless, she took a step backward, and very carefully extended her horse-touched senses toward the unapproachable inferno of divinity she knew as Molly. But Molly had changed. Or Caris had changed. What her senses encountered was not the crackling house afire she'd met before. What she sensed now was less forbidding, somehow, like a bonfire, maybe—still dangerous, but safe for a mortal to compass at a distance.

Molly tossed her head and stamped, and the bonfire of her presence flared.

Caris pulled her senses back a little and smiled. Molly was proud. She'd sensed Caris's touch and pushed back. Yet there was something else there as well. This…kinship she'd sensed. A new sense of herd—or, maybe more accurately, of *pack*, for a band of Phyros was anything but herd in the usual prey-animal sense. And pack-bond was a new notion. It surprised Caris that it did not repulse her. Instead, a potent mix of fear and excitement thrilled through her—a crackling bolt of possibility, of terrible, wonderful chance.

Rag let out a fearful whinny, and it drove a spike of shame through Caris. Withdrawing her senses entirely from Molly, she whirled about and hurried to her horse, reaching out with her mind to gentle her. To her horror, Rag had almost entirely walled her off; she could only sense the edges of Rag's mind, and even that shallow touch sent Rag into full-blown panic.

"No, please, Rag," she said. "It was her, not me. She forced it on me." But Rag did not understand. How could she? She knew only that Phyros fire had infected her friend despite promises. Withdrawing her senses from Rag, Caris hurried to her side and tried to calm her with gentle sounds and soothing gestures, but the mare reared and pulled at her tether, eyes rolling and showing their whites.

Tears streamed down Caris's cheeks. She got hold of the bridle and held Rag until she stopped panicking. After many long minutes, Rag calmed enough for Caris to stroke her and murmur comfort…the same as she'd done when she promised this would never happen again.

Promising again, she felt dirty and false, and her stomach sank into a mire of loneliness and self-loathing. *If she rejects me for good, I'd deserve it. But if she trusts me just once more…*

Willard rode past her. "Make haste. We have many miles ahead."

In time, Rag allowed Caris to climb into the saddle, and she followed Molly at a distance that Rag could accept without the calming influence of Caris's horse-touched senses. Far ahead, she could see Willard leaning over the front of his saddle to stroke Molly's scarred neck and speak to her, though Molly seemed more interested in stealing glares at Caris. A brief surge of pity rose in Caris for Willard. After ten lifetimes together, were he and Molly unravelling? First Willard had refused her Blood with his oath to grow old and die with the Lady Anna, and now Molly had blooded another warrior.

Heat rose in Caris again. She would not allow Molly to doom her as she had Willard. She would stay clear of Molly and the taint of the Blood would fade. Already, the brightness she'd noticed in the world around her and the thrumming of Molly's presence grew faint.

Her soul was steeped in shame on the ride back to their camp, but she made several decisions. First, she would stop bleeding Molly for Willard. Henceforth, he would have to bleed her himself, and Caris would stay well out of range of the monster's blood tooth. Second, she would guard her mind against temptation and mental ambush. If Rag then gave her the chance, Caris knew their closeness would return to the intimacy and trust they'd had before, but if she failed, she sensed she'd lose Rag forever.

She sighed, hoping that, in a day, none of this would even matter. For all her cares would end if Sir Bannus rode them down like a herd of frightened deer.

Much depended on the mad immortal following her false trail south. If he did not fall for it, he could be upon them before they saw another sunrise.

The Great Swords slew Phyros in the Cleansing. Willard's Belle.
Beldan's Karst. *Great axes earned names, but fewer survive to this
day. In the hands of Father Bundas, the axe named* Jack'a'nape *took
the head of Vichis. That axe rests high on a wall of the throne room
in Kingsport.*

— From A *Noble Historie of the Cleansing,* by Sir Gundon Pond

41

Worsic

Harric woke to a foul smell and something prodding his ribs.
"Wake up, Harric," said Father Kogan. "Near daylight, and the
chimpey seen a campfire in the valley. Need to be ready when Will
comes back."

Harric opened his eyes to see the priest's filthy bare foot—the source
of both the smell and the prodding—almost near enough to kiss. He sat
up, hoping it would encourage the priest to move farther away, but it
didn't. "Thought Bannus was following the false trail south," he said.

"Maybe he didn't. Or maybe he did. And maybe he has scouts
looking our way, too. Smart bastard like you oughta have a sense for a
hunt, and think of all the chances."

Harric nodded. Normally, he did have a sense. This morning, it
drowned in howling emptiness.

So you'll let this level you? he chided himself. *Let Bannus catch
you? Don't be a fool.*

"Willard taking the Blood?"

"Yep. What happened to your head?" said Kogan, peering at
Harric's bandage, but before Harric could dismiss it as nothing, the
priest evidently dismissed it himself; he turned and motioned for

Harric to follow. "Something I want to show you."

Harric stared at the giant's back as he lumbered toward the log circle they'd arranged at the center of camp. Probably no point in lying back down to sleep. The priest would only return to torment him again with his big toe until he rose. With a sigh, Harric put on his boots and rolled up his bedding. As soon as he'd stowed it with his pack, he joined Kogan.

He found Kogan on the largest of the logs in the camp circle. Across his knees laid his giant axe. As far as Harric knew, neither he nor any of the others had ever seen the blade of the weapon, for the priest had always kept it wrapped in oilcloth bound with rope. Now the oilcloth lay open to reveal a huge crescent wing of rusted steel counterbalanced by a hammer butt of solid iron, like an anvil.

As Harric took a seat, the priest transferred the head of the axe to Harric, and it felt like he'd laid a millstone across Harric's knees. Harric grimaced. "What is this thing?" The weapon seemed too large for anyone—even a giant like Kogan—to wield in battle. And it stunk of burned resin.

Kogan's small eyes sparked as he brought a lantern in close for Harric to examine the weapon.

Harric groaned inwardly. Just take this hunk of steel off my knees. I don't care what it is, or why you think it's special. But the priest kept smiling, and would probably make a pest of himself if Harric didn't oblige him. He made a show of examining the blade and hammer butt, and after a few moments—more or less by accident—he noticed a slight wiggle to the blade.

"Blade's loose," Harric said. He drew his finger down a seam between the stem of the blade and the block of the hammer. "I think the stem of the blade sits in a socket in the hammer butt."

Kogan gave a solemn nod. "Knew you'd see it." But he still didn't go away. If anything, the expectation in his eyes only grew, and he leaned closer, adding the scents of old sweat and mildewed smothercoat to the stink of burned resin.

Breathing through his mouth, Harric found a rusty bump on the hammer block. "I think this is a…pin," he said, picking at it. "It is. And here's another. The stem of the blade is held in a socket by pins."

"You're a good Arkendian lad, and this proves it. Now take her apart and answer your own question."

"My own question?"

"You asked it yourself: what is it?"

Harric stifled a sigh and wiggled first one and then the other pin until they came free. Kogan pulled on the blade until a short stem slid free of the socket. He set the blade aside, then rotated the hammer butt on Harric's lap, so Harric could examine the empty socket.

The stink of resin rose strongest from the socket, and as Kogan illuminated its depths, Harric caught the glint of brass workings inside. In spite of himself, his curiosity flickered to life. "The socket is meant for a resin charge," he said. "I can see flint wheels in there—three, it looks like—but the flints have fallen off their slots."

"I seen it." The priest's eyes had become intent. "Could you replace them lost bits? Fix her, maybe?"

Harric nodded. "Sure. Captain Gren gave me plenty of resin and flints."

Kogan's chin rose, and his chest seemed to swell. "Best do that later today, when we have more time." Retrieving the hammer butt on its haft, he slid the stem of the blade back into the socket. Then he pinched the pins between enormous fingers and lovingly returned them to their places.

"Well?" Kogan said, glancing up.

"It's...a Phyros axe?"

Kogan nodded. "You seen that walking stack of sticks round here?"

Harric stared as his brain tried to put "sticks" together with axe-heads and resin sockets in a way that made sense. "What...*what?*" he finally said.

"That shambling witch toy." Kogan glared about as if he expected to spy Mudruffle lurking in the ferns. "Caris told me he's back."

Harric suppressed a roll of the eyes. If the priest wanted to be mysterious about his axe, Harric couldn't care less. But he was in no mood for games. "He's at Caris's camp. With the horses."

"When I see him, I aim to keep my hands to myself, for Will's sake. Will and I is getting along so well, I don't want to go and spoil it by making a hash of the unholy stick puppet, but..." He grimaced. "I'd take it as a kindness if you keep it away from me. Not sure what I'll do if them spider fingers get to touching at me."

"I can do that."

A tension in Kogan's huge shoulders relaxed, and he laid a hand on Harric's shoulder. "You're a Maker, Harric."

"What is this *Maker?*" Brolli smiled as he crested the hillock and entered the camp. "Maker of what?"

Kogan's open expression turned to suspicion, but Brolli met his gaze with such polite curiosity that the priest grudgingly replied. "I says Harric is a Maker, not a Breaker. Means he helps those as needs it, even if it's a danger to him."

"Ah. Then it is a good phrase for a good thing." Brolli set his satchel beside Harric and studied Harric's bandaged head.

"Ran into a sharp branch," Harric said. "Not too bad." In fact, the wound hadn't hurt at all since he woke, so he'd almost forgotten about it. Fink had made him promise before he slept to wash it and bind it first, and apparently that had done some good.

"I will look," said Brolli.

"That's not necessary—" Harric began, but Brolli waved him off and began unwrapping the bandage.

"I miss my flock something terrible," said Kogan, his eyes on the unravelling bandage, but focused on nothing. "I think about them when it's quiet like this, and I wonder how Widda Larkin is making out without me." His small eyes flicked to Brolli. "You seen Bannus's fires in the valley...you reckon I'll ever see her again, or you reckon he'll catch us up?"

Brolli glanced to Kogan, then went back to his task. "I think the campfire is not for a large company. Squires and baggage, maybe, as Sir Bannus follows the false trail."

Kogan sighed through his nose. "My flock needs me. When I run off to help you and Will, I had half their coin with me, and they'll need it to pay passage on a boat up the Giant's Gap."

"Then you are a Maker, Father." Brolli held all the bandages in his hands now, but he turned his eyes upon the priest and gave him a small bow. "We need you, and you help us, though it give much danger."

A small smile softened Kogan's gaze. "Reckon so."

"And Willard is a Maker," said Brolli, as he turned his attention to Harric's wound, "for he drinks the Blood to protect us, though it harms him."

As Brolli studied Harric's scalp, gingerly parting the blood-crusted hair, Harric winced in anticipation and watched the Kwendi's expression. The expected pain did not come, and after some time, Brolli frowned and set about parting the hair less gently. Finally, he shook his head and handed Harric the bandages in such a way that he turned his back to Father Kogan. "There is no wound here," he whispered. "I think Mudruffle saw it before me."

Harric put a hand to the spot and found the wound gone without trace. Not even a scar.

"You wound needs no bandages, Harric," Brolli said, loud enough for Kogan to hear. "You may wish to bury them, since we are allowed no fire."

Harric wrapped the bandages in a tight wad as Brolli sat to write in his journal. He knew he should feel gratitude, but some pathetic and self-pitying part of him regretted that now the wound would never worsen and finish what Caris started.

Hoofbeats sounded from the north. From somewhere below their camp, Mudruffle honked, "It is Sir Willard and Caris."

The mention of her name sent a spike of dread through Harric. He took up a position behind the log circle, which would allow him a quick retreat if she went for her sword again. Or, for that matter, if Willard did, for if she'd told the old knight about Harric's pact with the Unseen, he'd probably do it himself.

Cobs. So be it. If they seized him, there'd be no point in resisting.

His heart jumped when he saw her riding toward the hillock, and when her eyes found his, it felt like javelins speared him through the eyes. In her iron gaze he saw no trace of remorse, no trace of apology, only intensity and judgment. When she finally pulled her gaze away, he felt as though he'd been dropped from a great height onto the hillock.

Limbs shaking, he sat back on the log.

Gods take it, I'm actually afraid of her.

A new idea came to his mind, and he looked down to her again as she rode around the skirt of the hill. Could Willard be feeding her the Blood? He saw no blue in her cheeks. But if she had taken the Blood, that would explain why she had attacked him that night—it would mean it wasn't actually *her* that attacked him, but the Blood rage. A tiny butterfly of hope fluttered up from the shreds of his heart.

Molly churned up the hill and into the camp, but Caris did not follow. She dismounted in the horse camp below and tied Rag with the other horses.

As soon as Willard hobbled Molly at the edge of their campsite, he strode toward them in the log circle. His eyes did not pause on Harric, which Harric took as a sign that Caris had not revealed his secret. Then again, Willard had changed so much with the Blood in the last days that Harric doubted he could accurately gauge him any longer. If it weren't for the tusk-like mustachio and the still-bald head—now stubbly—Harric might not have recognized him as the same man. Any soft lines and extra chins had vanished. His cheeks and jaw had gone angular, and cords of muscle now rippled in his neck.

Kogan evidently noticed this too, for he laughed and said, "Gods leave you, Will, you look like your own son!"

Brolli had stopped scribbling in his journal, and his mouth hung open as stared up at Willard.

"If you aren't ready to ride, pack up now," Willard announced. "We ride as soon as the girl is armed. Boy, hurry down and help her bring her armor up."

Harric's stomach shriveled. "I...don't know if that's a good idea, sir."

"She's given me her word she won't...object. So get off your lazy arse and help."

Harric rose, but tremors and nerves made him move like a badly strung marionette. "I'll help her," he said, but his voice failed him. He feigned a cough, trying to mask it, and at that moment, Caris crested the hillock with her sack of armor slung over her back.

"Think I can't carry my own armor?" she said. The look she gave Harric was so frosty it would shatter tree trunks, but her sword stayed in it scabbard. She dropped her armor beside the log and stood still as a mountain, eyes boring into Harric. "I don't regret a thing about last night, Harric. So don't you dare try to flatter me or pity me." Her eyes swept to Willard's and held the knight's gaze without flinching. "I am not stupid, and I'm not afraid. And I'm not the Caris you think you know. I'm not even the Caris I thought I knew."

Every pair of eyes in camp was on her.

Somewhere in the darkness, tiny birds chirped as if to say, *Here I am, where are you?*

Willard broke the tension with a snort. "About goddam time." He motioned to the spot beside him. "Take a seat, girl. I believe I remember how to lace a breastplate and tie a point."

"I'm not a *girl*," Caris said, making no move to sit. "Haven't been for some time."

Violet sparked in Willard's eyes. "Take a seat, *Caris*. We cannot ride till you're armed."

Caris turned her iron gaze around the fire, and when it found Harric, it took all his will to hold it. After what seemed like an eternity, she sat and indicated her gear bag. "Oiled the leather yesterday," she said as she picked up the quilted gambeson. "Shouldn't need any today." When she pulled the garment down over her head, the tension drained from the scene like wine from a punctured skin.

Willard plucked a plated vambrace from the bag and held it to Caris's left bicep so he could buckle it to the breastplate. "Listen close," he said, shifting abruptly to conversation. "We have more than one enemy. In addition to Bannus, we have the fire on the west ridge. Right now, the fire is driven north along the ridge by a south wind. But if the wind changes, the flames could jump the cliff into our valley and cross our path, and we'd be trapped between fire and Sir Bannus. To be safe, we need to get ahead of that fire. And if we don't make good time today, it won't matter what the fire does, because Bannus will be upon us."

Kogan nodded, his face uncharacteristically serious. "This is the time I been waiting for, Will. I got something for you."

Willard looked up from buckling. "Better make it quick."

Kogan lifted his axe from behind the log and laid it on his knees to peel back the oilcloth.

Willard scowled. "What in the name of Bannus's reeking socks is that?"

Kogan's voice dropped in reverence. "This axe—this very axe in the hands of Father Yonas—slew the Phyros stallion called Worsic."

"What man could lift it?" Brolli said. "This Yonas is a giant, yes?"

"He was a wandering priest, like Kogan," Willard said. "So, yes, a giant. And I thank Yonas for his deed, for Worsic and Sir Tighe were monsters. Beyond that, why should this hunk of awkward iron matter to me?"

"Because you're big enough to wield her now, Will," Kogan said. "And though you're still not a match for Bannus, this axe could make the difference."

Harric stiffened, expecting Willard to explode again at Kogan's statement.

But Willard merely ground his teeth and glared. When he finished Caris's left vambrace, he moved to her right side to attach the other. "It's a ridiculous axe. Looks like an ingot with a blade tacked on."

"She's special," Kogan said, as if it were an article of faith.

"Belle is also special. I'll use her."

"Does it have a name?" said Caris.

Kogan nodded. "Reckon her name's Worsic. Ain't that how it works? If she don't have a name yet, first kill names her."

"Worsic was a Phyros *stallion*," said Caris, "not a her."

"Can't be helped. Weapon's always a she."

Caris raised an eyebrow. Then she drew her sword, which made Harric's breath hitch. He didn't flee, and if he paled or flinched, she paid no attention. Instead, she angled the blade so the priest could see the crude inscription she'd etched there with a shoeing nail. *Mona.* She read the name aloud.

Kogan's beard split in a crack-toothed grin. "Well, I'm a stuffed pizzle. Already a name! Who was Mona?"

"A lady," Caris said. She dropped her eyes to the blade. "But I didn't kill her. I avenged her."

Willard practically rolled his eyes as he set to lacing the back of one of Caris's thigh cuisses, and it stirred Harric's anger, in spite of everything. Surely Willard would understand the reference to Mona Dionis, the horse-touched maiden who had hanged herself in the early years of Chasia's court. He'd been in court then, and any blockhead could guess the significance her name would hold for Caris.

"Powerful name," Harric said, keeping his attention fixed on the axe-head.

"Name yours yet, Harric?" said Kogan.

"Yes," said Harric. "*Sheath-seeker.*"

The priest let out a big "har!" and Brolli grinned. Willard curled a lip as if to say, *Always the knave.*

"The axe is special," Harric said, simply to cross Willard. "If you stuff a resin charge inside and then hit something with it, the charge explodes and shoves the axe blade deeper into your target. Probably right through it, judging by the size of charge she could hold."

Glowering, Willard finished the vambrace. "Let me see that."

Kogan smuggled Harric a wink as he removed the blade and handed the haft and hollow hammer butt to Willard.

The knight peered into the socket through a haze of ragleaf smoke. "This some kind of tooler gimmick?"

"The Arkendian alternative to magic, I think." Brolli grinned. "This fascinates."

Harric leaned in and indicated the brass flint wheels inside with a slender finger. "See *there*, and *there*. The flints have fallen off the slots beside the wheels, but I can replace them. When you hit something with the axe, the stem of the blade slides back in the socket and turns these flint wheels, which spark and ignite the resin and set of the charge. I'll get it working."

"If we *wanted* it working," said Willard. "God-touched thing could blow any second."

"No, that's what the pins are for," said Harric. "They prevent the blade from moving until you hit something hard enough to shear the pins away."

Willard's eyes narrowed at Harric. "How the Black Moon do you know that?"

Harric held his gaze with the strength of hollow indifference. "The toolers in Gallows Ferry made something like it to drive pilings at the landing. But any Northie could figure this out. Toolery's a pastime."

Willard snorted and turned his attentions back to Caris's armor. "It's a suicide axe. Recoil from the charge would send the blade forward and rip your arms off backward."

Kogan's face remained serious. "May come a time when we'd trade both arms for a crack at Bannus. I know I would." He stopped to reassemble the axe, then swaddled it in oilcloth and stood. "Best fix her tonight, Harric."

"Soon as we have time," Harric replied.

Kogan watched Willard for several long moments. "I'll keep her for now, Will. When Bannus sees you, he won't worry about you taking a chop at Gygon, because he'll see you don't have the power to cut an armored Phyros neck. But with Worsic here..." He patted the axe like it was a talisman. "She got the fire of righteousness, Will. Get her fixed and she'll chop a boulder, and Bannus won't never see it coming."

Willard's cheeks had turned purple during the speech, but aside from more forceful attentions to the points of Caris's armor, he controlled his anger. It wasn't until Kogan had returned the axe to the rest of his gear beside Geraldine that Willard threw up his hands and let the plates of Caris's cuisse hang loose from the breastplate. "My fingers are too big for this. Boy, lace her up, or we'll be here all day."

"Sir—" Caris began, cheeks darkening.

"Drop your foibles, both of you," Willard snapped. "He's not kissing you, girl, and he's the only one with fingers small enough to do it right. Do it now."

Willard stalked back to Molly with a look that dared anyone to object.

A glance at Caris confirmed to Harric that her jaw muscles bulged and her face had darkened with fury. He looked down, and the hole in his chest gave a terrific throb. *Great. Her thigh armor. Good decision, sir.* If the knight wasn't trying to get him killed, he was doing a good impersonation. But when he risked another glance at Caris's eyes, she gave a curt nod.

Kneeling behind her, he set to lacing the plates tightly to the back of her thighs as quickly as he could, making it his careful study not to nudge her buttocks.

Brolli looked up from his journal as if he noticed no unusual tension. "Lady Caris, how does one kill an immortal?"

"You don't," Caris said.

"Cut off their heads," said Kogan, from across the camp.

"We must cut off Sir Bannus's head?" said Brolli, brows climbing his forehead.

Caris gave an impatient shake of her head. "If you could, yes. But beheading an armored immortal is very difficult. It is easier to kill their Phyros. That's what they did in the Cleansing."

"That were the whole trick of the Cleansing," Kogan said. "No one ever attacked their Phyros before. But Will did. It was Will's idea, and it saved the kingdom, because once the Phyros is dead, it's only a matter of time before the rider's mortal. Most of all, Will broke the *spell*. Ten centuries of *Harm no holy Phyros* and *Raise no fire against them*, and Will threw it all away. Freed us from the yoke. He made everything possible."

Harric tied off the second cuisse, and Caris jerked away as if she'd anticipated the fraction of the instant he'd finish.

Willard mounted Molly. "To horse," he said. "We ride for our lives."

They all hurried to their mounts as Willard and Kogan rode down to the horse camp. While Caris loaded Rag, Harric went to Mudruffle, who waited by Idgit to be lifted to his saddle-basket. "Thank you," Harric said, laying a hand upon the site of his scalp wound and bowing deeply.

"I only do what I am sworn to do, Master Harric. I heal what needs healing. Though I do wonder at the source of the injury."

The tenderness in the golem's ridiculous voice was too much for Harric. The bubble of emptiness in his chest rose into his throat and choked off his words. As foolish tears came to his eyes, he bowed again so none would see.

"As I thought," said Mudruffle. "It is not Caris, Master Harric. It is the enchantments upon her."

Harric did not trust himself to speak, so he nodded and shrugged as if to say, *I'm not so sure, but I hope so.* Then he straightened and lifted the golem into his saddle-basket.

"Silence!" Willard said. All eyes turned to him, where he sat motionless in Molly's saddle, hand to his ear.

Very faintly in the distance to the south, Harric heard a deep, thrumming roar. It sounded like the rumble of a distant landslide mixed with a baritone bellow. It came and went again, and after several repetitions was joined by the unmistakable sound of horns— one louder and apparently nearer—answering and echoing from the hillsides. From the difference in pitch and volume, Harric identified four separate horns.

The group traded glances as Willard remained still, listening. Gradually, the roar dwindled, as if its source were moving away from them, though two of the nearer horns continued to sound.

Willard lowered his hand and sucked a lungful of ragleaf from a fresh roll. "Yoab. Big one, obviously."

Kogan chuckled. "You think Bannus mighta stumbled over that king yoab Caris seen?"

"We can hope. And if so, may he pass through its bowels before he hunts again. But these horns are the horns of his men, and from the sound of them, they are in several parts of the valley behind us, and the false trail only served to divert part of his force." Willard turned Molly abruptly. "Follow. We have no time to waste."

Before the Rule of Sir Anatos, those who drank of the Blood fell helpless to the Blood rage, which stripped from them all humanity. "Rage Slaves," Anatos named them, and, being one himself, labored to master it. … therefore, made he the Rule of Anatos, which is on two laws founded: the first is *Eat no Flesh of Any Beast, for All Flesh Feeds the Fire;* and the second is *Master the Blue Meditations and Make Them Your Continual Practice. …Upon this Rule, Anatos founded the Blue Order.*

—From A *History of Arkendian Immortality,* by Nicola Clouch

42

Yoab Maze

Willard set out at a swift pace and did not let up. The journey quickly blurred into a continuous stream of green forest, lumpy trails, and aching muscles. The horses blew and steamed with sweat, and Harric felt his limbs hardening in crooked shapes that he feared would never straighten if he were ever allowed to return to the ground.

But by midday, the relentless pace fell off as they entered what Mudruffle called the Yoab Maze. Though the highway that ran through the maze was generally wider and deeper and more clearly established than the runs of the maze, some of the crisscrossing offshoots and junctions were hard to distinguish from the highway itself. Even with Mudruffle's map and help, they had to backtrack several times when they discovered the run they thought was the highway ended abruptly or curved south.

"Like the maze in 'Willard and the Labyrinth,'" Kogan said, during a pause in which they consulted the map and argued. "Only instead of Blood Trophies, there's yoabs."

Harric did not find the reference humorous, since each time they had to backtrack, they lost ground against Bannus. At one point, they executed such a monumental reverse that he half expected them to come face to face with Sir Bannus as he rode up their trail.

And they encountered abundant evidence of recent yoab activity in the maze. In places, they found fields of raw, plowed soil, stripped of anything green—yoab feeding sites—checkering the forest floor for as far as they could see.

"These sites are fresh," Willard said, as they halted on a rise between two of these sites. "The yoab are definitely down from the hills for the winter. With luck, we won't meet one as big as Caris met. But regardless, this means the horses will be nervous as we pass through here. I advise we travel in strict silence today, to avoid unwanted attention." His eyes flicked to Mudruffle.

As if anticipating this, Mudruffle held a cloth to his little slit of a mouth. "Since my vocal apparatus is too simplistic for a whisper, I will endeavor to remain silent with this muffle applied to my mouth." His voice came through the cloth as a murmur. "Only in the event of an emergency will I speak without obstruction."

Willard managed a doubtful nod, and they forged on.

Whenever they reached a stretch where Mudruffle was confident of their direction, Willard rode ahead on scouting forays, and on occasion returned with reports that he'd been able to scare several younger yoab away from the highway. Another time, he spotted one asleep in the midst of one of these newly plowed fields beside the highway, and doubled back to ensure the group's silence as they circumnavigated its bed. What they passed looked exactly like a ferny hillock, with the difference that, unlike a hillock, it snored like a giant's bellows, so loudly that Harric doubted even Mudruffle could match its volume.

It was during one of Willard's absences that Kogan pointed out bright red blood on the highway. Blood had filled one of Molly's hoof prints. All around the bloody hoof print, it looked like Molly had been running in tight circles. Then her prints tore off up the road, and the blood followed in her wake, splashing the earth beside huge clawed prints. A yoab's prints. It looked like a yoab—and an injured yoab, too—had chased Molly and Willard up the run.

Unless the red blood is Willard's. Harric chewed his upper lip. No.

The knight's cheeks were now blue, which meant the blood in his veins must now be continuously blue. Willard must have injured it and led it on a chase away from the horses.

They followed the blood trail a quarter mile up the highway, and watched as it slowly dwindled until it terminated in the carcass of a yoab as big as a carriage.

The horses refused to approach with riders, but Caris calmed them enough that they allowed themselves to be led past on foot. As Harric guided Snapper and Idgit, Kogan followed with Geraldine and pointed to a wound behind the yoab's gigantic foreleg.

"Lance," Kogan said. "And this much blood must've been a heart wound." The priest shook his head and gave the stinking flesh a rub. "Ran half the valley with its heart split. Noble beast."

"Your spirit beast," Harric whispered.

Harric pushed Snapper hard on Willard's trail, but Molly proved impossible to match. She appeared to be tireless, and Harric often lost sight of Willard for long stretches. Sir Bannus's Phyros, Gygon, would be equally tireless, of course. And since Gygon had no mortal horses to slow him down—like Sir Willard did—it seemed he would catch up to them very quickly.

"But he does have mortal horses with him," Willard said, when Harric brought that up. "His men perform for him many tasks that are below the dignity of his Exalted and Celebrated Ur-Holiness. Mortal men get down and track for him. They wrangle abandoned horses for him. They cook the prodigious piles of meat he requires. They pitch his pavilion and adorn it with living captives." Willard rode in silence for a few long moments, then cast a grim glance at Harric. "So he was in the old days. And he's given me no reason to think he's changed."

"But he has dogs with him," Harric said, echoing Fink's point. "Once he finds our trail, he'll make time on us."

To that, Willard said nothing, but picked up the pace.

At around noon, the ancient trees and their canopy ended abruptly at the edge of a mudslide that descended the hillside and crossed their path like a mile-long tongue of mud. It spanned the hillside for about as far as a bowshot, straight across, and had leveled and swept away even the largest trees. As they paused at the edge of the trees, unfiltered sunshine dazzled their eyes, and the horses snorted and pricked their ears, alert and curious despite their long labor.

Nothing remained standing where the mudslide had passed. Trees, plants, all had been swept down the mountain and deposited in a heap of rubble as big as a castle, right on top of the river. The river had backed up behind it and formed a small lake before eventually finding its way around the west side, in a sharp bow.

Judging by the scarcity of the brush and fireweed on the slide, it was a new one. It must have slid during the previous winter. Fortunately for the horses, some enterprising young yoab had already reestablished the Yoab Highway across it. It wasn't the great rammed-through trough of the mature yoab highway, but at least the little cub had marked where it ought to go, and flattened the mud, knocking smaller obstacles from its way. Larger, older yoab would deepen the furrow and plow up the larger boulders and stray trunks.

Willard made them smother their armor and weapons in blankets before they crossed the open space, to prevent a stray glint of metal from revealing their location to any scouts on the opposite ridge. When they set out across it, Harric studied the western skyline, now blackened and smoking, and the fires to the northwest, where the ridge boiled with orange flame and the sky choked on columns of smoke.

"The fire is still ahead of us," Mudruffle honked, still muffled by a cloth at his mouth. "I fear if the wind remains from the south, the fire may descend into this valley at a place I named Many Rivers. We must make haste to arrive there tomorrow."

They crossed the clearing quickly and rode on, and when Harric believed Snapper would probably drop with exhaustion and his own body would never unbend from the saddle, Willard called them to a halt.

Willard had chosen a spot where a stream crossed the highway and paused just below it in a pool. "Rest and water the horses here," he said. "Have a swim, father. This northerly wind makes it hard to ride before you."

Harric dismounted with a groan. His pants stuck to his legs with sweat from the heat of Snapper's labor, and his back bent almost double with stiffness. Wincing with every step, he led the blowing gelding to the stream to drink. As the horse sucked at the water, Harric limped to the edge of the highway and looked down to the pool below. Blue, deep, and very likely a yoab wallow at one time, it was now a gorgeous swimming hole. He knew if he wanted to swim it, he ought to get in before Kogan's monumentally unwashed body fouled it. And he knew his body could use a bath, and that it might be good for his spirits, too.

But he couldn't summon the will to care.

The spot of sun on his shoulders gave him no pleasure. The water wouldn't refresh. And he knew he was being pathetic. He could practically hear Fink saying, *Feeling melodramatic today?* But he didn't care about that either. "It's all yours, father," he said. Maybe after Kogan had a good soak, Harric would summon the will to carve EVIL WATERS in a tree beside it, like they did for contaminated pools along the Free Road. But probably not.

"Caris and I will return within the hour," Willard said, pushing Molly onward up the highway. Caris still sat on Rag, well back on the trail, apparently waiting for Willard to move before she brought Rag to the stream. She'd maintained a greater distance than usual all day, and Rag had been strangely unmanageable. Despite his weariness, Harric noticed Rag's behavior seemed to upset Caris, too, and he worried it had something to do with Willard bringing her to bleed Molly.

"Come, Caris," said Willard.

It took a moment for Willard's intention to register for Harric, but when it did, he looked up in surprise. "You're leaving us again? I thought this was a short rest, and that we'd keep pushing on."

Willard ignored him.

"But, sir, you already took the Blood today—"

"And I'll bloody take it again!" Willard whirled Molly to face Harric. "If I do not take it, nothing will protect us from Sir Bannus when he finds us."

"An hour is long in our race with the fire," Mudruffle honked.

Willard's face darkened. For many moments, he pressed his lips together and clenched his jaw as if struggling against the urge to lay waste to those who questioned him. Harric glanced at Brolli for support, but the Kwendi still slept in the saddle under his blanket. His look was not lost upon Sir Willard, however, and this reminder of the ambassador's presence seemed to sober him.

"I would have you push ahead while I take the Blood, and then catch up to you, but I can't risk you meeting a yoab without me or Caris present. I will make this as quick as I can, but hurrying the process means that when we return to you, the rage will still be strong in me. To control it, I will be deep in the meditations of the Blue Men."

Kogan looked up from rummaging in his cheese bag.

"This is important," Willard said, "so listen closely to what I'm about to say. Especially you, Kogan. When we return, mount up and fall in line silently. Do not speak to me until you hear me speak. And it may be hours before I do. If you disrupt the meditation, you do so at your peril."

"Quiet as the grave, Will," Kogan said.

Willard turned Molly and rode north with Caris behind.

Harric watched as they disappeared into the darkness beneath the gigantic trees.

"I am uncertain of the wisdom in this," said Mudruffle.

"You and everyone," said Harric. "He acts like it's a sure thing that Bannus followed the horses south down the false trail, but he doesn't know any more than we do." He crossed his arms and hugged them in tight, startled by his own agitation—at the heartbeat that now drummed in his chest. But he'd seen what Bannus did to bastards, and he was scared. Death was one thing, eternal torture quite another.

"It's the Blood in him," said Kogan. Pungent odor announced the priest's arrival at Harric's side. "Once they start, it's all they think about. No worrying on it now."

Harric took a long breath and let it out. Then another. "I'll get Captain Gren's pack. You get Worsic. At least we can get her ready during the delay."

Caris shook her head and crossed her arms when Willard held out the razor and cup to her. "I can't cut her for you," she said. "She'll stab at me again. You'll have to draw the Blood yourself, then I'll bind you and give it to you."

They stood beside a fir at the edge of a ravine with a rattling stream at the bottom. The tree was close enough to the crumbling edge of the ravine to require care in navigating around it, lest she slide down the bank into the stream, but it was the only tree among the giant trunks that was small enough for the chains to reach around.

She took a step back from him, and Willard's brow wrinkled. "Your armor will protect you from her—"

"Not enough." She gave an emphatic shake of her head and stood her ground. All morning she'd silently rehearsed what she would say. "I'm not cutting Molly again. It's because of Rag. The merest touch of Molly's mind or Blood repels her. I can't lose her. I can't."

The Blood in her veins had prevented her from reaching out to Rag—it still burned in her; she could feel it—and her grief and loneliness steeled her resolve.

Willard licked his lips. "Girl, I don't...know if I can. I mean I don't know if I can stop myself from drinking it once the cup's full and in my hand." His eyes flicked up to hers, an expression in them she didn't recognize. "The *desire*."

She stared at him, frustrated that she couldn't tell what he was getting at. *Desire?* Did he mean the craving for the Blood? Impatient with herself, she shrugged. "If you try, I'll knock it from your lips." It was probably the wrong thing to say, but she was past caring; she was not going to cut for him.

Willard gave a grim laugh. "Yes, I'd wager you would. But it is unwise to come between the lion and his prey. Can't be sure I wouldn't bleed *you* if it came to that."

Heart thudding in her chest, she clamped her mouth shut and waited him out.

Willard sighed. "Very well." He turned toward Molly, still holding the cup and razor. "I'll try. But you might as well put on your moon-blasted helmet. Can't be too careful."

Caris did not have to knock the cup from his hands. Sweating and pale, he handed the brimming cup to her and allowed her to bind him before he drank. She gagged him as soon as he'd swallowed, and then walked back to Rag, whom she'd tethered so far away that they could barely hear his bellows in the distance. His noise would be enough to scare away most yoab, but if an old bull came to see what the noise was about, Molly's snarls would alert Caris.

Then...what? She had to smile. She'd lance it behind the foreleg, as Willard had done to the one on the road that day. Or she'd get it to chase her. She had experience with that.

As soon as Willard's bellowing ceased, Caris left Rag and trudged back to him. It hadn't even been half an hour, but he'd told her to test him when he fell silent. She found him sagging from the chains around the fir. Below the tree, the stream rattled in its channel, and she had to be careful not to step too close to the brink of the bank lest it crumble and she slide down.

"Sir Willard?"

"Mhm." He opened an eye. "Meditating," he said, very softly, as if speaking louder might disrupt the trance.

She nodded and released one arm, then the next. He stood, eyes still closed. "Be careful of the bank," she said, as she gathered up the chains and lifted them.

A wicked gleam in his eye revealed her mistake, and she barely got her arm up in time to deflect the hand snaking toward her throat. With a cry, she shoved the chains at him and knocked another fist aside. He lunged to his feet, but his boot slipped down the edge of the bank. As he windmilled to catch his balance, she put a boot on his hip and sent Willard-Krato sliding the rest of the way to the stream.

Bellows of rage filled the air, and Caris stared about in terror. Her first instinct was to run for Rag, but the moment he got on Molly's back, the race would be over, and Molly would tear Rag to pieces. And she couldn't lead Molly away from him on a string, like she could a regular horse. Her only real option was to mount Molly herself and ride away so Willard-Krato could not have her, and then keep her away until Willard had returned to normal.

But she couldn't. She had vowed, and she'd rather die with Rag than break it.

All this flashed through her mind in the space of two heartbeats. On the third beat, she turned from the tree and ran for Rag. She hadn't made four strides in her direction before Molly cut her off and reared before her, huge hooves pawing the air.

Caris skidded to a halt and whipped her sword from her sheath. "Back off," she spat, "and stay away! I'm done with you. And stop waving your fool hooves. You wouldn't have marked me just to kill me."

Molly snarled in fury, but Caris held her sword between them and circled around until she could back her way toward Rag. Molly rotated with her, stamping and glaring violet rage.

A groan from the ravine made Caris pause.

"What the Black Moon…?" Willard said. "Where am I? Girl! Girl, are you there? Are you all right?"

"Here. I'm fine."

Molly reared back and brought both front hooves down hard before Caris, as if demanding her attention. As Caris glared back, Molly presented her shoulder as if she wanted Caris to cut her, and a surge of guilty desire rose in Caris, accompanied by a pall of horror.

She could not—she would not—take the Blood. She had vowed.

And as she backed away, she sensed Molly's fury at the rejection, like the fury she surely harbored for Willard for all those years he would not bleed her because of the Lady Anna.

"I'm not climbing this blasted bank," Willard said. "Unhitch Molly and she'll bear me up."

Caris circled back around Molly to the edge of the ravine, keeping both eyes on the Phyros. A glance below showed her Willard standing at edge of the stream, mud caking parts of his armor. His face flushed violet-blue, and his shoulders rose and fell with as if still contending with the Blood rage. When he saw her, he stared up, unseeing.

"Willard?" she said. "How do I know it's you?"

He closed his eyes. "I take it I'm down here because of something *he* did?"

"Yes, sir."

Molly lunged, and Caris's heart did a flip inside her, but the beast soared past Caris and over the rim of the bank. The Phyros plowed to a stop at the knight's side, and Willard gave Caris a grim look. "You're lucky it's me and not Krato in my flesh," he said, as he climbed into the saddle. "Or this would be the end for you." As if to second his words, Molly glared murder at Caris, and Caris turned before Willard could notice the connection.

Gods take it, what's she trying to do?

She did not want to think of it. She ran for Rag. Molly made her feel dirty. But when she returned to Rag's side, she felt nothing but relief that she'd kept her vow and foiled Molly's efforts. She spent quiet minutes with the mare, nuzzling and hugging her, speaking quietly.

When Willard rode past her, he appeared to be deep in trance, eyes half closed. Caris pointedly ignored Molly's gaze, and mounted to follow with a long stretch of yoab run between them. She missed sharing senses and touching minds with Rag, but her heart warmed with the knowledge that she'd won that pass against Molly and kept her vow, even in a moment of crisis.

She grinned and rubbed Rag's mane.

Just as I'll win the next, and the next after that. I'm just as smart as you, monster. And I have more to lose, so I'm even more determined.

The moment they returned to the others, Caris saw Harric and Kogan scrambling to mount and ride. Kogan stashed Worsic, still wrapped in her oilcloth, on the musk auroch, and Harric stowed the spitfire pack behind Snapper's saddle. As he mounted, he glanced at her, which called up a hot flame of anger in her breast...not aching love, she realized, but good old *anger*.

She'd experienced this once before, when she'd touched Molly's mind in the stables back at the pass. On that day, the fires Molly's mind had somehow burned out the enchantment of the ring, and now they'd done it again.

She smiled. It felt good. She felt strong.

Questions swam in Harric's eyes as he watched her, and she stared back, her lip curling involuntarily. He looked like he'd been up all night—gray-faced and sunken—and she shrugged away a pulse of guilt. A different Caris. The true Caris. And it wasn't until he dropped his gaze that she realized she'd been touching eyes with him without pain or noticing.

She'd been doing that a lot.

Her heartbeat quickened as understanding dawned on her: Molly's fire was still in her from that morning, and not only did it snuff the ring's power, but it also snuffed her horse-touched aversion to touching eyes! Nothing had ever helped her with that aversion. Nothing but Harric's trick of looking at people's noses instead of their eyes, but that was just for hiding it, not a remedy.

The implications staggered her.

Molly's fire could be a cure for everything. It could make Caris whole as she'd never been.

She knew what happened if the touch was too strong, and she did not want that. But surely if she only touched Molly's mind a *little* each day, just enough to kindle her fire and keep it burning, so she wouldn't be overcome with rage, she'd be free her of the ring's tyranny, and free of her horse-touched anxieties and foibles. The evidence seemed clear: the ring's ache was gone, and in spite of the chaotic events of the morning, she had not once needed to reach out to any horse for comfort.

Gods leave me, I could be free.

Molly cast back a glare like a burning challenge, and it sent a shiver up Caris's gut. Molly changed her so she hardly recognized herself. She was a monster.

Changed for the better, part of her whispered.

She considered this and concluded it might be so. She had to admit it. But who said it was better to be free of the aversions she'd known all her life? Her aversions were part of who she was, part of what made her strong. And she knew beyond any doubt that her connection to Rag would not survive such change. Rag wanted nothing to do with the Phyros and couldn't bear the heat of the Phyros in Caris.

She buried her face in her hands. *Rag.* If she touched Molly's fire in any form, it would be nothing short of alienating and betraying her dearest friend for the sake of a misguided ambition.

Rag let out a worried whinny and Caris shook her head hard.

I will not forsake you! I have sworn it. You'll see.

And then she felt the last of Molly's fire dwindle to nothing, and the roar of horse-touched confusion rising between her ears. Her connection to Rag was too feeble to shield her from it, and as the roar grew in strength, she felt her world narrowing. Pain filled her head, and she had nowhere to hide.

Curling over her saddle, she squeezed her eyes shut and pressed her hands to her ears.

"You'll see," she whispered. "Just like before." And the storm overwhelmed her.

She returned to herself exhausted and dull. In her absence from herself, Rag had borne Caris faithfully at the rear of their procession, and the forest had gone gray with dusk and a smoke that hung heavy in the air beneath the canopy. She'd been lost in the roar for hours.

Rag glanced back at her and flicked her ears to acknowledge her. Behind her, Holly gave a nicker of greeting.

Caris smiled and murmured, "Yes, girls, I'm back."

Vaguely, she realized someone had just been speaking. It had been Willard. She searched her memory for conversation she'd been half listening to, like recalling a dream after waking. He'd said something about the wind shifting, which would explain the smoke.

"Is it in the valley, Will?"

"How could I know that? I see no better in smoke than you do. I see no choice but to ride on as we have been until we either see fire in our path or some view of where it's got to."

"We could be riding to our doom."

"Or to our salvation. I'll take even odds of fire before us over the certainty of Bannus behind."

They now rode at a walk between looming shadows of giant trees. Someone struck a light and held a lantern in the murk. The glow cast the hulking form of the priest in silhouette as he turned to peer back at Caris. She raised a hand in acknowledgement, and he gave her a slow nod and finally faced forward again.

She groaned inwardly. *Probably thinks I'm a natural fool, huddled on my saddle for hours. Hope I wasn't moaning the whole time.*

It was Harric, riding in front of Kogan, who held the lantern on a pole. He too glanced back at her, a hint of worry in his eye, and at the sight of him, her heart swelled with longing so strong that she had to choke back a cry of pain.

It felt like someone rammed a leatherman's awl through her sternum. *No. No.*

The ring was back. And beyond a doubt, she knew that the only thing that could make the pain stop was Harric. Embracing him. Squeezing him. Holding him. Kissing him.

No!

Like a woman on fire, she flung her senses at Rag as if the mare were the water that would quench her, but Rag still shied away. Flailing, feeling like she was suffocating, Caris flung her senses to Snapper and dove into him without preamble. The gelding snorted and startled and nearly threw Harric, but the combination of his Phyros conditioning and Caris's mastery allowed her to quickly restore his calm. The moment she did, she submerged her senses in his, leaving only a tiny connection to her own body as it hunched again over her saddle.

It took her some time for her to feel her heartbeat calming. And though Snapper allowed her in, he was not a comfortable host. His was a less sensitive awareness than Rag's, with harder edges, as might be expected of a Phyros-trained horse. He formed colder connections, and had less complex desires, as might be expected of a gelding. Nevertheless, he accepted her presence, and his even-tempered mind sheltered her from the worst effects of the ring.

When the combination of full dark and a blanket of smoke made it hard to see the path, she heard Willard speaking, and reluctantly returned half her concentration to her human ears.

"We don't dare continue," he said. "If we meet a yoab now, we'll be at a significant disadvantage. I see a knoll that will give us high ground for camp. Follow me there."

To Caris's relief, the ring's initial surge of longing had receded to a steady, miserable ache—and a persistent idiotic urge to make her bed with Harric. With half her concentration still in Snapper, she was able to tolerate and resist the urges.

The others took their horses to the top of the knoll, but she tethered Rag and Holly at the bottom, far from Molly. Willard instructed them to prepare their gear and saddles for departure at a moment's notice, and to sleep beside their horses. Caris did as told, and as soon as she fed and groomed the horses, she collapsed onto her bedroll. Too soon, she'd have to rise again to help Willard, but she did not want to. She felt as though she'd betrayed him, too, with Molly. And she felt cornered by the Phyros. Lured. She felt her integrity and honor being bent, and she no longer wanted to be near her at all. But she did not know how to tell Willard.

Too tired to think on it, she sent her senses into Rag, and though the mare's distrust allowed only a shallow and tentative connection, they were both so tired that they plunged into sleep.

Bright Mother, Mad Father, Hag.
A white maiden in a black bag.
Old crone
Old stone
Where did she go?
I'll never tell
She's in the well
As bright as newest snow.

—Arkendian Children's rhyme referring to the Bright Mother's eclipse
during Krato's Moon

43

Web Strands & Moon Spirits

Just as Harric's eyes began to win a tedious tug of war with his will, something pinched his arm. He looked for the source, but saw nothing. When he opened his oculus, he found Fink's nose jutting dangerously close to his eyes.

Fink clapped a hand over Harric's startled cry. "Time to work on that stamina we talked about," he whispered, and plucked at the top button of Harric's shirt to indicate he should strip and join him in the Unseen. With a nod in the direction of the horses, Fink mimed something like a jerking wooden puppet, which Harric guessed meant Mudruffle was scouting nearby.

Harric rose and walked out of camp as if to piss, then stripped and joined Fink in the Unseen.

When they were well away from camp, Fink finally spoke. "Yeah, twig boy is all fancy tonight. You should see him: his eyes bugged out, ears the size of soup bowls."

"What do you mean?"

"I mean he's playing watchman, so we need to be extra careful getting you in and out of camp."

"You mean he altered his…head? To see and hear better?"

Fink nodded, jiggling his numerous chins. "Think of a bug-eyed, bat-eared apple and you have the right idea."

"If Kogan sees that, it's the end for Mudruffle. Where is Mudruffle now?"

"Last I saw, he was off to the north, examining a circle of toadstools." Fink shuddered. "Souls, those White Moon spirits are creepy."

"Right. Because you and your sisters aren't creepy at all." Harric's brow wrinkled. "I almost forgot. I agreed to let your sister take a look at the ring."

"She isn't into toadstools."

"I mean Caris's ring. Are we in for the treat of seeing Missy tonight?"

Fink's talons clicked in a messy wringing motion. "Haven't been able to find her; she's out in the edges of the Web somewhere. But I sent messages. And I have three days, remember? She should be here by tomorrow or the next night."

An hour later, Harric was hiking south down the Yoab Highway in nothing but boots and shorts as Fink hop-flapped alongside. Smoke made a fog of essence in the Unseen, so Harric walked more slowly as he practiced holding himself in the Unseen while navigating the trees and boulders and keeping his oculus tightly shut. It was not easy, and though the late summer evening would normally require an extra jacket, the exertion was enough to keep him warm without a shirt.

"You're doing well," Fink said, "but you're making a racket like a one-man market up above us. It's like a dinner bell to the scavengers every time you move."

Harric blushed. "You only told me about a smooth entrance into the Unseen, not a smooth transit of the Unseen."

"You weren't ready." Fink grinned at some private humor, and drew Harric to a stop. "Now you're ready. Look behind you and see for yourself."

All around them, placid strands rose like ghostly sea grass, streaming to the sky. But where Harric had passed, the strands swirled and wavered as if thrashed by a rogue breeze.

Harric winced. "Oops. At least they're calming down, right? No harm done?"

"No, *up*, kid. Look up. See? You did that, too."

Harric looked up through the smoke to where the rising strands interlaced and joined to form thicker and thicker ribbons that banded together until they were as thick as the heavy cables that once held the thunder spire above Abellia's tower. Those seemed to be the main strands of the Web, and it was there among the thickest strands that the Web was in tumult.

Not only were the thicker strands swinging and oscillating, but each one appeared to surge and tug against the next, increasing the discord. And rather than dissipating like waves in a disturbed pool, these vibrations took longer to diminish.

Fink winced at the sight. "Pretty impressive in a not-good way." He raised a finger to one side of the sky. "There's why."

Harric followed his gaze and saw for the second time in his life the vulturelike creatures of shadow that he'd watched feeding on the ghosts of Bannus's army. Three of them. His blood turned to ice as the shadows drew near, sliding down strands of the Web like beads on a string, their hollow eyes staring at Harric.

"Moons, Fink," Harric said. "Can you make them go away?"

Fink shook his head, scowling. His taloned hands twisted together. "They won't come. They know my sisters."

Harric thought he heard doubt, and stepped behind the imp as the shadowy spirits reached a place in the Web no farther than a stone's throw above them.

"Fink? How sure are you that you're on good terms with your sisters? Because these things don't look friendly."

One of the vultures leaned down from a strand as if it would drop like a spider on their heads. A weirdly keening hiss emerged from its gaping beak. "Your man tears the Web."

"It must be stopped," whined another.

"We will devour it," said the third.

"The man learns," said Fink, white eyes flicking from one to the other. "He will not disturb the Web anymore."

"It will not disturb the Web because I shall consume it," said the second.

"*I* shall consume it!" said the first.

"We shall together," said the third.

In the next moment, the vultures were growing, falling, and Harric dove back. As he landed on his back and side, and Fink tumbled across him with his wings spread in a protective fan.

"Stop!" Fink said. "You idiots! This man is why you're fat as maggots. He is the one that filled the rocks with dead men. Show respect and there will be more."

The vultures froze. Twelve feet tall, they loomed above, three-fingered claws poised to grab. Their empty-eyed heads tilted to study Harric.

"That?" said the first.

The head of the second bobbed on a skinny neck. "It fed us well."

"I'm sorry!" Harric blurted. "I didn't know. Now I know. He was teaching me."

The three burst into eerie, creaking laughter. "It is bound to the imp," said the second. "An initiate. Let us go." The second and third slid up into the Web.

The first remained bent above them, fat as an autumn goose in its robe of dull feathers. "Not bound." It shook its empty head. "Not a true bond. A false bond. There is no blood pact here."

"What are you talking about?" Fink sneered. "You're as blind as you look. My sisters know it and approved it."

The creature let out an eerie laugh. "Your sisters cannot see as I. You tread on tradition, imp. You do not continue the pact, and you allow the unbound man to flout the Web."

Fink hissed, and his wings snapped to the side in anger. "You have no idea what is at stake here, you empty-headed gib-crow—things much greater than any pact, things dearer to our mother than any tradition. And you'd be wise to keep your crooked beak out of it or you'll find Mother herself looking into your dealings."

The vulture thing looked at Fink for a long moment then cocked its head to examine Harric. "There is some truth to what you say."

Fink jerked his head toward Harric. "You owe him."

The vulture spread its ragged wings and slid upward, without flapping, into the Web. A dry chuckle filtered down. "We shall see."

Fink watched until it disappeared high above them in the welter of spirit strands. His little arms trembled, and the fat of his new belly quivered. "Souls," he spat. The black tongue flicked across his teeth. "That could be a problem."

"It knew our pact wasn't right."

Fink's hands twisted around each other. "He won't do anything. He's bluffing."

"You sure?"

"He just wants a bigger share of the souls next time." Fink licked his teeth again and peered up into the Web. "When we're done here, I'll track him and make sure that's his price. Can't have him talking."

Harric lay back for a moment and let his heartbeat settle. "Moons, Fink. Those things scared the bones out of me."

Fink nodded, but said nothing, still wringing his talons and staring up in the Web.

Harric risked a quick scan of the Web. The disturbance he'd caused had settled to an agitated ripple. Before this night, he'd noticed disturbances in the Web and meant to ask Fink about them, but had been preoccupied with bigger things. Now it appeared such things were not details at all, but fundamentals that might spell the difference between life and death.

"You're about to do it again," Fink warned. "Look at your nexus."

Harric looked. A bright loop of the Web was dipping slowly, questing blindly toward his nexus. His first impression was of a glowing noose, which was appropriate, but it also reminded him of the slow, probing arm of a river star questing toward a mussel. Either way, his natural reaction was to withdraw.

Fink motioned for Harric to stay where he was. "It's all right. Let it touch your nexus. I've kept them away till now, because I wanted you to work on stamina without any help from the Web. You'll know what I mean in a second."

As it drew nearer, Harric felt a strange lessening of his burden in the Unseen. He looked at Fink, wondering if the imp had started carrying some of his load, but Fink only shook his head.

"That's not me you feel—it's the strand. We call that a Web Strand. Raw spiritual energy."

The instant the strand touched his nexus, Harric gasped. He felt suddenly buoyant, as if his burden had vanished entirely, and it even restored his lost strength. But he didn't dare move his hand or he might jerk the Web again and draw the vultures, and his heart began to drum in his chest. "Fink—what do I do?" His voice rose with panic. "I'm afraid I'll jerk the Web again—how do I get it off?"

"Look who suddenly cares about living again." Fink gave a wry grin. "The Unseen has that effect."

"Help me! I don't know what to do!"

"Relax. Just don't move. Feels good, right? All that weight lifted from you?"

Harric stood motionless, his gaze glued to Fink. "Yeah."

"To get one to come to you, all you have to do is stay put for a while. One will come find you. If you want to stay in the Unseen for a while without moving, it's a great resource: free power. But you have to stay *absolutely still*, see? If you decide to move without detaching it, you pull it like a harp string, and the whole Web is your instrument, singing your clumsiness."

"So how do I detach it?"

Fink shook his head. "It's not enough to detach one when you notice it's glommed on, kid. You have to learn to anticipate it happening and double-check before you move again after you've been standing still."

Harric ran a hand through his hair. The Unseen was as complex as the Seen, but in the Unseen he was an infant learning to walk, recognize shapes and colors, learning their meanings and to distinguish safety and danger, friend and foe. He blushed when he thought of his pride in learning to walk for a while by himself.

The Web Strand on the nexus now engulfed his hand, too, and a faint, feathery thrumming filled his arm. A similar flutter of fear filled his heart.

"How do I detach it?" he repeated, his voice hoarse.

"You don't. Not yet, anyway. I'll do it for you. What I want you to work on now is getting in the habit of noticing what's going on around you. See how you affect the Web, and how the Nexus affects the strands near it. You have to see these things like you would notice wind and weather in the Seen." Fink frowned again and twisted his talons together. "I let you go too long without teaching this. A result of the… unusual circumstances of our partnership. But that has to change. You saw why."

He passed a hand over his Nexus and the strand released and floated back upward with the Unseen tides. In the same instant, the burden of the spirit walk fell again upon Harric.

"Let's head back to your camp," Fink said. "But keep your eyes open whenever we stop moving."

Another Web Strand quested downward, seeking to anchor on the nexus. Harric moved away from it and kept moving. As long as he kept moving at a walking pace, the strand appeared to be too slow to catch him. And the rest of their hike, he never encountered one low enough to accidentally run into it. It seemed they stayed up in the lower edges of the Web until he paused, and then they came questing down.

A thrill of wonder rippled up his spine. The Web seemed almost alive.

When he saw the first glimmer of lantern light in the camp, he gathered up his stash of clothing and dressed. Fink left him, and Harric crawled into his bedroll, exhausted.

He was just drifting into sleep again when Fink whispered near his ear. It had the eerie quality of a voice coming from the Unseen, like someone speaking through a long drain pipe. "Kid. Take a look at your girl."

Harric opened his eyes. Fink was not visible, but Harric saw movement on the other side of his oculus, and opened it wider to look at Fink in the Unseen. "She's not mine or anyone else's, Fink."

"Souls, kid. Can you give the freedom thing a rest? Just take a look."

Something ominous in the imp's tone made Harric climb out of his blankets and follow the imp to the edge of the knoll for a view of Caris lying in her blankets by Rag.

The change in her was striking. Where before she had blazed with bright blue strands of spirit like tall, lazy flames, now there were violet and purple strands—whiplike and aggressive strands that lashed among them.

Phyros Blood. He'd been right. Nothing but Phyros Blood shone violet in the Unseen. A feeble hope kindled in him. Maybe it wasn't her that tried to kill him after all. Maybe it had been the Blood rage.

A huge gray cloud lifted from his heart.

"You getting turned on, kid?"

"Hush."

Almost as strange as the Phyros strands, it looked like Caris's strands stretched to Rag, but Rag's strands remained aloof from Caris's—almost timid, like the tentacles of a snail, easily frightened and retracting when the violet strands lashed too close. Just as evident were changes to the weaves of spirit from the wedding ring. The weaves were now ragged, as if the purple whips had shredded them, and they smoked as if the violet whips burned.

"Willard's been feeding her the Blood," Harric whispered.

"*Fed* her the Blood," Fink said. "It's fading."

A chill rippled up Harric's spine. Did Willard know the Blood would erode the weaves of the ring? Was that why he had her take the Blood? And did she know? It might work, since Harric had seen how weak the wing got when Caris was angry and her strands worked up in their own kind of frenzy. But it was a dangerous game to play, and with a high cost that he almost paid himself in the form of a sword to the head. A new anger kindled in his chest against Willard: if he really had fed her the stuff, the old goat had better have been honest with her about it.

"Fink, do you think if she had another draught of Blood, the weaves would crumble?"

"Hard to say. But that's not all I wanted you to see. Look at her head."

Harric peered at her head, and what he saw made his heart sink. Some of the strands emerging had been bent and diverted and twisted into what looked like a crudely shaped crown. The bright purple strands had distracted him, but now it was plain as day.

The ring's third weave. It had awakened.

"It's a Mind Compulsion," Fink said.

Harric's throat grew tight. He nodded. "But a compulsion to do *what?*"

Fink's tongue flicked across his teeth. He shook his head. "Only way to know is to watch and wait."

Harric studied the ugly band, the last of his hope draining away. Unlike the Opening and the Body Compulsion, the Mind Compulsion hadn't been burned and scored by the whips of Phyros strands when they had been strong; it became active when the Phyros Blood had faded and its strands were weak, so the weave shone bright and robust in the Unseen.

Harric shook his head. "That's it, Fink. The deal with Missy is off. We're leaving before she wakes and it pushes her at me."

"Hey, hey, slow down, kid." Fink held his hands out. "No need to be hasty. Give it a day. You don't know what it does."

"We don't *have* to know what it does. It's a Compulsion."

"But Missy might be able to mute it. Two nights more, that's all, and Missy will be here."

"That's not our agreement, Fink. I said three nights *unless something changes*."

"I'm begging you for your own sake, kid, wait and see."

Harric frowned and shook his head. "It won't matter what Missy offers, Fink. Caris won't even talk to me, and there's no way she'll agree to have Missy mess with her soul."

"Are you kidding me? You think the girl would say no to that? She was ready to chop her finger off a few days ago."

Harric grimaced. Fink might be right. Her hatred of the ring was at least as strong as her fear of magic and her rejection of dishonor. And she didn't have to accept Harric to accept the help.

He turned his gaze again to the crown of strands encircling Caris's head. The thing pulsed as if feeding. His stomach rolled over.

"All right," he said. "I'll wait and see what it is." Fink's bald head bobbed up and down. "But I make no promises, Fink. If it goes bad tomorrow, don't ask me to stay another day while she suffers."

Fink's black tongue darted across his teeth. "How bad would it have to be, kid? Some people live with Compulsions all their life and no one knows it. It might be subtle."

Harric ran his hand through his hair. "I don't know, Fink. I won't know till I see it."

It is not enough to learn how to ride; you must learn how to fall.

—Arkendian saying

44

Fever Fires

Abellia's mind slid in and out of consciousness. Fever dreams, warped and frenetic, tossed her mind like paper in wind. In one, she held tight to a horse's mane, its unfamiliar bulk beneath and between her legs as she spurred it for Mudruffle's fire road.

A wind rose above her with the sound of some giant's furnace. Color bleached from the landscape, pure white, as if the sun had come down to look at her tower, and a hammer of heat fell on her head. Horses screamed. Men screamed. Then the furnace roar drowned all other sound.

Her horse galloped with the speed of panic, and its mane burst into flame in her hands.

Her own hair, wet from a bath, hissed like it had turned into snakes and bit at her scalp before bursting in flames. Hot teeth tore at her neck and scalp. Red-hot claws tore at her back and shoulders.

She knew then it wasn't a dream at all, but real things remembered in dream, and sobs racked her in her sleep. She wept for the grandmother she couldn't save from Sir Bannus. She wept for the horses who were not responsible for the horrors of their riders.

Two sisters of her order paid a visit to her dream bed. They stood above her with fury in their eyes. Sister Magda and Sister Jine, who had taken their oaths on the same day with her.

"Your selfishness consumed a moon stone," said Jine.

"How could you do it?" said Magda.

"Say, rather, that the Bright Mother consumed *me!*" Abellia said. "Is a life worth less than a stone? I took back what was mine." The strength of her conviction in the face of her sisters surprised her. But even as she spoke, she heard the hollowness of her argument, for her nexus, had it survived, could yet save hundreds more lives.

The sisters' faces wrinkled in disgust. A disgust mirrored in

Abellia's heart.

As they turned their backs, she grieved. "I did not mean to break it. I didn't know. I only wished to have my life."

She woke to find herself lying upon a cot, on her stomach and naked to the waist. Her scalp and neck and back screamed as if still on fire. Before her, a semicircle of sun-browned faces looked down at her with brows wrinkled in concern. These were peasant faces. They were not unlike those of Iberg country folk, good and industrious. But unlike Iberg folk, they knew nothing of Bright Mother healing. These faces bore scars of diseases and injuries no Iberg farmer ever bore, for a sister would have mended them easily. These were the faces of those who suffered disease without hope. Who put their hope in hokum and quackeries worse than the disease itself.

"Leave me!" she screamed. She tried to rise and push them away, but her limbs were bound to the legs of the cot.

One said, "Butter's best for burns."

"Not butter," said another. "Red-clay mud."

"Where you going to find red clay?"

"Let me go!" Abellia said. "Leave me to die!"

The Arkendians made a stretcher of the cot. Someone touched her back, and her flesh erupted in fire. She screamed, and looked to see a crone hunched beside her, dressed in rags and stinking of urine, her old hands covered in butter.

"No!" Abellia cried. "You will kill me!"

But the old woman persisted, smearing butter over every raw surface, and it felt like she scoured with wire brushes.

Abellia fell into darkness again, and fever warped her dreams. The old peasant woman became a bear. Other peasant bears bound Abellia to a stake and rubbed butter on her. They chewed her at leisure, sometimes roasting her over a fire and nibbling ears or fingertips, other times raking long strips from her back and scalp, until a father bear with wise eyes said, "Too skinny."

The father bear had a horse and a boy cub called Farley, and the cub called the father bear Captain.

Captain and Farley took her from the peasant bears and put her on a horse.

"I take her to the gallows," Captain told the peasant bears, and they looked sad, as if hanging were a waste of good food.

"Slay me, please, end this," was all it could croak,
So slay it he did, with a merciful stroke,
Sad for the thing that once was a man
And bound to avenge it with Belle in his hand.

—Verse from the ballad "Sir Willard & the Halls of Sir Bannus"

45

Midsummer Night's Curse

Caris woke from dreams of weddings. Of her own wedding. Of wedding Harric.

These visions made her stomach hurt. It made her head ache. But she could not get them out of her mind. Nor did she want to. Whatever her stomach felt about them, her head and heart embraced them.

When Caris was little, her mother had talked of weddings. She'd gushed about flowers and gowns and cakes and dancing, gods leave her. She talked about it so often—trying to draw her little horse-touched daughter into a shared vision of her future—that Caris had asked if she could marry her horse. "That way we'd always be together," she'd said, "and run in the same fields and drink from the same streams."

Her mother had fainted, and all her maids had to revive her with draughts.

Caris sat up in her blankets and put on her boots. There was no reason to delay: today, if she had her way, she would wed Harric. She rolled up her blankets, and as she stowed them, she reconsidered the date. Maybe not today. To be done properly, it must be held in a Noble House, not a wilderness. She remembered that much from her mother's sermons. In any case, they'd marry at the first appropriate place they found. It was time.

Time to marry Harric? A tiny part of her rebelled. *What the Black Moon am I thinking?*

A wave of nausea swept through her guts and her stomach convulsed. Turning, she vomited in the ferns. The trees spun around her, and the wave washed back in her belly and bunched, threatening another surge. She steadied herself against a tree and cursed under her breath. Now her head throbbed as if her brain were stuck in a vise.

Gods take it, she'd taken ill. Must have eaten something foul. She'd tell Willard to check their rations. As she started toward Willard's camp, a wave of dizziness made her stop and sway over her boots, and when she recovered, she struggled to recall what she'd been doing.

Tell Willard... Tell him what?

Tell Willard that since her father was not present, that he—as her mentor—must give her hand to Harric. The dizziness cleared, but she did not set out to tell him. Willard was particular about things. He would want to know who would marry them, and where it would be held, and she didn't have the answers to those questions yet. Better to wait until she at least knew that Father Kogan could perform the ceremony.

Harric woke to an anxious tension in his gut, and wood smoke heavy in the air. Willard's voice had awakened him.

"Feed the horses and pack up," the knight said. "I won't bleed Molly this morning. We strike out as soon as we arm."

The speed of their departure left little room for interaction with Caris, but Harric watched her closely for sign of the Compulsion. In the few moments before mounting, she alternately smiled or looked ill at the sight of him.

Swallowing his worries, Harric fell in line behind Willard and rode. It wasn't as easy as it had been, because the smoke in the air made the horses skittish. "Riding into a fire," he muttered to Spook, who sat in his basket, grooming. "Should have cast your lot with a smarter man."

Whenever a gap in the trees and smoke allowed, he looked to the northwest, where he saw lowering clouds of smoke, but sometimes glimpsed shards of orange wildfire.

Willard pushed their pace even harder.

To the north, where smoke hadn't blocked the view, he caught glimpses of the Godswall. Shining faces of vertical stone flashed in the sun. Snow-capped peaks gleamed like the fabled white palaces of the Kwendi. Though still two days' travel hence, the mountains loomed huge and seemed near.

"We're clear of the Yoab Maze," Willard said, when they crossed an upthrust of granite bedrock. "Closer we get to the Godswall, the thinner and rockier the soil. Not enough soil for the beasts to eat. Less danger we meet them."

"I regret my map is now of less use," said Mudruffle, still speaking through the cloth. "It is my experience that yoab paths grow infrequent where soil is shallow."

But while the main Yoab Highway had ended, lesser yoab trails remained. These were less direct and sometimes wandered into dead ends, but their wide, flat surfaces made travel easy for horses, so it was worth a little backtracking to follow them.

As they picked their way through one of these runs, Harric heard Kogan say something that caught his attention.

"A wedding?" the priest said. He rode behind Harric, with Caris. "Course I can. I'm a priest, ain't I? Har! But only yesterday you looked like you was ready to kill the lad."

Harric stiffened. He turned his head slightly to better hear what the priest said, but all he heard was the sound of Caris throwing up again.

"You with child?" Kogan's voice shifted into a merry tone. "Puking in the morning and looking to marry quick. I know how this goes."

"That is not true, father, and you must not say so." Caris's tone was sharp.

As the priest fell over himself apologizing, Harric's mind whirled. Wedding? She'd asked about a *wedding?* His gut felt like a load of damp clay. Glancing back at Brolli, Harric saw the Kwendi asleep under his blanket, but Mudruffle met his gaze with sparkling black eyes.

"—been too long away from ladies, you'll pardon me," Kogan was saying. "But you're ill, girl. Eat a bad seed?"

When Caris failed to answer, Harric turned back and pretended to adjust a saddle pack, so he could look at her through a fall of hair over his eyes. She was frowning, looking ill and twisting the wedding ring on her finger.

The Compulsion. It had to be. Fink said it'd be easy to tell what the spell did, and he was right. There was nothing subtle about it. The third weave was a failsafe Compulsion to force a wedding.

"Maybe a bad seed," she murmured. "It's nothing. But what is your fee for a wedding, father?"

"*Fee-ee?*" Kogan said. "I don't fee. I marry peasants, and what peasant can afford a fee when they can't afford to eat?"

"But you'd marry a—someone who isn't a peasant?"

"Never did yet, but I'd be honored."

Harric snorted. *No you wouldn't, father.* If the priest knew of the magic wedding ring on her finger, he'd refuse outright. In fact, if Harric wanted to scuttle any chance of the priest wedding them, he'd only need to reveal the ring to Kogan. It was a tempting thought, but the wedding ring was Caris's secret, not his, and there was no telling how Kogan would react. Even in the best of circumstances, the hairy giant was a wild card.

Upon hearing Kogan's agreement to wed her, Caris groaned as if he'd socked her in the gut. Harric watched in alarm as she leaned from her saddle, dry-heaving.

"You sure you're well, milady?" Kogan said. "You want I should stop Geraldine and get you a mouthful of curds? Nothing like ox curd to calm a stomach."

Unable to speak, Caris shook her head.

Harric's gaze snapped back to the road ahead. *You're cobbing kidding me.* Though he couldn't be sure, his gut told him that in addition to forcing her feelings, the Compulsion was spurring her toward a quick resolution by making her physically sick if she resisted it.

He stared, and as the brutality of the weave sank in, his course of action finally became clear—he would leave her. Waiting for Missy was no longer in the cards because Caris needed his help now, and Fink said the ring's weaves weakened the farther he got away because the ring could no longer pull many of Harric's strands to it. That much he *could* control: he's strike out on his own, put distance between them, and the Compulsion would leave her alone.

The thought did nothing to ease the ache in his chest, though. On the contrary, it made the break feel more complete, for once he left, he might never see her again.

He slipped his hand into Spook's basket to stroke the little cat.

Fink would be upset when he learned of Harric's decision. He wished now that he hadn't agreed to let Fink invite Missy to look at a way to remove the ring. The more he thought of Missy's horrible hooded skull and the cold emptiness of her presence, the less he trusted her, even if Fink thought he could control her. Harric's gut was beginning to tell him that having Missy look at Caris's spirit might be worse than never getting the ring off.

Cob it. I never should have agreed. But he hadn't been thinking clearly, and Fink had been so persistent. Hopefully Missy's reaction wouldn't be worse than Fink's. She would be…what? Angry? Vengeful?

He swallowed. *So be it.* Let her exact her price from him, if that was how it must be. As long as Caris was free, he'd pay it.

Caris's voice penetrated his meditation again. "Then all we need is a Noble House to have the wedding. Once we get back to the river…I don't know if there might be one this far north. Maybe Mudruffle's marked it on his map…if so, we could have it there."

"A Noble House?" Kogan said the word *noble* like it meant *latrine*. "You don't need a fancy house to get married. All of Holy Nature's your house! Noble House is hot and crowded with puffed talk and ragleaf and perfume and never enough light in the place. About the *least* holy place you could find."

"The house in my father's country was a restful and spiritual place."

"Oh, pah," Kogan said. "Never seen a Noble House wasn't hot as any cave in the underworld, and all them liars put together in one spot—more spirit-*less* places I never seen, unless it were inside a noble's skull, and I seen a few o' them, too, so I oughta know."

It took Caris a few moments to respond. "I didn't ask for a sermon against nobles."

"No, I gave you that free," said Kogan, without irony. "But I can give a wedding, all right—don't take me wrong—and anywhere you likes. Maybe you wouldn't mind a Common House? Sure to be a Common House or two once we're back on the Free Road, though I still say a field or a bit a forest is hall enough, for the true wedding's in your hearts, or what's the use of marrying?"

Harric stared ahead into the morning gray, his mind spinning through scenarios in which Kogan convinced Caris to marry right there or at the first farmhouse they found.

Another reason to leave that night.

At a wide spot in the yoab runs, Caris overtook Harric to ride ahead and draw up beside Willard. Harric urged Snapper to trot after her, but he was still too far behind to hear everything she said. He caught the words "wedding" and "Kogan," and saw the knight look up from the depths of his meditation to give her a long, trancelike stare. Puffs of ragleaf gusted from his helmet when he cast a look back at Harric. Harric pointed emphatically at Caris, then at his ring finger, and made whirling motions beside his head with his other hand, to indicate the ring took her out of her mind.

Willard's eyes narrowed, and he turned back to Caris.

"No Noble House this far north," Willard said, and Harric caught a few phrases that followed: "...more appropriate... Kwendi palaces."

A wave of relief rinsed away some of Harric's dread. Willard was making a play for putting the wedding off as long as possible—until their arrival in the Kwendi capital, where their enchanters could remove the ring before she forced the wedding. Caris seemed to consider this.

Score one for the old strategist. Maybe meditation was restoring some of Willard's sanity.

Spook looked up and yawned—probably from boredom in the basket, as much as drowsiness—and Harric gave him a rub under his chin. "Gods leave it, I'd love to have as few worries as you do, Spook."

"I got songs I sing at weddings," Kogan called ahead. He'd ridden Geraldine up close behind Holly and Idgit. "It's called 'Throw Me Down on a Bed of Hay.' Want to hear it?"

"Not fit for a lady's ears," Willard called back. "And I daresay you know none that are."

"Course I do, Will."

"Name one."

"*Name* one?"

Harric glanced back to see Kogan sitting straight as a pole, chin thrust forward, as if Willard had questioned his ability to move in polite circles.

When Willard returned his attention to the trail ahead, Harric asked the priest, "Do you know 'The Gravedigger's Song'?" Kogan returned his gaze with a blank but urgent stare. Harric translated: "'The Ditch Digger's Ditty'?"

"'The Ditch Digger's Ditty'!" Kogan bellowed. "Real old and fancy words, too. Just right for a lady."

And before Willard could object, Kogan sang.

> O, the battle's done, the army's passed,
> The graves all filled with flesh,
> So I bucked my trowel and spade and set,
> to find the battle fresh.
>
> Beside the track I paused to piss,
> in dimsy dullness wrapped,
> And found a knight, full on his back,
> in rusting armor trapped.
>
> Quoth he in desert, cracking voice,
> "Fetch drink, thou varlet knave!
> A drop of beer or wine or blood!
> I've naught but dew for days!"
>
> My breeches down, my cob in hand,
> I froze and shook with dread.
> Had he not spoke, unknowing I'd
> have drained it on his head—

"Cobs and pissing are fit topics for ladies?" Willard glared back, and Harric had to bite his lip to not laugh. As he expected, Caris's concentration appeared to be upon Rag, not the song, and judging by her wrinkled brow, that task wasn't easy an easy one today.

Kogan noticed none of this, and bulled along at the top of his lungs.

> Quoth he, "My name is Rivenstaff.
> A knight I am, and bold.
> Fast fetch me drink, thou varlet knave,
> Or fast I'll see thee sold."
>
> At this his noble blue blood boiled,
> and rattled well his plates,

Which rust had welded each to each,
as fast as men to mates.

'Twas then I knew he did not rest,
but captive lay in steel,
Nor could he budge a fingerlet,
nor lift his head or heel.

"I have nor beer nor wine nor mead,
dread lord, but I have tea."
"Not hot, but warm," quoth I. Quoth he,
"Then look thou give it me!"

Then freely, glad, I loosed my stream
down through his visor slot,
And there he drank the stinging brew
my kidneys two had wrought.

I left him sputtering, that lord,
and whistled as I went.
For that's the only gold a lord
should ever get in rent.
O! For that's the only sort of gold
a lord should get in rent!

Kogan beamed like he'd won a singing contest. "Didn't I *say* I could sing? How'd you fancy it, lady?"

Caris looked back gave the priest a quick smile and a nod. Willard noticed this, and to his credit, the old knight said nothing and kept his gaze forward, quietly shaking his head.

Kogan seemed disappointed with the reception. "I remembered another whiles I was singing," he said. "It's called 'The Longest Lance of All.' Have a listen—"

"Thank you, father, that is enough," said Willard. "The knave has had his jest."

Harric let out a long breath and shrugged. "We needed something to smile about."

"Liked it, did you?" Kogan grinned.

"It was a good song, father."

But in truth, it only diverted Harric for as long as Kogan sang. The cold weight of clay guts returned, and no amount of sighing relieved it.

When they stopped at midday to rest beside a brook, Harric picketed the horses in his string in a patch of dry grass, but left the saddles on in case they needed to ride on a moment's notice. As he rose from checking Snapper's rear hooves, Willard stood before him. Startled, he had no time to speak before the knight's enormous hand seized Harric's collars and shoved him back against a tree.

"What—?" Harric winced against the rough bark jabbing his back.

"Did you get her with child?" Willard said. His eyes—only inches from Harric's—shone with violet fury. "Is that the morning sickness in her?"

"With *child?*" Anger flared like resin fire behind Harric's breastbone. "To do that I'd have to touch her, your Holy Righteousness, and I carefully avoid that. And not because you forbid it, but because *I* forbid it." Furious, he still managed to keep his voice to a fierce whisper, so Caris would not hear him across the clearing. "It's your god-touched *ring*, Sir Willard. Like I tried to tell you."

Willard held his glare for several long moments, breathing loudly through his nostrils. Harric tempted fate to speak so openly to this blue-furied Willard, but he couldn't stop himself. His grief and self-hatred boiled over.

Willard released Harric and stepped back. "If you take advantage of that ring..."

"The ring you were supposed to be protecting? The ring you gave me without telling me it was magic?" Harric stepped forward to look up in Willard's face. "You're the one who's hurt her, not me. I'm doing right by her."

"Sir, shall we go?" Caris called.

Willard held Harric's glare a moment longer, then snorted and gave Caris a curt nod.

"We just dismounted. I thought we were resting the horses." Harric looked from Willard to Caris and back. "You mean *you're* leaving us again?"

"Yes." Willard's ragleaf breath assailed Harric. And with that, he left Harric and mounted Molly.

"You're stopping everything so you can get another mouthful?" Harric said, once the knight had started Molly away. He couldn't keep the dismay and anger from his voice. "Is it no matter that every hour of daylight we lose is an hour Sir Bannus gains on us?"

Willard rode away without acknowledgement, and Caris fell in behind him. She glanced over her shoulder, eyes unmistakably amorous, and it punched a spike of guilt and helplessness through Harric's chest.

Turning away, he strode toward Idgit, where Brolli slept in his saddle.

"Time for some answers, ambassador," he muttered.

"Hope you don't mind, Master Harric," said Kogan, as Harric passed. The priest reclined against Geraldine, who lay in the grass, chewing cut. "Your cat was mewing something pitiful, so I took him for a bit of Geraldine's milk." Spook looked up from a cup where he'd buried his face, white flecks in his whiskers.

"Thank you, father," Harric said.

"You going to tell *him* about Willard going off?" The priest nodded toward Brolli.

"No. I…" Harric almost said, *I don't trust him,* but wasn't sure Brolli was truly asleep or listening. "No."

Kogan nodded. "I'll have a talk with Will, and he'll see sense. It ain't like Will to let the Blood make him sloppy like this."

"You?"

Kogan tossed a twig at Harric. "You'll see, you puppy. He'll listen to me."

Harric shrugged. "Better than me trying, that's for sure. But maybe work out what you're going to say before you say it?"

Kogan closed his eyes and stretched back to enjoy the sun. "Never did before. Probably jinx it if I do."

"Right. What could go wrong?"

Harric left him and strode up to Idgit, where he stripped from Brolli's head the blanket that acted as his artificial night. "I'm sorry to wake you, ambassador," he said, not bothering to veil his agitation, "but I need to know if you know anything else about that wedding ring."

Brolli blinked himself awake, huge gold eyes squinting against the light. "What is it?" he slurred. "What is— What?"

"It's Caris. She's throwing up," Harric said, keeping his anger in check but ignoring Brolli's irritation. "It's the wedding ring. I'm sure of it. It's making her talk about marrying me, and if she resists, it socks her in the gut until she pukes."

Brolli flipped his daylids down, frowning. "It…may be."

"So, let me get this straight," said Harric. "Your people thought the Lone Queen might need to force a mate? Thought he might need to be kicked in the gut until he wed her?"

Brolli frowned. "I am sorry for Caris. We had bad understanding of your people. My people have no mate for life. We do not have this thing called a 'wedding.'"

"Which is why you shouldn't have made a wedding ring!"

Behind the daylids, Brolli's face went stony. "It is unkind to retell this. We know this now."

Harric bit back on his frustration and ran a hand through his hair. "All I know is that Caris is now compelled to marry, and the wedding ring is hurting her. She can't endure this forever, Brolli. Is there nothing more you can tell me to help her? Do you have any idea how wrong that is for her? I don't think Willard can even *have* a married apprentice, and knighthood is everything to her."

Brolli was now like a statue of a Kwendi. Slowly, he shook his head. "How can I say I am sorry another way?"

Harric sighed. "You can't." He handed Brolli his blanket and turned away. "But please tell me if you think of any way to help her."

Any way other than me leaving.

Three things I've learned in Arkendia: fear the goat from the front, the horse from the rear, and a courtier from all sides.

—First Ambassador Brolli to his page escort on the day before he abandoned the court

46

Of Death & Revelation

In spite of himself, Harric slept in a spot of sun and did not wake until the sound of a snapping branch nearby woke him with a start.

Clambering to the top of a log, he peered down the run in the direction of the sound, where Caris and Willard rode into view. As before, the old knight sat upright, staring, and apparently deep in his trance of meditation. Caris remained in her saddle as well. She was clearly in communion with Rag and the other horses, for her gaze was about as remote as Willard's.

Harric hopped down from the log and crossed to the priest, who snored on his back with Spook asleep at the summit of his belly. Lifting Spook, Harric said, "Father," and kicked the dirt-black sole of the priest's bare foot. "It's time."

"Wha— I'm up."

Harric placed Spook in his basket as Willard passed, eerily quiet. Caris followed, gaze so inward that she barely regarded Harric. It seemed she was back in the world of horses and that whatever difficulty she'd had with Rag the day before had been resolved. It relieved him to know she could flee from the Compulsion into that world.

Harric mounted, and after a quick look to be certain the priest was on his feet and readying Geraldine, he rode after Willard, with Caris close behind.

Smoke hung like a haze in the great corridors of trees, making Harric's eyes and throat raw. Willard set a grueling pace without stopping for rest, and as night approached and they finally stopped to camp, both riders and horses were exhausted.

Spook ran straight for Geraldine, where Father Kogan milked her heavy udders.

Kogan stooped to fill a cup for Spook, and the cat swatted at his hanging beard. Chuckling, he said, "I'm like to steal your cat from you, Harric."

"You may well be a better friend to him than I. Let me loan you his basket, and see if he won't travel with you tomorrow."

"I wouldn't say no to that."

Harric watered Snapper, double-fed him, and rubbed down the gelding's steaming muscles. The poor horse wouldn't get much sleep tonight, for Harric would sneak him out of camp and leave as soon as he had an opportunity, and then he'd travel all night to get a head start.

When he'd finished checking Snapper's hooves and shoes, he packed for his departure by preparing two bags that he could carry on foot, in case he couldn't get Snapper out of camp without waking the others. The first was his mother's travel pack, where he stowed all essentials and a three-day supply of strong bread; the second was Captain Gren's spitfire pack.

As he finished with the packs, Willard called them together. Brolli and Mudruffle were already with him, holding up Mudruffle's map and pointing out features to Willard when Harric arrived.

"Take a good look at this map again, all of you." Willard pointed to their valley and to the adjacent valley where the fire burned. "So far, it seems this new wind has been our friend. It's blown the fire back on itself, so the fire is dying, starving for fuel. Brolli will keep watch for any chance the new wind blows the fire into our valley while we sleep, but the chances of that are dwindling."

"That is good news," Kogan said.

"Mudruffle has agreed to show us what he knows of our path tomorrow," said Willard. "And I want you to pay close attention, so you'll know where to go if we're separated." He nodded to Mudruffle, and the little golem stepped forward, gave a stiff bow, and laid his finger on the map.

"We are here now," he said, indicating a spot near the top of the map, just below a spot he'd named Toothed Canyon. Above the canyon, annotations were scarce, a shortcoming Harric guessed Mudruffle intended to remedy now. "The Toothed Canyon is only a half-mile long, but the cliffs there are so severe that I have found only one way through, and that way is hidden by the river for most of the year by powerful waters. We are fortunate that in summer the water is low enough to reveal it: it is a ledge of stone that runs along the edge of the river on this side."

"So it's a riverside trail?" said Harric.

"It is."

"Make no mistake," said Willard, "this canyon is a bottleneck in the valley, and if Bannus wishes to cut us off, he might have run up the other side of the river to meet us there. I think it unlikely, but we must be on our guard."

The others exchanged uneasy glances.

"So we follow the yoab runs from here to the canyon," said Harric, drawing a line north along the river with his finger, "and when we get to the canyon, we climb right down to the water to find the ledge, and follow the ledge up the canyon."

"That is correct." Mudruffle turned away from the map to face them. "When we are through, we will be near the Godswall, and we will turn west to find a pass back to the River Arkend."

"*If* there is no fire beyond the canyon," said Willard. "If there's fire in our valley or in the pass we want to take, we keep heading north for a pass along the feet of the Godswall."

"How likely is a pass west along the feet of the Godswall?" Harric said.

Willard snorted. "Less likely than dying in a burning pass, but I'll take my chances with the Godswall, all the same." The knight turned to Brolli. "If the fires enter our valley, wake us and we will flee."

"I will go to my watch now," said Brolli. "And I have seen fresh elk tracks. Tomorrow, Lady Molly will feast, or I am no hunter."

Willard nodded. "Harric will bring your nightly breakfast to you. Something hot. With all this smoke in the valley, no one will notice if we have a little cook fire. And one thing more." He gave Kogan a

long look, then stuffed a fresh ragleaf in his mouth. "Father Kogan has
convinced me of the wisdom of riding days and taking the Blood only
at night."

Harric looked up, but Willard avoided his gaze. Kogan smuggled
Harric a wink.

"Well, I'll be hanged," Harric muttered.

"Come, girl." Willard beckoned to Caris, and she acknowledged
with a nod. After her wedding discussion with Willard, she'd retreated
into the world of horses and scarcely come out.

"We will find a spot back on the road we took today," Willard said.
"As soon as I'm stable again, we return and you can get some sleep."

Willard rode, and Caris followed, holding a candle lantern high on
a pole. She did not look in Harric's direction.

"Farewell," he said, too soft for her to hear, for it could well be the
last he ever saw of her.

Harric picked up Spook, whose soft belly was as round and full of
milk as Fink's was full of souls, and sat by the fire to pet him as Mudruffle
boiled cakes of strong bread. Boiling the confection-like bread turned
it into a hot and delicious pudding, and the change was welcome to
Harric. With Spook in his lap, he wolfed two bowls. When finished, he
filled a bowl with Brolli's portion, and set out in the direction he'd seen
Brolli leave for his watch.

He found the Kwendi sitting atop a rock bluff some twenty fathoms
above the river. The view of the smoky valley and the scattered fires on
the opposite ridge was expansive, and though the waters rushed wide
and vigorous below, the bluff was high enough that its noise there was
little more than a sigh.

"Nights are getting cold," Harric said as he approached.

Brolli's head turned and his huge eyes flashed like a cat's eyes in the
silver light of the Bright Mother. He had bundled himself in his travel
cloak and seated himself on a boulder at the edge of the bluff. He held
below his nose a witch-silver cup full of steaming tea. Harric hadn't
seen that cup before, but the fact that it was witch-silver as much as
guaranteed it was enchanted.

"And here is the gliding frog among locusts," Brolli murmured. "Here is the only one to trust, for he has the most powerful aphrodisiac of the world, and does not use it."

Harric's shoulders stiffened and he bit back on a retort. Was that a jab or a compliment? Letting out a breath, he let it go; he had already snapped at the Kwendi that day, and he wanted to part on good terms. "Brolli, I am sorry for my rudeness today. The ring is not your fault."

Brolli looked up from his cup and stared at Harric for a long moment. "I thank you. And I thank you for the food." Brolli nodded at the bundle in Harric's hands. "You may put it down."

Harric set it on the boulder beside Brolli. An uncomfortable pause followed, while the Kwendi stared into his cup, which gave off a little puff of steam. Spook's big eyes were fixed on the puff as it rose, and he let out a sound that was half mew, half purr.

Brolli said something in Kwendi, and Harric's eyes narrowed. Was he talking to the cup? And was it talking *back*? Harric couldn't hear it saying anything, but something about it gave Harric the impression that Brolli was talking *through it* to someone. The mere possibility of such powerful magic set him aback. Not only had Brolli been learning Arkendian culture in the Queen's Court and with Willard on the road, but he could share it with someone back in the Kwendi cities…if they even *had* cities.

A faint chill passed through Harric's middle. Everything he knew of the Kwendi had come through Brolli, who could reveal as much or as little of the truth as he wanted. It made Harric feel toyed with and vulnerable. Of course, the balance of secrets between Arkendia and the Kwendi had always been in the Kwendi's favor—much like it had been in favor of Fink in Harric's relationship with the imp—but this changed everything. And now that Brolli was openly critical of Arkendia, it made Harric doubly uneasy.

"That is a very interesting cup," Harric said, wondering if someone else could hear him through the receptacle.

Brolli smiled. "We've shared many a night's beginning."

"You said something just now that made me think of something I hadn't thought of before."

"Mm? What is that?"

"You called the ring an *aphrodisiac,* and it occurred to me what an advanced vocabulary you have. Most Arkendians don't even know that word. They'd just say a 'love charm.'"

"Hear this!" the Kwendi said, the cup still under his nose. "I have advanced Arkendian words. That means strong."

"It just seems amazing that you speak our language so well when we only discovered your people last year."

Brolli's eyes flashed in the moonlight. "It's true. You knew nothing of us. But we have known of you for many years. Your knights have wandered our forests since before my mother's girlhood."

Harric stared. "You mean knights who went north on Redemption Quests?"

"You call them so, yes. I think instead of the banishing, a knight may take the Redemption Quest to bring back the horn of a spear dragon from our forest, yes? And if he succeeds, your queen forgives him his offense and the banishment."

Harric nodded. "But no one expects to come back. It's more of a way to die with honor. I don't think anyone has returned from one."

"That is so, because we capture these knights and from them learn much, including your language."

Harric blinked in surprise. It took a moment to be sure he'd heard the Kwendi correctly. Then a flame of anger flowered in his chest. All those knights never even had a chance to die in the way they'd chosen. "Why did you capture them? They weren't your enemies."

"Were they our friends?" The Kwendi gave Harric a sharp look and took another sip from his mug. "Would you let a strange creature crash through your farms without explanation? Before we knew the language, we did not know what they wanted. They just appeared and smashed through the forest. And if we let them disturb a dragon, our truce with the dragons would be lost, and the dragons could destroy us. That would be a greater tragedy than capturing a favor-less knight, yes?"

Harric knew his own anger was making him unreasonable. Nothing Brolli said was anything he might not have done himself, but it made him furious that the Kwendi people had known so much about Arkendia before the Arkendians knew anything of them.

"You could have turned them back to Arkendia," he said, looking for some moral basis for his anger. "You didn't have to capture them."

"How?" Brolli's tone bore no warmth or sympathy. "Even if we knew the language, how would we convince a banished knight to turn back home?" The cup spouted steam, and Spook, still staring at it, let out another purring mew.

"Before my mother's time, we killed the knights. Back then, your knights were rare. But in my lifetime, they came more and more often. We now know it was because of your queen's long peace and bad temper that so many were banished. It was my mother who decided to capture them and learn their language, so we could know what they wanted. Not all the clans liked this idea. But by capturing them, we have language for diplomacy with your people. It is law we learn to speak. If we had not done so, there would be no path but war."

Another chill passed through Harric. He felt like an ignorant child at the foot of a tutor.

Brolli's pointed canines flashed. "We are a nation of bastards, Harric. We, like you, do what we must to survive. I think we are good at it."

Bristling inwardly at the comparison, Harric forced himself to swallow his objection. "You had reasons," he said. "Even good ones." It was hard to admit it. Not only had the Kwendi fed back to him his own bastard survival philosophy, but by admitting the wisdom of the Kwendi, he admitted the ignorance of his own people.

Mercifully, something in the river caught Harric's eye, giving him an excuse to change the subject. He pointed to the moonlit rapids. "Look there. Are those milled boards?"

Brolli looked and nodded. "It is sawed planks. They are stuck in rocks."

"That means there's a settlement in this valley, upstream somewhere beyond the Toothed Canyon. And a settlement means a road." Harric smiled, relieved. His solo expedition didn't seem quite as terrifying as it had been a moment before.

"This is good," said Brolli. A puff of steam rose from his cup. Brolli glanced at Harric and gave him a wooden smile. "Thank you for the food," he said, as if dismissing him.

"Quiet watch." Harric left him to his post, but rather than returning to camp with a clear heart, he felt newly troubled. Before, it had seemed to Harric that the Kwendi were a wronged people struggling to make a quick peace with an invader. Now it appeared that they had far more cards in their hand than he'd supposed, and that the Queen's hand was much weaker. And he couldn't shake the sense that Brolli had ended their conversation so abruptly because he was up to something and impatient to get to it.

It might be as simple as Brolli wanting to throw the strong bread in the river and open his magic closet to eat a proper Kwendi snack. Or maybe Harric had interrupted a lover speaking to Brolli through his cup. But that hadn't been the mood Harric felt there. If he had to guess, he'd say he interrupted official business. Could Brolli make nightly reports to his people through the cup?

When he returned to their camp, Harric found it empty of all but the horses and Kogan, who lay beside the musk auroch, snoring like an overfed yoab. Caris and Willard were still somewhere to the south, bleeding Molly, and Mudruffle had gone east to map a fork of the yoab run. When Spook saw Kogan, he squirmed, and Harric walked him over to let him down on Geraldine's ample back, where he curled up for another nap.

"Farewell, Spook," Harric murmured. "You've been a good friend, but I leave you with a better provider. Stay safe."

A deep ache squeezed Harric's heart. Already he felt more alone than he had since the night of his last birthday, on which he'd been cursed to die.

Well. Farewells are a kind of death, too.

He left a note explaining his departure in terms of his concern for Caris, and his reasoning that putting distance between them would weaken the ring's influence. That it was what the real Caris would want him to do in this situation, in any case.

Then he took one last look at the camp, and led Snapper into the trees.

If Fate wants to kill you, she first makes you stupid.

—King Hamor, in *Apoligia for the Cleansing*

47

Revelation

Harric's plan was to take the horse north up the yoab trails and then down to the trail beside the Toothed Canyon. Once through the canyon, he'd look for the settlements on the other side. If he got through before dawn, he might be able to spot the morning cook fires. And a settlement would have information—and a road. Traveling alone, he'd be less conspicuous than the group with a Phyros-rider, auroch, wandering priest, and female knight.

Peering through his oculus into the Unseen, he led Snapper north along the main yoab run. A half-mile on, the run forked toward the river and the Toothed Canyon, just as Mudruffle's map predicted. There he walked Snapper off the run and into the labyrinth of logs and hummocks. When he found a mossy basin concealed by thimble berry and ferns, he hobbled Snapper and let the gelding go back to sleep.

"Fink, you here?" Harric whispered. Climbing to the top of a log so ancient it was now more hill than tree trunk, he peered about the spirit-lit forest.

"*Nebecci, Tasta, Tryst.*"

After a few heartbeats of waiting, he wondered if he had pronounced the words to the summoning incorrectly. Nebecci, *Jasta,* Tryst? But then a shadow of black smoke formed against the essence light of the moss, and Fink materialized.

His grin flashed as he looked around the grove, but when he saw Snapper saddled and packed, his wings drooped along with his expression. "Kid. What are you doing? What happened?"

"Hey, Fink." Harric shook his head apologetically. "I'm leaving. The Compulsion has her thinking of weddings and throwing up when she tries to resist it. It's hurting her, but if I get out of her sight, it should be better, like you said. I still want to help them for a while, though; I'll stay a day ahead and scout out danger on the roads."

While Harric spoke, Fink's talons twisted together like a tangle of fishhooks. His triple-chinned head shifted nervously from side to side. "Scouting ahead. That could work. Sort of with them but not with them. And we could take Missy back tomorrow night to take a look at the weaves."

Harric's gut knotted. "Maybe you should tell her to hold off a while—"

"Kid." Fink's voice hardened. "We don't tell Missy to wait." Behind the hardness, an edge of panic lurked in the imp's tone, and it set a burr of dread in Harric's heart.

"Then tell her it's off," Harric said. "That was our deal."

Fink cringed and twisted his talons. "That was *our* deal, kid, sure. But you don't offer Missy a deal like that."

"You mean you didn't tell her we'd call it off if something changed?"

Fink shook his head, jowls jiggling. "This is a mistake, kid."

"It's not. I know what I have to do." Harric sucked a deep breath and sighed. "I have other news, too. I just watched Brolli talking into a witch-silver teacup. And I think it talked back."

Fink's brow wrinkled. "Talking to it? What'd it say?"

"I couldn't hear it, but I think *he* could." Harric frowned. Some of Brolli's words—*locusts,* and *do what we must to survive*—came back to gall him. He made a decision. "Come on. I have a feeling about him tonight."

"So you're *not* leaving?"

"Not just yet."

A sound made them both freeze. A soft crack, like a boot on a rotten branch.

They both vanished into the Unseen.

The burden of maintaining himself in the spirit world fell on Harric so hard that he nearly fell to one knee.

"Your clothes, kid," Fink whispered. "Take off your clothes."

Harric glimpsed Brolli moving between trees not fifty paces away. "No time. Look." Brolli's huge Kwendi eyes turned in their direction as he hiked past, but he did not pause or change his direction.

As Fink lifted the burden of the Unseen from him, Harric rubbed the lucky jack card in his sleeve and willed Snapper to remain silent. It would be a very bad time for the horse to fart or snort or step on a twig. Thankfully, the gelding preferred to sleep, head down, and Brolli passed without noticing.

When they could no longer hear him, Harric nodded to Fink, and they followed.

Brolli avoided the yoab run and zigzagged through the log maze, sometimes over but usually around the seedling logs, and generally northward. Scouting their path to the Toothed Canyon, probably, or looking for a better vantage of the fire on the opposite side of the valley. Harric was glad he hadn't taken Snapper down the fork of the yoab run, or the Kwendi surely would have seen the hoof prints.

In the Unseen, the Kwendi's spirit looked different than those of Harric or the others. Instead of pale blue, it had a greenish tint, and instead of rising upward, his strands bent north. *North?* It looked almost like Brolli was following his strands northward.

Harric's brow wrinkled. Why wouldn't Brolli's strands go to the Unseen Moon, like everyone else's? He glanced to Fink, but didn't want to risk speaking out loud. He'd ask about that later. To keep up with Brolli, Harric had to concentrate intently on the forest floor in front of him, for it was not easy to move across it silently. Beneath the moss were twigs and branches that could snap as loud as a breaking bone, and he worried Brolli would lose them. But shortly after they'd crossed the fork of the yoab run, Brolli halted.

He had stopped in a sunken hollow between trees and logs, much like the one in which Harric had seen him with magic closet. Brolli set something in the moss beside him, and Harric recognized it as the cup he'd been talking into, only now it had a little lid on the top, and in the Unseen, Harric saw that many of Brolli's strands were caught up in it. Harric glanced at Fink and mimed talking into a cup, and Fink nodded. The imp's grin glittered, and his white eyes shone like little moons. *Bright Mother Moons*, Harric mused. Fink would hate the comparison.

From his satchel, Brolli produced a long rod of witch-silver, which looked like a rod of blackness in the Unseen. But the moment he drew it from its sheath, it seemed to suck Brolli's strands—almost all of his strands—into it, like a greedy mouth sucking in a plateful of noodles. As he set it the moss before him, the strands enwrapped the rod so tightly it began to blaze like a rod of solid lightning, hot and dangerous.

Fink's eyes widened.

Brolli removed the lid on his cup, releasing a puff of steam, and wrapped his hands around it. "I am ready." He spoke in Arkendian, and Harric instantly imagined an Arkendian listening at a cup like it somewhere else. This idea vanished when Brolli chuckled and said, "You do not practice your Stilty." After a pause, he chuckled again. "I am ready. Now."

Brolli stooped and grabbed the rod in its center, and then lifted it straight up from the ground, keeping it horizontal, until it was above his head; in the air below the rod now stood the dark rectangle of the magic closet. Brolli released the rod, but it remained where he left it—hovering above—like the lintel of a dark doorway. The black surface of the door glistened like liquid tar.

"Mother Doom…" Fink said. "That's a gate. Mortals can't do that."

"It's a closet," Harric whispered. "I saw it a couple nights ago. Meant to tell you. He keeps things in it."

The door rippled sleepily, as a Kwendi head poked through the tarry surface of the door, followed by the rest of him as he crawled to his feet on the moss.

Harric nearly fell over backward in surprise.

The new Kwendi reached back through the door and helped another climb through.

Both newcomers wore light clothing and bandolier satchels equipped with painted cudgels and hurling globes like Brolli's. They took up stations on either side of the doorway as a third came through. This last grinned roguishly at Brolli, like a brother, and swatted him on the arm. The two conversed briefly in Arkendian, but Harric was too far away to catch more than a few words, like *yoab*, *knights*, and maybe *big deer*. Brolli made some gestures to the east and the west and to the south when the other asked questions.

A new sense of danger and disbelief dawned in Harric. The magic closet was in fact a gate that led to Brolli's people. And apparently each night, while Willard and the others slept, the other Kwendi joined Brolli to help him with his scouting.

He blinked several times, mouth working mutely. *Gods leave it, he's been bluffing this whole time.*

And I fell for it.

Once the shock subsided and he was able to close his gaping mouth, some things became clear to Harric. First of all, the gate explained how Brolli had justified the unreasonable risk of striking out from the Queen's court on his own in the first place. Harric had always thought that strange, but it made more sense once he knew Brolli could gate home to safety once night fell. But this also meant the danger he and his friends endured had been unnecessary—and worse than that, Abellia had died for no reason. And what stopped Brolli from taking Caris through the gate to his people so they could remove the ring? Even if she refused to use the gate, Brolli could have brought a Kwendi magus to her!

A blaze of anger filled Harric's chest.

This gate also meant they could have agreed upon and signed the Queen's treaty by now. Brolli could have brought Willard through the magical doorway, or he could have brought the Kwendi officials here.

So why hadn't he?

The burn in Harric's chest cooled quickly, replaced by a hard lump of dread. Maybe they had no intention of signing a peace treaty with the Arkendians. Was this whole quest with Willard a ruse, a diversion, a farce? But if so, for what? To set them up for a surprise attack?

Harric's face burned with shame. Brolli had been playing him, and he hadn't sensed it. Whatever Brolli's game, in that instant he went from a practical politician and sometime friend to a treacherous foreign agent without scruple against harming Arkendians.

Harric crept toward the gate before another heartbeat passed.

It wouldn't be enough to simply expose Brolli's secret to the others. The ambassador could lie his way out of that, and the advantage of surprise would be lost. Surprise and the Unseen were the best cards in Harric's hand, and they were powerful cards. If he went all in, he could beat the Kwendi at his own game.

Brolli was not the trickster here. Harric was. A fact Brolli would learn the hard way.

Harric halted three paces from the door, with Fink tugging frantically at his shirttail.

The leader of the Kwendi scouts made a strange gesture to Brolli. Crouching forward on the knuckles of both hands, he bared his teeth in a forced, feral-looking grin. Was it some kind of salute? Brolli mirrored the grimace, then stepped through the gate and vanished as if he'd plunged into a vertical pool of tar.

Knocking Fink's hand from his shirttail, Harric took a step toward following, careful to approach it straight on so he could split the distance between the Kwendi standing to either side of it. The one on the right unslung his satchel and took from it a fast-running sandglass, which was already mostly drained. Judging by the amount of sand already passed, it measured the time the gate would remain open. If that were true, Harric had less than half a minute.

Fink gave up tugging Harric's shirt and clambered up his back to put his lipless mouth to Harric's ear. "Are you crazy? Don't go in there!" It was a plea. But Harric sensed something else, too—a hesitation, or reluctance, desire blunted by fear.

Heart hammering in his chest, Harric crouched to spring into the liquid darkness of the door. *I can do this. It's not a lightless pit. It's a door. I'll step from moss onto a tiled floor in a palace.*

He held up three fingers and caught Fink's eye. Then two fingers. Then one.

Fink clutched Harric's shoulders like the claws of a startled cat, and Harric leapt.

Into a void of silent, starless darkness where another gate hovered almost in reach.

Then he plummeted.

I am not fit for your queen's court, for I don't know how to lie.

— From First Ambassador Brolli's farewell note to his pageboy, Rilf

48

Fear And Trembling

Harric flailed an arm back to make a grab at the foot of the gate as he fell past it, but his leap had carried him too far away. Then, to his astonishment, he saw he hadn't fallen at all—or else the gates fell with him, for there they were, on either side of him, and no air whipped by—yet his stomach rose exactly as if he were falling. Weightless, he hung between the gates in a void of silent darkness, unable to reach either. If there had been a bridge between the gates, it seemed Brolli had taken it with him through the other gate, leaving Harric stranded.

Beyond the gate lay the quiet vision of an interior room with carpets and furniture. But Harric could not reach it. No matter how he moved his feet, there was nothing to push against, so he could not close the distance or move in any direction.

When he craned around to see the gate behind him, with its vision of green forest, that gate collapsed on itself and disappeared.

His heart began to flutter like a panicked dove. "Fink! I can't reach the gate!" he said, but the void ate the sound like he'd spoken into a pillow.

Move! Fink squeaked, not a voice, but a thought. *To the gate! Before it closes!*

Harric flailed. "It's not getting closer!" The thought of being left behind in that weird, weightless void without any anchoring reference set his mind roaring between his ears.

Reach out to it!

Harric reached with one hand, straining, and the doorway moved a little bit closer to him—or he toward it; there was no way to distinguish—but remained out of reach. He threw both hands out, reaching and grasping, and his hands passed through the liquid plane onto soft fur carpet. In that moment, spanning two spaces, he felt utterly out of place in the void—a foreign entity, a hated intrusion of space, time, light, and sound into nothingness.

As he pulled himself forward and passed through the pane, weight and light stunned him like a blow. Fink clapped both hands over Harric's mouth as he fell to hands and knees on a carpet of perfumed furs.

As Harric steadied himself on the fur rug, Fink released him and hopped aside, white eyes wide with fear. Spirit light illuminated the room, banishing the dark of the void. Strong smells of tar and unfamiliar spices assailed Harric's throat and nostrils, forcing him to swallow, lest he choke.

Above and behind him, the sound of silvery bells tinkled, and he looked up to see another witch-silver rod, suspended in air at the top of the weird black doorway from which he'd just emerged. The rod tinkled again, and then it dropped like a stone to the carpet, closing the gate as it fell.

Harric clambered to his feet and pressed his back against a wall to scan the room.

They'd landed in a huge cylindrical room, floored and paneled with wood, so in the Unseen it was bright with spirit essence. It reminded Harric of a drum tower, like Abellia's, but without floors above or stairways climbing up to them. Instead, the airy space was crisscrossed with countless branches, each as thick as his wrist and radiating from a pillar in the center to anchor in the surrounding walls. It was as if they'd built the drum around a spoke-limb tree made of polished wood. At various levels in the spokes above him hung enclosed wooden platforms, like tents or pavilions high in the branches. Harric counted at least a half-dozen, each at different levels and different sides of the central "tree." The nearest were three or four fathoms above, with the uppermost at ten or twelve fathoms before branches and platforms obscured further view.

Something thumped in one of the nearest pavilions, and Fink flung himself back against the wall beside Harric.

Straining to find the source of the noise in the glow of the essence, Harric saw greenish spirit strands so bright they could only be those of a Kwendi. The strands streamed from a large pavilion some six fathoms above, and dove down and into the ground.

"It feels good to be in armor again." It was Brolli's voice, from the pavilion.

He appeared on a branch beside the pavilion, wearing a strange, puffy quilted vest. Stepping from the limb, he descended amongst the multitude of branches in a kind of controlled fall, his hands and feet slapping and thumping on the branches as he passed them. Harric held his breath as Brolli stopped and hung from both hands right beside Harric and directly in front of Fink.

If either of them reached out with one hand, they could tweak Brolli's nose.

Brolli studied something on the wall beside Harric, his huge gold eyes intent. Harric turned his head slowly and craned his neck forward to see what it was. It appeared to be a tapestry or painting in a wooden frame, but he didn't dare lean out far enough to get a good look at it.

Brolli's puffy armor appeared to be the source of the tar smell. This close, Harric could actually taste it in his mouth. It appeared to be a heavy vest in which soft bricks of what he assumed must be tar had been stitched between layers of canvas. Each tar brick had deformed and sagged over the brick below, like bloated scales, and oils from the tar had saturated and discolored the fabric. The largest brick was the main chest "plate" of the armor, which was a thick pad of tar, while a ring of the bricks made a collar that nearly swallowed Brolli's head.

The whole thing gave him the look of a pinecone with arms and legs.

Brolli released his grip with one hand and reached out to the tapestry to walk his fingers across it. His brow furrowed as he counted each step.

A *map*, Harric realized.

"They move closer." Brolli scowled.

Harric wanted to sidestep away far enough that he could risk stepping out for a peek at the map, but he feared accidentally making a sound while so close to the Kwendi.

A voice answered in Kwendi from somewhere above. Then a Kwendi wearing the same sort of armor stepped out of the pavilion onto a branch. Speaking again in Kwendi, he descended the branches in the same kind of controlled plummet to hang beside Brolli, even closer to Harric.

Harric risked a careful step to the right, but something metal scraped the panel behind him and he froze. The Kwendi's eyes darted right through Harric, and Harric cursed himself inwardly. He'd forgotten that he wore his mother's traveling pack, and its buckle had scraped the wood.

"Where's your Stilty, Rurgich?" Brolli said, baring his teeth in a strangely over-wide grin.

Rurgich turned and delivered a sound like a cough to Brolli, which also sounded like a word—perhaps a rude one—followed by more Kwendi words.

"Not so," said Brolli. "Will Gredol learn if you do not? You show the example."

"You know our Stilty good," said Rurgich, in an accent so thick that Harric barely understood him. "We make talking time."

"It shows."

Their interaction was so strange, full of facial expressions involving teeth-baring and deliberate blinking, that Harric couldn't be sure if Brolli's last comment was meant to be ironic or an actual compliment.

"You have my lists?" said Brolli.

His companion held out a wooden tube, and Brolli stuffed it in a satchel at his waist. Together they swung hand to hand from the lowest branches until they got to a door at ground level of the drum. Above the door were other doors at intervals.

Rurgich flipped the door latch at the top of the door with one foot, opened the door with his feet, and swung through the doorway into a corridor similarly equipped with branches. Brolli paused by the door, where he reached out with a fingered foot and flipped a large sandglass that sat upon a table beside the door. Then he followed Rurgich into the hall and, with an agile foot, pulled the door shut behind him.

When their voices faded beyond the door, Fink collapsed to all fours, moaning. "What have you done? We have to get out of here, kid."

"Get out?" Harric looked at the door Brolli had just passed through. It hadn't even occurred to him they would hide in the room. "Fink, we have to follow Brolli. We need to see what his people are up to." He took off his pack as he crossed to the door, and then began stripping his shirt. For the first time since his near-brush with death at the hands of the woman he loved, something other than pain stirred inside him. The gray veil through which he'd been experiencing the world since that day had been torn asunder, and now bright, colorful light shone through.

What he'd just done mattered. Where he was and what he could do here mattered.

"This is the moment I was trained for, Fink. You're crazy if you think I'm staying here."

Fink whined. "You can't do it. You can't hold yourself in the Unseen."

"Then come with me. But *now*. Brolli looked like he was in a hurry."

"You don't understand. We've never been here before!"

"No kidding!"

"I mean my *moon* hasn't been here—*none* of us. It's too dangerous."

Harric stooped beside the door, which was much too short for him, and motioned to Fink with a finger to his lips. Opening it slowly, he peered down the corridor beyond. Cool air washed in and over his bare chest. Brolli and Rurgich were gone. Even in the Unseen, Harric could see nothing moving but dust motes. Swallowing his frustration, he turned toward Fink. "What's wrong with you, Fink? You're trembling like a leaf in the wind. What do you mean, 'too dangerous'?"

Fink hugged his knees to his chest and rocked himself back and forth. His hairless black head looked particularly hideous when he was frightened—a thousand-fanged rictus of fear amidst wrinkled black leather and white eyes bulging like boils. "We don't have anything to do with Kwendi souls, see?" said Fink. "We've known about them because they use our Web sometimes, and we've spied on them and tried to get in here—all the moons have—but nobody's got in, kid. Nobody! The *Aerie* is here." He spoke this word like a talisman of fear. "They're strong, kid. Terrible."

"Who are the Aerie?"

The imp waddled across the floor and clapped his claws around Harric's wrist like a snare. His triple chins waggled like turkey wattles. "*Spirits*. Strong spirits, but not of our moon. No one knows where they're from. They're like us, and like servants of the other moons, because they're tryst servants and guardians of the Kwendi. But they *don't have a moon.* They're some kind of throwback from the Making, I guess. But they're strong, kid. No one's ever got in. We can't get in."

"What are you talking about? We're *already* in. We came in the back door."

Fink's limbs quaked. "This is my end," he muttered, wringing his hands. "Why'd I let you go through that gate? Brolli might spare you, but I'm doomed. I'll be lunch for the Aerie. What a waste, too—no chance to enjoy this gorgeous belly."

Harric extracted his wrist from Fink's grip. He folded his shirt and took off his boots and socks, then crossed to where the witch-silver rods lay inert on the fur rug, and hid them behind a cabinet. He considered leaving his pants, too, but decided he might be cold in only his undershorts. The nexus he kept in the pouch around his neck.

"We've got to stay in this room, kid. If we wait here for Brolli, maybe the Aerie won't notice us, and we can leave the way we came, on Brolli's heels."

Harric hesitated. Till now he'd never seen any sign of weakness in Fink, even in front of his sisters. But he'd seen people too scared to think straight. He'd been in that situation with Fink before, when their roles were reversed, and he'd relied on Fink to help him through it.

"You have to trust me, Fink." He made a show of looking around the room. "None of the Aerie are here, right? Think of it for a second. They aren't here because they don't *know* we're here. They watch the *outside*, but we're on the inside."

Fink cringed as if Harric were pushing him toward the door. "Okay… But…" He groaned. "*Kid.* Don't do this to me."

"Fink, this is my art. Spying is what I was trained for, what I was born for. And this is our golden opportunity."

"Why do you care, kid? Who do you owe it to? No one!"

"I owe it to my queen, Fink. Because the Kwendi might be the real enemy, and if they are, then I need to find out and warn her."

"No one knows you're here. You don't have to prove anything to anyone."

"Oh, yes I do." And that was the bare truth of it, Harric realized. He cobbing well *did* have something to prove. Caris didn't accept his ways or approve of his techniques. Willard didn't approve. But Harric would make them acknowledge the results—results their swords could never have achieved—and they'd have to admit his way was every bit as vital to the Queen's survival. This was his best chance to prove himself.

"Plus, I have nothing to lose," said Harric. "If I die here, Caris is free, right?"

"Kid, that isn't funny."

"But she would be free."

Scowling, Fink nodded.

Harric grinned. "I haven't felt this great in a long time, Fink. I have a very good feeling about this."

Cracking the door again, Harric peered into the corridor in time to see a Kwendi swing past an intersection at the other end. His heart began to beat hard in his chest. It didn't look like Brolli, but maybe this Kwendi would lead him to Brolli.

"You coming, Fink?" he whispered over his shoulder.

From behind him came no sound of talons on wood. He glanced back to see Fink hugging his knees and muttering on the white fur rug.

Harric shoved his hair out of his eyes. "So, let me get this straight, Fink. All three of the moons have been trying to get in here for ages, and now that you find yourself in, you're going to hide like a puppy in a thunderstorm. I thought you wanted to impress your moon. How are you going to explain hiding in a corner to your sisters?"

Fink's tongue flicked across his teeth. "Kid, I have to tell you something." His voice came out hoarse and strained. "The Aerie could destroy me. *Destroy me*. Finished, killed, dead, gone. I'm not a true immortal, kid. I'm *demi*-mortal, which means I'm only immortal as long as nobody tears me to pieces." His voice quavered. He worried his giant nose absently with one clawed hand. "This isn't for me. This is for the major spirits."

Harric snorted. "Yeah, and I shouldn't be here either. I should let major players like Willard or my mother take care of it. Well, I say cob that. I have to go. But I think you're going to hate yourself later. Think this is an hourglass?" He nodded to the sandglass by the door. "Looks like maybe an hour-and-a-half-glass. I'll try to be back in an hour. If I'm not… Go back without me."

Fink just stared, face twisting as Harric put his empty pack on his back and stepped into the corridor. As he closed the door behind him, the weight of the Unseen fell on his consciousness like a load of sandbags.

He paused as the wave of headachy discomfort passed over him. If he left his mother's pack behind, it would lessen the strain, but he fancied he might need it to carry evidence or…things worth studying.

Staring down the strange corridor, he couldn't help but smile. He felt right at home, but not because of the architecture. The architecture was truly weird, with crazily high ceilings lined with trellises of branches like those inside the room.

He felt at home because he was sneaking. And he was good at it.

The corridor ran for about ten paces to a four-way intersection. When he looked back at the door through which he'd come, he saw another door two fathoms above it, accessed by the trellis.

Did Kwendi ever use the floor?

Another throb of pain washed over his brain. The strain of holding himself in the Unseen was still too much for him, and at this rate, he wouldn't get very far before he passed out. He considered creeping along in the Seen and only entering the Unseen when he saw a Kwendi, but he could tell by the scarcity and weakness of the lamps in the place that at best the corridors were lit dimly in the Seen, so any Kwendi in the halls would notice him long before he noticed them.

The lower door opened suddenly and Fink scrambled through it and into the corridor. The imp's shoulders relaxed as if he were relieved to see Harric still standing there, and Harric beckoned him over. Fink waddled toward him, belly swaying side to side.

"You're a very bad influence," Fink whispered. "My mother would hate you. Here." He tossed Harric's wadded socks at his feet. "Put these on. You know you want to."

Harric gave a soft laugh through his nose. With a silent apology to Mother Ganner—who had knitted them, and who would fall in a fit to see him use them so—he gratefully put them on. "Glad you changed your mind. Follow me."

"Wait." Fink held out a hand. "I take the nexus. If you yank on a Web Strand in here, the Aerie and everyone else will know it. In fact, there's one reaching for it right now."

Harric hesitated. "If I give this to you, you're not going to waddle back into that room and sit on it like a brooding chicken, are you? You're coming with me."

Fink grimaced. "I should do that, but I won't."

Harric took off the pouch from around his neck and dropped it in the imp's waiting hand, and the burden of the Unseen lifted immediately. His back was already slick with perspiration from his short time supporting himself in the Unseen.

"Thanks, Fink. Come on."

His senses on hyper-alert, Harric crept to the intersection with Fink lurking behind. At the intersection, he found a squat black mushroom lamp attached to the paneling. It cast a feeble circle of light from under its cap. One or two more shone in the distance in each direction.

"They like it dark," Harric whispered.

Peering behind the mushroom cap, he found a handful of glowing witch-silver globes the size of grapes. These he pocketed, leaving the lamp dark, to make it easier to identify the corridor that led to Brolli's room. Then he turned left at the intersection and set off at a jog after the Kwendi he'd seen. He passed numerous doors and counted eight intersections without a sign of any other living thing. A glance behind him revealed Fink had fallen far behind, and when Harric stopped, the imp caught his eye and beckoned frantically.

Harric ran back and stopped before the imp, his breath coming strangely hard. The Kwendi city must be at a higher altitude. Fink gasped and clutched at his plump chest like he might have a heart attack.

"Carry me." Fink reached up with both hands like an exhausted and hideous child.

"Gods leave it, Fink, you look like you weight five stone." But Harric wanted to move at a pace faster than a waddle, so he turned and motioned for Fink to climb up, and in a few moments, the imp clung to Harric's shoulders.

Harric staggered back into a jog. "Make that ten stone."

"That's power—you feel," Fink said between breaths. "And—we're going to need it."

"A fire can't throw a great light without burning something." This is what the Arkendians say when they wish to justify war. And yet what is the use of a great light if it burns you to make it?"

—From *Among the Stilties*, by Second Ambassador Chombi

49

A Failed Tryst

Harric glanced down each intersection they passed, hoping to notice movement or to hear sounds of Brolli or the Kwendi he'd glimpsed from the room. Seeing no sign of life in any of them, he hurried on, the limbs of the trellises flashing by above him as if he passed through some highly ordered orchard. When he'd crossed a total of eight intersections, the corridor opened abruptly onto a tiled square as wide as a stone's throw and open to the night sky.

A high and continuous trellis blanketed the entire square like the scaffolding for some broad and invisible building. Like the trellis in Brolli's map room, wooden platforms adorned various levels of the trellis, though here they supported no cloth partitions or pavilions. The trellis spilled over the edges of the square to climb the drum-shaped buildings just as ivy climbs trees.

A smile lifted one side of Harric's mouth. "They climb everywhere."

"Not here, they don't," Fink said. "Place is dead. Let's get out of here."

"Calm down. If it's dead, it can't hurt you."

But Fink was right. None of the usual signs of habitation presented themselves. The chimneys were cold. The windows were shuttered or dark. And the trellises were rotting and many fallen. The only sound or motion in the square was the splash and echo of a lonely central fountain and a steady sigh of wind through the trellis.

"What a shame," Fink said. "No Kwendi here. Guess we have to go back to that big room and wait for him to open the gate home."

"Nice try."

Harric began circling buildings to the right side of the square. "This way. It looks like there aren't any buildings on the far side, and maybe it opens onto a valley or something. I'd like to get a look at where we are."

As they passed the buildings, Harric examined them. Unlike drum towers in Arkendia, which rarely had windows bigger than an arrow slit, Kwendi drums supported numerous balconies, platforms, generous windows, and elevated doorways. Surely through one of these he should glimpse a Kwendi too old for the fields or a mother with children. Yet the place seemed cold and empty. Unlived in.

An uneasy feeling coiled in Harric's gut.

An inspiration to open a door and look inside died when he realized that none of the houses near him had front doors. At least, they didn't have ground-level front doors. Scanning the nearest building, he found what was probably the main entrance—a fancy porch and heavy double doors—some three fathoms up. He exhaled a puff of exasperation. He was not going to climb three fathoms of rotting trellis to a door that might be locked.

"This place is a graveyard," Fink said. "If they were here, we'd see their soul strands. I'm telling you, this place is a ghost town."

Harric said nothing. His own soul strands rose like a bonfire of spiritual light into the glorious Web of the Unseen. Where were the Kwendi's strands? Even if all Kwendi strands went to some terrestrial source, wouldn't they be visible as they made their way to ground? Hurrying to the open end of the square, he hoped a more expansive view of the area would reveal some sign of Brolli, or at least some Kwendi he could follow to a more populated area.

When he stepped past the last building, he found himself looking into a small valley no wider than a bowshot and shaped like a steep bowl. Dozens and dozens of Kwendi buildings ringed the inside of the bowl from bottom to top. And all of them stood as apparently cold and empty as the ones they'd passed in the square.

Harric stared in awe. "Where is everyone?"

The drum-houses were arranged in concentric terraces one atop the other from the bottom of the valley to the top. Harric and Fink

stood upon the second to the top terrace, with only one other above, and four below. Each of the ringing terraces had been cut into the side of the valley like rows of benches in the Iberg stadium in Samis.

Whatever they'd call it—township, village?—it was beautiful. And it was totally dead.

A shiver rippled up Harric's spine. Was this an entirely abandoned city? Ballads were sung of such places, burned by war and left behind as ruins. But these buildings weren't ruined. Their roofs and walls appeared sound. Yes, the paint peeled from doors and shutters, weeds clung to cracks, and the trellises sagged or rotted in places, but they weren't ruins. They seemed simply abandoned.

"Believe me now, kid?" Fink's talons gripped Harric's shoulder straps tighter. "We're in a tomb."

Then a barking laugh echoed somewhere in the distance to the right, and Harric turned in time to catch a glimmer of light—maybe of soul strands?—some twenty houses down the ring of the terrace.

"There, see that?" he whispered.

"I didn't see anything."

"That was a soul strand. Why don't their strands go to the moon?"

Fink clung tighter to the pack, drawing the straps so tight that they pinched Harric's shoulders. "It's the Aerie, I bet. Bet the Aerie eat their strands."

Harric glanced over his shoulder at the imp, whose eyes stared wide and white as goose eggs. "Can I trust anything you say right now, or are you just so scared you see Aerie in everything?"

Harric followed the terrace along the front side of the houses along a stone path. Each house stood still and cold, shuttered windows dark, but each had some version of the mushroom-shaped lamp by its second-floor front door. In the Unseen, the lamps appeared as dark blots in the ambient essence glow, but Harric imagined that in the Seen, the whole valley must glow in constellations of concentric rings.

As he passed the third or fourth door, Fink's claws hooked like a startled cat's into Harric's shoulders. Before Harric could protest, something huge and white flashed past a gap between roofs, and his heart nearly flew from his chest.

Whatever had passed was so big it had filled that band of sky.

Harric flattened himself against the front face of the nearest building, inadvertently smashing Fink behind him. Afraid to breathe lest he be heard, he sidestepped along the face of the house as quietly and quickly as he could, until he reached the side, and then slipped into a narrow alley extending back between houses, but the alley dead-ended at a high wall that rose to the next terrace. Only a trellis continued upward. Harric cowered against the dead-end wall and rolled his head back to look up for a glimpse of movement above the roof line.

"Aerie?" Harric whispered, barely making a sound.

Fink's talons pricked deeper. Then the imp let go with one hand and jabbed a crooked finger toward the right side of the alley, where an open archway beckoned from the concealment of a partially fallen trellis. Harric crept around the junked trellis and darted through the archway. He found himself in a tunnel that seemed to run beneath and behind the next house. Plunging forward, he put some distance between himself and the archway, navigating by the dim essence light of moisture and dust on the walls and floor.

When they were a good twenty paces in, they passed a door that must have gone into the basement of the house. Fink leapt from Harric's back and dove for it. With a frightened glance back the way they'd come, the imp clawed the latch at the top of the door and heaved it open. The hinges gave way with a rasping gasp that made Harric wince, but Fink plowed in, apparently oblivious, his fat chins shaking with fear.

Harric followed into a cellar lined with shelves of sealed pots and jars and walls stacked with urns. The space smelled of dust that now rose in glowing motes in the Unseen, disturbed by their feet on the floor. A wooden ramp climbed up from the floor to another door.

"Close the door, kid!" Fink practically squeaked.

Harric peeked out into the tunnel to be sure no one followed, then closed the door gently behind them.

Fink quaked like a freezing child. "Kid, how could you do this to me?" Eyes bugged from his bald head as he hunched on the floor, flabby arms hugging his knees. "How could I *let* you do this to me? They know I'm here, kid. I can feel it. They know."

"Fink, they don't know. If they knew, they would've grabbed you."

Fink shook his triple chins. "They're coming. We have to get out of here. I mean...we have to stay and hide. Maybe hide—" He put his hands on his head as if to keep it from flying apart.

Harric sighed and coaxed the nexus from Fink's talons. "I have to see what's out there. I have to see where Brolli went."

"This place is all wrong, kid." Fink's voice was barely a whisper. "No one's been in here for years. Full of food and drink and the things you mortals put in a tomb for the afterlife. As if that's what you're going to eat there." He gave a miserable wave at the jars. "This might as well be my tomb, but I can't eat any of that."

Harric cracked the door to peer back into the tunnel. "Fink, I'll be back. Just stay put."

"Souls, kid, don't let them see you. And hurry."

Harric stepped out and closed the door. He hadn't taken three steps before the weight of the Unseen pressed upon him like a suit of lead. Carrying Fink on his back had been a merely physical strain, and though it made him sweat, he could support it for a long time. Holding himself in the Unseen was carrying a spiritual weight, and it burdened him in ways that he struggled to understand. It was like diving after witch-stone nuggets in the deep pools in the river, where his breath felt too small, the icy water froze his temples, and a relentless pressure squeezed his lungs. It felt like the water itself wished to expel him, and the dives took careful concentration or he risked drowning or aborting the dive. But he still had no choice but to maintain himself in the Unseen or he risk being spotted by a night-seeing Kwendi.

The tunnel was wide enough for two men to walk side by side, but its ceiling was only a hand's breadth taller than Harric, and until he got used to it, he kept flinching and ducking for fear of knocking his head. The tunnel curved continuously under the ring of houses, passing many doors like the one to Fink's cellar, and crossing alleys every three or four houses.

He guessed he was in a servant's passage like the ones in Gallows Ferry, where cooks and maids moved supplies without disturbing residents. Whether the Kwendi had a similar kind of segregation of lords and servants, he had no real idea, but even without the segregation, it seemed likely the tunnels were for practical access. Ruts in the floor suggested carts moved through the passage with materials too heavy to move through a trellis, a suspicion confirmed when he passed an abandoned two-wheeled wheelbarrow.

At each alley, he stopped to listen and look up for evidence of the

Aerie or Kwendi before he passed beneath the brief band of open sky.

After a dozen alleys, he heard water ahead, and soon a glowing archway came into view, backlit by the brilliant blue-white spiritual essence of water. Beyond the archway lay a stone-vaulted reservoir. Or so he guessed it to be.

The room had no floor. Instead, it housed a square stone pit about eight paces to a side and five fathoms deep. Across the pit on the opposite side he could see another archway, connected to his side of the pit by an ancient trellis. From a pipe high in the right-hand wall poured a steady stream of water. In the Unseen, the stream shone like liquid lightning plunging into a pool of the same below. It wasn't exactly "running" water, but the whipping motion of the strands rising from the pool stung Harric's spirit body like nettles on sunburn.

He stepped back into the protection of the archway until the strands could no longer flog him, and from there examined what he could through the dazzling glare.

The room reminded Harric of the water tower on the cliff above Gallows Ferry, which provided the water for the inn; similarly, this cistern probably fed water to the Kwendi houses on the lower terraces. Something had happened to drain it, though, because it appeared to be only a fathom deep, at most. If it were full, he could simply strip down, toss his clothes across, and swim over. Drained as it was…

He stepped forward, enduring the sting of the water essence so he could get a better look at his options. The hand-bridge trellis looked like a ladder laid flat at a height just over Harric's head, and it looked about as trustworthy as any wooden structure left over a pit of water for years untended might look: slippery, and likely rotten in places. However, the Kwendi had also left a narrow ledge around the rim of the pit that he could probably sidestep to reach the other side, but if he fell into the pool below, he'd never get out.

He frowned and looked back the way he'd come. Another option was to retrace his steps to the last alley and then slip around the front of the buildings to the next one, but that would expose him to the risk of being seen by the Aerie. Or he could give up and go back to Fink.

Cobs. He did not want to go back empty-handed.

After a moment's study, he gritted his teeth against the burn of water essence leaned out above the pool, and grabbed each pole of the hand-bridge in his hands. He didn't trust the ancient bridge enough to hang from the rungs and swing across Kwendi style, because if even one rung broke as he hung from it, he'd probably fall. But if he first got *on top* of the trellis, he could crawl across on its back, and that way be secure enough on hands and knees to remain on its back if a rung broke loose beneath him.

Holding his breath, he gave a little jump and hoisted himself up between the first rungs. The support poles groaned, but held firm as levered his upper body above the rungs. Then the room echoed with a sharp *crack!* and the bridge gave a mighty shake and a tilt.

And Harric dropped.

O shall I fight, so weeping maids
May kiss my bleeding head?
Methinks such fame comes much too late
for me if I be dead.

— Sir Willard's eleventh squire, Corvil, in "Sir Willard at Broden Field"

50

Curiosity & The Cat

Harric's heart leapt into his throat as he swung from his right hand above the pit.

A stream of curses crowded his lips as he kicked his feet and struggled to get his other hand on the remaining support pole while the rotten one dangled by his ear. About the time he had cursed all Kwendi engineers and their mothers and fathers and offspring, he managed to get hold with both hands, kick his feet back onto the solid ground, and pull himself to safety.

He stumbled back into the tunnel and leaned against a wall to let his heart settle.

And may the rotting trellises of this rotting city catch fire and burn to ashes.

A vicious throb squeezed his head, reminding him of the precious few minutes he had in the Unseen.

Cob it. I'm going to get myself killed.

Rubbing an aching shoulder, he looked back the way he'd come. There'd be no shame in returning empty-handed. It would be the smart thing to do. It was certainly the safest thing to do.

On the other hand, he could sidestep the ledge around the edge of the reservoir and continue his search for the Kwendi. Surely he was close now to where he'd heard the Kwendi laugh. Stupid to give up now.

His feet took him back to the shining archway.

The sweaty walls of the reservoir were no different than the cliffs he'd grown up climbing above the river at Gallows Ferry. In some ways, this would be easier, because the stonework here was solid. He should have tried it to begin with.

The sunburn sting of whipping water strands resumed the moment he stepped out on the ledge, and again his head throbbed with the burden of sustaining himself there. But progress along the wall was easy. When he reached the first corner above the pit, however, voices echoed from one of the tunnels. One of the Kwendi laughed, and though the Unseen and the tunnels distorted the sound, it could easily have been the laugh of Brolli.

Heart drumming in his ears, Harric hurried his next step and set the ball of his sock-covered foot on a sharp pebble that made him lurch off balance. The gulf whirled around him as he teetered and felt himself leaning out too far. He shot a hand back to the other wall in the corner and managed to brace himself just long enough to reset his feet across the gap in the corner and restore balance.

Fool, he can't see you! He cursed himself. *You don't have to hurry this.*

As sounds of feet on stone grew louder, he forced himself to move slowly and deliberately. He still couldn't tell from which archway the sounds came, but he fancied they came from the archway he was heading toward.

And just as soon as they'd begun, the sounds of voices and footsteps ceased.

When he finally reached the safety of the other archway, Harric peeked around the corner and found nothing but more empty corridor. Picking up his pace, he resumed his quest down the tunnels and passed another alley, then another, before he once again heard what he'd been seeking: faint voices in conversation. He heard them echoing in the narrow confines of the third alley beyond the reservoir. By now his head throbbed with the effort of keeping himself in the Unseen, and sweat slicked his forehead and neck.

A quick look in the alley proved it empty, but a second-floor window stood open, and from it came the sound of voices. A male voice, possibly

Brolli, though the Unseen and the inflections of the Kwendi language made it impossible to know. If it was Brolli, Harric had to wonder what he was doing in this ghost village. Meeting with a ghostly official? Paying a visit to ghosts?

The houses spun around Harric and the weight of the Unseen forced him to his knees. Gasping, he released himself back into the Seen. His heart was racing like he'd just run up a hill.

The conversation above hitched and stopped.

Harric lurched to his feet and staggered back into the now-pitch-black tunnel, where he tried to catch his breath without wheezing or gasping.

When he finally regained control, he listened at the alley and once again heard that the voices had resumed their murmured conversation.

He hung his head in relief. That had been the longest he'd ever held himself in the Unseen without help. Nevertheless, it was clear to him he wouldn't be able to move through the Unseen on the way back. He'd be lucky if he had enough stamina left for a minute more in the spirit world, so he'd have to save that for an emergency.

Once more he considered turning back, but he'd come so far that he couldn't bear to retreat.

Cob it all. In for a penny, in for a queen.

Turning his back on the alley, he groped his way back down the passage, hand trailing along the right wall until he found the cellar door to the house and opened it.

Once inside, he brought out the glowing globes he'd taken from the mushroom lamp, and held them out for light. This cellar was much like the one he'd seen with Fink. Pots and jars burdened the shelves, sealed urns lined the walls, and a fine coat of dust carpeted everything. On the dusty floor, footprints of bare Kwendi feet crossed from the door to the shelves and from the shelves to the cellar ramp, up which they proceeded to an open door at the top.

Jackpot.

Faint sounds of conversation drifted down through the door.

Harric crept up the ramp and found himself in a stone kitchen with a hearth. A full complement of pots and pans adorned a few knee-high tables and a chopping block. Dried plants hung from the ceiling in clots of cobwebs. Dust and ash and long-dead spices scented the air.

Following the tracks, Harric moved from the kitchen to a vast drum-shaped room like Brolli's map room, with its central column and radiating branches. Among the branches at various levels lay wooden floors supporting soft-walled rooms like hanging pavilions. A few mushroom-shaped lamps on the floor cast a dim light upon a circle of cake-shaped leather cushions around a long, low table, like a bench.

Scanning the place through his oculus, it was impossible to miss the cascade of brilliant green soul strands pouring from a covered pavilion some two fathoms up and on the other side of the central column. The strands slanted downward across the room, wavering and undulating, full of life, and disappeared into the earth.

As he crept beneath the elevated pavilion, he studied the branches for a way to climb high enough to see into it. He imagined a Kwendi wouldn't think twice before flying up the abundant branches, but to him it looked like a treacherous climb. But on the far wall of the drum he found a ladder that passed within an easy step of the pavilion's platform, and he climbed it.

In that pavilion might lie the answers to his questions about the abandoned town. Understanding of what Brolli did each night.

As Harric crept out onto the platform, the voices went quiet. In a moment of panic, fearing he'd been heard and was about to be discovered, he clutched the nexus in its pouch and entered the Unseen.

The renewed burden hit him like a sandbag and blurred his vision, forcing him to hold to a trellis limb. Then, knowing he had only moments left, he staggered forward, parted the hangings, and peered into the pavilion.

The space inside seethed with the brilliant green-white soul light of two Kwendi—neither one Brolli and neither one wearing more than the clothes the gods gave them, male and female, at birth. That they were male and female he knew because their defining parts were quite visible. The female had her back to Harric as she sat atop the male, who lay on his back in a nest of furs and blankets. Despite the male's obvious distraction in that moment, he looked right at the gap Harric made as he parted the hangings, and his brow furrowed.

Harric froze. He couldn't back away or close the hangings without confirming that someone was there, but he had to re-enter the Seen before he blacked out.

As stars flashed across Harric's vision, the Kwendi's eyes widened in shock, and the female, seeing her partner's alarm, turned to look behind her. She let out a shout of surprise, tumbled to the carpeted floor, and hurled a mushroom lamp at Harric. The lamp exploded in fragments against the column beside Harric, sending glowing balls in all directions.

The male sprang to his knees, fists balled for a fight.

The fabric walls of the pavilion embraced Harric as he fell into darkness.

Arkendian infatuation with maleness manifests most strangely in naming offspring. Though a mother's identity is certain, and the father's identity equally uncertain, the child is considered to be of the father's clan. They think so little of women, that…in cases where the father is unknown, the offspring is considered "illegitimate," which means "outside the protection of the law," and is made to wear a badge of dishonor in the form of a belt. …and by this measure are we a race of illegitimates without knowledge of our fathers!

—From *Among the Stilties,* by Kwendi First Secretary Chombi

51

Flight

Dim, watery sounds drifted through a fog of pain, and Harric struggled to make sense of them. Yapping, barking. A cascade of jumbled syllables, like a cart of drums spilled down a cobblestone hill. His skull felt like a walnut under a boot. When he noticed a dim light moving in the fog, he opened his eyes to see frantic movement around him.

Brolli was pulling a shirt over his head. Strange words came from inside the shirt. Muffled. Brolli wore no pants, which was awkward.

But when Brolli's head emerged from the shirt, Harric noticed that he had a narrower face than Brolli, and a wider mouth, with a tangle of snaggleteeth at the front. Someone else shouted in the small space of the pavilion, and Harric turned to see another half-dressed Kwendi pointing and retreating into a corner.

Oh.

As his memory of the situation returned, embers of panic blazed into life in his stomach.

He surged to his hands and knees, only to fall over, tangled in a pile of furs and blankets. An infuriatingly irrelevant corner of his mind observed that he'd been lying half-naked on a bed with naked Kwendi.

Flailing, he leapt back and piled through the hangings, trailing blankets behind him.

Kwendi shouts pelted him as he fled down the ladder, but faded as he slammed through the kitchen and down the ramps to the cellar. Somehow he'd kept hold of his lamp globes, which he clutched like a life ring in one hand as he sprinted for all he was worth through the tunnel. Clutched in his hand, the globes gave almost no light, but he trusted to his knowledge that the corridor was clear and without impediment, and flew as fast as he could past alley after alley.

Until the floor dropped away.

And the opposite rim of the reservoir rushed toward him.

In an instant of desperation, he extended one arm as he fell past the rim. His palm hit the rim as pain shot through his ribs and knees, and the air *whoofed* from his lungs as he body-slammed the wall. He'd let go of the globes as he grabbed, so once again he plunged into near-complete darkness as he hung there.

Below him, the stolen spheres glowed like moons drowning in the pool.

Harric groaned, but dared not move lest he cause his single hand to lose its grip.

Shouts echoed down the tunnel behind him. The Kwendi had still been dressing when he fled, so he had a head start and now they couldn't know which way he'd gone. They might seek him in the wrong direction, or they could even leave the tunnel and seek him on the terrace in front of the houses.

Heart pounding in his ears, he listened until it was clear the shouts were growing louder.

Cursing, he strained upward with his left hand, only to find his reach well short of the rim. Gods take it, they would catch him. He considered dropping into the pool, trying to hide there in the Unseen. But then what? He'd be stuck while they raised the alarm. And if he passed out in the water, he'd drown.

Cobbing idiot. Too frightened to think straight, you squandered your cards.

He hadn't realized his feet had been scrabbling for purchase, but they must have been, because his sock-covered big toe found a mortar seam between stones and stuck. Hope rekindling, he put his weight on it, and though it hurt like the bite of a ragged tooth into the knuckle, it allowed for enough thrust for him to reach the rim with his other hand.

"Stop!" The heavily accented word echoed through the tunnel behind him. It was the female Kwendi's voice. The male echoed the command with an accent just as thick and an odd whistling note, and judging from the accompanying slap of running feet, they'd spotted him while still running up the corridor and would arrive at the reservoir in moments.

Harric's limbs seemed to move at half speed as he pulled and levered and scrabbled to get first one elbow and then the other over the rim and finally hump his torso onto the floor of the corridor like a seal onto a beachhead.

"You stop!" The female's voice bounced off the stone walls of the reservoir. She was in the archway.

As Harric scrambled to his knees, wood cracked and snapped behind him. He whirled in time to see the left pole of the trellis collapse and drop one of his pursuers into the darkness. She cried out, and then a loud splash echoed in the chamber. The male had already leapt out to grab the trellis when it broke, but in a display of terrifying agility, he somehow latched on the remaining pole and swung to its top, where he gripped the remaining pole with all four limbs like a possum on a branch. His maneuver had set the pole to bouncing, however, and at the bottom of each bounce, it emitted an ominous cracking sound.

The Kwendi froze, and Harric stared, mesmerized, but the pole did not break, and the bouncing settled. The male called down into the reservoir, and Harric noted an odd whistling to his voice. The female splashed below and responded with what sounded like cursing.

The male's golden eyes shone like a cat's as he fixed them on Harric, and fierce canines glinted in the dim light. Very slowly, he advanced a hand along the pole toward Harric, followed by a foot, then the other hand and the other foot, and the pole held fast.

Panicking, Harric leapt forward and shook the pole with both hands. Desperation gave him strength as he lifted it and hauled it down, instigating a chorus of crackling. The male snarled, freezing again on the pole. And then a flower of pain bloomed in Harric's side, like he'd been stabbed.

With a cry, he released the pole and staggered back into the archway. A glow stone bounced around the corridor behind him, and the female shouted in triumph.

The male took his opportunity and leapt, close enough to grab the edge of the corridor. But instead of thrusting himself forward, he thrust the pole down and past its breaking point. The whole structure collapsed, and he fell howling into the cistern. A tremendous splash resounded in the chamber, followed by spluttering and whistling curses.

Harric retreated farther into the tunnel. Rubbing the new welt on his side, he picked up the glow stone. *Moons, the Kwendi can throw.*

But they'd lost. They were trapped, and he was safe.

He crouched against a wall to catch his breath and take account of things. His chin and his knees stung and his ribs ached. The stone wall left scrapes all over him.

"You stop!" the male barked. "You bad! You not should be here!" Again the whistling note whenever he made an S sound. The tangle of teeth at the front of his mouth must make the whistle.

Harric said nothing.

"Who you are?" Whistler called. "Say!"

Harric stayed out of sight for fear of another whizzing glow globe. But a pang of worry prevented him from leaving. The two were truly trapped. They would not escape. The walls were too smooth, the pit too deep. And the bits of trellis that had fallen after them were too short to make a ladder. If he left them, would anyone find them? The city appeared to be deserted, after all. Others might search for them, but when? And how long would it take to find them?

Uncertain what to do, he lay on his stomach out of sight beyond the rim until the Kwendi gave up calling to him and began talking to each other in Kwendi. Then he inched forward and peered over the edge. The two stood on a shelf on the side opposite the falling water. The shelf was a foot above the water and a pace wide.

"You!" A shadowy figure pointed at him from the depths.

Harric retreated. "I'm sorry," he called. "I do not want to hurt you." In his head, he could hear his mother laughing. *Leave them, fool. They will starve or freeze in that consumptive pit, and no one will ever know you were here.*

Harric rubbed at a scrape on his chin. If they were rescued, the game would be up. Even assuming he got back through Brolli's magic gate without being seen, the next time Brolli returned to his people, the word would be out and Brolli would know exactly which Arkendian had followed him through the gate.

Let them die, said his mother's memory, *and no one will know you were here.*

After climbing to his feet, Harric opened the cellar door of the nearest home, gathered armloads of blankets and furs, and piled them at the rim of the cistern. After two trips, he'd amassed a huge pile. Without another word, he wadded them into tight bundles and tossed them down to the ledge where the Kwendi were stranded.

Without waiting to see how they received them, he returned to a cellar and opened one of the many sealed pots. The sweet scent of fruit rose from it, and he smiled, remembering Mother Ganner's plum preserves. A few of these pots ought to keep them fed until someone came looking for them. Gathering an armload, he took them to the rim and tossed them one at a time into the water. They splashed and plunked and bobbed. The Kwendi seemed to recognize what they were, because they gathered them in with long arms or with the use of one of the wooden rungs from the trellis. When several pots had been stacked on their ledge, the two bundled together in a nest of furs in one corner.

Harric stepped out of view. Had he missed anything? They had enough food and water for days. They'd be uncomfortable, maybe a little embarrassed, but he would not let himself feel guilty about that. They'd have imprisoned him if they'd caught him.

He returned to the cellar and found three fancy-looking dark glass bottles of what sounded like liquid. He guessed they must be wine or something like it. These he held it out above the water so the Kwendi could see it.

"Drink," he said. "Wine, I think?"

Silence from below. After several long moments, the female said a word in Kwendi. "Zisk. From honey."

"Ah! We call it mead."

She made a spitting sound.

Harric smiled and peeked down. In the light of the two glowing globes he'd lost in the cistern, he could see they were looking up.

"What do you want?" said Whistler.

Harric stepped back from the edge and wrapped the mead jars in a blanket. "Why are these houses empty?" he called. "Where are the people?"

"You pig Stilties kill them," Whistler snapped. "You—"

A bark from the female cut him short, and he spat something in Kwendi.

She said, "The Syne find you. Then we talk."

Syne? Was that the Kwendi word for Aerie? "How could we have killed your people?" Harric asked. "We have never been here."

More murmuring below, but nothing more.

The claim that Arkendians had killed so many Kwendi was preposterous. There had been no great battles with the Kwendi in the Free Lands, and those that occurred between settlers and Kwendi had been notable Kwendi victories.

Harric tossed the wrapped mead bottles into the water and left them.

It was only after he'd traversed several more blocks of tunnel back toward Fink that he realized the two may have been in the deserted city in order to keep their relationship secret, in which case he'd pretty thoroughly exposed them. He had to chuckle. It would be embarrassing, but since Kwendi had no marriage or lasting pair bonds, it wouldn't end with a jealous husband or wife leaving them there to starve.

Retracing his steps, he counted alleys until he found Fink's cellar, where the door stood slightly ajar. Knocking softly, he whispered, "Fink, it's me," so the imp wouldn't have a seizure, and pushed it open.

Shadows swung about the room as he shined the light from the glowing globes into each corner. "Fink?" he whispered. His voice echoed in the empty space. "Fink, come out. It's me."

Silence answered him.

Fink was gone.

*Old maladies plague the Free Road, and one malady never before
seen in Arkendia. Hoofrot and the crimson we know, as they flourish
wherever men and kine inhabit too little space for too long. This
new plague is ten-boil. It is like to the fiery pox in all but this regard:
when the number of boils reaches nine, say farewell to your lovies,
for the tenth boil will kill you.*

— From "Worse Than Chimpies," a tract criticizing the Queen's
Free Land policy in the north

52

Alone

Harric scanned the room for signs of struggle, and to his relief
found nothing. On the dusty floor he found the smudges of his
own stockinged feet, along with the imp's claw marks, but it was all too
muddled to be of much use. None of the dust on the cellar ramp had
been touched, however, so he knew the imp had not gone into to the
house above. That meant he'd gone back into the tunnel, and that he'd
probably gone back the way they'd come, or Harric would have met
him on his way back from the reservoir.

As he retrieved his pack and put his pants back on, he considered
whether Fink might have moved to a different cellar, for some reason, or
if he might have panicked and tried to find his way back to Brolli's map
room. When Harric stood again in the corridor, he stood still and listened
for the familiar click of talons on stone or the hiss of terrified breath, but
heard only the sigh of wind through a trellis in the nearby alley.

Did he dare Summon the imp? He chewed his lip for a second. No.
For all he knew, a summoning would be as much of a beacon to the
Aerie as it was to Fink. So he crept back down the tunnel toward the

square with its lonely fountain and scanned the dusty threshold of each cellar door, looking for signs the imp had entered one.

It bothered him that Fink had left no sign or message. He could at least have drawn an arrow in the dust to show which direction he'd gone.

When Harric reached the edge of the archway that opened onto the square, he peered out into the open space beyond. In the Seen, he could see only a few mushroom lights scattered among the high porches of the buildings on the other side, and the silhouettes of trellis everywhere. No movement anywhere. But what he saw when he looked at the same scene through his oculus made him suck a quick breath. On the trellises atop a building across the square perched a cluster of gigantic, moon-bright winged creatures.

Aerie.

A jolt of fear kicked his heart.

He counted four of the monsters, each a giant some two times the height of a man, even while hunched on a trellis. They looked like a cross between a snow owl and a giant Kwendi. Owl-headed, owl-winged, long-armed and short-legged, and bright as sun on snow.

Harric retreated into the tunnel. If those things had been there before, the sight of them would have given Fink a seizure. But their presence now might mean Fink was nearby. The Aerie had been drawn to Fink before; maybe Fink had relocated to a different building, and they'd been drawn to him. Maybe he was in that house where they perched.

If so, they didn't appear to be dismantling the house, or searching for the imp. Of course, there might be others that Harric couldn't see prying through the alleys while these four stood watch. Or they might already have captured the imp.

Harric's heartbeat thrummed in his ears.

Either way, that building was the best bet for Fink's location. If Fink hadn't been captured, he was probably gibbering in the corner of the cellar, and he'd need Harric to talk him back to sanity. If he had been captured… Well, no use thinking of it. Either way, Harric had to help.

He backtracked and looped through alleys to the foot of the square where they'd first entered the abandoned city. From around the corner of the last house, he discovered that from that angle, the Aerie's view of the foot of the square was obscured by taller buildings. That made it an easy matter for Harric to slip across the shadows at the foot of the square and dive into the tunnel under the front row of buildings.

In the mouth of the new tunnel, he paused to catch his breath and hug himself to stave off a chill. Autumn was much more advanced here than it had been in the forest he'd left behind. That difference and the fact that he could never quite get enough air in his lungs led him to believe the Kwendi city must be on a mountain.

Keep moving, stay warm.

He navigated by looking through his oculus, trusting to luck that there would be no Kwendi to see him moving through the Seen, and confident that the merest glimpse of an Aerie through his oculus would stand out like a beacon. When he judged the tunnel had taken him near Fink's hiding house, he scanned the threshold of each cellar door for signs of his passage. To his disappointment, the dust lay thick and pristine on each doorstep. Even the cobwebs across doors hung undisturbed, as if no one had opened these doors since abandonment.

After rechecking each door, he stopped at the archway opening into the next alley and chewed at his lip. There were more cellars where the tunnel continued across the alley, but he was almost certain that the four Aerie perched somewhere right above him. It would be very risky to step into an alley right below their perch. Even sneaking up to the edge of the alley and looking up would be dangerous, as an Aerie in the right position would be able to see his feet appear in the archway before Harric got his head around to peer up.

Swallowing back a curse, he got on his hands and knees and laid his already goose-bumped belly on the cold and gritty stone. Inching toward the arch, he peered up at the rooftops through his oculus. No Aerie. He was about to inch forward again and stick his head into the alley to peek directly above him, when a blazing white elbow and massive fist shifted into view just outside the archway. Harric's breath froze. The fist rested its knuckles on the stone of the alley as if its owner were standing guard beside the tunnel, and so close Harric dare not exhale, lest it feel his breath on its skin.

Heart slamming so hard he feared the creature would hear it, he inched backward.

The monster didn't move, but Harric's oculus began to burn and itch like he'd put his face in an anthill and the ants were swarming through his oculus into his brain. A bubble of panic threatened to burst in his chest. He wanted to slap his forehead. He wanted to run screaming.

Staring at the gigantic fist, he forced himself to concentrate on a slow retreat. One move at a time, telling himself that it was the presence of the Aerie that caused the sensation, and that the irresistible crawling behind his forehead was already diminishing as he retreated. Mercifully, when he finally climbed to his feet and fled down the tunnel, it ceased altogether.

Mother of moons…that was a thousand times worse than the cistern.

He imagined if he tried to enter the Unseen and slip by the creature, his whole body would erupt with invisible ants. And he was not about to find out.

But he could loop around through the tunnels under the next row of houses, and approach that alley from the other side.

Retracing his steps, he crossed over to the next row of houses and crept through it until he judged he was many houses past Fink's. Then he crossed back to the tunnel under Fink's row. Of course, if the monsters had trapped Fink, then there was probably another guard in the alley on this side, too.

Once again wishing he hadn't left his lucky jack in his shirt back in the map room, he kissed his fingers for luck and crept toward Fink's hiding place, scanning the thresholds of the cellar doors. No sign of Fink's passage. But when Harric's oculus began to crawl again, he knew he was nearing the alley with the Aerie.

And there it was.

Framed in the archway to the alley was the brilliant white flank of the creature. If it was the same creature, it had moved from its previous position. Now it crouched on taloned feet directly before the tunnel, a huge hip and leg filling the space, though its terrible owlish face still remained out of view to the right.

One cellar remained unchecked no more than twenty paces from the Aerie.

Harric pressed himself flat against the right-hand wall and proceeded very slowly on his stockinged feet. As he drew upon the cellar door, the Aerie stirred, and Harric froze. A bright strand of spirit had dipped lazily down beside the creature and curled against it. Harric stared for several long heartbeats before he recognized it as a Web Strand.

Cobs. He swallowed, hoping this one would not move toward him. He did not want to have to retreat. But the strand paid no attention to his nexus. It appeared to be floating around the Aerie and rubbing against it like a cat seeking attention.

Had the Aerie called it down? Maybe Aerie fed from them. Then a hopeful idea occurred to him: maybe Fink had drawn it there—either intentionally, or because he was in such a state of terror that he'd neglected to send it away. And if so, then maybe the Aerie weren't attracted to Fink at all, but to the Web Strands he unintentionally drew.

Emboldened by this notion, Harric stooped to examine the dust of the last threshold. Sure enough, there in the dust was the sharp line of a scrabbled claw.

Fink.

Relief bloomed in Harric, then wilted as he noticed dark liquid on one corner of the threshold. Did Fink have blood? Harric's breath stopped in his throat as he dabbed it with a finger and smelled it. It had a faint odor of fish. Rubbing it between his fingers, he found it slippery. Fish oil. Harric smiled as he imagined the scene as it must have unfolded: Fink clawing a jar open; Fink oiling the ancient hinges of the cellar door so heavily that he left a puddle.

Novice.

Silent hinges confirmed Harric's guess about the oil. He slipped inside then closed the door gently behind him, and the crawling sensation in his oculus stopped.

He found Fink huddled beneath a loaded shelf, staring and hugging his knees to his fat belly. He appeared to be alone. He was not bound. No Aerie pounced.

"Fink, it's me," Harric whispered as he crossed to the imp. "It's all right. They don't know where you are."

Fink stared at him, unseeing.

"Fink. Snap out of it. We can slip away from these things."

"Kid…" Fink's voice was barely audible. "You see them? You see them out there?"

"Yes. On top of this house, four stories up. And, well, one in the alley. But they don't know about you. I think they're here for Web Strands. Do you attract Web Strands?"

Fink dropped his forehead behind his knees and groaned. "They know."

Harric pressed his lips together, struggling for patience. "Fink. If they do know, they aren't stopping you, so let's get out of here." When Fink failed to respond, Harric took hold of one of Fink's wrists and pulled it gently from its death hug on his knees. Fink resisted at first, then let him take it. Harric clasped the imp's other hand and raised him to his feet.

"Come on," Harric said, turning around and stooping. "Climb aboard." After a long hesitation, Harric repeated himself, and Fink climbed onto his back, hooked his feet in the straps, and gripped Harric's shoulders. Harric handed Fink the nexus, and the imp took it without comment. Closing his eyes, Harric entered the bright world of the Unseen, and felt Fink shoulder the burden of it. "That's more like it," he said.

Fink's talons pricked Harric's shoulders. "What was that?"

"Ouch, Fink. Hold on to the straps. What was what?"

"Hush!" The prick of his talons did not let up. "What the White Moon was that sound?"

Harric froze and listened. Then an odd murmur stirred in his mind. It wasn't sound, exactly, because it didn't seem to come through his ears, but instead directly into his mind. In spite of that odd sensation, its source did have a direction, which was right beyond the door.

Heart suddenly leaping against his breastbone, Harric sprang for the cellar ramp and hurried up through the open door at the top, with Fink clutching tightly. Hoping to close the door at the top of the ramp behind them, Harric tested it by moving it fractionally, only to feel the hinges resist with the beginnings of a squeak of complaint.

Fink almost backflipped off the pack. "Leave it, kid!"

But Harric was already moving through the kitchen, which had a similar layout to the other he'd entered, and from there to a front room with an enormous trellis-tree in a great drum of stonework. This home had more windows and balconies perforating the drum at various levels, and Harric headed directly for one of these.

"We're dead, we're dead," Fink moaned. "They know. We're dead—"

A noise from somewhere seemed to confirm this—a thump, perhaps of a door?—but with Fink moaning in his ear, Harric couldn't tell if it came from above or back in the kitchen or cellar.

"Hush," Harric said. "I can't think."

"It's no use. We're dead."

Harric stopped before a pair of squat, windowed doors to the balcony, and peered through the dirty glass. The balcony beyond hung over a trellised walkway connecting houses. It wouldn't be a difficult climb down to find the tunnel below the next row of dwellings. But if the Aerie still perched above him, they would easily see him leave.

"Diversion," he muttered. "We need a diversion."

Biting his upper lip, he ran to another balcony on the opposite side of the great room and pushed open the doors. The hinges didn't squeak, but the door scraped across dirt from several weedy pots that had fallen from a railing. He opened it just far enough to reach through and shove a pot from the railing.

When it shattered below, he was already sprinting to the opposite balcony.

The odd murmur brushed across Harric's mind again. Aerie below him. In the cellar.

Turning the door latch, he shoved against the doors, but they wouldn't budge.

Another murmur moved through his mind, stronger this time, and it stirred a wave of nausea in him.

This time he hurled his weight against the door once, twice, and it finally opened enough for him to squeeze through, bumping Fink's wings on either side as he went. Without looking up to see of the Aerie were there—it wouldn't matter if they were, as he had no choice but flight—he leapt from the balcony into a gap in the trellis. Bars of trellises flew past him. He managed to get a hand on one or two, in a sloppy version of the controlled fall he'd seen Brolli do, and hit the ground upright.

Feet stinging from the landing, he darted across the gap between rows and into an alley.

During all of this, Fink emitted a faint but sustained whine, and it wasn't until Harric crouched inside the alley's service tunnel that he stopped.

Harric risked looking back for signs of Aerie, but saw nothing. None followed them into the tunnel. They must have left their perch to investigate the shattered pot on the other side. The diversion had worked.

Harric let out a long sigh of relief. "Fink. My shoulders. Hold the straps?"

He waited a moment, and then helped Fink unclasp first one hand, then the other, and replace them on the straps of Harric's pack. Tiny spots of blood smeared Harric's skin where the talons had bitten. "Tricked 'em, Fink. We're safe."

Fink's blank eyes stared.

"It's all *right*, Fink," Harric said. "We made it. They'll think it was Kwendi lovers looking for a place for a tryst."

He hoped. It had been a sloppy escape. If the Aerie understood tracks, they'd know the tracks he'd left were not from Kwendi feet. And in his hurry to cross the gap between houses, he'd left the balcony doors open, indicating the direction of their flight.

Time to move. He retraced his steps all the way to the foot of the square, checking for Aerie before crossing each alley, and finally peeked back around the last house to be sure the Aerie hadn't moved before they returned to the passage that brought them to the abandoned city in the first place.

But they had moved. The monsters had mounted into the air to circle above the house he'd just left. Harric jerked back behind the house.

"What is it?" Fink whispered, his voice so faint that Harric barely heard it.

"Uh. Probably nothing. They just left their roost."

"They're coming for me!"

Harric peered around the corner again. The Aerie's circling flight had expanded, each pass drawing steadily nearer. "Moons, Fink! Did you take the strand with us?" Harric scanned the sky, and sure enough, one of the bright Web Strands drifted toward them across the empty square like a filament of spider silk on a breeze.

Biting off a curse, Harric crept from behind the house and beelined across the square for the passage. The arch was only thirty paces away. He reasoned that even if the Aerie could see the Unseen, they still might not see him from that distance. But if he hesitated and let them take up a new roost at the foot of the square, he and Fink would never get by.

He hadn't gone four steps before one of the creatures veered from its circling path and landed with a thump on the house he'd just left. Harric's heart nearly leapt from his throat as another departed its circle and dove directly at Harric. He dove to the ground, gritting his teeth in anticipation of impact. But the thing merely swooped. Its wingtip passed directly overhead, followed by a rush of soft wind.

"They can't see us," Harric whispered.

Fink answered by jerking frantically at the straps, and Harric sprinted for the archway. Only ten strides to the corridor. A glance back showed all the Aerie circling closer, and the Web Strand drifting lazily after Fink. But Harric's fear had already begun to subside, for he now knew one thing for certain: that the Aerie could not see them in the Unseen.

When he'd put a good fifty strides behind them down the passage, he slowed. "Moons, those things are weird," he said between panted breaths. "Fink? You there? We did it. We got away. They can't see us in the Unseen."

Fink said nothing. The imp clutched the pack straps with a grip like death.

After eight intersections, Harric found himself back at the map room's corridor, which he'd marked with the lightless mushroom lamp.

Fink extended a trembling hand and pointed to the map room.

Harric shook his head. "Fink, I'm sorry, but I haven't seen where Brolli went. I can't leave yet. He must have gone down one of these other two passages."

"You were gone all that time and you didn't find him?" Fink's voice rose to a squeak. "What the White Moon were you doing?"

"Heh. Tell you some other time. A little surprised I made it back to you at all."

Fink groaned.

"Come on, Fink, you have to admit it: the Aerie were so close, but still didn't know you were there. They were there for the Web Strands. Did you attract the strands?"

Fink groaned again. "Maybe. Yes, sure. That makes sense."

"You have to pull yourself together, Fink. That kind of mistake will get us killed."

Harric began scanning for clues to the way Brolli had gone. "Come. Let's try again. This is your chance to impress your moon if they still have you on probation or whatever. Or you can stay and wait in the map room for me. But decide now, because I'm going to find Brolli."

As bluffs went, it was a pretty thin one. To do any reasonable exploration, Harric would need to be in the Unseen for a long time, and much longer than he could support himself. Fink knew it too, but he did not climb down. Harric felt him take a couple of shuddering breaths and shift his weight on the pack straps.

"You're right, kid. Can't face my sisters without learning something here. Maybe if we learn something, Missy won't be so mad when we stand her up."

"And the Aerie?"

Fink let out a hissing breath. "You're going to make me say it? All right, they can't see us."

Harric nodded. "I'm glad you're coming."

"Wouldn't get far without me."

Harric grinned, but his eyes flicked back toward the empty city, where he'd left two Kwendi who could blow their cover. But those two were days from help, their cries muffled deep in a cistern underground. And he needn't tell Fink about it yet. No need to worry him more.

"Where to?" Fink said.

"Not sure." The floors here weren't so dusty, and Brolli didn't use the floor anyway. Harric reached up and ran a finger along a rung of the trellis from both of the corridors they hadn't yet explored. The one opposite the map room came away with a small smudge, but the other came back with a fur of gray dust. Another unused corridor. Harric couldn't help but wonder if it led to another valley of empty houses.

"This way," he said, trotting down the hall with Fink on his back, and in a couple of minutes they stood at the edge of another a deserted square—only this one was actually circular, with its fountain in the middle of a ring of deserted houses.

"Don't go out there, kid," the imp whispered. "We know what's there: nothing, and no one but Aerie."

Harric stared in wonder. Not one abandoned township, but two. How many more might there be? The explanation that the Arkendians had killed entire cities worth of Kwendi now seemed even more preposterous. The scale of slaughter required to exterminate so many—and not just warriors, but women and children and elders, too—was unthinkable. There simply weren't enough Arkendian warriors among the settlers of the north to make the sort of army required. And as Harric understood it,

Arkendians in the Free Lands had been on the defensive against Kwendi until the current truce was declared.

When they returned to the intersection, he faced the only passage they had yet to explore.

"Now we get some answers," he said. "Last one's lucky."

"Way to jinx it, kid."

There is no secret so close as that between a rider and her mount.
How much more, and yet less, between rider and Phyros.

—Sad Bella

53

Fireflies

Caris rode down the yoab run behind Willard through the dark and smoky halls of the forest. The giant boles of the trees loomed out of the murk in the light of her lantern. In some ways, the movement of the lantern on its pole threw more confusion than light, but it was enough for Rag to see by. She'd known some horses that were unable to travel by firelight because the flickering made every root seem a snake.

She leaned forward to rub Rag's chestnut neck. The mare glanced back and watched her. She had opened to Caris a little. But it seemed she was testing Caris, and her trust would not come easy. Nevertheless, it was enough for Caris to submerge herself in the mare's senses when she needed, and the gradual closing of the rift gave her hope it would indeed be mended.

"You'll see," she murmured often, stroking Rag's mane.

Willard's pole lantern bobbed above him on the trail ahead like a will-o'-the-wisp. He still hunched over his saddle, silent since they'd left camp.

When they'd set out, she'd intended to return to the topic of the wedding with him. It had been the first thing on her mind. But now it couldn't be farther from her mind—indeed, it made her sick to think about, though she couldn't guess why. She hadn't touched Molly's mind. She hadn't been blooded. In one moment she'd decided to wed at the first Common House they found, and in the next, the wedding fever vanished, and she knew instantly the influence of the ring had been bending her to wed.

I will never marry that deceitful roach.

A wave of nausea crossed her stomach, and she recognized it as the enchantment of the ring, but this time it was weak. Nothing like the stomach-wrenching convulsions she'd known that morning whenever she resisted its power.

Shame washed over her as she recalled how the ring had turned her into a single-minded wedding fool in front of Kogan and Willard that day; how she'd accosted them one after the other, like she'd picked up some new horse-touched fixation. And this brought back other shames, like when her mother tried to explain love and marriage to one person for life as something like the bond between a horse and rider, and Caris fixated on marrying Rag.

Her cheeks heated and she let out a small sound of disgust.

So why had the ring suddenly weakened and allowed her this clarity on the matter? It couldn't be the nearness to Molly, because Caris had ridden beside Molly that very day during the height of her wedding fixation. And it wasn't because she was far from Harric, either, for he was only a mile away, sleeping next to Snapper, and that sort of distance had never affected it before.

She shook her head and sighed. Whatever it was, she needed to discover it, so she could employ it in lieu of Molly's touch.

Willard chose a tree for his binding and tied Molly's lead to another. Without a word, he laid out the iron hobbles Caris would bind him with, and set about bleeding his Phyros.

Caris watched, chewing her lower lip as Molly resisted him. The Phyros reared or pulled away so he couldn't cut the vein, and Willard responded by hauling down on her halter and pummeling her mouth with brutal blows of his fisted gauntlet. Even more disconcerting was the indifference with which Molly greeted these measures, and the fact that, through it all, her gaze never budged from Caris.

"Girl! Give me some space." Willard sent her a dart of a glance, and it pierced a cord of guilt in Caris.

He'd seen Molly's look, and he blamed Caris for his Phyros's resistance. Maybe that was Molly's game, to torment Willard and make him jealous or enraged against Caris. Just as likely, she was trying to make the task of bleeding her so difficult that he'd insist Caris do it, which would give her another at blooding her.

Despite everything, the urge to touch the fire in Molly stirred in her, and she had to tear herself from it—to physically turn herself from the Phyros—before Rag could sense it and doubt her all over. Sending her mind back to Rag, she concentrated on sharing senses with her, and coaxing her to trust.

You see, I am here. I am not with Molly.

"It's done, gods take you," Willard snarled. "Get this out of my hand before I drink it unbound!"

Caris hurried to him, and she had to lay her hands on his wrists to keep him from gulping it before should could take away. A small amount spilled as they struggled, and he hissed with fury.

"I'll give it right back," she said, not daring to meet his eyes. But she did dare to reach out with her senses and smooth any of the anger, lest the Blood further taint her. "I'll hold it for you. That's all."

Willard uncurled his fingers from the cup as if each finger had frozen and he fought iron stiffness. When it was safe in her hands, he stalked to the tree, where he sat and reached his arms behind him. "You'd better bloody make it quick."

The muffled roars of Willard-Krato dwindled behind Caris as she rode Rag toward a smooth dome of rock they'd passed on their way up the run. After tying Rag at the base, she climbed to its summit and gained a view between trees of a narrow slice of the sky and river valley. She sat against a small tree and let out a long sigh, which the north wind echoed in the trees. A few stars winked through the haze of smoke still smothering the valley, and some reflected off the surface of the river, like a line of fireflies.

Her brow furrowed at that, for the river here was swift and frothy, too rough to reflect starlight. She stared hard at the line of lights, trying in vain to make sense of them with respect to the river and the valley, but the moonlight was dull and indirect, smothered behind a cloud.

As if answering her need, the Bright Mother peeked out for a moment and gave enough light for her to finally see the rapids of the river and to reveal that the fireflies lay above the line of the river, and therefore beyond it, in the distance. The lights winked in and out, colored yellow-orange by the haze from the wildfires until she recognized them for what they were, and her blood froze.

Torches, not fireflies.

Bannus's men, riding with torches up the other side of the river, to intercept them.

"Her Majesty will never marry, for now she is both king and queen, and if she marries, she will be but queen."

—The Queen's Lady Anna to the Duke Arcenon
upon his third and final courtship visit

54

Preparations

As Harric hurried down the last unexplored corridor, he passed numerous intersections with smaller passages. He'd passed a half-dozen of these before he began to hear the sounds of life echoing from some of them: Kwendi voices, thumping doors, muffled laughter.

Unwilling to make any turns that would be hard to remember later, he passed these and kept on until the main corridor made a sharp turn to the right. He had just paused at the corner when he heard something approaching from the other side, and a moment later pressed himself against the wall as a Kwendi swooped past them on the lowest branches of the trellis. The Kwendi blazed with streaming green strands as he moved easily from rung to rung, his feet holding tight to the handles of a basket smelling of berries.

"Mother of moons," Fink said, when the passage stood vacant again. "These things give me chills. I'll keep an eye out, and if one sneaks up from behind, I'll rap the back of your head."

"Good plan. You rap, I duck."

Around the corner, the corridor grew wider and louder as Kwendi appeared in the trellis from doors high on the wall, many wearing long, many-pocketed vests and bizarre hats like wooly cones. A welter of bright green soul strands filled the air as the Kwendi barked and grinned and blinked at each other, and swooped away on the upper swing-ways with satchels of belongings beside them or clutched in feet. Harric couldn't be certain, but it appeared that these Kwendi were men and children, and that he hadn't seen a Kwendi woman since the reservoir.

Navigating the floor of the passage was relatively easy despite the crowds, because very few Kwendi moved on the ground. A few pushed carts full of baskets or boxes too heavy to carry, but those were slow-moving and easy to avoid, and once he saw a gray-haired Kwendi knuckle-walking between doors, but these elders were neither numerous nor swift-moving.

Soon the corridor fed into an open-air square like the one in the ghost town, only the trellises here were well maintained and full of roosting Kwendi men and children. Even the ground beneath the trellises was packed with them, so that their soul strands filled the space like a brilliant green sea. If he'd seen such a crowd at Gallows Ferry, it would be for the hanging of a witch or a horse thief, but these Kwendi appeared to be listening to a speaker somewhere in their midst in the trellises, for they all faced the center, from which a lone voice rose.

"Look at all these Kwendi," Harric whispered. "Their clothes look nothing like Brolli's."

"Did you expect them to look like Arkendians?"

"Well…yeah. Brolli wore Arkendian clothes." It bothered Harric that he hadn't questioned why Brolli's clothes had borne all the marks of an Arkendian tailor, down to the style of buttons and fabrics and the range of colors muted by the dictates of blood rank.

These Kwendi—the real Kwendi—stood out in stark contrast, favoring bushy fur vests over loose, brightly colored breeches or wraps, with exotic-colored sashes. Aside from bare feet, the only thing Brolli had retained from his people's style was the long, braided locks, which appeared to be universal among Kwendi men.

But even there Brolli had muted the expression of Kwendi tastes, for most of these Kwendi had stones or witch-silver worked into their braids with colored ribbons, and just as many tied them up in huge piles atop their crowns or wrapped them in cloths. Brolli had also worn no jewelry, whereas loops of witch-silver festooned these men, piercing their ears and dangling on forearms. Similarly, ink or colored paint adorned their skin.

Brolli had clearly adopted Arkendian mannerisms and fashion to portray a very Arkendian-seeming image of his people, and from it Harric had foolishly imagined a whole culture of Kwendi who were more or less like Arkendians.

"There's one trying to look Arkendian," Fink said. "Why would anyone want to do that?"

He pointed to a young Kwendi in the nearest trellis, dressed in the scarlet tones of what had surely once been the doublet of an Arkendian of umber blood rank. The sleeves had been removed to create a passable vest, but to Harric's eye, its velvet and cut looked out of place with its new owner's beaded braids and sashes.

But now that he knew to look for it, he saw these bits of Arkendian fashion on younger Kwendi throughout the crowd. One wore the high hat of a spitfire tooler, and among the children he spotted page caps in all colors of the blood rank. But whether they'd been taken as trophies from dead Arkendian settlers, or won in trade, he couldn't tell.

The speaker in the middle of the crowd shouted something, and the crowd exploded, hooting and waving their long arms above their heads and slapping feet against trellises. Since the hooting reminded Harric of the way Brolli laughed, he judged the crowd must approve of the speaker, but he could not interpret their animated grimaces and blinks.

"Hey, Fink," Harric said. "Can you get down for a while? My shoulders are killing me."

When Fink said nothing in response, Harric turned his head to look back.

The imp blinked his pupil-less eyes and then stretched his lipless mouth in hideous imitation of a Kwendi. "What's wrong, kid? You don't speak Kwendi Face Spasm?"

Harric smiled. "That's the Fink I know. Welcome back."

"Seriously, what's wrong with their faces? Think they ate bad clams?"

"I'm sure that's it exactly." Harric nodded to the ground beside them. "Climb down?"

Fink hesitated, apparently anxious despite the return of his humor, but ultimately climbed down and hooked a talon in Harric's belt, as if he feared Harric might abandon him again.

"This way," Harric said. Sidestepping along the outer edge of the square, he found a gap in the crowd through which he could see the speaker at the center. "Brolli!" he whispered to Fink. "We found him."

As Harric watched, Brolli barked something in Kwendi, and the crowd reacted in the same boisterous way.

In the trellis below Brolli stood Rurgich and a half-dozen sharply dressed warriors in bright red uniforms and oddly shaped felt hats. The musculature of these Kwendi was nothing short of astounding, rippling with corded muscle, as if some drunk god had taken Willard's top half and attached it to the legs of a prentice. Heavy bandoliers of hurling globes and cudgels hung from their shoulders.

After the final burst of clamor, the crowd dispersed and Brolli descended the trellis to stand beside a central fountain with his escort. One of the warriors handed him several sheets of parchment. He perused them and issued several crisp orders, then the warriors climbed up the trellises and swooped away in various directions.

Harric frowned. "How do you account for our friendly ambassador?"

"How do you mean?"

"Rousing speeches, orders to warriors. More than your basic ambassador's authority, don't you think? I think maybe he's more than just that."

Fink made a noncommittal noise. A glance down confirmed the imp had gone back to scanning the roofs at the edges of the square.

"Just keep those Web Strands away," said Harric, "and that will keep the Aerie away."

"Easy for you to say. Barely holding myself together."

"You're doing great. Sense of humor back and everything."

"Gallows humor."

Rurgich had disappeared in the hubbub of the square, which Harric saw was a market of sorts. He now emerged from the scrum with steaming skewers of meat for himself and Brolli, and the sight made Harric's stomach rumble. He'd have to snag some food when he had a chance, but the square was too busy and chaotic to risk navigating in the Unseen.

Brolli and Rurgich wolfed their meat sticks and ascended the trellises, and before Harric could lean away from the wall, they swooped away into a passage between buildings on the opposite side of the square.

"Get on," Harric whispered, and as soon as Fink climbed aboard, Harric dove into the market, dodging Kwendi and weaving through stacks of baskets and handcarts until he made it to the passage Brolli had taken.

High in the trellis and far down the passage, he spotted Brolli and Rurgich and followed at a lumbering jog. For a long minute, he barely kept them in sight until a soldier in red armor stopped them at an intersection.

Just as Harric caught up to them, they resumed swinging in their original direction, but they were halted so often by messengers who appeared to be seeking them that Harric was able to reclaim some of his breath.

Everywhere Brolli went, the respect and love and command he held over the soldiers and servants was evident. Despite the strange grimaces Harric couldn't interpret, he thought he recognized a few signs. Small dips of their heads to Brolli, like little bows, coupled with wider grins and a slightly higher pitch to their voices when speaking with him. And he seemed calmer, less demonstrative, like a well-liked leader who knew his station but didn't flaunt it.

Ambassador, my filthy socks. More like a general.

When Brolli halted at a pair of huge double doors, Harric staggered to a halt and hung back, so the Kwendi wouldn't hear him panting. Two of the red-clad guards in the oddly shaped hats flanked the doors, their lower lips thrust out in a deliberate and sustained pout. Was that supposed be intimidating? Welcoming? When Brolli whirled down a ladder beside them, the warriors' pouts vanished, and they bared their teeth in something like a grimace of pain.

"Before we leave," Fink whispered, "I want a hat that looks like a constipated toad."

The guards opened the great doors for Brolli, admitting cool outdoor air into the corridor along with the sounds of battle and brilliant daylight.

Daylight?

Brolli and Rurgich flipped their daylids down and stepped out onto what appeared to be a broad, trellised balcony crowded with Kwendi. Just as strange as daylight at night, the brilliant glare came from *below* the balcony, not from above, where Harric saw the night sky of the Unseen, with the swirling strands of the web.

Harric dodged the few Kwendi on the floor of the balcony and pressed against the back wall. Cool air laden with smells of earth and forest brought blessed relief to his sweating body.

Brolli and Rurgich joined a huge figure in crimson armor who stood at the edge of the balcony below numerous Kwendi who sat in the trellis to watch something in the daylight below. This Kwendi's hair was silvered and his face aged and deeply cratered with pox scars. When he saw Brolli, the two embraced.

"You wear your armor," said the elder, in perfect Arkendian. "That is good."

Brolli shook his head. "I have lost my breath for it, uncle."

"What do you think of the new machine?"

Brolli looked down into the bright light. "Yes. It's good, that one. It simulates well. Are there others?"

"Another will be complete soon. This one is used without stopping, night and day."

"Good."

The elder turned his pocked face to Brolli. "We are strong enough for war," he said, with a grim change in tone. "There is no treaty."

Brolli nodded as if he already knew this. As the two stared at the bright scene below, the sounds of battle redoubled, and Harric felt his heart shrinking like a punctured wineskin.

No treaty. War.

Though he'd suspected this to the point of believing it, confirmation hurt. His mind drifted back over the last weeks with Brolli and Willard, trying to make sense of Brolli's game. If there was to be no treaty, what was the point of stringing Willard along? The only reason Harric could imagine was for Brolli to continue to milk Willard of his understanding of Arkendian war craft. Indeed, what better source than Sir Willard? Battle tactics, strategy—these were the constant subjects of discussion between them during all those nights in Abellia's tower. Brolli had been fascinated with the coordination of mounted lances and archer squads, of spitfire teams and foot brigades and the use of signal banners and trumpets. He'd scribbled it all in his journal. And hadn't he recently asked how to kill an immortal?

As the scale of the Kwendi's betrayal became clear, Harric felt his throat tightening, his chest squeezing his breath. And if this were so, then surely Brolli never intended to remove the rings from Caris.

Fists trembling, Harric barely restrained himself from shoving

Brolli over the railing.

You gutless, mother-cobbing liar. You stinking traitor. Caris is suffering, and you lie and give her false hope. I'll make you pay for this. I will find a way.

Harric took several deep breaths to calm himself and then crept to the edge of the balcony to look down. The light shone up from large white balls suspended on poles. In a garden of shrubs and small trees below were a dozen goggled Kwendi in the heavy tar-bag armor, bearing even heavier-looking tar-bag shields and helms. They formed two ranks: the first rank was a shield wall with cudgels in hand; the second rank had shields on their backs and hurling globes in their hands. Together the two ranks moved against a very strange opponent, which Harric recognized immediately.

It was a bulky wooden contraption mounted on wheels and powered by giant springs of twisted rope like those that powered Arkendian catapults. The machine was clearly meant to resemble an oversized war-horse with a long, blunted lance mounted on its head. The "charge" was a strike of incredible speed in which the beast lunged forward and knocked a soldier in the shield wall spinning. Two Kwendi on the machine guided the lance strikes and reset the mechanisms, while others manipulated its orientation by pushing and pulling against long levers.

The Kwendi were preparing to fight against mounted lances.

The Kwendi warriors' tactic was simple. Their tactic consisted of waiting for the knight to charge them with a lance, at which time the first rank aimed cudgel blows and the second rank lobbed heavy hurling globes at the beast's head.

Even more horrifying to Harric, however, was that there was no mistaking the design of the contraption as *Arkendian*. The rope-wheels, the levers, the gears—the sheer ingenuity of it—was the purest example of Arkendian toolery. The Kwendi had enslaved some captured knight, Harric guessed—or more likely a knight's squire, as it wasn't a gentleman's pastime—and that Arkendian was still here, in captivity, building for the Kwendi.

Could such knights have turned traitor out of spite for their banishment?

Harric chewed the inside of his cheek. More likely they had been forced to make it, or they had been lied to. It wasn't a master tooler's work, in any case: though it simulated the moment of impact and force of a mounted lance, it in no way reproduced the follow-through of a charging war-horse. Harric could see this flaw immediately, though the Kwendi did not seem to notice it. The contraption also moved from side to side around the slow-moving shield wall—a loss of momentum no lancer would allow. Nor would a knight fight alone like that unless separated from the others.

It was strange to Harric that Brolli had seen the charge of a cavalry line in action, yet seemed content with this flawed mechanism.

Harric studied the training, furious that Brolli would talk peace out of one side of his mouth and yet prepare for war out of the other. He counted heads in the first and second ranks, and noted how a leader in rear rank shouted commands to the front, the way the two ranks moved together and how the warriors in each rank moved, and every detail of intelligence he might gather for Willard.

The contraption circled and feinted, and circled again. When a soldier was knocked down by a lance strike, the front rank of Kwendi surged forward to cover him while the second rank reclaimed the injured and redoubled harassment with hurling globes.

Then the lance impaled itself dead center in a soldier's tar-bag shield and stuck fast. As soon as the lance attempted to jerk back for another strike (another flaw, for a mounted lance did not recoil after striking, but drove through the target or splintered on impact), the tar of the shield held it fast, so it couldn't retract. The lance merely jerked the soldier forward to his knees as thick black tar oozed from the shield. The stricken soldier dropped his cudgel and clung to the shaft with both hands and feet as if his life depended upon it. As his added weight dragged the lance down farther, the shield wall surrounded the horse's "head" and showered it with cudgel blows.

A cheer went up from the balcony.

Attacking the horse. Had they learned that from Willard's tactics in the Cleansing?

But this was a flawed, foolish tactic for mounted knights. An actual knight would simply drop his lance if it stuck in a shield, and whoever had designed this simulacrum had not provided the Kwendi with a useful training tool at all. In fact, Harric began to appreciate that the Arkendian responsible had effectively sabotaged the Kwendi perception of mounted lances. When they met the real thing, in force, their strategy would be almost useless.

A fierce pride of kinship with the architect flared in Harric. Though forced to build for the Kwendi, that nameless man had done real damage to their war effort.

A bell rang, and the balcony exploded with hooting and howls. The squads below looked up and grimaced, waving long arms. One of them shouted something about "Stilty warriors," and another chorus of howls went up.

A flash of white caught Harric's eye in the open sky above the open courtyard. Fink saw it too, and dropped from Harric's back to drag him back against the wall.

"*Aerie!*" Fink said, his trembling renewed.

The monster disappeared above the building, but a moment later, its claws curled over the edge of the roof above them, as if it had perched there. In the Unseen, Harric had no oculus to erupt in irritation, but its presence resonated in the spirit world around him like the thundering vibration of a waterfall, and it made his entire spirit body *itch*. An instant later, another landed beside the first, and the vibration grew to such an intolerable pitch that Harric jumped, letting out a cry of surprise and distress. Without looking to see if any Kwendi had heard him, Harric bolted for the doors, only to find them closed fast and flanked by pouty toad-hat guards.

"Close the shutters!" said the pockmarked elder, in his perfect Arkendian. Harric turned to see soldiers slamming doors over the balcony, and Kwendi flipping up their daylids. The shutters also closed out Harric's view of the talons on the roof, and the itch receded to a level that didn't make him want to tear off his own skin.

"Kid, you okay?"

"No."

Brolli turned to leave with the elder, and the guards swung the doors wide for them to pass. A handful of armored Kwendi accompanied them, and Harric followed them all as close as he dared. As soon as he could, he won free of the crowd and pressed himself against an out-of-the-way wall, rubbing his arms as if to swipe away biting ants. Fink cringed at his side, white eyes darting about.

Harric said through clenched teeth, "You forgot to mind the Web Strands, didn't you?"

"Lot on my mind."

Brolli exchanged grimaces with the elder and swung away down the corridor, while the elder returned to the balcony.

"Come on," Harric whispered, before Fink could whine about the map room. "We'll stay away from windows and balconies."

I ran a wagon caravan for His Lordship in the Free Lands… never guessed it would end as it did. Surveyors picked a lovely spot, I can tell you — high hills and green waters, trees tall as the sky and just begging to be milled. I hauled grain there all summer from His Lordship's plantations down south, and my last job come when leaves was turning. …been a hard, dry road, and I was ready for a hot meal and a bunk. But as I come over the last falls below the place, I smelled smoke. And when I come to the manor…well, it was gone. All burned, and my mates was corpses. One man — Davey, he was, and a stout carpenter, too — still lived, but barely. "Who done it?" I says. "Was it Westies?" His eyes was wide, like he seen impits everywhere. "Chimpies," he says. "Painted chimpies come out of the trees."

— "Testimony of Marto Bulls in H.M.'s Court," after the Bright Massacre, first evidence the northlands were not "uninhabited"

55

Witch-Silver Depths

Harric followed Brolli past smithies full of huge-armed Kwendi smiths, and armories that stunk to the moons of boiling tar. These places they dared not enter lest the smoke reveal their unseen bodies, "like a specter, perfectly detailed," Fink said. They passed courtyards full of Kwendi children racing through trellises, orchards full of fruit smells and the squawk of birds, and halls full of Kwendi working leather or painting or weaving on looms.

When they passed a kitchen where the Kwendi smoked what smelled like salmon, Harric's stomach growled again.

"Hush it, kid, you'll give us away."

"I'm starving."

"*You're* starving? Kid. Look what this has done to my luscious belly."

Fink clambered down from Harric's back, and Harric turned to see the imp almost as scrawny as he'd been when first they met.

Harric gaped. "You've shrunk!"

Fink nodded, wings sagging. In his hands he cradled a tiny, round belly the size of a melon—all that was left of his tremendous surplus of souls. "Takes a lot to keep you in the Unseen, kid. Hate to cut this pleasant tour short, but we need to turn back."

Harric glanced after Brolli to be sure the ambassador was still in sight, then looked back the way they'd come. "Do you think you could remember the way back?"

Fink went very still. "Are you saying you don't know how to get back to the map room?"

"Um, well, it's been a complicated path." Harric's cheeks flushed hot. "Sure, I think I know, but…I just figure if we stay with Brolli, then we don't have to risk getting lost; he has to get back before long."

Fink's gaze hardened. "If I get low enough," he said, very slowly, "I'll need to feed off you. You understand?"

Harric's stomach felt suddenly heavy, but he nodded. If he thought he could find his way back through the maze of corridors and courtyards and halls, he would turn back right then. But there was a chance he could get lost and not find the way to the map room before Brolli opened the gate. And he wanted to see more—needed to see as much as he could of the Kwendi preparations.

He motioned for Fink to climb aboard, and as soon he was set, Harric followed Brolli.

Brolli picked up his pace, and his path took them downward in spiraling ramps. When Harric guessed they must be several floors below the surface, Brolli passed through a set of tall, thick doors made of the blackest night. Harric stared at them, barely able to see them in the Unseen.

"Witch-silver," Fink said. "No presence in the Unseen."

Harric ran a hand along the face of a door. It felt cool and hard and heavy, like solid metal. Like the doors to a treasure vault.

His heartbeat quickened, and a wry smile lifted one side of his mouth. "This is it, Fink."

The corridor beyond was just as black in the Unseen, lit only by the essence glow of the wooden trellis, for the floors, walls, and ceiling were all of witch-silver. It was like the passage had been carved from a mountain of the stuff, or as if some magic had turned the stone to the mystical metal. If it weren't for the glow of the trellis, it would be like the void they'd traversed in Brolli's gate.

Harric's gut tightened at the memory, so he kept his eyes on the trellis as he passed through the door. Once inside, he noticed a trace of glowing essence from dust on the walls and floors, and that helped him to keep his feet and bearings.

From then on, doors they encountered were closed and guarded by pairs of guards in special black uniforms and toad hats. These guards did not display the elaborate grimaces that others had for Brolli, and Harric guessed that they were independent of Brolli's direct command. Slipping through these doors was difficult, as the guards closed them after Brolli, so Harric had to stay close on his heels. At the first of these encounters, when the guard started to close the door, Harric had to lunge through, causing him to run into Brolli's tar-armored back. Fortunately, Brolli said nothing, assuming perhaps that a guard had bumped him.

Their descent ended at the top of a wide ramp descending to the floor of a vast hall housing numerous spoke-limb trellises and teeming with Kwendi.

The floors and walls here were also of witch-silver and totally lightless in the spirit world. Like the spiraling ramps, however, the lightless floors and walls were crowded with wooden tables and shelves and trellises that gave a substantial essence glow, and this—combined with the brilliant pale green strands of the Kwendi—lent the place enough volume and dimension to stave off memories of the gate void.

As Brolli paused in the archway at the top of the ramp, Harric pressed against the wall.

Fink's talons squeezed tighter at the straps of his pack. "The women," Fink whispered at Harric's ear. "It's the Chimpey women."

Harric paid closer attention to the clamor of the Kwendi below, and realized Fink was right. The timbre of their voices was brighter and clearer. Looking closer, he saw that their faces, without the harshness of the male teeth and whiskers, had a definite softness. There were differences in clothing, and their braids appeared to be adorned and arranged differently. Most surprising, however, was the fact that Kwendi females were as flat-chested as the males.

Fink tapped Harric's shoulder frantically and pointed into the hall. "What in the White Moon is that?"

Something huge and dark moved in front of the glowing wooden pillar of a spoke-limb trellis. Whatever it was had no more essence or spirit to it than the witch-silver, so it all but vanished when it moved out over the floor. Harric froze, eyes searching the area where it disappeared until it appeared again in silhouette against a wall of shelves. Shaped vaguely like a Kwendi, it stood twice as high as a man, yet its body was without claw or hair or notable musculature beyond the mere mass and the thickness of its limbs.

"It's a tryst servant," Fink said breathlessly. "Like Mudwhistle."

"Made of witch-silver?"

Fink nodded. "*Bendy* witch-silver. No idea how they do that."

Two smaller forms leapt from the creature onto the shelves, but whether they leapt out of the creature, or had simply been clinging to it, Harric couldn't tell, for they too gave no spirit light. They were shaped like spidery little Kwendi, and easily climbed to the top shelves, where they fetched globes of witch-silver. One of these leapt from the shelf into a trellis and began to swing rung by rung across the hall and up the ramp toward Brolli, until it hung by both arms in front of him.

After a short conversation with Brolli in Kwendi, the creature whirled about and swung back into the depths of the hall.

"These ones can't see us either," Harric whispered.

"This place is a freak show, kid. We have to get out of here."

"We have to wait until Brolli leads us out, Fink. And just look at all this witch-silver, and the tryst servants. Don't you see? This is where they make their secret magic. This is where you earn out of your probation, and I find a way to help my queen."

*Arkendian courtship ritual is not designed to facilitate mating,
but to discourage it…because of the need to identify the father of
a child, and because children are… raised by the father's family…
Therefore, they attempt to confine mating to a single, well-known
mate. In my estimation, however, Arkendians esteem the act no
less pleasant than we…so it is no surprise that illicit mating is
common…nor that the island is abundant with "illegitimate"
children they call bastards.*

—From *Arkendian Mating Mysteries*, First Ambassador Brolli

56

Witches

A loud voice trumpeted Brolli's name from the bottom of the ramp.
Brolli grinned and descended the trellis to the source of the
voice. "Mima!" he called.

The owner of the voice was a gray-haired Kwendi matron with a
sooty and pox-scarred face. She grinned with what seemed like genuine
pleasure, and when Brolli joined her, she drew him into an embrace.

Harric descended the ramp with Fink clinging tightly to his pack,
and stood behind Brolli.

Mima's announcement of Brolli's arrival caused the hall to surge
with excitement. Shrill cheers erupted from various parts of the hall,
and dozens of beaming female faces converged toward him, flashing
teeth and craning necks for a look. Love and admiration radiated from
them. The cheers spread to distant parts of the hall, and repeated
several times before the place returned to some semblance of its former
business.

One of the smaller tryst servants approached Mima and swung to a stop beside her. In its feet it carried a heavy bandolier of witch-silver hurlers, which Mima took and presented to Brolli.

"Ah! I need these," said Brolli, speaking slowly and deliberately in Arkendian. "I used some of your last batch. They were excellent."

Mima said something in Kwendi as she wiped her hands on a leather apron so sooty that it seemed unlikely it could accept any more from her hands. Patches of perspiration stained the long vest and short pants under the apron, leaving pox-scarred arms and legs quite bare.

"Still no Stilty, eh, Mima?" Brolli chuckled.

She made a sound of distaste and turned away into the hall, beckoning Brolli to follow.

"But you understand it well enough."

She did not respond. Now that the initial excitement of his visit had subsided, she seemed weary, as if at the end of a long working day.

Mima led Brolli into the aisles of tables, and Harric followed as closely as he could, but Brolli attracted the younger Kwendi women, which made it dicey to stay too close to him. Wherever he went, weary faces lit, and when he passed, they worked with renewed purpose.

Soon it appeared to Harric that Mima was parading Brolli about for that very reason. She brought him to every corner of the hall, and in each one he was greeted by other matrons, distinguished from their apprentices not only by their gray hair, but by leather aprons, while their helpers wore aprons of cloth.

Each matron also wore a belt and keys and what looked like a hoop of marbled stone as big around as a tea saucer. These they wore behind their aprons on cords from their necks. The matrons kept one hand on them almost at all times, for they were heavy. But Harric caught a good look at a couple of them, which appeared to be carved from white stone marbled with veins of red and black.

Harric flinched as something bright moved near him in the side of his vision. A strand of spirit quested toward him from high in the trellis, moving downward like a blind worm.

"Fink!" Harric said. He ducked and backed away from the strand, almost knocking over a shelf of witch-silver bowls in the process. "A Web Strand!"

"Can't be," Fink whispered. But a breath later, the imp let out a low hiss and said, "Mother of moons. How'd that get here? Web Strands don't go underground." Then the hiss sounded more like anger, and a tone of menace entered his voice. "That's part of the Unseen. They're tapping into *our moon*." When Harric backed far enough away, the strand appeared to lose interest in Fink and the nexus stone in his talons, and instead drifted toward a nearby matron.

Harric was watching to see what would happen when it reached her, when a piercing screech split the air.

A door in one of the long side walls burst open on its hinges. The explosion sent a shuddering vibration through the floor and a thick billow of smoke into the room.

For a heartbeat, a paralyzed hush filled the room, then clamor erupted. Mima shouted; Kwendi women hurried past Harric and bumped hard into Fink without stopping. Witch-silver servants rushed to the smoking room and disappeared inside.

Fink dove under a table while Harric jumped on top, knocking a stack of bowls to the floor. From his vantage, Harric saw one of the huge witch-silver servants emerge from the smoke with two matrons in its arms. One of the matrons choked and coughed and nodded repeatedly, as if to say she was unharmed. The other lay limp and did not open her eyes.

The servant laid them side by side on a table only ten paces from Harric and stepped back as other matrons surrounded them. As the second matron opened her eyes and tried to wave them off, a fire flickered to life in her hair, and the witch-silver giant snuffed it with a gentle hand.

When it was certain both matrons were conscious, Mima exploded in what sounded like a scathing rebuke. Pointing and gesticulating, she stormed around the table bearing the injured matrons. Most of the smoke had risen high into the trellises, but the hall now stunk of burned metal. Harric saw then that the smoking chamber was one of many adorning the long wall of the hall, and that each bore scorch marks or soot streaks from similar accidents.

When Mima finished her tirade, she stood fuming beside Brolli. The two spoke in Kwendi, and Mima motioned to the tired, dirty girls in aprons and the drooping matrons.

Two of the huge tryst servants lifted the table with the injured matrons and carried it like a stretcher to a small trellis tree hung with heavy cloth partitions, on the opposite side of the hall. Mima turned to go in the opposite direction toward the smoking chamber. Before she left, she spoke to Brolli and pointed to the ground where he stood, as if instructing him to stay put in her absence.

Brolli stayed put for a few heartbeats, then he swung into the lowest branches of the trellis and headed toward the partitioned trellis tree. Harric slipped to the ground to follow, and instantly regretted it, as the younger Kwendi women moved toward Brolli like iron filings to a lodestone.

Diving under a table, Harric skinned his knee. The women surrounded Brolli, voices loud and chittering like squirrels. Fink skittered over from an adjacent table and hugged Harric's leg. As a Kwendi prentice passed, the imp's talons flicked out like a striking snake and hooked a brilliant strand of spirit. The strand whipped into his mouth and disappeared down his throat like he'd sucked up a noodle. She kept walking, but slapped at her hip where the strand had been attached, as if swatting a biting insect.

"Fink!" Harric gasped. "What are you doing?"

"Feeding myself. What the souls you think I'm doing?" Fink spat, white eyes glaring like taut boils. "I'm starving."

"You can't just do that."

"Oh? Then can I feed off *your* strands? I have to eat something."

The viciousness in his tone took Harric aback.

"Or maybe you'll kill a Kwendi for me?" Fink said. "You have to *feed* me—you said you would, but now look at me! You're burning me up like a tallow candle. I'm ribs."

The imp's gauntness was shocking. He was skin and bones. Harric had seen starved children that looked better. The imp seemed dried up. Mummified.

Fink's eyes gleamed with hatred—or desperation. "We have to go. Now. Or you have to feed me on your strands. It can't wait."

Harric's mouth moved without sound. He swallowed. "Ah—I—my strands?"

"They grow back. They always grow back. And it's that or I die, and without me, you die."

Harric felt the weight of the Unseen flicker above him, pressing on his shoulders and then releasing, as if Fink were losing strength. And whether or not the imp had purposefully manipulated the burden to persuade Harric, Fink's gaunt frame said it all. He wasn't faking this.

"I understand," Harric said. "But I don't want you feeding off anyone else. This was my choice. No one else pays for it."

Harric swept his arm under Fink's nose and steeled himself. One of the bright strands rising from his arm swirled and curled before the imp's eye like a weightless ribbon of sugar taffy. Talons flashed, and Fink sucked it in his needled jaws. Desperate greed flashed in his expression as he swallowed, and his gaunt face swelled. The entire strand—many fathoms of glowing ribbon—whipped down from the sky into Fink, and Harric watched as flesh poured over Fink's ribs and filled the hollow of his belly. As the end of the strand whipped into his mouth, the root tugged from Harric's arm like a plucked feather.

The imp gasped and closed his eyes, and Harric fought back a wave of nausea.

Before the imp could ask for more, Harric ducked out from under the table and climbed on top. His arm stung where the strand had been, and already it swelled like a circular burn. As he rubbed it, his heart thumped hard behind his breastbone. He had no idea how long it took for strands to grow back, or what would happen if he died before it could. Spirit strands were what lifted a soul to the Unseen Moon when it left its body. They were like wings that way. If he lost one, would he still have enough to lift him? He had no idea how many it would take to lift a soul, or how many he could spare and still rise.

He took a deep, shuddering breath. The welt began to pucker as he rubbed it, like the bump from a plucked feather, or a nipple.

The thought froze him in place. His mouth hung open as he studied the lesion.

It's a Witch's Teat.

He'd seen marks like it on some of the witches they'd hung in Gallows Ferry. Witch hunters claimed it was an identifying mark. They claimed it was the site on the witch where her familiar nursed from her.

Now he knew it was true. And he wished he'd chosen a less obvious spot than his forearm.

I know ten words for "looting" and each one is music to me.
— Jack-a-Knave, in "Sir Willard & the Treasure Fair"

57

Stranded

As Harric watched Brolli swing away toward the partitioned trellis where they'd taken the injured matrons, a realization hit him hard enough to pierce his worries.

The injured matrons.

It was a realization of opportunity. A recognition that he could be saboteur as well as spy.

Climbing down from the table, he beckoned Fink to follow, but Fink merely stared at him. His eyes were no longer wild, but Harric could still see anger in them. The imp shook his head, eyes narrowed.

Harric held out a hand. "Then I need the nexus. I'll just be a minute."

After a moment, Fink extended his trembling hand and laid the stone in Harric's. "I can't hold you in the Unseen when you leave me here."

"I know, but I have to try."

"Keep away from Web Strands. If one attaches, *don't move.* I'll find you."

Even as Fink said it, one of the glowing strings quested toward Harric from the trellis above.

He gave Fink a nod and left, quickly outdistancing the strand. Fink still carried the weight of the Unseen for him, but Harric steeled himself for the moment he got too far from the imp and the weight fell fully on his shoulders. He'd closed half the distance to his destination when it crushed down on him and he realized he might only last a minute.

Discarding stealth, he stumbled into a run to close the distance quickly and dove behind the heavy partitions. He found himself in what appeared to be a rest area, judging by the many the whispered conversations of women there. Many enclosed pavilions floated in the branches above, but there were also a few round and slightly bowl-shaped nests of blankets underneath them on the ground. Among these beds, Harric found Brolli sitting and conversing in hushed tones with a black-haired matron and a half-dozen of the younger women. In the Unseen, the Kwendi's pale green strands bent into the floor, but a single bright blue strand rose from the matron's breast. It took Harric a moment to realize it was a Web Strand, and that the thing had latched on to the hoop around her neck.

Harric stared, his head aching with the weight of the Unseen, his mind spinning.

So the loops were like a nexus. That meant this matron must craft Unseen magic, like the wedding ring on Caris's finger, and that her hoop attracted Web Strands like Harric's nexus. It seemed obvious now that the black marbling in the hoops must be of the same material as the nexus stone in his hand. He shook his head in amazement. If that were so, then the red marbling must be of the Mad Moon, and the white of the Bright Mother. Did that mean the Kwendi had stolen nexuses from the moons? And if so, how had they melted and marbled them together?

Creeping closer, Harric saw that Brolli and the others sat vigil beside the injured matrons' beds, and that both were already fast asleep. Heavy fur blankets had been drawn up to the matrons' armpits. Their long arms rested outside the blankets, and each rested a long-fingered hand on their strange, marbled hoops.

Jackpot.

Harric had just stopped between the beds of the two matrons when his head gave a vicious throb, and his vision darkened as it had before he'd collapsed on the Kwendi lovers.

Cobbing moons, not now!

He dropped to his belly and pushed past the overhanging blankets into the space under one of the matrons' beds, only to find that Kwendi beds did not have legs like Arkendian beds, but stood on a kind of pedestal, which left only a rim around the edges in which to hide.

Cursing, he curved his body around the pedestal as best he could, but his head and shoulders were just inside the rim of overhanging blankets.

It was insane. He was trapped, and they would find him easily.

As his vision faded, he released himself into the Seen, and everything went dark.

It took him a moment to realize he hadn't passed out again, but that it was simply very dark in the Seen under the bed. He held still, listening as Brolli spoke in low tones, performing one of his small miracles of morale and apparently captivating the circle of women.

Harric closed his eyes and allowed his breathing and heartbeat to settle. *Now what, genius?*

Arching his neck, he peeked through his oculus from under the curtain of blankets. The Kwendi women still sat with their backs to him. He could just see the bottoms of their cushions and a few of their feet between them. He could not see Brolli.

The injured matron on the bed above Harric murmured and moved so the ropes supporting the mattress creaked and nudged his shoulder. Brolli stopped speaking for a moment, and one of the Kwendi women rose and knuckle-walked to the bed until her foot stopped inches from Harric's face. The ropes creaked and bumped his shoulder again as the woman attended to the matron, murmuring comforting words.

The matron settled, but then the attendant set about tucking up the edge of the blanket where it draped over the edge of the bed.

No! Go away! Leave the blankets!

The curtains lifted on Harric's legs, and if she stepped back, she'd easily see him. In seconds, she would tuck up the blankets before his face, exposing him to Brolli and the others.

Absurd possibilities flashed through Harric's mind. He could pin the tail of the blanket to the ground so she couldn't lift it. He could grab her foot and hope she thought it a rat or a prank by one of the others. He could push upward against the mattress to lift the resting matron and then drop her suddenly so she appeared to convulse.

That might work.

He'd just set his shoulder against the mattress for this last plan when another glowing foot dropped before his face. Only this time, it wasn't a foot. The blind, blunt end of a Web Strand quested along the edge of the bed like a fat and lazy glowworm.

Harric thrust his nexus into the strand and dove through his oculus just as the attendant pulled up the furs before his face. For an instant, the Unseen crushed him like a bug beneath a boot, then the pressure vanished and he felt as light as cork in water. The Web Strand hummed, sending a vibration like a thousand singing voices through his being. He let out a long, quiet sigh of relief, and watched as the attendant tucked the last of the blanket and gave Harric a full view of Brolli and the others.

Moons, I love the Unseen.

But now he had a Web Strand stuck to his nexus, and he did not know how to detach it.

No matter. He'd deal with that later.

Crawling out from under the bed, he knelt on the mattress beside the matron and examined the position of her hoop. As luck would have it, her hand had slipped from it, but he could not see an easy way to lift the cord from her neck and around all her braids without waking her. If he'd brought his purse knife, it would be easy, but he'd left it with his shirt back in the map room. Then he noticed a missing segment in the leather cord. Peering closer, he realized it was a witch-silver clasp, which appeared as a black gap in the Unseen.

Identifying it by touch, he unfastened it and slipped the cord from the loop. Then he waited until a moment when it seemed Brolli had fully occupied the attention of the attendants gathered around him, and lifted the hoop from the blankets.

Harric wasn't sure how much the hoop would add to the burden of holding him in the Unseen—or if Fink would notice it when he took over—but the Web Strand gave no sign of strain when he lifted it into the Unseen and stuffed it in his pack. The empty cord ends that lay on the matron's chest screamed of the theft, so he tucked them under the blankets in such a way that, at first glance, it would look like the hoop had been tucked underneath.

This process he repeated with the second matron, and if anyone noticed the blankets moving, they said nothing, probably assuming the matrons simply moved in their sleep.

Standing off a bit, he gave each matron a courtly bow. *Apologies, good ladies, but these trinkets will prove useful one way or another. Plus, I have a love charm to remove, and these may prove useful bargaining chips.*

The Web Strand still clung like a leech to his nexus, radiant, light as air, and humming brightly. On second thought, *he* was the leech, drawing off *its* energy. And if that were the case, there must be a way for him to "un-bite" the strand, only he could not imagine how. He tried to shake it free, but only managed to send whipping vibrations up its length.

Oops.

Well, the matrons couldn't see what effect they had on the strands, so they must walk around all the time with the things dragging behind. Surely if he dragged it down the hall, it would look like trade as usual among the matrons.

Surely.

He hoped.

Pushing his way through the partitions, he left the scene before someone could notice the missing hoops, and dragged the Web Strand with him. As soon as he had a view of the hall, he climbed a table and scanned for Fink. The imp was easy to spot, waving his hands wildly and gesturing for Harric to stay where he was.

"Sorry," Harric whispered, when the imp crow-hopped up to his side. "I had no choice."

Fink snatched the nexus and detached the strand. "You want to bring the Aerie to us?"

A low *boom* shuddered through the place and resonated through the hall. It was like the sound of a giant's tread above, and its vibration rattled the shelves and shivered the trellises.

Every Kwendi in the room stopped moving and talking and exchanged startled looks.

Fink's eyes widened to the point where Harric wondered if they'd fall from his skull. Snatching Harric's hand in his, Fink began dragging him toward the exit.

"I get it, we're leaving. Stop and get on my pack and we'll move faster."

They found Mima at the foot of the ramp, conversing in serious tones with several other matrons. Two of these she sent hurrying up the ramp as Brolli descended a trellis beside her.

Brolli spoke with her then pulled an hourglass from his satchel and winced. Mima said something in Kwendi and pointed him to the door. For an instant, their gazes met and a grim look passed between them, then he leapt into the trellis and fled the way he'd come, Harric hurrying beneath him.

...in governance, Arkendians are not a rational people. Their kings are hated by many they rule. Worse, they are succeeded in power by heredity of the eldest male, not election...even when the eldest male is a well-known fool, incompetent, cruel, or insane. This method is sacred, and the very people who suffer by it defend it with their lives.

—From *Notes on Stilty Governance,* written in Kwendi, by Second Ambassador Chombi

58

Locked & Barred

Harric followed as Brolli swung without pause through the complex of upper corridors. He now stuck to the highest of trellises, which were used by fewer Kwendi. The few Kwendi he met moved at top speed, faces anxious and set, and did not stop to speak. Periodically, the deep, booming vibration would repeat itself somewhere in the complex, seeming louder with each repetition.

It soon became clear to Harric that Brolli was not returning by the same route back to the upper floors that he had taken to come down. On this new path, he passed living quarters with great halls, and several of the corridors they passed breathed cool night air on Harric's perspiring skin. This perplexed him at first, for how could there be open windows or doors to the outside if they were underground? But then it occurred to him that what he had imagined basements or subterranean floors might abut a cliff face where windows and balconies could look out from the side of the mountain, over valleys.

Brolli entered none of these, following a path that took him higher in the complex and clearly in one direction. When they'd risen several steep ramps to the point that Harric guessed they must be very near the floor on which they'd started, a commotion stopped Brolli short. Swinging up to an archway, Brolli peered into a courtyard from which fresh night air poured into the corridor. Whatever he saw beyond made him curse and retreat from the archway. Hanging by one hand, he checked again the sandglass in his satchel, cursed once more, and turned back the way he'd come.

Harric risked a peek through the arch before following, and saw a courtyard like the one in which Brolli had given his speech to the crowd. The commotion came from Kwendi merchants hurriedly packing their wares and hurrying away from three huge, owl-faced Aerie, which perched upon the trellises only thirty paces away.

"Kid! He's getting away!" Fink tugged on Harric's pack straps.

"Keep an eye on him," Harric whispered.

Harric withdrew before Fink could see the Aerie, and was about to follow Brolli when he heard a whistling tone from a Kwendi near the archway, and he froze.

Unless there was another whistling Kwendi, the two in the cistern had escaped.

"He went that way!" Fink said, pointing after Brolli. "Catch him!"

Barely hearing the imp, Harric peered around the corner again, and saw two Kwendi—a male and a female—accompanied by a half-dozen of the black-clad warriors in toad hats, who brought them before the Aerie. The female's braids were plastered to her face, soaking wet, and the male spoke urgently in whistling tones.

Harric pulled his head back and bolted after Brolli.

Brolli had picked up his pace, but Harric caught up to him easily because he knew where he was now: the courtyard was the same where Brolli gave his speech, and the path he took now simply skirted around it to avoid the toad hats.

"You almost lost him," Fink said. "What were you looking at?"

"What do you think?" Harric said.

Before they reached the corridor leading to the map room, Harric saw several more detachments of the black-armored guards moving purposefully down hallways and ushering Kwendi from the main corridors. But Brolli had already slipped the net, and Harric, unseen, passed easily beneath the trellises.

Harric could not fathom how the couple had escaped the reservoir.

Maybe an Aerie followed their strands back to the spot. It was, of course, possible that they'd simply found a way to build a ladder with the blankets and bits of wood that had fallen into the water. He could hear his mother's mockery in his mind. *Take pity on an enemy at your own peril.*

And now the game was up. Not just for this night, but for all nights. But he'd made it, and he got what he came for. Let them lay traps for him to return—he'd disappoint them.

When Brolli finally turned down the corridor to the map room, Harric's legs burned and wobbled with weakness, and drips of sweat ran down his sides. Rurgich waited in the open doorway as if he'd been waiting a long time.

"Brolli," he said, brow creased. "You go through?"

"I must." Brolli dropped from the trellis and knuckle-walked through the door. Harric slipped through while Rurgich stared after his friend.

"What is the alarm?" said Rurgich.

"I do not know." Brolli grunted as he ascended the trellis to the platform. "Help me with this armor. I cannot let the Syne delay me."

Rurgich closed the door and followed into the trellis.

Harric and Fink crossed to the fluffy white fur where the gate rod still lay, and Harric retrieved his shirt and boots and stuffed them in his pack atop the hoops. Fink cringed against the wall. When Harric donned his pack, Fink clambered back on top and leaned close to Harric's ear.

"I saw it, kid," he said, voice tight with excitement. "I watched them do it."

"Do what?"

"I saw the way they make their toys. It's the big hoop at their neck. They use the hoops."

"How did you see it?"

"When you were gone. I ran from my table. I ended up in one of those rooms. Like the one where the door exploded. I saw them do it. They use those big loops somehow."

Harric let out a long breath. If he took a hoop out of his pack right there, the imp would probably pop. But this was not something he would share with Fink. Not yet. Maybe not ever. The notion made him uneasy, and he needed time to think it through. Some of what he'd seen that night unsettled him. Plus, he'd learned that secrets were leverage in the Unseen, and that Harric himself possessed precious few of those. The fact that Fink had revealed what he'd seen to Harric was probably not an indication of trust, but of how panicked the imp was.

Either way, the hoops would stay secret for now.

Brolli thumped to the floor below the trellis with his new bandolier of hurling globes slung from one shoulder. With Rurgich on his tail, he crossed to the witch-silver rod and stooped to grasp each end. Brolli muttered something then lifted the rod in both hands, and again the weird, liquid tar opening stood before them with the rod above, like a lintel. In the vacuous space beyond, Harric thought he could see another door, and figures moving dimly in the quasi-distance.

A Kwendi filled the other door, and then he emerged onto the white fur rug, where Brolli and Rurgich helped him to his feet. One after another followed until there were four newcomers, the scent of the forest strong upon them.

"Gredol," Brolli said to the first one. "The Syne have sounded the alarm. I do not know why."

Gredol's eyes flicked to Rurgich and back to Brolli. A hiss of anxious breath escaped the other three.

"Report quickly," said Brolli.

Gredol looked about in confusion. "This—bad—" He stumbled over the words, and made a sound like a curse before making his report in Kwendi.

Brolli's face slackened in surprise as he listened. Then he cursed in Kwendi and pointed Gredol and the others toward the door to the corridor. A distant *boom* shuddered the ground, and the newcomers all leapt into the trellis and swung for the door. Brolli settled the bandolier on his shoulder and, without so much as a "Gods leave you" to Rurgich, leapt into the gate.

Rurgich stepped up to the gate before Harric could follow, and grasped both ends of the witch-silver rod of the lintel, as if he'd hang from it. Filling the gate in this way, he watched Brolli as if he would follow.

What are you waiting for? Go!

Harric bobbed to one side, then the other, looking for a gap to squeeze past, but the Kwendi's broad back filled the gap. Fink began to tug frantically at Harric's pack straps, but Harric could not see a way past. Beyond Rurgich's shoulder, Harric saw the outline of the other gate, like a window into the bright spirit light of the southern forest. Then Brolli climbed from the void into the forest. He stood to wave back at Rurgich, and then collapsed his gate.

There was nothing now but void beyond Rurgich's gate.

"*Hy-ot*," Rurgich muttered, and, with a single motion, dragged the witch-silver rod down to the carpet. Once he'd set the rod in the nearest cabinet, he leapt into the trellises and hurried from the room.

Gods help us, the Queen's a woman!

—A West Isle boy upon his first viewing of the Queen

59

Hooves In The Night

Caris half ran and half skidded down the stone slope of the viewpoint and back into the shelter of the silent trees. Grabbing her lantern pole, she mounted Rag and spurred her back toward Willard.

He was probably still in the midst of his rage, but she had to ride to him in hope that maybe—just maybe—he'd be back to himself and could ride. She'd spilled some of the Blood that night, after all, so he hadn't drunk as much as usual. Surely, if he hadn't drunk as much, then the rage wouldn't last as long.

As Rag cantered down the ill-lit run, Caris felt herself breathing quick, shallow breaths of fear, and forced herself to slow it down and draw a deep lungful, but her heart continued to pound as if she were entering combat.

Before they saw Willard's candle lantern, they heard Molly blowing and stamping, rattling her lead chain like a mad dog at a stake. Caris knew Molly was as unridable after bleeding as Willard was unreliable, but she'd never come back so early after the drinking, so she had no way of knowing if this was her usual reaction to bleeding, or if she sensed her brother, Gygon, on the other side of the river.

Caris tied Rag a good two hundred paces from the Phyros, took the lantern from its pole, and hurried to Willard. As she approached, it seemed like Molly would pull the tree over if someone didn't set her free. But that someone would not be Caris.

Willard howled incoherently into his gag when he saw her, and her heart dropped. Krato still blazed in his glare, and he continued to gnaw through the kerchief. Gabbling and choking, he slung saliva and rolled his eyeballs.

Caris set her jaw. She'd have to wait, but she would not wait there. She'd turned to go back to Rag when she sensed something had changed in Willard-Krato. His eyes were shining…with laughter? An unpleasant sensation prickled the back of her neck. Yes. The incoherent gabble was hateful laughter. Willard-Krato threw his head back against the tree trunk, then rolled his head to leer at Molly, and back to Caris, choking on laughter.

Caris raised the light to look at Molly and saw the violet eyes burning like immortal fires. Her scars glowed with purple light as she jerked at her chain and pulled at the tree until her rump faced Caris, tail high.

And all the blood drained from Caris's heart.

"No…" The word escaped as the merest breath, and it sent Willard-Krato into another fit of laughter.

Molly was in season. Gygon had set her in heat.

Caris could see the god's plans in Willard-Krato's eyes: Molly, mating with Gygon; Molly, siring a new breed of home-grown Phyros; Molly's offspring, reviving the Old Ones.

And now Bannus and Gygon had ridden ahead of them to cut them off.

Caris ran back to Rag, climbed into the saddle, and rode back toward the camp as fast as the poor light of the lantern allowed. Willard wouldn't be sane for an hour, but she couldn't wait that long to warn the others of Bannus. She would wake them and set them in motion, and then she would return and release Willard.

The torches she'd seen would be well ahead of them by now, and if Sir Bannus knew of the canyon, he would cut them off there. And then what? Would Willard order they turn back?

She bit back a scream of frustration and urged Rag to greater and greater speeds.

When she finally rode into camp, she found no sign of Harric, Mudruffle, or Brolli, only Kogan, fast asleep with Geraldine and Harric's tiny cat. Dismounting, she shoved the priest's shoulder with her boot. "Father Kogan, wake up."

The priest did not stir, but the musk auroch lifted her tremendous head, and the cat looked at Caris with sleepy green eyes. Caris shoved Kogan again, harder, and his small eyes fluttered and stared from under heavy lids.

"Where is Brolli?" she said. "Where are Mudruffle and Harric? Are you the only one here?"

Kogan gave a sleepy grunt. His eyes closed. "Let's talk about weddings in the morning."

"Sir *Bannus* is here," she said, "and we have to move now."

The priest's eyes grew wide and he stared as if half in a dream, but he climbed to his feet. "Bannus. Does Will got Worsic?"

"Willard is full of the Blood and still tied to his tree. I can't let him loose until he's himself. But you have to pack—"

"Can't ride without Will."

"I'll ride back for Willard, but you all need to be ready when we return, and the others aren't even here. You have to find them."

Kogan squinted around the camp. "Harric with Will? His horse ain't here."

Snapper was gone, and so was Harric's gear, and it took Caris a moment to think that through. So he'd ridden off—left for good, she guessed. And since she hadn't crossed paths with him on the yoab run, he must have ridden ahead toward the canyon.

Gods leave the fool. He's running right to Sir Bannus.

He was a jack and a knave, but he didn't deserve that fate.

"Reckon he don't want to marry?" Kogan said, looking sympathetic. "I seen cold feet before, lady, and don't you worry. He'll warm up. And if he got you with child, we'll warm him up for you."

Caris clenched her teeth. "If he got me with child, there'd be nothing left to warm."

Turning away, she stomped toward Brolli's lookout, boots crunching sticks like brittle bones, lantern tossing shadows to the sides. "I'll get Brolli," she called over her shoulder. "You pack and saddle the animals."

Her jaw hurt from clenching. *Had* Harric run off because of the marriage? She snorted. "Well, good riddance," she muttered. Then, after a moment, "And good luck."

At the lookout, she found Brolli's bowl, but no Brolli. Below the overlook, the river rattled tirelessly, but she saw no winking fireflies beyond it. Bannus had moved ahead. Walking back into the shelter of the trees, she called for Brolli, but the mossy vastness seemed to swallow her voice as it left her lips and she gave up.

"Father Kogan," she said, when she found him cinching Idgit's saddle. "if I don't get back in time, you must lead Idgit and Holly."

Kogan did not acknowledge her. He was glaring across the camp to where Mudruffle approached from the yoab run. The golem waved a spidery hand and called out in his honking voice, "Lady Caris, the good father delivers ill tidings."

"Yes," she said, relieved to see him. "I'm glad you returned, Mudruffle. Let me put you in your basket so you can fasten the belts."

"I may be of more service searching for Brolli."

Caris chewed her lip. She did not like giving orders, but someone had to do it. "Can you see in the dark?"

"I require light to see."

"Then I think it would be best if we got you in your basket. I know it takes time to strap in, and you may not have time when I return."

Mudruffle looked at her, black eyes glittering. Then he bowed from his waist. "You speak wisely, Lady Caris. It shall be as you say." The little golem stalked up to her in his jerking gait and raised his arms so she could pick him up.

By the time Caris returned to Willard, Molly had settled, which probably indicated that Gygon was no longer near. Molly glared at her. It seemed to Caris that the ancient mare was daring her to reach out and make contact again, and again the desire to feel the fire swelled in Caris, but this time she rejected it immediately and tore her gaze away. Since their return to camp, she sensed Rag opening to her ever so slightly again, and it spawned such frantic hope in her that she drew considerable resolution from it. She would not spoil it by touching Molly.

Willard—or Willard-Krato—sagged against his chains, chest rising and falling in apparent exhausted slumber. He'd spat out the gag, though this time the kerchief was not entirely gnawed through. A foolish corner of her mind wondered how many kerchiefs the old knight had packed in his bags, how many more he had to spare.

Reaching out with her horse-touched senses, she felt around the edges of his consciousness. She had not noticed what she thought of as the "hex-presence" since the first day she'd bled Molly and shackled Willard and sensed it swimming beneath the surface of his consciousness. Whatever it had been, the thing was too canny to be caught twice, for she sensed no trace of it now. And that relieved her, because the bizarre thing had unnerved her, and she could not afford to be distracted while she attempted to sense if Krato was lurking in ambush again.

She flitted her senses around the edges of his consciousness like a feather duster around a crystal candleholder with a candle still burning inside it. She didn't dare come too close to his mind or it would set her own mind alight and dismay Rag all over again; instead, she only drew close enough to sense its heat from a distance. If she sensed a burning fury crouching beneath the surface and waiting to pounce, then she'd know it was Krato-Willard, and that she had to wait longer.

To her relief, she sensed no raging fire, only a subdued but steady glow of anger.

She nudged the heel of Willard's boot with the toe of hers. "Sir Willard. We are in haste."

His eyes opened, clear and alert. When they lit on her, they narrowed. "What haste?"

She told him as she unfastened his chains. His eyes flashed and his nostrils flared as he stood to face her. He drew the chains through one hand. "You did well."

"She's in heat," Caris said, before he approached Molly.

He continued to stare, eyes smoldering violet, and Caris was overcome with the sense that this was no longer the Willard she'd known. Some huge, young *other* filled the immortal armor. He'd shed the bombast of stuffing he'd used to fill the plates, and what lurked there now was hard, corded, masculine muscle.

His chest rose and the muscles of his jaw pulsed as he stood and stared at her. "Her Blood is in me," he said, winding the chains in his hands. He pronounced each word very clearly and slowly. "I feel her heat in me."

Caris's tongue seemed to stick in her jaw. Her feet took her back a step, and she clasped her hands together to keep from resting one on her sword. She forced a quick bow, turned, and strode calmly back to

Rag, but her heart felt like it was throwing itself against her breastplate.

Gods leave me, is he touched with Molly's heat?

She listened closely to the rattle of the chains, which told her Willard was still where she left him—that he hadn't pursued her. She reached out to Rag, and this time found the mare calm and open enough to help steady her nerves. But it wasn't until she reached the mare's side and heard Willard speaking to Molly that she allowed herself a long breath of relief.

Hands trembling, Caris untied Rag's lead from the tree, then mounted and followed Willard. Slowly the fear that spurred her heartbeat drained away. After some time, it seemed clear to her that while Molly remained in season, the bloodlettings would be more dangerous, and next time she released Willard from his chains, she would ride away the moment she unclasped the first manacle and let him unlock the others while she fled.

It was not a thing she wished to discuss with him. She would simply do it that way.

Chewing at her lip, she tracked the bob of his lantern as he topped a rise, and his silhouette appeared for a moment against the bole of a tree. Broad-shouldered, straight-backed, radiating power and strength. Enough to face Bannus yet? Maybe. But she wondered if the change in Molly's Blood would affect whether he could control a heat-maddened Molly when Gygon was near.

If you must trust, then trust your mother, or those who need you. Your mother has no choice but to want the best for you; the same for those who need you. Suspect all others.

— From *To Those Bound For Court*, advice, by Lady Tickle Mehoney

60

Trapped

Panic threatened to slip past Harric's lips in a wail. As he hurried to the cabinet where Rurgich had stowed the gate rod, it threatened to escape like a breath held too long.

Fink crouched alongside him, his trembling reaching a new peak.

Flinging the cabinet open, Harric snatched up the rod and almost dropped it, for it was much heavier than he anticipated—surely solid witch-silver. In the Unseen, it appeared as a lightless black line, but bright pearl had been laid along its length in letters of an unfamiliar script. Instructions, maybe? Passwords?

He set it on the fur carpet, his breath coming in rapid, shallow puffs.

Another *boom* shuddered the complex, rattling a trellis above.

"Hurry..." Fink breathed the word as if his lungs were paralyzed with fear.

Harric grasped the rod at each end, like he'd seen Rurgich do, and lifted it vertically.

No gate appeared beneath it.

"Try it again!" Fink squeaked.

A tremor of vibrations, like giant wings above, pulsed down from beyond the ceiling, followed by a thump on a roof high above. Harric imagined a giant, glowing snow-owl Kwendi lifting the roof like the lid of a basket and snatching them in cruel talons.

Harric tried again with the same results.

"Say the word!" Fink said. "He said a word. Say it!"

The booming repeated, louder. Nearer. Harric heard outside the door the now-familiar sound of Kwendi hands slapping trellises. Lots of Kwendi hands.

"Hy-ta!" Harric lifted the rod.

No gate.

"Hy-*tu*. Hy-*to*. Hu-*ty*. I wasn't listening, Fink. I don't remember!"

Fink reached for the rod and Harric released it. The instant Fink touched it, he froze, then his face went slack with surprise. Closing his eyes, he lifted the rod from the rug, and the tarred gate rose below it, but his skinny arms buckled when it reached the height of his knees.

"Help me!" he gasped.

Harric laid his hands over Fink's and lifted. The already heavy rod had tripled or quadrupled its weight, as if the gate itself were indeed a curtain of heavy tar.

As soon as Harric had pushed it to the height of his chest, he stared into the void beyond and panicked. "There's no forest gate! Where is it?"

Fink shoved Harric from behind with his small hands. "Go! Go!"

Somewhere high above them, the complaining shriek of metallic hinges erupted, and a breath of air stirred in the room. A beautiful baritone voice filled Harric's mind in a language he did not understand. Harric stood in fascination. He wanted to hear the musical tones again, but something slammed into his back and he stumbled through the doorway.

And the world disappeared.

Falling, he flailed, trying to catch himself, but there was no ground. Everything but the doorway beside him had vanished, and that remained beside him—despite his sensation of falling—falling with him. A soundless window upon Fink in Brolli's map room. Fink dove at Harric, collided with him.

Then the imp's snakelike tail hooked the rod at the top of the door and slammed it down behind them.

Harric clutched Fink's tail as if it were his only hold on sanity. In the immensity of the void around him, there were no Web lines, no moons, no stars, no winds, no clouds—not even a mote of dust to lend a glimmer of dimension or external existence. In that limitless darkness, only three things existed: himself, Fink, and his soul strands, which appeared severed and drifting in messy tangles, like broken anchor lines in slack water.

Where are we? he said, but there were no words, only thought.

Fink shook his head, peering about. He looked everywhere but at Harric, and it sent a lance of panic through Harric's middle. Why wouldn't he look at him? Were they in trouble? What was wrong?

We're nowhere, kid. The imp's voice rasped in Harric's head, terrifyingly intimate. *Stop jerking around. You're tangling your strands.*

Harric stared in horror at the little pool of soul strands. He wanted to gather them about himself like a blanket of comfort in that limitless sea of nothing. Or was it infinite? Maybe it was merely a lightless casket, its walls just beyond reach. The thought filled him with claustrophobic terror.

How long had he been there?

Fink had instructed him not to move. But he could not tell how long ago. Moments. Days. There was no way to measure time except in the sequence of the memories of thoughts and conversations that created a history. But in the void, every thought or conversation swung free, out of sequence with other memories. The moment he thought a thing, it became unrelated to the thoughts before and after. Memories floated loose like bubbles in the sea, in no particular order. He struggled to huddle them together into some kind of sense, but his mind was now a net with a weave too wide to hold anything.

Fink, get us out of here! The thought escaped like a gasp. *You can gate. That's what you do when I Summon you, right?*

Fink nodded. His eyes still swept up and around the welter of Harric's strands, looking anywhere but at Harric. *Gating isn't our problem, kid. A gate's just a weave, like Spirit Walking. Problem is, you can't just gate anywhere you want, only someplace you know like it's part of you, like your home.*

So?

Fink's eyes finally rested on Harric. *So, my home's the Unseen Moon.*

Harric stared. He felt his throat contracting.

Yeah. Full of black fumes you can't breathe and spirits like my sisters. Fink's needled jaws stretched downward. *So our choice is this: I could try to gate you to one of the places I've seen in Arkendia, and risk sending you* to the bottom of some lake or a mile above a mountain, or we stay here and hope we see another Kwendi gate open near us. Not great choices.

Harric sucked in a convulsive breath, and somehow he could not exhale, like his lungs kept trying to draw air, even after they could draw no more.

He felt as though he were submerged in still sea beneath a starless night sky. Somewhere near him, the surface lurked—beyond his reach, invisible—and beyond that surface lay time and space and order. But he had no idea where to find it. And as Fink stopped talking, the sea around Harric filled with disordered bubbles of thought and memory.

Talk to me, Fink—! he finally gasped. I'm—a—a—!

Afraid. Yeah. Fink stared at him, unblinking, and Harric felt a cold wave of fear wash over him. It was as if the imp weren't looking at Harric, but at some fat, unclaimed soul he'd found in the void—like a moon cat might look at a rat still alive in a trap: idly curious, waiting for appetite to develop.

Gods leave me if he wants my soul—the way he's looking at me—

Opening that gate took a lot out of me, kid. Fink's black tongue flicked over his teeth. *I'm starving again. But…no worry.* He turned his gaze on Harric's strands, and the tongue flicked out again.

Fink—

Fink raised his hands in a calming gesture. *It's that whole mortality thing, kid. It scares you. Infinity scares you. But you want to know something funny? The opposite is true, too. I was terrified in that Kwendi hive. Before today, I never understood why you mortals fear death. To me, it's a natural part of the cycle. And I'm one of the ministers of that cycle.* He snorted and tugged at his enormous nose. *But there's no end to the names you mortals pin on us. Slavers. Devourers. Deceivers. Monsters. All because you don't know what death is and what we're for.*

But today it was me they could have destroyed. I'm not used to that. What happens to a spirit when you destroy it? Is there rebirth? Oblivion? And what are the Aerie? Just like you poor suckers, I fear the unknown.

Harric felt the pressure of a sob building in his chest, and tried to swallow it back.

Yeah, I can smell it on you. You're terrified of me. Think I'm going to go back on our agreement. The needle jaws spread in a grin. *No need to fear.*

Harric fixated on Fink's every word, grasping for solid reference and distraction.

Fink nodded. *That's it. Better.*

Don't stop talking, Harric blurted. *Tell me—what you saw in the fortress.*

Fink gave a sly look from narrowed eyes. *The magic. Now, that was a wonder. And I owe it all to you. But souls, was I scared. If I had the right anatomy, I'd have laid an egg.*

Don't stop talking! I don't think I can wait a day for a gate. I—I'll go mad.

Fink frowned. *You have to keep it together, kid. Next time Brolli and his friends open their gates, we go for Brolli's. If we get to it before his friends enter, we can pop out at his feet and run while he's surprised. But if the others enter first, they'll see us here, and they'll have time to get over their surprise.* He shook his head, looking past Harric.

What is it? What aren't you telling me?

Fink frowned. *Truth is, we may never see their gates again. They may not open up where we can see them, kid. There's no consistency in this place.*

Fink!

I know. I'm sorry. Fink's brow pinched as he continued to look past Harric. *That's odd. Look at your strands.* The imp pointed.

Harric tore his eyes from Fink to see that his strands had oriented all in the same direction, as if some invisible current had caught them and straightened them in its flow like strands of river grass in a stream.

What is it?

Fink's eyes lit up. *Don't move. I can crawl your strands. Mother of moons, kid. I think this is our way out. Just don't move!*

Fink crawled up Harric's body, talons gripping his clothing, and then released him and slid away on Harric's strands. Against the black of nothing, Fink's dark skin vanished, and only where he obscured Harric's strands could Harric glimpse parts of the imp.

It's here! Fink said, his voice just as loud in Harric's mind as if he were beside him. The imp's laughter rang with relief. *Follow your strands to me. Think it—will it. Like the first time we were here.*

Harric's heartbeat drummed like a rabbit's, but willing himself down the strands came easily, and he found himself rapidly gliding down the glowing stream toward the imp's fly-on-a-window silhouette. For a moment, he worried he did not know how to stop, but the instant he thought it, he stopped gliding, still short of Fink. He willed himself across the remaining distance and Fink grabbed his hand as he stopped. Fink had hooked his hand on something in space—a line in the dark, like the crack under a door. All Harric's strands had gathered at the crack as if someone had shut a door on them.

Fink's grin radiated triumph. *When you came through the gate the first time, it cut off your strands. Now they want to connect with their other halves, see? They led us right to Brolli's gate stick. That little line is it. It's back in time somewhere.*

Harric felt his mind scattering. He pressed his hands to his temples. *Get me out of here, Fink. Please.*

Fink nodded. *Since I can see this rod, I think I can gate you to wherever it is, just like I know the place. But remember, Brolli has this rod. I'll try to drop you near him but not on him. Still, you need to be ready to hide or run or lie you head off.*

You're not coming with me?

Fink shook his head. *How would you lie me away? I'll gate to my moon and meet you later.* He extended a hand and stuffed the nexus in Harric's pants pocket. *Summon me.*

Good. Fine. Just do it.

Fink's grin glittered in the light of Harric's strands. *Your wish is my command.*

Arkendians believe the north of their island is inhabited by beasts and mythological monsters, including their creator god Arkus, who uses the site for his bath. A curious god indeed, who values such privacy and requires such minimal creature comforts. We would call such a fellow a hermit and crackpot. There, he's a god.

—From *A Merry Stay in a Backward Land*, Iberg, circa before the Kwendi Emergence

61

Lies

Brolli stepped from the world gate and looked around the slopes of the mossy grotto in which it stood. Night cloaked the forest. The moons had set, and smoke hugged the land. Somewhere in the distance, a yoab croaked. He could see Rurgich through the world gate, small and worried. He waved, then closed the gate.

Alone again in the silence of the southern forest, he paused. Something had happened to rouse the Aerie, and it couldn't have been a Spear Dragon attack, because dawn was still far away. He let out a breath laden with vague anxieties and looked down at the buck Gredol had taken. It stared back with dull eyes already crawling with flies.

"Better get you to Molly before you spoil," he muttered.

He'd just finished the ritual of thanks to the beast when he heard a voice and froze, listening. Again it sounded, like a bellowing ox. The Stilty priest. He was shouting Brolli's name, along with something else that sounded insulting.

Should lob a flasher near him. He'd soil his pants. Not that he'd smell any worse.

Cupping his hands to his mouth, he called back. Then he hoisted the deer over his shoulders and set off toward the sound.

A thump in the ferns behind him gave him a start. He dropped the deer and tumbled to one side, expecting a young yoab or bear coming for the buck, but saw instead Harric. The young man knelt at the rim of the grotto, no more than ten paces away.

Brolli's gut tightened. Moments before, the world gate had been there in plain view where Harric would have seen it. Hand tight on the haft of his cudgel, he stared at Harric.

The young Stilty wore no shirt, just a floppy back-sack, and he remained on hands and knees as if he'd tripped and fallen. Now he stared about, unseeing, his eyes wide and white as turtle eggs. A wave of relief washed through Brolli as he realized Harric couldn't see his hand in front of his face at night, much less a black gate at the bottom of a grotto. He must have gotten lost when his light went out.

Or he's been trying to spy and knew light would give him away...

Brolli shifted his cudgel between hands, eyes narrowing. But as he studied Harric, he realized the lad was weeping. The young man had hung his head. Hair concealed his face, but his shoulders convulsed, and Brolli heard faint sobbing. Harric's fists clutched at the moss as if it were the only thing anchoring him to the earth.

Taken aback, Brolli watched in silence, and then he felt embarrassment for Harric. This was not the reaction Brolli would expect if Harric had just seen the world gate. Something else must trouble him. Brolli's instinct was to give privacy—to creep away before Harric knew he was there—but he couldn't leave without knowing for certain that Harric hadn't seen anything.

"Harric," Brolli said with as neutral a tone as he could manage. "Are you well?"

Harric looked up as if surprised. Strings of hair stuck to tears on his face, concealing much of his expression. He rose on his knees and wiped his eyes with the palms of his hands. He nodded. On one forearm, Brolli spotted a raised, angry weal, like a nasty spider bite.

"Your arm. You are injured. No, the other arm."

Harric found the wound with a groping hand and winced. "I— It's a burn. I meant to wrap it." His voice came out hoarse and jittery.

"Do you have light?" Brolli said. "We must return to camp. Bannus is near."

Harric's mouth dropped open. He closed it and stood. "I—I'm—" He swallowed. "Yes. I'll be along. Go ahead."

"Is there anything wrong?"

Harric coughed. "Caris. It's nothing."

Brolli winced inwardly, but his worry finally dissolved. *The moon-cursed wedding ring. Will there ever be an end to the misery it causes? Damn Willard's hex for landing it in the boy's hand to begin with.* "I am sorry."

Father Kogan bellowed like a dying yoab. *"Brolli and be hanged!"*

Brolli smiled. "Wash your face and come. I think we must ride."

"Tonight?"

"Yes. Soon."

Harric nodded. "Thank you." The young Stilty slung his pack from his shoulders and sat to recover his shirt and his boots from it. The fool had been running about shirtless in dirty stockings. Brolli paused as a nagging doubt tugged at the edges of his mind, but he could not put his finger on it.

He shook his head and slung the buck over his shoulders again.

Love makes idiots of us all. Stilty and Kwendi alike.

Sir Willard's helm had shattered,
But the giant's heart was rent.
Said Willard, "Moll', I've got a job
For you beneath this dent."

—From "Sir Willard and the Giant of Winty Crack"

62

Unholy Fire

Harric led Snapper up the yoab run toward the canyon, determined to get as far ahead of the others as possible, but any excitement of striking out on his own had been strangled in its crib. Memory of the Nothing and its terrifying eternity still reverberated in him like the peal of a giant iron bell. On top of that, he now bore the serious duty of passing on to Willard what he'd learned of Brolli, and that meant his departure would not be the clean break he'd planned, for sooner or later he'd have to go back to meet the old knight or wait for him somewhere ahead.

He mulled over the matter as he plodded along without light, using his spirit vision to navigate. He could announce Brolli's betrayal to the entire group. That would take Brolli by surprise and maybe force a confession. But such a confrontation could also get messy. Brolli could interrupt him, muddy the issue, feign outrage, or say Harric must be ill and hallucinating. He'd demand evidence, and Harric would be forced to either back down or reveal his own magic.

Snapper snorted, and Harric looked up at the gelding, who had stopped because Harric had stopped. "Sorry," he muttered, and resumed walking. "Afraid I might be slightly mad, now."

Through small gaps in the trees, Harric caught glimpses of the far side of the valley, now bathed in silver moonlight. On the wind, he caught the scent of green things and only the faintest touch of wood smoke. With luck, that meant that the wildfire had died and not spread into the valley. One less thing to worry about.

Something stung his forearm, and he gave it an unconscious rub, only to yelp as the spot flared like a live burn. *Cobs.* He'd forgotten about the Witch's Teat. He pulled up his sleeve to examine the ugly pucker, and found it looked exactly like a fat and angry teat. With the tip of a finger he explored it, gingerly, and pain flared like he'd poked an angry burn. Disgust and revulsion swelled in his stomach.

Cursing, he fished a length of linen bandage from his bags and bound it as tightly as he could, to protect and hide it. If a wandering priest or a witch hunter saw it, they'd search him for his witch-stone, and that would be the end of his ballad.

When the run northward grew difficult, he judged he must be approaching the canyon and turned down a smaller run that sloped toward the river.

In the Unseen, the spiritual essence of the river shone like blinding sunlight through the gaps in the trees, and when he crossed a particularly large gap, it stung his oculus like the water of the cistern had done. If he squinted his oculus and peered closely, he could discern in it thousands and thousands of thrashing ribbons—like soul strands, only thinner and hotter and whipping madly with the motion of the torrent below.

He closed his oculus and opened his eyes, which were now well adjusted to the dark and capable of navigating in more frequent spots of moonlight near the edge of the forest. The roar of the river grew louder with every step, until he came to a stop in a depression that may have been another yoab bed. From its edge, he could see the white foam of the river some twenty fathoms below.

Looking back the way he'd come, he let out a long breath. No sign of Willard and the others yet, of course, which was good. But they were riding already, and he did not want to meet them until he knew what he was going to say. If they overtook him, they'd think him inept—that he had muffed his getaway—or that he was weak and cowardly and had second thoughts.

No. Better if he rode ahead and waited to meet them at some stop beyond the canyon, where it would look like he'd stopped deliberately to deliver a message. Then he'd ask to speak with Willard alone, and once he'd revealed what he knew, the knight could do with it what he pleased, and Harric would ride to tell the Queen himself.

That decision dissolved the knot of tension in his chest, and he felt his shoulders loosening.

He'd just turned back to the trail when a distant shout broke up his thoughts and he froze, uncertain where it had come from. Peering through the trees above the river, he tried to scan the opposite bank, but the trees there limited his view.

For a long moment, he heard nothing but the roar of the river below him. Then he heard hoofbeats and another shout went up from across the river.

A knife of fear slipped between his ribs. *Cobbing moons. It's Bannus.*

After tying Snapper's lead to a branch, Harric crept down an elk trail that slanted down from the yoab bed toward the river. In the imperfect light, he stumbled over roots and stones until he came to a wider break in the trees where he could crouch in a well of shadow. Torches bobbed in the forest beyond the river. Soon the riders that carried the torches emerged onto the margin of the river. A dozen riders, perhaps, drew up across from his position.

Torch and moonlight glittered on the back of the rushing water and from the polished armor of the knights. The ranks of knights parted to make way for a rider in deep black or possibly purple robes. From the depths of a cowl, the robed one surveyed the river, looking upstream, then downstream. As he turned to look downstream, a ray of moonlight gleamed from his alabaster mask, and Harric's breath snagged in his chest.

The Faceless One. Sir Bannus's shield bearer.

Sinking farther into the shadow of the hill, Harric made himself very small. His hand went to the side of his neck to find the scar left when the creature had cut him and begged his master for Harric's skin. He saw—or rather felt—himself naked and helpless all over again—saw the raw red flesh behind the mask, the red-shot, lidless eyes. And his guts seemed to turn to water inside him.

The Faceless One pulled back the cowl of his purple robes and turned his masked face to the Bright Mother, as if her silver light on the mask might cool the burning flesh beneath. Other riders emerged from the trees to gather at a distance. Then the huge shape of a Phyros-rider loomed behind them and came to a stop beside the Faceless One. Yet the Phyros-rider was not Sir Bannus. This rider wore no armor. Instead, he wore a wide robe or smothercoat that made him look if anything bigger than Sir Bannus. And the robe looked…alive somehow, as if composed of living serpents.

Ballads were sung of Phyros-riders who used the Blood to sculpt and augment their bodies with the flesh of vanquished enemies. Was this such a one? Were the serpents the living trophies of fallen foes, or a kind of living armor?

The deep notes of an immortal's voice reached Harric over the roar of the river. The Phyros-rider appeared to be speaking to the Faceless One, who still faced the moon. Even in the moonlight, Harric had difficulty making sense of the Phyros-rider's figure, especially what seemed like an impossibly thick neck—or maybe no neck at all—or thick braids, like ropes, in a bunching mane.

The Faceless One returned the cowl to his head and motioned to the south. The gathered knights spurred their horses and rode, and the Faceless One followed, leaving this new and unfamiliar Phyros-rider alone on the bank.

Gods leave us, they're on the wrong side of the river. They have to backtrack to a crossing.

As the sounds of horses and gear submerged in the roar of the river, the immortal sat in his saddle, his attention seemingly fixed on the water, and Harric imagined he gauged whether his Phyros could swim the torrent. Every particle of Harric's body froze like a petrified prey animal. If the rider crossed, Harric was dead.

The immortal's mane and robe stirred like shadows on dark water. After what seemed an eternity, the Phyros turned downstream and followed the others.

Harric let out a long, shuddering breath. Cold sweat had soaked the hair at the back of his neck, and as he stood, his knees quaked.

It seemed clear to him that Sir Bannus's shield bearer and this new Phyros-rider would ride south only far enough to find a place where the river widened and slowed enough for them to cross. Harric didn't know how far downstream that would be, and he didn't know if Mudruffle's map would show the nearest crossing.

Cursing, he scrambled up the trail to Snapper, and hauled him around to face back the way he'd come. Harric had no choice but to return to Willard and the others now. They were in much greater danger than they knew, and he had to warn them.

He mounted Snapper, and with his back now to the river, he opened his oculus and navigated using his spirit vision. As he rode, it occurred to him that Sir Bannus was still unaccounted for. Halting, he looked back, cursing himself for panicking and leaving so quickly. If he went back and waited a little longer, Bannus might well emerge from the trees like the other Phyros-rider had. No, Harric decided, resuming his trek. If Bannus was riding with them, they'd have waited on the bank and not run ahead without him. Bannus was elsewhere, and this was a scouting party or a second flank.

Harric hadn't gone far before he spotted the bobbing lanterns of his former companions in the gloom ahead, and realized he'd look suspicious without a light source of his own, but it was too late to light one. If they asked him about it, he'd say he doused it for fear of the enemies so near.

Molly sensed him first and growled just as he said, "It's me, Harric," but Willard's sword was out and Molly upon him in the instant. Willard loomed over him, standing high in his stirrups as if he'd chop Harric in two from crown to crotch, then lowered his blade.

"*You,*" Willard spat. "What the Black Moon do you mean by lurking on the trail like a bandit? Thought you were gone for good. Having second thoughts? Or do you return on some other whim?"

The stink of Blood gusted to Harric on Molly's breath. He recoiled and steered Snapper to the side so he could breathe, and waited as the others reined in beside them.

Caris's gaze traveled across him, unseeing and distant, her mind clearly in the world of horses, but the sight of her tugged at his heart. She led Idgit and Holly, and both Brolli and Mudruffle strained to see Harric from their seats on the mare's back. He had to keep his eyes off Brolli to keep himself from glaring, and instead focused on Willard.

"It was for Caris's sake that I left," Harric said. "And I had no intention of returning, but I saw something that you should know of." He proceeded to describe to them what he'd seen of the riders and the Faceless One, and concluded with a description of the new Phyros-rider.

Willard chewed a stub of unlit ragleaf through the account, but his jaw stopped moving when Harric described the thick, misshapen form of the new Phyros-rider. "You're sure about his robe? It moved. Like serpents."

Harric swallowed. "Like a smothercoat of ropes. Was it—"

"You didn't imagine it." Willard flicked his gaze back toward Brolli and frowned at Harric, as if to say, *Say no more of this before the ambassador.* Rag had turned her head and blocked Harric's view of Brolli, but when he saw him again, Brolli appeared to be listening intently.

"You saw nothing of Bannus?" Willard said.

Harric shook his head. "Nothing."

"Then Bannus has either found a way up the other side—a way the others couldn't follow—or he has already gone south to find the nearest ford to cross onto our side, and will soon appear on our tails."

Mudruffle's shining head poked from the basket behind Brolli, flat eyes glittering. "There is no way through the valley on the west side. High cliffs prevent it. You will see when we enter the canyon."

"Then he is behind us and we must fly." Willard urged Molly past Harric and gave him a grudging nod. "Well met. Fall in behind Caris."

As Caris rode past Harric with Brolli and Mudruffle in tow, Harric avoided their eyes by busying himself with maneuvering Snapper, but he felt their gazes on his face like heat from a torch. They would judge his sudden departure and return without understanding, and there was no point in explaining anything. The only explaining he planned to do was to Willard as soon as he could get the knight alone.

"I don't like this," Kogan said, as Harric fell in behind the lumbering musk auroch. "If Bannus got up the canyon ahead of us, it'll be a trap. Bannus ahead, the others behind." He spat. "Don't care what that honking hat rack says."

"I doubt even Bannus could cross the river," Harric said. "That other Phyros-rider seemed to consider it, but he turned south with the rest of them. Wait till you see the water, here, and you'll understand. It wouldn't drown a Phyros, of course, but the water would dash it miles downstream before it found a spot to climb out. And anyway, the only thing we know for sure is what we'll find if we go back."

The sky lightened with the feathery gray of dawn as they descended the elk trail to the flat rock ledge that ran along the edge of the river. Hooves clattering on the stone, they rode for the dark cliff at the head of the valley.

In the predawn gloom, the mouth of the canyon yawned in the face of the cliff like the open gate of some giant's stone keep. So steep and straight were the canyon's sides that it seemed they'd been cut with a potter's wire when the rock was clay. From it, the river tumbled swift and cold and brawny, deeper than a man was tall and thirty paces wide. In places, it rose in standing waves that bunched and broke like the crests of a gigantic serpent.

Willard rode into the throat of the canyon, Molly's iron shoes ringing and echoing from its walls, each horse adding to the din. Harric felt like an ant crossing the threshold of a castle.

As Mudruffle predicted, the low autumn water had exposed a wide shelf along their side of the river, right along the base of the steep canyon wall. Also as he'd predicted, there was no bank or ledge on the opposite side, where the water deeply undercut the sandstone wall. They were on the only path through the canyon.

The shelf proved passable, if difficult. At times, it rose a full fathom above the torrent, but just as often dipped under the swirling water to depths well over the horses' ankles. Other times, the canyon wall retreated from the water's edge, giving them a path as wide as a carriage, but more often it squeezed them against the river so badly that they had to unpack the saddlebags from Molly and Geraldine and lead them through by hand. Twice in the first hours, the cliff overhung the path so low that all riders but those on Idgit had to dismount to pass beneath.

Above them, the high walls pinched the dawn sky to nothing more than a jagged ribbon of gray, and Harric watched as a hawk dipped low enough to get a good look at them, probably wondering at the line of lanterns glittering off the water. By the time the amber light of sunrise gilt the opposite rim of the canyon, however, the canyon walls relaxed and widened into a steep V crowded with the standing trunks of dead trees. It seemed the forest had succumbed to some plague or other in this part of the canyon, leaving nothing but rank upon rank of sun-bleached white trunks, like bare and sterile fangs.

"Toothed Canyon, I'll wager," Harric said, though Kogan didn't appear to hear him.

Farther up the canyon, the dead spikes gave way to swaths of lodge-pole pine. These crowded the slopes all the way to the river's edge, where their dry silver underskirts overhung the water like brittle lace.

Luck grant Sir Bannus can't scale such crags as these, Harric thought, looking up at the crown of cliffs above the wooded slopes. It occurred to him then that if Bannus did confront them in the canyon, the river would prevent Harric from hiding in the Unseen even if the sun had already set. He ran a hand through his hair and chewed at his lower lip. If it came down to it, he'd jump in the river. No one would follow him. And better to be swept away and die than allow himself to be taken by Bannus.

That'd be odd. Survive the Kwendi city and the void, only to drown in a river.

But it would also clear him of any trouble with Missy.

Thought of her summoned a cold hand upon his heart. This was the night Fink had arranged for Missy to meet them regarding the ring on Caris. Unless it was the night before… And now Harric couldn't remember if Fink said he'd called it off with Missy or not. With all the excitement of the gate and the Kwendi city, the matter had been buried in the shuffle. And lack of sleep had made his brain foggy.

If she *had* come that last night—say, after they'd entered the gate and gone halfway across the continent to the Kwendi lands—then she'd have found no sign of them. Surely that would raise questions. And when she saw Fink's chubby soul belly had returned overnight to his usual half-starved scarecrow self, that would raise questions. What would he say when she demanded to know what great task had drained so much from him?

Harric chewed at the inside of his cheek.

Gods take it, Fink. You better be ready with a good lie.

Three things one never forgets: a first love, a first loss,
and a first horse.

— Barwell, Stabler to Earl Bright

63

Heart Sacrifice

Caris raised her eyes to the red-orange crags across the river and squinted against the setting sun. The low angle of the light sent long shadows down the cliffs, skeletal fingers that seemed to reach for her from the heights. Seemed like the shadows were always grasping for her, and none greater than Molly's. She looked past Harric, who had taken up the position behind Willard, and watched Molly walk, her enormous haunches rippling and flexing with each step. The dark strength of the immortal beast called to her, tempted her to reach out for just a light brush against the flame—

She shuddered. *Gods leave me, is this what Willard feels? Is this addiction?*

Tearing her eyes from the Phyros, she patted Rag's sweaty shoulder and murmured praise. Rag shook her mane and her steps grew noticeably lighter, as they did when she was happy or playful. The change was so sudden and unexpected that it roused a laugh from Caris. Rag let out a chuckling whinny, and Caris—hoping against hope—sent her senses into Rag and found the mare's heart once again open and trusting.

Tears of joy streaked Caris's cheeks. "Thank you, girl… Thank you."

Rag was back. Their bond was back. Rag was family again.

Halting, Rag let out a soft snort, and Caris looked up to see that Harric had stopped Snapper because Willard had called a halt. The stone path before him had dropped below the surface of the water, and the cliff beside it had squeezed it to a strip barely wide enough for Molly to pass without a rider.

Willard dismounted, took Molly's lead, and led her onto the flooded ledge. As water piled against his boots and sucked at Molly's ankles, he called back, "Slippery. Take care."

Caris caught Harric looking back at her as he dismounted, and the touch of his gaze sent another pulse of longing through her. A groan welled inside her. The night before, she'd felt so good and so free, as if the ring had finally given up. But that morning, the ache had returned with renewed vigor and the theme of *wedding*, like some idiot ballad she couldn't shake from her head. Tears stung her eyes, and before another swell of longing could bewitch her, she buried herself deeper in Rag's senses.

When Harric disappeared around a bend in the ledge, she sighed and dismounted.

"Come on, girl."

Holding both Idgit's and Rag's leads in one hand, Caris braced her other hand against the sun-warmed cliff and followed. The river pushed against her boots, and at once the freezing water kissed her toes and soaked her stockings. Evening sunlight dazzled off the surface of the water, redoubling the heat on her cheeks, but a steady breeze rode down the canyon on the back of the river to counter it. She moved slowly up the ledge, first probing with her boot, then setting it, and finally transferring weight before repeating with the other foot. Each boot became a bucket of icy water and each foot so numb she had to stamp to feel anything.

Harric led Snapper some forty paces on the submerged path and disappeared around a bend in the cliff. Once he was clear, she started after, and had reached about halfway to the bend when a peculiar whinny from Molly drifted back to Caris on the breeze. The sound drained all the warmth from her middle, because it came from Molly, and she'd heard it before: it was a whinny of mating urges and frustrated needs.

Gygon. She senses Gygon.

Caris's heart thumped in her ears. If Molly scented Gygon, it meant he and Sir Bannus were upwind—ahead of them—and they were walking into a trap.

"Sir Willard!" she called, but the roar of the river swallowed the words. *Piles!* The path was too narrow and treacherous to try to turn around, and she couldn't back more than one horse at once, so her only option was to push on till they came to a place wide enough to turn.

Tugging Rag after her, she continued her painstaking steps.

"What is the trouble?" Brolli said, leaning out so he could see around Rag from his saddle on Idgit.

She bit her lip. "I heard—"

The rest was a cry of surprise as her boot slipped and she sat down hard in hip-deep water. Icy fingers invaded her armor and shoved her downstream toward Rag's hooves. Rag whinnied and tossed her head, eyes rolling. In that instant, Caris saw herself sliding into Rag, taking her hooves out from under her, and dragging the whole line of horses into the flood.

Arching her back, she pushed off the ledge with one hand and staggered upright. One boot caught a lip in the rock, halting her slide, but the other continued to slip, and she windmilled on the edge of the deep water.

"Got you!" Brolli grabbed her by an arm and held tight until she braced herself against Rag and got her boots set. When she finally caught her breath and looked up, Rag was giving her the look she normally reserved for noisy stable hands who woke her before her hour. Brolli was hanging half on, half off her saddle, one hand firmly in her mane.

He flashed his huge canines. "I stand in the saddle. This makes me a trick rider, no?"

Caris let out a tight laugh. "You climbed from Idgit onto Rag?"

"Your beast is wise and patient."

Caris pressed her head against Rag's neck and caught her breath. "Yes, she is."

"Are you safe, Lady Caris?" Mudruffle called from his basket on Idgit. "If I were not hindered by these straps, I would have endeavored to do as Brolli did, though my construction somewhat limits my agility."

"Yes, thank you, Mudruffle. Thank you, ambassador."

"It is my pleasure." Brolli released her arm, but remained dangling from the mane and saddle to watch, as if he expected her to fall again. *Which isn't unlikely*, she thought, since she had no feeling in her feet.

Forcing herself to be patient in spite of her fears of Gygon, she resumed the push against the stream. When she finally rounded the end of outcrop, the narrow ledge rose from the water and opened onto a broad pan of sunbaked sandstone. The pan stood a good fathom above the river and spanned forty paces across, hemmed by cliffs and water on three sides, and steep woods on the other—the first time they'd had trees on their side of the river. After the claustrophobic ledge, it seemed like acres, and plenty of room to turn horses.

As soon as she stepped clear of the water on dry ground, her eyes went to Molly, where Willard had stopped her in the middle of the pan. To Caris's surprise, Molly appeared calm. At least, as calm as any Phyros ever was, which meant snorting and glaring as at invisible enemies. And Willard, too, seemed unworried. He sat back against the rear cantle of his saddle, smoking and staring at a chute of rapids that cut down through the cliff at the head of the pan. Harric had ridden all the way to the head to get a look at the rapids.

Caris exhaled a sigh of relief. False alarm. Something about the roar of the river in the canyon must have warped the sound of Molly's whinny. Or maybe it had been Snapper she heard.

As soon as all three of the horses in her train stood on dry land, she mounted Rag and rode to join the others.

"Here is the end of our stone path," Mudruffle announced. The golem extended a spidery finger toward the slope of lodge-pole pines that marched to the edge of the pan, replacing the cliff to their right all day. "There is an elk trail through the trees, and that is our trail now."

Caris rode to where he pointed, and frowned at what she saw. Though the trail appeared wide enough for them, the trees in that part of the canyon had grown so dense that it seemed as if generations of dead ones still stood among the living, and their bleached silver branches gleamed like claws that would tear at a careless horse or rider.

"How much farther till we're out of this canyon, Mudruffle?" Willard said.

"Here begins the end of the canyon," the golem replied. "You see it grows wider here. In one mile up this trail, we enter a new valley, almost at the feet of the Godswall."

Father Kogan emerged from the gap at the foot of the pan, splashing and dragging Geraldine behind him. He led the dripping musk auroch to the foot of the elk trail and peered up it. "This our trail?"

Caris nodded.

A strained whinny from Molly shattered the peace and sent a shudder of nerves through the rest of the horses. Rag skittered sideways into Geraldine, whose bulk easily withstood the check. And then Willard was cursing and struggling against Molly as the Phyros reared and whinnied and danced in a circle. As her tail spun past, Caris caught sight of winking flesh, and knew that she hadn't imagined the nature of the earlier whinny.

"If you don't fancy being stepped on by the mad wench, follow me," said Kogan, starting up the trail.

"It's Gygon," Caris said.

Father Kogan stopped in his tracks.

"Yes, he's done it, gods take him." Willard hauled Molly's head to one side to halt her rearing. "The monster found a way around."

"What monster?" said Brolli.

"Bannus. He's near. Probably above these rapids."

Kogan now looked up the trail as if it might lead to a dragon. He backed Geraldine away. "You sure, Will?"

"Wind's from up the gorge."

"Then we must flee back down the canyon," Brolli said. "Better face his men than Bannus."

Willard could not respond, for Molly began a series of violent, twisting leaps that took all his skill to survive in the saddle. Rag shied sideways from Molly's fit, and both Idgit and Holly, still trailing behind Rag, crowded Rag's rear, increasing her irritation.

"Father, turn around," Brolli said. "We must go back."

The priest did not appear to hear; he was squinting up at the cliffs across the river, and his face had gone slack. He pointed a thick finger. "There," he said, breaking into a crack-toothed smile. "The fool's on the wrong side of the river."

Across the river, the red-stone cliff rose into the sky like a series of broken towers peppered with pine trees. On a ledge directly across from them and some twenty fathoms up, Sir Bannus sat upon Gygon, watching them like a bird of prey over a chicken pen. The Phyros stallion's violet scars glowed in the rays of the setting sun, and Sir Bannus's soot-marred armor gleamed dully. How they'd traversed the cliffs and slopes to reach that point, Caris could only wonder. But the

priest was right, gods leave him. Bannus was stuck on the other side of the river. And in that moment, though she had cursed the water many times that day, she blessed it with all her heart.

When Molly saw Gygon, she ceased all struggle and stared at him, nostrils flaring.

Willard chuckled. "Sir Bannus, you look the fool today. There is no crossing here, and there is no passage north. You must return the way you came, and we shall escape you."

Even at that distance, Caris could see that Bannus's armor seemed had been badly scorched, and of his once glorious Crown of Horns, only burned stumps remained. It had to have been resin fire from Abellia's fire-cones to have burned them so quickly. Gygon must have fled the conflagration even as the white-hot flames outraced his strides, for the stallion's once magnificent fetlocks, his glorious stallion mane, and his glossy wine-black coat had been scorched to the skin, leaving sheets of violet scar. Surely his rump and flanks were the same, and his tail a naked whip.

A swell of pride and triumph for Abellia rose in Caris like a shout.

Bannus's immortal voice boomed over the river. "Hear, Abominator. My hunt has been long, and I have grown impatient, so I tell you briefly. Three things I require. The ambassador. His ring. Your head. I shall not leave until I have them."

"Words, Sir Bannus," said Willard, his own voice taking on immortal volume and girth. "I say again, you have failed. Go back to your bootlicking slaves. They will tell you how puissant you are, and how wise."

The scars of Bannus's face writhed. "I see you have returned to the Blood! That is good. I have waited for this day. The day you might give me satisfaction—not as a withered husk of mortal weakness, but as a true immortal—in just combat. Indeed, you satisfy me in part already, for in taking the Blood, you break yet another sacred oath—the oath to your lady—and once again prove yourself unworthy in all affairs. Willard Oath Breaker. Willard the Untrue."

The mad gaze flicked to Brolli. "Do you not guess you are lied to, foolish ambassador? This man is as faithless as his bitch queen. When they betray you, you will find the Old Ones your allies against them."

Brolli snorted. "I like not your kind of faith."

White teeth flashed inside Bannus's helm. "Then you deserve your fate."

Gygon's upper lip lifted as he caught Molly's scent and snorted. Molly whinnied and pawed the sun-heated pan beneath her hooves as if beckoning to Gygon.

"Yes," said Bannus. "Gygon shows us a miracle. The famed Molly will breed in Arkendia!" He lifted his face to the sky and spread his arms in prayer. "How wise you are, Lord Krato. How good and wise. For you make him who betrayed us into the vessel of your rebirth in Arkendia. See, Worsic! See, Malgus! See, lost brothers, our god's revenge!"

He leveled a finger at Willard. "Gygon shall take Molly while you sit in her saddle. Then you shall watch as your bond mate revives the Old Ones in this land."

"Spare us your stale fantasies," said Willard. "You shall have nothing, and only your words will reach us today."

"I bring reckoning, Sir Willard. And sooner than you believe."

Bannus turned Gygon from the brink and disappeared behind the lip of the ledge.

Caris started breathing again; it came in short bites. "Gods leave us," she muttered. Bannus knew Molly was in heat, and he knew that she could breed on Arkendia. But he didn't know she *already had* a Phyros foal. He hadn't noticed Holly.

"Terrifying even when impotent," Harric said.

"Yes." Willard almost seemed to be laughing. "But he will seek a way to ride north, and therefore we must ride north faster. Come."

A clatter of falling rocks or hoofbeats echoed between the cliffs, and Willard looked up. In the next instant, the unmistakable sound of hoofbeats grew louder, and Caris glimpsed the tips of Gygon's ears as he galloped toward the brink of the ledge.

Willard's mouth went slack and the ragleaf dropped from his lips.

In the next instant, Gygon and Bannus rose into view. Caris had not imagined there might be space enough behind the ledge for Gygon to rise into a gallop—none of them had—but there he was on the cusp of an all-out run as he approached the brink. A black sword flashed in Bannus's hand, and Gygon bunched as if to spring across the river.

And in that instant, Caris knew he would succeed—with Sir Bannus on his back—and crash among them like a thunderbolt. "No!" she screamed, and stabbed her hand at the stallion as if she could hold him back with her will—as if she could stop and push him back where he'd come from.

And Gygon balked.

In that instant, the stallion's eyes found Caris, and his violet rage transfixed her mind like a red-hot spike through her skull. The fire flashed through her connection with Rag, and Rag squealed in pain and terror.

"No!" Caris screamed, but could not tear her eyes from the furious stallion. "Rag!"

But in that moment of hesitation, Gygon's weight shifted forward over his enormous front hooves and skidded out over the brink. The mighty Phyros wrenched his gaze free as he toppled. Too late, he thrust his hind legs in a tremendous buck—an attempt, perhaps, to salvage the leap—and flipped heels over head above the river. Twisting and snarling, he struck the water flat on his back with a tremendous clap.

A spire of water shot to the sky. Then the river drank it back and swept the Phyros away.

Caris could not tear her eyes from Sir Bannus. He had been pitched from the saddle like a stone from a listing catapult, but most of Gygon's momentum had gone into sending him—not Gygon—over the river. Limbs flailing, sword flashing in one hand.

He seemed to hang for a moment at the apex of his flight. The great sword gleamed, a dark promise. Then he fell like a stone down a well and crashed behind her with an impact she felt in her bones.

The horses went berserk.

Rag bucked like her mane was on fire. Molly whirled away as if she wished to leap in the river after Gygon. Holly and Idgit were screaming on the ground—either on their side or on their back—hooves flailing and eyes rolling white with terror. It appeared that both had been knocked or wrenched from their feet when Bannus's armored bulk landed between them on Holly's lead. Sir Bannus now lay upon the lead, effectively pinning Holly's nose to the stone.

"Brolli!" Harric shouted. "Brolli's down!"

Caris struggled to keep her saddle, but she glimpsed the ambassador sprawled among the roots of a lodge pole. Blood drenched his shirt and his huge eyes were closed—visible now because his daylids had been knocked from his face.

The sight struck like a fist to the jaw. *Brolli!*

Drawing her saddle knife, she cut Holly and Idgit's lead so she could focus her attention on Rag. The immortal hadn't stirred since impact, and his hard landing had mashed and twisted his helmet over his face, probably blinding him. Nevertheless, he lay within arm's reach of the ambassador, and Caris had to get to Brolli before Bannus stirred. But Rag's terror was overwhelming. The more Caris tried to calm her, the more the mare's terror threatened to infect her own mind.

As she struggled with Rag, he watched helplessly as Bannus lurched and pushed himself up with both hands, then drew a knee up beneath him. When he raised his head, a torrent of violet blood cascaded from his ruined helmet.

"Take Brolli!" Harric shouted. "Kogan, take Brolli!"

Caris redoubled her efforts and pushed her senses deep into Rag… only to find that Rag was wasn't there. To Caris's horse-touched senses, there simply was no Rag.

She tried again, concentrating harder and groping with her senses, but she couldn't feel the mare at all.

An empty gulf opened inside her, and her voice caught in her throat. "Rag, come back!" She threw herself into the connection and thrust herself at Rag—or where Rag *should* have been—but all she could feel was a surface, not a mind. Rag had closed herself entirely. To Caris's senses, she might have been any horse. A frightened, unfamiliar horse.

A sob burst from Caris. She hadn't meant to touch Gygon. She hadn't meant to do anything; she'd just reacted, unthinking. And though it had robbed Bannus of his Phyros and may have saved their lives, she sensed without any doubt that, in touching the stallion, she'd lost her dearest friend, forever.

Eyes streaming, she managed Rag like she would any unknown horse—like some common rebellious beast—forcing her submission and breaking her will.

When Molly rump-checked Rag, Caris realized Willard was struggling as much to control Molly as she was to control Rag. She felt like screaming at Willard to kill Bannus while the Old One remained on his knees, but it appeared to take all of Willard's skill just to stay in the saddle. Molly bucked and whirled as if she wished to cast Willard to the stone. Between jumps, she lunged for the river, squealing for Gygon, ready to swim after him. And though Willard was strong, she had the strength of estrus, and each whirling jump took them closer to the water.

With a wordless cry, Caris stabbed into Molly's mind as she had done Gygon's.

And a lance of violet fire struck back through the connection. Molly could not be surprised like Gygon. She'd felt this trick before, and countered fiercely.

If Caris had tried this trick an hour before, Molly's counterattack might have knocked her from her feet, might have burned out her mind like a nut on a stove. But Gygon's fire had already primed Caris's mind. Coupled with Caris's anger at the loss of Rag, the two blew up into a tempest of fury: fury at herself for betraying Rag; fury at losing her best friend; fury at the immortals who forced the loss upon her. Violet fire streaked down the channel between them, shattering Molly's lance and stabbing deep in the mare's startled mind.

Molly faltered, and it gave Willard a chance to grab a mace from his gear and stun her with a blow to the back of her head. A mortal horse would have fallen from the blow, but Molly only staggered. Yet it was enough for Willard to win control and force her back from the brink.

By then, Bannus had risen to his feet. Now with one hand, he tore away his helm and tossed it aside; with the other hand, he held fast to Holly's bridle, and now he drew her between himself and Willard as a shield and barrier.

Once again master of Molly, Willard called, "Ride!" to Caris, and confronted Sir Bannus, Belle flashing in his hand.

"But Brolli—"

"Ride! I say, ride!"

Two men commit the same crime
And face a different fate:
That man gets rack and gallows,
This one crown and state.

— From Arkendia Corrupted, stage play suppressed during King Harnor's reign

64

Knight Of Krato

Harric managed to stay in his saddle. He and Snapper had been closer to the head of the pan near the rapids when the mayhem began. From there, he'd watched the drama unfold like a tragedy performed in the courtyard of an inn, complete with the appearance of a tyrant king in a balcony above.

Now as Caris whipped Rag up the hillside through the trees, she cried to him, "Ride!" but he kept Snapper where he was; Caris might be under orders from Willard, but Harric was not. And though Brolli was a traitor and perhaps deserved death, Harric couldn't abandon him to be captured by Sir Bannus.

After snatching Captain Gren's pack from his luggage, Harric leapt from Snapper's saddle to the bare stone stage. Calm as Snapper generally was, when Harric tried to tie him to one of the trees at the edge, he surprised Harric by pulling away and bolting after Caris.

Cursing, Harric let him go and pushed into the pines to scramble up the steep slope above the pan. When he reached the game trail that Kogan and Caris had taken, he crept down until he could see the lower half of the pan and the foot of the trail, where Brolli lay in the brush. Bannus stood with his back to Brolli as he held Holly between himself and Willard. The immortal was laughing.

"It seems mortality has dulled your wit, Abominator."

Sir Bannus began slowly sidestepping away from Brolli, along the edge of the trees. He was moving toward the foot of the pan, keeping Holly always between himself and Willard. In his free hand, he held his black sword high. "Did you think I did not know the god had sent us another mare? Did you think he would not tell me? Why do you doubt my prophecies?"

Pounding footfalls approached Harric from up the trail, and he turned to see Father Kogan running toward him, smothercoat flapping, with the enormous Phyros axe in one hand. Breezing by Harric, he skidded to a halt some ten paces from Bannus, axe held high. "Will!"

Without breaking gaze with Bannus, Willard waved it off. "See to Brolli."

Kogan faltered. He looked at the bloody Kwendi, then back to Willard. For a moment, it seemed as if he'd toss Willard the axe, but Willard's attention was on Bannus, who had stopped only a couple strides from Brolli to gather up Holly's lead.

"Wait! Not yet!" Harric said, though the priest gave no sign of hearing him. Harric pulled a spitfire from the pack and tried to move to the uphill side of the trail for an angle where he wouldn't risk hitting the priest instead of Bannus, but the corridor of open space between the trees was narrow, and moving didn't improve his chances. "Father—"

But Kogan let out a snort, lowered the axe, and strode to Brolli. Keeping himself to the side farthest from Bannus, he scooped up the ambassador in one arm and then whirled to retreat up the trail.

Harric tried to find an angle on Bannus for a shot, but Kogan was too big and the spitfire too inaccurate to risk it. And then it was too late.

Bannus struck like a snake, and blood fanned from Kogan's neck.

The immortal had made a simple fencer's lunge, a move impossible for any mortal in plate armor. He'd shot out to full extension over one knee, sword forward and Holly's lead in the hand behind him. The black blade had whipped under Kogan's beard and rung out on something iron. Then he recovered the lunge as fast as he'd struck.

Kogan's eyes flew wide. He did not drop Brolli. He turned and rushed him up the trail.

A pained cry died in Harric's throat. He was dimly aware of immortal swords clashing below, but his eyes were on the blood spurting from

Kogan's beard. Blood. There was so much blood. On Brolli. On Kogan. On the trail. As the priest labored past, he shifted the Kwendi's limp body into the crook of the arm with the axe, and pressed his free hand to the wound. Eyes intent on the trail before him, he did not appear to see Harric at all.

Frantic, Harric whirled toward the foot of the trail and raised the spitfire to keep Bannus from following, but the immortal was sidestepping away toward the gap at the foot of the pan, with the terrified Holly as a shield. Hands trembling, Harric took aim, then lowered his weapon with a curse as he realized that now a shot was just as likely to hit Willard or Holly.

"Stand, Sir Bannus," Willard said. "And only one of us shall leave this place."

A drunkard's grin split Bannus's scars. Coupled with the wreckage of burns and facial amputations, the sight drained the blood from Harric's legs.

"Do you think I've come for you, Abominator? Indeed, these many days, that was my aim. But today the god spoke to me. He reminded me you and I have eternity to embrace, and that today our prize is much greater. Lord Krato sends his thanks for her foaling, and I thank you for your arrogance, which was the bait for my trap."

Willard's eyes blazed violet, but to Harric it seemed his face grew pale. With a wordless roar, he launched Molly at Bannus. Belle flashed and clashed against Bannus's parry. The black blade countered and struck home under Willard's arm. Violet blood flew. Molly drove into Holly, but Bannus appeared to anticipate the attack and moved with immortal speed, retreating and retreating as she pressed, and keeping Holly always between himself and his attackers.

Harric matched their movement by advancing to the foot of the trail, but abandoned hope for a clear shot unless Bannus somehow got clear of the others.

Molly attacked with the ferocity of a mother protecting her offspring, but her iron shoes slipped and scrabbled on the smooth stone, and Bannus outraced her. It wasn't until they approached the gap at the foot of the pan that she grew desperate. She slammed into Holly from behind in an effort to topple and stand over her. And in normal circumstances it would have worked, but Bannus anticipated her again and buttressed

Holly with his own great strength, keeping them both upright, and the impact slid both Holly and Bannus backward, speeding their retreat to the path.

Swords flashed and clashed again as Bannus backed onto the path, his boots ankle-deep in rushing water. As he pulled Holly into the gap, behind him, Willard feinted as if he'd slash Holly's lead line, and when Bannus moved to parry, he twisted his wrist to cut at Bannus's throat. Unable to block it, Bannus shrugged a shoulder and lowered his head so his pauldron deflected the blade up and into his jaw. Bone split. Teeth and blood flew. But Bannus kept his feet. Jaw hanging, he retreated into the gap until both he and Holly stood in the rushing water on the path.

"She is not for you!" Willard roared. "She is not for you!"

Molly pranced in the gap, snarling in rage for her lost foal, but Willard held her back. The path was too low and narrow to follow while still upon her back. He would have to dismount and lead her on the treacherous path, single file.

Well out of range of Belle or Molly, Sir Bannus held his jaw together with one hand, and violet blood streamed down his arm and from his elbow. When he dropped his hand a moment later, the blood had stopped, and a new rope of livid scar shone on his jaw line. He let out a clattering laugh.

"How do you reckon things now, Sir Willard?" His voice slurred slightly from his injury. "You thought me incapable of craft? A fool is he who learns naught from his foe, and I learned from the craftiest of foes. Yet I fear you have smoked so much ragleaf and your wits have grown dull, for it seems much too easy."

Harric could not see Willard's face from his angle. But it was clear that Sir Bannus had won. Willard could not follow or engage Sir Bannus without dismounting, and if he left Molly on her own, she might as well leap in the river after Gygon, and then Bannus would have two Phyros mares.

"See, brothers!" Bannus shouted to the sky. "Already it has begun. Already Molly restores the herd. Now shall Krato sire Phyros in Arkendia, and new brothers shall ride them—yea, and the first shall be my shield bearer, Titus. I name this foal Trochus, bearer of Titus, and mother of herds."

Harric stared as comprehension dawned upon him that Holly was a

Phyros and that Molly was her dam. She had neither the violet eyes of her dam, nor the blood tooth, nor any other outward sign, but Bannus clearly recognized her, and Willard's reaction confirmed it. Molly had foaled Holly in Arkendia, and far from Willard reducing the number of Phyros, as he'd done in the Cleansing, he had just given the Old Ones the means to sire more.

A horn sounded deep in the canyon. A long, silvery note, trailing away. The sound sent a quill of dread up Harric's spine. Bannus's men. The Faceless One and the other strange Phyros-rider were coming. They might be a mile away. And once Gygon washed out of the roaring canyon, the Phyros stallion would be no more than a half-day behind.

Without a word, Willard turned Molly and rode back up the pan. Harric saw something he'd never seen, and it nearly unstrung his courage. It was only there a moment before it was masked in that grim, controlled rage, but Harric recognized it as despair.

Molly's iron shoes struck a hollow clatter against the stone. When she climbed the trail, Harric dodged into the trees to make way. It wasn't until he'd passed that he realized Willard wasn't stopping, and Harric now stood alone in the canyon.

A spear of panic hit him full in the chest. If Bannus wanted to add a skewered bastard to his triumphs, here was one within easy reach.

Hands trembling, Harric raised the spitfire and knelt in the path to sight the mouth of the narrows. Bannus had retreated around the bend in the path, but his laughter echoed in the canyon. Snatches of triumphant shouts reached Harric's ears, and in them he caught the words "Krato" and "glory."

What the Black Moon are you doing, Harric? Think you'll stop him by yourself? He licked a bead of sweat from his lip. Then he lowered the spitfire.

"Cob this," he muttered, and fled after the others.

The wise will be shocked to learn that explorations of the northern fastness, long held to be the sole abode of the god Arkus, yield no sign of the reclusive god. Arkus has not appeared to frighten our usurping settlers back down the river, nor to toss them back over the Godswall. Neither do we find reports of him stealing knights or sturdy peasants to make more of his pestilent priests. For this, at least, we can be thankful, for the Wandering Fathers already swarm the Free Lands as thick as the fleas in the rags of the rabbles they lead...

— From News of the Free Lands, gossip rag printed and released in Kingsport

65

Priest Of Arkus

Harric pounded up the trail, spitfire in hand, the weight of the resin in his pack bouncing on his back. The trail climbed steeply, winding between the half-dead pines. As his boots crunched silver twigs and needles, every step took him past new splashes of blood. Red blood painted the roots. Red blood colored the stones. It looked as if someone had run up the trail with sloshing buckets of the stuff, and it made Harric's heart squeeze in on itself.

When he finally crested the hill above the waterfall, his lungs and legs burned and the empty trail stretched before him with no sign of Snapper or anyone else. Cursing, he stumbled onward, following the dwindling track of blood.

The trail traversed the wooded hillside about fifteen fathoms above the rushing water. Through occasional gaps in the trees, he glimpsed the opposite side, which was just as steep and choked with pines. But farther ahead, the canyon's ridges appeared to dwindle, and no more than a mile ahead, it seemed to open into a valley.

Forcing his nerveless legs to run, Harric followed the dwindling blood track, and as he rounded each bend, he dreaded what he might find on the other side.

Hunting horns sounded again, and he guessed from their volume that they couldn't be far below the falls. *Moons, I need a horse.* He would never escape on foot. Where in the Black Moon was Snapper? Had no one thought to catch him and bring him back to Harric, or had the beast run wild?

A harsh, graveled horn blast ripped through the canyon behind him. Bannus's horn. There was no mistaking it. And it was much louder and nearer than the others.

But how can that be? Bannus's gear had been lost with Gygon in the river. The only explanation, of course, was that the stallion had not only escaped the roaring waters much sooner than Harric thought possible, but that he'd found his way back to Bannus with equally improbable speed.

We're cobbed. Sir Bannus would catch Harric before he got far in the valley.

Stopping at a gap in the trees, he looked up at the ridge above the opposite side of the canyon. The western sky was still bright, but the sun had disappeared behind the mountain, which meant it was officially night where he stood…

A spark of hope sprang to life in his chest as he fumbled for his nexus and tried to gauge whether he was far enough from the river to enter the Unseen. Was this trail higher than the one on the previous night? He couldn't tell. But he had to try. As soon as the glassy stone cooled the palm of his hand, he closed his eyes and relaxed his oculus just enough to open it a crack.

Bright strands erupted through his oculus like lashes of fire. He cried out, blinded, and clapped his hands to his forehead, but the strands continued to sting like hot needles. His oculus went numb with pain, unresponsive to his efforts to close it.

His knees hit the trail. He fell forward and pressed his forehead to the ground, wishing he could bury his head…and the light and pain faded. He gasped in relief. The earth, it seemed, blocked the river strands. A few still flicked in around the edges, but by comparison it was no worse than the stinging sunburn he'd felt in the Kwendi reservoir.

Bannus's horn ripped through the air somewhere down the trail, and Harric nearly jumped, but he dared not lift his forehead. If his oculus didn't recover and close, Bannus would find him with his face in the trail and his arse in the air, just waiting for a swift kick or a lance. *Hurry up and close!* he willed it. *Hurry!* Blood slammed in his temples as he strained against its numbness, but it barely closed.

With every passing moment, sensation returned, he closed it a little more, and Bannus rode nearer. When it seemed Harric'd had his arse in the air for hours, his oculus finally sealed tight.

Panting and blinking away tears, he staggered to his feet and glanced back to be sure his enemies weren't right there, holding their laughter till he turned. But the trail behind him remained empty.

He whirled and ran, once again following the blood trail, and he must have run another half-mile before it looked as if the final bend approached. By then his lungs felt like he'd been breathing flame, and his legs felt like jelly. But now the wide valley beckoned through the trees, and in the absence of a good creek bed to hide in, he ran for it. If he reached the valley before Bannus caught him, he could leave the trail and cut away from the river until he was far enough to enter the Unseen.

What he found around the last bend was what he'd hoped to find, and what he dreaded. Only a hundred paces hence, the canyon walls fell away and the trees descended into a meadowy valley flanked by more distant ridges. At the north end, the valley ended at the Godswall, whose icy peaks still shone in the last light of day.

And only ten paces hence lay Father Kogan.

Harric stopped at the priest's feet and stared in dismay. Geraldine, who stood watch at Kogan's side, looked up at Harric through wooly locks and let out a mournful groan.

"Kogan," Harric whispered, afraid to wake him.

The priest lay on his back, head propped against a boulder, his smothercoat dark with blood. One hand remained at his throat as if to keep the blood in, though Harric doubted much could be left inside. The great Phyros axe lay abandoned on the trail.

Like the yoab that took a spear to the heart and ran a mile before expiring, Kogan had carried Brolli until he collapsed on the trail. Someone—Willard or Caris—had taken Brolli.

Harric saw a glimmer through Kogan's narrowed lids. His mouth moved.

Dropping to his knees at Kogan's side, Harric took up the giant's heavy hand in both of his.

"Moons, I have plasters!" he said with a start. "Willard gave them to me!" As he plunged his fingers in to grab one of the dried-up scabs, Kogan laid the giant hand on his.

The glassy eyes gleamed. "Blood of Krato..." he murmured. "Never."

Harric's heart sank. Willard had probably already offered, but of course Kogan wouldn't take it. Just as he must have refused Mudfruffle's healing. "I understand," Harric said.

Kogan drew him closer. His voice came faint, with pause for shallow breaths between words. "Will come. Took...Brolli...body."

"Body?" The word struck Harric like a slap.

The priest's gaze drifted up to Harric's. "Limp...as a...chimpey doll. Bled out." His cracked teeth showed for a moment. "Bannus... done it. Like...he got me."

"Didn't they try to heal him? Will must have tried plasters. And Mudruffle—"

Kogan nodded, a movement so small it was barely noticeable. "Too late. Will took him. Must've...forgot the axe." He held Harric's gaze for a moment. "Take it to him."

"Yes, I will, father."

"Tell him keep it. Use it. Make...him promise."

"I will."

A dribble of blood leaked from beneath the hand Kogan held to his throat. With his other hand, he reached under his beard and, with some effort, pulled something away. His head fell back and his eyes closed as if he'd lost consciousness. Then the eyes opened a crack, and from the bloody wool of his beard he drew forth a double bend of thick iron, and after a moment's confusion, Harric recognized it as Kogan's priest collar. It was the iron ring said to be placed on every wandering priest by the hand of Arkus himself.

The band had been cloven, and Kogan had bent it open to remove it. Now he laid the twist of bloody metal in Harric's hands. "Mustn't let..." His voice hitched on a weak cough.

"...let Bannus capture this?" Harric said. "I won't."

Kogan's mouth twitched in the beginnings of a smile.

"Yeah. I'm a Maker," Harric said. "You don't have to say it."

A silent *har* died on Kogan's lips, but his eyes glittered.

Bannus's horn rattled in the distance, sending a jolt through Harric.

Kogan groped Harric's arm. A stab of panic hit Harric as he imagined the priest knew of Witch's Teat under the bandage, but the hand found the stock of the spitfire jutting from the pack and drew it toward Kogan. Brown eyes glistening, he laid it in his lap as if he'd keep it to fight off Bannus when the immortal arrived.

"You keep it," Harric said.

Kogan gripped it like a pistol and directed its pipe at a tree that leaned out over the trail by his feet. "Bannus don't...get my head neither."

The flint wheel sparked, and the weapon belched a wad of flaming resin into the tree, transforming it into a giant torch.

When Harric flinched in surprise, the great mound of Kogan's belly shook with silent laughter. His eyes widened and he dropped the empty spitfire to grasp Harric's hand.

"Tell...Widda Larkin..." His eyes glistened, and he fell still.

Harric's throat constricted. "I will," he said.

Geraldine stirred. Her huge head had hovered near them through the whole exchange. Now she set her huge pink tongue to Kogan's bloodied face and cleaned it like she would a newborn calf.

Therefore, bury your dead upon islands in rivers that run the year round, for running water is purifying fire to an unquiet spirit. And since no specter will dare it, ye shall sleep untroubled… You must beware those who say "bury me at the end of the lane," or "bury me in the yard," for they surely be witches, and these shall ye hang over water and leave them for the crows.

— Town Ordinance VIII "Regarding Burying of the Dead," Arditch-on-the-Spyre

66

A Cure For Fleas

Harric stood. He couldn't breathe. It felt like someone had set a huge stone on his sternum.

Numbly, he picked up the spitfire and stared at the blazing tree, which had already spread its fire to several beside it.

A funeral pyre. To keep his body from capture.

He let out a rueful laugh as the fire crackled and spread in the thick tinder beneath the trees. Kogan had chosen the whole cobbing forest for his pyre. And as the heat of it warmed Harric's face, the north wind cooled his back and sent a shiver up his spine.

The north wind—the blessed north wind!—would push this fire away down the canyon toward Bannus. And if the entire hillside blazed, Bannus would have to turn back.

Suddenly alert to possibility, Harric scanned above and below the trail. Kogan's fire would not spread fast enough to spread up and down the whole hillside before Bannus arrived—there would be plenty of room above or below the fire for the immortal to skirt it by bushwhacking.

Unless Harric finished the job.

Grinning like a madman, he drew the second spitfire from the pack and aimed it between the trees below Kogan. If he got lucky, the wad would race between a dozen trees, spattering them all before it hit one full-on. He squeezed the lever and the stock bucked against his shoulder, spitting the wad past a half-dozen trees before it crashed against an age-silvered pine.

Bannus's horn sounded again, but much louder than before, as if he had finally climbed above the rapids and onto his trail. Then the clear notes of hunting horns joined in the mocking tune of "Hang High, Father."

The heat from the fire was already uncomfortably hot, forcing Harric to grab his pack to move it farther up the trail. As he passed the father and Geraldine, he tripped over the axe.

"Geraldine, you've got to get out of here."

Harric dropped the pack and spitfires a few paces up the road, then returned to pick up the axe, which was already growing hot to the touch in the glare of Kogan's fire. When Harric heaved the enormous weapon onto Geraldine's back, it nearly mashed the little basket there.

"Spook!"

The lid jumped as if the little cat were trying to get out, but the priest had fastened its strings so it wouldn't open.

"Not much longer, boy," Harric said, as he shifted the axe and lashed it to the saddle. "You'll be safer in there."

Spook mewed, but Harric ignored him.

Despite Harric's coaxing, Geraldine did not want to leave Kogan, and his efforts to drag her enormous head around went almost unnoticed. He'd almost given up when one of the trees beside Kogan's fire went up with a whoosh that sent a tremor through her. Then she turned with little urging, and he was able to slap her rump and send her cantering up the trail.

Heat hammered Harric's bare cheeks as he recovered his pack and followed Geraldine to a comfortable distance. As he reamed and reloaded the spitfires, he judged that the blaze had already doubled in size. The dry wood seemed greedy for fire, and the north wind just as eager to feed it. As soon as the spitfires were loaded, he sent blazing comets into the trunks above and below Kogan's resting place.

Harric reamed and fired, reamed and fired, extending the wall of flames above and below, and when the trumpet end of one spitfire began to flame like a resin torch, he grabbed his gear and climbed the hillside, setting it to every tree he passed. By now the hillside was an almost continuous wall of flame, and he had to retreat again from the ferocity of the heat.

Horns sounded, so close he thought they must be rounding the last bend, but he could no longer see the trail beyond a raging wall of fire and smoke.

When he was confident the upper hillside was impassable, he hurried down to finish the job below. Before he even reached the trail, the heat beat him back another ten paces and a steady stream of sweat began to blur his vision. He was now a good sixty paces from the flames, and whole trees were blooming spontaneously into torches. The roar of the flames grew deafening.

When he struck the trail, he paused to catch his breath and retreat another five paces from the heat. Beyond the wall of flames, he imagined he glimpsed men and horses and heard shouts and whinnying. Then a tree engulfed in flames crashed down across the trail where Kogan lay, and sent a gout of sparks into the sky.

Bannus's horn ripped the air so near that it made Harric's heart skip. Through an eddy in the smoke, he glimpsed the immortal on Gygon, thundering up the trail straight toward the fallen tree as if they'd leap it and trample Harric.

Fingers fumbling, Harric stuffed a double charge of resin in one spitfire and sighted down the trail, aiming right between the violet eyes.

The double-charged weapon bucked so hard it knocked Harric backward.

A pair of shrieking comets corkscrewed toward the immortal like javelins of fire. Bannus roared and Gygon veered off the trail and into the trees below it with a tremendous crash. Another flaming tree fell, this one beyond the fire, and Harric thought he heard screams of confusion from man and horse alike.

Harric yelled in fear and triumph, "Run! Flee, you stinking cobs!" but the roar of the fire had reached such deafening pitch that he doubted any but himself could hear it. As if in answer, a tree below exploded with a report like a resin charge.

A spot of heat at his cheek startled him, and then he felt a sizzle and burn at his ear.

Cursing, he dropped the spitfire and swatted at the flames in his hair. A burning glob of resin dropped to the ground, and some burned the skin on the back of a finger. By the time he wiped it off with a handful of dirt, it left a burn the size of a small coin on the finger. Touching gingerly, he guessed a similar blister adorned his ear.

Stupid. The overloaded weapon had spat back a burning hornet of resin, and he hadn't been wearing his spitfire mask.

Harric imagined he heard Sir Bannus howl in rage, now much lower on the hillside, and it sent shard of panic through his stomach. He hadn't seen to the lower flank of the fire yet, so Bannus might yet find a place to ride through.

Reaming and loading a spitfire, he shouldered his pack and dove down the slope, careless of the clawing branches. When he finally approached the edge of the cliff above the river, however, he found that the dry forest and the north wind had done the work for him. Flames in the lower flank roared ten fathoms high with no gaps for Bannus to cross, and now the roar of the flames was so great that Harric couldn't hear his own panting breaths.

"We did it," he said, though even he couldn't hear it. "We cobbing did it."

Cheeks stinging, he retreated to a stone upthrust and climbed atop it to survey the fiery maelstrom. It was solid flame and smoke. Nothing of the canyon beyond was visible through the conflagration.

Twisting shapes rose in it like fiery dust devils—spirits of the Mad Moon, they seemed, wild and mad with triumph. Banshee wails pierced the general roar, and despite the heat, Harric felt a shiver run up his spine. Were they not spirits of that moon? Fink would know. One of these whorls rose high above the blazing crown of the trees—a giant of twisting flames—and from its out-flung limbs rained flaming branches and cones to the opposite side of the canyon.

Spots of fire rose in the dark trees on that side of the river.

Soon the whole canyon would be a furnace of whirling spirits.

Peering up at the trail, he sought the mound of Father Kogan in the blaze, and imagined he saw the priest standing in his smothercoat amid the flames, head thrown back in laughter.

The fire was Kogan's victory. Bannus got Holly and he killed both Brolli and Kogan, but Kogan had denied the immortal his trophies and driven him back with his tail between his legs. "Plus, it's a sure cure for fleas, father," Harric said.

As the flames rose higher and the heat became once again unbearable, Harric climbed down from his viewpoint and hiked to a comfortable distance of at least a hundred paces, then climbed back up to the trail. The north wind now rushed to join the fire, sucked forward by the heat rising from the inferno, and as he turned his back, its touch cooled the sweat of his body.

He now stood at the end of the canyon. For the next half-mile northward, the steep slopes on either side of the river melted into a wide-bottomed valley. The sight further lifted his spirits. Soon it would be easy to remove himself far enough from the river to enter the Unseen.

Later. There was no longer any rush, and leaden weariness now infused his limbs. He sat heavily on a log by the trail and drained his waterskin without pausing to breathe.

The thunder of hooves approached from ahead. Molly, Harric guessed.

Rousing himself, he stood and carried his pack and weapons into the first trees above the trail in order to give the beast space. His pack was light now. He'd spent all but a few resin wads, which he'd have to conserve now.

Willard reined in beside Harric but did not acknowledge him. He glared down the trail at the fire, huge body tight as a bowstring. Red light gleamed from Belle in his hand. Fury boiled behind his eyes. And again Harric thought he saw the shadow of despair he'd seen on the pan.

The roar of the fire was now as loud as the rapids of the river, the heat of it strong on Harric's face. "The fire was Kogan's last act—" he said, and his voice cracked as he said it. Stupid. He always looked weak in front of Willard. "His pyre."

The knight's eyes remained on the fire. Harric wasn't sure if Willard heard him over the flames. In any case, the knight was probably angry. The Blood probably made him want to face Bannus—to win Holly back—and the fire prevented him.

"Bannus?" said Willard.

"Stopped. He— I think he turned back."

Tension drained from Willard's shoulders, and he sighed. "Yes.

He would turn back. This blazing conflagration is Kogan's parting gift to us. Stinking, big-hearted fool."

He pulled a roll of ragleaf from his gauntlet and stuck it between his teeth. As he lit the roll with his flint wheel, his violet eyes turned to Harric without him turning his head, and his gaze rested on the deflated resin pack and still-smoking spitfires. When the ragleaf caught fire, he blew a gust of smoke from his nostrils and gave Harric a slow nod of acknowledgement.

"Might be the wisest thing Kogan ever did. And you did well to further his wishes."

In spite of himself, Harric experienced a small wave of gratitude. "As long as we have this north wind, the fire will chase them down the canyon. Might buy a couple days."

"At least."

"He also sent the axe along on Geraldine. Did you see?"

Willard snorted. "I saw."

"I think he thought you left it on purpose. Told me to make you promise you would take it and use it. Told me to tell you it was his dying wish."

Willard's shoulder plates rose and fell in little jerks. He was laughing quietly, and the silent shake of his barrel chest built to a deep chuckle. "Very well, Kogan," he called into the fire. "By this hand, if I can use your fool axe, I will!"

From one of his many saddlebags, he pulled a tarnished brass horn that Harric had never seen. In the ballads, Willard had blown a horn called Gold Throat as he went into battle. It had been a gift from the Queen when he was her champion, and Harric wondered if this could be the same horn.

"Farewell, Kogan," Willard shouted to the flames. He lifted the horn to his lips and blew a long, clear, soaring note. He blew it again, and again, his immortal lungs imparting a ringing power that hung loud and pure and glowing in the air. Harric took satisfaction in the thought that Bannus's men were sucking too much smoke now to wind theirs in defiance.

"Call it 'The Good Father's Cavalcade,'" said Willard, as he lowered the horn.

He smoked quietly for many long heartbeats, and the roaring silence seemed tribute to Kogan.

"I failed, this day," Willard said, still watching the fire. "Sir Bannus outplayed me and outwitted me." He rubbed his face. "Seems my disciplines are no longer as sharp as they once were, and I let the Blood cloud my judgment. Nor did I think his mad brains had the wit for strategy any more. Nor the sanctity for prophecy." He leaned to one side and spat. "He let me believe it was me he wanted, and under that pretense took two of our company and Holly."

"I'm sorry for Brolli," Harric said.

The roar of the fire devoured the words, and Willard lifted his eyes again to the fire.

"Mudruffle has preserved the ambassador's body with the magic of his moon," said Willard. "And I will return him to his people. I owe him that. And such a gesture may be our only hope of salvaging this disaster. I fear our quest is lost. I fear that when they see their slain ambassador, there will be war. Still, I must try, for the Queen needs allies, not enemies. And we must hope."

A huge tree collapsed in the wall of fire, sending a fountain of orange sparks to the sky.

"Sir Willard, I must tell you something about Brolli. This is a bad time, because what I have to say is not flattering to his memory, but you must know before I leave. It may change your mind and plans."

Willard turned his violet eyes on Harric, and his jaw muscles bulged.

The sound of hoofbeats drew Harric's attention up the trail, and there he saw Caris riding toward them on Idgit—a sight as ridiculous as when Willard rode her—which made him wonder if Rag had been injured.

As Idgit slowed to a walk and Caris drew near, Willard snorted. "Well, boy? Out with it."

"I'm sorry, Sir Willard. But this is only for your ears."

Willard sucked hard at the ragleaf. "Very well. But if what you have to tell me is some new knavery to get back at Brolli for an imagined slight, I shall know it, and I shall chain you and leave you for Bannus."

You judge men by the color of their garments and call it wisdom.
But any child knows it's a fool who judges a horse by its saddle.

—Queen Chasia to First Herald Timus
when he denounced her removal of the sumptuary laws

67

Separations

Harric risked a look at Caris as she stared in awe of the raging flames.
"We are safe? They are turned back?"

Willard nodded. "Why do you ride the pony? Is your mount hurt?"

She looked down. A lock of hair fell about her face, but Harric saw a
tear leave a track in the dust on her cheek. "She won't let me near her,"
she said, voice hoarse. "Can't contact her. Can't…" She gave her head
a shake as if casting off weakness. "Can't control her anymore."

"I'm sorry," said Willard, and the gentleness of his voice surprised
Harric.

"Mudruffle asks for your attention, Sir Willard. Something to do
with Brolli."

Willard's jaw pulsed, and he glanced at Harric. He acknowledged
Caris with a nod, and Molly began to move up the trail. To Harric, he
said, "Find me when you're ready."

When Willard had left them, Caris dismounted on the opposite
side of Idgit from Harric and stared at the howling inferno. Wind raced
past, sucked in by the towering flames, blowing her hair forward and
once again concealing her face.

"Brolli…" Her voice choked off.

"I know."

"There will be war with the Kwendi, Harric. We failed. And Holly is gone. Gods leave us, it's like the Chaos Moon is coming."

Harric nodded, but said nothing.

"Kogan's in there?" She was staring at the fire.

"Set the fire himself. It's his pyre."

A small smile bent her lips upward, and she bowed her head.

"I'm sorry about Rag," Harric said. "You should take Snapper. He's a good horse. And Phyros-trained. I won't need a Phyros-trained horse any longer."

She pulled the hair back and tucked it behind her ear to look at him, and her gaze—her dispassionate, *unattached* gaze—sent a tremor of doubt through him. It was a look of frank regard that he had not seen from her for a very long time. Not since Gallows Ferry. Not since before the ring.

"So you're leaving," she said.

He nodded, studying her closely now. "It's best. And I could take Rag, if that's what you want."

"It's too late for what I want." She looked back to the fire, and the wind whipped her hair back over her face.

Harric put a hand over his oculus as if he were merely shading his eyes from the glare of the fires. Since the river was bending away, it might be possible to crack his oculus open for a look at her spirit. Of course, if it wasn't, he'd end up slamming his face to the ground, which would be awkward. But he had to try. It would be his last chance.

The sunburn itch began the moment it opened, but this time it was bearable. He let out a quiet sigh and dropped his hands to his side. Then he closed his eyes and turned his spirit vision on Caris.

Bright Phyros violet startled him. Streaks of the stuff mingled among her brilliant blue strands and looped off toward Willard and Molly. *Gods leave her, Willard made her drink from Molly.* He still found it hard to believe, and anger pinched in his heart. But this would certainly explain why Rag had rejected Caris so absolutely. Rag hated being near Molly, and if Molly's blood was in Caris... Could the old knight not see what that took from Caris? And then Harric noticed other strands of violet stretching south through the fire, and he stared for several long moments, trying to make sense of it. Surely there was no attachment to Gygon. But could that be an attachment to Holly?

But even more shocking were the weaves of the ring.

Because they were gone.

His jaw dropped as he set to studying more closely. He hadn't been mistaken. The weaves were gone. He could hardly believe it, but the Phyros fire had done it. She was free. And a new lightness filled his heart, like a joyful wind lifting a paper lantern.

"What are you doing?" Caris's voice was hard.

Harric's eyes snapped open and he closed his oculus to find her glaring like she was about to reach across Idgit's back and slap him.

He blinked, mouth moving mutely. "You're *free...*" He breathed. "Can't you feel it? You're free."

She clenched her jaw, eyes boring into him. Then they flicked to the side as her attention went inward. After a moment, she blinked several times, and her brow furrowed. "It's…it's gone." Her teeth shone in a rare smile, but when she grabbed the ring to pull it from her finger, the smile faltered.

"It still won't come off. It's gone—I mean, *inside* it's gone. But it still won't come off."

Harric rubbed his stubbly chin. He didn't know about the stuck-on-your-hand part of the enchantment. At least, he couldn't see that part of it in the Unseen. But the Kwendi used magic of all three moons, so he guessed it was possible that part of the enchantment was from the Mad Moon or the Bright Mother, which might not show up in the Unseen.

"But your heart is clear now?" he asked. "Your head is clear?"

She nodded, but her eyes had narrowed and her lips were pressed in a hard line. "How do you know all this? It's that…*creature*, isn't it?"

Harric gave her a cautious nod. "I can see your spirit. I can see that the magic of the ring is gone. But I don't know why it's gone. I only know that I didn't break it. I think you did it yourself. Something to do with…the Phyros Blood, maybe?"

Her nostrils flared and her eyes grew bright. A tear rolled down her cheek, pushed sideways by the rushing wind, and she wiped it with the back of her hand. Above the roar of the fire, he thought he heard her say, "Molly." She looked back the way Willard had taken the Phyros. "Molly and Gygon," she said, louder. "I touched them and they… burned me. Burned Rag."

"Burned out the ring."

She nodded, hair now streaming behind her. An empty ache tugged at Harric's heart as he took in her profile. The lines of her neck. The honesty of her gaze. *Moons, I'll miss you,* he thought. He already missed her.

Somewhere behind that ache, however, was the bittersweet realization that with her freedom came his own freedom. That he was no longer beholden to the ring or to Caris, no longer beholden to Willard for Caris's sake. Of course, it was also true that he no longer needed to leave, in order to put distance between himself and Caris to weaken the weaves, either. But that only illuminated the fact that he didn't *want* to stay. That he'd changed and was ready to leave. That Willard and Caris would never see good in magic and they didn't see good in him.

Realizing this lifted something like a stone cap from his heart.

"One last thing before I go, Caris. I owe you an apology."

She looked at him. Looked right in his eyes, not at his nose.

"I'm sorry I asked you to keep my secret for me, Caris. About the magic. It wasn't fair, and I want to take it back."

She nodded, but her gaze remained hard. He comforted himself with the thought that even though she didn't respect his choices, she had kept his secret. It might have had something to do with the ring's enchantment, but he hoped it was also an acknowledgement that she knew they'd helped each other—that on some level they were truly friends—and that whether or not they liked it, they were part of each other.

He gave her a deep bow. "Thank you, Caris. Luck grace your trail."

"And yours." Her jaw muscles clenched as if she didn't trust herself to say more. Then she mounted and rode Idgit back toward Willard and Mudruffle.

Harric watched her go. Then, with a deep sigh, he reamed and loaded his spitfires, stowed them, and followed her back toward the others. He stopped when he saw Sir Willard walking toward him up the trail, the red eye of a lit ragleaf pulsing in the fire-reddened dusk. Behind him, a hundred paces up the trail, a couple of lantern lights glowed beside the horses.

"You're making camp," Harric said.

The gigantic knight stopped before him and squinted as he studied Harric's face against the bright backdrop of the fire. "Horses need rest.

Forced march for nearly two days. A wonder none went lame." He pulled the ragleaf from his mouth and exhaled smoke. "Out with it. What must you tell me?"

Harric gave a small bow. "Several things. First, I must depart tonight, as I originally planned. I have given Caris my horse, Snapper, who is Phyros-trained. I'll take Rag."

"She approves this?"

Harric nodded.

"Well, I don't, you selfish knave. The girl's enchanted to love you. What in the Black Moon do you think it will do to her if you leave? I need her competent to fight, not blubbering in a puddle of foolishness."

"The ring is broken. Ask her. It doesn't affect her any longer."

Bushy eyebrows bristled over the knight's violet eyes. "How is that possible? How do you know that?"

"Ask her," Harric repeated. "She'll tell you."

Willard took several long tugs on his ragleaf, smoke gusting from his nostrils. "By all the damned gods, you'd better not have hurt her, or I'll wring your neck and—"

"If I had hurt her, I'd deserve it. But I haven't. Will you listen?"

Willard clamped hard on the ragleaf, eyes blazing.

Harric forced his shoulders to relax. "Sir Willard, if she says otherwise, I will stay. But she won't. Just ask her."

"I will."

"And now that she's free, I've decided I must go to the Queen. Someone must."

Willard snorted. "If you want my approval, you have it, and good riddance. Was that what you wanted to tell me?"

"No, there's more." Harric took a deep breath in preparation to speak, but then hesitated. Standing so close, he'd become acutely aware of Willard's restrained anger. The Blood in his veins and the misfortunes of the day had the knight wound up and ready to pop. Indeed, just now he'd nearly burst a vein in his forehead over Harric's *good* news about the ring; the rest of his news might be too much for the knight's restraint.

Harric exhaled and made a decision. "The lore songs say that you and the Blue Order would occasionally grant a short truce to the Old Ones, a time of open speech and meeting without blows."

"A New Moons Truce. Three days. What of it?"

"I ask for such a truce, if I may, before I share what I know."

"You've done something so heinous you must ask for such a thing?"

Harric made a small, ironic bow. "I do not think so, but you and I have disagreed on such things before."

Willard's eyes smoldered. He sucked at the ragleaf until its coal burned bright and white smoke obscured his eyes. "I give you one day."

"I accept."

Nevertheless, Harric retreated half a step under the pretenses of glancing back at the fire behind him. "There is no easy way to say this, Sir Willard. And it gives me no pleasure to say it, especially now that Brolli is no longer with us. But Ambassador Brolli was not all he seemed. Of course, we knew and accepted that he had secrets, as we all do. But I discovered the scale of his secrets last night when I saw him using some Kwendi magic to open a door in the air."

The rag roll went still between Willard's lips. "A magic door? What foolishness is this? Would you slander him now that he's gone and cannot refute you?"

"I do not make this up. Why would I?" He then told Willard how Brolli had gone through the door and that Harric had followed. He told Willard he heard the Kwendi elder say there would be no treaty. He described the Kwendi warriors training to fight mounted knights, and the magic of the Kwendi women.

When he'd finished, Willard stood still as stone. Abruptly, his hands squeezed into fists at his sides.

"Truce, remember," said Harric.

When Willard finally spoke, his voice grated like iron on stone. "Magic doors. Peeking and spying. These lies are as vile as the sneaking jack that spawned them."

"Sir Willard, I saw all of this. You must believe me. You will be in danger if you go to the Kwendi lands."

In one quick motion, Willard seized Harric by the collar and lifted him until he barely stood upon his toes. "Lies." Rag smoke gusted in Harric's face. "Vile, faithless lies. Or have you gone mad? None could do and see as you claim."

Harric felt a calm that he normally only felt at the card table. "I can, and I did. Let me show you how."

"Show me this magic door?"

Harric thought about it for a moment. "I hadn't thought of that. But yes. If you let me look through Brolli's things, I could show you the rod he used to do it—"

Willard shook Harric so hard that the collar burned the skin at the back of his neck. "So that's your game. You hope to get at the dead ambassador's toys. I should fling you into the fire."

"You asked—" Harric choked. "You asked if I could show you the door, and I answered honestly. But I can show you in another way. Let me go and I'll show you how I know." Willard shook him again, and again, as if trying to knock different words from him, and Harric gasped between shakes: "We—have—a truce—!"

Willard released him, and Harric stumbled back. The immortal's eyes burned violet, and his skin darkened with the Blood. "If you do not produce a miracle, I shall not be accountable for my actions."

Harric rubbed his neck and smoothed his collar. Then he took a few steps back and drew himself up, watching Willard. "You will not be disappointed." Slipping his hand into his shirt, he removed his nexus from the pouch and held it before Willard. Its glassy surface swallowed all light that fell upon it, like Harric held in his hand a hole in the very air.

Softly, Harric said, "*Nebecci, Tasta, Tryst.*"

Fink materialized on Harric's shoulders and looked down in surprise. His wings whipped out for balance. "Oh hey, kid. What's the trouble?" A sharp intake of breath from Willard drew Fink's attention, and the imp's white eyes widened in surprise. "Moons, kid. Didn't know I was meeting the parents. I would have dressed up."

Belle flashed from her scabbard in Willard's hand, and Fink dropped behind Harric with a squeak.

"You traffic with a *god?*" Willard snarled.

Fink peeked around Harric's leg. "What? Did he just call me a god?"

"Sir Willard, you gave me your truce," Harric said.

"I did not give *that thing* my truce."

"He is my friend, and if you harm him, you harm me."

Willard ground his teeth, chest heaving, but stood his ground.

Fink tugged at Harric's pant leg. "Can we just note that this man said 'god'?"

"Fink, this is an important moment, and not because he said god," Harric replied.

"Sorry."

Harric gave a slow nod to Willard, whose eyes were now wide with outraged horror. "Now I will show you how I was able to learn all I did about Brolli. Don't be alarmed. When you see—or rather, don't see—you'll understand." Then Harric opened his oculus and entered the Unseen.

Willard's form seemed to explode with blinding violet spirit strands. As the old knight stared at the space where Harric stood, he made the sign of the heart in the air before himself.

"This is how I know, Sir Willard. I can move unseen through the spirit world. Even Kwendi eyes can't see me, but I see them. I followed Brolli through the magic door, and I saw everything I told you about. I do not wish to speak ill of the dead, but the ambassador was betraying you, leading you uselessly north, probably to imprison you, like the others. They are preparing for war, and you have to warn the Queen."

"Kid." Fink pointed up the trail to where Mudruffle stood motionless in the tall grass, about ten paces away. In the Unseen, the clay of the golem's body shone only faintly, so he stood out like a dark silhouette against the glowing strands of the vegetation. Fink hopped up on Harric's pack and held to the straps.

"Sir Willard, Master Harric is charmed!" the golem called. "The imp speaks through him to sow dissension between us. It wishes to ruin your mission of peace so its foul kin can feed on the slaughter of war."

Anger flared in Harric. "You have no idea what you're talking about."

"I know all too well, young Harric."

Mudruffle swept his hand in a high arc toward Harric, as if casting dust upon him. Half an instant later, Fink hissed and slapped both hands over Harric's oculus.

A warm and heavy weariness had fallen over Harric's limbs as Mudruffle finished his gesture. It draped him like a heavy, comforting blanket, and his vision blurred. He felt himself swaying over his feet, wanting desperately to lie down and sleep. But Fink's hands seemed to wake him, and then the sensation passed as quickly as it came.

As he stabilized his balance, Harric saw Willard lying flat on his face.

Mudruffle was hurrying toward Harric's location in jerking strides.

In the next moment, Willard was on his feet and moving almost too fast to track. Then Mudruffle was flying back into the brush from which he'd emerged, and Willard stood seething, teeth clenched, and trembling with rage.

"Touch me—with magic—again," he said between what seemed like painful efforts at restraint, "and it shall be—the last thing you do in this world."

"You must bind him," said Mudruffle, now struggling to right himself in a tangle of greenery.

Willard picked up the sword he'd dropped during Mudruffle's spell and scanned the area where Harric still stood in the Unseen. "The boy has my truce and I am bound to protect him. Do not test me in this, Mudruffle. Do not harm him or his"—Willard glared—"his…"

"His *god*," Fink supplied.

"False god!" Mudruffle honked. "Spirit of darkness!"

"Fink," Harric said. "Don't make this harder than it has to be."

"Like how, show myself?" said Fink. "You already did that."

"Enough!" Willard bellowed. "Show yourself, Harric. You have made your point."

Harric re-entered the Seen, and Willard's eyes snapped to him.

The knight's chest heaved with labored breaths. "Leave us. You have told me what you intended. Now leave. And never return."

"I am not under a spell," Harric said. "Please believe what I told you about Brolli."

Motion drew Harric's eyes twenty paces behind Mudruffle, where Caris led Rag down the trail. Her brow wrinkled as if she was wondering what all the yelling was about, and her eyes were on Willard, who had bellowed the loudest. When she saw Harric and Fink, she stopped cold and her eyes widened to the size of duck eggs. The horror in her eyes as she looked at him smote Harric in ways he couldn't define.

Willard took Rag's lead from her and turned the mare around. Slapping the saddle, he said to Harric, "Mount and ride while you have my protection."

Harric climbed aboard as if moving in a dream. Caris had fastened Spook's basket to the saddle bow, and must have let the little moon cat out for a while, because he wasn't mewing inconsolably.

"Sir Willard, this is a grave mistake," Mudruffle honked.

"Put a cob in it, Mudwizzle," said Fink.

Willard took the lantern from Caris, handed it to Harric, and slapped Rag's rump. As the Rag bore him past Caris, her eyes filled with tears. Not for him, Harric knew, but for her oldest friend, lost to forces beyond her control.

"I'll take good care of her. I promise you," he said.

Before they drew out of speaking distance, Harric reined Rag and turned to face them. The three stood watching, silent as standing stones and silhouetted by the blaze of the wildfire behind. Mudruffle's shiny black eyes glittered in his lantern's light.

"There are no lies between us now," Harric said. "I leave with a clean conscience. I am no longer your man, Sir Willard. I am no longer beholden to the wedding ring, nor to the strictures of the two laws. I am the Queen's man. And though you may think only swords can serve Her Majesty, I will prove you wrong."

Willard spat and made the sign of the heart.

Harric turned Rag and rode. As he passed the camp where Brolli's body lay, Snapper whinnied and Geraldine let out a mournful bellow, and for some foolish reason, the sounds brought stinging tears to Harric's eyes.

Harric and Fink rode in silence out from the trees of the canyon into a wide, grassy valley. Harric cradled Spook, scratching behind the cat's ears and letting the vibration of the animal's purr calm the turbulence in his heart.

In the light of the Bright Mother, the valley seemed a silver sea, the breezes moving in gentle waves among the grasses. Rag tossed her head and snuffed the open air as if in approval, and Harric felt a new energy to her gait. Dark, forested ridges bound the sea on either side, and ahead, the moonlit ramparts of the Godswall towered over its shores, no more than a day and half's ride away.

As the river curved away to the left to run up the west side of the valley, Harric steered Rag north to cut directly across the grasses.

It wasn't until much later, when the Mad Moon peeked above the rim of the world, and the Bright Mother rode the western sky, that Fink spoke. "You did well back there, kid. I'm impressed. Or I guess I should say that I did that well, since the whole time I was controlling you like a puppet."

When Harric laughed, the imp leaned around from behind, his bald head cocked. In a conspiratorial whisper, he said, *"Price of heroes."*

"Yeah."

Fink nodded to the gear behind Harric. "You got something in that pack you want to tell me about, kid?"

Harric felt his guts tighten, but maintained a careful mask of calm. Fink couldn't know of the hoops; Harric had stashed them well. Unless…unless the imp had searched the pack when Harric was asleep.

Cobs.

"What do you mean?" he said, avoiding Fink's intent gaze, and stroking Rag's neck.

"Look for yourself."

Harric craned himself about and turned his oculus on the pack. The bulk of it glowed softly with smoke-blue strands of spirit essence rising upward toward the moon, but one side of it sizzled with long purple strands that flickered horizontally westward, like the flames of a campfire in a wind. Relief washed over him. "Phyros plasters. Willard gave them to me."

Fink's nose wrinkled. "He gave you Phyros turds?"

"No, *plasters*. Scabs from dried Phyros Blood. You put them on wounds. Willard gave them to me."

Fink's eyes widened. "You have the blood of a god in your bag."

"Blood of a cob-head god, yes."

"I thought Sir What's-his-Bugger didn't approve of magic."

"It's not magic, it's Blood."

"God magic isn't magic?"

"It's not moon magic, so it isn't magic."

"You're making a jest. You stole these or something."

"No. It's the truth."

After a long moment in which Fink appeared to study Harric's face intently, he said, "I'll never understand this stupid island."

"Which reminds me," Harric said, displaying the bandage he'd wrapped around his forearm. "Thanks so much for this nice new plague boil on my arm. You didn't tell me this was coming when you took my strand."

"Wasn't time."

"You should know that in Arkendia, people are hung for these things. They know what they are—call them Witch's Teats—and I'll be hung if anyone sees it on the road."

Fink cringed a little. "Sorry, kid."

"How long will it last?"

"Month or two, longer if you let me nurse off it—"

"That's revolting in more than one way."

Fink bristled, wings and chin jutting. "And starving isn't revolting?"

Harric raised a placating hand and looked into the imp's scowling face. "I don't ever want you to starve again, Fink. But I really don't want to hang, either. Arkendian witch hunters look for these things, and some of the best will look under bandages. They know."

"We did what we had to. It was feed on you, feed on the Kwendi ladies, or be caught, and you wouldn't let me feed on them."

"That's true. And I would do the same thing all over again. But if it ever comes to that again, could you pick a spot on my back?"

Fink's wings sagged. "Yeah. Sorry about that. I wasn't in my right head. Guess it's best if you don't let me get so desperate next time."

"It's a deal." Harric smiled.

Fink's black tongue flicked over his teeth. "Speaking of deals," he said, glancing into the sky. "I'd love to sit on this horse's back end all night, but I need to find Missy and tell her the deal's off." His face screwed up in what might have been a grimace of worry, and he twisted his talons like he was wringing them out. "Anyway, you seem all right on your own right now."

Harric nodded. "Probably better alone right now, actually."

"In the Unseen, you're not better alone. Fire like that draws vultures looking for fire kills. And there's no Phyros with you to scare them off."

"Then why don't you stay?"

Fink's face twisted again. "Better I find Missy before she finds us. Maybe stay near the river, just to be sure. I'll be back as soon as I have news."

Fink vanished. Harric sighed and gave Spook another rub behind the ears.

Far to the left, across the moonlit sea of grass, he saw the dark line of willows marking the edge of the river. As he steered Rag toward it, raindrops kissed the skin of his hands and face, and whispered in the dry grass around them. The first rain of autumn, and enough to stir up the scents of dry grass and wildflowers. Spook let out a mewing complaint and shook his ears, so Harric put him back in his basket, and turned his face to the sky.

Alone. Unknown. Only Spook's purr and Rag's breath and cadenced steps for company.

Behind him, the Bright Mother had risen to fill the valley with light, and his shadow stretched before him toward the darkness of approaching clouds.

"Price of heroes?" he murmured to the cat. He shook his head. "Freedom isn't a price. It's a prize."

There was triumph in that. There was birth.

And the ache in his heart made it truth.

Epilogue

Fink writhed and gasped for breath as Missy's iron-cold talons squeezed tight around his skinny neck. The black mists of the moon enveloped them, hiding them from prying eyes.

"He is mine," said Missy, in her mournful, owl-song voice. "And you are mine. Your game is done."

"No—" he gasped. "You—don't understand—"

"You have no blood-soul pact. The boy is rogue. You are rogue. I will consume you both."

Fink squeaked as she lifted him effortlessly from the ground. The vulture had told her, just as it promised. The poisonous, ungrateful corpse-eater had ruined everything. "Mother—will decide that." He gasped in pain, prying at her talons with his claws. "You can't—decide that. I know—things!"

She held him before her like a rat on a stick. Then she drew him, very slowly, upward toward the emptiness behind her hood.

"The Kwendi!" Fink said. "I know things!"

"You know nothing."

"Stop! I do! I saw the magic! I was there!"

"You saw the Kwendi put weaves in the stone?"

"A different Kwendi—a woman Kwendi—in the Kwendi land—"

Missy hissed and drew him to the brim of her hood. Fink squealed in terror. "You lie."

"A magic door! Through a door!"

"What door?"

"Every night—let me show!"

His slow progress to the hood halted, but she did not lower him. Silence reigned for long moments in which Fink whined, the cold void inches away, but knew better than utter a word. Soft owl notes echoed from deep in the hood, as if it housed some vast subterranean cavern. Her breath made frost on Fink's nose. "You will show me," she said. "You will tell everything."

Fink writhed and made tiny, frantic nods. "Yes!" But inside, he seethed. He felt like a bug on a pin—helpless, desperate. If he showed her, she would consume him anyway and claim the discovery for herself; she would justify his destruction with the revelation that he had no pact with Harric. If he didn't show her, she would torture him, or imprison him in some lost nest in the Web until he dwindled to nothing or confessed.

He had to reach Mother before she could act.

Missy lowered him to the ground, but she did not release his throat. Her breath was the sigh of wind over hollow bones. "Show me."

Fink shivered and nodded, and she released him. As he led her into the Web to lead her, he sent a thought down a strand to Harric.

She knows, kid. Get to the river. Now. It's your only chance.

BACKERS

To the believers who backed The Unseen Moon trilogy: thank you!

Don Crowe
Stone Gossard
Kathryn Rogers
Rodney Taber
Scott Merlino
Alex Anderson
David Dewine
Todd Floyd
Vikram Prakash
Jane Tomlinson
Pat Perkins
Katherine Swenson
Lynn Rambaldini
Steph Judy
Don Crowe
Norma Patterson
David Baugh
Brandy Coward
John Tomlinson, Jr.
Corinne OFlynn
Matt Newland
Tracey Tomlinson
Rachel Gleeson
John & Danya
Schwab
Renee Ruhl
Jo Eike
Lucas Virgili
Craig Holt
Glenn Rotton
Brenda & Don
Mallett
Niki

Pam Stucky
Stephen Spech
Dennis
Reichenbach
Jim Rogers, Jr.
Marlys Gerber
Jules Hughes
Mark Hauge
Juliana Groisman
Lucinda Payne
Santiago
Ryan Niman
Jeff Seymour
Sue Constan
Jodi Ryzowski
Amy Raby
Ace Forsythe
Charla Lemoine
Katherine Nolte
Anne Belen
Anne LaChasse
Alison Rambaldini
Kirsten Fitzgerald
Dick Vitulli
Charlotte Bushue
Katherine Van Slyke
Quinn Roberts
John Joynt
Heron Prior
Steve Viles
Brian Senter
Scott Maynard
Emma Major

Paul Hughes
Peter
Gail Mitchell
Janka Hobbs
Kathrina Simonen
Fiona Robertson
Richard Sundberg
Ed Almquist
Steve Gurr
Kai Ichikawa
Lisa Floyd
Barbara Bender
Anthony
Betsy Lee
Mariann Krizsan
Stefan Marmion
Brett Frosaker
Gabriela Fulcher
Brainiac187
James Arnold
J.S. Elliot
Rob Rose-Leigh
Delaney Ruston
Thomas Cleland
Ross Bowen
Ricciardi Luc
Christy Shaver
Jim Tomlinson
Larry Couch
Arne Radtke
Cathleen King
Phoebe Copeland
Jim Naeger

Alan Hellie
Ashli Black
Rob H. Stevens
Joshua Haynes
Ian Wright
Brad Karr
Becca Morris
Jeff Miller
Deirdre Hancock
Nancy Katims
Brandon Smith
Evan Roberts
Roman Pauer
Stephanie Hahn-
Wagner
Delaney Hancock
Tye & Ann Swiftney
Laura Yeats
Cole Krause
Rebecca Carr
Boo Edmunds
Michael Downey
Derek Freeman
Austin Warawa
Michael Frost
Jeanne McGuire
Alexander John
Aristotle
Kimball Tamara
Towers
Brian Karr

Author's Note

While *The Jack of Ruin* is still fresh in your mind,
please take time to leave a review or even a couple words
on Amazon and/or Goodreads.
For updates or announcements on the release dates for book three,
subscribe to my newsletter at stephenmerlino.com, follow
@stephenmerlino, or on Facebook, Stephen Merlino. For a look at
my random interests or doings, look me up on Pinterest—Stephen
Merlino—and on Instagram—wordbender.

Thanks again, and happy reading.

ABOUT THE AUTHOR

Stephen Merlino lives in Seattle, Washington, where he writes,
plays, and teaches high school English. In 2014, *The Jack of Souls* won
the Pacific Northwest Writers Association award for fantasy,
and in 2016, a chapter taken from the novel won a place in
Writers of the Future anthology, volume 32.
Stephen cohabits with the most desirable woman in the world,
two fabulous children, one cat, and three attack chickens.

CPSIA information can be obtained
at www.ICGtesting.com
Printed in the USA
BVHW031817070419
544866BV00002B/2/P